I0650733

ARROWS

THROUGH

TIME

A TIME TRAVEL TALE OF ADVENTURE, COURAGE, AND FAITH

DEBRA & DAVID LAWRENCE

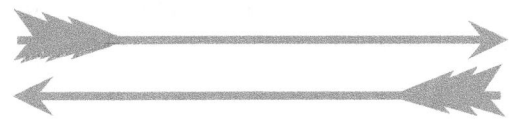

GlacierDog Publishing

A Division of

GlacierDog Intergalactica

Anchorage, Alaska

~ Arrows Through Time ~

A Time Travel Tale of Adventure, Courage, and Faith

Copyright 2009 Debra Anne Ross Lawrence and David Allen Lawrence

ISBN 978-0-9797459-2-8
ISBN 0-9797459-2-6

Library of Congress Control Number: 2009924426

All rights reserved. No part of this book may be reproduced or transmitted in any form or by any means, graphic, electronic, or mechanical, including photocopying, recording, taping, Web distribution, or any information storage and retrieval systems, without permission in writing from the publisher.

Notice to the Reader

Arrows Through Time is a work of fiction. Names, characters, places, and incidents are the products of the authors' imagination or are used fictitiously. Any resemblance to actual events, locales, or persons, living or dead, is entirely coincidental.

TABLE OF CONTENTS

Acknowledgements

We express deep appreciation to our wonderful friends, Professor Channing Robertson, Reverend Peter Loughman, and Professor Melanie McNeil, for reading our manuscript and providing insightful comments.

We especially thank our special friend, Betty Skladal, for her encouragement and her careful and detailed editing.

We are very grateful to our friend and mother, Marguerite Ross, for her enthusiastic support, multiple edits, and valuable comments, which helped us refine the manuscript.

~ Dedication ~

TO MARGUERITE ROSS

ADVENTUROUS SOUL
PERSEVERING, TRIUMPHANT
INTREPID ... AND FUN!

PREVIEWS

Immediately, she felt herself being sucked down deep into the Earth by an irresistible force. She could not breathe! She panicked! This must be the beginning of the severe and painful death she used to overhear her people say she would surely endure. She was accelerating downward at a speed she thought impossible. It was too dark to know where she was or what was surrounding her. *The life is being sucked out of me. I'm dying.* She thought of Yachay. What would he think when he came looking for her and she was gone? Would he think she had been killed in the jungle and never made it? No, he would find her tracks and see that she *had* made it. And then, would he step through the elusive wall and die too? She could feel the blackness. The air was being sucked out of her body. She was flying, flying through a tunnel. She felt herself gasping when...SMASH...she slammed into something hard and lost consciousness.

Kawsay's breath had returned to her. She awoke suddenly with the feeling someone, or something, had nudged her. It was very dim, but not totally black. The air was damp and smelled earthy. Her legs hurt. *I wonder how far I fell. I must have ended up at a lower level of the cave.* But it felt different somehow. She must figure out where she is now.

She slowly stood up and felt stiff, as if her joints had all frozen and refused to bend. She felt as if someone or something was watching her. She looked toward the dark recesses of the small chamber and thought she detected movement. She became fully alert and then became aware of a different smell, an animal smell. *This can't be good.* She slowly turned around and saw what looked like a doorway. She realized the dim light was coming through the doorway behind a huge animal. *Oh no! A great jaguar has followed me and trapped me here!* But this monster was bigger than any jaguar she had ever seen. She could feel the blood slowly drain out of her head and thought she was now experiencing her first real test of courage, her first encounter with true danger. Would she be a coward and faint? Against her will, Kawsay felt her body turn to jelly as she slowly slumped into a puddle of human fear on the cold rock floor. In the safety of unconsciousness she dreamed about hugging the neck of the Chief's jaguar stool. She could feel its warmth.

Slowing awakening and trying to get her bearings, she became aware she was again someplace new. The air was damp and earthy, though, and she could still smell the beast. She slowly opened her eyes, squinting to see and wondering if she would be pounced on, torn to shreds, and devoured. She could see an enormous ceiling sparkling above the huge, dimly lit room. Kawsay opened her eyes wider and was amazed at the stalactites, stalagmites, and vast arrays of twisting helictite crystals surrounding her. She was in a giant sparkling jewel box. This must be the jewels of the Earth her grandparents had told her about! She thought she could stay there forever, lost in its spectacular beauty. The ceiling was laced with crystalline vines, many of which looked to be as long as she was tall. She heard a stream. She lay there listening to it for a moment while taking in the luminous beauty above her. *At least I will be looking into the heavens when I die.*

The girls looked closely at Yachay and giggled louder. "It's not Halloween yet! Halloween! Halloween!"

Yachay had no idea what they were saying, but it was not threatening. In the moonlight Yachay could see that one of the girls looked about six years old and the other maybe eight. They had yellow hair and pale skin. Yachay had heard of yellow hair and just yesterday he had seen pale skin. He wondered why the girls seemed to think he was so funny. They were now jumping around saying, "Ug, ug, ug." Yachay looked back up the side of the boat at the luminous sky. His arm was crusted with dried blood and was still oozing. The girls were jumping on stools that were against the low fence that protected them from falling into the water. They climbed from the stools up to the top of the fence, looked down at the water, then jumped back onto the deck giggling. Yachay did not think it was safe for the young yellow-haired girls to jump around on the edge of a huge boat. They looked at Yachay, giggled, and then climbed back up to the fence whispering. Yachay was keeping an eye on the girls. He decided to take off his sling and tuck his spear as far into it as possible. He realized he was dressed very differently from anyone he had seen and decided the spear would not help. He secured the pointed end of his spear into his sling along with the pouches that were tied around his waist. He wanted to keep all his possessions and weapons together and safely in his sling. There was not much he could do about his tunic and bare legs.

As he was about to strap the sling across his back, a loud booming horn pierced through the rumble. His eyes darted over to the girls, and he saw the younger one fly off the fence and down toward the dark water. In a single motion, Yachay dropped his sling, grabbed the older girl, whose scream joined the horn, and pointed her toward the front of the boat where the people were. He shouted "Yanapay!" as his momentum joined with a push-off from his feet and carried him off the stern of the boat right behind the small yellow-haired girl. Yachay had anticipated this type of accident so he was braced for it. The girl glided on the wind and splashed into frigid water, which silenced her scream. Yachay's arms were outstretched – he could almost touch her. Just as the force of her body hitting the water halted her flight, Yachay's hands reached her and his arms engulfed her small body. He did not want her to get away from him in the moonlit darkness. He clutched her to his chest as they both plunged beneath the frigid surface. He held his breath and hoped he had not knocked the air out of her small lungs as he landed on top of her.

He could not believe how cold the water was! It felt like icy daggers slicing his body. He needed to get her out. But first he needed to get her up to the surface. Yachay held her with one arm and fought to get to the surface with the other. He looked around under the dark, frigid water. There was enough moonlight to illuminate the bubbles on the water's surface, and he could feel the roughed-up turbulence from the boat's wake. He swam toward the faintly lit bubbles. His head broke the surface, and he took a breath. While kicking hard with his legs, he held the girl's head out of the frigid water. He could not tell if she was breathing. Yachay shook her shoulders. He did not know what to do. She coughed. Yachay could see her face in the moonlight. He could also see the huge boat moving away. The girl was sobbing. *A good sign,* Yachay thought. Yachay knew he needed to get the child out of the frigid water. He wanted her up on his shoulders. But how could he communicate that to her when he could not speak her language?

CHAPTER 1.

KAWSAY

YEAR 1596
SMALL VILLAGE NEAR VILCABAMBA, PERU

NO PLACE AND NO TIME
IS TOO SMALL OR TOO REMOTE
TO RESCUE ONE LIFE.

"Please let my baby live!" she pleaded as tears began welling up in her eyes. Sumaq was sitting on the straw floor of the Chief's hut clutching her newborn. As she nervously adjusted her baby's brightly colored woven blanket, her eyes rested on the Chief's jaguar-shaped carved stool. She envisioned it coming to life and biting him if he denied her honorable request. Sumaq had always loved and respected the Chief, but this was about life and death – the life and death of her second child and first daughter. She was the last child Sumaq would ever have with her now forever-gone husband.

"Please permit me to nurture and train this child until her thirteenth birthday so she can learn about the jungle," Sumaq pressed her case. "Then she can be sent off to live there on her own, banished from our village forever. If the gods help her and she survives, she can dwell in the jungle for the rest of her days, but if she dies, it will be the judgment of the gods." Sumaq anxiously looked from face to face at the private late-night gathering of the most senior elders of her small tribe. With her long dark hair and light brown eyes, Sumaq, just twenty-two herself, looked like a wounded child. She had recently suffered the loss of her beloved husband and now, just two months later, faced the required sacrificial death of her newborn daughter, Kawsay.

"We have discussed this matter at great length," the Chief said, moving his hands in a broad arc toward the somber elders. "Because a short time ago you suffered the death of your husband, we have decided to grant your unusual request to let your daughter remain with the tribe until her thirteenth birthday. But there are conditions. She will not be permitted to participate in tribal activities or interact with the other children. You must also understand that after she leaves, she will never be permitted to return. If your daughter is to learn the ways of the jungle, it will be from you and your family," the Chief concluded.

The Chief knew that allowing this baby to live would engender great resentment among other families who had been required to sacrifice their own deformed newborns. Kawsay had been born with a cleft lip. By the tradition of her small tribe, all deformed babies were to be sacrificed on the first full moon following their birth. The Chief understood the expediency of this custom. Since the Invaders destroyed the Inca Empire, this small group of survivors was ill equipped to care for anyone born with great needs. Yet, the Chief had never had peace about a practice he considered child sacrifice.

The next afternoon the Chief prepared for the tribal meeting. Walking among the excavated terraces of corn, potatoes, beans, and peppers, he struggled for the words to convince his people that the right and just decision had been made in sparing little Kawsay's life. As he watched the orange Sun slide toward the mountaintops, he hoped the great sun god, Inti, would give his words power and authority. The Chief looked down at his llama hide sandals and realized he had dressed in his finest knee-length tunic and brightly colored vicuña wool cloak, accented with ruby red parrot feathers. He had been so preoccupied by that little innocent Kawsay, it was difficult to concentrate on anything else.

When the Chief arrived at the tribal meeting he noticed everyone was present except, as he had instructed, Kawsay's mother, brother, and grandmother, who were noticeably absent. Scanning the faces of his people in the dusky firelight, some curious and some livid, he began speaking. "As you all know, our dear young friend, Sumaq's beloved husband, was taken from us only two months ago." The Chief motioned toward the broad, intricately cut stairs leading down to where they were all seated.

The Chief continued, "Already a great stonecutter, our dear friend did not even get the chance to meet his precious little baby daughter, Kawsay. As you also know, our dear little Kawsay has a miniscule dimple in her upper lip. If it were not for the tragic loss of our dear brother, the child's father, we would be announcing the decision of the elders whether this particular abnormality, this tiny dot on the child's lip, requires a sacrifice. However, in light of the family's situation, we, the elders and I, fear the great Inti will punish all of us if we take little Kawsay from her grieving mother and now fatherless brother, Yachay. Their beloved father is in the afterlife undoubtedly making beautiful stone works for our great and just Inti."

The Chief looked around to see if his people were buying his downplay of Kawsay's lip and diversion to her deceased father. He noticed a half-smile on Kawsay's grandfather's face, and that the curious faces looked more placid and the formerly livid faces were merely shades of pink rather than the crimson color of the sunset sky. Rumors had already passed through the tribe that Sumaq had given birth to a deformed baby, and its life would be spared.

The Chief continued, "In order to be just to both Sumaq's family as well as those who have sacrificed their own babies for similar, albeit more severe, abnormalities, we have decided that the child will be raised and trained to survive in the jungle by her family until her thirteenth birthday, at which time she will be sent there permanently where her survival will be determined by the gods. For those of you who believe this child should be sacrificed, in spite of the insignificance of her abnormality, you will be comforted by the likelihood that her death will simply be postponed and undoubtedly will be a severe and painful death alone in the jungle by starvation, by fever, or in the jaws of the great jaguar. It will very likely be much worse than a painless and merciful sacrifice as an unaware infant." As the harshness of this prediction impacted his listeners, the Chief, looking beyond them toward the cloud-draped darkening peaks of the surrounding Andes Mountains, abruptly asked, "Now, is there any other business to attend to before we are finished here?"

Kawsay was to spend the next thirteen years with her small tribe hidden high in the Andes in an area that is now modern day Peru. Her tribe had been formed by a group of survivors who escaped from domination after the Inca Empire was dismantled in 1532 at the hands of Spanish conquerors led by Francisco Pizarro. The members of the tribe had cloistered themselves just trying to survive, believing the outside world was hostile.

CHAPTER 2.

NATE

JUNE – THREE YEARS IN THE FUTURE
MENLO PARK, CALIFORNIA

OUR SMALL FAMILY
WILL THERE BE A SECOND CHANCE
TO BE TOGETHER?

Nathaniel topped the dune and scrambled down to a deserted campsite. The tent door flapped in the gathering wind. "Dad! Where are you?" The howling wind answered, stinging his eyes with sand. "Dad! I'm here. Please be OK!" Looking around in desperation, he saw a figure receding into the dusty air across the valley. Sprinting in pursuit, he began to discern the awful form of a Philistine giant – the largest he had seen – carrying his manacled father over a hulking shoulder. *No!* he screamed to himself. *We've already lost Mom. I need to rescue Dad!* Nathaniel caught up with the giant and began pelting his back with rocks. The giant turned and sneered. He reached down flung Nathaniel through the air. Nathaniel braced for a hard impact, but instead splashed into a cold, swift stream. Struggling to swim, he was rapidly carried away by the current. He heard the roar of a waterfall and in an instant was again airborne. He looked down between flailing legs to sharp rocks far below. "Dad! Help!" His thoughts raced. *Who will take care of Dad? Mom is gone. He needs me and I need him. Dad! Dad!!!* Nate accelerated toward impact. Thud!

The front door closed loudly, jolting Nate awake. His eyes tried to focus. *Dad! Thank God he's home. I must have dozed off. What a dream!* Nate was comforted by the familiar sound of his father dropping a heavy briefcase and humming as he checked the mail. "Hi Dad," Nate called out, still shaken by his dream. He reached up and felt the imprint of his laptop keyboard on his cheek. Nate recalled he had finished his regular homework and had been searching the Internet, trying to wring additional meaning from the Hebrew word usually translated as "deliverer". He had gathered that a deliverer rescues, provides a way of escape, or brings someone to a place of safety.

After warming a plate of weekend leftovers, John Diamond hurried upstairs to see what his son was up to. His tie was loose, his light brown hair was a little mussed, and he was dark around his light blue eyes, but his hawk-like gaze missed nothing. He was not surprised to see Nate immersed in one of his special projects. "How are you, Son? Sorry I'm late again. Tomorrow we hope to close the genetics company deal I've been telling you about."

"I'm great, Dad. Glad things are working out. I had a great day! Found out that I aced the Calc AP exam. I think I'm the only sophomore who took the test." Nate stretched and ran his fingers through his slightly shaggy blonde hair. "Guess that means I can pick up the martial arts training again, right?"

"Great! Sure. A deal's a deal. I still wonder what to do with you after the next school year. Hard to select the right college when we're not sure what you really want to study." John sat down on the edge of the bed and continued shoveling in the late dinner. He put his iced tea on the night stand.

"Well, Dad, I'm already studying what I care about. I don't know how to take it to the bank, but languages, Biblical history, archeology – that's what grabs me. My friends can't imagine why I find all that interesting."

John was happy his son was unique in so many positive ways, but was not sure exactly where he would find his niche. "Nate, you know how I feel about all that. There's a great difference between hobbies and vocations," John said between bites. "Just like I love golf and sailing, but it's my venture capital business that keeps us afloat."

"I know, Dad, but can you really see me working in an office like yours?" Nate associated offices with prisons.

"You'd be fantastic at anything you put your mind to. I'm just waiting to see where your compass points once you finish growing up."

Nate had been feeling more grown up these days. With his father absorbed in his demanding investment business, Nate had learned to take care of all his domestic chores, set his daily schedule, and even find answers online to a young man's almost endless questions. Yet he knew he was still a work in progress and often looked in the mirror and wondered who was gazing back. He also knew he must really love his dad because he missed him when he was cloistered at the office in Palo Alto with his business partners as they tried to find the next big hit. "Yeah, I wonder about that too," Nate mused. "It's funny how much alike we are in some ways and how different in others."

"You know, Nate, it's the differences that I value in you the most. No really!" John continued holding up his hand. "So many of your special traits remind me of your mother." He paused and fought back his emotions. "It's been twelve years now. Even though you were only four, I'm grateful you remember so much. There's not a day I don't think about her, about our loss. God I hate cancer! Why can't one of these darn start-up companies find a cure?"

Nate wanted to comfort his father. "Dad, you've been great. Sure, I wish she was here too, but you've been like two parents to me. You know that whole rebellion thing? Know why I've not given you a hard time like most teens?" This new thought had just occurred to Nate. "It's because you have challenged me to be the person I was created to be. Despite all your advice, and I know you only want the best for me, you have never told me what I 'should' do, at least since I was a kid. You've just made sure I thought about all the possible consequences of whatever I was thinking about doing. There's nothing to rebel against! You're not just 'Dad'. You're the best friend I could ever have."

After a thoughtful pause, John said, "Nate, I was so worried when you had that car accident a few months ago. When I first got the call, I had this sudden fear that you had been killed; that I'd lost you. I don't think I could take losing your mother then you. What would I have left to live for?"

"Funny thing, but all the time I was in the car hanging upside down by my seat belt, I just knew it wasn't my time. But you're right that it was a close call. If that Morrow guy hadn't been right there to pull me out, I would have been burned to a crisp." Nate paused.

"You know what's even more weird? When you took me over to thank him, he appreciated it and all that and wondered how I was doing, but he swore we'd met before and that he should be thanking me! I had no idea what he was talking about."

"Who knows? The mind can play tricks. You probably reminded him of someone," John suggested, keeping to himself the fact that Morrow *had* met his son on another occasion.

"Yeah. Well, he didn't remind me of anyone I've ever met. He looked like an angel – and not just because he was helping me. He had this really light blonde hair, almost white, and really striking light green eyes. I'll never forget him," Nate recalled. "He also had a funny scar in the middle of his forehead."

"I'm just so glad you were able to get out of there alive. It's great to have you around!" John said, trying to lighten things up. He was aware that he was giving too little time to Nate, the only person left in the world he really cared about. His company always seemed to trump his plans for spending time with Nate. While he knew this had to change, he also realized his day-by-day input into Nate's life was paying off, and Nate was getting to a level of maturity where he would not need his dad at all. John finished the last bite and set the plate down. He looked up at his son.

"Nate, I really regret cancelling last year's trip. I know you were excited about it, and I really let you down. I came across the old brochures last Saturday and made some calls today. I've secured the same boat we were going to rent last year and got us some plane tickets to Nassau. Can we get ready in 5 days?"

"I know a no-brainer when I hear one, Dad. I can be ready in five minutes!" he exclaimed, becoming animated. "I don't think I ever unpacked that waterproof sea bag you got for me last year."

"Well, I think we're both overdue for this. Are you sure you can tear yourself away from the ancient sands of the Middle East for some sandy beaches in the Caribbean?" John asked with a wink.

"Look, Dad. I know I'm a little obsessive, and I know King David was no sailor, but remember, I'm your son. I'm sure we had nautical ancestors."

"That's right, mate. Maybe pirates! Arrrrgh!" John said, recalling some of the role-play games of Nate's youth. "Seriously, Nate, are you sure you want to leave your research projects for three weeks and gunkhole around with me? I sometimes wonder if you really belong to an ancient civilization because you seem so drawn to them."

"No, don't you see? We're both obsessive, just in different ways. I have to admit, though, that I sometimes wish I could live more than one life – one here with you in the modern world and another during some exciting time in history. It's frustrating, you know, to try to really capture what life was like for people thousands of years ago. No matter how much I research, all I hear is an echo. I can't picture what it was like. I can't really see it, touch it, taste it. I guess you just had to have been there!"

"Well, Nate, I know that you'll follow your heart. Maybe you're destined to be the greatest archeologist or historian in the world. You know I'll always be with you all the way." Before his eyes could betray an intense inner sadness and a large dose of fear, John looked away. "I better resurrect that packing list and get started."

CHAPTER 3

LIFE IN TRAINING

YEAR 1598
SMALL VILLAGE NEAR VILCABAMBA, PERU

A FAMILY'S LOVE
INSTILLS STRENGTH, COURAGE, AND HOPE
AGAINST HOPELESS ODDS.

Kawsay's grandmother, Asiri, looked out the doorway of her modest home at her husband, Kusi, who was holding his two-year-old granddaughter in the morning sunshine. She turned back and smiled at her daughter, Sumaq. "Don't worry, Sumaq. We will spend every day preparing Kawsay." Sumaq was flaccidly slumped on a stone stool her deceased husband had made for her. Asiri had been trying to encourage her daughter daily since the Chief's decision to let Kawsay live. "Sumaq, Yachay is a fine boy and will teach his little sister to track animals, scavenge food, fight, run, swim, climb trees and cliffs, and obtain shelter."

"Yes, but Yachay is just a boy himself, only three years her senior," countered a discouraged Sumaq.

"But your father, the boy's grandfather, is already teaching him. Yachay is a wise boy, as his name signifies," insisted Asiri.

The older woman looked tired as she began preparing a meal of roasted corn and potatoes for her husband, daughter, and two grandchildren on the small clay oven in the center of their stone-studded adobe hut. It seemed like just yesterday that her daughter and son-in-law were happily anticipating their second child, and now that joyful young woman had been transformed into a defeated widow with a young child doomed to a life of difficulty and possibly early death.

Sumaq pondered her mother's wise words for some time. "You are right, Mother!" Sumaq almost shouted as she sprang up. "It is time for me to be strong for my babies! We will train both of them to be fierce warriors so they can protect each other and themselves." Sumaq knew that her son, Yachay, had already become the protector of his sister and would never allow her to remain in the jungle by herself, but would somehow follow and help her. Sumaq also knew she would always be in close contact with her daughter, even if it meant abandoning the tribe and living in the jungle with Kawsay.

"Ah, my daughter is back!" said Asiri as Sumaq's mood seemed instantly transformed from gloominess to one of strength, exhibiting her characteristic resiliency.

When Kawsay was four years old, her brother, just a boy of seven years himself, began taking her into the jungle for long walks during the day. He pointed out food and warned of danger, and they ran as fast as her small legs would permit. Kawsay squealed with delight thinking it was all a game. Some days Grandfather went with them, bestowing his wisdom of the jungle and passing on tales from his youth. Although she had a dimple in her upper lip, Yachay thought his little sister was pretty. He could not understand why the other children made ugly faces at her whenever they caught a glimpse of her running up and down the terraces of corn and potatoes or in and out of the edge of the jungle near their small house.

When Kawsay was six years old her brother began taking her out during the night for survival training. Late, after the village was quiet, her brother guided her into the jungle so she could become familiar with the sounds of darkness. "That is the bat catching her dinner! That is the great jaguar calling his mate! That is the water running and running, which you will do one day to a safe place, my little Kawsay," Yachay would whisper. Their grandfather, who stealthily followed alongside them, always out of sight so as to not insult Yachay, thought his grandson's teaching and encouragement of his sister were remarkable. Kusi always told his wife and daughter of their nightly adventures, and of how Yachay enthusiastically instructed and encouraged his little sister.

"How do you know all these things?" Kawsay asked her brother as they were walking along the edge of the jungle one sparkling morning after an all-night caper.

"Grandfather taught me everything," he said proudly, "and he still teaches me when you are with Mother watching her weave."

Thinking she spotted a great cat beyond the trees, Kawsay screamed, "Cat, cat, cat!" and ran into the sun-specked jungle hoping to catch a glimpse of the great jungle cat. She had loved the jaguar-shaped carved stool in the Chief's house since she had first laid eyes on it and had spent many hours hanging over it with her arms wrapped around its neck. Often when Kawsay could not be found, her mother would find her asleep in the Chief's house wrapped around her beloved jaguar stool.

"Cat, cat, cat!" was what the other children often shouted at her in their mocking tones. Kawsay thought they were just yelling about the jungle cats as she had. But as she grew older she realized they had always been ridiculing her cat-like mouth. The truth was, the children not only made fun of her because of her lip and the fact she looked a little different, but also because they dared not go near the Chief's house, while Kawsay was welcomed by the Chief any time she chose. It was their jealousy that made them hate her, not her lip.

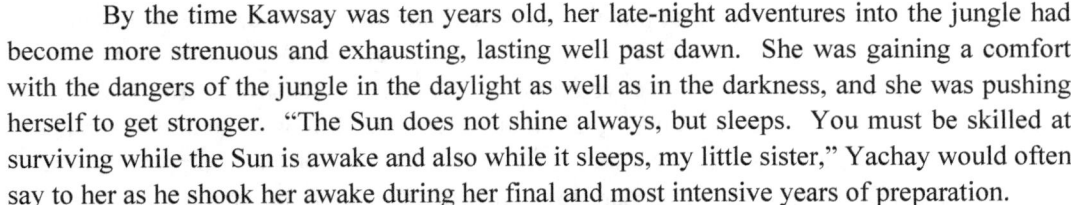

By the time Kawsay was ten years old, her late-night adventures into the jungle had become more strenuous and exhausting, lasting well past dawn. She was gaining a comfort with the dangers of the jungle in the daylight as well as in the darkness, and she was pushing herself to get stronger. "The Sun does not shine always, but sleeps. You must be skilled at surviving while the Sun is awake and also while it sleeps, my little sister," Yachay would often say to her as he shook her awake during her final and most intensive years of preparation.

"But brother! If the Sun sleeps, why can't I?" Kawsay sighed in return, as she dragged herself from bed in the middle of the night.

Approximately a year before Kawsay's thirteenth birthday Asiri made a special meal of roasted corn, potatoes, and quinoa bean soup. Kawsay sensed that something was happening, and felt the funny pang in her stomach that arose whenever the conversation steered toward her upcoming departure. Her life was unusual, but she was happy and loved her family. Grandfather had a serious look on his face signaling something important was on his mind. His usual demeanor was entertaining and a little goofy. Kawsay had always thought this was a technique Grandfather used to disarm people and make them comfortable so they would speak freely, allowing him to stay abreast of all the happenings and gossip of his small community. Grandfather often said it was important to know what was going on around them.

"Well," Kusi began, looking at his granddaughter and sensing her growing discomfort. He lowered his voice almost to a whisper. "I, ah we, your mother, grandmother, and I, believe you would greatly benefit from a practice trip to the secret caves. You will no doubt be feeling a little anxious when the day of your departure arrives and will have enough on your mind without the added disquiet of never having traveled there before. Such a trip would need to be kept completely secret from everyone outside the family because we do not want anyone to know where you will be living after you leave. Do you understand the importance and reason why absolutely no one can know your location, Kawsay?"

"Yes," Kawsay said, nodding. They had been over this many times before. "Because there may be someone who resents that I was allowed to live when others have been sacrificed for similar but greater ugliness."

"No, well yes, you are correct that others may resent that you are alive, but there is nothing ugly about you. On the contrary you are truly a beautiful girl. We just don't want someone to know your whereabouts who may be a little crazy and believes you should have been sacrificed as a baby. You know we find this practice repugnant and are slowly working to change it. Some believe it is merciful to sacrifice babies who cannot live a normal, healthy life. They believe they are protecting such babies from a life of struggle and unhappiness. But everyone has difficulties in life, and we can't sacrifice everyone!" Grandfather consciously lowered his voice again as this subject always upset him. "If we travel quickly, we should be able to get to our destination and back in less than ten days. That is a long time to be away, and we don't want people to realize we are gone, so Grandmother, Yachay, and your mother will make a presence here for us as we leave quietly."

"What?" Yachay protested.

"You are in training with the other boys your age, and your absence for so long would be noticed. It would raise difficult questions," Kusi responded in a measured, soft voice. "I have been known to disappear for periods of time, and people would assume I am either on an errand for the Chief or continuing to practice being a good warrior. Your sister is usually out of sight anyway, so her absence probably would not be noticed at all. You, Yachay, will be the man here and I expect you to protect your mother and grandmother from harm. It is a most important job." Turning back to Kawsay, Grandfather continued, now in an almost inaudible voice. "I think we should go sooner rather than later. There is not much happening here in our village for many days, and your departure is far enough in the future that no one is paying much attention to you yet. They will become more curious about your behavior as the time grows near."

Kawsay's mind was beset with conflicting thoughts. She had spent her whole life preparing to leave, but somehow it still seemed impossible that she would be forced to actually go. Her family always became visibly nervous each time a woman was about to give birth. If the baby was deformed, it would again draw attention to her situation and undoubtedly cause people to become angry with her. With that thought, maybe it *was* better she would be going soon. *But how will I survive without my family? It will be terrible!* She realized that Grandfather was right – it was better that she take this test trip now and get some idea where she would be going.

A few nights later, Kawsay's mother dressed her in layers of clothing and helped her strap food bags and weapons to her waist. Kawsay and Grandfather snuck out of their hut and into the jungle. It seemed to be pulsating with nighttime sounds. She had been sneaking out for as long as she could remember, but somehow tonight the jungle felt a little different. Maybe it was because Yachay was not there. Had she ever been in the jungle at night without Yachay? No, never. She did trust Grandfather more than anyone, though. He was strong and experienced, and much revered by the members of her tribe.

They didn't speak until they were far away from the village, just as she and Yachay had done. Grandfather moved lightly and quickly in front of her without disturbing any leaves or twigs as he glided along the ground. *Amazing*, Kawsay thought. She had never noticed him move like that before. At a safe distance from the village, Grandfather finally began to speak, using a voice audible only to her and to the night.

"Kawsay, you have learned to travel quickly and silently, and that is good. In less than five days we will be at the caves. You will see the dangerous vertical pathway leading to the hidden entrance, and you may hear the singing voices. I have never learned what they mean, but I sense they are not evil, though very mysterious. You may eventually discover what they are." Kawsay could only take this in and could not formulate a response.

Over the next few days, they continued over the varied terrain. Kawsay struggled to pay close attention as Grandfather explained how next year she would need to follow the same path. She reminded herself that the next time she traveled this route she would be taller and stronger. She paid close attention to the important landmarks that would need to guide her toward the correct branches as she navigated upstream. She also made mental notes of where they camped. Kawsay was thankful for Grandfather's foresight to make this practice journey with her. She was beginning to realize how vast and lonely her new world would be and tried to keep herself from feeling too overwhelmed.

Late on the fourth night of their journey, they arrived at the cliffs housing the secret caves. Grandfather suggested they camp at the base of the cliff and leave for home early in the morning. He did not want to be away too many days. Sometime after she fell asleep Kawsay was awakened by a faint, soft singing sound. She realized she had finally heard the wailing lady for herself. Just after dawn Grandfather pointed out the best route up the vertical cliff. He described the shelf about half way up that held the entrance to the secret cave. She could see it was a well-camouflaged location that would not easily be found by others.

"You will be safe up there, Kawsay. There is water and protection. It will be a good home for you, and we will know where you are," Kusi said as he meticulously smoothed the dirt concealing their campsite.

One night during their trip home, she and Grandfather were huddled by a tiny fire, talking about the night sounds that echoed around them. Grandfather spoke of ideas that were beyond her personal experience. "From the experiences of our elders and our ancestors, we have knowledge of the world outside our village. Our people used to maintain travel and trade routes beyond the mountains into the endless jungle to the east and down the slopes toward the west to the endless salt lake. Now that the Empire has been destroyed by the Invaders, we fear traveling too far from our homes. But we know there is a world beyond that is almost without end. It has strange foreign tribes that are not like us at all. Because we will send you outside our village, I am not able to prepare you for everything you may find and everyone you may meet. What you have learned from your family will be valuable, but you will face challenges we are not able to foresee. You will only have your own wisdom and courage to rely upon, along with whatever powers the gods give to you. While I fear for your future in so dangerous a world, I also envy you as well for your life's adventure may exceed that of us all."

Kawsay smiled at Grandfather in the flickering light. She appreciated the depth of Grandfather's ideas and the way he spoke to her as if she were grown up.

As Kawsay's thirteenth birthday drew near, the reality of her future began to weigh heavily on her mind. One night when she was feeling particularly discouraged with her plight – a seeming death sentence – she said to her brother, "What's the use anyway? We both know the jungle is too dangerous for a young girl alone."

"Don't let those sissies make you afraid. You are stronger and more astute than any boy in this tribe," Yachay responded, knowing that the other kids spoke loudly about her future demise when they thought she would overhear them. *Why were they so mean?* he wondered. Yachay loved his little sister and feared the day she would be sent away, but knew he would follow her to help her when she needed him.

During the long afternoons, Yachay had been studying for his tests with the other boys his age. It was customary for boys at age sixteen to be tested on knowledge of math, religion, history, battle tactics, oratory, strength, skill, courage, and pain endurance. Yachay's desire to care for his sister made him excel at all of these subjects, and he had become the strongest and smartest young man in his tribe. The other boys admired his abilities, but pitied him for all the time he spent with his little sister – and they did not even know about the all-night training sessions.

In addition to her jungle survival training by her brother, Kawsay was also taught the medicinal techniques of her people by her grandmother, Asiri. "Use this plant if you cut your skin. Use this plant if your stomach is upset," Asiri said with a twinkle in her eye one afternoon as she pointed to the array of plants she had carefully laid out on the woven blanket between them. "And when that special day comes and you go off to begin your new life, you must run many days toward the morning Sun to the great cliffs. In the month of your birthday, the cliffs will be just in front of the rising Sun, my Kawsay. Then, when you get to the cliffs, you must be very quiet and listen for the sound of the 'wailing lady' from the high caves. You must climb toward her voice to the secret caves above. There you will be safe."

"If the caves are secret, then how do you know about them?" Kawsay asked with a confused look on her face.

"Your grandfather's grandfather took him there when he was about your age. And your grandfather took me there when we were young."

"You mean you have been to the secret caves? That is very exciting! What is so special about them? And who is the wailing lady?" Kawsay probed with new excitement, realizing for the first time Grandmother had actually seen the caves.

"There were legends … ah, people found things … things that did not seem to belong here. And being an adventuresome type, your great great grandfather decided to go in search of where these, ah, things had come from."

"Exactly what 'things'?" Kawsay asked.

"Weapons, tools, dead people wearing strange clothing. Apparently they have been found in and around the caves. They looked different from us, and different from each other. They seemed to turn up over time. At least those are the stories that have been passed down. Nobody talks about it openly, and not very many people even know or have known."

One night as that final day approached, Yachay was testing Kawsay on identifying all the sounds and scents of the jungle she had learned during their many long excursions. As they went deeper into the jungle, Yachay tested her on fighting. He pretended to be a great cat about to pounce. Kawsay pulled out her bola with lightening speed and hurled the three stones connected by llama tendon lengths at his legs. He fell laughing in pain from a high over-hanging branch and praised her on her skill. It had been at night when Yachay usually taught her to fight, so she could protect herself even if she could not see her enemy.

They also practiced climbing rocks and trees, as their grandmother had told them many times that Kawsay would one day need to climb a special cliff. Later that night, during a particularly difficult rock climb, while hanging from the side of a cliff, Yachay was sure he sensed and heard something below and to the side of them. Reaching over to still Kawsay, he whispered, "Get your spear and throw it at whatever is following us." He pointed down toward where he thought he heard something.

"No, not good! It's Grandfather!" hollered Kusi as he waved his free arm while hanging from the side of the cliff below them.

"Grandfather? What…?" squealed Kawsay, delighted that her grandfather had joined them.

"I thought I sensed you following us for a little while the other night, but didn't realize you were here tonight," Yachay announced, proud he had known of Grandfather's presence in the past, but disappointed he had not known tonight.

"What other night, and how did you know I was there? I must be losing my stealth skills," laughed Kusi, still hanging on the moonlit cliff by one hand.

"No, I just learned from the best," Yachay said, beaming down at his teacher. "Maybe we should continue this conversation standing or sitting, rather than hanging."

"Up to the top or down to the bottom?" Grandfather asked.

"Up!" Kawsay shouted.

As they all reached the top of the broad-faced cliff, Yachay looked at his grandfather seriously and asked, "How many times have you followed us?"

"Oh, a few," Grandfather said looking away as if he was distracted by something.

"No, seriously," Yachay said, catching the glint in Kusi's moonlit eye.

"Seriously? I haven't slept since you first began going into the jungle at night. It is a very dangerous place. I know now that you are both ready and can survive alone. Besides, I needed to practice my own skills as apparently you have caught me!" Grandfather continued, looking slightly embarrassed. "Therefore, if you can detect the great master himself, you are ready for anything."

"Wow, you mean you've always been here with us?" Kawsay was amazed.

"Always," Kusi smiled. "Come now, let's go home and get some breakfast." They climbed down the cliff face and hurried home.

As they reached the edge of the jungle, they caught sight of two silhouettes approaching them in the dawn. "It's Mother and Grandmother!" Kawsay exclaimed, running toward them.

"What are you two doing up so early?" Grandfather inquired.

"Kawsay has her final medicine test today," Asiri said. "She needs to be able to identify important plants."

They walked back to their house together, where a pot of potato soup was warming on the small clay oven in the center of the room. Kawsay sat on a woolen blanket on the straw-covered floor and stared at Mother's wooden cups and bowls painted brightly with animals and birds, and at her favorite decorated ceramic vase. Kawsay looked around at the oven, the wicker baskets, the woven wall decorations, and the gold and silver dishes, and wondered how her new world would look, smell, and feel. She could smell the familiar aroma of the potato soup combined with the burning dried llama dung and twigs that fueled their stove. New llama hide sandals with modestly-colored plaited wool fibers that Mother had made were laid out for her. Next to those were a new knee-length tunic with drawings of plants and birds dyed into it and a green and brown camouflage rectangular wool cloak. Women usually wore long ankle-length tunics, but Yachay said his sister couldn't climb unless it was short.

She looked through the intricate trapezoidal stone doorway her father had made, and wondered if the cloud-wreathed mountains would appear the same from the secret caves that would soon be her new home. Although their stone and adobe home was modest, her father and grandfather had made them feel wealthy with Father's impressive stonework doorway and oddly-shaped stone stools, and Grandfather's gold and silver masks, plaques, and animal figurines. She couldn't help but smile when she looked at the Chief's jaguar-shaped carved stool that he had given her on her 10th birthday. He said it was an awkward height for him and made his back hurt, so she may as well enjoy it, but she knew he had been looking for an excuse to give it to her for many years. She wondered if the sun god, moon goddess, and earth mother would protect her during her journey to the secret caves.

Grandmother sat down and laid out an array of plants and herbs for her final medicine test. "You know, Kawsay, your mother's name, Sumaq, means beautiful, good, and wonderful. We named her that because we knew she would be all that and more. She named your brother Yachay, which means 'to know', because she and your father could tell he was wise beyond his years, even while he was yet a small baby. Your mother named you Kawsay, which means 'to live', because she wanted you to live and knew that if the Chief and elders gave you the chance, you would live a long and full life. It is just a few days before your great adventure begins, and I truly believe you will do very well."

CHAPTER 4.

A LONG DAY BEGINS

1018 B.C.
NEAR GIBEAH, ISRAEL

ONCE ARROWS ARE LAUNCHED
THEY ARC TOWARD THEIR DESTINED MARKS
AND RARELY RETURN.

Shimon awoke early again. He groaned. *That rooster next door will find itself on our spit if it continues to crow while the Sun yet rests!* His young muscles were sore from military training, especially his sword arm. Barely seventeen years old, he already was shield-bearer for the King's son and soon would be a soldier in his own right. But he was glad to have a day off from his exercises.

Shimon pried himself from his sleeping mat, put on his cloak, and climbed down the rough stairs to the main level of his parents' home. His father was away with the flocks, but he found his mother in the courtyard preparing the first meal of the day. It was crisp and clear. The last stars were fading in the west and a half moon stood overhead. Shimon often pondered its regular, inexplicable phases.

His mother looked up and smiled. "Good morning, my son. I hope you slept well. Can you find your brother? We will eat soon."

Before Shimon could answer, the outside door flew open and his younger brother appeared, excited and panting. He was already dressed in his usual brown cloak. He ran past his mother, tore off a piece from the bread that rested on a small table, and began to chomp on it enthusiastically.

Tirzah thought she had taught her twelve-year old son better manners. "Stop that! We will eat soon. Please wait a few moments."

"I must hurry, Mother," the boy replied with a full mouth. "The Prince sent for me this morning. Did you not hear the messenger at the door? I just talked with the Prince. He needs my assistance on an important mission east of Gibeah today."

"What missions is that?" Shimon asked mockingly. "What need does he have of a young boy like you, Yamin?"

The younger boy stuck out his chin. "He did not say, but who are you to question his commands? And I have told you many times, Shimon. Stop calling me Yamin! I am twelve years old and deserve to be treated like a man."

Before the exchange could escalate, Tirzah deftly intervened. "Here, son. I will wrap some figs and bread for you to take along. Take this flask also. On an important mission you will need nourishment. Do not keep the Prince waiting. Eat while you are traveling."

The young boy brightened. "Thank you, Mother. I am not sure how long I will be gone, but will be sure to return well before sunset." He took the food and water and gave his mother a hug. After giving his older brother a sideways look, he flew out the door, leaving it open.

The King's Palace was only a short distance down the street near the center of the city. The young boy was running quickly toward the main door when he heard his name called.

"Yamin! I am over here, ready to depart."

The boy stopped in his tracks and saw the Prince standing in the recess of a side door of the Palace. He ran to the Prince, oblivious to the use of his nickname. The Prince was tall and strong, and seeing him always inspired the boy. But today he appeared tired and distraught, and he kept looking up and down the street. The boy spoke loudly. "I see you have your new bow and a full quiver. Are we going on a hunt?"

Without answering, the Prince quickly ushered him around a corner and toward the small eastern gate of the city. They walked quickly through the empty streets without being seen. Once outside the city wall, they increased their pace. They moved past nearby rock outcroppings and out of sight of the guard towers.

The Prince stopped. "We will not be hunting today, my young helper. I merely want to try out this new bow and the special arrows I recently acquired. I should like to see if they fly as straight and true as promised. I will need you to find all the arrows and bring them back to me. Come. It is some distance to the newly cut wheat field where we can perform this test."

The boy knew it was not time to ask questions, but only to obey. He hurried along in the wake of his master. Their trailing shadows were very long as they hurried toward the rising Sun. The young boy loved the feeling of adventure, and was sure this would be a day to remember. If he served well, perhaps in a year or two he could replace Shimon as shield-bearer when his older brother advances in rank!

CHAPTER 5

FUTURE UNKNOWN

I AM NOW READY
IS THIS A NEW BEGINNING
OR THE END OF ME?

On the evening before Kawsay's thirteenth birthday, her mother, brother, and grandparents sat outside around a small fire and reminisced about all the happy times and adventures of the past thirteen years. Kusi told many stories of Kawsay and Yachay's all-night adventures he had observed when they were unaware of his presence. With his animated gestures and voice, he pretended to move stealthily around his small family and acted out Yachay teaching Kawsay to hunt, listen, fight, and climb. He made sure to point out he had always been known for his stealthy tracking skills, and no one would have been able to detect him, not even a great jaguar. Yet Yachay had eventually detected his presence.

As she stared into the fire, Kawsay's mother, Sumaq, told stories about her husband that Kawsay had never heard before. She spent hours telling everything she knew about her husband's childhood, their wedding, his devotion to his son, and his eager anticipation of his second child. Sumaq surprised her daughter when she suddenly took on a serious tone, looked Kawsay in the eyes, and said, "I never want you to forget this one fact, Kawsay. Our Chief was wise and let you live, but if the elders had decided you should be sacrificed, I had planned to take you into the jungle and escape with you. The two of us would have lived or died together, but I would not have gone through with the sacrifice. Never."

"What about me?" Yachay looked taken aback.

"We all would have gone together," Grandfather said quietly.

"Perhaps we should all go together this time as well," Yachay whispered.

"You know that would draw entirely too much attention, which would certainly put your sister's life in jeopardy," Asiri said quietly. "There are better ways. We can check on Kawsay. She will be safer without the whole community chasing us."

As the evening concluded, Kawsay's grandfather affirmed what her grandmother had told her many times – that she would be safe in the secret caves because they are difficult to find, and those who know the legends would avoid them. There was water there and the opening was midway up a cliff and difficult to get to, so she would not be bothered. He also went on to say that there were treasures in the caves that may prove useful as she grew older. When Kawsay pressed him on what he meant, he simply said, "You never know when something you may find that is of rare value may be useful to you. I don't know what your future holds, but it never hurts to have an invaluable item to trade for your life if the need arises."

That night Kawsay stayed at home rather than going out into the jungle. She was wide awake most of the night trying to imagine what lay ahead and what her new life would be like. It would soon be the dawn of her thirteenth birthday and she would be sent off to survive, or to perish, on her own. During the thirteen years of her life, no deformed babies had been born into their small tribe. For this, she heard, the Chief thanked the gods with each new birth! She was told that her departure was to be unceremonious because the Chief did not want to draw attention to her unique situation. Nevertheless, the Chief, who was growing older, had recently told her privately, "Kawsay, I will be very sad to see you go. We have been special friends. Yet I have wondered if the gods might have some important mission for you." More for Kawsay to ponder.

The predawn morning was still cool as a new day and a new life for Kawsay was beginning. She and her mother and brother arose while it was still dark. Kawsay's mother dressed her in layers of light clothing beginning with the colors of the jungle by day and then overlaid them with a heavier cloak of darker colors to get her though cooler nights. Sumaq stroked Kawsay's warm brown skin and almost black hair that reached nearly to her waist.

"You are a beautiful girl, Kawsay," Sumaq said. "Your lip is a tiny thing. Isn't that right, Yachay?"

"Of course she is beautiful, but she is also strong. Because of her lip she has learned to survive in the jungle better than any man.   Kawsay is a warrior and will be able to protect herself," Yachay responded with conviction.

"Yes, Kawsay, your name means 'to live', and you will," Sumaq said, still adjusting her clothes.

But Kawsay was remembering the many times the children in the village taunted her from afar, calling her "cat-face".

As dawn was breaking and the sky was beginning to glow, her mother, brother, grandparents, and the Chief gathered at the edge of the small village to see her off and give her final words of advice. She had mentally prepared for this moment all of her conscious life and promised herself she would not cry. She knew that at her mother's request, the Chief had given her a chance at life. She wanted to show respect and gratitude and also display the self-confidence she wished she had. Her brother had tears running down his handsome, angular face. He had Kawsay's large eyes and straight nose, but was nearly a head taller and more muscular.

"Run to the secret caves where you will find shelter," Sumaq said softly as she leaned down, adjusting the many belts and bags hanging from her daughter's small frame. "There are many caves in the mountains, but the *secret caves* are deserted and safe, with plenty of water, hidden caverns, and the jewels of the Earth."

"Yes I will," Kawsay assured her mother, wondering what the jewels of the Earth would look like.

The Chief doubted she would find the secret caves, but agreed that if she found them, she would not be bothered by other people in such a desolate and forbidding part of the mountains.

"When you believe you are very close to the secret caves, you should be very quiet and listen for the sound of the wailing lady up in the cliffs. A sound unlike any you have ever heard will guide you. Then, you must climb up and up to reach the opening into the caves," Asiri reminded her in a quiet whisper.

Kawsay nodded, thinking she had heard every sound the jungle could make. When she and Grandfather had camped at the base of the cliffs the previous year, she thought she *had* heard the soft wailing sound.

Her mother was again adjusting the bags and small clay containers that were tied to her. She was equipped with beans, corn, dehydrated potatoes, cereal, water, a wooden cup, a brightly painted bowl with birds, and a knife.

"This was given to me by my grandfather when I became a man. Even though you are a sweet young girl, you must also be a man." Grandfather reverently handed her a strangely-shaped, glittering, jeweled dagger with some small intricate markings. "*This* is one of the jewels of the Earth. You may find more where you are going. It is not of our people."

Yachay, still fighting back tears, handed her a spear and paraphernalia for fishing and hunting. "This is my first lucky spear. As you know, I am now using another lucky spear that is sized for a grown man." He leaned over her and whispered softly, "I have my tests in a few days; then I will come and find you." Stepping back he said, "I have made you a superior llama wool woven sling and here are a few good stones to fill it. And here is my favorite bola," he said, handing her three stones attached to lengths of llama tendons. "Remember, if the great cat threatens you, spin this in the air and propel it toward his legs before he leaps. He will become entangled and powerless and at your mercy. You just twirl and release, my sister, and you can land anything." Yachay knew she had thrown a bola expertly countless times, but he wanted to encourage her and psych her up for her journey.

"When possible, I will – in secret – come and find you to see if you are all right," Sumaq whispered through tears she could no longer hold back. "I will also send your brother after he finishes his tests."

The Chief pretended not to hear any of the whispered words from Kawsay's family about future contact. "You must not return to the village or make contact with your family, Kawsay. This was the pact I made with the tribe and especially those who have had to sacrifice their newborns. You must survive without help. The gods will determine your fate," the Chief said loudly, as much for the benefit of any eavesdropping tribe members as for Kawsay and her family. In a soft voice the Chief said, "And you, the members of Kawsay's family, must all make yourselves clearly visible to the tribe members for several days so that no one suspects you have gone with her into the jungle."

After final hugs from her grandfather, grandmother, brother, mother, and even the tearful Chief, Kawsay hesitated for just a moment and then took off in a sprint into the jungle without looking back. She was sure if anything slowed her down, it would not be a great jaguar, poisonous snake, or monster of the jungle, but rather the luggage she carried on her slim body. With a sense of excitement laced with fear, she ran as fast as she could in the direction prescribed by her grandparents. She was thankful Grandfather had taken her to the caves in the not-too-distant past, so at least she had some memory of how to find them.

The early morning jungle felt wet and cool, and she sensed things grabbing at her legs, arms, and head. She used Yachay's lucky spear to open the foliage before her as she ran through it. Her adrenaline denied any fatigue, but as the hours passed and the Sun rose overhead filtering through the treetops, she wondered how long she could continue before collapsing under the weight of her clothes, food, and weapons.

How long had she been running? The sweat had been pouring into her eyes for hours, and she felt frightened and anxious. No, she was not frightened. She had been running though this jungle her whole life. She was not afraid of anything. But why did she feel so different compared to every day and every night during the past ten years? Since she first could walk, she walked here. Since she first could run, she ran here. But now it seemed so strange, so foreign, so different, so … alone. No Yachay teaching her. No Grandfather secretly stalking her. Had she always known Grandfather was close by? Had she always somehow felt his presence? There was no one with her now. It was just Kawsay and the jungle.

As the day began to cool, she finally stopped to eat, rest, and get her bearings. There were bugs everywhere. Why had she not noticed how thick they were before? She looked around and realized she had climbed higher. She also could see that the Sun was slipping quickly down as the shadows across the valley rose upward. It was growing darker on the forest floor. She decided to walk toward her destination, still following the directions of her grandparents and watching for the landmarks from her last journey.

As she continued in a daze, she realized it was dark and she was running again. She became cognizant that she was hearing a noise, though she did not know if it had just begun or had been going on all evening. *Is that the wailing lady – or just a wild beast stalking me for dinner? Maybe I'm delirious!* She looked for a large tree to climb up for the night. She spotted a grand tree, climbed nearly half way up, found a comfortable niche, and fell instantly into a deep, dreamless sleep.

Shriek! Squawk! Squawk!

Kawsay leaped up out of a dead sleep and then quickly grabbed her branch as she remembered that she was lodged high in the air. She grasped her belongings as a large, brightly-colored bird shrieked down at her from an overhanging branch. She was not happy to be awakened in such a manner, but thanked her colorful neighbor for not letting her sleep away the day. *Is this a good omen*? she wondered. *A brightly-colored bird very close and waking me up.* If only she had been able to gather together with the other people in her village during the evenings when they told their stories and passed along legends to the next generation, then she would know what this meant. Yachay said she was not missing much, and people who murder their own babies are not worth listening to anyway. She had strained to listen from afar behind trees when she was little, but the panpipe music usually masked the voices. As she grew older and her night training became more rigorous, she used the early evenings to sleep so when her brother woke her after the village was quiet, she would be strong and awake to face the jungle at night.

She slid down from the tree and was off in a run, too excited for any thought of food. As the Sun rose in the sky and she felt the perspiration begin to make its way into her eyes, she remembered Yachay's words: "Eat and drink, little one, eat and drink. A warrior needs her strength!" Kawsay decided she would eat and drink – but keep running at the same time. She needed more water, so she decided she must look for the stream again. She saw it this morning; where was it and which way was it running? *Well I haven't crossed it, so I must be running at least somewhat parallel to it unless it bent away from me. How stupid I am!*

Grandfather said many times to keep track of the water. She stopped and listened. It was beginning to rain. She could hear the dripping. If she did not locate the stream quickly, the rain would make too much noise for her to find it, and she wanted to fill her water jugs. She thought of Yachay. He would know where to find the water. Suddenly, she felt sad and alone. She began to cry. She stood alone in the dripping forest for a long while, as her spirit seemed to dissolve in the warm rain.

Kawsay realized the danger of this kind of thinking and declared firmly out loud, "My family did not raise me to give up, but to be courageous and strong!" She closed her eyes and tried to hear any noise suggesting water. She thought maybe she could hear a rushing sound to her right. She slowly walked in that direction and saw a thick cloud of mosquitoes. She moved toward it and the ground became softer and wetter. *The stream must be here, and once I find it I should make sure I know where it is as I move toward the caves. Not only is the water a source of life, but the stream will guide me upward toward the base of the cliffs. How long have I been traveling? Was it just yesterday morning that I left?* She knew she had been moving faster than she and Grandfather had on their journey to the caves, but the trip would still take her several days.

She finally heard rushing water. "There it is!" she said aloud. Kawsay found a spot where the water was rushing over rocks. She expertly filled her small water jugs and tried to get her bearings. *Now I will continue my trek to the secret caves while monitoring the steam.*

The following two days she walked and ran in the direction of the sunrise, slept in trees, ate her dehydrated potatoes as she ran, and visited the stream for water, which mostly paralleled her route. The terrain was rough, and she had climbed up and slid down so many times she could not tell if she was ascending or descending in elevation. During much of the day, it was difficult for her to determine if she was even moving in the right direction.

On the morning of the fourth day of her trip, while she was getting her bearings at sunrise from high in a tree, she thought she caught sight of some steep cliffs, but the jungle was too dense to know for sure. She did not know how many days she had been running, but her food supply was noticeably shrinking. The day grew hot and the jungle was damp and thick. She had been climbing higher and higher. By evening she reached broad, sheer cliffs, which seemed strangely familiar and may be the ones she visited with Grandfather. *I will sit very quietly as the darkness falls and wait for the sound of the wailing lady to guide me to the secret caves.* She was weary and overtaken by thirst after the anguish of her journey. Kawsay drank as much water as she could hold and fell asleep.

She found herself standing behind a tree, listening to the haunting five-tone melody of the wooden panpipe instruments of her people. They were gathered around a huge fire. *What are they saying? I can't hear them. They're not talking, they're singing. Someone is singing!* Kawsay slowly awoke from this dream and realized she actually could hear a soft, strange, metallic moaning sound. *How long had it been going on?* she wondered. *Am I still asleep? Where was it coming from exactly?* She looked up the cliff in the light of an almost full Moon, closed her eyes, held her breath, and listened intently. *If these are the sounds of the wailing lady, and perhaps she only sings at night, then surely I will have to ascend the cliff tonight ... in the dark. I may not hear the lady sing tomorrow during the day or even tomorrow night.* Kawsay remembered climbing countless trees and small cliffs during her nights of training with her brother. If Yachay were here, he would definitely tell her to climb now.

Kawsay packed up her food, water, weapons, and all that she now owned, and she strapped them securely to her back. She listened again, eyes closed, moving side to side along the cliff until she was certain the sound was directly above her head. At that point she began to negotiate a path up the sheer cliff toward the sound. She tried to look up as she climbed, but could not see if the shelf Grandfather described was directly above her in her path. Her fingers hurt, and her legs and arms began to tremble with fatigue. *You are impervious to pain. You are stronger than any man.* Kawsay repeated Yachay's words to herself over and over. After what felt like hours of a grueling climb, with bloody fingers, her back breaking under the weight of her belongings, and her eyes and mouth full of sweat and pebbles, Kawsay reached a crevice in the cliff that she was certain was the location of the voice of the wailing lady.

The sheer sides of the crevice were bridged by a flat area of rock forming a shelf. The moonlight cast dramatic shadows across the ledge and revealed part of a small opening at the farthest point of the shelf. *That must be the cave entrance! This is certainly a safe place to live, with sheer faces of rock above, below, and to the sides.* She only hoped no one else already inhabited the cave, except the wailing lady, whom Kawsay was sure would be harmless. She was more than curious about what may await her in the cave but, on the off-chance it was unfriendly, decided she was too weary to venture into the darkness and face what could be lurking inside. Kawsay gently placed her belongings between the cave entrance and the cliff's edge and fell into a deep sleep.

At first light, Kawsay awoke and drank the last of her water, hoping that the cave would offer some sort of spring or run-off from the mountain above. She picked up her gear and crossed the threshold of the cave.

It was pitch black. *Of course*, she thought, *I must find some means of light if I am to live here.* She could hear dripping in the recesses of the interior. *Definitely a good sign.* She decided to slowly move toward the dripping. The air was cool and dank, but it would be a great place to be during the hot afternoons, she assured herself. There was an earthy, hard-to-describe smell and no sound except the dripping. She wondered where the bats were; surely there must be bats in here!

Suddenly, she heard the strange metallic sound of the wailing lady, although it seemed softer than last night. She crept closer toward the sound as her eyes slowly adjusted to the darkness. As she moved along, there appeared to be caverns and tunnels off to the sides. The sound was just in front of her now; it seemed to be coming through a solid rock wall. Or was it really a wall? It seemed elusive, shimmering. She studied it carefully, wondering if it was safe to touch. Then she realized that she had, in fact, been able to see, albeit dimly, since just after entering the cave. There was faint, diffuse light barely illuminating the halls and caverns she had passed by on her way toward the sound and the elusive wall. The cave must be very porous, and she wondered if all this light coming in was good or bad for her future safety and comfort. *Back to the wall. Is it safe to touch its shimmering surface? Oh well, what have I got to lose*? she thought, reaching toward the "wall".

As her fingers reached the wall they felt a light touch, but nothing solid. They kept going forward until her entire hand began to disappear! Quickly she jerked it back! Her pulse accelerated. *What is going on? Maybe I'm hallucinating! Grandmother warned of the bad spirits who caused hallucinations. Perhaps something got in my mouth when I was running. No, I began running through the jungle days ago! It would have affected me earlier. Well, maybe it didn't get into me until late last night.* Kawsay took a deep, slow breath. She held Yachay's lucky spear out in front of her and slowly stuck it into the wall. It too began to disappear as it entered! She decided this would be a good time to go find the dripping water and return to this mysterious "wall" later. She needed time to think. *Think before you do...think before you do.* That is what Grandfather always said.

As she continued walking beyond the elusive wall, Kawsay heard louder and louder drips. She entered a small cavern and faintly saw a pond, which was fed by a stream trickling down a carved-out rock. *This is a good time to fill my water jugs and clean the dirt and blood from my fingers.* She slowly approached the pond, wondering if there was anything living below its innocent-looking surface. She smacked the surface of the water and it splashed up. Then she waited. *No monsters.* She closed her eyes and stuck her fingers into the water. The water felt cold and smooth between her fingers. It smelled fresh, better than the streams along the trail. She carefully filled her jugs and washed her hands and face, swirling her hands around in the shallow water. *What's this?* Kawsay felt something wrap itself around her little finger. As she jerked out her hand, it brought along an object. She immediately realized it was not alive and then, feeling it carefully, perceived it was a string of oddly-shaped metal beads. *How strange! Why would a necklace be in this pond? Maybe this is one of the jewels of the Earth!* Instinctively she slipped it over her head, rose up, and stood there for a while.

"Hmm, now it's time to contend with the weird wall, or whatever it is," she said out loud as she turned around and began retracing her steps. She slowly approached the ever-so-faint sound. *This is definitely where the sound is coming from – the wall.* She decided to examine it again. It appeared to be very black and gauzy, yet somehow shimmering. The wailing increased, but then became almost inaudible. She timidly poked her spear through and back ... and through and back ... through and back ... through and back ... at least a hundred times until her arm got tired. *What to do? This is so strange. This is clearly a doorway to somewhere. How can I live here for the rest of my life and not know where this goes? Sooner or later I need to know what is in here – why not now? Besides, what's the worst that can happen? Can my life get any worse?* She bundled up her belongings and stepped tentatively through the elusive wall – a shimmering passage through the fabric of space and time.

Immediately, she felt herself being sucked down deep into the Earth by an irresistible force. She could not breathe! She panicked. This must be the beginning of the severe and painful death she used to overhear her people say she would surely endure once she was out on her own. She accelerated downward at a speed she thought impossible. It was too dark to know where she was or what was surrounding her. *The life is being sucked out of me. I'm dying.* She thought of Yachay. What would he think when he came looking for her and she was gone? Would he think she had been killed in the jungle and never made it? No, he would find her tracks and see that she *had* made it. And then, would he step through the elusive wall and die too? She could feel the blackness. She felt something holding tightly around her ankle. The air was being sucked out of her body. She was flying, flying through a tunnel. She felt herself gasping when...SMASH...she slammed into something hard and lost consciousness.

CHAPTER 6

SECOND CHANCE

A JOURNEY BEGINS
WHO CAN FORESEE THE OUTCOME
AS THE WAVES ENGULF.

"What a perfect day," Nate said, smiling at his father who was steering the 32-foot sloop *Second Chance* they had chartered for their 21-day tour of Caribbean islands and coves. It was the first full day of their voyage, and they were equipped with scuba and snorkel gear and two lockers of basic provisions.

"Could the water be a more spectacular shade of aqua?" John mused. "I wonder if the weather will hold for the whole trip."

"There's absolutely no one around – it's like we are the only people in the world!" Nate said, lifting his sunglasses and slowly looking about the sparkling sea.

"Seems so. It will give us some privacy and time to talk," John said, feeling very reluctant to broach the topic that would cause his son great distress.

"Right, privacy," said Nate absentmindedly. "There are a few dark clouds way out there. See 'em, Dad?"

"Yeah, there are a few dark ones out there."

There was a lull, but before John could introduce his topic, Nate spoke up. "Dad, do you think I'm going to grow more? You're pretty tall, and I'm getting worried that I won't catch up."

"Well, Nate, you never know. I grew a few more inches after I was your age, but then your mother and her family were on the short side. Does it bother you?"

"Yes and no. I mean, for a long time all the girls were taller than me, and at least I've caught up, but all guys wish they were taller. That martial arts training helped me feel more tough and all that, but, well, who wants to be short all his life?"

John turned to look at his son. "Honestly, Nate, I don't think you should count on being over six feet like me, but five nine or ten is very possible. You know history better than I do. Weren't there many great men who were huge on the inside regardless of their stature?"

"Yeah, I know. And there were some tall men in history who were not big heroes."

"You mean giants like Goliath?" John asked.

"No. I was thinking of King Saul. He was a head taller than everyone else and looked like a king. But he was kinda empty inside – didn't have the character to pull off the job. I really admire his successor, though – David had it all together."

"I admire King David too, but he had more than his share of problems. Seems his heart was right, though," John said.

"Your right, Dad. I wonder how tall he was," mused Nate.

Another lull. John knew he needed to return to his topic. He felt like he was acting in his own movie, and he did not like the plot. Seeing the gathering clouds, he knew he had to get it out before things got crazy.

"Nate."

"Yeah Dad?" Nate was again watching the approaching weather.

"I'm serious. There's, ah, something we should talk about," John said.

Seeing the furrows in his dad's forehead, Nate said, "Sure Dad, let's furl the sails and drift for a while. I'll get some water."

After dithering around the deck nervously, John finally sat down facing his son. He secured the wheel for a straight course. They both took generous sips from their bottles.

"Nate, you're sixteen now. You're not a boy anymore; you're a young man. You're not only the brightest kid I know, but you're unusually mature for your age."

"Thank you, Dad," Nate said, still distracted by the gathering black clouds.

"You remember when your mother died, she was so worried that you were too young to understand that she wasn't abandoning you. She wanted to make sure that I always told you how much she loved you."

"I know, Dad. It's not like she wanted to die. She is in heaven with the Lord waiting for us. I know you really care about me and will always be there for me no matter what. I'll always be there for you too." Nate sensed the wind pick up a little, but John was preoccupied with his difficult task.

"Thank you, Nate. I really appreciate that and believe you. You know, God has blessed us with this prosperous business I have and your genius intellect, so we've had a pretty good life even with your mother gone. I mean, how many sixteen-year-olds have all the credits they need to graduate high school? We have money put away for your college and graduate education. Anything you decide to do – no problem."

"I know, Dad, I really appreciate it, but what are you saying? I think it's going to rain." The sky seemed to reflect the fear Nate was starting to feel from his father's demeanor.

After looking down at his new deck shoes for what seemed like five minutes, John looked directly at his son and said words he had rehearsed carefully. "I went to see your Uncle Jack a few weeks ago ... in his office."

"Why would you go to Uncle Jack's office? He's a brain doc!" Nate pulled off the sunglasses he no longer needed, revealing growing concern in his dark green eyes. "What are you getting at, Dad?"

"Things don't look so good. And I think it is only fair to be honest with you. I, ah…" John trailed off as he noticed the storm had sneaked up and now towered over their heads.

"You mean cancer?" Nate asked. "Is that what you're saying?" John said nothing, but his steady eyes held the answer. Nate continued, growing agitated. "There must be something they can do! So what if it's cancer? Cancer doesn't have to be a death sentence these days!"

"And it wouldn't have been if I had only known earlier," John said shaking his head. "But I didn't have symptoms. I didn't even have many headaches."

"You never told me you were having headaches. You didn't say *anything* to me about it! Why didn't you trust me?" Nate was beginning to scream now, but so was the wind. Then tears began to fill his eyes and pour down his cheeks, mixing with the pellets of slanting rain. "Why didn't you go see Uncle Jack earlier? There must be something they can do! Massive chemo! Massive radiation! Some new genetic drug! You know – something!"

"When we get home I am going to do just that. I will try anything. I don't want me to die either. I just wanted to enjoy this vacation with you since it may be our last," John said evenly, as he swiveled around in the swaying vessel and hit the starter button on the diesel engine. He had played his part well and waited for the inevitable.

"When we get home? We've gotta get home right now, Dad! Please! We can't waste one minute when you could be getting treatment!"

"Fine, but right now we've got to get to shelter, Nate. No time to lose. These clouds are too dark. They don't look right. And this wind is getting to be way too much," John shouted into the gale.

At that moment, lightning struck the mast of the sloop, issuing a piercing crack and exploding the cabin roof. Nate was catapulted overboard. John heard a splash and realized his only son was in the water. Nate was dazed, but quickly became conscious of looking up toward the surface of the troubled sea. His dad was swimming down toward him. Nate knew he was deep in the water.

John swam strongly down toward what he thought was his son's blond head, but it seemed that Nate kept moving deeper and further away. John wanted to scream, but knew he would lose the little air remaining in his lungs.

Nate struggled up toward his father, but felt himself being pulled down by something like an undertow. But that made no sense since he was out in deep water. What was sucking him down? He could see his father fighting his way down toward him, and he thought he could make out an anguished look on his dad's face. But that was impossible. It was too dark. He must be imagining his face. He must be imagining all of this!

It feels like I'm entering a wind tunnel, a dark wind tunnel. I'm being stretched. I'm not breathing. The life is being sucked out of me. I'm dying. Here I come, Mom. Here I come, God. Am I breathing? Dad! Help me. Nate thought he felt something ripple past him in the opposite direction. Nate was shouting either in his mind or with his mouth, he couldn't tell which. He saw his mom when he was a boy before she died. She had long blond hair and green eyes like his. There was his dad smiling beside her. They were standing in front of a birthday cake with four candles on it. It was his cake. What a happy day! Nate thought he must be unconscious, only he could feel the air being sucked from his lungs and could perceive a swirling blackness. He felt like he was flying, flying through a tunnel...then suddenly twisting… SMASH! He slammed into something hard.

John had almost reached his son when Nate suddenly just disappeared from his sight. He looked around, his lungs bursting. He refused to give up, yet had no idea which way to swim to find his Nate. *Need more air, more air.* He kicked hard back to the surface, only to be rocked by a wave just as he was gasping for air. He came up once more, coughing, overwhelmed by the power of the angry sea. He caught sight of the *Second Chance*, smoking from the lightning hit and hopelessly blowing further and further away. He dove downward in a last attempt, hoping Nate would return to him, but he saw nothing. *Where is my son?*

CHAPTER 7.

LIFE ANEW

MAY – PRESENT YEAR
SIERRAS, CALIFORNIA

MY SOUL IS ADRIFT
IN THE SEA OF CREATION
IN SEARCH OF ITS HOME.

Kawsay's breath had returned to her. She awoke suddenly with the feeling someone, or something, had nudged her. It was very dim, but not totally black. The air was damp and smelled earthy. Her legs hurt. *I wonder how far I fell. I must have ended up at a lower level of the cave.* But it felt different somehow. It appeared that she was in some sort of chamber, maybe twice the size of her house in the village. Would she ever see home again? She remembered that she no longer had a home. She must figure out where she is now.

She slowly stood up and felt stiff, as if her joints had all frozen and refused to bend. She felt as if someone or something was watching her. She looked toward the dark recesses of the small chamber and thought she detected movement. She became fully alert and then became aware of a different smell, an animal smell. *This can't be good.* She slowly turned around and saw what looked like a doorway. She realized the dim light in the chamber was coming through the doorway behind some kind of huge animal. *Oh no! A great jaguar has followed me and trapped me here!* But this monster was bigger than any jaguar she had ever seen. It had a bulky head, a long snout, and shaggy fur. She could feel the blood slowly drain out of her head and thought she was now experiencing her first real test of courage, her first encounter with true danger. Would she be a coward and faint? Against her will, Kawsay felt her body turn to jelly as she slowly slumped into a puddle of human fear on the cold rock floor. In the safety of unconsciousness she dreamed about hugging the neck of the Chief's jaguar stool. She could feel its warmth.

Slowing awakening and trying to get her bearings, she became aware she was again someplace new. The air was damp and earthy, though, and she could still smell the beast. She slowly opened her eyes, squinting to see and wondering if she would be pounced on, torn to shreds, and devoured. She could see an enormous ceiling sparkling above the huge, dimly lit room. Kawsay opened her eyes wider and was amazed at the stalactites, stalagmites, and vast arrays of twisting helictite crystals surrounding her. She was in a giant sparkling jewel box. This must be the jewels of the Earth her grandparents had told her about! She thought she could stay there forever, lost in its spectacular beauty. The ceiling was laced with crystalline vines, many of which looked to be as long as she was tall. She heard a stream. She lay there listening to it for a moment while taking in the luminous beauty above her. *At least I will be looking into the heavens when I die.*

"Mhh. Mhh." Kawsay heard someone, or something, clear its throat. *Oh yes, the monster.* She turned her head ever-so-slightly to the left and peeked out of the corner of her eye. To her surprise the great beast was sitting about ten paces away staring at her. Its eyes seemed compassionate, almost loving. She suspected it may be waiting for her to faint again. It was shimmering silver against the sparkling background, but appeared monstrously powerful. It definitely was not a jaguar, not cat-like at all. From where she lay, it looked more like some kind of giant dog! Just sitting there, it seemed to be as tall as she was.

"You're safe. Do not fear," said the beast in a soft, deeply resonant voice. Kawsay had never heard English spoken before and interpreted this as a muffled growl. Kawsay had given into fear earlier after she awoke from that awful sucking tunnel experience, and she vowed she would no longer, not ever, be a victim of fear again. Besides, if this silver beast had wanted to devour her, it surely would have by now, so at least she had that in her favor. She slowly sat up so as not to make any fast movements and provoke the predator's chase instincts.

The silver beast just continued to sit there watching her with intelligent light blue eyes as she cautiously rose up to a sitting position. Then the beast yawned and stretched out lazily on the cave floor. It could relax now that she had demonstrated she had survived her travels and appeared to be functional. She stared at it uneasily as it stared back at her calmly but with curiosity. *All right, now it is time to stand up, slowly, and see if I can get free of my guard, if indeed escape is possible. I will need food, and I want to see the Sun again.*

Kawsay gently rose to a standing position. The beast remained still. Now that she was standing, she could get a look at this magnificent, massive cavern. She must be very deep below ground because the ceiling was so high above her, or perhaps she was in a hollow mountain. Kawsay had never seen anything like this amazing world of sparkling, glittering rock, if that's what it was. Ah, now she could see the water – a subterranean stream, skirted by clear, sparkling pools, running along the far end of the great room. She slowly walked toward the stream and noticed that the wall along the far side was glistening. There was a thin sheet of water cascading down the wall feeding into the stream. She moved along the stream and its pools in the direction of its apparent origin. It appeared the stream was fed not only from the glistening sheet of water, but also from below in a rounded corner of the cavern. As she was trying to examine where the stream was bubbling up from, she wished there was more light so she could see better. *Where is the light coming from anyway?* "Ah, two tiny vents up near the edge of the ceiling are letting in dim streams of light," she whispered in a barely audible voice. The tiny jets of light that came in from above were amplified as they reflected off the crystalline ceiling and walls, resulting in a diffuse luminous glow. She looked over at the beast to verify that it had not moved. It was still there, thankfully, big and commanding, but apparently unconcerned with her.

A giant silver dog who seems friendly. A sparkling, glittering, heavenly place. What is really going on here? Kawsay wondered. *Maybe I am dead after all. I am so very sleepy and weary.* She had not slept much during the preceding days and was famished. Kawsay sensed her weakness and decided to try to get some rest. She could figure this all out later. She would need food, and she would need to understand where she was and what was real and what she may be imagining. She wondered where her belongings were as she slipped into a much-needed sleep next to the stream.

Kawsay dreamed she was safe and warm in the Chief's tent, again hugging the neck of his carved jaguar stool, only it was much larger, warmer, and softer. While holding on she began to float up a long tunnel, up and up and around from side to side. She definitely was not experiencing the horrible sucking tunnel. This was a smooth, warm, peaceful ride on the back of the Chief's stool. Or was it? It was too large and warm to be a wooden stool. Was she really dreaming? The next thing Kawsay became aware of was voices, new voices – with faces – looking down at her! It was nighttime, and she was in the open air in the doorway of some large structure. Two people were looking down at her. They did not seem threatening, but they did not look like any people she had ever seen before either. She contemplated her options. *I can run, or fight, or speak, or…*

The strange people bent down and spoke to her in a peculiar language she had never heard before. "Are you OK, honey?" the woman said.

Alison Hunter had been sitting in bed beside her sleeping husband, thumbing through the latest issue of the *American Journal of Archaeology*. She looked down at Ben. He looked so peaceful. He had a slight smile on his face. Ben always smiled when he looked at Alison. *Maybe he's dreaming about me.* She admired his ruggedly handsome looks with wavy dark brown hair and olive skin. She remembered the first time he looked at her under his bushy eyebrows – those light brown eyes with gold sunburst centers. He was tall and athletic and appeared younger than his forty-two years, but Alison didn't look her thirty-nine years either.

Ben often said he "married well". Alison was a strong, yet gentle, woman with an intelligent and curious mind. She was petite with a slim, athletic build. Her wavy, medium-length, light brown hair framed a pretty oval face with dark blue eyes and a spray of freckles.

They had been married three years, yet he was still something of a mystery to Alison with his ever-so-slight accent she could not place. Ben's brother, Helmut, had described how Ben was adopted into the family. Alison thought Ben was generally a happy person, but noticed a bit of sadness hiding in his soul. Alison looked over at her bedside table at the latest haikus he had written to her and hidden in her bathroom drawer just that morning. *What a romantic he is – I love him so deeply.* She picked up the poems to read again and put into her little book where she kept them.

My darling Alison:

Thank you for waiting
Your faith in God's provision
Has brought me to you.

My forest retreat
Did not become my true home
'Til it was our home.

Beyond "I love you"
Only one more truth exists:
You are my soul mate.

Alison decided to pen some haikus for Ben. *Where would be a good spot to leave these so I can surprise him in the morning?*   She began writing:

My beautiful Ben
My life began when we met
I love your sweet soul.

THUD … THUD … THUD.   Suddenly she was startled – it was as if an enormous hand was banging against their strong wooden door. One night last week a couple of raccoons fought over her prized tomato plant at midnight on the front deck, but this did not sound like raccoons sparring.

THUD …THUD …THUD.

Alison dropped her pen, her eyes wide.

"Ben. Wake up!" she whispered urgently as she gently shook is arm.

"Huh? I'm awake," her husband responded in a crackly voice.

"You always say that when you're sleeping."

"I do?"

THUD … THUD … THUD.

"I hear it," Ben said jumping out of bed and to his feet faster than his wife's eyes could track him. "Maybe it's a neighbor."

"We don't have any neighbors," Alison whispered loudly back while hopping out of bed behind her husband and reaching for an old Roman sword artfully displayed on the bedroom wall.

Ben lifted one of his eyebrows at her, turned, and headed for the living room.

THUD …THUD … THUD.

Ben swiftly crossed the living room, turned on the porch light, and peeked through the eye-level, miniature round window embedded in the door.

"I can't see anything," he mumbled. "That's funny. Wait a minute, it looks like something down on the ground – just lying there." He looked back at Alison who was holding the long Roman sword up in the air. *Why the sword instead of the shotgun?* he wondered. "You look cute with that sword, Alison." Ben smiled at her.

Alison and Ben cautiously opened the front door to find a petite young girl lying in a heap on the porch. "How could such a fragile girl make all that pounding noise?" Alison asked. The girl opened her eyes and looked up at them, revealing a mix of fear and curiosity.

"Are you OK, honey?" Alison said as she knelt down next to the girl.

Kawsay froze. *They seem friendly. What should I do?* Kawsay wanted to trust someone and feel safe after the past several days of running through the jungle, falling through a sucking tunnel that nearly killed her, and then encountering the mysterious silver beast.

Alison and Ben saw the girl begin to relax, and they gently reached out to her as Alison said, "Come on inside, honey, and let's get you something to eat." Ben noticed the look of fear and confusion on her face and motioned with his hand and mouth as if he was eating.

Kawsay cautiously responded to their kind gesture and began to sit up. Alison and Ben helped her into the house, across the living room, and through a large doorway into a grand kitchen. As Ben flipped on the switch and the room lit up, Kawsay squinted from the bright light. She had never seen any house this big and bright. There were shiny pots and pans hanging from the ceiling, giant shiny surfaces, and almost endless unfamiliar objects. *I know I shouldn't trust these peculiar people, but Grandfather always said to rely on my instincts. They do seem harmless, and I'm so tired.*

"Come on, honey. Sit down, and we'll get you some good food. This is my favorite chair," said Alison in her most nurturing voice as she patted the back of a beautifully carved chair. They had the opportunity to see her more clearly in the bright interior light. The girl was not large, only about five feet tall, but lean and strong. She was very striking, with a straight nose, high cheekbones, and long brown, almost black hair. They quickly noticed a cleft upper lip.

"I'm pretty sure she doesn't understand us," said Ben as he began rooting through the refrigerator looking for the leftovers from their lasagna lunch. "She looks Hispanic. Maybe she is a new immigrant from Mexico or South America and got separated from her parents. Ah, there's the lasagna."

Ben set the lasagna on the counter, walked over to the table, gently squeezed Alison's shoulder, and sat down next to the girl. "¿Habla usted Español?" he asked her in his best Spanish.

Kawsay understood that these strange people were trying to communicate with her, but she did not know how to respond. She had lived a life of people shunning her because of her lip and did not understand why these people were not ignoring her, as had everyone she ever knew except her family and the Chief. She reached up with her right hand and touched her deformed lip as if to assure herself that she was still repulsive.

"Well, let's just have some lemonade and lasagna and talk later," Alison said as she softly patted the girl's shoulder and walked over to the counter where her husband had left the lasagna.

"There are other languages spoken in South America," Ben said. "We can call Herschel Rhodes tomorrow; he knows every language under the Sun. She must be very poor, or someone would have corrected her cleft lip many years ago."

Kawsay saw the kind woman pick up the bright blue container the man had set down, and place it inside a white box. There was a soft hum followed by a high startling ring. Then the woman took the container back out of the box. It was steaming and smelled wonderful! The woman then opened a larger box, withdrew a container of yellow liquid, and poured it into three cups. She scooped the steaming food onto three plates and brought them over to the large flat table with four beautifully carved legs. Kawsay watched the strange people slowly begin to eat the appetizing food and decided to do the same. The food, whatever it was, was delicious and she decided to not think, but to just enjoy a warm meal. They ate in silence.

"I think I'll take her into the bathroom for a nice hot bath," Alison said as she was finishing her snack. "The poor thing looks like she hasn't bathed for weeks."

"I'll clean up the dishes," Ben said getting up from the table. He noticed the girl looking around the room as if she had never seen a modern kitchen before in her life.

Kawsay was trying to understand her new surroundings – all the colors, textures, and objects. Some resembled things she had seen before, like the ceramic cup across the room, and yet some objects looked strange and foreign. The nice woman was speaking and wanting her to go someplace. Kawsay felt hesitant for a moment, but then decided to go with the woman. *What's the worst that can happen?*

Alison led the girl through the back of the kitchen and into a long hall that led to the back bedrooms and bathrooms. The house was a giant log cabin that had been augmented with new rooms several times. Alison had requested a bright modern kitchen when she married Ben three years ago and began spending weekends and summers there. "Ah, here we are," Alison said as she guided the girl into a large bathroom and turned on the lights. The room had a white tile floor accented with cobalt blue tiles, white walls mostly covered with mirrors, and a cobalt blue tile counter with two cobalt sinks. Alison thought it was a stunning room. "Here," she said, pointing to the over-sized, antique claw-foot tub in the far corner of the room. Alison crossed the room and began filling the tub with crystal clear hot water. "Let's get you a big fluffy towel," she said, opening a floor-to-ceiling closet and retrieving a cobalt blue towel and handing it to the girl. Alison saw the perplexed look on the young girl's face. Kawsay was examining every detail of the bathroom with curious eyes. Alison noticed her staring at the toilet and wondered if she knew how to use it. "Here," she said lifting the toilet lid and flushing it to show the girl how it worked. The girl seemed surprised at the flushing event. "You just sit on it and voila… Oh dear."

Kawsay was in awe of the giant house with all the pretty rooms and unusual objects everywhere. This was almost as stunning as the giant, jewel-filled cavern she first arrived in after the elusive wall and the sucking tunnel. The woman was motioning her to come over to the tub, splashing her hand in the water. The women helped her with her tunic and sandals and assisted her into the hot water. Alison noticed the girl was wearing a necklace that looked like it belonged in a museum. It had oddly-shaped gold and silver beads. *They look like peanuts! I need to get a good look at that later.*

"There you go. Just sit there and relax. I'll put these clothes in the wash and get you something clean to wear. Here's some nice soap and shampoo." Alison smiled at the girl genuinely and then decided to demonstrate the soap by rubbing it on her own skin. She then held the shampoo while pointing at her head. Just to be sure, she also gave a short pantomime of Toilet 101. She then stepped out of the room, closing the door behind her, but leaving it slightly ajar.

Kawsay slowly slid into the warm, foamy water. She was beginning to relax when she realized with a pang of fear that she did not know where all her belongings had gone – Yachay's old spear, Grandfather's jeweled dagger, her cloak, bola, sling, bags, small clay containers carrying what remained of her food, as well as her wooden cup, brightly painted bowl, and knife. All she had was her new necklace that she inspected more closely for the first time in the bright light. Kawsay felt too warm and full to worry about all that now, although the idea that she lost her belongings was disturbing. She wondered who these pale strangers were, with their funny clothes, and why they were being so nice to her. Didn't they realize no one was allowed to speak to her except her family?

"How's the girl?" Ben kissed his wife as she entered the kitchen.

Alison smiled. She could tell her husband was curious about their visitor. He loved solving problems, and the girl certainly was an unknown. "Did you see this interesting tunic?

And those sandals? Her clothing looks like something from an ancient culture," Alison said showing her husband the camouflage-printed tunic Kawsay's mother had made for her journey. "And don't you think it's odd that we heard all that pounding on the door, and then the girl was asleep on the porch? It's as if someone knocked until the light went on and then took off and just left her there."

Ben was examining the tunic. "But we're in the middle of nowhere. Why would someone bring her all the way up here?"

"Maybe we should call the sheriff and see if there's a missing persons report," said Alison.

"If she doesn't speak English, she probably isn't an American citizen and wouldn't have been reported," Ben said looking at his wife.

"Maybe she's deaf or doesn't speak," Alison mused. "We need to make a noise behind her and see if she responds. She *is* self-conscious about her lip, though. Did you see her touching it earlier?"

"I did. We need to figure out if she does speak and hear, and if so, what language. I'll give Herschel a call and see if he can come up and meet her."

Bark! Bark! Bark! Their Great Dane puppy came galloping into the kitchen.

"Hey, Junior, where were you when we needed you? Did you break out of your doggie-door earlier tonight? I don't want you running around the forest at night – there are mountain lions out there. I am going to have to work on his doggie door again," Ben said as he cradled Junior's face in his hands and looked into the puppy's happy eyes.

"I'd better go check on the girl. She may have been startled by Junior tromping down the hall." Alison patted Junior and kissed Ben's forehead. "You're enjoying this; aren't you, honey?" she said with a smile as she left the kitchen. Alison stopped by her room to retrieve a clean nightgown and robe and then knocked as she stepped into the bathroom. The girl was standing in front of the sink wrapped in a cobalt towel looking toward the door. "Hi." Alison smiled as she presented a mint green nightgown and robe to Kawsay. Alison placed the robe on the counter and held the nightgown out so it fell open in front of the girl. "I'll drain the tub while you get dressed. I see you liked the soap."

Indeed Kawsay did enjoy the fragrant, slippery bar that seemed to lighten her skin appreciably, but now she was focused on the delicate lacy nightgown. She examined it thoroughly before pulling it over her head. It fell almost to the floor on her small frame. She lifted the robe off the counter and looked at its tiny, perfect stitching. *The thread is so fine and delicate*, she thought as she slipped her arms into the soft sleeves.

Alison had been watching the girl carefully examine the robe. Alison pulled a hairbrush and some detangler out of a drawer next to the sink and began slowly brushing Kawsay's long hair. *This could take a while,* she thought as she noticed the many snarls. *The girl seems to be used to having someone brush her hair – she has a mother who brushes her hair, but didn't find a way to fix her lip? How odd...*

The girl's back was toward the door as Alison heard Junior romping down the hall in the direction of the bathroom. Kawsay suddenly stiffened and abruptly turned toward the door with concern in her eyes. Her face was tight, and her eyes were round. At that moment Junior plowed his way through the unlatched door with his tail wagging and the "traveling chalkboard" in his mouth. "That's Junior!" Alison set the hairbrush down as Junior trotted over to her. "Here boy, let's see what you've got." Alison slipped the smooth wooden stick from Junior's mouth. There was a short link chain attaching a miniature, six-inch square chalkboard. "Let's see, what did Daddy write on this?" The small chalkboard had the words **"Hot Chocolate!"** written on it. "This is how Ben and I send messages to each other because Junior always knows where we both are." Alison brought the puppy closer to Kawsay and said "Junior" as she touched his back with both hands. "Junior," she said again looking at the girl.

Kawsay stared at the obviously harmless canine for a moment, realizing how silly it would be to regard it as she would a wild jungle animal. Her muscles relaxed and a slight smile washed over her face – the first smile she felt from herself in what seemed like a very long time.

"It's OK, you can pet him," Alison said as she gently shoved Junior closer to the girl. Kawsay tentatively reached out toward him as Junior lifted his head to sniff her fingertips. Kawsay felt happy.

"Well, let's go get some hot chocolate," Alison said, patting Junior and ushering the girl into the hallway.

As they entered the kitchen, Ben was sitting at the table with the three hot drinks. Ben had been running all the possibilities of the girl's background through his mind.

"She *can* hear," Alison said casually, answering one of their earlier questions. "She could hear Junior running down the hallway before he barged into the bathroom."

"Has she said anything at all?" Ben asked as he motioned for Kawsay to sit in front of one of the steaming cups.

"No, but let's see if she will. I think she likes Junior," Alison said as she presented Junior to the girl and repeated "Junior, Junior" while nodding her head and looking at Kawsay. "Junior. Can you say that, dear?" Alison gently took Kawsay's hand and placed it on Junior's head and repeated his name slowly three times.

Kawsay smiled tentatively and made a "Ju" sound, but then stopped abruptly at the foreign sound of her own voice. She had not spoken aloud to any human being since she was sent away from her family.

"Good! That's good," said Alison, smiling encouragingly. "That's enough for now. Let's just enjoy some cocoa and then get some sleep. I bet you're exhausted. You've probably come a long way."

Kawsay was amazed how good her hot drink tasted, and she felt warm and relieved that these strangers were so kind to her. She suppressed any suspicious feelings that may have been lurking in the back of her mind toward them and instead thought of their kindness. She made a conscious effort to not think any bad thoughts or entertain any of her worries about her things, her brother following her, or where she was. As the two strange people chatted away, she quietly sipped her wonderful hot drink and examined the bright kitchen and what she could see through the doorways into other rooms.

After they finished, Alison led the girl into one of the bedrooms off the main hallway. The room was as big as the kitchen and furnished mostly in white and gold with warm green accents. The walls were made of logs that had been sanded and polished to a smooth fawn color. Kawsay was so weary and overwhelmed with all that had happened to her, she did not even notice the soft fluffy bed the nice woman was helping her crawl into. Kawsay was asleep before Alison gently closed the door to the guest room.

"Herschel Rhodes here," the professor said absentmindedly as he picked up his phone.

"I had a feeling I'd catch you in the office on a Saturday morning when you should be antique shopping with your wife," laughed Ben into the carved mahogany speakerphone Herschel had given him the previous Christmas.

"Are you using that expensive phone I gave you to harass me, Professor Hunter?" Herschel responded. "We in the linguistics department actually come to school and do some work on occasion, unlike you archaeology types who always seem to be digging around someplace else."

"Speaking of which, Alison and I dug up something, or someone, mysterious last night that I thought your vast knowledge and expertise might be able to resolve for us. This someone is a young girl whom we discovered sleeping on our front porch after we heard some loud thuds on the front door. She looks Hispanic or something, but doesn't speak English or Spanish." Ben paused. "I was hoping to get you two together sometime soon since you know every language ever spoken under the Sun."

"That's it; butter me up a little bit, old friend," Herschel laughed.

Alison barged into their home office and unloaded her arms onto the large carved desk. "Look at this, will you dear? I was looking for Junior, and all this stuff was on the porch. It couldn't have been there last night or we would have seen it."

"Hi Alison!" Herschel's voice came though the speakerphone.

Ben began to examine the brightly colored artifacts displayed before him. "Wow, you found these things on the porch?"

"What's going on over there, you two?" Herschel chimed in.

"Hi Herschel," Alison called out. "We found a young girl and now this stuff. Wait a minute ... that looks Mayan ... no, wait! That's an Inca bola, but that jeweled dagger doesn't look like it belongs with the rest of the items. What would this young girl be doing with something so exquisite?"

"Herschel, you really need to see this," Ben said enthusiastically.

"I'm on my way; this sounds too good to miss. I'll bring some picture books and language books from Central and South America for the girl. We can see if she recognizes anything," Herschel said. Herschel had detected an excited tone in his old college roommate's voice that he had not heard for a very long time.

"You're welcome to bring Grace, and you two can stay the night if you like," Alison called out to the speakerphone.

"Drive safely," Ben mumbled as he was carefully examining each item. "This stuff is amazing. I'm glad you're coming."

"Thanks. We'll see you up there in a few hours. I'll go kidnap Grace from choir practice and bring her along."

"Wait! I almost forgot – there's one more thing I found. Wolf prints around the front of the house. Really big ones," Alison recounted, suddenly very serious.

"A timber wolf around here?" asked Ben with a concerned look.

"They're way too big," Alison responded. "I'd say about twice the size of any wolf print I've ever seen."

"You two stay safe indoors. We'll be up there ASAP." Herschel clicked off.

"I think I better go check on the girl," Alison said.

Alison slowly cracked open the guest room door trying not to wake the girl if she was still asleep, when she realized the bed was empty and the window was wide open. Pushing open the door, Alison entered the room to see if the girl was anywhere inside. After looking in both closets, the adjoining bathroom, and under the bed, she left the room, hollered for her husband, and ran down the hall through the living room and out the front door. "Hello, hello! Where are you?" Alison called out.

Across the landscaped yard about seventy-five feet away from the house, Junior barked once. He was standing directly under one of their tallest Douglas fir trees, enthusiastically wagging his tail. Alison jogged over to join Junior under the tree where she could view the yard and forest from the dog's perspective. "What is it, boy?" she asked, patting his shoulder and looking around. Junior barked again, looking up to her eyes and then over her head. Alison looked up following Junior's eyes and saw that the girl was perched high up in the tree where the branches were dangerously thin. "Oh my," she murmured. Then she shouted, "Ben, I think we need Helmut's helicopter!"

Ben heard his wife call him and was now jogging over to join her at the bottom of the tree.

"My crazy brother with his homemade chopper? He's probably out somewhere hunting Bigfoot!"

"Oh come on, dear. You two love each other. How in the world do you think she got up there?" Alison asked pointing up to the small figure of a girl teetering a hundred feet over their heads.

"He'd probably blow up the tree trying to rescue her," Ben answered, still thinking about his nutty brother, but contemplating how to rescue the small girl in his tree. "How in the world did she get up there is the operative question. But she *did* get up there somehow, and maybe she can climb back down."

"Well, either she's like a kitten and climbed up but can't get back down, or she is capable of both and just needs some encouragement – like breakfast," Alison suggested.

"Anyone who could climb straight up that tree deserves some sort of reward," said Ben, in awe that the girl could actually get that far up without a crane.

Kawsay had awakened with the tree-filtered sunlight streaming into her window and for a moment had forgotten where she was. She had not really seen the beautiful room the night before, but as she looked around in the morning light, she was struck by the beautiful fabrics, textures, and strange objects surrounding her, including a huge overstuffed green chair. She spotted her tunic folded neatly just inside the door on a lace-covered white dresser. Kawsay slid out of bed, walked slowly over to a large window, and parted the sheers. She tapped her fingers on the glass and moved them in large circles, wondering how such a thing could be made so clear and big. Beyond the window was a forest that seemed familiar, yet was somehow different from her home. It felt different, and through the partly opened window, she could tell that it smelled different as well. *I need to explore this place and determine if I may be close to home.* She had no idea that her home was not only far away, but in a different time altogether – a concept she would have trouble grasping. Kawsay turned to retrieve her tunic, dressed herself, neatly folded the mint green nightgown, and returned to the window. She examined the screen covering the open section of the window and slid the glass to expose more of this strange mesh material. She began pushing and pulling the screen in all possible directions until she saw that it could be slightly raised and pushed out. The screen fell to the deck and startled Junior, who had been resting in a warm spot where the sun made its way through the tall forest trees. The puppy trotted over to investigate.

Kawsay jumped up onto the window ledge and down to the deck in a single fluid motion. She looked around at the groomed yard encircled by tall trees and then down at Junior expectantly wagging his tail. Kawsay ducked under the railing, jumped to the ground, and cautiously proceeded across the front yard to the edge of the forest. She looked up at a tall tree and decided she could view the terrain much better if she were at the top. At that thought, Kawsay clambered straight up the trunk of the tree. Beautiful statuesque pines, cedars, and firs surrounded her – this was not her jungle. Kawsay wondered where in the world she had ended up. *Everything looked so different. Where is Yachay? Did he follow me? Are Mother, Grandmother, and Grandfather worried about me?* Kawsay began to feel tears well up in her eyes and immediately berated herself for not being able to suppress them. She heard a noise coming from the house, saw the door fling open, and heard the nice woman call loudly. Junior barked, and the woman came over to her tree. Kawsay wondered if she should try to hide her presence. At that moment, the man came out of the house and ran over to stand with the woman. Junior betrayed her location, and she knew she had been found. At that moment, the man began making eating motions with his hand and mouth, which Kawsay could see from her high perch, and he was saying something loudly to her. *This doesn't look or feel anything like home! Where am I? Why am I looking for home anyway? I have no home anymore.* Feeling hungry and overwhelmed, she decided to descend, which she did with amazing speed and grace.

"Wow!" Alison gasped as she grabbed Ben's arm and watched the girl literally glide down the tree. "She moves like a monkey! How can she even hold on to the trunk, let alone climb, or should I say slide, down it? I would have cuts and bruises all over me if I tried that."

"I'd be dead if I tried that," Ben said.

Kawsay noticed the astonished look on their faces and wondered if they had now, for the first time, gotten a clear look at her lip and realized what a mistake they made by being nice to her. She looked down at the ground and contemplated whether or not she should run away now or wait for a full stomach, that is, if they still wanted her to eat with them.

"Come on, dear, let's get you something good for breakfast. Mmmm, what should we have?" Alison said as she put her hand gently on the girl's shoulder, and they began walking toward the house. The late spring air felt soft with just a hint of moisture and diffused an earthy smell. Kawsay wondered where she was and began to feel her heart ache for her family.

"How about whole wheat waffles with blueberries along with some scrambled eggs with spinach and cheese?" Ben suggested, beginning to realize how hungry he felt. The three of them walked back to the house in the morning sunlight that danced through the tall pines and firs surrounding the old log cabin. They had forgotten about the fearsome wolf tracks. Kawsay felt secure, at least for now. Once in the kitchen, Alison stirred up the scrambled eggs while Ben made blueberry waffles in his chrome-plated waffle iron. Kawsay felt happy and grateful that she found nice people. She wished she could somehow let her family know she was being cared for and tell them about all the wondrous things she was seeing and experiencing. *But Yachay probably followed me to the secret caves and couldn't find me. They probably think I'm dead!*

Alison had been talking nonstop since they arrived in the kitchen. Kawsay could not understand her, but the chatter was somehow soothing – like Grandmother who also talked constantly even when she thought she was alone.

Ben was deep in his own thoughts, wondering what to do about the girl. *If Herschel can figure out her language and we can use her belongings and language to find her home, we should get her back as soon as possible. Her family must be terribly worried, unless she was abandoned. But she seems so sweet; no decent person would abandon her.* He could tell Alison was as concerned as he was because she always chattered faster and faster the more nervous she became. It was one of her personality traits he thought was so endearing. "What are you saying, honey?" Ben asked in a voice he hoped would not alert her to the fact that he had not heard a thing she said.

"I was just explaining why some spices are so healthy to our young guest and wondering out loud if she uses any of the spices we use at her home even though I know full well she can't understand a word I'm saying. I know, I know, dear. You know how I babble when I'm trying to work things out in my head," Alison said in one breath and then made a conscious effort to stop talking.

The food was delicious, and there was so much of it that Kawsay was happy to just sit and eat while she continued her curious examination of everything she could see in the kitchen. She could also see through the doorway into the huge, rustic living room, which had log walls and a high ceiling crisscrossed with climbable rafters. The nice man and woman were smiling a lot at each other and talking in their strange language. They seemed to really enjoy each other and touched each other a lot.

After breakfast, Alison offered Kawsay a flowered T-shirt and some leggings she had recently bought for herself and not yet worn. While Alison outweighed Kawsay by about fifteen pounds, she thought the clothes would still fit. Kawsay was happy to have something new and different to wear and eagerly changed into the new outfit.

Once Kawsay was dressed, Alison took her on a tour of the house, hoping it would make her young guest feel more comfortable. Alison explained that each room had its own unique character, beginning with the living room, which was the original cabin. A massive rock fireplace and hearth took up most of one wall in an otherwise log room with a high open-beam ceiling. There were three doorways off the living room. One doorway led to a large sunroom covered on two sides with windows. The room had sliders to the deck and three large skylights. This was the original bedroom of Ben's eccentric brother, Helmut. The second doorway off the living room, opposite the front door, opened into a long hall that ran to the back of the cabin. The third doorway, next to the hallway, opened into the huge chef's kitchen and dining area. Off the hallway there were several guest rooms, each with small bathrooms, and the main guest bathroom where Kawsay had bathed. At the end of the hall were Alison and Ben's large office and master suite. Also off the main hall was a circular stairwell leading up to a large library and modest museum containing various artifacts they had collected on their archeological adventures.

Alison was slowly walking around the library museum with Kawsay when the girl stopped and stared at an old arrow Ben had with his Holy Land collection.

That arrow looks exactly like Yachay's arrow. Could Yachay have been here? Kawsay's brow furrowed as she wondered how Yachay's arrow could be here. *The nice woman doesn't seem to make any connection between the arrow and me. Wouldn't she know that Yachay and I are related? Wouldn't she have hidden the arrow from me if she was hiding Yachay?*

Alison noticed the girl look at the arrow, then at her, then back at the arrow. *Why would the girl be interested in a Holy Land arrow?* Alison smiled at the girl and led her out of the library museum and back downstairs. Alison noticed that Ben had astutely put away the girl's belongings from his desktop in the office so they could present them to her properly. *How in the world did her effects end up on the porch this morning?* Alison again wondered.

"OK, dear, now that we've seen the inside, let's take you outside and walk around a bit." Alison motioned for the girl to follow her down the hall, into the living room, and out the door. "Isn't this just beautiful? This property has been in Ben's family for many generations."

Kawsay thought the nice woman reminded her more and more of her grandmother. The woman seemed so interested in her comfort. The man was different from Grandfather though, as he did not seem as funny or as happy. The man was very nice, but seemed very serious too. He did have interesting light brown eyes with centers of gold and must have put a lot of effort into building and maintaining this amazing house. Once outside, Kawsay felt lighter and closer to home. The nice woman had taken her into the forest and was still chattering away and pointing at things.

"…and there's a sugar pine over there, and there's a Douglas fir," Alison was pointing to the left. "And this is a cedar. What kinds of trees are near your home I wonder? Do any of these look familiar? And animals, we have foxes, skunks, coyotes, bobcats, deer, and even mountain lions and bear. We have many beautiful birds too. Let's see. Maybe we can find one for you. We have too many annoying woodpeckers; what a nuisance they can be! Also many other birds, such as chickadees, quail, sparrows, flycatchers, and warblers."

The ground felt spongy and slightly damp. Kawsay was intrigued with all the unfamiliar trees and shrubbery. This was definitely not near home. She was used to macaws, parrots, tanagers, and monkeys flying through the trees. There must be something here that she recognized. Just then Junior caught up with them and began nuzzling Kawsay and licking her hand. She could not help giggling.

Then Junior stopped and looked at her as if to ask, "What next, friend?"

Kawsay looked up at Alison and had an idea. She put her hand on the dog's furry shoulder and stated authoritatively, "Allqu. Allqu!"

Alison hesitated, surprised to hear the girl speak. Then she realized that Kawsay was trying to teach her in return. She turned to face Kawsay and put her larger hand over Kawsay's. She looked deeply into Kawsay's eyes and said, "All cue?"

Kawsay smiled and shook her head. "All-qu."

Alison tried again. "All coo?"

Kawsay beamed back. They paused for a moment. Then Alison pointed to herself and said "Al-i-son. Alison"

Kawsay readily understood and quickly repeated, "Alison. Alison!" with surprising fidelity. Then Alison pointed right at Kawsay.

Kawsay hesitated, wondering if it was right to give away her name to this unusual but completely kind woman. She went with her instincts and declared her identity for the first time in over 400 years. "Kawsay. Kaw-say."

Now it was Alison's turn. "Kawsay?" Kawsay's name sounded wonderful to her ear. They both instinctively reached across Junior – and across time and space – and embraced, almost like mother and daughter.

A short distance away across a ravine, a huge silver wolf crouched in the shadows, watching their every move. He thought, *I brought her to the right place. She will do well here. This family of the forest will know what to do.* Satisfied, he finished his meal of grass and leaves before disappearing into the forest. He was far older than Kawsay.

CHAPTER 8.

CROSSED PATHS

1018 B.C.
NEAR GIBEAH, ISRAEL

LIFE IS AN ARROW
FLYING AN UNCERTAIN COURSE
DESTINED FOR ITS MARK.

Nate was stunned for a moment, tried to stand, only to return to the rock floor with a bout of vertigo. While he had lost his breath, he had not inhaled seawater. His light-colored cotton sailing clothes were soaked, and he began to shiver. His head was spinning, and he could not think straight. It was too dark to see anything. Then he remembered: *Sailing, storm, lightning, Dad!*

Nate's instincts were to save his dad, but where *was* his dad? Where was *he*? *I'm not in the middle of the ocean!* Had he been washed up on some dark shore? Was his dad here too? Finally, his survival instincts brought his brain into focus.

He looked around. It was dark, but not black, and very faint light was coming in several feet up and to his left. *Maybe I've washed up into a sea cave.* Nate thought he heard a sound like deep breathing from the darkness behind him. The hairs on the back of his neck stood up. *I don't think I should stay in here.* Nate rose to a crouch and carefully inched his way up toward the light. It was brighter here, but still no direct light. Continuing toward the light, he meandered along in the near darkness. As he rounded one more serpentine bend he finally saw a small craggy opening several feet beyond. It was only three feet by three feet, but large enough for him. He felt warmer air as he approached the opening. Cautiously, he poked his wet head out and inhaled the wonderful scent – of a wheat field. The stubble from a recent cutting was damp with dew. *So, wherever I am, it's morning.* As his eyes adjusted further, he noticed how rocky the area was. Large rock piles dotted the field like giant tortoises. His vantage point was from an opening in a long cliff that defined one border of the field. The only trees were in the distance and reminded him of olive trees he had seen on a trip to Spain several years ago.

Nate hesitated. His heart was still racing, and he was crazy with worry about his dad. "Dad! Where are you," Nate whispered to himself. He heard a rustling sound and looked up, ducking and raising his arm to cover his head as a hawk-like bird sped by his hiding place. *What should I do? I can always return to this little cave, but I should see what kind of island this is. Maybe if I can get to the shore I can signal for help.*

Cautiously, Nate emerged from the bottom of the rock cliff into the early morning light. The rays did little to relieve the chill of the wet cotton clinging to his body. *The Sun seems too low in the sky.* Nate looked around. *Which way should I go? Where is Dad?* He trotted to the nearest rock pile and climbed up for a better view. Even five feet of elevation helped. He surveyed the low hills surrounding the field and the larger hills beyond. His heart sank when he realized that this terrain persisted wherever he looked – there was no Caribbean nearby. *How could this be?*

He saw a movement from across the field, or thought he did. Had a person just darted behind one of the rock piles? It was worth checking out. Maybe he could learn where he was. Quickly, Nate jumped from the rock pile and ran across the field toward the place where he thought he saw the person. Coming around the side of a large rock pile, he passed a young man crouched against it, as if hiding. He stopped abruptly, and each stared at the other in surprise and disbelief. The young man was dressed in a beautiful but dirty robe. His long dark hair was matted. It was wavy, almost curly. He was wearing sandals with bindings that disappeared up his calf. There was an intense, fearless look in the young man's eyes, which were taking Nate's measure in a calculating manner. Neither spoke.

Then their attention was diverted by voices at the far end of the field. Nate and the stranger adjourned their staring contest long enough to see the approach of two people – one a tall, regal-looking man and the other a boy about twelve years old. The boy was carrying what appeared to be a longbow and a quiver of arrows. The stranger uttered something that sounded a bit familiar, but Nate could not quite make it out. It was immediately clear, though, the stranger wanted Nate to leave and to do so quickly. He pulled a dagger out of his garment and waved it at Nate, pointing back toward the cliff with his other hand. He took a step toward Nate, who took a step back.

Again their attention was diverted, this time by a whirring sound. *Another hawk?* There was a faint thudding sound. They saw that an arrow had landed about thirty feet from their rock pile shelter. *Is the archer shooting at us?* Then Nate noticed that the boy, no longer carrying the weapons, was running toward them. The stranger again signaled Nate to get away. He heard another arrow flying in their direction, then hitting even closer than the first. Confused and panicked, he needed no more encouragement. Nate took off at full speed toward the cliff.

He made it a short distance, almost to the protection of the next rock pile, when he felt a stab of pain in the back of his left leg. He went down, bouncing his head off the hard ground, and tumbled out of sight behind the rocks. Nate was dazed, but conscious. His light-colored slacks showed an alarming circle of red, and emerging from the center was the tail of a long wooden arrow. Even more shocking was the aggressive metal tip, which emerged with streaks of blood from his inner thigh. *God help me! I have to get out of here – they're trying to kill me!*

The tall archer was shouting something that sounded like Hebrew. *I really am losing my mind.* Ignoring the pain, Nate took off again for the safety of the cliff, holding the tail of the arrow to keep it from jerking. He was hobbling as each step on his left leg produced an agonizing jolt of pain. *If I can only reach the little hole, maybe I can hide out.* Despite his total focus on his objective, Nate became aware that the young boy who had arrived with the archer was now chasing him, rapidly closing the gap. In the distance he could hear the tall archer shouting again, this time something that sounded like "Yah minn! Yah minn!"

The boy was getting closer. He was not armed, but was carrying two of the fearsome arrows in his hand, swinging them wildly as he closed in, his long brown cloak flapping behind him. Nate panicked when he realized the small opening of the cave was not apparent. But for the trail he had left in the wet stubble, he would not have located the well-hidden entrance. Nate reached the entrance only a few seconds ahead of the boy. Ignoring the pain, he crawled through the hole and began to feel his way down the passageway. The boy entered the cave behind Nate, temporarily blocking the light. Nate stealthily pushed further into the winding dark passage. *Maybe the boy will be afraid of the dark and just go away.* Nate kept retreating around corners and under low-hanging rocks. He was expecting to eventually run into the back wall, at which point he would be trapped. But there was no back wall.

There was no floor either. Nate felt himself in free fall, unable to see or touch anything as he flailed his three good limbs. He needed air after running and limping across the field in a near panic, but could not inhale. *Oh, no. This is just like what grabbed me under the water. What is happening to ...?* Nate hit a solid barrier and fell mercifully unconscious.

Back in the dark cave, arrows still in hand, the young boy was determined not to let the odd, light-haired stranger get away. He did not realize the stranger was not stealing the arrow, but had been pierced in the leg. After his hot pursuit of Nate across the wheat field, Yamin had lunged into the little cave and felt his way along, eyes useless after the bright morning light. The young boy called out, "Hey, I just want my arrow back. Please?" No answer. Not one who easily gives up, the young boy continued feeling his way forward. He froze a moment as a wave of fear passed through his body and just listened. He knew his Master, Jonathan, would expect to get all the arrows back. *Where is that light-haired arrow thief?* He heard the sound of moving air. *Is that someone breathing?* "Hello?" Still crouching, he followed the passage downward through several twists and turns. Hearing a sound like wind or breathing, he took one more step, tripped over an unseen rock, and fell forward. He braced for the inevitable impact with a rough floor or wall, but there was no floor or wall to stop him. Screaming in terror, the boy not only fell, but was sucked into a seamless tunnel, accelerating so quickly it took his breath away. He expected to hit bottom and be smashed, but kept going faster. He could not see anything. Still gasping for air he was launched across a rough rock floor, skidding to a stop against a solid barrier. The impact dazed him.

The boy was young, though, with a strong resilient body. He got to his hands and knees and shook his head to clear his thoughts. He reminded himself he still needed to get the arrow and return it to his Master. The boy mentally checked himself for breaks and gashes and decided he had survived the long fall intact. *Just some bruises – I am fortunate! How do I get out of here? My Master will surely come to find me and help.* He also heard an odd high-pitched singing or wailing sound and thought his ears must be ringing. Seeing what he thought was the opening back to the field, he stood up, the two arrows still in his tight fist. He made his way toward the light and seemed to enter a larger and lighter underground room. He suddenly stopped, sensing he was not alone. Then he sensed movement to his right. Maybe it was the older boy with the other arrow. He turned and was about to speak when he sucked in his breath, startled by what must be an apparition!

He had never seen such a being. It was fearsome, with a painted face, a rough cloak adorned with some unusual designs, and long, straight hair laced with colorful feathers. Even more unnerving, it had large, shiny gold earrings and a necklace made from what appeared to be human teeth. It stood still as stone for a moment, not blinking an eye. Then it slowly grew a wide grin, revealing large gleaming teeth. *This guy is scarier than any Philistine*! *May the Lord deliver me!* The boy took a cautious step back, then another. The grin remained, now more comic than frightening. The being seemed to laugh a bit and offer some unknown words of greeting. *He better keep his distance! Where is my Master when I need him?*

The young boy moved toward the light until his back was to the opening from which the light was entering the otherwise dark room. From this vantage point, the strange vision was surrounded by the dark depths of the cave. *I should just run away toward the light!* As he was about to bolt, he heard footsteps behind him beyond the opening. *Maybe it's the boy who took my arrow. No, it looks like a woman.* The first apparition called out to the second as it appeared in the opening, silhouetted against the light. Now surrounded, the boy instinctively dropped to a crouch and held an arrow in each hand, one pointing sword-like at each intruder. His position was untenable. He needed to hide – to find a dark place where he could defend himself.

The grin had disappeared, and in its place was a grim frown. A dagger appeared from under the cloak. The boy moved left, and his armed adversary circled in the opposite direction. The boy moved further left as the adversary continued to circle. This tense dance continued until their positions had reversed, and both apparitions were between the boy and the lighted opening. To distract them, the boy reached back and flung an arrow with all his might at the adversary, who yelped and jumped aside. The arrow clattered harmlessly on the cave floor, but it was enough of a distraction. As the apparition went to retrieve the arrow, the boy scurried back into the darkness, seeking a place to hide with only one arrow left for protection. He kept his arms in front to shield himself from outcroppings.

The young boy ran down a corridor looking for a niche where he could hide. He wondered if the older boy who had taken his arrow was hiding somewhere in the cave. He spotted a darker place in the rock and stepped into it. He felt himself step off into space and begin to fall, just as he had a short time before. He emitted a surprised "Aaaah!" before his breath again was sucked away. He accelerated out of control, sure that his life must be over as he made his way to the nether world. When his lungs felt like bursting, his head like exploding, he felt a deceleration. He slid along a solid mass and collided with a hard surface. This time, he did not get up – or move.

But the boy was quite alive. The impact had added to the bruises a slight concussion. Within an hour, though, the boy revived with a splitting headache and incoherent thoughts. *The frightening apparition. The older boy who stole my Master's arrow! My Master Jonathan! Where am I now? Am I alive?* Slowly he put the events of this unusual morning together, not budging from his prone position. Unsure what might await him next, the boy gathered the courage to inspect his newest environment. He was pleasantly surprised. *No apparitions. No noises. No feelings of being watched. Dim light entering from an opening!*

He cautiously walked from the small cavern though a rough doorway into a larger cavern. The light was not from any easy exit, but from an array of openings in a vast ceiling. *The night sky? No, a roof of jewels! Sparkling shapes. Could the place of the dead be so beautiful?* After absorbing this enchanting place for a short time, the boy realized he could not stay. His Master would be looking for him, and his family would expect him for the next meal. Besides, he was thirsty and wanted to tell his friends of his amazing adventures. *Is there a way out of here?*

He saw no obvious exit and certainly could not reach the passageways in the ceiling. Turning this way and that, not knowing which direction to prefer, he felt a light zephyr on his cheek. He inhaled and sensed a hint of dryer air. Following his nose, he came to a dark opening at the far end of the room and determined it to be the source of the drier air. The opening was wide enough for two people to walk through without bending down. He entered the dark passage, feeling his way very slowly and cautiously. *I don't want to fall through another hole!* The passage turned left, then right, then left again, all the while the air growing warmer and drier. He continued for a while and then realized it was getting lighter. One more right turn and he saw it – a spot of blue sky through a rough but large opening. *Thank you, Lord!*

Confident that his ordeal was over, he strode to the exit, but then stopped just short of it. *After all that has happened, I need to be careful.* He poked his head around the edge of the opening to survey his surroundings. He saw enormous trees and rocks, but they did not look "right". There were towering evergreen trees as tall as forty men, but not like the cedars he knew. The terrain was rugged. There were a variety of shrubs growing from the moist forest floor, none of which he recognized. It was beautiful country, but it did not look like his home in Gibeah or any other place he had ever imagined.

The opening was part way up a steep incline, but a subtle pathway seemed to lead away to the right and downward. He had no choice but to begin following it. *I need to remember my way back.* He carefully followed the path for a while, until he heard the inviting sound of a mountain stream below. After a few more steps, he could see it through the green branches. *A drink of cool water would be wonderful!*

Reaching the stream and getting down on one knee, he cupped his hands and brought the first sip up to his lips. He drank many more times, always keeping his eyes vigilant. Then he washed his cuts and bruises, enduring the sting. *Must keep moving.* The path then followed the side of the stream with occasional detours around boulders and large trees. He heard unfamiliar bird calls, but looked in vain for the sources.

The boy, refreshed by the water and warmed by the sun glinting down through the trees, gained some spring in his step. His attractive surroundings temporarily distracted him from the thought that he had no idea where he was going. The path then turned and crossed the rushing stream on a wooden bridge. *A bridge?* He knew bridges, but could not help noticing that this one was held together by shiny metal spikes, which were round on one end and six-sided on the other. *What wonderful craftsmanship. I must tell Father about this!*

Across the bridge the vista opened up into a broad field, but not the familiar wheat field near Gibeah. There was, though, a similar low escarpment like the one where he had followed the older boy into the hole. *Familiar, but all different. Where does this path lead?* It led close to the base of the cliff, which was about four times his height.

Suddenly, a piercing yell, alternating between normal and falsetto tones, cascaded down to him from the top of the low escarpment, accompanied by the sound of pounding feet. Then he saw it. *A giant bird!* The bird had taken off from the cliff above the boy and was frantically flapping its odd wings as its yelling changed more to a scream of terror. The boy ducked involuntarily as the bird's shadow passed over him. Then, without further ceremony the bird crashed to the ground, skidded, spun around, and stopped in a cloud of dust. All went quiet.

The young boy had already weathered a lot of new experiences in the last few hours, but this one was just weird! Not more than five steps from him was the crumpled form of an enormous bird – not looking much like a bird at all. There were pieces of metal, some thin strips of wood, torn pieces of papyri, and even a few ornamental feathers. But in the center of the chaotic remains was a human form lying spread-eagle on its back, dressed in tight-fitting clothing – a green, brown, and black shirt tucked into tan leggings, hard black coverings on the feet, and a brown leather helmet. The upturned face sported eye coverings with shiny transparent crystals. Nothing moved except the last remnants of the dust. There was no sound until a low groan arose from the form in the middle.

The boy no longer feared the giant bird, but was concerned about the fallen angel in obvious pain. He walked over to take a closer look and noticed a little blood at the corner of the birdman's mouth. *This is no birdman. It's a boy about my age!* He cautiously bent over him and looked at the eyes. Through the crystal eye coverings the eyes blinked open to reveal dazzling blue eyes. Neither boy moved, though both pairs of eyes were wide open. A few seconds passed, and then the bloody mouth curled into a grin, or was it a grimace? The bird-boy squawked in a quavering voice, "Awk! Can you help me back to my nest?"

CHAPTER 9.

NEW LIPS SPEAK NEW TONGUE

MAY – PRESENT YEAR
SIERRAS, CALIFORNIA

A NEW BEGINNING
MY IMAGINATION SOARS
DO I DARE TO DREAM?

Alison and Kawsay walked back to the house with a sense of connection. *It's interesting how Junior helped us communicate*, Alison thought, looking at Junior's perpetually wagging tail. *Where is this sweet girl from? Herschel should be here soon; hope his well of languages includes hers.* Alison thought the back deck would be a good place for Kawsay to talk to Herschel. *The girl seems to be comfortable outside, and meeting with Herschel would be another new experience for her.* Alison patted a comfortable chair next to the patio table for Kawsay and motioned she would go and get drinks for them. Kawsay smiled back and began petting Junior. The deck wrapped around the back and sides of the house. Kawsay liked sitting up high where she could look into the forest.

As she entered the house, Alison heard Herschel's car arriving. She hurried to join Ben to receive their guests.

"How is your sabbatical going?" Grace asked, as Ben opened the front door. The front wall was set with two huge windows that made the otherwise dark log room bright. It always reminded Grace of the old meeting room where her church held weekend retreats.

"Our sabbatical has been restful until the excitement of the past twelve hours," Ben answered, shaking Herschel's hand as Grace and Alison gave each other a warm hug. Herschel, like Ben, was forty-two years old and about six feet tall. He had dark skin, short thick hair, and light brown eyes surrounded by round, metal-rimmed spectacles that gave him an appropriately scholarly look. Grace, a successful psychologist, had slightly lighter skin than her husband and dark brown eyes that were understanding and engaging. She was five-six with an average build, short dark hair, a gentle kind face, and perfect Southern manners.

"Well, you two lovebirds look no worse for the wear," Herschel said as he turned to Alison for a hug. "And where is this young mystery girl?"

"We have learned her name is Kawsay." Allison slipped her hand into Ben's. "She is on the back deck with Junior. Why don't I take Grace out to meet her first while Ben shows you her belongings? At least we *think* they're hers. She doesn't know we have them yet. Perhaps we can introduce them to her in front of you, Herschel, and if you can communicate with her ... well, we could learn a lot by how she responds to all those amazing artifacts." Alison's mind was racing as she wondered how such an innocent, sweet girl could possess such an amazing array of weapons and other odd objects. *Looks like she raided a museum.*

"Good idea." Ben squeezed Alison's hand and turned to Herschel. "OK, my friend, we'll take a detour to my office to look at what showed up with our young guest. I have an idea what may be going on here. Can I get you something to drink first?"

"You have an idea about what?" Alison raised an eyebrow at Ben. "Grace and I will grab some iced tea and bring it to the deck."

Ben winked at his wife. "I will share my thoughts after Herschel establishes some communication and learns what he can."

Ben gently closed the office door behind Herschel and removed the contents of a box that was hidden under his desk. As he placed each item on the desk, Herschel's eyes grew wider. Herschel picked up each artifact and softly recited what he held. "Ah, bags and small clay containers holding what was left of … it smells like beans, … corn, … potatoes, maybe cereal, and water. Next we have a wool cloak, a wooden cup, a brightly painted bowl with birds on it, a knife, a strangely-shaped jeweled dagger. Would you look at that!" Herschel was turning the sparkling dagger under the light. "A warrior's spear, paraphernalia for fishing and hunting, a woven sling, a few round stones, and a bola. You have yourself quite a collection, Professor Hunter. If all this showed up with our mystery girl, I am certainly ready to meet her. It's interesting that while these look ancient, they are not very used or worn."

"Alison and I noticed that as well. Come on, I'll take you out to the deck."

Alison had led Grace through the house and slid open the door to the deck. They stepped into the warm forest air. The sunlight was speckling through the tall trees, dancing on the deck. Kawsay looked surprised when she saw that Alison was not alone. Alison, sensing Kawsay's concern, quickly said, "Hi Kawsay, hi Junior," and smiled reassuringly.

Kawsay was curious about this new, dark-skinned woman. Grace sat next to Kawsay and began petting Junior.

"This is Kawsay," Alison said to Grace as she pointed at Kawsay. "And this is Grace." Alison looked at Kawsay and pointed at Grace.

"Hi Kawsay," Grace said smiling warmly at Kawsay.

Alison repeated, "Grace," pointing at Grace and looking at Kawsay.

Kawsay touched her lip self-consciously, wondering if the new stranger would accept her repulsiveness as had her light-skinned caretakers. She suddenly had that old familiar wave of self-deprecating fear that she was about to be shunned, and deservedly so.

Grace reached over gently, took the hand Kawsay had used to touch her lip, and smiled. "It's OK. You are a beautiful girl, Kawsay. We will figure out how to get your lip fixed." Grace looked over at Alison. "She is so self conscious about her lip. It pains me to think about how the young girl must feel when she looks at herself. Where must she have come from that her family would not have had this fixed?"

Kawsay had gotten a good look at herself in the bathroom mirror after breakfast. She had seen herself in polished metal and water before, but she had never encountered such a reflective surface as the bathroom mirror, and the bright fire-lamps overhead made her image more pronounced and easy to see. She knew how bad she looked before, but now she could see every painful detail of her deformed upper lip.

"Ben and I talked about this late last night. Regardless of where she is from and who her family is, we will pay to have her lip fixed as soon as possible so she does not have to endure its effect on her self-image any longer. She must come from a very poor family, perhaps illegal immigrants. If we can figure out what language she speaks, it will help to identify who her family is and where she belongs." Alison felt upset that Kawsay had endured this for all these years. "I don't even know how old she is, Grace."

"I'd guess she's about thirteen," Grace suggested, again smiling at the girl.

Kawsay liked the sound of Grace's voice. It was soft and soothing and full of compassion. She wondered why Grace was here. Was she coming to take her away from her pale-skinned caretakers? Does she know where Yachay is? Her head was beginning to swirl.

Ben and Herschel stepped out onto the deck, and Kawsay froze. *These people have come to take me away! I knew all this kindness was too good to be true.*

Junior trotted over to Herschel as Herschel stooped down to greet his canine friend. Junior misjudged his speed and plowed Herschel over backwards, and then began licking his face. The adults began laughing as Ben pulled Junior off Herschel.

"This crazy puppy is still expressing his gratitude to you for rescuing him from the freeway and bringing him to us when he was just a tiny little guy." Ben rubbed Junior's back.

Kawsay forgot herself and could not help laughing at the sight of Junior knocking the dark-skinned man onto his back. *He looks pretty harmless with Junior licking his face. The dog must know these people to behave this way. The dog is totally at ease with them.*

Alison had been watching Kawsay's reaction to Herschel and, again, noted how this silly puppy had put Kawsay at ease. She motioned for everyone to sit down and pointed at Herschel saying, "Herschel. Her-shel." Alison pointed again at each person. "Herschel. Her-shel. Grace. Grace. Ben. Ben. Alison." She then pointed at the girl and said, "Kawsay"

"Hi Kawsay," Herschel said in his calmest voice, sensing the trepidation in the young girl. "I need to get her talking so I can figure out her language and dialect."

Kawsay liked Alison and Ben and wanted to stay with them, at least until she could figure out where she was and what had happened to her. *I am a warrior not a victim. I need to take charge of this situation as much as possible and not keep getting knocked around by circumstances, funny sucking tunnels, giant silver dogs....*

Junior interrupted her thoughts with a bark. He saw a squirrel in the yard, leaped off the deck, and disappeared into the forest.

Before Kawsay could catch herself she called out, "Junior!"

Alison, surprised and happy, chimed in, "Yes, Junior!" She pointed again at herself and said, "Alison," then pointing at Kawsay, said "Kawsay!" She went around the table again saying everyone's name. She pointed at Kawsay again and looked expectantly.

"Kawsay," the girl responded. Kawsay then pointed at Alison and said tentatively, "Al-i-son." Kawsay followed Alison's pointing hand around the table and timidly repeated each person's name after Alison said them slowly.

Herschel slid a replica of an Inca quipu out of a satchel he had filled with Inca and other South American trinkets and books after their telephone conversation that morning.

That captured Kawsay's full attention. *Finally something familiar.* "That looks like Grandfather's quipu!" she blurted out in her native Quechua language. But it was not Grandfather's, just similar.

"That's the most I've heard her say!" Alison said excitedly.

"What is that?" Grace asked curiously.

"Instead of writing, ancient Incas used this for record keeping." Herschel held up the quipu. "This woven system of knots recorded births, deaths, weapons, food, crops, and livestock production. Quipu-keepers had perhaps hundreds of quipus stored coiled up in jars. They were made of up to hundreds of strands of cotton or wool of varying lengths. You two hit the nail on the head when you mentioned you found Inca artifacts on your porch. She certainly recognizes this quipu." Herschel laid the quipu in front of Kawsay. She had spoken so fast he was not able to make out her language. In English he said, "What can you tell me about this? I need to hear more from you."

Kawsay stared at the quipu, not sure what to do. *Why are they giving this to me? Do they want me to record something?* "Grandfather keeps the quipu. Grandfather keeps the quipu." She began to feel her eyes well up with tears. "Where am I? Where is Yachay?" The tears began running down her face.

"That sounds like the Quechua language. It is used in the Andes, Peru, Ecuador, and Bolivia. It originated in Cuzco, but is still used by Andean people today. I think we're getting somewhere," Herschel said hopefully.

"Oh, that reminds me, Herschel," Alison blurted out, mad at herself for not mentioning it earlier. "Kawsay taught me her word for dog this morning; it's Allqu!"

"Well, that is certainly a Quechua word."

"Do you speak the Quechua language well enough to communicate with her?" Grace asked her husband. "She really must feel very alone if she cannot understand anything we are saying in English."

"There are many dialects within the Quechua language, and hers is unfamiliar to me. If we can speak slowly and perhaps use some pictures, perhaps we can communicate. And you're right, Grace, she must feel very isolated. It sounded like she said 'Where am I'."

"I think now is the time for me to get the stuff we found on the porch," Ben said as he got up.

"Good idea, dear." Alison smiled at Kawsay. "Herschel, tell her as best you can that we found some things in the same place we found her – on the porch."

Herschel looked into Kawsay's eyes and, using the most common dialect in the Quechua language he knew, said very slowly, enunciating each word, "Your, Kawsay's, belongings were found on the porch."

Kawsay understood they found something, her belongings. *Is that what he said? This dark man can communicate with me? This is fantastic! He can help me learn where I am!* Kawsay thought.

Just then Ben stepped out on the deck carrying the box of Kawsay's effects and set them gently next to the patio table. The spear Yachay had given her was sticking out of the box and was the first item she saw. Kawsay's face lit up. "Yachay's old spear!" She jumped up from her chair, knelt next to the box, and began removing the contents and laying them on the deck. She felt more comfortable sitting on the deck than in a chair.

Herschel slid out of his chair and sat on the deck next to Kawsay. He pointed to the items and did his best to name what they were. Kawsay corrected him, as she could tell he was trying to communicate with her. She wanted to encourage him to understand her since their language was so foreign, and he seemed to understand hers to some extent. Kawsay told

Herschel about each item. "Mother's wooden cup and bags. Her clay containers that held food – beans, corn, dehydrated potatoes, cereal, and water. Grandmother painted this bowl with birds. The knife had been Father's." She told Herschel her father died before she was born. That is why they let her live.

"What do you mean 'let you live'?" Herschel asked in what was close enough to Kawsay's Quechua dialect that she could mostly make it out.

"My lip. Deformed babies are sacrificed to Inti since our small tribe cannot properly take care of them and their lives would be unbearable. They think they are doing it to be compassionate. Yachay thinks it is barbaric."

"Yachay is your brother?"

"What is she saying?" Alison whispered, not wanting to loudly interrupt Herschel's obvious progress.

"Sorry, I should be translating for you. I just got into her story and forgot."

"Where is Yachay?" Herschel continued.

Kawsay looked at Alison, remembering the arrow in the museum that looked like Yachay's. "I am afraid he may have followed me through the sucking tunnel and something bad happened to him."

Herschel raised his eyebrows and took a deep breath. "Are there any mental institutions anywhere nearby?" he asked, wondering if she may have escaped from an asylum.

"Do you think she's nuts?" Ben looked disappointed.

"I don't know what I think. She doesn't seem nuts, but she mentioned something about her 'tribe' sacrificing babies with deformities. Then she talked about what I think was a 'sucking tunnel'."

"Perhaps the dialect is so different you're not fully understanding her," Alison suggested.

"Good point, Alison. I'll keep going." Herschel looked back at Kawsay and picked up the strangely-shaped, dazzling jeweled dagger that had caught his attention when he first saw it. In his best Quechua he slowly said to Kawsay, "This dagger looks different from your other belongings."

Kawsay sensed his suspicion of her. She decided to be as honest as possible. She wanted to be understood. "Grandfather gave it to me before I left. He said he got it in the secret caves."

Herschel was trying not to make any judgments. "This looks like an Inca bola."

"A bola?" Grace asked.

"It's a weapon with three stones attached to lengths of llama tendons," Alison answered.

"A sling," Herschel said, holding up the last item, not noticing Kawsay's strange look.

"You said 'Inca'. That was the name of our great leaders. That was before the Invaders came."

Herschel translated this response. Ben was particularly intrigued by what it might mean. "Let's see what she knows about the Incas," Ben suggested.

Nodding, Herschel pulled out a book he had on the Inca Empire. He laid it open on the deck between them. "Where are you from?"

"The jungle." Kawsay showed no interest in the book.

"Where, what jungle?" Herschel pressed.

"Near Vilcabamba." She remembered Grandmother explaining how her small tribe came to be where they lived.

Herschel finally felt like he was getting somewhere with just simple, basic questions. "What does your family do?"

"My family grows food. Father used to carve stone. He made great steps, buildings, many things." Kawsay looked sad. "They were also training and preparing me."

Herschel was translating Kawsay's and his words back to Grace and his friends.

"What were they training and preparing her for?" Ben jumped in.

Herschel asked her.

"So I can survive alone in the jungle."

"Why must you survive in the jungle alone?"

"Because of my defect. I cannot stay with my people because of my lip. That was the agreement Mother made with the Chief and he made with the tribe: that I would leave at age thirteen and either live or die in the jungle alone. It was the will of the gods that would keep me alive or let me die. So I went to the secret caves where Grandfather showed me to go. And then,… then I stepped into the sucking tunnel. Now I am here."

Herschel related this to his friends. They stared at each other in silence.

"Ask her if she has ever seen white people before," Ben requested.

Herschel related the question to Kawsay.

The girl crossed her arms, slouched a little, and said she had only heard of them.

Herschel asked her what white people she had heard of and continued to relate the conversation.

Kawsay thought and said, "Francisco Pizarro," in a strong accent.

Herschel repeated what he thought she said, "Francisco Pizarro?"

"Yes," she responded with disdain.

"What god do your people worship?"

"Inti," Kawsay said proudly.

"Wow!" said Alison. "She worships Inti?"

Herschel leaned back against the leg of a chair. "Let's see. She worships Inti, her people sacrifice babies with defects, she speaks sort of Quechua, and the only white man she ever heard of is Francisco Pizarro." He paused and then proceeded with gravity. "This girl appears to have just stepped out of the remains of the Inca empire post-Pizarro! *Where* did you find her?"

Kawsay had questions too, and this seemed to be the time to ask.

"Where am I? Where is Yachay? Why do you have Yachay's arrow? Can you help me get home? What is going to happen to me? Why don't the nice, pale people shun me because of my lip? Your skin is darker like mine. Is your home near mine? You know my language. Where did you learn it? Do you know my tribe? Where did all this stuff come from – it is all so different!"

"Please, Kawsay. One question at a time." Herschel smiled at the young girl's boldness.

"Where am I?"

"You are in the United States in the Sierra Mountains at Alison and Ben's home."

This meant nothing to Kawsay. "What is United States and Sierras?"

"You have never heard of the United States of America?"

"No." Kawsay decided to move on for the time being. "Where is Yachay? Why do you have Yachay's arrow?"

Ben and Alison looked at each other. "She noticed an arrow upstairs in our little museum," Alison explained, noting Ben's pensive expression.

Herschel responded to Kawsay. "We haven't seen your brother. The arrow must just look similar to one he has." Herschel wondered how her brother could have something similar to what he recalled being in Ben and Alison's museum.

"Can you help me get home?" Kawsay realized finding home would answer a lot of her questions, such as where Yachay is and if he still has his arrow.

"We will try to help you get to your home. That is why I am asking you all these questions – so we can help you find your family."

"Your skin is darker like mine, is your home near mine? You know my language. Where did you learn it? Do you know my tribe?"

"I learned your language in school, but I live near here. Your language is spoken by people who live far away. Maybe that is where your home is, or was…" Herschel was trying to put his thoughts together. *Inti, sacrifice, Inca bolas, Inca artifacts, and the only white man she ever heard of is Francisco Pizarro… What is going on here? Didn't I read about some untouched tribes still living in Peru?*

Kawsay interrupted Herschel's thoughts. "There are many objects in this house I do not recognize – it is all so different!"

"It is just the way we live. Craftsmen made all these things we use. It makes life easier." He was perplexed how to answer all her strange questions.

"Why don't the nice, pale people shun me because of my lip?"

"They don't mind your lip, but they will help you fix it if it bothers you."

That was the first Kawsay had heard of fixing her lip. "How could that happen?"

"We have healers that can completely repair it."

Repair my lip – is that really possible? Kawsay's thoughts drifted as she thought of all the implications of repairing her lip.

Herschel repeated his thoughts to his wife and friends. "Inti, sacrifice, Inca bolas, Inca artifacts, she lives in a tribe, the only white man she ever heard of is Francisco Pizarro, she has never heard of the United States of America, nothing is familiar to her… What is going on here?" Herschel stared into the forest. "What was she wearing when she arrived?"

Alison reached over to Herschel's Inca book and thumbed through until she got to a picture of a short tunic and sandals. Pointing, she said, "It was quite similar to that."

"You're not saying you think she is from the Inca Empire… I mean *really* from that time period, are you dear?" Grace's brow was furrowed.

"That would be sometime after 1532." Alison's gaze fixed intently on Kawsay – at her features and long dark hair. *Could that hair have never been brushed by a modern hairbrush until last night?*

Kawsay was transfixed on the idea of "repairing" her lip. *Would I be able to rejoin my family – rejoin my tribe? Would they accept me? Do I want to go back and live among the very people who wanted me dead? I need to find Yachay.*

"What do you think, Ben? You haven't said much. You said earlier you might have an idea." Alison nudged her husband playfully, then rested her hand on his.

Ben was staring blankly at the patio table in front of him. He did not know what to say. He was reluctant to believe the young girl was, in fact, from the Inca Empire. *Maybe her family was poor and somehow obtained her clothing and trinkets from a museum somewhere, and then something happened to them. But why didn't they fix her lip?* "Things just don't add up," Ben mumbled, not planning to say that out loud. "I mean, we should check missing person's reports – that's a given."

"You're not thinking about calling the police are you, dear? Isn't there another way to find out if anyone has filed a missing person's report? She *only* seems to be concerned about her brother following her." Alison was worried about getting police involved until they knew more.

Herschel shared his thoughts. "From what I could understand, she said her father had died and only mentioned her mother and grandparents in the context of what they gave her. While she thinks her brother may have followed her, she has said nothing about her other family members doing the same. She says she wants to get to them and to her home. There is no indication they all traveled someplace near here and then got separated. She said she was sent away by her 'tribe', went to the 'secret caves', and fell into a 'sucking tunnel'. Unless she has a vivid imagination and is some kind of a run-away, it does not appear she got lost on some vacation to the U.S. Heck, she hasn't even heard of the U.S. or the Sierra Mountains. If she was on vacation here or immigrated here, she certainly would have heard of the United States of America! I think we should wait on the police. If we report her being here, then child protective services will get involved, and I'm pretty sure they don't speak her Quechua dialect." Herschel looked tired and a little frazzled. He had not expected this meeting to get so weird. He spent his career studying ancient languages, but never expected to stumble across someone speaking an ancient language who was from that language's ancient time!

"We can check Internet sites for missing kids and look for signs posted on nearby roads. If someone is looking for her, they would get her name out locally," Alison suggested.

Ben recalled Alison's report of large dog or wolf prints and wondered if there was some reason for her being here. "I agree, we'll check missing person's reports and look for signs, but I doubt we'll find anyone looking for her. Unless we believe she *is* from the past, we shouldn't suggest it to her. She's been through enough already. I think we should break for lunch and get you two settled into our second guest bedroom."

"Good suggestion, Ben. I'll help Alison in the kitchen, and you two can use your masculinity to get our bags out of the car." Grace was trying to lighten things up. "Oh, can you tell Kawsay that Alison and I request her assistance and perhaps guidance in the kitchen?" Grace reached over and squeezed Herschel's hand.

In his best Quechua and with a half smile, which reminded the girl of her grandfather, Herschel told Kawsay that Alison and Grace needed her to show them how to fix lunch.

Still pondering how to go forward, Ben scanned his friends' faces. "We should keep her presence a secret until we figure all this out."

After just a little encouragement from Alison and Grace, Kawsay orchestrated the preparation of a meal of roasted corn and potatoes along with a stew containing beans and a variety of vegetables Alison had on hand. During lunch, Kawsay pointed to certain items and said her Quechua word for each. She started with numbers by holding up her fingers.

"Hoq, iskay, kinsa," she said,

Herschel translated slowly, "One, two, three."

Kawsay repeated, "One, two, three." Kawsay then said "Qari, warmi, allqu."

Herschel translated, "Man, woman, dog."

Kawsay slowly repeated, "Man, woman, dog."

Pointing to her mouth and glass, Kawsay said, "Mikhuy, yaku."

Herschel repeated Kawsay and translated, "Eat, water."

Kawsay giggled at Herschel's mispronunciation of Mikhuy and suggested she could help him talk better in exchange for him helping her communicate with Ben and Alison. Grace got up and walked around the room pointing at items for Kawsay to say in Quechua. Grace, Ben, and Alison repeated Kawsay's words, and then Herschel helped Kawsay say the English words. This game went on for over an hour as they finished eating and ventured beyond the kitchen and the house.

After walking around the house and property naming various items, the four adults and Kawsay found their way back to the deck. Alison was feeling happy about their young visitor, but was mystified by the idea she could be from the Inca Empire. She asked Herschel to press Kawsay a little further on her home and "tribe".

Kawsay explained what she knew about Pizarro's destruction of her people, how some fled and were captured and killed, and how her tribe members were a splinter group that traveled far into the jungle for many weeks. She recounted that only a few of the tribe's elders had a living memory of what happened and had seen Pizarro's army. She went on to describe daily life in her tribe. She said her people were farmers – they excavated terraces for corn, potatoes, sugarcane, beans, peppers, tamarillos, and gooseberries. When she noticed Grace's wedding ring, she said her people had gold and silver masks and figurines that they managed to take when they escaped. She recounted how she had listened from behind a tree to panpipe instruments playing haunting melodies in the evenings. She talked about her grandfather's earplugs, explaining they were gold disks pressed into a hole in the earlobe. She also told about how funny he was and how he had stalked her and Yachay every night when she was out being trained. She told them about the Chief and his jaguar stool that she loved and how he finally gave it to her for her tenth birthday, pretending it hurt his back. While touching her lip, she talked about how everyone shunned her and how the other children made fun of her and hated her because she was repulsive, but that Yachay said they were just jealous of her because she was welcome in the Chief's tent. Her mother had told her that the adults resented her because she was allowed to live when other people's babies did not.

Ben tried to sum up everyone's thoughts. "Unless you believe her to be an artful liar with a deviously creative mind, after her description of her life, don't you find it difficult to believe she *isn't* what she says she is." Ben stood up to stretch his legs and excused himself. He needed time to think. He proceeded into the master bathroom to wash his face. When he got there, he noticed a haiku wedged between the bristles of his toothbrush that Alison must have written in the past couple of hours.

> *Our little Kawsay*
> *We don't know from where she comes*
> *We must protect her.*

Ben pulled out a pen and small notepad he kept in his bathroom drawer for these occasions and wrote back to her:

> *Traveling through time*
> *Is it really possible?*
> *Do you believe it?*

He placed the haiku in the bristles of Alison's toothbrush as he heard the phone ring.

"Hello?" Ben grabbed the phone on his nightstand.

"It's your crazy brother. I'm in Borneo! You know that mysterious carnivore species I mentioned that was spotted in the central forests of Borneo? Well, I had to see it for myself."

"Well, did you see it?" Ben was always intrigued by Helmut's adventures, but loved to rib him about his pursuits.

"I finally caught a glimpse of it. It's a mammal slightly larger than a domestic cat with dark red fur, a long bushy tail, and large hind legs. It looks like a cross between a fox and a cat. It could be the first time a new carnivore has been discovered on the island in more than a century! It may be an entirely new species or just a new species of marten or civet cat." Helmut's voice was animated.

"We have something exciting going on right here at the old Hunter estate. In fact, I was thinking about you just a few minutes ago. Do you know any good plastic surgeons who wouldn't ask questions about where a patient may be from?"

"So you're finally going to take my advice and have your face rearranged?" Helmut laughed at his own wittiness.

"You do enjoy yourself, don't you Helmut – and often at my expense! Too bad you're the only one who finds you funny. Seriously, when are you coming home? I do want to make contact with a good plastic surgeon."

Sensing his brother's serious tone, Helmut changed gears. "If it's an emergency, I can get home right away."

"Thanks. Well, we got this visitor last night. A young girl showed up on the porch. She doesn't speak English, so Herschel and Grace are here. Herschel discovered she speaks Quechua. Anyway, she's about thirteen and has a cleft lip. Alison and I want to fix it."

"Wow, that's even more interesting than my fox-cat. Quechua is spoken in South America, isn't it? Does she have parents? How would they feel about you having surgery done on their daughter?"

"Clearly, the first order of business is to try to locate her family, but I'm not optimistic we will find them." Ben did not want to get too deep into Kawsay's mysterious background.

Helmut was speechless – a rare status for him. "I do know a good plastic surgeon. Very bright – and a woman. She would put your Quechua girl at ease. Sounds rather exciting around there. I think I can be home in a few days. I'll call you later after I get things sorted out. I think I've had about all the fun I can stand down here, for the time being anyway."

"You're the man, Helmut. I can always count on you to help when weird things happen."

"That's what I thrive on, brother."

Ben heard the line cut off. While he was not yet ready to divulge his suspicions about Kawsay to Helmut, he was glad his brother was coming home. Stepping onto the deck, Ben was happy to see the language lessons had continued between Herschel and Kawsay. Alison and Grace were also working on pronouncing Quechua words. Ben smiled at Kawsay and laid a hand on Herschel's shoulder. "Tell her I believe she will be speaking English better than we do within a few weeks!"

After Herschel translated his remark to a smiling Kawsay, Ben continued, "I just spoke to Helmut. He's in Borneo, of all places, chasing some mysterious fox-cat creature – sounds pretty normal for him. Helmut has an MD and a zoology PhD from an elite school, and this is what he does with his time? Anyway, he does know a good plastic surgeon and will be home in a few days to set everything up. In the meantime we should make darn sure there is not a family looking for her that may not appreciate our generous deed to fix her lip. Alison and I are prepared to put up the cash. If we are unable to find her family and decide to believe the unbelievable – that she is from the past – we'll be left with the fact that she has no legal guardian. In that instance I think it would be safe to proceed with the operation. After what she has said over the past several hours, I just cannot believe how a child could say what she says about her life in the manner in which she presents it, and have it all be a scam."

Herschel looked up at Ben, "I listened to her very closely; I watched her body language. She believes what she said. If she was insane, she could not possibly know all the facts about the Incas that she knows – how they lived, what happened to their empire. Her knowledge is too vast. While I'm not an archeologist like you two, I have learned quite a bit about South American cultures during the years I have studied their ancient languages. What she says about her life and the history of her people is right on target. Could an insane thirteen-year-old have memorized all that information so perfectly and then present it so flawlessly and believably? I don't think so." Herschel took a deep breath. "What do you think, Grace, being a counselor and all? Aren't there some telltale signs that indicate whether a person is telling the truth?"

"Well, I was actually studying her as you were relaying all that fantastical information she was saying. While there are no absolute telltale signs of a lie, there are general behaviors you can look for. For example, liars tend to move their arms, hands, and fingers less and blink less than truth tellers. This is especially important if a person normally gesticulates, but we don't know that about her. Her body seemed relaxed and animated as she relayed different aspects of her life and described her belongings and environment. She showed what seemed to be appropriate physical expression and body language toward things she liked as well at what she seemed to resent or disdain. She seemed completely 'in the moment', not rigid and calculating. Further, liars' voices tend to become more tense or high-pitched. Kawsay's voice was all over the place, depending on what she was describing or relaying. Liars may pause more during speech – probably to calculate their next story. Kawsay seemed to think for a second after you asked her something, which was undoubtedly to translate your imperfect use of her language, then blurted out a response – hardly a sign of calculating a lie. Let's see, liars make fewer speech errors and rarely backtrack to fill in forgotten or incorrect details. Well, who knows if she was making speech errors, but from listening to your translations she seemed to be progressing forward with each answer. I didn't hear any 'wait let me backtrack, I forgot to say something'. Another thing we look for in liars is that their stories may seem too good to be true. I'm not sure what this young girl could get out of telling this story to us except a ticket to the police station or local insane asylum – so I can imagine no benefit to her in concocting this. Finally, liars sometimes make micro-expressions from feelings of fear, guilt, or delight at fooling people. Again, she seemed animated in a smooth and natural manner. I saw no twitches or quick probing glances to see what type of effect her remarks were having on us. She just seemed natural and, as I said, appropriately animated for what she was saying."

"Good grief you're good, Grace! I've not heard such a succinct and insightful analysis in – I can't remember when!" Alison exclaimed. "Poor Herschel, he can't get away with anything!"

Kawsay wondered what all the fuss was about and what Grace had been saying for so long. *She smiled warmly at me during her speech, so I don't think it was anything bad.*

"Herschel, tell her we are saying good things about her and how impressed we are with how articulate she was in communicating her life to you," Grace urged.

With each hour, Ben, Herschel, Alison, and Grace were becoming more and more convinced of Kawsay's past. But what seemed to dawn on each of them at about the same time was what Alison finally verbalized as the five of them were taking a walk through the forest at twilight. "How in the world did she get *here*?"

"She kept mentioning a 'sucking tunnel' and then 'here I was'," Herschel replied. She apparently went through some kind of tunnel. Then she also mentioned something about a jeweled, sparkling cave and a giant silver dog who she thinks must have brought her to your house and delivered her belongings. She seems somewhat fuzzy with her memory after arriving in the *cave*. Is there a cave on your property, Ben?" It was growing darker outside, and Herschel could not see his friends' features anymore.

"Oh, that reminds me! We saw huge paw prints the next morning off the porch." Alison was noticing how dark it was getting and wondering who owned those prints.

"I think we better get back to the house," Ben said. "Come on, Junior. You've been such a good boy all day, and we've been mostly ignoring you." Ben herded his friends, wife, and Kawsay back to the house. Ben did not want to talk about that particular cave. "Oh, there are many caves around this area."

Kawsay had been thoroughly enjoying their walk in the forest. It was different from her jungle, but being out at night with the trees, animals, and earthy smells reminded her of Yachay and their nighttime training. She was also listening to their conversations, imagining much of it must be about her. "What is going to happen to me?" she finally asked Herschel as they stepped onto the front porch. "I like it here, but I miss Yachay. I wish I knew where he was. Are you going to stay here? How will I communicate if you leave?"

Herschel noticed that Kawsay's questions often came in bursts. *She must have floods of thoughts of her family in between her curiosity about her new environment.* Herschel looked out at the cool spring night, turned to Kawsay, and answered in her language, "We are beginning to understand where you are from. We are going to help you learn to speak our language, English, so you can easily communicate. Ben and Alison are going to get your lip repaired. You can stay with them as long as you like or until we find your family."

Turning to his friends and switching to English, Herschel said, "We ought to get on the internet tonight and look for missing persons reports and also check tomorrow for posted signs and newspaper ads or stories – just to be absolutely sure we're not overlooking something. Once we satisfy ourselves of the obvious, we need to tell her where and when she is from. I would like to be involved in that. I don't have any classes on Monday, and Grace doesn't see patients on Mondays. If it's OK with Grace, I think we can stay until Monday if you want to wait until then to reveal our thoughts to her."

"I think that's a good idea if our hosts don't think we're overstaying our welcome. By then you will have had more time to work with Kawsay on language, and she will have been here a little longer before we lay something too heavy on her." Grace squeezed Herschel's hand as they all entered the house.

"We would love to have you stay as long as you can," Alison assured them.

For the next two days, the four adults launched an exhaustive search for anyone who might be looking for Kawsay – short of calling the police. Alison and Grace went to the closest police stations, which were not very close, and inquired about a missing handbag while looking for missing person flyers. Nothing. No one was looking for Kawsay. Kawsay was also getting intensive training in English and giving Herschel invaluable lessons in the Quechua language and Incan people. Kawsay had already mastered dozens of useful English words. By Monday night, it was time for Herschel to explain, based upon her accounts, where and when she was from – the late Inca Empire.

They all sat around the kitchen table. Herschel had books laid out that pictorially showed Kawsay a time progression from a little before the Inca Empire to the present. He also had a globe and a number of maps to show her where her family had lived and where she is located now. The toughest part, the part he dreaded, was telling her everyone she knew had been dead for hundreds of years.

Kawsay went through every feeling and emotion – disbelief, curiosity, exuberance, deep sadness, then back to disbelief – at least disbelief that her family was dead. "They were all going to follow me. Not just Yachay, but Mother, Grandmother, and Grandfather. Grandfather always follows me – always! If they did not follow me, then I must go and get them and bring them to this amazing place where lips can be repaired and lights go on and off instantly." Kawsay jumped up and ran out of the kitchen, through the living room, and out the front door.

Ben was behind her before anyone saw him get up.

"Gee wiz that man is fast," Herschel said getting up and following.

Alison and Grace were close behind Herschel. Junior had already caught up with Kawsay.

Ben knew Kawsay was heading for the cave, except he was pretty sure she did not know how to find it. "Kawsay! Kawsay!"

Kawsay heard Ben's voice and realized she did not know where she was going. "Cave, cave." That was one word she had made sure she learned in English from Herschel.

Ben caught up with her and said. "I will show you but not now." He made motions with his hands as he spoke.

She understood he said 'I' and 'you', but was not sure of the rest.

Just then Herschel trotted up and Ben said, "Tell her I will show her but not now."

"Show her what?" Herschel asked.

Ben hesitated and looked down.

Wondering what was going on, but respecting his friend, Herschel related Ben's words to Kawsay.

Kawsay felt satisfied but also tired and overwhelmed by the past three days. She patted Junior's head and walked back to the house with her new adult friends who all appeared to accept her and her repulsiveness unconditionally. They genuinely seemed to want to help her. She decided to be thankful and let them take care of her, at least for the time being.

Herschel and Grace had loaded up the car before the big conversation with Kawsay. "Well, my young friend, I am giving you my cell phone number." He handed Kawsay a piece of paper with his number and pulled the cell phone out of his shirt pocket to show her what it looked like. "Alison and Ben will show you how to call me on the telephone. If you get frustrated with English or just want to talk to someone who sort of speaks your language, call me. I would enjoy taking with you anytime. I have learned a lot from you the past few days, and you have enriched my life and Grace's life too. We both like you very much and look forward to spending some more time here with you until you feel comfortable with the English language. Ben and Alison like you a lot also and will take good care of you."

"Tell her about Helmut," Ben requested.

"Ben's brother, Helmut, lives here too, though he is gone a lot. He will be returning home in a few days and is going to help you get your lip fixed by a doctor. He is also a doctor, but does not repair lips." Touching his car, Herschel continued, "Now you have seen our car and the way it sounds and moves – like a jaguar with wheels, I think you described it. Well, Helmut has a car that flies like a bird or insect. It is big and very noisy and is called a 'helicopter'. Don't worry when you see and hear it. Also, Helmut is kind of a big, strong guy, but he is gentle and will take care of you just like Ben and Alison."

Kawsay held Herschel's phone and was intrigued by the lighted window and number keys. Herschel took it back and pretended he was talking into it and explained a little how it worked. He said it was like yelling to someone far away, except it allows you to communicate without raising your voice. He told her that one day she would enjoy the telephone as most girls her age do. Herschel realized Kawsay would benefit greatly from a quick phone demonstration. "Go into the house with Alison for a minute, and I'll show you how this telephone works."

Alison took Kawsay into the house just in time to hear the phone ring. She picked it up and held it to Kawsay's ear and mouth.

"Hi Kawsay, this is Herschel. Can you hear me?" Herschel said in Quechua.

Kawsay took the phone and held it out in front of her and looked at it. "Herschel! Are you in there? How did you get inside there?"

Alison could hear Herschel laughing. She put the cordless phone back against Kawsay's ear and led her to the front door so she could see Herschel speaking into his cell phone.

"Hi Kawsay. I can see you," Herschel said as he waved at Kawsay from the driveway.

Alison showed Kawsay which button to push to hang up the phone as they stepped off the porch to join Herschel, Grace, and Ben. Herschel gave Kawsay a hug, and Grace followed with a long, warm hug.

"Call us any time, Kawsay," Herschel said, pointing to the phone Alison was holding. They got into the car and disappeared around a bend in the driveway.

Three days after Herschel and Grace left, Ben heard Helmut's helicopter approach. Kawsay and Alison were out on the deck, and the patio table was covered with an array of photos, each having nothing to do with the others. Alison was naming things from pictures and Kawsay was repeating after her. Then Alison pointed to the pictures to see if Kawsay could remember the English words without prompting.

They heard the helicopter land in its usual spot, which was a small meadow behind Helmut's cabin. Ben and Alison led Kawsay over to meet him. Helmut's cabin was about two hundred yards from the main house. Even though Helmut had a bedroom in the main house, he kept most of his belongings in his cabin and preferred to sleep there. By the time Ben, Alison, and Kawsay reached Helmut's cabin, he was already inside with his travel bags, petting Junior.

Ben introduced Kawsay to Helmut as Helmut extended his hand to warmly shake hers. Kawsay was not sure what that meant and thought he was handing her something. Alison grabbed both of their hands and slowly said Helmut's name for Kawsay to repeat.

"Hi, Kawsay, how are you?" Helmut said slowly.

"I am fine." Kawsay had already memorized basic greetings. She was impressed with his six-two height, broad shoulders, thick dark hair, and strong facial features. Kawsay was momentarily transfixed by his intense blue eyes. *He would be a fearsome warrior, but is a little bulky.*

"I called Sandra Salazar, the plastic surgeon. I said we have some very special friends from South America who are dirt poor and never had their daughter's cleft lip fixed. I see it's not a bad deformity. It should heal up nicely, and within a year no one will know it was there. We can call Sandy and set up the surgery as soon as you like." Helmut smiled at the girl.

"You are a prince, Helmut!" Alison turned to Kawsay and, using a few English words and pantomime, she explained that Helmut talked to a lip doctor who can repair her lip.

Kawsay was visibly excited and asked, "Now?" She had a sense that her lip did not repulse Helmut. Herschel had explained that Helmut would help her.

"Very soon." Alison knew Kawsay did not understand her and at that moment decided Herschel would need to be with Kawsay the day of the surgery to talk her through what would be a new and potentially scary experience. "Herschel should be with us on the day of her surgery. Perhaps we can coordinate with him when we schedule with Dr. Salazar."

"Ben already mentioned that would be a good idea." Helmut was petting Junior's head as he spoke. "Sandy's office is pretty close to Herschel's home and work. We can fly down early, and Herschel and Grace can pick us up at my favorite landing pad off Sand Hill Road near Stanford. Sandy is set up to do this type of surgery in her office, so Kawsay won't need to interact with anyone but her office staff."

"I know you two brothers have had conversations by phone about all this. Kawsay has already spoken with Herschel on the phone three times in the past few days, and he has been trying to prepare her for the surgery and aftermath. I've noticed her looking at her lip closely in the mirror. I cannot imagine what she must think about what has happened to her in the past week." Alison stroked Kawsay's long hair.

"I imagine it all seems somewhat surreal to her," Helmut mused. "On another subject, I spoke to some friends who specialize in immunology about how someone from a remote village could be protected from common, modern diseases. I've put together a little vaccine program for Kawsay. I'd like to get Herschel on the phone to explain the vaccines to her. Kawsay may not like the needles, but compared to surgery, it won't seem like much. Oh. One more thing. I looked in on your apartment down near campus. Everything looked fine, and the mail seemed to be forwarding up here just fine."

Beep ... Beep ... Beep ... Beep. *I can't stand alarm clocks.* Beep ... Beep ... *Why hasn't Ben turned it off?* Beep ... Beep ... Alison looked over to see Ben had already gotten up. Beep ... Beep ... She reached over and turned off the alarm.

"I brought us some toast with nut butter," Ben whispered as he gently closed the bedroom door behind him. He had a large ceramic plate with four pieces of toast and a giant mug of coffee. "Kawsay can't eat anything this morning because of her surgery, and it would be cruel to eat in front of her, so I sneaked this for us before we get her up."

"You are sweet, thoughtful, brilliant, and handsome." Alison had a huge smile on her face as she thought about how lucky she was to have met and married Ben. "I waited my whole life to meet you and I am soooo happy I finally found you under those rocks in Israel."

"There are worse things you could have dug up, honey. I thought we could share the coffee." Ben sat on the edge of the bed, handing Alison the mug and eating one of the toasts.

After she and Ben enjoyed their intimate breakfast, Alison went into the bathroom, opened her drawer, and found that her husband had again surprised her with two haikus.

My love, life, and heart
You own them dear Alison
Please hold them always.

Kawsay's life will change
Her mother vindicated
Today is the day.

Alison knocked and opened Kawsay's door. She was up and dressed in loose stretch pants and a light sweater. Alison had thought that would be a comfortable outfit for her on such a day. "Hi, dear, did you sleep?" Alison spoke and used pantomime.

"No, little sleep." Kawsay looked worried.

"I think we need to get you to the doctor soon and just get this over with," Alison smiled, knowing Kawsay could not understand much of what she said.

"Doc-tor now? Heli-cop-ter now?"

"Yes, first helicopter ride."

"Your airborne limo awaits! Time to go." Helmut barged though the front door. "Is Junior staying in the house while we're gone today or in his run?"

"He's going in his run." Ben came down the hall. "You ladies ready?"

"We're here." Alison and Kawsay emerged from Kawsay's room.

Kawsay was about to be totally amazed by her first flying experience. The helicopter engine began with a lot of noise. Herschel had warned her it would be loud, but Kawsay was unprepared for just *how* loud – and the shaking and shuddering. *Yikes*! she thought.

Kawsay was sitting in the front seat next to Helmut. He could see her tenseness and pulled earphones out of a metal box on the floor and gave them to her. He also handed sets of earphones back to Alison and Ben.

Kawsay could hear Helmut talking through the earphones. She could also hear Alison's and Ben's voices. *Wow! This is like the telephone.* After she fully scrutinized the inside of the six-seat helicopter, Kawsay turned her attention to the front window. Then the helicopter noise increased, and they rose straight up! Kawsay felt her stomach tingle, and she sucked in her breath. It made her think of the sucking tunnel, yet compared to the tunnel it seemed relatively tame. She quickly noticed they were flying over treetops! *This is amazing!* she thought, exhaling. Kawsay loved the perspective of looking down on the forest. The sky seemed to go on forever!

Soon the helicopter approached the central valley of California. Kawsay could see the fields of vegetables and fruits. Helmut was pointing at everything, rattling off what they were seeing. Even though Kawsay did not understand all he was saying, she knew Helmut was doing his best to put her at ease with his chatter. As they drew nearer to the Bay Area, she became fixated on the cars and freeways. She asked Helmut at least three times, "Where go car?" She pointed down at the cars on the freeways. Kawsay was taking in so much new information, and this was such a momentous experience for her, that she was not thinking about her empty stomach or the imminent surgery.

As they drew near their destination, she remembered what this exciting ride was all about. She wanted to keep flying and skip the surgery, except she was looking forward to the results. This was one of the few times in her life that she felt apprehensive about something she wanted to do. Usually she just wanted to do something or she did not want to do it, and that was that. But this time she wanted the results but not what came between now and when she was finally healed.

They landed in a field at the corner of a large parking lot. Herschel and Grace were waiting in a large van they borrowed from a friend to take them to Dr. Salazar's office. During the drive, Herschel spoke to Kawsay in Quechua about everything that was about to happen. He said Dr. Salazar would give her some medicine that would put her to sleep while she repaired the lip. Then Kawsay would wake up, and it would all be done. He told her what the office would probably look like, and that there would be nurses and equipment. He talked almost continuously until they arrived at the office.

Kawsay was glad Herschel and Grace were both with them. Kawsay had noticed all the cars, people, huge buildings, bicycles, dogs on leashes – it was overwhelming! As they entered the office, Kawsay could instantly smell a very strange odor. She wrinkled her nose. There was a woman in white behind a window. Helmut took charge once they entered the office. Kawsay recognized a number of words spoken between Helmut and the woman. Then a door opened, and another woman in white ushered all of them into a hallway and back to a pre-op waiting room. The woman in white left the room and immediately another woman wearing light green pajamas entered. *She has light brown skin, dark brown eyes, and dark brown hair – like me!* The adults all spoke with each other.

"Hi, Kawsay, my name is Sandra Salazar. You can call me Sandy." Dr. Salazar took Kawsay's hand and gave Kawsay her full attention.

"Hi, Sandy," Kawsay said in the strongest voice she could manufacture.

"We are going to get started now. You need to change." Looking at Grace and Alison, Dr. Salazar said, "Let's take her into the next room and get her changed into a gown."

Herschel said a few more words to Kawsay in Quechua. He told her not to worry, to just drift off to sleep, that it would be over when she woke up, and they would all be there waiting. He also warned her that Sandy would put a "needle" in her arm before she went to sleep and not to worry.

In the next room, Grace and Alison helped Kawsay into the gown and onto a table. A warm blanket was placed over Kawsay and an IV inserted into her arm. Dr. Salazar let Alison and Grace remain in the room until Kawsay drifted into an anesthetized sleep. Helmut gave Dr. Salazar's receptionist his cell phone number, and they walked down the street for a more substantial breakfast.

Later that night, Kawsay was safely home at the Hunter estate after a successful and uneventful surgery. Ben had held Kawsay during their flight home as Alison kept Kawsay's IV secure. Helmut decided to stay in his childhood room in the house rather than sleep in his cabin so that he could be near Kawsay during the first days after surgery. She was to remain on IV for the night, then she could use a straw to drink fluids for the next ten days. After that, she would be able to eat soft foods. Helmut used his quiet time with Ben and Alison to show them the photos from his latest adventure in Borneo with the fox-cat creature and to look at their newest archeological artifacts. They also pondered together what they should do with Kawsay, since it did not appear possible to return her to her home. Helmut was not sure what to think about Kawsay's mysterious origin.

Over the next three months, Helmut, with Alison's assistance when he was away, cared for Kawsay's lip, making sure there were no infections and healing was going well. Herschel and Grace visited on most weekends. Herschel felt he was learning as much from

Kawsay as she was from him, although he was impressed how quickly she was learning English. Ben and Alison were thankful they were on sabbatical during this extraordinary time when Kawsay entered their lives and needed them. As Kawsay's lip healed, she concentrated on learning English. As her language skills improved, she was able to tell her new friends the details of her upbringing. She loved reminiscing about her all-night training sessions with Yachay. She giggled when she spoke of Grandfather and how he had stealthily followed them at night. She talked about Grandmother teaching her about herbs and medicinal plants so she could always be able to heal herself. Helmut was particularly interested in that topic. She spoke of how wonderful her mother was and how she missed her. As the weeks went by Kawsay was amazed at her lip and her face. She looked normal. She could even begin to see why her mother and brother had always told her she was beautiful, though she would never see herself that way.

She reminded Ben that he had said he would take her to the cave. She realized that if Yachay had followed her, the great silver dog probably would have delivered him to the house as he had her. She just wanted to see the cave again. Ben assured Kawsay he would take her to the cave, but it was dark and had protruding walls in places, and he wanted her lip completely healed in case she tripped or was bumped in the face. Kawsay accepted that and believed he would soon take her.

Alison and Ben became like parents to her. She felt she could truly trust them. They spent hours teaching her about the world by showing her pictures and explaining to her what she was seeing. As her ability to understand English grew, she learned more and more about her new world – about telephones, helicopters, airplanes, cars, plumbing, electricity, microwave ovens, radio, television, washing machines, spaceships, other countries and peoples, and a bit about history and her people's place in it.

She adored Herschel and Grace, and between their weekend visits, Kawsay spoke with them regularly on the telephone. As Kawsay's speaking improved, Herschel began teaching her to write. Helmut was in and out, but always available when needed as her personal physician. He flew her back to Dr. Salazar's office two times for post-op check-ups, but they did not linger because Helmut was worried about her immune system.

Kawsay felt very fortunate she had ended up here with these wonderful people. On the morning of her thirteenth birthday, as she left her mother, brother, grandparents, and Chief standing at the junction between her village and the edge of the jungle, she never, in her wildest dreams, could have imagined this world and this life. In her quiet moments, she missed her family desperately, and knew they would be looking for her in vain. She wished that she could let them know that she was doing well. She wished she could tell her family about her new world. She felt conflicted; she wanted to be with her family again, but not back in the village from which she had been banished.

CHAPTER 10.

THE WOUNDED TRAVELER

AUGUST – PRESENT YEAR
SIERRAS, CALIFORNIA

REACHING SAFE HARBOR
STRANGERS BECOMING ALLIES
A TIMELY REFUGE.

It all left Nate very weak: Dad's health news, the storm, being blown into the sea, the unnerving events in the wheat field, the young boy chasing him into the cave, the arrow shot through his leg, the loss of blood, and two breath-taking falls through the tunnels, both with hard landings. As he slowly regained consciousness and tried to move, he flinched in pain as the wayward arrow tortured him anew. That pain was the only part of his world he was certain was real. He was becoming delirious, his extremities getting colder by the minute. *Do I dare open my eyes this time? Is there anyone who can help me?*

The last time that thought crossed his mind was earlier that year as he hung bat-like from the seatbelt of his friend Jake's pickup truck that had flipped into a ditch on the way home from a football game. It must have been some drunk that crossed the center line and forced them off the road only a few miles from home. They were not hurt, but the crushed roof kept the doors from opening, and the nearly full gas tank had ruptured.

Nate was now smelling something odd, moist and close, certainly not gasoline. Squinting his eyes open, he looked up, but saw only pitch black. Yet in his imagination he saw Morrow, the fireman-trainee who had just "happened" to see the truck flip and "happened" to have his jaws-of-life in his vehicle at the time. Nate struggled to speak. "Morrow … am I glad to see you. How … how do you always show up at the right time? You got Jake and me out of the truck just before it exploded. Can't ever … thank you enough. It's my leg … I'm hurt. Need a doc this time." His mind drifted. He closed his eyes. He dreamed he was floating.

When he opened them again, Morrow was still there, not doing or saying anything. As he looked up, he could now see stars … and maybe moonlight. *Still that moist smell – is it someone's breath?* It was then Nate realized it wasn't Morrow. It wasn't anyone at all. It was a beast, the largest dog he had ever seen – or was it a wolf – poised over him. He had to get away somehow, but was too weak to move. He could only lie paralyzed with galloping fear. *What more could happen to me today?* The beast's eyes seemed to gleam with an inner light, as they calmly regarded his pitiful and vulnerable condition. Nate could hear the beast's slow respiration. It took in a deeper breath and began to emit a low growling sound.

But it was not a menacing growl. It was a low, measured, intelligible voice. "Fear not. All will end well. You are not alone."

Nate was about to muster a suitable response, but he could not form a cogent thought.

His heart, racing toward shock, was fluttering out of control. *Too much, ... I can't deal with ...* He lapsed into unconsciousness.

"Kawsay is an amazing young woman," Alison declared, finally climbing into bed. She knew Ben was not really asleep even though his eyes were closed. "Since Herschel got her started with English, she's been after me to teach her more and more. I think the teacher is more worn out than the student!" Alison snuggled under the comforter.

"It's great to see the two of you together," Ben responded, mumbling only slightly. "I think she really likes being with us – almost like family. Of course, she's been with us for three months now."

"You know, I think you're right. Perhaps this is starting to feel like home to her, though she's obviously worried about her mother, brother, and grandparents. It's been fun having her help me with the garden and other chores, especially in the kitchen. That veggie dish we had yesterday afternoon was mostly an Inca recipe."

"Really? It was quite good. Maybe we should just hand over kitchen duties to her full time!"

"Well, Ben, we do need to figure out what to do with her, but whatever her future is, it's not as our cook."

Ben rolled over, opened his eyes, and gave her his full attention. "Alison, we are responsible, but what *can* we do with her? If the press got hold of this, things could totally get out of control. It would be a circus. And they'd ask us where we got her and if we believed she came from the past. What would we tell them that wouldn't make us look crazy?"

"Well, Ben, do *you* think Herschel is right – that she is a living relic of, what did he call it, 'a post-Inca Empire splinter group'? You haven't really said."

"You have to admit, honey, if you put aside what we 'know' is impossible, the evidence supports Herschel's theory," Ben answered. "What evidence do we have that her story is *not* possible? Maybe it's happened to other people, and we just don't know about it."

"Ben, I understand your logic, but the whole idea is just ridiculous. Have you thought about the implications?"

"Actually, Alison, I've thought about it a lot, and I think the implications are a little scary. If it happened once, it could happen again. Where would it end?"

"I see what you mean, but don't you think it's a little exciting too?" Alison's mind churned through the possibilities. "I mean, in our work we're always trying to figure out the past from little pieces left in the ground – pottery and tools, even garbage. Imagine how much more we'd learn if we could actually talk to the ancients! They could teach us so much!"

"Like good organic recipes?" Ben joked.

"Not a bad start! I think they could teach us a lot about herbal remedies and interesting natural diets. There's a lot of wisdom that has been lost. Anyway, it's late, and Kawsay's likely to be up early with more questions."

"You really like her, don't you, honey?" Ben asked, watching her eyes.

"Don't you? She's so sharp and, well, not spoiled like kids today. She appreciates everything so much." Alison grew quiet for a moment. "Ben, you know how sometimes you just *know* something, not from logic, but from something deeper?" Ben just looked at her with a little grin. "Well, there's something about all this. I just feel that Kawsay really is just what she appears to be – a little visitor from the past. It scares me, but at the same time it's absolutely wonderful."

"I'm really glad she's here too. It's been fascinating getting to know her. Let's get some sleep. Didn't Helmut say he was planning on leaving in the morning?" They extinguished the lamps and quickly fell asleep.

THUD … THUD … THUD.

This time they awoke together with only a few cobwebs to clear. They listened.

THUD … THUD … THUD.

Ben grabbed his robe. "Let's check this out, but this time, please get the shotgun." He and Alison quickly made their way across the large living room to the front door. Kawsay came scurrying down the hall to join them. Junior was right behind her, helping out with short barks and squeals. Alison corralled the large puppy by the collar.

"Who is here?" Kawsay asked.

"We don't know," Alison answered in a hushed tone.

Ben switched on the porch light and looked through the small window in the large bear-proof door. He immediately saw a human form lying on the porch in the same place they had found Kawsay three months earlier. But just beyond the edge of the circle of light he also saw two large light blue eyes shining back at him. Ben flicked the light off for a second and then back on, and the eyes were gone. "Alison, put Junior in the kitchen, please!" Ben directed. After Junior was secure, Ben hastily unbolted the door and rushed forward, followed closely by Alison and Kawsay. All three knelt down around the unmoving figure.

Their eyes took in the details. Young man, blonde, not too tall, lightweight, damp clothing. "He is hurt! Arrow!" Kawsay was the first to notice the wound.

Alison quickly checked the boy's vitals. Clammy skin, eyes rolled upward, racing pulse. "Let's get Helmut, fast!" Ben and Kawsay took off down the path to Helmut's cabin. Alison remained with the unconscious boy and covered him with her thick robe to conserve what body heat was left in him, careful not to jar the protruding arrow. The boy's face was eerily pale in the dim porch light. *Nice looking. Not a hunter, wrong clothes. Why was this wounded boy delivered here – like Kawsay a few months ago?* After a while, she heard them pounding up the path.

Helmut immediately took over, and Alison stepped back. Ben put his arm around Alison, and she put hers around Kawsay. Helmut began issuing commands. "Need to get him to a warm and light place. Lost too much blood. Need to stabilize. Must get this filthy arrow out. I'll have to break off the tail and pull it through."

They slipped their arms under him, Ben at the head, Alison at the feet, and Helmut in the middle, guarding the leg from further damage. They carried the young man carefully down to Helmut's cabin where he kept a small arsenal of medical supplies. As they entered the cabin and turned on the main light, Ben got a good look at the still ashen face. He retrieved Alison's bathrobe as Helmut began to cut away the blood-stained trouser leg. *This boy seems familiar,* Ben thought. *But I can't place him.*

"Ben, Alison and I can handle this. She has the training." Helmut was hooking up an

IV and pulling out various surgical weapons.

"Yes, please take Kawsay back to the house and see if you can settle her into bed," Alison suggested. "I'll call you as soon as we know something."

Ben had been dismissed, but knew that the patient was in good hands.

"Come, Kawsay," Ben said quietly, "Let us go back to the house and put you back to bed. We will learn more in the morning."

Kawsay and Ben left reluctantly. As they approached the house, they noticed the front door had been left open, and Junior had somehow escaped. He was nervously skimming the ground in front of the house, excited about some new scent. Seeing them approach, he broke off the investigation and bounded over.

Ben and Kawsay each scratched an ear. "C'mon, Junior, it's not safe out here," Ben said, guiding him inside.

Ben led Kawsay back to her room. She jumped into her bed. "Try to sleep, Kawsay. So much going on."

"Yes. I will." Ben kissed her forehead and began to leave. "Ben?"

"Yes, Kawsay?"

"You saw the arrow?"

"Yes. Poor boy."

"The arrow is same as your arrow."

"What?" Ben asked. "Same as what arrow?"

"Same as arrow in your big book room upstairs."

Ben looked at Kawsay with surprise. "Are you sure?"

She nodded. Ben nodded back and gave her a brief smile. "Thank you. Try to sleep. Enough excitement for one night." He left quietly and softly retreated up to his library. He had a lot of thinking to do.

Ben was still there at 6:00 a.m. when Helmut found him, head down on his great desk, asleep. Helmut had burst into the room with important news, and it was too late to leave quietly. Ben had awakened at Helmut's heavy footfalls and noticed a crick in his neck. "Oh. Helmut. Hi. Guess I fell asleep while studying. How did things go with the boy? Is he OK?"

Helmut was breathing heavily from hustling up the path from the cabin. "Bro, we need to talk about this," he panted.

"Is the kid OK? Don't keep me in suspense."

"Nathaniel. His name is Nathaniel Diamond. Lives down in Menlo Park. See, here's his driver's license."

"Good. As soon as the Sun is up, we can call his parents. I'm sure they're worried. But Helmut, is he going to be all right?" Ben persisted.

"Yeah, he's out of any danger. But take a close look at this license." Helmut continued to hold it out to Ben, one eyebrow raised.

Ben gave it a once-over. Now his eyebrows lifted a bit. "Doesn't look like mine. There's some hi-tech photo thing and a different design. Is it a fake or something?"

"Keep looking."

Ben scanned the plastic again. This time his eyebrows went quite a bit higher. "You mean the birth date? It says February 14th, um." Ben paused. "So, that would make him a bit over thirteen. I see – I would have guessed more like sixteen or so."

"Ben, you're still asleep. Don't you get it? Last time I checked, this state wasn't in the habit of allowing thirteen-year-old kids to drive. Has that changed? Also, the issue date on the license is in late February three years from now!"

Ben was quiet. Helmut was right as usual. This didn't make sense.

"There's more. Take a look at this." Helmut held out the two pieces of the arrow he had extracted from the boy's leg. "Sorry I had to break off the tail, but I'm sure you understand that it was important not to drag the tip or the tail through all that raw flesh. Infection is a great enough danger with puncture wounds."

"It's just an arrow; what does it matter? What's important is how – what was the name, Nathaniel? – how bad is his wound?"

"He'll be fine. No major damage to vessels or nerves, I'd say. Mostly a loss of blood. Antibiotics should take care of whatever I couldn't wash out. Probably should stay off the leg for a while, though. Mercifully, he's asleep now. When he wakes up, maybe he can help us with his little mystery."

"You mean the license?" Ben asked.

"Ben! Please! Just look at the arrow."

Ben took the pieces from his brother and examined them under his desk lamp. He had been thinking about the arrow all night, but his heart quickened when he actually touched it. Ben did not want to have this conversation with his brother, at least not right now. Kawsay had been right about the arrow, of course, but Ben had hoped Helmut would not notice. "Hmmm. This looks similar to the one I have in my collection."

"Right, just like the one that you had when you visited my Big Bird crash scene."

"This can't be!" Ben protested. "How could a thirteen-year-old, or sixteen, whatever, California kid have one of those arrows?"

"Well, I was kinda hoping you could tell me. We never did find out exactly where you got your arrow either, did we? Maybe this kid can shed some light on where you came from? Do you think so?"

Ben hesitated. "Sure, when he comes to. Can you stay a few more days until he's out of danger?"

"Yeah, no problem. I wasn't too keen on leaving here just yet as it was. This is the only place I really feel at home and where all the good memories live, and I need to rest and recharge. Besides, it's getting really interesting. First the Inca girl, and now the kid with the impossible driver's license and the familiar arrow. What's your next surprise for me?"

"Well, I wish I knew, I really do. Somehow, though, I think there's more to come." Ben got up and gingerly placed the arrow on the shelf near its mate. Then he went to shower and get dressed. Helmut watched him leave and slowly shook his head.

"Ben, I like the way you help me with breakfasts. In fact, I *really* like it when you have it all ready for me when I show up in the kitchen a little late." Alison looked great today in her jeans and T-shirt that said "*Shalom* – We Dig You", a souvenir of the archeological dig north of Shechem where they had first met. "Looks like our friend Kawsay is sleeping in after last night's excitement. I didn't get to bed until after three. I saw the note on my pillow saying you'd be down when you were done. I'm sorry I didn't come and retrieve you; I must have fallen asleep. What were you studying upstairs so late?"

"Trying to figure some things out. What did you learn about our new arrival?" Ben asked, diverting the discussion.

"Nice looking boy. Scary wound. But it could have been much worse. He lost lots of blood, but Helmut thinks there's no major damage. I wonder who would shoot him and then leave him? He could have bled to death!"

"Looks like we have two young mysteries," Ben said. "I have some ideas I want to bounce off you later today, but first I'd like to talk with Nathaniel when he wakes up."

"That would be great. We're usually good at figuring things out when we put our heads together. I didn't wait all those years to find you to be on the outside looking in."

"Thanks," Ben said. "How about a hike to our favorite overlook? It's been a while."

Before Alison could answer, the intercom from the cabin beeped. "Ben, you there? Thought you'd want to know. My patient is awake and agitated. Wants to call his dad. You still want to talk to him? Maybe you can calm him down."

"Thanks, Helmut. Be right down." Ben quickly finished his cereal. Grabbing his jacket, Ben gave a bewildered Alison a short hug, and she reeled him in for a much longer kiss. "I'll be back soon. Let's take our walk about eleven. Can we bring some cheese sandwiches? Seems that's our tradition."

"Do you want me to come along with you now?" Alison asked.

"Thanks, but I really need to talk to young Nathaniel alone. I'll explain later." He rushed out the door and virtually sprinted down the path. He was quickly at the door of Helmut's cabin, a smaller version of the big house made by the same local log home master. He did not wait to be invited in and found Helmut cleaning up his dining room, which doubled as his operating room. "Can I see him?"

"I'd tell you not to upset him, but it's too late. See if you can calm him down – he's still light-headed." Helmut pointed toward the extra bedroom in the back. Ben strode over to the door and peeked inside. The bedside lamp was on, and the young man was wide awake.

"May I come in? My name is Ben Hunter. I found you by my front door last night."

"Sure. Maybe you can help me."

"I hope I can. Maybe you can help me too, Nathaniel."

"Just 'Nate'. That's what everyone calls me."

"That was a bad wound. Good thing you got here when you did – you were going into shock."

"Yeah, I was pretty far gone. I wasn't sure what was real and what was not. Where am I anyway? The doctor didn't want to tell me anything. Said I needed to talk with you."

"The doctor is my brother, Helmut. We're lucky he was here last night. He tells me that you'll be fine in a few weeks, though you won't be up for a marathon for a while." Ben smiled, trying to ease Nate's mind.

"That's not what's worrying me. I need to call my dad, or try to. I don't know if he's home or actually if he's even alive."

"Why, what happened to your dad?"

"Last I saw him – was it yesterday or a few days ago? I've lost track of time. He was drowning in a storm in the Bahamas. I couldn't save him 'cause I got sucked under, then I woke up in a cave by a wheat field, got shot with that arrow, and ended up in another cave. Let's see... Oh, yeah. I was pretty out of it! Then, unless I dreamed it, a giant wolf or something brought me to your house. I know this sounds crazy, but I just need to understand what's happened to me. If my dad's alive, he probably is as worried about me as I am about him." Nate finally took a breath so Ben could get in a word.

"Nate, let's just slow down. Maybe we can sort this out. You're not crazy, at least no more than I am." Ben smiled; Nate relaxed a little and smiled back. "Here, have some more of this wonderful elixir my brother concocted for you." Nate took a deep draw on the straw.

"OK, Mr. Hunter. So where am I exactly?" Nate scanned the room for clues.

"You're at the Hunter family estate, a little in-holding in the National Forest, a few hours east of your home. It's been in the family for years. I spent most of my growing-up years here." Ben relaxed, leaning against the wall by the window.

"So this is your house?"

"No, the whole property is owned by a family trust. This is Helmut's cabin. He moved down here after I got married a few years ago. Alison and I live just up the path in a larger house."

"I was wondering how often this cabin is used. That calendar is pretty out of date."

Ben looked where Nate's eyes had traveled. A current-year calendar with helicopter action photos was hanging on the far wall. "What do you mean? I just gave it to Helmut for Christmas."

"What? Why would you give him a calendar that's three years out of date? You must have gotten a real bargain," Nate remarked.

Ben felt a shiver up and down his spine. *First the driver's license – now the calendar! Another late night delivery from the cave.* He had to think fast. "Yeah, I suppose so." Ben needed to know one more thing. "Nate, who shot you?"

"I'm not sure, but I think it was maybe an accident. It's part of what's jumbled in my mind." Nate could see that this was important to his host. "Remember I mentioned a wheat field? I was running back to the hole in the cliff where I had come from when the arrow hit me. A kid was chasing me, and somehow I made it back to the cave. But he isn't the one who shot the arrow. There was a tall man who was yelling at the kid. He shot me."

"Interesting. Do you remember anything about the kid?" Ben asked warily.

"Not too much. It all happened so fast. He had dark hair and a long brown cloak. The tall guy was yelling something at him like 'Yaw mean'."

Why did this happen, and to this particular boy, Ben wondered. *There must be something special about him.* Ben decided to probe. "Nate, do you have an interest in history?"

"Yeah, my dad says I'm obsessive, especially about the ancient Middle East. Don't know why, but I guess he's right."

"What about languages?" Ben prompted.

"Well, I've learned a little about European languages in school, and I've been teaching myself Greek and Hebrew because of my interest in the Bible. Why do you ask?" Nate responded.

"That's fine, Nate. Just one more question." Ben smiled and took a breath. "Was the kid carrying anything?"

"He was just running after me ... I don't know ... Well ... Yeah. He was running with two arrows in his hand. Funny how the mind works. There I was with an arrow in my leg and I wondered if his teacher had ever told him not to run with sharp objects."

Ben had heard enough. He needed time to integrate all of this. Whether Nate was from the future or the past, he was part of the key to something that had been on Ben's mind all these years. "Nate, please promise me one thing, OK?"

"Sure. What?" Nate knew he owed these people his life.

Ben drew near, looked Nate gently in the eyes, and spoke quietly. "Just don't do anything for a few days. Don't try to go anywhere or call anyone. You know what I mean? When you regain some strength, we'll talk more about this." Ben saw that Nate understood. "I think I can help you understand what's happened, but my talented brother would probably think you're a little crazy. Remember, you're *not*, but that's because I know you're telling the truth. Thanks for telling me what you remember. All this is very important."

"OK, Mr. Hunter. But see if you can find out about my dad. Please?"

"Fine, Nate. That's fair. Oh, there a few more people you need to meet later. My sweetheart, Alison – a fellow archeologist – and our little visitor from Peru, Kawsay. She had some plastic surgery on her lip a few months ago, so she'll be interested in your bandages."

"Are you really archeologists? Both of you? That's a field that I'm thinking of getting into. Gee, I want to know all about it."

Ben realized he'd hit on one of Nate's hot buttons, and as a result failed to calm him down at all like Helmut had requested. "We'll have plenty of time for that. Good to meet you, Nate. I'm glad you're here. See you later. Helmut's a great doctor, so do whatever he tells you. Remember, what you most need now is rest – you've been through a lot." Ben patted Nate's arm and quietly slipped out.

Neat guy, but why was he so interested in the wheat field? Nate wondered.

Helmut had not been right at the door, but had overheard quite a bit as he finished cleaning up. "So, did you manage to ease his mind like I asked you to?"

"I don't know that I did. Sorry. He's looking pretty good, though, considering. I told him to cool it for a few days. Hope that helps."

Helmut ushered Ben out the front door and asked him in hushed tones, "What do you make of the whole thing?"

"I have some ideas I want to bounce off you later. I promised Alison a short hike and picnic. Let's connect later this afternoon, OK?" He could see Helmut's exasperation with being put off again. Ben continued in a low voice. "One thing you should know, though. Nate – that's what he goes by – thinks it's three years in the future. We'll have to tell him before too long that it's not, and I don't know how he'll react. Learning that right now definitely would not calm him down."

"There I agree with you. Have a nice walk with Alison. We can talk later." As Ben was leaving, Helmut put a hand on Ben's shoulder and added, "You know, Bro, I think it's great the way you and Alison relate together. I really envy you. I thought you were a bachelor for life, but she's really brought out the best in you. I don't know how you do it, but the honeymoon doesn't seem to be ending."

"Helmut, it's not. It just keeps getting better. She's just amazing."

Something had clicked in Alison's mind. From time to time, Ben had written her Haikus that seemed unusual, as if he was attempting to communicate to her something he could not bring himself to say out loud. She had put them aside in a special place for future reference. Alison picked up her book of Ben's haikus. She sat by their bed, reviewing them from a new perspective.

I am love's arrow
Launched across the centuries
Whose mark is your heart.

There's one of those mysterious haikus again. She had been slipping the unusual ones into the front pocket. *Where are the others like that? There they are…* She began leafing through them.

I have journeyed far
Left my life and world behind
So I could find you.

Neither time nor space
Not even hectic careers
Could keep us apart.

Of all the relics
That you have or will unearth
Only one loves you.

The will of our God
Whose bridges fly beyond time
Willed us to be one.

Alison thought these haikus were beautiful, even if they did not make sense to her. She decided the time had come to ask Ben what he was trying to tell her.

CHAPTER 11.

BEN'S STORY

AUGUST – PRESENT YEAR
SIERRAS, CALIFORNIA

WHEN YOU HEAR MY TALE
WILL YOU STILL BELIEVE IN ME
WILL WE BE THE SAME?

The Sierra peaks do not give up their beauty to the casual visitor. The west slope roads and rivers follow V-shaped valleys, and long vistas of distant peaks are rare. And so it was with the Hunter property, with the exception of one high escarpment, a rocky outcropping scoured bare by harsh winter gales. There Ben had spent many wonderful hours during his teenage years studying, contemplating his life, and seeking answers. He called it his "Window to Heaven". When he first brought Alison home with him from the Middle East as his new bride, Ben insisted that they visit his special place on their first day. Once she got over a slight bout of vertigo, Alison, a flatlander from the rolling grasslands of southwestern Minnesota, declared that Ben's "Window" was one of the most beautiful and peaceful places on Earth. Today, Ben and Alison briskly climbed the switchback trail to what was now *their* Window, over 1,000 feet above the rushing mountain stream.

They chose a perfect day, with a warm sun in and out of light clouds contrasting with a refreshing breeze. Arriving at the overlook, Ben spread a small tarp on the ground by the lone gnarled tree only a few feet from the precipice. Alison always wondered why Ben seemed so heedless of the danger, but had given up sounding warnings about falling. A boulder provided them a backrest just the width of their porch loveseat. "If I'd known about all of this," Alison gestured to the panorama before them, "I'd have married you sooner."

"What do you mean? We'd been together less than two weeks when I proposed. Wasn't that fast enough?" Ben liked the theme of their unusual courtship.

"No it wasn't. I was losing patience and thought about telling you to forget it!"

"Well, I think our timing was just fine. I remember our colleagues telling us we were nuts to get married on the spot, but every day we prove them more and more wrong," Ben said. "I wouldn't advise young people to marry so hastily, but we were fully-formed adults and had a lot of lost time to make up!"

"We'd only been together for that first week when I had to go back home for my grandmother's funeral. I hate funerals and felt bad that I hadn't been with her at the end. You'd been keeping me up late every night, and I used the time back home to rest. It seemed you and I had endless things to talk about – not just our life histories, but our views on politics, religion, UFOs – all those really important things."

"I think it was providential that we had those ten days apart. It gave us both time to think," Ben said.

"Think?" Alison turned to him and put her nose an inch from his. "I wasn't *thinking*, I was going crazy! When I thought of you so far away, I could hardly breathe. My family didn't want me to return because they thought I'd caught something!"

"Well you had – you'd caught me! I had one good rest after you left and then started falling behind on sleep again, staying up late, writing you extremely candid e-mails." Ben's nose was now touching hers.

"You were more than candid. Do you realize the number of pages we filled?" she asked. "We were strangers on the surface, but I got to know your essence, your soul. It was obvious to me that despite what my mind was telling me, I couldn't *not* be with you."

"Alison," Ben's nose retreated a bit so he could see her eyes more clearly. "I liked that you were a strong woman who didn't need anyone to take care of her, but during that time of separation, I felt like I'd been given a new job as your protector."

They embraced and kissed. Ben hesitated, not sure how to proceed. He had known that this moment would arrive someday, but had never been sure how to handle it.

Alison helped him. "Ben, there's something important you need to tell me, isn't there?" No response, as Ben looked away across the canyon, retreating within himself. "It's about your past, isn't it?" Alison was the intuitive thinker in the family.

"Yeah, it is. I've figured out some things, or to be truthful, come to a point where you might actually believe me when I tell you."

"I thought our understanding was that we would not keep secrets, except about Christmas presents." Alison tried to keep things light, but knew this was about a missing piece of their foundation.

"I wanted to tell you from the beginning, but sensed that if we got into it when we first met, you'd think I was nuts."

"Look, I already know you're nuts. But you're the finest man in the world, and if you're nuts, then we're nuts together." Alison knew how to draw Ben out.

"The more time passed, the harder it was to talk about it because you'd wonder why I'd waited so long. Now I know it's time because I think you might believe me now. The last few months prove that it's all true."

Alison settled back and looked at the passing clouds, not wanting to press Ben too hard. "On a day like this, nothing you tell me could upset me. How can this place be so peaceful? … Look at those cirrus clouds," Alison said pointing high over the far western ridge. "They look like arrows with those little swooshes on the end."

"That's the key, Alison – the arrows." He was more confident now. "Did you notice anything unusual about the arrow Helmut took out of our latest visitor?" She shook her head. "You were probably too busy with the surgery to look closely. Helmut brought it to me before breakfast. It's on my shelf now. It's just like the one that's already there – the one I had when I first met Helmut thirty years ago." He let that sink in.

"Now that you mention it," she replied, "I did wonder about it. It's not like the arrows hunters use today."

"No, not at all. Hunters don't use arrows with Hebrew inscriptions," Ben suggested. "And they don't shoot at young boys who fall off sailboats."

"Just a minute, Ben, slow down. Give this to me in little bites. An inscription about a sailboat?"

"Right. I mean no, not about a sailboat." Ben took a breath and started again. "Alison, we both know Hebrew very well. The inscription on both arrows shows that they are special recreational arrows, not war arrows. Did you ever notice what it says? 'House of Saul'."

"That *is* strange. What could it mean? And how could Nathaniel have the same type of arrow as you did?" Alison was getting into this mystery.

"I hope you can help me figure it out; I have a theory. By the way, he goes by 'Nate', and there's something else about him that's very unusual. He thinks it's three years in the future."

"What? What makes him think that?" Alison asked, now totally engaged.

"Helmut showed me Nate's California driver's license, and if it's to be believed, Nate was born a little over thirteen years ago. The license was – or will be – issued in February three years from now."

"Well, it's obviously a fake of some kind. He'd have to be at least sixteen to get a license."

"He *is* sixteen, honey. You saw him. Even with growth hormones, thirteen-year-olds don't look like that. I think he got lost in time like Kawsay, except that he came to us from the opposite direction." They both let a moment of silence pass.

"So, you no longer have any doubt that Kawsay is from the past?" Alison asked.

"Are you finding that hard to accept?" Ben countered.

"Well, doesn't it all seem a bit strange?" Alison piled on a third unanswered question.

Ben ended the question game. He adjusted his posture, turning more toward Alison. "Well, all the evidence supports Herschel's original theory. Except there's just one problem – everyone knows that it's impossible, so there must be another explanation," Ben stated.

"If it's impossible, how do *you* explain Nate's license?" challenged Alison.

"I don't. I think we now have two strong pieces of corroborating evidence staring us right in the face, and we need to reconsider the presupposition that their narratives are not possible." Ben found that multi-syllabic words made this easier to talk about.

"Well," Alison said, "I know that you've done some reading on the subject of time. What do you think? And what about Nate's arrow? How does that fit in?"

"Right, the arrow. Well, that's what's so strange. How could he have an arrow from the distant past if he came from the future?" Ben asked another stalling question.

Alison challenged, "How do you *know* it's from the distant past?" Alison had arrived at the nub of the matter.

"Well, we have Kawsay and Nate. There's a third piece of evidence that settles the matter."

"There is?" Alison furrowed her brow. "What might that be?" She really didn't know what to expect, but was prepared for almost anything by this point.

Ben took a deep breath and exhaled slowly. "Yeah. The inscription. It means exactly what it says. The arrows belonged to the King of Israel, or actually his son."

"What do you mean? Israel hasn't had a king since, well, almost forever."

"Almost. I'm talking about the first king – Saul, David's predecessor. Remember his son, Jonathan?"

"Sure, I know those stories as well as you do," Alison responded, not liking her intelligence insulted.

"Actually, honey, you don't. I know them better than you might imagine."

"But we've both studied archaeology," Alison said. "There's no doubt about Saul's historicity. After all, we've visited Tel el-Ful and looked at what is generally accepted to be his small fortress, though I understand there is still some debate whether that site is historical Gibeah."

"Well, I've looked at the surrounding countryside and am confident that it *is* historical Gibeah," Ben added.

"Fine, but how did you get one of Saul's arrows, if that's where it came from."

"I had it with me the morning I met Nate."

"What do you mean? You met him last night," Alison responded, starting to lose patience with Ben's loopy travelogue.

"Sorry. Please. This is hard for me." Ben paused. "I'm not sure yet why Nate was there. I don't think he should have been. He messed up the whole story. But I know I was there, and I know where I came from. It's time you knew."

"I agree. Are you talking about the third piece of evidence?" Alison braced herself. She felt like Ben had been removing a bandage millimeter by millimeter.

"Yes. I'm the third piece. If you believe Kawsay's and Nate's stories, maybe you can believe mine too," Ben said, finally arriving at the moment he had so long avoided. "I was Jonathan's helper. My older brother, Shimon, was his shield-bearer. Our father, Jokim, was a leading herdsman under Saul's chief herdsman, Doeg."

Alison, taking this all in, noticed that Ben obviously did not like Doeg. "So what is your real name?" Alison thought it a fair question in light of the surreal nature of their conversation.

"Benjamin, or Binyamin in Hebrew, same thing."

Alison searched his eyes, making sure her Ben was still in there. "I don't doubt that you believe your own story, but can you be sure it's all true, that you didn't just dream it or something? I thought you had some kind of amnesia when the Hunters found you. Your subconscious may have embroidered all of this." Alison was reluctant to accept Ben's "third piece" of evidence because it was so frightening, so bizarre. She looked out at the clouds and allowed her mind to consider whether her Ben may truly be a bit crazy. *But what about Kawsay and Nate? I don't know what is real anymore.*

"My mind didn't embroider the arrows, and it didn't embroider your Bible either. You have told me you wish you could meet Bible characters. I'm pretty minor, but I'm in there."

"In where?" Alison returned her gaze to Ben, trying to calm herself and listen to the whole story.

"In 1 Samuel Chapter 20." He noticed Alison's eyes riveted on his. "After I arrived here, I mean in the Sierras thirty years ago, I had no idea where I was. Helmut took me home to his family. I was afraid and disoriented. Of course, I was desperate to return to my original home, but later learned that I could not. I knew the Hunters didn't speak my language, so I barely spoke to them at all. I tried to learn their language and their culture. A twelve-year-old learns quickly, but it took me a long time to piece things together. They thought I was a little slow because I did not talk about my past even after I learned English. They tried to find my family through police and private investigators. They finally just accepted me as a big bundle from heaven and gave up trying to figure it all out. By that time, Helmut and I were like brothers, so they just adopted me into the family. I was still trying to understand where I was from, and I asked for some language books."

Ben paused to gather his thoughts. "It's interesting, but my discovery of my past came from a spiritual quest. The Hunter family wasn't much for attending church – there just aren't any near here – but they did have devotions and had Bibles around. After I learned to read, I had my own spiritual awakening and was trying to find God. It was a real challenge to reconcile what I had already learned about God from my original family with the Hunters' New Testament stories that were totally new to me. One long winter day when Helmut was off with his, I mean, our dad, I was flipping through some of the historical books when I came across Samuel anointing King Saul. It wasn't until then that I began to realize what had happened to me. Until then I didn't know if I was just in some other country or maybe another planet. It hadn't occurred to me that I was really in another time, about 3,000 years after my birth."

Alison, despite the immensity of his tale, couldn't resist adding some humor. "Honey, I keep telling you that you don't look your age."

Ben laughed nervously before continuing. "Anyway, I kept reading until the chapter in 1 Samuel I mentioned, and then it came back to me in Technicolor. I was a refugee from the Bible, AWOL from my place in history. My little story didn't just talk about me, but it explained the arrows too. I could not get around it; it couldn't be a coincidence. I was all excited and thought I should run and tell everyone about it, but then I realized it was ridiculous. I knew no one would believe me, and even if they did, what could they do about it? So I just let it go. I think you can understand, though, why I showed an early interest in archeology."

"So, what is your story? I remember something about Jonathan signaling David with some arrows." Alison was trying to reserve judgment. She wanted Ben to always be open with her and did not want to reproach him when he was obviously being sincere – even if it seemed fantastical.

"Right. Here, let me read it to you." Ben pulled out the small Bible he had brought along in the pack. "You remember how Saul was losing his mind and alternating between treating David like his son-in-law and like his enemy, trying to kill him?" Alison nodded. "Well, my master, Jonathan, was a close friend of David, closer than a brother, and did not want to believe that his father was trying to kill David. So they found a way for Jonathan to test Saul, and then for him to signal David whether it was safe for him to stay around or not. Jonathan was supposed to go out to the place where David was hiding, a rocky field outside of town, and shoot three arrows. He brought me along to help him, but I didn't know about the plan to signal David. I just thought it was a fun outing. As the Bible explains, the plan was that if it was safe for David to remain in King Saul's house, then when I went out to retrieve the arrows, Jonathan would yell something about the arrows being off to my side. Conversely, if it wasn't safe for David to remain, then Jonathan would yell that the arrows were beyond me. Here, let me read it to you. The key part begins in verse 35:

And it came to pass in the morning, that Jonathan went out into the field at the time appointed with David, and a little lad with him. And he said to his lad, Run, find out now the arrows which I shoot. And as the lad ran, he shot an arrow beyond him. And when the lad was come to the place of the arrow which Jonathan had shot, Jonathan cried after the lad, and said, Is not the arrow beyond thee? And Jonathan cried after the lad, Make speed, haste, stay not. And Jonathan's lad gathered up the arrows, and came to his master. But the lad knew not any thing: only Jonathan and David knew the matter. And Jonathan gave his artillery unto his lad, and said unto him, Go, carry them into the city.

"According to the account, after I left, Jonathan talked with David and agreed that he had to get away and hide."

"I remember the scene now – a real turning point for the future king. You played a very important role!" Alison was beginning to adjust to Ben's story, and even felt proud of him. "Are you mentioned anywhere else in the Bible?"

"No, and neither is my family. The only other people I recognize that I knew well are my brother's best friend, Ittai, and his father, Ribai, who are mentioned in both 2 Samuel 23:29 and I Chronicles 11:31. It seems that even though Ittai was from Gibeah like my family, at some point he transferred his loyalty from Saul to David and became an important leader in David's army. I remember he was always interested in military training, but then my brother was too. I worry about what happened to my family when Saul lost the kingdom. A lot of his people were killed."

"Well, that's over now. Ancient history. There's nothing that can be done about it now." Alison paused, still struggling to believe Ben's story.

"Well, it's not that simple. Something went wrong, terribly wrong."

"What do you mean, Ben? Sounds like David got his warning and got away."

"But that's not like it happened. I never returned with the arrows. Nate took one of them, and I chased him into a cave and never returned them to Jonathan. Other than what I read in the Biblical account, I don't know what happened next to David and Jonathan."

"What Nate? Our new visitor? I didn't hear him mentioned there? I thought he was a California boy." Alison felt Ben leading her into deep weeds again.

"Yes, Nate." *This is not an easy story to explain. Did I do the right thing bringing this all up?* Ben wondered. "I don't know what he was doing there either. He doesn't realize where he was, but that third arrow – I thought he took it. I tried to catch him and get it back. I didn't know it had accidently stuck in his leg, but he disappeared into a cave at the edge of the field."

"Did you get it back? Did you find him?" Alison was trying to make sense of all this.

"Yes, I did. I got it back this morning when Helmut gave it to me. You see, when I got into the little cave at the edge of the field, I was too late. Nate was already gone."

"Gone where?"

"Gone to here. Don't you see? There was some kind of connection. Nate fell through time. There was some opening in the cave, and he fell into the future just like Kawsay did, I suppose. Me too. I stumbled in the dark trying to find the boy who took my arrow and fell into the same hole after Nate did. Only I didn't arrive in the same place, or more correctly, in the same time. I entered the tunnel a few minutes after Nate, but after a little detour, I arrived here about thirty years *earlier*. I don't know why, but that must be what happened. That's when I met Helmut jumping off a cliff in a bird suit – a fitting end to my day – and his family took me in."

"But the Bible doesn't say anything about all this," Alison objected. "Are you saying the Bible is wrong?" Ben's story seemed to be getting even more convoluted.

"I'd never say that. I think it has to be right, somehow. It's Nate that seems wrong – like he wasn't supposed to be there. He messed it all up, though it wasn't his fault. He had just arrived there that same morning. Seems like he had quite a day too. He says he got sucked down a hole in the ocean off the Bahamas and turned up in Saul's wheat field just in time to run in front of Jonathan's arrow. What I've struggled with all these years, besides being exiled from my world, is how to undo that accident. I'm afraid of what may happen if I don't fix it, but I don't know how. Yet somehow it must get fixed, or has already gotten fixed. I just don't know how."

"Well, maybe you can return the arrows," Alison proposed.

"Maybe, but there are several problems with that. First, how could I get back there? Even if I jumped back into the tunnel, who knows where I'd end up? Second, how could I complete the story? I'm not a little boy any more. Jonathan would know something was wrong. Finally, there were three arrows. I brought one with me. Nate brought another arrow. I'd need to get the third."

"Do you know where it is?"

"I fear it is lost. See, I made a detour. On my way here from Gibeah I made a stop somewhere in another cave. There was this weird guy there – face paint, feathers in his hair, a necklace of human teeth, big earrings, and a goofy grin. He scared me half to death! To get away, I threw one of the arrows at him and jumped back into the time tunnel. I can't imagine how I could ever retrieve the third arrow."

Ben didn't know what else to add to his revelation. "So, Alison, do you have something about your history that you need to tell me?" He had the little smile that he used when he knew he was shamelessly diverting a conversation.

"Oh, Ben, there are a lot of black sheep in my family, but no lost sheep like you. Well, it must have been really traumatic for you to suddenly be separated from your family, from your entire world. I think you've done amazingly well in your new life. I'm tempted to be really mad at you for keeping this from me, but I understand the dilemma you were in. Until Kawsay arrived, and now Nate, I don't know if I *could* have accepted your story. Even now it's really difficult, but you leave me no choice. Three displaced persons under my care! If Kawsay can bridge several centuries, so can you. Who am I to deny what you say? I have to trust you. You took a long time to tell me this, but I know that you're not a liar or a lunatic, so what's left?" She processed Ben's story a little more. "We know the Bible is true, and archeology has shown that a lot of its history is accurate, even in small details. I have to believe something will happen to fix your episode. It's not your fault. You didn't do anything wrong. God's in charge and He'll have to find a way to fix it. Apparently He already has, or the Bible story would read differently."

"Maybe you're right, but I'm worried that there's some unfinished business that may take me back there, away from you. I wonder if all this – our wonderful life here – is some kind of mistake, and one day I'll awaken, and it will all have been a dream. That thought weighs heavily on me. If anything took me away from you, … well, I just couldn't go on. I also worry about what happened to my family, my original family. They must have been sick with worry about me."

Alison saw the deep concern in Ben's eyes, and her heart went out to him. "Ben, dear Benjamin, I don't know what all this means, but I know without any doubt one thing for sure. We were created for each other, and God brought us together for one purpose beyond all others – to care for each other forever. Nothing can ever take us away from each other, not even temporary inconveniences like death and tunnels through time. Nothing."

Ben could not speak. A small tear appeared in the corner of each eye. Alison was blinking away tears too, and they could only embrace one another, first gently, and then fiercely, as if to signal to the entire universe that they would never be separated, no matter what. After several minutes, first with sobbing, then with laughter at their extreme drama, they let go and gave each other happy grins. Ben broke the silence. "I knew we'd have this discussion sometime, and I feared it more and more as time passed. I never imagined it would be one more episode that would strengthen our bonds. This soul mate thing is such a mystery."

"Ben, every time we've gone through a crisis we have come through it closer than ever," Alison said. "There is nothing we can't face together. Oh, by the way, you've solved one of my mysteries. Thank you!"

"What mystery? What are you talking about?"

Alison had her little quizzical grin. "You know I save all the poetry we write to each other. Some of the ones you'd written I just wasn't sure about. You know the ones. They talked about crossing time and space, leaving yourself behind, bridges flying beyond time, … oh, and that one about you being an old relic! Really, Ben!"

"Well, see, I was trying to tell you about me. I was just being a little cryptic," Ben said, thinking himself pretty clever.

"Just a little, I'd say."

"Alison, what about the others?" Ben asked, returning to a serious tone.

"What do you mean?"

"I need your advice. What do I tell Helmut? What do we tell Nate and Kawsay? Where does it end? We could all get locked up in an asylum if we ever tell our stories!"

Alison pondered the problem. "Look, there are people running loose – especially here in California – with far stranger tales than yours, Kawsay's and Nate's, and no one's locked them up. They call into that all-night AM radio show all the time, claiming they are from other galaxies. How could you compete with them?" They both laughed. "But, I think publicity of any kind would be terrible. Sure, some people would think you three are crazy, but it could be worse if you *were* believed. It could be like a circus – or a fishbowl. How could Kawsay ever have a normal life? Maybe you and I could handle it, but not young people. At least for now, this has to be kept quiet."

"I can't keep it from Helmut; he's already more than suspicious. I think he's partly figured it all out. And it won't take Nate long to figure out that he's been displaced too. Kawsay won't accept the fact that her family has been gone for four-hundred years. She still is waiting for them to follow her."

"OK," Alison agreed. "Let's start with Helmut. I'll vouch for you if he gives you any trouble. Then we can deal with Nate. Kawsay, well, that may be the least of our problems. Herschel shared his theory with her as best he could early on, and she seems to be adjusting pretty well. But she still expects Yachay will find her any day now."

"Sounds like a good plan. We might have to bring Herschel and Grace inside the loop eventually, but let's take things a step at a time." Ben stopped and looked at Alison ominously. "There's one more thing before we leave our beautiful 'Window'."

"No, please, I don't know if I can bear any more revelations in one day!" Alison wasn't kidding.

"Ah!" Ben let his Hebrew accent come out as he slowly pulled two Ziplocs out of his pack. "Let me reveal to you, all the way from the twenty-first century, the greatest cheese sandwiches in the history of the world!"

Alison giggled. She inspected both packets. "This one is yours," she said, pointing.

They looked alike to Ben, until he saw the slightly damp little note in the one identified as his. He smiled as he slipped it out and read it:

It's not where we start
It's where we are now, my love
And where we're going.

Ben had to wonder, *Did she suspect all along?* It was a picnic they would never forget. It would become part of their unfolding story.

"Doctor Hunter?" Nate called out.

Helmut put down the Stephen Hawking book with a chapter about time travel he had retrieved an hour ago from Ben's library. The physics of time was a topic he and Ben had always found fascinating. He poked his head into Nate's room. "Hi, partner. Feeling better?"

"Yeah, thanks to your handiwork. Do you do a lot of arrow extractions?" asked Nate with a smile.

"Sure, all the time. A guy could get rich that way. Getting hungry? I think you're ready for solids."

"Famished. I don't know when I last ate. I'm a growing boy, you know!" Nate was in good spirits.

"Right. At your age you'll heal quickly too. What sounds good?"

Nate responded without hesitation, "What about peanut butter – the staff of life?"

"I'll join you. Hmmm. Looks like I'll have to borrow a jar from Ben. I won't be long."

"One more thing doc. What day is this?"

"You mean the date?" asked Helmut a little defensively.

"No, I mean the day of the week?"

"Oh, it's Saturday. Best day of the week."

Nate listened as Helmut banged around for a few minutes and then shut the door on his way out. This was his chance! He slowly, painfully, carefully uncovered his legs, noting the white wrappings on his left thigh. He swung his legs over the side of the bed. While the wound was only through the edge of his hamstring, any flexing produced a sharp pain. *Hope he got all of that arrow out of me!* Using the furniture and door knob as crutches, Nate hobbled into the kitchen, looking for a phone. *Nothing on the wall or counter. Darn.* Then he saw a satellite phone sitting on a duffel bag in the corner. He had to reach it!

Nate flipped it on. He dialed a familiar number. As it rang, he gingerly sat down on a kitchen chair.

"Hello." It was a young voice, trying to sound mature.

"Is my, er, is Mr. Diamond home, please?" Nate asked.

"Sure, just a minute please." Nate heard feet running away. As seconds passed, he felt his damp palms.

"Hello?" asked John Diamond. "Hello?"

"Ah, hello Mr. Diamond … it's good to hear your voice. When did you get back from the Bahamas?"

"I haven't been there for years. Are you sure you have the right number?" John asked impatiently.

"I think so. Who answered the phone?" asked Nate, disguising his voice a little.

"My son, why?"

"Oh, I must have the wrong number then. The person I'm looking for doesn't have a son." Nate clicked off hastily, his mind reeling. *Did I just talk to myself? My dad only has one son! Who does that make me?* He heard footsteps returning down the path. Nate quickly replaced the phone and worked his way back to his bed. He was around the corner before Helmut entered the cabin.

"What do you want with your sandwich?" Helmut called in to Nate.

"Oh, just some fruit and milk," Nate said, trying to calm his voice.

"What about chocolate rice milk? Tastes great and better for the system," Helmut suggested.

"Fine." Nate waited a minute before asking again. "What did you say the date was again?"

"I didn't." Helmut consulted his fancy aviation watch. "It's August 16."

"Right," Nate responded. He needed to know. "What year?"

Before he could stop himself, Helmut rattled off the current year. *Crud – that was stupid.*

"Thanks, doc," came a quiet voice from the next room.

In a few minutes, Helmut brought Nate his lunch, but retreated with minimal conversation. He wanted to collaborate with his brother before proceeding with this time issue. He wasn't sure what Ben knew, but it was more than he did. *Need to gather all the facts before venturing a diagnosis.*

Nate was grateful for the lunch, but was lost in his thoughts, not yet ready to ask more questions. *How can I tell them they are living three years in the past? How can I prove that I'm even myself. They'll find out that I already exist, at least a younger version of me. They will think I'm messing with them somehow. But I have to do something!* Nate continued thinking as the nourishment reached his blood and began to give him some much-needed strength. *Whatever else I do, I need to find some way to warn my dad. He needs to see Uncle Jack soon for an exam to catch that brain cancer early. He just has to believe me!*

Helmut inserted his head into the room. "Nate, Ben and Alison are back from their walk. Ben wanted to see me about something. Think you can get some rest?"

"That's all you doctors ever seem to say," Nate said. "Sure, I'll rest. No one wants me to get healed up more than I do!" Helmut took off quickly, leaving Nate alone with his thoughts. Nate was bright, but nothing in his prior experience had prepared him for his current muddle. *Maybe I'll need some help; maybe this is bigger than me.*

Nate was not alone for very long. He heard quiet footsteps in the next room and pricked up his ears. Then he saw a dark head with two big round, brown eyes peer around the corner at him. The owner of the eyes saw that the intrusion had been detected, and the rest of the form slowly emerged into view.

CHAPTER 12.

ANSWERS BEGET QUESTIONS

AUGUST – PRESENT YEAR
SIERRAS, CALIFORNIA

OUR WORLDS LEFT BEHIND
WHAT SEEMED LIKE THE END GAVE US
OUR NEW BEGINNINGS.

Nate was ready for a distraction. Trying to piece his shattered life together while full of painkillers was yielding more questions than answers. But he was not prepared for this particular distraction.

Kawsay was naturally curious, particularly about a mysterious boy who arrived at night like she did sporting what could be an arrow from her brother, Yachay. She assumed Yachay had tried to follow her, but even with his tracking skills he may not be able to find her here. She also wondered if a new person would notice her repaired lip. So there was a lot on her mind when she slipped down to the cabin to extend her hospitality to Nate.

After Kawsay finished entering the room, a few inches at a time, the two travelers stared at one another for a while, blinking but not saying anything. Nate did not have Kawsay's shyness, a result of her years of being shunned, but he was not accomplished with girls either. He started with a smile. No reaction. He tried the only line he knew. "Hi." No answer. "I'm Nate. You must be …," He had forgotten the name Ben had mentioned, but assumed she was the Peruvian girl.

"I am Kawsay. It means 'to live'," Kawsay said matter-of-factly.

"My name, Nathaniel, means 'God has given'."

"That is nice. God gave us both life!" Kawsay summed things up.

"Hey, that's right. God almost took my life away last night. It is good to be alive today." Nate thought her unique accent was very cute. Kawsay looked very together. Nate took a quick inventory. She was wearing the khaki slacks and a denim shirt Alison had gotten for her from the trading post down by the highway. She was barefoot. Her straight, waist-length, nearly black hair was parted in the middle and held back with two oval turquoise barrettes. Her posture was impeccable, her complexion a smooth tan, her eyes sparkling and intelligent. Nate felt a little self-conscious in Helmut's oversize pajamas and his hair still full of salt water grunge. "You speak English very well. Did you study it in school?"

"Please, Nate, speak slow. I begin English when I came to here. Professor Herschel teaches, Alison also. You understand my words?"

Nate admired her linguistic acumen, but agreed under the circumstances he should speak plainly. "Yes, Kawsay. You are a great student. I know many languages. I like learning them."

Kawsay took off in a streak in her native tongue, telling Nate how wonderful it was to find someone to talk with, until he waved his hands.

"Hold it, hold on. What are you saying?"

Kawsay stopped, looking very disappointed. "You do not speak my language. I am sorry. Professor Herschel calls it Quechua. You not know it?"

"I've heard of it. Is it one of Peru's native languages that is dying?"

"That is what they call my home – Peru. I do not know that name. They say I am Inca. But my people are Tahuantinsuya." She paused. "What means language dying?"

"The native people of Peru use old languages less now. More speak Spanish, Español."

"No, no. All people in my village speak like me. Our words not dying!"

Nate had not meant to upset the girl. *Better back up and try again.* "Hey, I'm a terrible host. Want to sit down?" He motioned her to the foot of his bed. She eased onto the corner of his bedspread. Nate noticed her feet. Not long, but broad at the toes and thickly calloused. "Kawsay, how did you get here from Pe … from your home?"

Kawsay came to get answers, not to give them, but she decided to wait her turn. "I do not know. I leave my village near Vilcabamba and go to secret cave to be safe. I find wall that sings and fall down and down. Hit bottom. Wake up in beautiful place with big silver dog. Think big dog bring me here. You come here that way also?"

Nate had not seen this coming. "A big dog? Like a wolf?" He made a motion indicating a long snout, and then he panted. She nodded. "Did the wolf hurt you?" Nate asked.

"No, not like a beast from jungle. I think big wolf likes me. Everyone here likes me."

"I thought I was dreaming. But I think a big wolf may have carried me here too." They both thought about this coincidence for a moment. "Kawsay, how old are you?"

She counted through her new numbering system. "Thirteen. I leave my village when I come to thirteen. How old are you Nate?"

"Oh, I'm sixteen."

"Like Yachay!" Kawsay wondered if there was a link. Maybe he had trained in the jungle with Yachay. *No, he's not from home.*

"Who?"

"Yachay, my brother. He is man now, strong warrior and hunter," Kawsay answered. "Do you know Yachay?"

Nate had to laugh. "No, I don't think we have met. Did he come here with you?"

"I do not know where he is, but maybe he is near here."

"When did you see him last?" Nate inquired.

"When I leave my village. I think he follow. He maybe cannot find me." Her hopes for an arrow connection were waning, but it was worth making sure. "Yachay has arrow like one in your leg. Yachay did not put arrow in your leg?"

"What? I do not think so. A tall man shot arrow at me. Maybe accident. A boy had arrows too, but he was not sixteen. He was younger."

Kawsay sensed the trail was cold. She had one more angle. "Ben also has arrow like arrow in your leg. Maybe he got arrow from Yachay?" Kawsay suggested.

No wonder Mr. Hunter was so interested in the arrow and where I got it! Nate thought.   "Really? Let's ask him where it came from. Maybe he can help find Yachay. Maybe he can help both of us," Nate said.

"You do not tell me where you from and how you come here." Kawsay was back on offense.

"Oh, I am from Menlo Park. It is about a three-hour drive from here."

"You have family?"

"Yes, very small. Just me and my father. My mother died when I was only four."

A very sad look came to Kawsay's eyes. Her lips trembled a bit. In a moment, though, she was composed. "My father die, died, before I came to live. My mother alone now, but has Yachay and Grandmother and Grandfather."

"I understand," Nate said quietly. He wanted her to know that someone cared. "I am sorry, Kawsay. Are you lonely?"

"Do not know 'lonely'. I am sad. I wish to see my family, but not allowed."

"What do you mean, not allowed?" *Are they in prison or something?*

"My lip." Kawsay pointed to her almost healed scar. "Before Doctor Salazar change my lip, it open here. In my village they kill baby when body not all good. Mother tell Chief my problem very small and my father gone, so please have Kawsay live. Our Chief and old men decide I live, but must go away when thirteen and not come again. My family can never see me again. So if we meet, must be secret."

This girl's story is off the wall, but no more than mine. She tells me everything. I feel I can tell her anything too. "That is not right! It's not fair. Besides, your lip is just fine!" Nate's sense of justice was offended by her story.

"You like my lip now? Does it look good?" Kawsay was smiling from ear to ear and had learned not to hold up her hand when she did so.

"Sure.   You look great.   No problem."   Nate thought he was pretty good at compliments.

Kawsay had never been admired by a boy, other than by Yachay and Grandfather for being like a boy. It felt very nice. She basked in the glow for a moment. She looked at Nate with new eyes, not for what she could learn from him, but just for himself. "You look great too!" she ventured. They both laughed. *Why do I feel so good being here? Nate is like part of my family. No, not like Yachay. When Nate looks at me, I feel special. He is special too.* Kawsay looked down, wondering if her face betrayed her thoughts.

Nate sensed her embarrassment. "Thank you for visiting me, Kawsay. Can we be friends?"

"Yes, we must be friends. You lose mother, and I lose father. We both need doctors and come here at night asleep with big wolf." Kawsay liked having this affinity with Nate.

"You were asleep when you came here?" asked Nate, interested in this coincidence. "Were you hurt too?"

"No, not hurt. Just very tired. And I hit rock very hard," she responded.

"You fell?"

"In secret cave went through wall. Something pull, pulled me down and down. Could not …," She mimed taking a breath.

"Breathe?" offered Nate.

"Yes! Could not breathe. Then – I told you hit hard. Saw big dog. Fell asleep. When I wake up, I see Alison and Ben. They give, gave me a bath!"

Nate started to realize there was a greater affinity than he could have imagined. *Sounds like she went through a tunnel like mine! Could she be from the future?* "Kawsay, are you from the future, from a different time?"

She eyed him warily. She did not know what "future" meant. "This is not easy to know. Professor Herschel talk many hours with me. He thinks maybe I come from long time before. Many many years. Time after Francisco Pizarro. He tells me keep this secret from people I do not know, but I like to tell you, Nate."

Nate motioned for Kawsay to come closer. She moved up the bed. Nate reached out and took her hand in his. He had been sitting up against the headboard and pulled her even closer. He spoke in a very quiet voice. "Kawsay, I have a strange story too. May I tell you my story?" Her eyes assured him. "I came like you. Not exactly. I started in the future." She furrowed her brow. "Not time before, time after. Three years. I was on a boat with my father. I fell into the water in a big storm. I was pulled under the water but came to a cave somewhere. I think it may be many, many years before. I do not know where it was, but I was there only a short time. That is where I was shot with the arrow." Her eyes widened. "Like I said, I don't think it was your brother. I did not stay long. I went back to the cave and went into the tunnel again. I could not breathe. I landed hard, and I was hurt. I saw the big silver wolf." Her eyes were still wide, and she was nodding her head slowly, encouraging him to keep talking. "I think the same huge wolf brought me here. I wonder why. Wolves usually do not help people."

"The big dog, wolf, was good to me. He tried to talk to me, but he did not know my language," Kawsay added as if it happened every day.

"It's all so crazy! I think the wolf talked to me and told me everything would be all right – that I should not worry." Nate thought a bit. "Maybe there is some reason we are here together. Maybe we will find out. I think Mr. Hunter knows a lot. Do you think he can help us?"

"They care for us, not hurt us. I will help you, Nate. And you will help me." Kawsay wound her forearm around Nate's and firmly grasped his hand in hers. Her grip was strong, her hand calloused.

Nate knew this had some solemn significance. He felt the bond. "Yes, Kawsay."

"I go now. Please be strong fast. I have many places to show you in the forest. You climb trees?"

"I suppose so. Do you know martial arts?" He made some Karate gestures.

"Oh, I see," she said delightedly. "Yachay teach me to fight like warrior!"

"Maybe you better go now. I promised the doctor I would rest, not get into a fight. Will you come again to visit?"

"Yes, every day until you come and see me at the big house." With that she slipped off the bed and glided to the door. She stopped half way out and leaned back for one last glance. Her eyes looked older than her years. They mirrored Nate's hopes.

While Kawsay was fact-finding down at the cabin, Helmut was caucusing with Ben and Alison in his old bedroom off the living room of the big house. He had found them putting away their hiking and picnic paraphernalia and asked Ben if this was a good time to talk. They settled around Helmut's old work table, bare but for a pitcher of ice water and three glasses, all on a wooden tray that had been in the family for years.

"Nice day for a picnic. And such a romantic spot. Did you remember to eat your lunch?" Helmut smiled knowingly.

"We did," answered Alison, who had learned not to take Helmut too seriously. "But we spent most of the time talking. I'm glad we went."

"Anything new with Nate?" Ben asked.

"It's all good, I think," Helmut answered. "He tore through some sandwiches and fruit in no time. I'm sure his leg is tender, but I didn't overdose on the painkillers so his mind is sharp. He even tricked me into telling him what year this is, even though I didn't intend to, at least not yet."

"Hmmm. How did he react to that?" Ben inquired, putting his glass down and leaning toward Helmut.

"He just thanked me quietly and then didn't bring it up again. Why is that so important anyway? Do you have a theory about the driver's license thing?"

"We think he might be like Kawsay," Alison said, recalling how they had explained Herschel's theory to him. She knew that Helmut's impatience did not mix well with Ben's reticence. "He probably came through time like she did, just in the other direction. And they both arrived at our front door in the same inexplicable way."

Helmut smiled. "Indeed they did. Ben, you've studied this concept more than I have. What's your take on it? You agree with Alison?"

Ben was grateful for Alison's lead and now came to her aid. "I don't see any other explanation. I see you have Hawking's book. I looked at it and others last night before I crashed. There's no scientific support for the feasibility of time migration; they especially see going backwards as problematic. But all the physicists and others seem to have one important thing in common." Helmut did not venture to guess, but just waited. Ben continued, "They don't speak from experience. It's like speculating about life in other galaxies without leaving campus."

"And we have Kawsay and Nate here with us – imagine what they could tell us!" Alison added.

"Guys, they're just kids," Helmut objected. "They can relate their experiences, but we can't expect them to interpret the evidence for us. Plus, finding out that they've been dislocated from their worlds might be a little hard on them, don't you think?"

Alison readily agreed. "Of course, it's a lot for them to take in, so we need to help them cope and adjust. But Kawsay pretty much knows and accepts what Herschel told her. After all, she's the one that went through the experience."

"Well, Alison, I think Nate has already added two and two and has more than a few suspicions," Helmut asserted. "Before we drop this on him don't we need to be sure that it *is* the truth, not just our supposition?"

"Helmut, it's the truth. It *has* to be. Their stories are similar, and it all checks out,"

Ben said.

Helmut narrowed his eyes and tilted back his head, giving Ben a knowing and suspicious look. "I'm sure it does, bro. Can you give me the particulars? I know you want to help me out, right?"

"Yes, I do, and I'm sorry if I've seemed a little furtive," Ben apologized. "I hope you'll just cut me some slack, OK?" Helmut exhaled and seemed to deflate. Alison put her hand on Ben's as he continued. "I don't know if these experiences are limited to young people, but I wonder. After seeing the bloody arrow this morning and then debriefing Nate down at the cabin, I became certain that I had an encounter with him a while ago. You see, before Nate arrived here – I mean now – you know what I mean – he detoured to the past. That's where he picked up the arrow, and that's where I remember him from. He wasn't supposed to have the arrow."

Helmut prompted Ben. "Must have been a while ago, since you had one just like it when I almost landed on you thirty years ago."

"Yeah, it was. It was the same day I arrived here. Well, actually it was where I started that day in a wheat field outside my hometown of Gibeah." Ben saw Helmut shift uneasily and sensed his exasperation. "OK, here's the deal. I know what happened to the kids because the same thing happened to me when I was a kid, when I was twelve."

"So, you've know all these years where you were from – what did you call it, Gibbey Yaw?" Helmut asked. "Where in the world is that?"

"Ben and I are pretty sure it's about 4 miles north of Jerusalem, on the way to the airport," said Alison, trying to help things along."

"Helmut, I didn't figure things out for a while, and by then it didn't matter because you and Mom and Dad were my family. Would you have believed me if I told you?" Ben asked reasonably, shrugging.

"Told me *what*, exactly!" Helmut tried again.

"That Ben was…" Alison began but Ben cut her off.

"That I had traveled almost 3,000 years from ancient Israel to witness you try to kill yourself in a bird suit. Or would our parents have thought I was almost as daft as you?"

"You got me there," Helmut admitted. "No, really, you really did all that? How do you know for sure when or where you came from? Did you bring your driver's license?"

"No, but something just as good – the arrow," Ben said. "Helmut, remember how quickly I picked up Hebrew on my own? Well, I cheated a little – I already knew it, though not in modern form. Remember the inscription on that arrow I had? Maybe not. It translates 'House of Saul', which is the name of the outfit I worked for."

"Sounds like a line of women's fashion or something," quipped Helmut. *Ben's really serious! Why am I making light of this?*

"Helmut, the arrow reminded me of who I was and where I was from, and confirmed that I wasn't crazy to have memories of places that didn't seem to exist. It was Grandma's old Bible, though, that lit up my past for me and told who I was, or had been."

"Oh, so you're Benjamin, Joseph's little brother, Jacob's youngest son?" Helmut remembered the Patriarchs.

"No, but that is my tribe. As I was telling Alison up at the 'Window' today, I found myself in the book of 1 Samuel in the middle of a scene between David and Jonathan. That's where I also saw Nate, but he wasn't supposed to be there." Ben thought he was being clear, but Helmut held up his hands to slow down the barrage of odd facts. Alison knew that Ben was not the best narrator when he was agitated, so she stepped in and untangled the fantastic story Ben had told her earlier, including the outline of Nate's untimely intrusion. She also read 1 Samuel 20 aloud for Helmut's benefit.

When she finished and Ben nodded and then shrugged innocently, Helmut slouched back, ran his fingers through his thick dark hair, rubbed the back of his neck, and gave out a long, low whistle. "You know, Ben, I had a lot of off-the-wall ideas about your past, but I must admit that my imagination was way inadequate. And, I have to admire you for pulling it off all these years. If I hadn't seen Nate and the duplicate arrow with my own eyes, along with his driver's license, I'd have walked out of here halfway through your story. So, I can't judge you for what you did." He thought more about how he felt. "You know, those missing pieces about you always created a barrier between us because I knew you were not telling me everything. That hurt because it suggested you didn't trust me. I'm really glad to clear the air. I've never been happier to have a brother than right now. I look forward to hearing all about your first twelve years." He paused again. "But that has to wait for now; we have more immediate problems – Kawsay and Nate, especially Nate. What are we going to tell him?"

Ben was glad he was not the topic any more, and that he'd successfully crossed another big canyon today, this time with Helmut. "It's not so much what we're going to tell him that has me concerned, it's what we're going to *do* with him."

"What do you mean, honey? We have to keep Kawsay, but doesn't Nate have a family? Don't we need to contact them?" Alison asked, tilting her head. Ben often got distracted when he looked at her blue eyes. She saw him smiling at her and smiled back.

Ben poured himself some more water and topped off the others. "I'm glad you're both here to think this through with me. I don't think it's simple at all. The theoreticians who write about the possibility, or impossibility, of time migration make a distinction between forward and backward movement. Take Kawsay, for instance. She may be displaced, but she can't affect her past, at least not without visiting her 'sucking tunnel' again. Whatever she does here will only affect the here and now and what comes after. It won't change her past. But Nate is *in* the past, or at least his past. What he does will affect the future he came from." He could see the problem registering with his listeners. Ben continued, "For example, suppose Nate unintentionally does something that causes his younger self down in Menlo Park to die in an accident. What would happen to the Nate who is here now? That's the problem."

"You mean that he could erase himself or something?" Alison asked.

Helmut weighed in. "I'm on this, Ben. If Nate went down to visit his dad, he wouldn't only freak out his dad, but he could meet himself."

"Bingo. Who knows what would happen? And the fallout could affect more than just Nate; there's no way to tell. Until we sort this out, we need to keep Nate away from his family." They all nodded silently. "But I don't know if we can. We can't lock him up. And, from what he told me, he is frantic to contact his dad."

"That's only natural," Alison said.

"Yes, and no." Ben said. "Remember Nate's story about being sucked under the ocean. That was three years from now near the Bahamas. Seems his dad was there with him and he's worried that his dad drowned, or that his dad didn't drown but will think his son did."

"But that's no reason to talk to his dad right now. He needs to talk to his dad before they take their sailing trip in three years," Helmet suggested.

"Well, Nate is pretty mature and very bright," Ben stated. "Did I tell you he wanted to be an archeologist, and that he's quite a linguist – including Hebrew? I think we need to level with him and explain why he needs to be careful."

"Even if we convince him to be careful," Alison said, "we still need to help him decide what to do next. We can't just buy him a bus ticket and wish him well."

"But we can't keep him with us either if he doesn't want to stay," Ben responded. "Helmut, if you were in Nate's shoes right now and believed that your time vector had folded backwards three years, what would you do?"

"Well, I could say that I'd get rich betting in the stock market, but I think I'd find some terrible things about to happen and try to prevent them," Helmut answered.

"Wouldn't you be afraid of messing something up?" Alison asked. "Maybe you'd make many other worse things happen." Alison thought she'd do the same thing as Helmut, but would be worried about unforeseen consequences.

"I know what you're saying," Helmut mused. "But if I knew someone was about to be killed and didn't try to prevent it, I'd feel responsible. Who knows? I might wonder if I'd been brought back here with that special knowledge in order to prevent the harm."

Helmut's insight challenged Ben whose more cautious nature might give him second thoughts in the same situation. Their speculations were curtailed by the slamming of the front door and almost immediate appearance of Kawsay. She ran up and gave Alison a hug.

"Hi, Kawsay. Where have you been? How are you doing?" Alison asked.

Kawsay started to answer, then stopped, then started again. "I talk with Nate. We talk about coming to this place. He saw big wolf like me. Nate is my good friend."

"That's wonderful, honey," Alison said, smoothing Kawsay's hair. "I hope you and Nate can be friends."

Ben was smiling too, but heard something the others seemed to have missed. *Today was hard enough, but how am I going to tell Alison and Helmut about Zevél?*

The weather turned cloudy and cool toward evening, and a rare summer rain threatened. Nate had slept away the rest of the afternoon, and he appreciated the hot plate of stir-fried vegetables and toasted multigrain bread Helmut had dropped off. He wondered, though, when he might see a burger.

Alison set up Kawsay with lined paper to practice her letters and other lessons Herschel had created for her and also with unlined paper for drawing with her colored pencils. She had created surprisingly beautiful and realistic scenes of her village. It helped her deal with the bouts of homesickness that still bothered her.

"We're going down to the cabin to see Nate for about an hour. Will you be all right here with Junior?" Alison asked.

Kawsay was already planning her next few hours and did not listen too closely. When

Alison lingered, Kawsay finally answered, "I am fine. May I also visit Nate?"

"Yes, of course – tomorrow." Alison slipped on a light sweater and joined the two men as they left the house.

They were on an important mission. They did not want to overwhelm Nate. "Let me start it out, OK?" Ben requested as they approached the cabin. No dissents.

When they arrived at the cabin, they found Nate finishing his yogurt dessert, looking perkier than the adults. His room was too small for all of them so they gathered in the living room, giving Nate the recliner to support his leg.

"Nate, this is Alison, the love of my life," Ben broke the ice.

"Good to meet you when I'm awake, Mrs. Hunter. Thanks for helping to get that arrow out of my leg – and for the nice dinner."

"Good to meet you too, Nate, now that you're conscious," Alison responded, grasping his hand warmly. "Kawsay had a big hand in the dinner too. I'll let her know you liked it. Good nourishment is important to your healing."

"The leg will be pretty tender for a few more days, Nate," the doctor opined. "After that, if you don't overdo it, it should show steady progress. I'd say you will be walking around pretty well in about a week."

"The sooner the better. When can I get rid of the bandages and take a shower? I feel really grungy," Nate said.

"Yeah, I can see that," Helmut agreed, taking the side chair as Ben and Alison went for the small couch. "Let's stick with sponge baths for a few days. Then you can shower."

"Kawsay has learned to like showers!" Alison added. "I don't think she'd ever seen one before. She remarked to Herschel about having a hot waterfall inside our house." Everyone laughed a bit except Nate.

"Don't they have showers in Peru?" Nate asked, not letting on all he had learned earlier from Kawsay.

"Not in her part of the country," Ben answered.

"And who is Herschel? Another guest?" asked Nate, smiling this time.

"Well, not exactly," Alison answered. "Herschel and Grace Rhodes are two of our best friends. Herschel is a linguistics professor from Stanford and has been helping Kawsay learn English. She's made wonderful progress in the three months she's been here."

"Wow!" Nate interjected. "Hearing her talk I never would have guessed that she'd only been at it for a few months!"

Ben explained further. "Alison has been helping her every day, and Herschel has been up here almost every weekend. It's been a challenge because Kawsay didn't have the concept of written words and letters, so he had to start from the beginning. If he didn't know her Quechua language, he probably would not have been able to get her started so quickly. I have to give Kawsay a lot of credit, though. Not only has she been an attentive student, but she's been training the great Professor Rhodes to speak her language correctly. I think he's as excited about the two-way lessons as she is."

"But we know that he can't keep on coming up here after fall classes start," Alison added. "And I don't want her to lose momentum."

Nate's interest was aroused. "I'm really good at languages too. I could take over. It would be fun. Did you say Quechua? Isn't that a dead language?"

"Not entirely," Ben answered, wondering how to get back to the intended purpose of the meeting. "It is still spoken in many of the remote areas of Peru, Bolivia, and Ecuador, though Kawsay's dialect may no longer exist."

Helmut was keeping his patience this time. He was proud of Ben for finally leveling with him and Alison and was content to just observe for now.

Nate gave a confused look and quickly asked, "If her dialect doesn't exist, how did she learn it?"

Alison attempted an answer. "Well, Nate, we're pretty sure that she learned it from her family. She has a mother, brother, and grandparents that she left behind. She came here with only what she could carry. We had no way of knowing where she was from, but with Herschel's help we think we have solved the Kawsay mystery."

Nate was the impatient one. "She was down here earlier today. We had a nice visit. She told me she came from the past. From what she told me, it sounded like over 400 years ago when the Spanish conquered South America. Do you believe her? Do you think time travel is really possible? I always thought it was strictly sci-fi."

Ben turned his head to rub an imaginary itch on his right ear lobe. "Well, Nate, I think it may be since it happened to me a long time ago. I think Kawsay and I arrived here through the same time tunnel, just at different times from different places."

"Did people believe your story, Mr. Hunter?" Nate asked.

"I didn't tell anyone at first," Ben answered softly.

"What he means," added helpful Helmut, "is that until today he didn't tell Alison or me." He folded his arms and gave Ben a prodding nod.

"So … why did you wait so long, why today?" Nate pushed.

"I had my reasons," Ben explained. "I didn't know for a while where I had come from. I told them today because I knew they'd have to believe me, thanks to you."

"Me? What did I have to do with it?" Nate asked, claiming innocence.

Alison replied gently, "After having you and Kawsay arrive here like you did, Ben knew that we'd have to believe his story too." She leaned forward. "Nate, Ben and Helmut tell me you're a bright young man. It sounded to Ben from what you told him that you'd had an experience like Kawsay's or maybe even more unusual. You apparently already have figured out you are three years in the past and probably have a lot of questions. Maybe we can help."

Nate's plan to hold onto his secret had just dissolved in Alison's understanding and empathy. He could tell she cared, and he also realized that she wanted help him. *After all they've done for me, I owe them the truth – especially since they already know.* "I do need help. I don't know what to do."

Ben shifted and looked into Nate's eyes. "We came down here tonight to offer you our assistance, but we're not entirely sure what to do either. Don't worry about getting well. You can stay here until you're fully recovered. We just need to think about what to do after that."

Alison sensed Nate's agitation. "If you're not up to talking about that right now, we understand, considering all you've been through. There's no hurry to …"

Nate cut her off. "But I *am* in a hurry. I need to warn my dad. But how can I warn him when I don't exist."

They all looked at him in confusion. Alison began, "Of course you exist."

"No, I really don't. When I called my home today my dad and his son were home. Sorry doc, I borrowed your phone while you were out. I'll pay for the call. Don't you see? I'm his only son, or was, and there's no place for me. It's like I don't exist!"

Ben's alarm bell was deafening in his ears. He looked at Nate incredulously and blurted, "You didn't tell them it was you, I hope! There's no telling what might happen. You can't contact them at all!"

"No, Mr. Hunter, honest. I hung up when I realized that I really had come back here from our sailing trip. I just wanted to see if my dad was all right and let him know that I was too, but then I realized that it was ridiculous. It couldn't make sense to him."

Helmut needed to calm Ben down. "See, Ben, no harm done."

"I wish I could be sure. I hope so." Ben began to relax and turned again to Nate. "Sorry. You see, Nate, unlike Kawsay and me, you traveled back in time, or actually way back and then most of the way forward again. We'll talk more about that in a minute. From what I've read, that may create problems because what you do now could affect not just others but you too. For example, what if you did something now that prevents you from falling into the time tunnel in three years? Then you wouldn't be here to do what you just did. Would it make you disappear or what? Some physicists have conjectured that because of these conundrums, backward time migration is impossible, but you've blown away their theories."

"Maybe after the arrow and the wheat field I was supposed to get back to the storm in the Caribbean three years from now and just fell a few years short," Nate theorized. "Maybe I can still get back where I belong."

"Maybe, but I don't exactly understand how these time tunnels work and can't recommend jumping into them – who knows where you'd come out," Ben added. "I never wanted to take that chance myself."

Helmut had not let his attention drift one degree. "Do you know where and how to find these tunnels?"

"I know where two of them are," Ben confessed. "The one we all arrived in is only a short distance from where you and I first met, part way up a steep incline. There's a large cavern with some side rooms. It's quite a beautiful place. I hid the entrance a few months after I arrived so that no one would find it. I was concerned about it."

"And the others are in Israel and Peru," Helmut added.

Nate's attention was diverted from his predicament by this new revelation. "In Israel? That's really neat. What can you tell me about it?"

"Well, Nate," Ben related, "it's where I began my journey. It was at the base of a long low cliff at the edge of a rocky wheat field inside a small cave."

"Sounds like where I got chased by the boy with the arrows," observed Nate, not realizing what he had just stumbled upon.

"It *is* the same place." Ben arose and fetched a small folded blanket with what looked like cedar chips stuck to it. He had brought it along to show Nate. He unwrapped it carefully to expose a brown cloak with white laces down its front. He laid it on the coffee table without comment.

They all kept quiet as Nate looked at it, his thoughts flitting around as he attempted to distill what it all meant. He looked back and forth between Ben and the cloak a few times before speaking. "This reminds me of what the boy who chased me was wearing. How did you..." The light of recognition finally glowed bright. "Do you know, ... Are you...?"

Ben nodded slowly. "You got it, Nate. When I first saw you last night, you looked familiar, but I couldn't place you. Remember all my questions this morning? You confirmed that we had met before. By the way, I want to apologize for Jonathan shooting you. I'm sure he didn't see you; it was an accident."

Nate furrowed his brow and scratched his chin, continuing to study Ben. "So, where were we? When?"

"We were near the city of Gibeah in Israel, about 3,000 years ago. I'm sure of it." Ben then related to Nate how he discovered his origin by way of Biblical history.

Nate was enthralled to be talking to someone from the very time in history that so interested him. *I'll never run out of questions for this guy. This is better than any dream!*

When Ben finished his story and a reading of the pertinent verses in 1 Samuel from Helmut's slightly dusty Bible, Nate selected one of his questions. "So who was the guy behind the rock that chased me away?"

"You mean you saw David?" Ben was surprised. "What did he look like?" Ben listened to Nate's description. "Yes, that's David. No one was supposed to know he was there or what was going on, not even me," Ben said.

"Wow, I actually met King David. I didn't even have the time to talk with him! Bummer!"

Alison quietly got up. "It's getting a little late. I need to check on Kawsay and get her to bed. Nate, it's wonderful to have you here. I just know you're here for an important reason. Maybe together we will discover what it all means. Good night." She slipped out the door noiselessly.

Helmut used this as a segue to turn Nate toward bed. "Probably should get my patient to bed soon. I'll change your dressings and help you get ready. Then I'll be right here in the front bedroom if you need anything." He began to get up, as did Ben.

"Just a minute, doc. I think I know why I'm here, or at least one reason." The two men were very interested and sat back down. Nate continued with his thought. "It's my dad. Remember how it all started on the sailing trip? Well, my dad wanted to take me on that trip because he thought it might be our last. My Uncle Jack – he's a doctor too, a neurosurgeon – had just told Dad that he had an inoperable brain tumor, and Dad wanted to spend time with me while he could. My mom died when I was four, so my dad only has me. Dad is great, but he is also super busy. He's a venture capitalist. He often feels guilty about not spending enough time with me. Guess he was too busy to take care of himself too, because by the time he went to see my uncle, it was too late. I don't think he was given much time to live."

"From what you told me, Nate," Ben said, "he may have drowned in that storm."

"Well, I've been thinking about that. If it hadn't been for the cancer, maybe we wouldn't have taken the sailing trip when we did, and maybe the lightning wouldn't have hit the boat, and maybe..."

Ben interrupted, "…and maybe you wouldn't be here telling me all this, but you *are* here."

"Yeah, I know. But maybe it's not just a coincidence or a mistake. Maybe I'm here to warn my dad, to tell him to get a checkup so that he has a chance to beat the cancer. If I don't tell him he's going to die, then his son – me – will have no parents at all. I can't let that happen! I just can't!" Nate's eyes were filling with tears as fast as he could blink them away.

Ben was watching Nate, and Helmut was watching Ben. "But Nate," Ben protested, "if you talk to your dad, you could, or would, change the future, including your future, which could prevent you from being here to talk to your dad. There's no way to know what would happen. What if you met yourself? Maybe …"

Helmut had heard enough. "Ben, hold on!" Ben obeyed. "Look, … Ben, let me ask you something. Suppose Alison was diagnosed with terminal cancer, it was far advanced, and there was nothing you could do except pray. Now suppose you wake up the next day, you find out it's last year, and your other self is away on business or something. What would you tell Alison? Would you just look in the window at her after dark and then walk away? Could you let Alison die when you might be able to save her life?"

Ben looked at Helmut tragically, imagining the role he'd suggested.

"Would you let some theoretical physicist publishing his little suppositions keep you from saving Alison?" Helmut added.

Ben knew Helmut was right. He knew his "theoretical" concerns were legitimate, but he also knew what it meant to be human and to love.

Helmut was not done. "You have Alison. Nate here has his dad. Isn't their relationship just as important as yours?"

Ben surrendered and sat back, looking tired. "OK, Helmut, you're right. I think we'll be taking a huge risk, but if we do nothing, Nate's dad hasn't a chance. Maybe Nate is right about his purpose. But we've got to be careful," Ben stated, remaining cautious. "We have to be sure that Nate doesn't meet himself. And we need to make sure Nate still travels back here from three years in the future." Ben shared another concern. "One more thing – it's another problem with traveling backwards in time. Nate, two of you are alive at the same time, living not all that far apart. We don't know if there is any precedent for one person to be living in two bodies at the same time."

Nate looked concerned. "I wonder which body has my soul!"

There was a long silence. No one knew the answer as Nate looked from Ben to Helmut and back.

Finally Helmut said, "I'm sure you still have a soul Nate." Helmut had been troubled by one other aspect of the time travel stories. "I don't understand why all the openings to the tunnels seem to be located on the surface of the Earth in caves that are accessible but well-hidden. It all seems too convenient. The openings seem to be in fixed locations; but actually, relative to the rest of the universe, they're spinning and gyrating through space along with the rest of the planet. And why aren't the entrances and exits in the center of the Earth, up in the air, on other planets, inside a star, in other galaxies, or in deep space?"

"My first entrance was underwater near the Bermuda Triangle," Nate offered.

"Right," Ben responded. "Helmut, I've wondered about that too. You're more a physicist than I am – you tell me. Maybe the gravitational and magnetic fields around the Earth keep the tunnel network localized. Maybe there *are* connections to the places you mentioned. I certainly wouldn't want to enter a tunnel and pop out in deep space or inside the Sun! It also is possible, however, that the tunnels are not just random physical anomalies, but were installed for a purpose. In other words, their 'convenience', as you put it, may not be just coincidental."

"I hope you're right, Mr. Hunter," Nate added, "because that might mean that I'm not here because of some weird accident but for some important reason."

"Nate," Ben said, looking at him with admiration. "You're an amazing young man. It took me a long time to adjust after my arrival. You've been here less than twenty-four hours and were seriously injured, but you seem to have taken it all in stride."

"Believe me, Mr. Hunter, I'm pretty torn up inside. I'm concerned for Kawsay too."

"She said she'd visited you, and you two are good friends," Ben said.

"She cheered me up a lot. It was neat finding someone who had been through something like I had. But I wonder what will happen to her."

Helmut noticed that Nate really seemed to like his new friend. "I believe visitors help a patient recover faster. I prescribe daily visits!" Helmut winked.

Nate did not know what to make of the wink, but had an idea. "With the fall term beginning, the language Prof won't be able to keep up with her lessons, right? I was wondering, well, as long as I'm here, maybe I can take over that job. I'm really into languages and I think I could help her keep learning. I could also help her learn how to be a real American kid."

Ben liked the idea a lot. "Brilliant! She'll be thrilled. But a word of warning." Ben sounded ominous, but then smiled. "Don't be surprised if she wants to teach you her language too, and she'll probably try to turn you into an Inca warrior like her brother, Yachay."

CHAPTER 13

YACHAY'S SEARCH BEGINS

YEAR 1609
SMALL VILLAGE NEAR VILCABAMBA, PERU

A NEEDED WARNING
AN UNDETECTED RESCUE
HISTORY PRESERVED.

"**B**ut I need to go. I'll sneak out late tonight. I can follow the path Kawsay described and the directions Grandfather told me. I will find Grandfather and be back before I am missed. Besides, the Chief won't let anyone bother you. You can tell people Grandfather was so distraught over what the tribe did to Kawsay – sending her away alone – that he probably got lost out in the jungle." Yachay's nostrils flared out as he spoke. He felt he was failing his sister by not being with her. Why did he let everyone convince him to let her go alone? Mother had said the tribe would hunt her down and kill her if any of us went with her. *Are they really that barbaric*? Yachay wondered.

"No one will believe that your grandfather could get lost – even if he tried." Sumaq looked worried as she stirred the soup and pretended everything was fine. "The people will send out searchers looking for him. Then who knows what they will do if they find him helping Kawsay; they could kill both of them."

"Don't say that, Sumaq," said her mother. "Your father has only been gone for ten days. I am sure he found Kawsay and is helping her get settled in the caves. I told the Chief just yesterday that he has been out in the jungle on and off, like always. Your father often goes out into the jungle – it's just what he does and who he is. The Chief seemed to accept that." Sumaq's mother was good at smoothing things over and making any crisis seem less bad.

"Oh Mother, you know as well as I do the tension is rising in our village. The Chief is the only decent person in this whole tribe!"

"Don't forget it was not only the Chief but also the elders who agreed to let Kawsay live," Asiri responded.

"You're right, Mother, but many of them are dead. There are very few decent people left in this tribe." Sumaq was too depressed to finish the soup. She handed the wooden utensil to her mother and sat down next to her son.

Yachay had made up his mind he was going after his sister and grandfather before he ever introduced this conversation. He wanted his mother and grandmother to air their concerns – but he was going no matter what. He realized he needed to be firm, but sensitive. "I have already packed what I need for my journey to find Grandfather and Kawsay. I, too, am sure they are together and probably fine. It is just that Grandfather has been gone longer than he said. It is possible he ran into trouble on the way back home and is waiting for me to assist him. I would not want to disappoint him if he needs help."

"You are learning your convincing style from the Chief, young Yachay." Grandmother smiled. "Very good tactics. Your grandfather said you will one day soon be as good as he is in navigating the jungle. He is very proud of you and said your mother and I should not worry about you when you are out – that you are quite astute and strong."

"That settles it. I will leave tonight." Yachay sensed victory. He knew something needed to be done. The boys his age were taunting him about his sister being gone, saying, "No one was supposed to help her, yet your grandfather disappeared two days after she left and hasn't been seen since." Yachay knew he needed to go find Grandfather and realized his mother and grandmother knew it as well.

"I just don't know, Yachay. Your father is gone, your sister is gone, your grandfather is now missing, and you want me to give you permission to go as well?" Sumaq looked small sitting on a colorful woolen blanket on the floor of their modest house.

"I am not going to *be* another problem; I am going to solve a problem! I will find Grandfather and bring him home. I will find out how my sister is and make sure she is set up until my next visit when things settle down around here and people are not looking so closely at us. You know I am right and must go before the talk about Grandfather's whereabouts escalates into action, and people go in search." Yachay nailed his argument with a final tactic. "Don't you trust me? Grandfather taught me everything. I placed the best in the tribe on my tests. No one is more capable than I am to rescue Grandfather, if he needs rescuing, and check on Kawsay." Yachay's steady, confident stare penetrated deep into the eyes of his mother and grandmother.

Sumaq sighed. "Go quickly to the secret cave and quickly return. I will prepare food for you. If you are not back in eight days, your grandmother and I will come after you. There will be no need for us to remain here anyway if you do not return. Our tribe has not accepted us since Kawsay was born and we, in essence, became like outsiders. Go sleep now. The day is still early. Sleep all day. You will need strength for your journey. If I know you, son, you will not sleep much on your quest to find Grandfather and Kawsay."

Sumaq's mother was surprised at her daughter, but knew there was no other way. Looking at her daughter, she said, "While Yachay is gone, we will collect our most valuable items and provisions for a journey to the caves in case he does not return within eight days and we must go. There could be much tension around here as the days go by." Turning to her grandson she cautioned, "Count the days carefully, Yachay. If you cannot make it back within eight days, then do not return at all. Your mother and I will go to the caves on our own and meet you there. Do you understand?"

"I understand, Grandmother."

Asiri waited up, listening carefully until her little village was quiet. She was glad Yachay was asleep. *The sign of a true warrior*, she thought. *He can sleep during a tense time and gain strength for whatever may lie ahead.* She gently touched Yachay's shoulder and whispered, "Time to go, Yachay."

Sumaq was busy preparing Yachay's provisions. She wished they were all going. She dreaded the false explanations she and her mother would need to make in the days ahead. She wondered if they could all join Kawsay and escape from the tribe. She had begun to agree with her son that the tribe had become an increasingly barbaric group. The children and grandchildren of the village founders were becoming less, rather than more, civilized. They seemed to be filled with suspicion and strife. The founders had escaped from the Invaders. They had been such strong and decent people. *What had become of their children and grandchildren? Why could they not have compassion on poor Kawsay? The dimple in her lip was so miniscule.* Yachay interrupted her thoughts.

"I love you, Mother. I will return. I promise." Yachay stood tall with his camouflage tunic, sandals, food and water in bags, and a llama hide sling securely holding his knife, bola, and small spear in which he embedded the lucky arrow Grandfather had given him. He fastened the sling diagonally across his back, kissed his mother and grandmother, noiselessly slipped out of the small hut, and stealthily exited the village.

Yachay ran through the jungle effortlessly. He was glad he had slept most of the day and evening. He was ready for whatever lay ahead of him. He moved quickly and quietly, but periodically made the cry of the macaw to signal Grandfather if he was near. They had agreed many years ago that would be a signal they would use in the jungle. Yachay pictured his sister running along this same route just two days before Grandfather left, or twelve days ago. He was to run to the stream, then mostly follow it toward the sunrise to the cliffs. It should take several days, but he would run fast. Grandfather left two days after Kawsay and was planning to catch up with her by sleeping less than her. *I wonder if he did? Of course, never doubt Grandfathers ability – he is the best.* As it grew light, Yachay began looking for signs of his sister's trail. He figured Grandfather would be more stealthy and impossible to track.

Yachay ran through the days and most of the nights. He refilled his water in the stream and slowed to a walk only to pull food out of his bags and check for signs of Kawsay's trail. She had left only a few signs – broken branches in the brush and a few patterns of smashed leaves. *What had she been thinking about during her journey? Did she feel abandoned? Did she understand that we had to let her go alone in order to protect her from people who resented her very life? What should we do going forward? Let her live alone in the caves for the rest of her life – sneaking up to visit her now and then? What kind of a lonely life is that? Why do we even stay in this village? The five of us could live without the tribe, couldn't we?*

Within a few days, Yachay reached the bottom of the cliff. It was almost dark, and the cliff was steep. He could not see the top. In the dim light he could see where someone had begun a climb. There were small ledges where pebbles and dirt were shoved aside by what were undoubtedly Kawsay's and Grandfather's hands and feet. This was the place. He made sure his llama hide sling was secure across his back and began his climb. *What is that?* He heard a wailing noise from above. *Ah, so that's what it sounds like. The "wailing lady" is guiding me to the secret caves.*

Yachay continued his rapid ascent until he reached a crevice in the cliff, which must be the location of the unearthly voice. The crevice had sheer sides with a flat area of rock between them forming a shelf. It was almost dark, but at the farthest point from the edge he could see a small opening of what must be the cave entrance. Yachay stuck his head through the opening. It was hauntingly black inside. The sound grew louder. *Should I sleep here and wait for morning light to make exploring easier or just follow the sound? What would Kawsay have done?* He decided to call out to Kawsay and Grandfather. First he whispered, "Kawsay? Grandfather?" Nothing. He stepped inside. "Kawsay?" Silence. Then more wailing. Louder wailing. *This is ridiculous!* "Kawsay? Grandfather?" he shouted. *This is stupid.*

He stepped further inside toward the metallic wailing sound. He could hear dripping in the distance. It smelled earthy, yet strange. The air was cool and dank. "Kawsay? Grandfather? Where are you?" Yachay had his hands out in front and to the sides with his right hand running along cool rock. He was heading toward the dripping sound, thinking Kawsay might make her camp near a pool of water. The rock wall to his right ended. He still had his hand out. Instead of feeling a slight breeze or dead air, his hand tingled. He froze with his hand still outstretched. *It doesn't feel like just another passage.* He listened. His hand tingled. The dripping was still ahead of him. "Kawsay? Grandfather?" He felt something at his feet. He kicked it. *Metal scraping on rock.* He reached down, feeling a knife – the blade and distinctive open oval handle. His fingers traced the oval in the dark. *Yes, three jewels! That's Grandfather's dagger. He must have left it on purpose for me to find.*

Yachay secured Grandfather's dagger in his sling and tightened the sling around his back. *This is where I turn – the passage I must take – even though it does not feel like an ordinary passage. Grandfather would not leave his precious dagger here by accident. He must be leaving me a sign. Grandfather was here, which means Kawsay was here – in this very spot.* A loud wail burst through his fingers. He jumped and turned toward the sound. It trailed off. He stepped forward grabbing in front of him. Suddenly he was sucked down.

He couldn't breathe! *The life is being sucked out of me. I'm dying. Kawsay must be dead! Grandfather must be dead! Mother and Grandmother! Who will take care of them? I promised I would return – I promised!*

Thud! Yachay slammed hard into a solid rock wall. "Ow! My shoulder. What is going on?" Yachay was not happy and was telling anyone who might be listening, except it was pitch black and he was alone. Yachay was lying on cold rock. He put his arms out to the sides and rotated them around. He felt the rock wall he slammed into. He traced up the wall as he stood. He stood very still, thinking that if there was a way out, he should feel at least a slight breeze. Nothing but dead air. He began walking with his arms outstretched running his right hand along a rock wall. He needed to figure out how large of a chamber he was in. He seemed to be going in a circle. He knew this because he encountered the funny part of the rock that made his fingers tingle just a bit. *That must be where I came in.*

There seemed to be no way out. Yachay sat down on the cold rock to think. He started to lean back and remembered his sling across his back. He reached back and could feel that everything was still securely in place. *That's surprising – everything is still right where it should be even after that fall. Maybe I didn't go that far. I must have fallen to a lower chamber of the cave. Could Kawsay and Grandfather be here?* He whispered urgently, "Kawsay? Grandfather?" Nothing. He reached to the side in frustration and felt a rock. It felt like a stool.

He stood slowly and climbed up onto the rock and felt around. He felt handholds in the wall in front of him. He pulled himself up and felt a ledge. *Now I'm getting somewhere.*

He climbed up onto the ledge. His hands explored the rock around and in front of him. He felt a void opposite the ledge. He crawled forward into a narrow passageway that seemed to incline upward, and then it angled more steeply upward. The passage stopped abruptly, and Yachay's head butted against a wall. *Ow.* Yachay ran his hands over the end of the passage and noticed that it was not smooth rock like the walls. It felt like flat rectangular stones a little bigger than his hands. They seemed to be of uniform size. *This can't be part of the cave wall.*

He pushed on the flat stones. They did not move. He decided to feel each one and individually push on it. As he pushed on each stone he found a couple at the top that slightly moved. He pushed harder, then pounded until he moved two of them outward. They finally gave way and fell a short distance onto what sounded like more rock. Yachay did not think Kawsay and Grandfather would have knocked these flat stones out and then put them back. *I don't think they are here, but I should figure out where I am. I know they went through the tingling wall because Grandfather left his dagger for me.*

Yachay slowly removed enough of the flat stones to make a hole big enough to shimmy through. He felt around and realized he was in yet another passageway. The ceiling was low, but he could almost stand up. The passage wound to the right until he came to a small room with a very low ceiling. There was a hint of light. Yachay was curious and continued toward the light. It was coming through what felt like very straight pieces of wood in the ceiling. He pushed up, but it was another barrier. He pounded. A slat of wood loosened, and he pushed it up and to the side. Yachay pushed two more slats.

He stuck his head through the opening he had made and peered into a dimly lit room. He pulled himself through the opening and saw what appeared to be light flickering. Yachay found himself in a massive room. His eyes widened to take in the dimly lit walls, floor, and towering ceiling – so high he almost could not see it in the flickering light. The walls were stark white, there were objects suspended from the ceiling, and there were huge pieces of what looked like wood apparently holding up the ceiling. *This looks like some type of temple. Grandfather said our people once had great temples. And what is that – large openings with some type of transparent material?*

Yachay's thoughts were interrupted by footsteps. He saw a rectangular opening set into the wall. There was just enough room for him to climb up and crawl out. He effortlessly and silently climbed out the hole and jumped down to the ground. It was dark, but people had set out unusual torches. The air was cool, but not too cold. Yachay could smell just a hint of flowers. He hid behind a bush and reconnoitered. He noticed a wide path covered with small, round stones and structures made of stone and wood.

What a strange place. Where in the world am I? Yachay was mesmerized by the strange world he had entered. *What would Kawsay think if she was here? She'd be terrified. I must find her wherever she is. I hope Grandfather has found her, and they are together. What? Someone else sneaking around?* Yachay's attention was quickly drawn to a man with pale skin and brown hair that looked like it was pulled back. He was wearing strange clothes; he was covered by fabric from head to toe! His feet were encased. His body was covered by something that certainly was not a tunic! But beyond his strange attire, Yachay was most curious that this man was clearly acting stealthily!

If anyone around here would have seen Kawsay and Grandfather, it was certainly this strangely-dressed stealthy man. I must talk with him. Yachay began surreptitiously following the man down the road. He could see what looked like a river ahead. The man moved smoothly and swiftly, as if he knew where he was going. Yachay was less than thirty feet behind him when he noticed two men off to the left. They were following the man too! *This is getting weird.* The men moved cautiously. They clearly did not want the first man to see them. They were closing on him – maybe twenty feet away. Yachay then noticed the glint of a knife in one man's hand. The other had a knife too! *What is going on here? Are these cowards going to attack this stealthy man from behind? What cowards! They're coming at his back. Men fight face to face in battle.* Yachay was incensed.

While Yachay had only just encountered the stealthy man, he somehow sensed the man was good. He needed to protect him. Yachay reached into a pouch and pulled out his bola. The cowards began a fast approach toward the stealthy man. *The time is now.* He launched his bola at the closer man's legs, which resulted in the man landing on his face. Yachay jumped on the other coward. The two of them fell onto the first coward who was still lying face down. Yachay had the element of surprise in his favor, but knew it would not last. He grabbed a rock and hit each man in the head. Neither moved. Yachay unwrapped his bola, put it in his pouch, and returned his attention to the stealthy man – the man he protected from perhaps mortal harm. The intended victim had no idea all this happened. Yachay saw him step into a small boat with some other men. Yachay ran to the shore of the river. He sat near the water's edge to think while he watched the boat cross the river. He looked at the ground where the stealthy man had stepped into the boat and noticed something shiny on the ground. He picked it up. It was a small, oddly shaped metal object with some sort of marking on it:

"You dropped something. Have you seen Kawsay and Grandfather?" Yachay called out before he realized what he was doing. He quickly ducked down and stuffed the object into a small pouch. Yachay then heard rustling behind him. *Smart move Yachay – you woke the two cowards.* He decided to return to the temple structure in which he arrived. He sensed that Kawsay was not anywhere near here. Nothing felt right. His thoughts were interrupted as the cowards started yelling, "Indian. Indian." Yachay took off running up the hill. He looked up and noticed an extremely tall pointed structure sticking up from the roof of the temple. Suddenly, two lights shone from the top of the structure. *That's strange.* Yachay stopped briefly to observe the two lights. *This must be a signal. Would Grandfather do this? No. They are not here. I just don't feel them here. Besides, they would not have put the rectangular stones back in that first passageway if they had climbed through and were on this side. They would have left an opening for themselves to return if needed.* Then, as he stood looking at the two lights, they suddenly went dark. *They were there, and then they were gone. What does it mean?*

Yachay again heard the two cowards yelling, "Indian. Indian." He ran toward the temple. "Church! Church! The Indian is running toward the church!" The cowards were shouting something again. *Oh no, there are more of them.* Yachay saw two more men wearing bright red tunics, white fabric on their legs, black headdresses, and black foot coverings. He ran swiftly and smoothly to the temple, saw the opening in its side where he had jumped out, and silently jumped back in. It was darker inside than when he left and very quiet. He held his breath and could faintly hear someone creeping toward him. *Someone else sneaking around – what's with this place?*

He dropped to the floor in the near darkness and began crawling toward where he had climbed up into this great and massive white-walled room. He found the slats he had removed and shimmied down to the room below. He wanted to cover his tracks. He reached up and silently repositioned the three slats he had removed. He slowly and quietly adjusted each one into position. He felt sharp-pointed metal pegs that had held the slats in place. Yachay heard someone moving around above. He wanted to do a perfect job of hiding where he was. He was beginning to sweat.

Now in total darkness, he returned his thoughts to where he was and how to navigate back. *This was the room with the passageway leading to the opening I made by removing the rectangular stones. Kawsay is not here. I must find her.* Yachay felt his way into and along the passageway until his foot hit something. *It is one of those rectangular stones.* He felt to the front and ran his fingers over the wall of rectangular stones. He carefully crawled through the opening he had made earlier when he crawled out. He reached down and brought the stones to his side of the wall. Yachay carefully positioned the rectangular stones back into place, reforming the wall. His eyes felt strange in the total blackness of the small passageway. He was still perspiring. He crawled down the narrow passage slowly as it steeply declined and then began to level out. He knew the ledge would be upon him at any moment and felt for it with his hands. The rock was cool on his hands and knees.

Ah, there's the drop off. Yachay turned and let his legs down. He lowered himself until he felt his foot brush the rock he had used to climb up. Yachay stood securely on the rock and then stepped down to the small room he had first entered. He ran his hands along the walls. He wondered if the two men were still chasing him, and if they found the boarded up hole he climbed down in the large white room. He knew Kawsay and Grandfather were not here – and never had been.

He needed to find them. *I am a man and I need to protect my sister and my grandfather from whatever they may be facing. Whatever it is, it's not here. I do wonder what the stealthy man I followed was sneaking around doing, where the boat was going, and where this world is. But it doesn't feel like a place I need to remain. Maybe I can climb back up to the secret caves. Or maybe if I step back through this magic wall, I can go to where Kawsay and Grandfather are now.* With that thought Yachay felt for the tingling wall, secured the pouches that hung on his waist, removed his spear, and secured the sling across his back. Holding his spear tightly in his fist, Yachay stepped through the tingling wall once more.

CHAPTER 14.

ANCIENT WISDOM

LATE AUGUST – PRESENT YEAR
SIERRAS, CALIFORNIA

IN WAYS WE KNOW NOT
OUR PATHS ARE CAREFULLY AIMED
TOWARD OUR DESTINY.

Helmut was busy plotting his next expedition. It would be funded by his earnings from many challenging weekends spent keeping his skills sharp in the hospital emergency room near his Bay Area flat. Alison and Ben had quickly adjusted to having the two travelers with them and to the unusual recent revelations of Ben's boyhood. While they were dealing with the challenges created by first Kawsay's and then Nate's arrival, they also found some time to work on the purpose of their sabbatical – to sift through and organize the results of their latest Holy Land expedition. They had persuaded Nate to rest and heal before attempting to contact his father. As a result, Nate and Kawsay were at liberty to follow their imaginations.

For the first few days after his arrival, Nate restlessly remained at the cabin, trying not to stress his leg. Kawsay spent mornings at his bedside or with him in the living room in informal language training and introductory lessons in American youth culture. A short-wave radio and an Atlas allowed Nate to include some geography, while also adding in some basic math. In the afternoon, it was Kawsay's turn to impart stories of her people and lessons in her Quechua language. Junior liked to sleep in the puddle of sun on the floor nearby, enjoying their company, but hoping for more kinetic games. In the evenings, they devised a question and answer game where they *had* to answer truthfully, with the realization that the inquiry could be turned back on the questioner. Nate showed Kawsay the games of checkers and chess when time and energy at the end of the day permitted. When Alison insisted that she leave him alone to rest, Kawsay rejoined the adults, helping in the kitchen, garden, or anywhere else she could.

By the Wednesday following his unusual arrival, Nate was able to move around unaided and with much less pain and had begun showering on his own. Ben had picked up some clothing in Nate's size and loaned him a beginner shaver. All this improved Nate's appearance, which Kawsay readily noticed. Nate often caught her staring at him with a rapt look on her face, but he could not object as she found him doing the same to her. The only disruption of this pleasant routine occurred at night, when Nate was alone with his dreams.

On Thursday after a hearty breakfast together, Helmut told Nate of changes that were in store. "I'll be leaving this afternoon for my other place. I'll be working the next two weekends and then will be away for at least two weeks. I will be reachable by satellite phone and will check on you, but I'm pretty sure you're out of any danger. I'll leave the meds you need and detailed instructions with Alison."

Nate liked living in the cabin with Helmut and especially enjoyed the stories of his past expeditions to find and document unusual new animal species. He was fascinated that Helmut was both an M.D. and some kind of extreme zoologist. It made him think that he could pursue more than just one of his many interests too. "Where will I be staying while you're gone?"

"We talked about that last night. You can use my old room in the front of the big house; it's sunny and pleasant. It might be more convenient for you to stay up there," Helmut replied.

"More convenient for Alison and Ben too. I should start helping out around the place. I owe them a lot – you too, doc."

"I'm sure they will welcome your help as soon as you're up to it," Helmut said. "Actually, I was going to suggest that you start to expand your rehab exercises today. Why don't you try taking a short walk outside and see how it feels. After a certain point, the damage from inactivity becomes greater than the danger of re-injury."

"Doc, may I ask you something?" Helmut nodded and Nate continued. "Have you heard me making any noises at night – like talking in my sleep?"

"Yes, but it hasn't bothered me too much. Do you always do that?" Helmut asked. "Do you remember what's disturbing your sleep?"

Nate reflected. "I'm not a sleep walker or anything like that. I usually sleep very well, which is why I'm worried about these dreams."

"Tell me about the dreams."

"Well, they're so real. It's almost like I'm reliving events from my life in detail, way beyond what I can remember. Here's an example. You know how in dreams you can't read anything? You try, but you can't see the words on the page? Well, in these dreams I *do* see the words on the page, and they're not goofy like dreams usually are. Like last night, I dreamed I was reading the sports page in the San Jose Mercury – that's the local paper my dad gets. I could see all the scores and game descriptions. We don't get that paper up here, do we?"

"No. We don't get any papers up here; we just use the internet," Helmut responded, suddenly interested in this strange report.

"That's what I thought, so I checked the paper's web page on your laptop and found the articles that I'd just dreamed about. How could all that information get into my head? And that's not all. I dreamed about a conversation with my friend Joe Knight, who used to live next door, just like it happened yesterday. But he moved away in, let's see, it will be next year, and we've lost contact. Why would I have such a detailed discussion with him?" Nate wondered.

"Remember, Nate, it's not next year yet, so he hasn't moved. Let me ask you a question. Was Joe your age?" Nate nodded. "How old was he in the dream?" Helmut asked.

"Just like I remember him – about thirteen or fourteen."

"So, it's like this conversation was happening right now, while you're thirteen. Another question, partner. You look like you haven't been sleeping too well. Do you remember any other time in your life when you had trouble with dreams and fitful sleep?"

Nate was about to answer "no" when he stopped himself and thought for a moment. "Yeah, there was a time a few years ago when, for several weeks, I kept waking up after weird dreams. It got so bad my dad took me in for a checkup, but I was fine. The doctor thought it might be related to puberty or something."

"Do you remember when it was exactly?" Helmut pressed.

"Is it important? Let's see." Nate puzzled for a while. "I think it was right around the start of eighth grade. That's when my voice was changing and everything."

"Which would have been what year?"

Nate counted backwards. "This year, just before school started."

The two looked at each other for a while, each with darting thoughts. Helmut asked one more question. "Nate, do you remember anything about the dreams you had when you were thirteen? Anything at all?"

"It's hard to remember dreams, but I remember telling my dad about some of them. He didn't seem as troubled about them as I was. Let's see…" Nate rummaged for a while. Then his eyes riveted on Helmut's, and Nate slowly shook his head. "Doc, you're not going to believe this. But I do remember some of them. It's like a *déjà vu*, only backwards. I've been wondering why everything here seems familiar to me in some weird way – like we've all met somewhere before. Everything – the buildings, pathways, trees, and even the furniture is just where it should be. I think in all those dreams I was here, or at least saw little clips or episodes of what we're doing here. I already knew what Kawsay looked like before she visited me the first time last Saturday morning. Isn't that odd? I don't know what to make of it." Nate was troubled, and his lack of sleep was not helping.

"I have a theory, Nate, but before we delve into it, I want to talk it over with Ben and Alison. Since I'm leaving soon, I want to brief them on your symptoms and make sure they are primed to help in any way they can." Helmut was ending the interview, but Nate was not.

"That's fine, but please don't put me off like that. Just tell me what you think," Nate implored.

Helmut had a practice of being totally straight with his patients if he thought they had could handle the truth. "Nate, all I have is a theory. Actually it started with Ben's concern about you living in the same time as your younger self. I dismissed his concerns at first, but he keeps bringing it up. It is possible that what you're experiencing confirms his theory. If he's right, then it's not just some theory, but a real problem – one we don't know how to solve right now."

"Right. I remember he told me not to meet myself, and I agreed. I only want to meet my dad and warn him."

"We've been talking about that too, and maybe we can arrange something with your dad soon. I'll be back up here with the helicopter next week to pack up some gear for an Alaska expedition. Maybe we can fly down and see him."

"I hadn't heard exactly where you were going. What's the deal?" asked Nate.

Helmut did not talk much about his work with unusual or mythical animals, but he knew Nate's interest was genuine. "Maybe you've read about this somewhere. There have been sightings of previously unknown birds in Alaska, mostly in remote southwestern parts of the state, and mostly by bush pilots, but a few from the ground too. According to the reports, the birds are larger than any known species, even larger than the great albatross. If the reports are at all accurate, I may be on the path of the largest flying animal since the pterodactyl. People have estimated a wingspan of about fourteen feet. Way too big to be a sea eagle!"

"You think there's something to it? Not just some hoax?" Nate was intrigued.

"Too many independent sightings by 'normal' people to be a hoax. There's no way to know for sure without more investigation and evidence, like photos, tracks, or a nest. Leads like this can be long shots, but they sure get me excited." Helmut had a bit of a glaze on his eyes. "Anyway, keep it under your hat. There are enough people that think I'm just a dreamer."

Nate remembered his own dreams and turned Helmut back to the topic at hand. "So, what is the theory you want to talk to Ben about?"

"Well, my friend, it's just this. We've talked about how backward time travel could be a problem because a person could affect his own future in an endlessly circular way. This is somewhat related. I'm concerned that it could be unhealthy for a person to live in two bodies in the same time frame. You see, you're not a clone of yourself, Nate, you're really yourself. There has never been a 'you' before in history, and there will never be another 'you'. A clone has a separate identity, just like an identical twin. Right now you have two hearts and two heads, but what's bothering me is that you can't have two souls. I'm concerned that in the current situation, your soul, your spirit, has to do double duty living in two places in two bodies. Ben has expressed similar concerns. I think you get the idea."

"And the dreams...?"

"It fits the facts. Don't you see? It's possible that your dreams are more than dreams. They could be your soul integrating the day's experience from your younger self down there in Menlo Park into your mind. And the dreams and sleeplessness you experienced when you were entering eighth grade may be the same thing happening in reverse – your younger self integrating the experiences you are having here right now. Your being here may be causing the weeks of troubled sleep you remember having three years ago." Helmut stopped because that was as far as his thinking had progressed. He was worried how Nate might react to this theory.

Nate took it in his usual way. He turned thoughtful. "Doc, if all this is true, then I can't stay here, at least not for long. Maybe if I went to another place or to another time. You guys need to help me figure this out. I know I need to talk to my dad, but after that..." Nate's voice trailed away.

Helmut tried to help. "We won't do anything until we have a plan. Maybe there's a way we can put everything back together." Helmut paused and thought of one more diagnostic question. "Nate, tell me. Those dreams when you were thirteen. Did they stop?"

Nate thought briefly and then smiled with a small hopeful glint in his eye. "Actually, they did. They went on for a while, and it was really getting to me. Got so bad my dad and I finally prayed about it. Guess we should have tried that earlier, but after we prayed, the dreams just stopped. I think I slept most of the next day. Makes me think that maybe we will find a solution."

Helmut smiled back and pondered this additional information. "I'll fill in Ben on what we've talked about. Maybe you two can figure this out while I'm away."

"Good plan, doc. Thanks for leveling with me. I don't know what I'd do without you and Ben and Alison."

"What about Kawsay?" Helmut had to ask.

"She's been great! She's the reason I've been a good patient. I have a hard time sitting still, but it's been fun teaching her and also learning about her world. You know, she's really smart. I can hardly wait until I can move around because there are a lot of places she wants to show me. I don't think I'm going to climb to the top of a 200-foot Douglas fir, though. I'm not that brave."

"Nate, I think you are brave, and somehow I think you'll need that quality in the days ahead," Helmut said. "I don't think your adventure is over quite yet."

In the early afternoon, Ben helped Helmut move Nate's small stash of new belongings up to the big house. Nate insisted on traveling under his own power with a little help from a walking stick, but was relieved when the big house came into view. He liked the way it nestled under the tall trees and had to smile at the greeting committee of Alison, Kawsay, and Junior who had gathered by the front door to herald his arrival. The scene was perfect. *Maybe it looks "right" because I remember a dream,* Nate considered.

Kawsay ran down to meet him. "Nate, you now walk well."

Nate was slightly embarrassed by the attention. "I'm feeling really good, but it still hurts a little to walk. Alison, Ben, this place is great!"

Alison replied, "We'll put your things in Helmut's room to the left of the door here. I think Kawsay wants to show you around."

Ben added, "You kids go ahead. Helmut and I need to talk before he leaves."

"Yeah, I really do need to get going," Helmut said, looking at his watch. "Nate, I'll download to Ben what we were discussing this morning. He and Alison can take it from there."

The adults disappeared down the hall into Ben's office, while Kawsay tugged gently but insistently at Nate's sleeve. Her tour included the upstairs library and museum where Nate got reacquainted with the arrow that punctuated his arrival. By the time they came to his new bedroom, he was eager to sit and rest. "My leg feels pretty good, Kawsay, but being in bed for several days really makes you weak."

"No, I am not weak. You are weak Nate, but I will help you be strong again fast," Kawsay replied, correcting Nate.

"Tell me, Kawsay," Nate shifted the subject, speaking just above a whisper, "has Ben agreed to take us to the cave?"

"Yes, but it is long walk with big hill. Ben wants you more strong first. Maybe after one more week."

"Did he say any more about the silver wolf?" Nate was still speaking quietly.

"He said we talk later. He also says do not tell others. Maybe the wolf make them afraid?" Kawsay asked.

"I think he does not want others to know, at least not yet," Nate suggested.

"Now I can speak English, and I want to thank the wolf for helping me," Kawsay proposed.

Their whispering was interrupted by noise in the hallway. They heard Helmut saying goodbye and promising to return the following Tuesday or Wednesday. They heard footsteps approaching, and then Ben's head appeared at the door. "Hope you like your new room," Ben said.

"Sure, it's great. Thanks," Nate replied. "It won't be the same around here without your brother."

"We're accustomed to his comings and goings. You may have heard he'll be back next week. I asked if he could fly you down to visit your father. Think you'll be up to it?"

Nate felt a surge of excitement accompanied by apprehension. "Of course I want to see him, but I don't want to freak him out. Don't we need to talk to him before he sees me so he knows I'm coming?"

"Absolutely. I think we need to explain what's been going on and then arrange a place to meet," Ben said.

"May I meet Nate's father?" Kawsay asked.

"I'm sure you will," Ben replied, "but on this first visit, Mr. Diamond will have a lot on his mind. We will tell him about your adventure after he understands about Nate."

Kawsay heard Alison call her name, and she slipped silently out the door. Ben gently closed it after she had gone. He took one matching chair by the window and gestured to Nate to take the other. Ben cranked open a side window to let in the fragrant and warm afternoon breeze. "I'm sure you'll sleep well here. Sorry you've been having those dreams. Helmut told me about them. Seems to confirm my theory."

Nate wanted to talk more about his father. "When can we call my dad?"

"I want to give it a few more days." Ben saw Nate begin to object. "No, I have my reasons. Listen. First, I think you need to meet with him, just the two of you. There's a lot for him to take in, and I don't want to add to his worries by having you limping around like you are right now. More important, though, this isn't just a social call. We need to plan what to say. We are going to need your dad's help."

"I know he's going to be, well, shocked to see me. Who wouldn't be?" Nate said. "But once he gets over what's happened to me, what's so hard about telling him to see Uncle Jack for a checkup right away?"

Ben shook his head and leaned forward, elbows on knees, chin on hands. "Nate, don't worry, we'll warn your dad about cancer, and I'm sure he will take the necessary medical steps to preserve his health. It's you I'm concerned about. Helmut and I talked over your dream experience, or I should say, *experiences*. Do you really understand the significance of all this, if my theory is right?"

"I think so. I shouldn't meet myself or do anything that might prevent myself from coming here to warn my dad," Nate answered, thinking he had it down.

"There's more. Listen, Nate. I agree we need to make sure we don't do anything that prevents you in the future from coming back here. Think about it. You are here because of the storm, and you were in the storm because of the cancer. Your father wanted one last sailing trip with you. Now, if we tell him how to avoid the cancer, will that mean you don't take the sailing trip into the storm so you won't get drawn into the tunnel under the water, ..."

"I get it!" Nate interrupted. "Then I wouldn't be here to warn him, so where would that leave us? We could go around and around."

"I don't think we'd go around and around. I don't believe there are multiple strands of reality. I think there is just a single life experience for each of us. Everything that happens to us only happens once, even if we jump on and off some universal timeline. We need to find a way to make sure that your younger self takes that sailing trip in three years and arrives here worrying about his father's cancer, because you're here and that's what you're worrying about."

"Why? He won't get cancer because I'm going to warn him!" Nate protested.

"Yes, but don't you see?" Ben was looking into his eyes for the glimmer of understanding. "When your thirteen-year-old self grows to become your sixteen-year-old you, he needs to come here to warn his father, and he needs to come here worried about his dad because that's what has happened. It has to happen this way. There is no other reality. Somehow these events have to unfold as they have. We shouldn't, or perhaps we can't, change them."

"Are you saying that we don't need to warn my dad?" asked Nate, struggling.

"No, just the opposite," Ben persisted. "If there is a reason for your time migration, it may be just for the purpose of warning him or maybe for that and *other* purposes."

"What other purposes?" Nate wondered out loud.

"I don't know yet. Time will tell." Ben smiled and shrugged. "Take my situation – why did I come all this way through time? I know one big reason was to live life with Alison. We both believe that in our hearts. Maybe there are other reasons too – maybe to help you and Kawsay or to somehow help my original family."

Nate thought a while before asking more questions. "Well, if you're here to help me, maybe I'm here to help you in some way too," he suggested logically.

"Interesting," Ben responded. *Maybe there are hidden purposes to our time experiences.* "I'll think about that. You're already helping Kawsay. Without you, she would not be making such good progress and might spend too much time missing her family."

"Right! And her being here helps me. Kinda amazing." Nate paused and frowned. "So what *do* we tell my dad?" Nate returned to the main topic.

"Well, we have a few days to work out the details, but here's my idea. He needs to get medical treatment, but he needs to not mention it to you, that is, your young self. Then he needs to take you on the sailing trip in three years, tell you about the cancer, and let the storm happen. You need to fall into the tunnel under the ocean, just like it happened."

Nate was holding up his hands as if to stop traffic. "Wait a minute, wait a minute! Ben, what's the sense in that? Why save him from cancer and then let him drown? We need to warn him *not* to go sailing, at least on that day."

Ben was still a few steps ahead of him. "And then have you not come here to warn him? I know it seems crazy at first, but it has to happen like it did happen. How do we know that he'll drown? Did you see him drown?"

"No, I just saw him trying to save me," Nate admitted, brow furrowed. "But the storm was really bad, and our sailboat had been hit by lightning." Nate puzzled a little longer. He sat back in his chair and looked out the window. He saw Alison and Kawsay harvesting some produce from the garden down in the clearing. They looked happy together. Then he remembered another *déjà vu*. He had seen this scene somewhere before! *Must have been in one of those dreams when I was thirteen.*

His reverie was disturbed by the sound of Helmut's helicopter starting and warming up. Within a minute, the motor noise increased and the unusual craft rose above the trees and banked westward. Silence slowly returned. Nate turned to Ben with a troubled look. "This is awful. I mean it's wonderful being here, but I don't think I can stay. I have nowhere to go, but I can't just stay here either. These dreams I'm having, and that I had – they have to end, or they did end. Where do I go next?"

Ben realized they had reached the critical part of the discussion. He liked having Nate here and was growing attached to him, but knew it was not a stable or enduring arrangement. *If I ever write an article about all this, I'm going to advise people against turning their time arrow back into their earlier life!* Ben mused. "Let me make a suggestion. Nate, you know that part of you is eternal."

"Sure," Nate responded on somewhat familiar ground. "Some call it the spirit, some the soul. I plan to live forever."

"Me too, but not here on Earth," Ben responded. "The Bible doesn't mention whether people ever travel through time. There are many unusual occurrences – being translated a great distance in a flash, Old Testament prophets appearing at the Transfiguration, and people seeing the future. Unless I missed something, though, there's nothing about time travel."

"I think God exists outside of time," Nate contributed, "and that time is part of creation, so God can see and do things in the past, present, and future without being limited by time."

Ben was surprised at Nate's insight. "I totally agree. But that doesn't solve your situation. I was rummaging around last night and came across Hebrews 9:27, which says, '…it is appointed for men to die once, but after this the judgment….' Unless you have an exemption from this, Nate, I have to conclude that you cannot, you will not, continue very long living at the same time as your younger self. If you did, then this verse would not be true. Your younger self down in Menlo Park could get hit by a truck tomorrow and be killed. Where would that leave you?"

Nate's eyes were saucers as he absorbed Ben's reasoning. "Could that happen?" Nate paused. "Actually it almost did, or will happen! A few months before the sailing trip I was almost killed in my friend's truck, but was rescued by a guy named Morrow just before it exploded." He paused again. "But isn't my being here now sort of a guarantee that my younger self *won't* die before the sailing trip?" He paused yet again. "But these vivid dreams are too much. How can I get back together to being one person? How can I stop being split like this?"

"Nate, if I knew for sure, I'd tell you." Ben had a bewildered look. "I believe it will happen, and I'll do anything I can to make it happen. But it's beyond my limited understanding. Just because I'm over 3,000 years old doesn't mean I know everything." Ben displayed a wry smile. "But I know someone even older who may be able to help us find the answer."

Nate protested. "Hey, there's no one older than you. No offense, Ben."

"No offense taken. I'm talking about Zevél. You already met him."

"I did? Here? I thought I knew everyone here. Is there someone I missed?" Nate was learning that following Ben's train of thought was sometimes difficult, as Helmut had warned.

"No, you *did* meet him. Zevél means Wolf of God. He's that big fellow who brought you here Friday night and probably saved your life. If you get the chance, you should thank him." Ben smiled to see Nate's furrowed brows rise up toward his hairline.

"I forgot about that. We never really talked about it, did we? You mean I didn't dream it?"

"C'mon, Nate. I know you and Kawsay compared notes."

"I remember some big creature tell me all would be well," Nate reported.

Ben smiled. "So far it's turned out that way, wouldn't you say?" Ben had waited to deal with this part of Nate's arrival until the proper time.

"C'mon Ben, this is serious! My arrow wound is healing, but now I'm worried about my soul!" Nate was clearly troubled.

Ben leaned over and put his hand on Nate's shoulder, looking him in the eye. "I'm sorry, Nate, it's not something to trifle about. I can hardly imagine how you must feel. What you're going through must be more difficult than my experience. I really do think my old friend might help us if anyone can."

Nate could only muster a weak, "Really?"

"Really," Ben said assuringly. He leaned back and took a deep breath. "It's funny how he just appears when I need his help. Let me tell you about the first time I met Zevél. After I arrived here as a kid, I sometimes slipped away to the cave, wondering if I could get back home. The Hunters were wonderful to me, but at that time they hadn't become 'family' yet. Several times I almost jumped back through the wall. I hoped to go back home, but was unsure if I could. I was worried that I might go back to the other cave where I saw the strange man with the feathers in his hair!" Nate seemed fascinated by this account, and Ben continued. "Well, one time I had a bad case of homesickness and probably would have jumped into the tunnel when I heard a deep voice behind me. It said, 'You are to stay here. Your family is doing well without you. You are needed here.' I thought someone had followed me up the path. I spun around to see who it was. That's when I saw Zevél standing not ten feet from me with an inscrutable look on his face, virtually filling the passageway. Before I could panic, he said, 'I am your friend. I come from the time of beginnings. I, too, travel the time tunnels.' I was wary and felt prickles on my neck, but at the same time knew that this apparition was good, not evil. Then it struck me; it was speaking my native language, Hebrew, not English."

Nate hated to interrupt. "Have you told Kawsay about this? She really wants to meet the silver wolf who delivered her here. I'd like to see him again too. It still seems totally unreal."

"Nate, I can't make him appear," Ben said, "but he seems to show up at about the right time. Until you and Kawsay arrived, I hadn't seen or talked with Zevél for many years. During my first years here, I saw him many times at the cave. I could talk to him about my time travel experience when no person knew about it. It was like talking to a grandparent. He is wise and encouraged me to find my purpose here. He never answered all my questions, but helped me think about what to do next. I don't think he's shown up again now for my benefit, but for yours and Kawsay's."

"So you think we should look for him? Does he live in the cave?"

"No, Nate, he *uses* the cave. See, he has mastered the tunnels. He seems to move through time like we did, except that he seems to know where he's going and doesn't land as hard. I guess he lands on his feet." Ben smiled, but was serious about Zevél's skill. "Maybe he can help you navigate to wherever you need to go."

Nate was pleased for this ray of hope, odd as it was. "So, we don't look for him? We just go and see if he's there?"

"That's about it," Ben replied. "This is mostly a mystery to me. But I think we should go up to the cave this weekend before we contact your father."

"Can Kawsay come with us?"

"Yes, I think that would be good," Ben replied. "She may want to ask him about her situation too, now that she's learned English. You see, Zevél is very good with human languages, but he probably hasn't learned Quechua."

That evening Nate took Kawsay aside and filled her in on the possibility of a cave trip on Saturday. She was fascinated to learn more about the unusual animal she had met three months ago and wondered if the wolf might know Yachay's whereabouts.

The same evening at bedtime, Ben asked Alison if she remembered the large paw prints she saw the morning after Kawsay arrived.

"Yes, how could I forget!" she replied. "I've been nervous about letting Junior out of my sight. I didn't think canines got anywhere near that big."

Ben wanted to allay her concern. "There's one more part of my story that you need to know about. It's probably the strangest part of all, but may also be the key to solving Nate's and Kawsay's problems – maybe mine too."

"I know that Nate has the dream and split-soul problem, and Kawsay wants to contact her family and is worried about her brother. But what problem do *you* have right now?" Alison asked.

They were up talking until 2:00 a.m. They pushed the envelope a little further on the question of how to set things up with Nate's father. They also went over the various options regarding Kawsay, always coming back to the idea of just keeping her and letting time heal her fractured life. Ben reminded Alison of his lingering concern about the missing arrow and the requirement that the marred episode in the wheat field somehow be set right. Finally, after much temporizing, he stated, "Our two visitors were carried here by a very large wolf, though unlike any wolf you may be familiar with. He is older than I am, speaks several languages including English and Hebrew, and knows the time tunnels as well as you know the pathways around our property."

Alison was fairly sure Ben was kidding, but said nothing.

Ben then described his earliest contacts with Zevél and his hope of meeting with him again soon.

Alison felt very uneasy at the thought of a giant wolf prowling around her house no matter what language he spoke. "Well, then it's a good thing I've kept Junior close to home!"

Alison exclaimed.

Ben explained that Zevél was not a threat to Junior or any other animals since he was a herbivore. Alison had never been so close to throwing a net over her husband. Undaunted by her look of incredulity, Ben plowed ahead. He explained that he believed, based on the wolf's diet and other things Zevél had said, that he came from the earliest time in recorded history, before the beginning of the era of tooth-and-claw.

"You mean before the Fall?" Alison asked with a dubious look.

"Why not? He could have escaped through a time tunnel before acquiring a taste for blood," Ben answered. "I don't know what Helmut would make of him, but he'd probably think he'd found the Holy Grail of critter research!"

Alison was too tired to absorb any more revelations. She would ponder all this later.

After they finally turned out the lights, Alison nudged Ben and offered one more idea. "Honey, remember how Kawsay was so interested in those arrows? She seemed to think that her grandfather or her brother had one like them. Is that possible?"

Ben thought for a while. "Well, I had assumed she was excited to see an arrow and maybe it reminded her of her people and their weapons."

"I don't think so," Alison objected. "Kawsay doesn't miss much, and I don't think some generic arrow would excite her like that. Besides, from what I read today, I don't know that her people used bows and arrows, though the conquistadors had crossbows. We have to admit to the possibility that she really *has* seen an arrow like the two upstairs. They are distinctive."

"But how could she? Arrows like that just did not exist in ancient Peru, they come from, …" Ben stopped himself and drew in a breath.

"Yes? Ben, what is it?"

"No, it's too far-fetched. Too much of a coincidence."

"Honey, you are always suspicious that coincidences are God's thumbprint," Alison reminded him.

"Well, don't get your hopes up, but could it be possible that Kawsay has some connection to the funny guy with the feathers and tooth necklace?"

"That would surprise me less than meeting your big multi-lingual fuzzy friend," Alison retorted. "Knowing you is endlessly fascinating."

With that, they finally fell silent, but each continued to process the fruits of their consultation for quite a while before sleep finally reigned.

The last Saturday of August arrived quietly at the Hunter estate, with light dew and stillness in the trees. The four residents stirred awake from their separate worlds of sleep, each experiencing a flood of excitement as they remembered this would be an important day of discovery. Without an appointment, they planned to look for Zevél, bringing a large bowl of salad as a token of friendship. The forecast had been for quickly warming temperatures, and all donned hiking shorts and loose shirts.

At breakfast Ben broached the topic already on everyone's minds. "We're all hopeful that Zevél will be around today. In the past, I usually found him resting in the main part of the cave, the large room with the crystals in the ceiling. I think he forages at night and rests during the day, probably to avoid being seen."

"How should we act around him? Will he know us?" Alison asked.

"He knows who we are. We only need to ask if he will talk with us. If so, I expect he will mostly listen; that's how it always seems to go," Ben responded.

Nate joined the conversation. "I know the point is to talk about our situations, but can I ask him about, well, himself? There's so much I'd like to know."

"I don't think he'll object to questions, but he usually tells me only what he thinks I need to know," Ben said.

Kawsay kept her own counsel, but hoped to learn if Zevél had seen Yachay.

After cleaning up the breakfast dishes and placing a salad in a large container, they gathered outside the front door. Nate had a ski pole in hand to use as a crutch. "Shouldn't we take Junior along with us?" Alison asked. "Maybe he's already met the wolf and hasn't told us about it."

"I know Junior at least caught the scent of Zevél after the late-night deliveries," Ben said. "Might be best for them to meet and decide who's the Alpha." They decided to bring Junior and get him used to being on a leash.

Ben led the hikers down the path, through various trail intersections, past Helmut's big bird crash site, and across the bridge with the shiny hardware, now more tarnished and rusty. Finally the trail angled upward. He had hoped to see an occasional large paw print in the soft places in the trail, but found none. Much to his consternation, however, he found an occasional human print, not of a hiking boot but smooth, more like a sandal. *Whose could those be?* he wondered. The forest had remained quiet, which made the occasional bird calls seem amplified.

The cave entrance was partially obscured. It was not visible from below, but could easily be reached from the narrow hillside path. The short column of trekkers entered single file, first Ben, flashlight in hand, followed by Nate, Kawsay, and finally Alison with a leashed Junior. He led them carefully through the serpentine passageways. They eventually rounded the last bend that led directly to the beautiful crystal room with the natural skylights. Kawsay remembered the room, but it was new to Alison and also to Nate since he had only been there at night. They momentarily forgot about the main purpose of the visit, as they were absorbed by the unique beauty of the chamber.

"It's no wonder the wolf likes to spend time here – it's just beautiful," Alison observed. "There are even small pools of water along the back wall. Oh, look! There's a curtain of water coming down the wall from above – how wonderful!"

"It's almost as if it was carefully designed for occupancy. There's enough ventilation so it's not as cold as most caves, or as dank," Ben added. "I remember spending many interesting hours here. I used to sit on that little rock formation over there. It had a perfect contour for me when I was smaller."

"Is this where I came through?" asked Nate as he looked high and low. "It doesn't look familiar."

"The tunnel entrance is down that corridor in a smaller chamber," Ben said.

Junior also was interested, exploring mostly with his nose. He sensed something unusual and gave out a small whimper.

"How did Zevél get me to your house? I'm pretty heavy," Nate wondered aloud.

"Have you forgotten how big he is? He must weigh nearly five hundred pounds. I imagine he just took your belt is his mouth and, ..." There was a noticeable THUD from the corridor beyond, and Ben immediately lost his audience.

Alison felt her scalp prickle with excitement, and the two young people drew in their breaths. Junior's ears were at full attention as he tensed up. They instinctively huddled close to Ben, flanking him to the rear. Their anticipation was short-lived, as soft footfalls became audible.

A large black nose poked into the room, followed by two huge light blue eyes set in an enormous, majestic silver face. The eyes blinked, taking in the small group. Zevél completed his entrance and stepped up to Ben and his friends. His luxurious silver coat shimmered in the indirect light. He sat down, head remaining almost as high as Ben's, and extended a right paw that must have been at least nine inches across, adorned with impressive claws. Junior signaled unconditional submission, tail between legs, as he crouched low behind Alison. Ben reached out and shook the giant paw.

After the brief greeting, Zevél made steady eye contact with each visitor. He seemed to smile and emit a very deep rumble, more felt than heard. He then opened his enormous jaws and spoke slowly with a pleasing, resonant voice. "Shalom, Binyamin. It pleases me you all are here." With long fluid strides he moved to a place under the crystals, well-lit from fissures in the rock ceiling, adjacent to Ben's old rock throne. He laid down to continue the interview in comfort. Ben led the group to the small outcrop and offered Kawsay his comfortable old seat. They all found suitable perches.

"Thank you for bringing these two travelers to our home," Ben began. "This is Kawsay. She traveled four hundred years and many thousands of miles from the Andes Mountains of South America."

"Thank you for helping me," Kawsay said cautiously.

"And this is Nathaniel," Ben continued, "who came from three years in the future, but stopped in my wheat field outside Gibeah on the way, where he took one of my arrows."

Nate tried his Hebrew. "You saved my life. Thank you, 'Wolf of God'."

This seemed to please the listener, who nodded and responded in kind, "You are welcome, 'God Has Given'. So, you are the young man Binyamin followed into the cave in Israel." Finally, he turned his massive head and looked at Alison.

Ben completed the introductions. "This is my beloved Alison. She did not travel through time, but waited many years for her soul mate. Alison, this is my friend, Zevél. I am happy you two can finally meet."

Alison hesitated before beginning her first-ever conversation with a creature of this pedigree. Then she realized that she talked to Junior constantly even if he wasn't quite as fluent. "It is wonderful, actually amazing, to meet you." She was momentarily speechless. "We brought you some salad, as you are a special neighbor to us."

Zevél gave a rare chuckle, which echoed around the chamber. He responded in a soft and deep tone. "You are gracious, Alison. Binyamin realizes why he belongs in this century. Thank you for protecting me from the carnivorous beast cowering behind you." Zevél seemed amused at his last remark and appeared to smile.

Knowing his friend used words economically, Ben quickly turned to the matters of greatest importance. "Zevél, we seek your advice on matters that concern us all. May I explain?" Zevél's silence and slight nod indicated assent.

"You have told me that events usually have a purpose that may at first be hidden," Ben began. "We have talked about what it means to walk by faith, and how I find that a challenge. The arrival of Kawsay and Nate raises many questions, and it is difficult to know what to do."

Zevél had some idea what was on Ben's mind and was prepared to offer his best suggestions. "Perhaps it is easier for me to follow the lead of my Master, Elohim, since I come from before the great division. But you live after the great healing. You also can experience His presence. But remember I am but a wolf, not a priest."

Ben remembered Zevél's humility and that he responded best to simple friendship. "You have mastered the time tunnels, and we have not. We need instruction so we can travel to exact times and places. We cannot jump blindly into the dark, not knowing where we are heading." The entire group was curious about this.

Zevél tilted his head a bit in thought. "Why do you assume your past travels have been blind and unplanned? Do you believe Elohim oversees all that befalls you? Might you all be here for ordained purposes?"

Ben was reminded of Zevél's sometimes annoying yet challenging way of answering him with insightful questions. "Are you suggesting that Kawsay falling through a cave in Peru, Nate being sucked down in the ocean, and my time dislocation were part of a divine plan?"

"Do you not already know this? Have you not discovered a unity of purpose? Do you not expect more visitors?" Zevél answered with more questions.

Ben's ears caught the final comment. "Do I, … What more visitors?"

"Count the arrows, Binyamin," Zevél added, without a question.

Ben went silent. *Of course. I told Zevél of my wheat field adventure and the need to fix the outcome.* Then Ben spoke. "You probably noticed the arrow lodged in Nathaniel's leg. After he and I talked, we discovered that it is the second arrow, and that he was the stranger in the wheat field who wasn't supposed to be there."

Zevél nodded. "There were three arrows according to your account," he prompted.

Ben had not planned to get sidetracked talking about the arrows, but to focus on Kawsay's and Nate's concerns. But they were already into it this far. "I fear the last arrow is lost. There may be no way to find it," Ben lamented.

"I have seen arrow like your two arrows," Kawsay interjected quietly.

"Are you certain of this?" Ben asked, quickly turning to her. "It is a very special arrow, different from others."

"Yes. It has same markings and is made from same metal and wood," Kawsay spoke with complete confidence. "That is reason I had big interest in the arrow upstairs and the arrow in Nate's leg."

Ben wanted to believe her. Alison knew this was an important development. "Kawsay," Alison ventured, "do you know where the third arrow is?" Even Zevél was watching her with heightened interest.

"Yachay has it. Grandfather gave it to him when he became fourteen years to help him. He carries it with him now inside his spear."

Ben's hopes sank. Even if accurate, what good was this information when Yachay was hundreds of years and thousands of miles away?

Alison continued her prompting. "How can we find Yachay? Is he with your family?"

"My brother is wonderful hunter and tracker," Kawsay announced with pride. "We have plan that he will follow me to the secret caves and report to my family. He will help me if I find trouble. I hope he finds me here and learns I am not in trouble. If Yachay comes here, he will bring arrow."

Zevél offered an observation. "If brother Yachay entered the time tunnel touching you, he would come to the same time and place. If not, he may travel to a different time and place. You did not arrive alone, Kawsay, but your fellow traveler was not your brother. Of this I will say no more."

Ben and Kawsay now despaired of ever finding Yachay and the elusive third arrow – they could be anywhere and any time. Ben knew, however, Zevél had foreclosed further discussion of this topic for now and redirected the discussion. "Today you arrived through the time tunnel while we were waiting for you, Zevél," Ben stated. "Did you know we needed your help? How do you control the place and time of your travel?"

Zevél could keep secrets, but here he had none to keep. "I exercise no control. I simply choose obedience to Elohim's will. I sense in my spirit when I am to travel and step through with confidence that I will be delivered to the intended destination. Obedience need not be a struggle."

Nate picked up on the idea. "It sounds like what my pastor calls 'stepping out in faith'. He says it's scary at first, but after a while we can learn to trust God. I'm not so sure, though, that getting blown out of a boat in the middle of the ocean during an electrical storm involved much obedience!"

"I just stumbled in the dark and fell while trying to find Nate and the arrow," Ben added.

"And I stepped through the singing wall because there was no place in my world for me," Kawsay stated objectively. "Maybe your God saved me and brought me to a better world."

Zevél appreciated their confusion. "My exit from the beautiful garden surprised me too. Leaping across a chasm, I intersected with an invisible tunnel opening and emerged near the end of time. In that fearsome place I learned great lessons. Now Elohim uses me in different times and places. I cannot return to my place of origin. Where I began life, we knew no sickness or death, and I took these strengths with me."

This was more than Ben had learned during his many earlier discussions with Zevél. It helped him understand why his friend seemed to be of another world.

Alison's curiosity got the better of her. "Zevél, do many people, animals too … travel like this? I am the only one here with no story to tell."

The great animal seemed to shrug. "I have encountered others, but have no knowledge of the numbers. Perhaps you hear accounts of many who disappear. Why do you assume they have met death?"

Nate had experienced another difficult night of dreams and had a question of his own. "Something weird has been happening to me. Ben thinks it is because I traveled backward a short time and am living at the same time as my younger self."

Zevél ruminated. "Nathaniel, your experience is unusual and does not continue long. Do you want to return to your point of departure?"

"Well, I like it here, but if I cannot stay, where else do I belong? Ben thinks I need to return so I can complete my life as one person," Nate responded.

Ben rejoined the discussion. "That's right. I think it's the only way for Nate, but I don't know how it will be done. We don't know how to get him back."

Alison had synthesized an idea. "Honey, maybe we don't need to know exactly how to do it, but just need to be ready to take a 'step' when the time is right."

Zevél smiled because Binyamin had found a woman of wisdom. He needed to add only one more thought. "Just as your arrows must return and fulfill the historical account, Nathaniel must return and continue his life. Your heart will tell you this is true. Do not presume you can plan all events. It is enough to step forward with the light you have. What you call a detour may be a divine appointment."

Ben's nature was to attempt logical analysis and plan all events. "But how will we know exactly what to do and when? We cannot leave Nate's or anyone's life to chance!"

Zevél grew impatient when Ben spoke primarily from his human brain. "You speak of chance as part of your reality. It is not part of mine. You speak of chance to fill a gap in your understanding, but it has no meaning, no reality. Without Elohim upholding you every moment, you would not live. The truth you see with your heart you do not see with your physical eyes, yet it is firm and enduring."

Kawsay was trying to follow this theological discourse and raised a question that had grown large in her heart as she grew close to her new friends. "My people teach that Inti made us, that Inti rules over us. Did Inti make you?"

Ben and Alison had not expected this from Kawsay, though she and Nate had ranged into religious questions in some of their discussions. Zevél did not shrink from her honest inquiry. "Our Creator is given many names, but not all names are His. He is above all gods that are made by hands and minds. What do you know of Inti?"

Kawsay remembered her people's beliefs. "Inti warms the sky each day. Inti is too powerful for my eyes." She stopped and wrinkled her nose. "Inti does not care for me. Inti made me ugly. I was left to die. There is no love, only fear. Did your God bring me here?"

Alison was overcome with compassion for her little orphan and turned to embrace her with tears in her eyes. "Oh, Kawsay, yes! God brought you here as a safe place for you. He loves you. He has put that love in all of us. We all love you very much."

Kawsay felt warmed to the core of her being. These were not her family, yet they loved her like her family. The rest of her tribe had hated her. "Alison, please teach me of your God. He is kind to me and cares for me. It is a new feeling."

Ben sensed the discussion was drawing to a close. "Zevél, I have one more question. How do you manage to avoid hurting yourself when you exit a time tunnel? We all seem to get badly bruised!"

Zevél provided the second resonant chuckle of the morning. "I always land on my four feet. Think like a cat."

They all enjoyed the humor, but maybe it was sound advice. Nate also had a question for his new friend. "Zevél, how did you learn speech?"

"From my earliest days I was able to speak with humans and other animals. Later, after the number of languages multiplied, I found I had a knack for learning them. I also have a little friend who is quite gifted and enjoys teaching me new languages."

"May we visit you again, especially if we have more questions?" Nate asked.

"We may talk again before your journey home, Nathaniel. I have been honored to meet you all today. Enjoy your adventures. Now I will rest." With that Zevél turned slowly, walked to the rear of the great chamber, and began to lap at the cool water.

Alison popped the lid of the salad container and left it by the outcropping, not imagining that it would be returned overnight to the drop-off spot outside her front door. Having been dismissed, the group quietly filed out of the beautiful cavern and found their way back into the warm noontime air. Once down the hill they fanned out along the trail and talked quietly about their recent encounter with the ancient animal. Junior slowly recovered from his perplexing encounter with a distant cousin.

"I'm never sure until the next day whether I really understand all that Zevél has told me," Ben offered. "Why is it that simple things can be so deep?"

Alison was not feeling all that confused. "I think it's pretty clear, honey. We move ahead with our plans, do all we can, and trust God for the rest."

"Like I said, honey, simple is hard for me." He gave her a wink, feeling thankful for her daily help. So many of her skills and traits were complementary to his.

Kawsay suddenly let out a little yelp, turned, and ran a short distance into the forest. Junior strained at his leash. The others had no idea what had startled her, but quickly joined her in a small clearing.

Alison asked, "What is it, Kawsay? Did you see something?"

"Yes!" she proclaimed. "Someone was following us and watching us. When I turned, he disappeared."

They all stared blankly into a wall of trunks, needles, and leaves. They listened, but heard only insects. Whoever or whatever it had been was gone. They returned to the path and continued back to the house, contemplating different facets of their amazing morning. It felt good to return to their regular activities and enjoy a beautiful late summer day.

That night, as Ben laid his head on his pillow, he heard a crinkle of paper under his ear. Reaching into the pillow case, he pulled out a small piece of note paper. He had not received one of these communiqués for a while. Alison was still brushing her teeth, so he had a chance to read it alone. There was his name, not Ben but Binyamin, and the date. At the bottom was a little drawing of a dog or wolf sitting with three arrows at his feet. In between were these words:

I am filled with awe
As I ponder the great deeds
For which we were made.

Ben propped himself up on one elbow and leaned over to place the message in the bottom drawer of his nightstand, where it joined many similar slips of paper, each speaking love in one of its many forms. As she returned, Alison saw him filing the haiku and smiled inwardly. As he turned back to lie down, Ben saw her watching him. He smiled outwardly. "Honey, thank you for being there today. I'm glad you met Zevél and were part of our talk with him. In the weeks ahead, I will need you more than ever."

"I will need you too," she said, slipping into bed with her usual icy feet. "The greatest deed for which we were made is to love each other. It's a grand undertaking, but I'm not getting cold feet."

CHAPTER 15.

THE REALITY OF DREAMS

AUGUST 30 – PRESENT YEAR
MENLO PARK, CALIFORNIA

A NEW TRUTH ARRIVES
VIOLATING PRESUMPTIONS
RANSACKING THE MIND.

John Diamond could never sleep in. His internal clock was set to 6:00 a.m. and did not care that it was Sunday. Rather than spring up and prepare for another day of parenting his business and his thirteen-year-old son, he allowed himself the luxury of staying in bed, reading the newspaper, and sipping some coffee. He had a few hours before church, and he did not want to disturb Nate. Nate was in a growth spurt and needed his sleep. Once Nate's eighth grade classes started, they both would again be driven by alarm clocks. He was only a few pages into the A Section when he heard Nate calling out from his room down the hall. He was quickly at his son's side.

"Nate, Nate, I'm here. Everything's fine. You're just dreaming again." The blanket and sheet were in disarray, and his young son was repeating, "He's so huge, so huge." He was not upset, but seemed to be involved in a very vivid dream.

The father's presence seemed to break the spell. Nate quieted down and then opened his eyes to a squint. After a moment, he opened them a little more, staring at his father's caring face. Nate furrowed his brows in contemplation, deciding which reality to accept.

"Hi, son. It's Sunday, no hurry to get up. We don't have to leave for over two hours. What sounds good for breakfast?" John asked gently.

This reality was attractive to Nate. "Hi, Dad. Was I talking in my sleep again?"

"Yes, but only just now. I hope you got some good rest."

"I think so. I feel OK." Nate paused, remembering shards of his dream. "Guess what? I saw another huge wolf in my dream. Remember the big one I thought was going to eat me? Well, this time he was just standing there with my dream friends. But that's not all. He was talking to us!"

"Too bad they don't give Oscars for best imagination," John said with a chuckle. "Maybe you should write some of this down in case your English teacher asks the class to write a creative short story."

"Yeah, I suppose so, but I'm not sure that I remember enough details. I don't mind dreams, you know, but the ones I've had this week are over the top! They feel as real as talking to you right now. I want them to stop. It kinda scares me."

John tried to imagine how Nate felt, but had no clue what to do for him. "Not as scary as that dream you had a little over a week ago about some kind of wound in your leg."

"Actually this new dream wasn't bad," Nate responded. "What's scary is that it was so real. It felt like I was really living it."

John was growing more concerned with each episode. "Nate, I'm not sure what to do. If it keeps up, I'll have to take you to the doctor. In fact, I think I better make an appointment tomorrow. Best thing right now is to come and help me with breakfast. Have you decided what you want?"

An idea popped into Nate's mind. "How about some Malt-o-Meal?"

"Whatever made you think of that? I don't think we've had that in the house for years. I'll just let you pick the cereal you want."

The remainder of the morning was normal and pleasant. Nate enjoyed the service and his church friends. He was probably the only youngster who took notes on the sermon. He enjoyed reviewing the scriptures later in the day in his interlinear testament. Occasionally he found something in the original language text that intrigued him and prompted him to e-mail ideas and questions to Pastor McQuade.

When they returned home after having lunch at Nate's favorite fish'n'chips restaurant, John called his office number to check for messages. There was one message. *Has my workweek started already?* He began listening while rummaging for a pen that might work.

"Good morning, Mr. Diamond. This is Professor Benjamin Hunter. I'm an archeologist from Stanford, but I'm on sabbatical at my home in the Sierras right now. There's an important matter I need your help with and wonder if there's a time this week, maybe on Wednesday, when we could meet? I might be able to give you some insights into your son's dreams." The message ended with a phone number and, "I look forward to hearing from you as soon as possible."

John had jotted down the name and number, but his pulse was suddenly racing. *How could this guy know about Nate's dreams? I haven't told anyone.* Before returning the call, John detoured to Nate's room where his young son was already looking over his sermon notes. "Nate, have you told anyone about your dreams? Anyone at all?"

"No, Dad. Remember, you told me not to," he answered casually. "Do you think I should?"

"No, that's fine. Just wondering." John liked to get questions answered quickly and directly. *There must be some explanation!* He went into his home office, closed the door, and took out the note with the phone number. He quickly stabbed in the numbers.

"Hello?" It was a woman's voice.

"Hello. This is John Diamond. I am returning Professor Hunter's call."

"Hello Mr. Diamond. Ben was hoping he'd hear from you today. I'll get him, he's with … I'll get him." The phone was quiet for a moment. John heard one receiver pick up and another click off.

"This is Ben Hunter. Mr. Diamond?"

"Yes, I'm returning your call."

"Thank you. Is this a good time to talk? It may take more than a few minutes."

"I have time right now. Your message concerned me because it referred to my son. What is this all about?" John was feeling some anger at the intrusion. He was also somewhat suspicious and detected a slight accent he could not place.

"I apologize for the cryptic remark about dreams, but it was essential that we talk.

And, like I said, I do think I can help you understand the dreams that..."

John quickly interrupted. "What interest do you have in my son?"

Ben was apprehensive at John's tone. *This is beginning badly, but I can't blame him.* "I care about you and your son. I know this may be upsetting, but please hear what I have to say. It is extremely important." Silence. Ben continued, "I'll come right to the point." He tried to sound friendly.

"I'm sorry I jumped at you, Professor Hunter. I'm very protective of my family."

"That's quite all right; I completely understand," Ben said, pleased to defuse the situation. He took a deep breath. "What I'm going to tell you will seem preposterous, and you'll be tempted to dismiss me as a crank or a lunatic. If you first want to check my credentials, I'll give you websites for my publications and my university standing."

"No, that won't be necessary. I am interested in whatever you have to say."

"Well, before I proceed I want to validate my message in another way. You keep your old stamp collection on the top right shelf of your den closet, and you'd like to travel in Earth orbit."

John was shocked to hear this. *Who does he think he is prying into my business? But how could he know these things? I've only told Nate about them.* "Professor, I have no idea how you got this information, but I hope you have not been bothering my son."

"Mr. Diamond, I did receive this private information from your son, Nate. I asked him to tell me something that would prove to you that he had been talking to me."

"I always believe what Nate tells me," John protested. "I don't need any proof. Should I go and ask him about his conversations with you?"

"Once I explain, you will see that is unnecessary. I met Nate just over a week ago. He arrived late Friday night at our house. He was wounded. My brother, Dr. Helmut Hunter, was here and treated him. He's doing fine. The story he told me the next day will be very difficult for you to believe, but I know it's true as sure as I'm sitting here."

"Professor Hunter, what you are saying is ridiculous!" John blurted out. "Nate has not been away from home since July when we drove down the coast."

Ben realized that he needed to tell the story quickly. "Mr. Diamond, let me relate to you the story Nate told me. As I understand it, you and he were on a sailing trip in the Caribbean three years from now in June. You had just told him that your brother, Jack, had diagnosed you with inoperable brain cancer. A storm came up, and lightning hit your vessel. Nate was launched overboard and began to sink. You were swimming down after him when he was sucked under out of your reach. After an intervening experience we can go into another time, he ended up in a cave on our property. He's here right now and would like to talk to you. He remembers the vivid dreams he had just before the start of eighth grade. Sir, your son has traveled back in time from three years in the future, is now sixteen, and wants you to get a cancer checkup before it's too late." Ben had gotten the unusual truth out on the table. He waited for John's reaction, not knowing what to expect. He added, "Please, Nate loves you and wants you to live."

John was indecisive – rare for him. He wanted to hang up as he would for a kook, but this was not a kook. It was the *message* that was beyond absurd. This was leading nowhere, so he decided to take control. "Is he there – this sixteen-year-old boy?"

"Yes, he's in the next room. I'll let you two talk." Ben set the phone down and opened the office door. "Nate, your dad wants to talk with you now. I told him a little, but I don't think he accepted it as truth. Who can blame him?" Nate was up like a shot, but stopped cold before entering the office. He looked up at Ben with concern in his eyes. He was not sure what to say. Ben read his face and encouraged him. "Nate, it's just your dad, your best friend. Just speak from your heart."

Nate nodded and entered the office quietly, taking a seat in the large well-worn office chair. He looked small and vulnerable, and he seemed to view the receiver like a dangerous snake. Ben gave him a thumbs-up and closed the door as he exited.

John was also apprehensive. He was trying to think of a way to explain away this call, or at least to test its authenticity. Then he heard a somewhat familiar voice, like Nate's, only much lower.

"Dad? It's Nate. Really, it's me. I miss you."

John responded the only way he knew how. "My son, Nate, is in his bedroom down the hall. I just talked to him. Who are you?"

"Dad, I'm scared. This is hard for me too. I know I'm there. I'm probably looking over this morning's sermon notes. That's what I usually did. Are you in your office right now? Are you sitting in your black hi-tech chair in front of Grandfather's old oak desk? Is that picture of you and Mom and me from our last trip to Muir Woods before she died sitting to the right of your computer screen?" Nate was tearing up, desperate for his father to acknowledge his existence. "She was so sick, but she just had to see the big trees one more time. On the way back I was afraid you'd drive off the road because you kept tearing up. Dad," Nate sobbed, "it's really me. I love you. Please!"

John looked out his window to see if someone was looking in at him. He knew his son intimately, and this did sound like his Nate. *The voice is deeper, but could it be Nate? No, it has to be a prank.* "I don't know who you are. You sound like my son, but my son is here. I'm not sure what you want." John wondered in his heart if this could be Nate, but his mind was objecting to the entire premise.

"It's really me. I know it seems crazy. Getting sucked into a time tunnel is crazy. Those things don't really happen. But it did. You just have to believe me. If you see me, you'll know it's me." *Please God, let him recognize his only son! How can I help him if he won't believe me?*

"I... I don't understand what is going on." John paused. "I will agree to meet you. If you are Nate, then I know you understand why it is difficult for me to believe something like this."

After hearing his name on his father's lips, Nate lost it and began to cry. Nate tried to calm himself. "You have to believe me. Dad, it's really me. I don't understand everything that has happened, but I know who I am. I also know that if I don't warn you, you're going to die in three years. I don't want to be an orphan. We just can't let cancer destroy what's left of our family."

John's mind wanted to follow his heart, but it could not. His mind was too strong. He needed to get control of this situation and of himself. "I need to see you, um, Nate. This is just too unbelievable. When can I see you? Where are you?"

"I'm at the Hunters' place in the Sierras. I guess it's a pretty long drive from home. Ben's brother, Helmut – he's a great doctor and did a great job with my wound. Well, he's coming back in a few days with his helicopter and said he'd fly me down to see you. I think Ben wants to come along. Maybe Alison too."

John did not take in much after the word "wound". "What's this about a wound? Are you hurt?"

Nate thought Ben had told him. "Don't worry, Dad, I'm fine. I was lucky. I guess, it could have been a lot worse."

"*What* could have been worse?" John demanded.

"It was an accident. An arrow went through the back of my leg."

"An accident? Who shot you? If this Ben person has hurt you in any way…"

"No, Dad, Ben had nothing to do with it, well, at least not directly." *How can I explain all this?* "Look Dad, that part of my story is even crazier than the first part. I'll tell you all about it when we get together. Can I see you this week?"

John found himself consulting his appointment calendar as he would for a new acquisition prospect. It was reassuring to do something familiar in the midst of a sea of mental turmoil. "When did you say they'd bring you down?"

"I think Helmut said Wednesday would be best."

"Well, that should be good." *I had a closing scheduled, but last Friday it was deferred so my schedule opened up.* "Let's see, public school started last week, but your academy doesn't start until Wednesday. Oh, just a minute. With school in session, how can you come down here Wednesday?"

"Dad, you're confusing me with my younger self. I'm not starting school," Nate assured him. "Wednesday is perfect because Ben tells me it's important that I don't meet myself. There's no telling what might happen."

John's mind again was starting to object to this absurd conversation, making him impatient. "Look, I don't want to leave this hanging for three days. Why don't I just drive up there right now?"

"I'm eager to see you too, but Ben and I need to figure out some more things so we can work on a plan with you. It will take us a day or two."

"I don't know what you're talking about. What kind of plan?" John asked warily. "Just what is this professor planning?"

"Dad, once we get into this with you, I think you'll see that I can't stay here, and I need to get back to where I came from three years in the future. Those dreams that I had, or that I'm having, are just a symptom. And that's not all. It's not enough that you get checked out by Uncle Jack right away. We also need to make sure you and I don't end up drowning in the storm. I don't know if we can pull it off, but we want to let you in on our plan and see what you think."

John was comfortable in the role of a consultant. "Well, I'd like to hear what you have to say, and of course I'll give you my take on it …"

"Great!" Nate interrupted. He was relieved to get his dad on board. "Look, let's meet by my favorite pizza place in the fast food area at the Stanford Shopping Center. I'll try to get there a little before noon, OK?"

John wanted to object to the entire concept, but realized that he had no choice. "Well, what can I do to prepare? What should I be doing in the meantime?" John asked.

Nate knew his dad very well. "Just come hungry and bring some money. They don't do pizza up here, and I think I'll order a large."

John found himself laughing despite everything. "Sure, I'm buying."

"Oh, and one more thing. Read over 1 Samuel 20. It's part of my story. It's where I met Ben, though only he's mentioned there."

John had had enough. He did not want to go there now; he had enough to think about. "Fine, whatever. And you said I shouldn't mention this to … well, to your younger self?"

"Right. Ben will explain his theories about this, but when you think it over, you'll realize why," Nate answered. "Did you want to talk to Ben again?"

"No, that's fine, but we should talk Tuesday night to confirm."

"OK. Just call after I go to bed. We'll be here."

John was still confused, but talking to this voice felt exactly like talking to his son. It had to be his son. But how? Why? "As you might imagine, this is very, well, unbelievable and confusing."

"I know. I was pretty confused when I found out what had happened to me. But I've gotten past that. And it's been interesting being up here. The Hunters are archeologists and know a lot about the Holy Land. There's a girl staying up here from the Inca Empire four hundred years ago. She's really nice. She's trying to find her brother who has the third arrow that Ben was supposed to retrieve in 1 Samuel 20, and we're also trying to figure out how to bring all three back to Israel about 1000 B.C." Nate stopped, realizing that all this was probably not helping dispel his father's confusion.

John's mind already had been sufficiently numbed by the surreal conversation that he was immune to further damage. "That's fine. I'm looking forward to meeting with you and getting this all sorted out." He paused, thinking. "Will I know you? What will you be wearing?"

"Of course you'll know me. Well, I've grown about four inches and my hair's kinda long. But don't worry. I'll know you, right?"

"Right. I'll call Tuesday night to confirm."

"Great. Thanks, Dad. It's been good to talk with you. Last time I saw you, I thought you were either dying of cancer or drowning."

"I feel like I'm drowning. I've got some thinking to do."

"One more thing, Dad. Be nice to your son. He's a great guy and loves you a lot."

John smiled at Nate's familiar sense of humor. "Sure. Will do. I love him too. Goodnight, Nate."

"See ya, Dad." Nate replaced the receiver and sat back. The unease he had felt about his dad – the cancer, the storm – had begun to subside, if only by a few notches. He felt a small ray of optimism that there may be a solution. But he remembered what his dad often said about his venture capital deals: The devil is in the details.

John also sat back after the call and took stock. He felt like he was living in two realities, one that made sense and one that did not. He did a quick Internet check to verify Ben and Alison Hunter's credentials. He needed to make sure his son was still in his room to confirm at least one reality. As he walked down the hall, he could hear the reassuring click of computer keys. He looked in the partially open door.

Nate looked up. "Hi, Dad. I was just e-mailing the pastor. Do you think he likes having a kid like me ask all these questions?"

John was relieved to find his son as he had left him. "I know for a fact that he appreciates your notes very much – and not just because it proves at least one person was listening. We learn a lot more from people who challenge us than from empty compliments."

"I know, but I hope he doesn't take it as criticism. Hey, want to hear something funny? I was typing away here and BAM! Out of the blue, guess what I thought about?"

"I have no idea. What?"

Nate leaned back and clasped his hands behind his neck. "I suddenly thought about that new pizza place at the shopping center. I saw you sitting there in a suit like you were waiting for someone. Funny, huh? You don't even like pizza that much."

"Yeah, funny." John was starting to understand why they needed a plan. "It's a nice afternoon, and summer's about over. Let's change clothes and throw a baseball around in the back yard."

"Sure. Good idea. I'll get the mitts."

I need to spend more time with Nate, John thought. *He won't be young forever.*

Ben and Alison wanted to hear all about Nate's conversation with his father. Nate reported that he may not have entirely persuaded his dad that he really was himself, but his dad did agree to meet on Wednesday. Ben was pleased that they had forged this critical link. He and Alison felt responsible for Nate and Kawsay. They had spent many hours discussing how to help the young people figure out where and when they belong.

Ben put a hand on Nate's shoulder. "It's been an intense morning. We need to work on our plan, but maybe we all need some down time. Kawsay wants to take you around to some of her favorite places in the forest. Are you up to it?"

"Sure," Nate replied. "I need to get out. I'm amazed at how quickly my leg is healing."

Kawsay heard the mention of her name from where she was sitting on the living room couch. She had been looking through a stack of coffee table picture books. She was constantly studying, drawing, or contemplating her new world, which endlessly fascinated her. If there were any words she overused, they were: who, what, where, when, how, and why. She preferred being outdoors. On her walks she studied the small plants, relentlessly looking for the medicinal and spice herbs Grandmother used. She also enjoyed spying on an entirely new set of animals.

"We begin our walks today, Nate. I have much to show to you," she called out. "We stay on the ground until you are more strong."

Nate saw Ben nod permission to go. "When should we be back?" Nate inquired.

Alison looked at her watch. "Well, it's almost two o'clock already. Let's heat up the rest of yesterday's stir-fry and eat before you go. There will be plenty of light after that."

Nate and Kawsay readily agreed. They set the table and washed some fruit, cutting it into a community bowl. Part way through the meal, Nate brought up something he had been wondering about since he arrived. "I notice that you don't eat on a normal schedule around here. How come?"

"It's normal for us," Ben replied. "We've been doing it this way for about a year."

Alison provided a more complete explanation. "We used to eat the way most people do – light breakfast and lunch, followed by a heavy dinner. We were starting to add a little weight here and there."

"So, what happened?" Nate asked, remembering how his hosts had been encouraging him to improve his nutrition.

"We found a book with a lot of good ideas," Ben answered, "one of which is not to eat late in the day or evening because our bodies store the calories as fat while we sleep."

"Don't you get hungry at night?" Nate asked.

"No," Ben answered. "Actually, on occasions when we need to eat late, I feel too stuffed to sleep."

Alison did not want Nate to feel compelled to change his habits to suit them. "It's OK that you want snacks later in the day. Ben does the same thing, but he thinks I don't notice."

"What do you mean?" Ben protested. "I rarely grab a midnight snack. In fact, I can't remember the last time I did."

"Oh, come on, honey, you think I haven't noticed?" Alison responded with an incredulous look. "I don't count the slices of bread or pieces of fruit, but I've been noticing food disappearing from the kitchen all summer." *No need for the kids to listen to this discussion,* she thought. "Why don't you two get started on your explorations? Ben and I will clean up."

Kawsay and Nate looked at each other with conspiratorial smiles and made a beeline out the front door. Kawsay immediately re-entered and retrieved some of her "weapons" from her room and quickly disappeared again.

Ben returned to the food mystery. "What exactly have you noticed, Alison. You never mentioned anything to me."

"It's OK. I'm sorry I brought it up," Alison said, dismissing the matter.

Ben tried to put Alison at ease. "Please, tell me what you've observed, honey. I'd like to know."

Alison realized Ben was serious. "Well, I started noticing that things were missing, not every day but sometimes. I asked Kawsay if she was taking some extra food, but she said no, so I assumed it was you. It wasn't just fruit and bread but also veggies from the fridge and the remains of cereal boxes. The gooey butter cake even disappeared unusually fast."

Ben liked a mystery but not in his own house. He quickly considered the possibilities. *Could someone be coming in here at night? I wonder if anything else is missing?* "I always check the front and back door before turning in." He furrowed his brows. "What about the laundry room door? Have you been keeping it locked?"

Alison rarely worried about door locks – that was Ben's department. "I know you check all the doors before we go away for vacation or down to the city …." They both realized that their security had been lax. "You don't think someone has been breaking in here, do you?"

Before Alison could finish speaking, Ben was striding across the kitchen toward the laundry room. He called back, "Well, it's not locked right now." She heard him open and close the door and then turn the bolt. "Hey, what's all this?" Alison heard the concern in his voice and was at his side in a flash.

Ben was on his toes, straining to see what was on the upper storage shelf to the right of the door. He brought down an animal carved from wood. It was about seven inches long. "Look at this," Ben said, holding out the unexpected object in two cupped hands.

Alison drew in her breath. She looked at the carving, then at Ben, and then back at the carving. It was an intricately carved mountain lion – or was it a leopard or jaguar? "It's beautiful, but what is it? And what's it doing here?" she asked.

Ben did not answer, but handed her the object and reached up on the shelf for another. This one was more easily identified as a llama, carved from the same fine wood. Ben sniffed it. "It smells like fir. The wood is still fresh and aromatic. There's no chemical finish on it."

Alison put the cat down and took the llama, turning it over looking for some identification. There was none. She offered her opinion. "These are very nicely done, probably not mass produced. Where could they have come from?"

Ben shook his head. "Wait, there are more." He gathered several more carved objects, set them in a row on the washer, and turned on the harsh fluorescent lights. As they looked down the lineup, they became more mystified and astonished. The complete collection included what looked like a tapir, a deer, some kind of monkey, and a soaring condor. There were also a dog and a large wolf. "Some of these are not California animals," Ben observed. "They look South American."

Alison scrutinized each of them closely. She picked up the dog last. "Funny, but this dog carving looks like Junior." She handed it to Ben.

He examined it closely and then held it out to Alison, pointing to the dog's collar. His voice sounded ominous. "Alison, this *is* Junior. Look at the tiny chalkboard dangling from his mouth! Someone has carved Junior. And this wolf – doesn't it look like Zevél?"

She grew concerned too. "Who would do that? And when? Is this some kind of prank or something?" Ben turned to look at the upper shelf to see if there was anything else. He found one more suspicious item – the box that Kawsay's athletic shoes had come in. "I thought we weren't saving these boxes any more," he said. "Wait, there's something in it." He set it down and opened the lid. There was something wrapped in the tissue paper. It was another carving, this time of a person. It was a young girl.

They stared at it, speechless. It was about nine inches high and a striking likeness of Kawsay wearing the tunic she wore on the night she arrived. They looked at each other. Alison spoke first. "Who could carve Kawsay wearing those clothes? She hasn't had them on since she arrived?"

Ben silently pondered the mystery. "I have an idea," he said, putting the carvings back on the shelf. "Do you think there might be a connection between the food disappearing and these figures appearing?"

"Why should there be any connection?" Alison asked.

"Well, maybe there isn't any, but they are right next to the door we've been leaving unlocked, and they've obviously been created by someone who has seen Kawsay and Junior, and probably the rest of us too."

"And," Alison added, "both events are unsolved mysteries." She paused. "So what's your idea – hide here and catch whoever it is?"

Ben thought some more. "Well, we could, but that could be dangerous, and whoever it is could return any time on any night. What about making a tape? We have a video camera. Maybe we could rig a switch to turn it on when this door is opened. If the intruder meant harm, it probably would have happened by now."

"I don't know. I'm not comfortable knowing that someone is in my house at night," Alison responded. "And we need to check for other items that might be missing."

"I agree. If nothing else has been taken, we'll just all lock our bedroom doors tonight. We can keep a weapon close by," Ben suggested. "Let's give it a try. I don't sense that this is a dangerous person, but I really wonder who it is that has been sneaking in here."

Alison was not completely comfortable with the idea, but decided to give Ben's plan a chance. "Let's not tell the kids. It might upset them. I'm surprised Junior hasn't sounded an alarm. I thought you told me he'd be a good watch dog."

"He is a good watch dog. You know he has really sharp ears. Our intruder must be really quiet!" Ben said. "Late tonight I will rig a switch by the laundry room door and run a wire to my small video camera. I'll set the tripod where it can get a broad view of the kitchen and the exit to the laundry room. We can set out some bananas and bread on the counter and leave on the dim light over the range to insure the pixels will record any interesting events."

Kawsay and Nate were busy elsewhere, oblivious to the brewing mystery. Kawsay had explored most of the trails that laced the Hunter property and many trails beyond since there were few boundary markers. She had brought along her bola and lucky spear. Nate brought along the ski pole again to assist in walking though his leg felt surprisingly much better.

They followed the stream down about a mile and then turned through a particularly large stand of firs next to a small secluded group of sequoias. Nate had not expected to see the big trees around there, thinking they only grew in the national park. Kawsay was on the lookout for whomever – or whatever – she had seen the day before while returning from the cave. To Nate, the forest seemed very close and seemed to be watching them.

Finally, they came to a clearing left over from logging many years earlier. Kawsay thought this would be a good place to try the bola. "Nate, my bola is good to catch a running animal. I swing it like this." She began to rotate the ungainly amalgamation of stones and sinew over her head and suddenly let it fly toward a small unsuspecting tree. It wrapped its tentacles around the tree with the stones whipping against the trunk with loud cracks.

It happened fast and startled Nate. He was impressed. "Where did you learn to do that?" he asked.

"Yachay and Grandfather are my teachers. They say I must be able to live alone in the jungle and hunt and fight like a man."

"I've never seen a bola in action. May I try it?"

"Yes, I want to teach you to be a man too." Kawsay offered. She retrieved her weapon and brought it to Nate. She showed him how to hold and twirl it. "You must let bola go at right time. Then bola will find the animal."

Nate had no idea what the "right time" would be, but remembered how to throw a ball. His first attempt resulted in the bola skittering to the right and tangling itself in a bush.

Kawsay had to laugh, but then remembered her first failed attempts. "Please watch me throw bola one more time," she encouraged Nate. "Watch when I let it go."

This time Nate paid closer attention to her throwing technique. The bola flew straight to the same tree and grasped it a few feet higher. Nate loped over and unwound the bola, eager to take another turn. "I think I know what I did wrong," he said. He began to spin the bola around and released it at a more opportune moment. He saw it take a high trajectory and wrap itself around a branch about thirty feet above their heads. Kawsay again laughed, shaking her head at Nate, who could not help but join her. "Sorry Kawsay. How will we get it down?"

She did not answer, but jogged over to the tree and jumped up, grabbing the lowest branch. She deftly swung herself up onto the branch and effortlessly made her way up the side of the tree to the bola-decorated branch. She slithered out the branch with her legs wrapped securely around it and dislodged the weapon, tossing it down to Nate. "Nate, try throwing bola more times. First let me get far from the tree!"

He tried several more throws with Kawsay's coaching and encouragement. After he managed to partially wrap the trunk on successive throws, his teacher said, "You learn fast. That is good for today. Let us try my spear."

Nate felt more confident in the spear-chucking competition, but let Kawsay go first. She apparently had it in for this particular little tree because, after walking about fifteen paces away from it, she turned and flung the spear in its direction. Kawsay was pleased that she had not lost her touch, as the spear lodged only a few inches to the left of center. Again her quick, cat-like movements startled and impressed Nate. He had not realized that a young girl could be so fearsomely deadly.

Nate ran to pry it out of the tree. The spear was a little less than three feet long. The shaft was a straight piece of very hard wood. The tip was made of shiny black stone with a surprisingly sharp serrated edge. It was set into the shaft and secured with some kind of gut or sinew. He hefted it like an Olympic champion, eager to please the crowd. He saw Kawsay watching him as if ready for more comedy.

"I'll give it a try," he said. Nate took several long strides, turned, and launched the spear with all his might toward the hapless tree. His injured leg slightly buckled, and he tumbled over onto his back, unable to see where the spear ended up. Looking up, he saw Kawsay kneeling over him, her eyes dancing with mirth and her hands covering her mouth. *Oh no,* he thought, *I blew it again.* He gave a shrug and then joined her in the laughter.

It felt good be a kid at that moment, regardless of where the spear might be. As the laughter died away, they both continued to look at one another, and their eyes locked for a long moment. Kawsay was admiring the dark green color of his eyes, a color so unlike that of her people. Nate was admiring her deep brown eyes with their ever-watchful gaze. They enjoyed a moment of quiet closeness. He reached up and touched the side of her head and lightly stroked her hair. He ran his hand across her cheek and under her chin while his eyes searched her face.

She stiffened at the thought of her lip being observed so closely. With a troubled look in her eyes, she said, "You do not find me ugly."

Nate could not tell if it was a question or a statement, but he understood that she had spent a lifetime being shunned. "Kawsay, no. I find you beautiful. You are amazing. You are very special to me."

Kawsay felt a rush of emotion from deep within, which made her both smile and show a tear in each eye. She looked even more deeply into Nate's eyes, wanting to believe his words.

"Really, it's true," he tried to assure her.

Kawsay let out a few small sobs and then took one of Nate's hands in both of hers, kissing it repeatedly. This was new for them both and a little frightening. Nate rolled to his side and assumed a kneeling position, mirroring hers. Again he stroked her hair, this time its entire length, and then ran his fingers along her bronze cheek and jaw. His finger then moved to her scar where it rested for a moment. This time she did not grow stiff, but she waited holding her breath. Nate put his arms around his special teacher and friend, his fellow traveler, contemplating the miracles it took to bring them together in this place at this time. He slowly enfolded her in his arms and gently rocked her back and forth. She felt small and vulnerable in his arms.

When the magical moment passed, they drew apart, looking down. Their eyes slowly rose to meet again, and they both recognized a wonderful sense of belonging. Kawsay smiled, remembering the spear. "You throw spear very well, Nate."

"I do?" he responded. She pointed at the tree. Nate grabbed her hand, and they strode over to the tree. The tip was buried very deeply, a few inches below the scar of Kawsay's earlier throw. Nate smiled and gave a short bow. Kawsay began laboring to dislodge her special spear. Nate helped her wiggle it free.

"I am a great teacher," Kawsay boasted with amusement. "Next time we will bring my sling."

"And we can kill giants!" Nate exulted. As they continued their trek, he told her the story of the great battle between David and Goliath. She admired the young shepherd's skill with his sling and his courage even more.

They soon turned back toward their new home, with Nate offering to hold her hand every time they came to a large rock or small stream. Kawsay enjoyed his chivalry and readily accepted his help, even though she had no need of it. He had helped her in a more important way – to feel beautiful and accepted. She had helped him too. He was standing taller and feeling an excitement in his heart that exceeded anything his books and studies had ever brought.

Kawsay and Nate returned about six o'clock as the sun was beginning to filter through the trees across the clearing. They reported that they had enjoyed their nature walk. Nate explained that he threw the spear well, but that mastering the bola would take time.

Later that night, Nate had a question for Ben and Alison. "You have a great place. I can see why you like to spend as much time up here as possible! Are there any neighbors?"

Alison responded, "Well, it depends on your definition of neighbors. There are no other holdings for several miles in all directions. When we see someone, it's usually a hiker. Did you and Kawsay see anyone?"

"No, but Kawsay kept watching. You know she thought she saw someone when we were returning from the cave yesterday," Nate reported. "I had a feeling that we were being watched today. You know how that feels."

Ben turned and looked at Alison, then at Nate. "Yeah, we know the feeling. Can't explain it, but you never know. It could be a person or an animal."

The household slept soundly, including Junior. Nate had partly adjusted to the vivid dreams. It helped to know the cause, and he found it interesting to relive some of his earlier days, but he felt a little tired and stressed.

Ben was up first and initially did not remember that they had rigged the camera. When he arrived in the kitchen to start breakfast, he noticed the range hood light and it all came back to him. He quickly checked the camera and was excited to find it had been tripped. He looked around and determined that some food was missing. He could not wait to view the tape, so he rewound it and hit the play button. He viewed it on the tiny screen that flipped out from the side of the instrument.

The useful segment was not long, only about a minute or two. The lighting was low and the image was indistinct on the small screen. All he could make out was a figure entering the kitchen from the laundry room, first a head warily looking around, then slowly the rest of the body. It methodically filled a small pouch with some fruit and bread and then looked in the refrigerator, removing a few items Ben could not see. Finally, it skimmed some nuts and dried fruit from the cupboard. The intruder obviously knew its way around. The quantity removed was not large, perhaps to avoid causing anyone to miss the items. Then, ever so silently, the figure slipped back out. The tape continued showing the empty room. Sensing there would be no more action, Ben stopped the camera and rewound.

Who was this? Some hermit? He replayed the cut, this time paying attention to the figure itself. The thief was of moderate height, had hair at least to the shoulders, and was wearing jewelry and a shapeless dress. *Is this a man or woman?* Ben decided he needed a bigger screen to get a better look.

As he was packing up the tripod and finding the cords for a feed to the television, Kawsay arrived with Junior. Junior was a wonderful addition to her life, and she enjoyed giving him food and treats. She let him out the laundry room door for his first sniff-fest of the day. She was already dressed as if ready for another trek.

"Good morning, Kawsay. Sleep well?" Ben asked as she returned to the kitchen.

"Yes, thank you. What is our breakfast this day? I will help you."

"We're a little low on supplies. I was thinking of a yogurt-granola mixture, toast with almond or tahini butter, and some bananas," Ben responded. "Sound good?"

"Yes, it will be very good." She busied herself getting out the ingredients for the meal.

Ben watched her move silently and efficiently around the large kitchen. He noticed that since her arrival at the start of the summer, Kawsay had grown, both in height and maturity. *Maybe Alison should have one of those talks with her,* he wondered. With the two of them working together, the meal was soon ready. As Ben was setting out juice glasses, Junior barked to come in. Kawsay ran to open the laundry room door, and Junior came bounding through in search of Alison, almost knocking Nate over as he entered the kitchen.

"Good morning," Nate said sleepily. "Did I miss breakfast?"

"We'd never let you do that, partner," Ben answered. "Come on and have a seat."

Kawsay and Nate eyed one another, but did not exchange words. Each was wondering how the other felt about the prior day's events. Nate noticed that she was dressed in hiking clothes and asked, "So, Kawsay, is today my sling lesson?"

Her smile reassured him that she was feeling as wonderful as he was. "Yes, Nate, if you like."

Ben was filling Junior's dish when the puppy returned with Alison. She was dressed in jeans and a fleece top to dispel the morning chill, her hair brushed and gleaming. "Sorry I'm poky." Alison looked at Ben questioningly and made the little charades hand motion for "movie".

Ben understood and nodded. "Let's eat first," he proposed.

During breakfast, Ben reminded Nate they needed to give priority to preparing for the upcoming visit with Nate's father. The conversation turned to Kawsay's progress on language and geography, some artifacts from the last dig, and the fact that Ben and Alison's sabbatical would be ending in a few months. As they finished eating, Ben brought up the subject of the intruder, explaining that someone had been sneaking into the kitchen at night and taking food. He wanted everyone to look at the tape. Alison was impatient to see it.

"Maybe together we can figure out who this person is. This happened last night while we were sleeping," Ben said. "Also, I want everyone to be on the lookout. I don't think this person is dangerous, but we never know. Meanwhile, I'll be locking all the doors at night and when we leave. We're pretty sure the intruder has been coming in the laundry room door."

Ben readied the equipment while his audience perched on the leather couch. "This only lasts a short time. See what you think." He hit the play button.

On the large screen the details of the empty kitchen were more visible. In a few seconds, the head appeared and looked around. It was clearly a male with sharp darting eyes. *So what's with the jewelry and dress?* Ben wondered. As the figure on the screen emerged, their attention was diverted to Kawsay, who had become very agitated and was leaning forward, wide-eyed. Then she covered her open mouth with one hand and pointed at the screen with the other.

As the brief scene continued, she moved in front of the screen, touching it with her hand. When it was over, she turned them, looking very distraught. She saw three questioning faces. "Taytaku," she said quietly. She received blank stares. Then louder, "Taytaku! It is Grandfather." It was difficult to know who was the most surprised. She let out a burst of questions. "When did camera see him? How did he get here? Where is he now?"

Alison reminded her of the discussion the day before about food disappearing and their concern that someone might be coming into the house at night.

Kawsay was shaking her head. "Grandfather does not steal," she said somberly.

Then Ben remembered the carvings. "Just a minute, Kawsay, there's something else we want you to see," he said, heading toward the laundry room. He returned with an armful of wooden carvings and a shoebox. Sitting on the floor, he arrayed the little animals on the coffee table.

Kawsay slid over, fascinated at what she saw. Nate and Alison drew close to her. Kawsay picked up each figure and examined it closely. She slowly spoke. "Alpaca. Luwichu. Kuntur, Sacha. Allqu, no Junior! And Zevél!" She looked at Alison and Ben and smiled. "Grandfather does not steal. See, he give you wood animals. He makes nice things from wood with knife. He thanks you for food."

She had solved both mysteries, only to open a larger one. Ben handed Kawsay the shoebox with an encouraging nod. She wondered why they were giving her more shoes. She opened the lid carefully and found a figure inside. She broke into a huge smile. "See, Nate," she held it out for him to see, "this is Kawsay." Nate took it carefully from her, cradling it in his hands.

"It looks just like you," he observed. "It's perfect."

Then Kawsay reached inside the box again. She extracted another larger figure that had not been there the day before. It was similar to the Kawsay carving, but was obviously a male. Kawsay held it up before her face with a desperate look in her eyes. Then she held it to her breast, enfolding it in her arms. "Yachay. Yachay," she murmured over and over, her eyes closed. Then she remembered the others and looked at them with tear-filled eyes. "This is my turay, my Yachay."

"May I see it?" Alison asked. She took the new carving from Kawsay and examined its features. "He looks like you Kawsay. He is very handsome."

Nate had moved over next to Alison to get a better look. "I wonder if Yachay is here."

Kawsay was suddenly energized and on her feet. It finally registered that Grandfather and maybe Yachay were nearby. *I had almost given up hope! Could they really be here? I must go and find them!* Kawsay ran from the room and flew out of the house leaving the door open. Ben, Alison, and Nate jumped up to follow her, but by the time they were outside, she was disappearing into the forest. They heard her voice pierce the calm of the morning. "Yachay! Taytaku! Yachay! Taytaku!"

Ben shouted after her, "Kawsay, come back. We will help! Come back!" But she was gone – in another world, her old world.

"Ben, let's go after her!" Alison appeared very anxious.

"We can't go in our slippers. Nate, hold down the fort. Helmut would kill me if I let you go running through the woods. C'mon, honey. Let's find our running shoes." They hustled back into the house. Ben and Alison were out the door in less than a minute, running in the same direction as Kawsay.

Nate watched them disappear into the dark shade of the trees as they called out her name. He knew they were no match for Kawsay. She would be long gone. He was angry that his leg was not yet strong enough to join the chase, but what could he do? He decided to clean up the breakfast dishes. As he finished, he remembered the carvings and went over to them. He admired each skillfully-made animal. Then he picked up Yachay. *He looks a little scary, like a warrior,* Nate thought. Turning to the last figure, he held it up and looked into its eyes.

He spoke to it. "Kawsay, come back, come back."

Nate heard the big front door open and quickly set down the figure. Ben and Alison came in, damp and out of breath. But they looked more worried than tired.

"Did you find her?" Nate asked without optimism.

"Not a sign," Ben lamented. "I'm no tracker, and she is. She could be anywhere."

"Well," Nate suggested, "maybe she can track down her grandfather. If he's here, why would he hide from her anyway?"

Alison was wondering the same thing. "I first noticed food disappearing about the time Kawsay came here. Considering that and all these carvings, I think her grandfather has been around here quite a while."

"Why would he keep himself secret?" Ben wondered. "What is he up to?"

"Maybe he's afraid of what might happen. No one has explained to him where he is and what's going on. He must be mystified and frightened," Alison said.

"I agree. He probably feels lost and doesn't know how to get home," Ben stated, remembering that Zevél had blocked him from returning through the tunnel.

"The poor man. We've got to find him!" Alison proclaimed.

"I don't think we'll be able to unless he wants to be found. If anyone can find him, it's Kawsay," Ben posited. "If she doesn't come back soon, though, I don't know what we'll do. It's a big forest out there."

"And a big world," Alison added. "What if she wanders too far away and other people find her?"

"They might think she's an illegal and deport her or something," Nate conjectured.

"Let's not let our imaginations get the better of us," Ben said. "I think all we can do is wait and see. She knows the area as well as any of us. If she's not back by afternoon, we'll have to go looking again, though I fear that might be futile. If she's not back by dark, we ..."

"Let's wait a while and then check the cave," Alison interrupted. "Her grandfather came here the same way she did, so maybe he's staying there."

CHAPTER 16.

IMPROBABLE REUNIONS

AUGUST 31 – PRESENT YEAR
SIERRAS, CALIFORNIA

WHEN WE ARE APART
PART OF ME DIES, BUT REVIVES
WHEN WE TOUCH AGAIN.

Kawsay was unaware of the worry she was causing her new friends. She was completely focused on finding her family, whichever members were in her new world. She ran on instinct, not randomly but methodically, looking for signs of human passage through the brush. She noticed that Junior had come along to help, but if he had tracking skills, he was not using them as he invited her to stop and play. "No, Junior. No time to play. We find Taytaku. We find Grandfather." Junior only partially comprehended.

She thought she had picked up Grandfather's trail a few times, but it disappeared. Watching the ground and not paying attention to the larger landmarks, she became disoriented and was in danger of getting lost. She stopped to think and sat down on a flat rock. Junior sat down too and accepted an ear scratch. Speaking her native tongue, she enlisted his help. "Junior, you must help me find Grandfather. He has brown skin like mine and big gold ear disks. He likes dogs. Maybe together we can find where he lives now." Junior seemed pleased to hear all this.

Kawsay stood up and looked around. She knew she had traveled far from the big house in the last hour. The immediate surroundings were not familiar. A pang of fear arose within her chest, but having Junior with her was reassuring. *Junior and I will find home later. I must think like Grandfather.* She sat back down, this time on a log. *If I knew what he was trying to do, I would know where he is.* She remembered that when she and Yachay were training in the jungle, Grandfather had been nearby but out of sight. *He always watches over me. I wonder if he followed me to the secret cave. Of course, he would want to be sure I got there.* She heard bees circling an array of late summer wildflowers blooming at her feet. Junior had finished claiming several trees and returned, rolling and squirming on the ground, itching his back, a smile on his face. She kept on thinking. *I suppose he wanted me to find a safe place to be. He must have followed me through the singing wall!*

She stood up, startling Junior, who immediately came to attention. Again, she addressed him in Quechua. "I remember something holding my ankle when I went down the time tunnel. Junior, that must be how Grandfather got here!" She had not seen him in the cave when she arrived. *I think I remember something or someone else moving in the cave, but I was very groggy. Grandfather must have been there if he traveled with me. I wonder if he saw Zevél?* Kawsay was beside herself about Grandfather being nearby. Then she remembered. Zevél had told her that she had not traveled alone. "The wolf must have been talking about Grandfather!" she informed Junior. He wagged his tail in agreement.

A dark cloud passed over Kawsay's face. *Zevél also told me Yachay was not here. I will not find Yachay.* She missed her wonderful and brave brother so much. She also missed her Mother and Grandmother. Kawsay had been fighting bouts of homesickness, but she had no word for it. She only knew it hurt a lot. Junior was becoming impatient to get moving. *Where could Grandfather be?* At last she fit the pieces together.

"Of course, Junior! Grandfather came to the wolf's cave like me, and Zevél knows he is here. He must be staying in the cave. It is safe and has good water. And it is close to the big house." Junior's Quechua was too rudimentary to catch all she said, but he was happy to see his friend running again. Kawsay retraced their steps, and Junior soon took the lead since he was not disoriented at all. When they reached the stream, she headed for the bridge. They flew over the span and turned toward the cave. Kawsay's pulse was racing now, not so much from exertion as from anticipation. She felt sure Grandfather would be in the beautiful cavern!

The air had become warm, but retained the stillness of the morning. The excited searchers kept running until they reached the cave entrance. Kawsay paused at the dark opening, wondering if Grandfather would be there and what story he would tell her. She had so much to tell him! *Where will we begin? He has been watching me. He must tell me everything first.* She entered cautiously, but Junior zipped by her. She hurried along to keep up. As Junior disappeared around the last bend, he began barking. Kawsay heard a human voice and stopped to listen.

"Good morning, my furry friend! I am sorry I have no meat for you today. I will hunt later. You are hot from running. Here, have some water from this bowl." Kawsay recognized the voice and the language. It was like a flash from another world, yet it was here and now! She surged ahead heedless of the walls and uneven floor. Rounding the last corner before the lighted crystal room, she spied Junior back by the clear water pools next to a person in familiar garb.

"Grandfather," Kawsay whispered to herself in recognition. She ran forward. "Grandfather! I found you!" Her voice pierced the dim cavern and left a ringing echo. Grandfather turned toward the sound, but she was upon him before her identity registered. He was able to brace himself against her impact and barely avoided being knocked onto his back. Her strong, desperate embrace told him all he needed to know.

"Kawsay, Kawsay, my little Kawsay," he murmured. "My brave and beautiful little one!" She continued to hold onto him as if to prevent him from ever going away from her again. A moment passed before he spoke again. "Dear Kawsay, why are you here? You should be with your new family."

Kawsay still would not let go. "Oh, Grandfather! Until this morning, I did not know you were with me. But I should have known that you always watch over me." Junior had been watching the reunion happily and now wanted to get in on the action. He let out a few squeals and then a sharp bark. Grandfather brought his four-legged friend into the huddle. Then Kawsay realized that Junior had known all along. "Grandfather, you and Junior are friends!"

"Yes," he laughed, "We met soon after I arrived and quickly became friends. When I gave him some of my meat, he liked me even more." Grandfather finally was free of

Kawsay's grip and held her at a distance by the shoulders. "You look very nice in these new clothes. And you have grown during your time here. Your new family is taking very good care of you."

"Alison and Ben are wonderful people and have been very kind to me. They have given me new clothes, and they have taught me their language and how to use symbols for words. But, Grandfather, do not call them my new family. You and Mother and Grandmother and Yachay are my family."

"Yes, we are your family, but remember, you cannot live with us. I followed you to see if you would do well. I did not expect you would find new people who would accept you. I thought you would live alone in the jungle and the secret cave." Grandfather's eye was caught by a glint of light reflected from Kawsay's necklace. He reached out and examined it with his hand and squinted to see it in the dim light. "Kawsay," he asked in a hushed tone, "where did you get this necklace?"

Kawsay had forgotten about it because she wore it everywhere. "I found it in the water pool near the singing wall," Kawsay responded. "I was filling my water pouch and washing blood from my hands after climbing up the cliff."

Kusi thought, *It must have fallen out of my sack!* "It is very valuable," he said. "Be careful not to lose it."

"Why do you speak of jewelry at this time? I want to know how you got here," she urged. "Did you come alone?"

"I am alone," Kusi said dejectedly, looking down at the cold stone floor. "When I fell through the singing wall – remember I was holding your ankle – I thought we were dying. When I hit the bottom, I must have hurt my head because I was unconscious for a long time."

"I never saw you. Why didn't you tell me you were here?" Kawsay asked, offended that Grandfather would hide from her.

"Kawsay, I only came to make sure you were safe, not to prevent your independence. Well, when I came to, I did look for you. When I entered this room, I saw a huge silver wolf sitting by you. You were asleep. The beast did not harm you. He saw me and walked over to me, saying words I did not know. I spoke to him in our language, but he seemed not to understand. So, I spoke to him in the only other language of which I had any knowledge, Español, the language of Pizarro. I pointed to you and then at me and said, 'Abuelo.' He seemed to understand this and replied, 'Me llamo Zevél, servidor a usted.' The big wolf then walked over to you and gently nosed you onto his broad back and took you out of the cavern."

"You knew that he would not hurt me?"

"I did not know, so I followed him, ready to attack with my small weapons if he tried to harm you. But he left you by your new house. I saw the light-skinned people come outside and find you. I watched through the openings in the side of their big house as they fed you and helped you become clean. You appeared to be safe, and soon everything went dark. I watched for a long time. All these days I have been living here, hunting in the forest. I have continued to watch you every day. These are good people, and they have such strange and wonderful inventions. I have never seen such amazing things." Kusi was looking more closely at her face. It was covered with sweat and dirt from her frantic morning search, but it was also changed. He reached out to examine her lip. His arm recoiled as if shocked. "What magic is this? What happened to your lip?" Grandfather had seen Kawsay with her bandages after the operation, but had not seen her up close since they arrived.

"It is not magic," Kawsay explained. "A good healer in a gigantic city fixed my lip so it looks almost perfect. I flew to her in the large metal bird with the spinning wings. I have wondered if I can return to our village now that I am not ugly. But maybe it is right that I stay here." She had once hoped to return to her village, but was not sure it was possible. Also, she had to face the truth – her new friends were wonderful. They loved her even when she was ugly, just like her family had. And she liked living here more than in an isolated village in 1609 where she had already learned almost everything there was to know. And there was her new special friend, Nate.

"This healer must be very powerful. You were always beautiful to me, but it is amazing to see you with this change. Inti has been good to you."

Kawsay looked down shaking her head. "No, Grandfather, Inti did not help me. You know this to be true. Our village did not help me. They all hated me and wanted me dead. The God of Ben, Alison, Nate, and Zevél loves me and has helped me. I think I should never go back to our village. To me it is a place of hopelessness and darkness."

Kusi could not dispute her words. He did not know about this new god that Kawsay mentioned, so he took another tack. "Then you know Zevél? He sometimes comes here through the tunnel, but mostly I am alone."

"Yes, I remember he brought me to Ben and Alison's home. We came to this cave two days ago and talked with him. Zevél speaks many languages, but does not know our language." She remembered another event of that day. "I did not see you in the cave during that visit, but I think I did see you in the forest as we returned to the big house."

"Yes, I was there watching. But I did not mean for you to see me." Kusi looked tired and not as strong as in the past. "I think your new family is good for you. Maybe you do not need me any more."

"What do you mean?" Kawsay protested. "I will always need you. You and Yachay taught me everything. I love you. We are family." She was very distressed that he would even think of leaving her.

"Kawsay, you do not understand!" he corrected her. "We taught you so you could live *without* us after you were sent away. You know what a danger it is for any of us to be away for very long because we are not supposed to help you. Even if you did need me, think of the others, of Grandmother, your mother, and your brother. I fear the village will harm them when I do not return. And I have been gone a very long time. Is it not more important that I go to them and protect them?"

Kawsay thought this over, and the same concern grew in her heart. *I am being selfish. The rest of the family needs him to return, or there will be suspicions.* "I understand that you must return. You are right. It is not safe for them when you are away. Do you know if they are all right?"

Grandfather, usually a very happy person, appeared uncommonly sad. He looked down and shook his head slowly and helplessly. "I know nothing of them all the time we have been here. Two days after you left our village, I left to follow you. They expected me back within days. But I did not return, and I am sure that Yachay went looking for me. I do not know if he also went through the singing wall, but he has not come to this place. I have wondered if I should leave you here and return to our village. I had seen Zevél come and go through the back of this cave. One day when he was here, I tried to go back into the tunnel, but he stopped me. I said to him 'Debo volver a mi familia.' He stopped me and shook his head, saying, 'No, Señor. No está para que usted vaya.' I decided that he understood the tunnel better than me, and he was very large and persuasive, so I did not argue. But now I think I will try to return when he is not here to stop me. Things could be very bad in our village."

Kawsay pondered all Grandfather said. She wished they could let everyone know that they were fine. But there was something important that Grandfather needed to understand. "Grandfather, do you know where we are?"

"No, I am not sure. There must be something mystical about the tunnel, though, because this place is so strange. The first night I noticed that the stars were different, though the moon was the same. I observed that the Sun does not pass overhead, but stays closer to the hills. The animals and plants sometimes look familiar, but when I study them closely, they are all different. This tells me we may be very far away, yet I do not understand how we could travel so far just by falling."

Kawsay would do her best to explain something she could not fully comprehend. She faced him, sitting cross-legged. "Grandfather, you have interpreted the signs correctly. We are *very* far from home. Across much of the world and far to the north and west of our village. Ben tells me it would take a person more than a year to walk to our village from here, and we would encounter people who would try to stop us."

"But that would be too late! I must get there very quickly. I do not know how to go. Can Ben show us the way? We must try." Kusi was very concerned about the need for haste.

"Please, Grandfather, it is impossible … I mean there is no reason to try to walk there. Our village does not exist at this time." He looked totally confused. Kawsay took a deep breath. *How will Grandfather take this news?* "I have learned that the sucking tunnel did not just move us across the world, it also moved us across time. We are living in the future, four hundred years from the time when we fell through the singing wall." She watched his face as he just stared at her blankly.

He knew that the gods moved beyond time, but he had never heard of people doing this. His loneliness was turning to despair, as he thought of his wife long dead. Everyone dead. His lingering hope of returning to his home was evaporating as she watched. Kawsay's heart was breaking for him. She knew well the feeling of being severed from everything in the world that you love.

"If this is true…" he began. "Oh, Kawsay! What have we done? What are we doing here? I am worse than dead!" he moaned.

"No, Grandfather, I am here. I will never leave you." Kawsay embraced her dear grandfather. It was a new feeling to be comforting him when he had always been the strong one. Grandfather had never before seemed so old to her. Never so sad and hopeless. "Do not give up hope. I believe all will be well. Maybe Zevél can help you return."

"No, Kawsay, I feel I am a lost man. Better you should return to your new family. I must now leave you in their care. You do not need me. I am tired."

Kawsay realized that Grandfather was dying inside, even if he had been getting enough food. "Grandfather, you must come with me today. Right now I want my new friends to meet you. They will like you, and maybe Ben and Alison can help you." Grandfather was looking again at her with a dead stare that frightened her. Then she thought she detected a glimmer of hope. "I also want you to meet my new friend, Nate. He told me I was beautiful."

Grandfather was interested in this. "He is the young boy with yellow hair that came recently to this place?" Kawsay nodded. "I remember the night he arrived. I had been asleep, but I awoke and followed Zevél as he brought the boy up to the big house. He had been hurt by an arrow."

"Yes, Ben's brother is a good healer and removed the arrow. Nate is healing quickly."

"I know that, Kawsay. I saw him trying to throw a bola and a spear. He is not what I would call a warrior!" Grandfather had to laugh at the memory of Nate and the bola.

Kawsay felt her neck and ears warm, but her embarrassment was not visible in the dim light of the cavern. "Grandfather, you were spying on us!" Kawsay protested.

"I was there in case you needed me. Did you know that in this forest there is a dangerous cat much like the jaguar of our jungle? During one of your walks alone in the forest not long after you arrived, one was stalking you. I chased it away." Kusi was glad he had been there to protect her and remembered how it had felt to be needed. "Do not be embarrassed that you and Nate have an interest in one another. You are reaching an age when you will find young men interesting and will have special feelings toward them, different from those you feel for your brother."

Kawsay was about to protest, but could not. She and Yachay were as close as siblings could be, but her feelings toward Nate were new and different and were growing stronger. Yet she still missed Yachay so much! Kawsay suddenly stood up with her hands over her mouth, remembering something very important about Yachay.

"Grandfather, listen! I must tell you this. The arrow that injured my friend Nate was exactly like the lucky arrow you gave to Yachay. I investigated this because I thought maybe Yachay was here and had shot the arrow into Nate. That is not what happened, though. Wait, there is more. There is another arrow that Ben has in the big house. At first I wondered if he got it from Yachay, but he did not."

Grandfather was immediately engaged by this story. It was not just because he was looking for hints of Yachay's whereabouts, but because of the unusual way he had first acquired the arrow he later gave to his grandson. He felt energized. "I would like to find out more about these arrows."

"Yes, Grandfather, I want you to come and meet Ben and Alison." Kawsay saw this new discussion was reviving Grandfather. His brain seemed to be whirring again. "Ben will be eager to talk with you about the arrows. He believes it is important for him to gather all three arrows to complete an old story. You see, Ben is like you and me and Nate. He came from another time too. Nate is from the future, but Ben is from a time long before ours. Ben wants to find Yachay almost as much as we do so he can get the third arrow."

Grandfather resisted her proposal. "No, Kawsay, they must not know I am here. They might be afraid of me, or else they may try to hurt me or make me a prisoner. Also, I do not speak their language so I could not talk to them."

Kawsay was a little exasperated with his excuses. "Grandfather, please, what you say does not make sense." She stopped, surprised that she would speak to him disrespectfully. "I am sorry, but please listen to what I have to say. They have a friend, a man of learning named Herschel. He has very dark skin. I met him the first day I was here."

Kusi was listening. "Yes, I remember seeing him."

"Good. Well, he speaks our language, not perfectly, but well enough to understand my story and to explain what happened. He and his wife are wonderful people. I know they would be very honored and thrilled to meet you and talk with you. They would be very disappointed if you refused to meet them." Kawsay saw that her remarks were having an impact. She pressed her point. "Also, we all have been thinking of ways to travel in the tunnels. Ben thinks it may be possible for my friend Nate to go back to his place and time in the future. It may be possible for you to return home too. If Ben and Alison can help you return to our place and time, you may yet be able to help our family. Do you have a better plan?"

As Grandfather considered all this, he was looking at his granddaughter with new respect. He had one more objection before allowing himself to be persuaded. "But I am not clean, and I do not know their customs. I would not know how to act."

"You are right to wonder about their customs. It took me time to understand them and fit in." She reached out and took his hand. "But, Grandfather, you know what is most interesting? In their hearts they are just like us. They help others. They care about each other. They work hard. They sometimes laugh and sometimes cry."

Grandfather almost agreed with her. "Kawsay, there is one important difference as I see it. They welcomed you and helped you after our own people rejected you and wanted you dead."

Kawsay nodded. "That's one more reason you ought to meet them – to thank them for their kindness."

"You are a wise young woman." Grandfather smiled admiringly. "What gift shall I bring to them?"

"Meeting my wonderful grandfather who tells great stories and laughs often, that is the gift *I* will bring to them. And the carvings you already gave to them are very beautiful gifts."

Grandfather suddenly looked worried. "They found the carvings?"

"Yes. That is how I knew you were here," Kawsay replied. "Also, they have an invention that makes pictures which can be seen later. They have pictures of you coming for food last night. I saw you in the kitchen. But do not worry. I assured them that you are not a thief. They know that you have generously paid for the food. It is not a problem."

"I hope that is true, but I must apologize. I *am* sorry. I have not been able to find normal foods to eat in this forest. It is so different from our jungle. I have been able to capture some animals, but a person needs good plants to eat too."

Kawsay again looked at him and realized that he had become very thin. She also knew that the nights were getting colder, and Grandfather did not have warm clothing. "Then it is settled." Kawsay took charge. "You will come with me to meet Ben and Alison. You can thank them for caring for me and thank them also for the food. We will ask them to help you return to our village. You can talk with Ben about the third arrow. I have been learning their language and will help you speak with them. Also, I want you to meet my new friend, Nate."

Kusi had been wondering about that boy. "He is not a trained warrior. What is wrong with him?"

Kawsay understood his concern. "Nate is very different from Yachay because his world is very different. You are right that he is no warrior, but I am going to train him. He wants to learn. But, Grandfather, he knows so many things and is very wise."

"Just what *does* he know?" Grandfather asked with some disdain. "Can he hunt? Can he fight? Can he protect you?"

Kawsay came to Nate's defense. "He *is* brave and strong. He did not complain of the pain of his arrow wound. His mother died when he was four. He is here to save his father from a great sickness. He knows many languages and is learning our language. He knows about the world, the Sun, the Moon, and the stars. Did you know that all the stars in our sky are like the Sun, except very much further away?"

Grandfather was not impressed with Nate's supposed knowledge. "There is only one Inti!"

"No, Grandfather, there are more suns than could be counted in a lifetime. And they are not gods; they are great fireballs." She picked up a large rock and a small rock. "Our world is a smaller ball of rock and water and air. It spins around the Sun one time every year and turns around like this." She demonstrated rotation and revolution. "The Moon is another round rock that goes around our world, lit by light coming from the Sun. Did you know that men from this empire have made voyages from our world to the Moon and returned with pieces of it? You see their amazing inventions. I thought they were magic, but they are not. People of great learning have figured out how to make all these inventions. They do this to make their lives easier, to go places very fast, and sometimes just to enjoy themselves. They can see and talk to people far beyond the mountains. They can fly through the air. They have buildings taller than many trees and boats larger than our entire village. They cook food without fire in a very short time. They have weapons that can turn mountains to dust. But," she paused deliberately, "they also can heal the lip of a small girl who was hated by her village. Grandfather, they teach me of a God who made Inti and all the other suns and stars, who is greater than all other gods." She rested her case.

Grandfather was beginning to feel overwhelmed. "I fear they have no respect for the old ways. They must think we are very stupid people."

"You might assume that, but that is not true of Ben and Alison. They are teachers who study the past. They spend time on the other side of the world digging up cities that died before the first of our people came to the mountains. They believe much can be learned from history and that people from the past often had greater wisdom and character than the people alive at this time." Kawsay caught her breath. "When they met me, a person from the past, they were as filled with wonder as I was at meeting them! It will be the same with you. They will be extremely interested in your stories – far more than were the silly people in our village."

"Do Ben and Alison know what became of all our scattered people after the Invaders destroyed the empire? Are they all dead?"

"No, Grandfather, descendants of our people continue to live together in the same place. Many still speak our language and remember some of our ways. But they have changed after all this time and have limited understanding of their own history. Many have intermarried with the Invaders. They all live together in a new empire that is called 'Peru'. There is no emperor, no 'Inca'. All the people together choose their leader and their local chiefs. There is one more interesting fact that I found out," Kawsay said, changing the subject. "People near here have brought llamas and vicuñas from Peru. They use their wool like we do, and they use llamas to protect other animals from the dangerous cats. Remember how llamas would scare away jaguars?"

Of course Grandfather remembered. He was trying to grasp all the information Kawsay was giving him. She had learned so much in so short a time. Her new friends must have spent much time teaching her like he had. "Kawsay, I will not argue with you. You have changed. Before, you were strong in body and full of courage and skill. You now also have grown wise and confident. Once you hid your face. Now you speak very strong words from your heart. I am ready to meet these new people and bring them greetings from our world."

They stood up to depart. Junior, who had dozed off during the private discussion, scrambled to his feet. Grandfather insisted on taking his bola and spear in case a mountain lion or other danger arose. He also took his small pack of other supplies which he carried strapped to his back. He did not know when he would return to the beautiful cavern and wanted to be prepared for whatever was next. Kawsay led the way out of the cavern that had been her grandfather's home for over three months. Once outside, Grandfather took the lead and Kawsay followed, but Junior ran ahead.

Alison had been looking outside every few minutes. It was past noon, and Kawsay had not returned. Alison saw Ben and Nate distracting themselves with maps of the area around Gibeah where Ben grew up. Ben was pointing out landmarks that had endured over the millennia. *Maybe they can concentrate, but I'm worried enough for all of us!* Alison thought. "I can't wait any longer. I think we need to go out looking for Kawsay again. We should check the cave first. Maybe that's where her grandfather has been staying."

Ben looked at his watch and stood up quickly. "You're right, honey. Kawsay should have returned by now. Nate, why don't you come along this time? We can fan out and cover more territory. I'll get us all some whistles and other signaling devices so we can find each other if necessary." Ben was opening the door of the gear closet when they all heard a single bark. They looked at one another only an instant and then in unison broke for the front door.

As they stepped into the sun, they heard another bark that sounded like Junior. It came from the forest in the direction of the trail to the cave. A few seconds later Junior burst into the clearing and ran toward them, looking all rested and happy. Then they saw Kawsay emerge along the path with a smile on her face.

Thank God she's all right! Thank God she's back! Alison thought. She ran over to Kawsay and embraced her like a lost sheep. "Oh, Kawsay, I'm so glad you're here and safe!

We were so worried about you."

Ben and Nate joined them. Kawsay looked at Alison, then at Ben. She realized that she had caused much distress. "I am sorry that you worry about me. I was very excited to find Grandfather."

They looked up to see a striking man walking slowly toward them as if out of history. Despite his worn tunic and matted hair, he had nobility in his bearing. There was no face paint or feathers in the hair, but he had gold ear disks the size of quarters and a necklace of human teeth. As he arrived at the gathering, he stopped behind Kawsay and put a hand on her shoulder, looking into Ben's eyes, then Alison's, then Nate's. He gave them a completely friendly, almost comic grin. Then the grin disappeared, and he spoke earnestly, stopping after each phrase to allow Kawsay time to translate. "I am Kusi, grandfather of Kawsay. It is my honor to meet you. I am here to give thanks to you for caring for Kawsay and for healing her lip. For that I am in your debt. I express sorrow for taking food from your house. I gave you wood carvings. I hope you will enjoy them. I have information about the arrow. I seek your help so I can return to my village and help my family."

All three just stared at Grandfather for a moment, as they might at an exotic creature. Ben seemed immobilized, with his jaw fixed in the open position. Alison nudged him back to the present.

Ben stepped forward and extended a hand. Grandfather looked at Kawsay, who nodded. Kusi grasped Ben's hand in both of his and offered another large grin, which Ben returned.

"Welcome, Kusi." Ben was in awe of the moment. "I am Ben Hunter. This is my wife Alison." She smiled and gave a small nod. "And this is Nate Diamond." Nate also shook Kusi's hand. After the greeting ceremony, Ben said, "Kawsay, tell your grandfather we also are honored to meet him and welcome him to our home. And please invite him to our afternoon meal." Kawsay related this to her patriarch.

Through Kawsay he replied, "I will eat a meal with you, Ben Hunter. After we eat, we have much to talk over." Then she added for herself, "I am so happy to see Grandfather. He came through the tunnel with me. He stayed in the beautiful cave and watched me all the time I am here. Also, he is good friend of Junior." She tugged Grandfather toward the house.

Upon entering, Grandfather looked around with curiosity. He had not had the opportunity to inspect the interior in the daylight. He was particularly taken with the large picture window, which he tapped several times with a fingertip. "Kawsay, it is like solid air." He noticed the floors. "See the smooth and shiny floor, wood as flat as a calm lake." Kawsay thought, *Wait until he sees the bathroom!*

Alison intervened to get things organized. "Kawsay, would you and Nate show Kusi some of the features of the house? He seems very interested. Ben and I will prepare a meal for the five of us. What kind of food does he most like?"

"Oh, he likes fish and corn and peanuts. He has been eating too many squirrels, so he needs vegetables," Kawsay prescribed.

As they worked on the meal, Ben thought out loud, "Isn't it exciting to have so special a guest? He came a long way to join us!"

"I was *so* relieved that Kawsay came back," Alison stated, taking her ulu knife to the fresh vegetables. "Can you believe that her grandfather has been here all this time living in the cave? It's no wonder he was hungry!"

When he was sure the others were out of ear range, Ben came and stood close to Alison and put an arm around her shoulder and spoke softly into her ear. "This is the man I saw in the cave on the way here from the past, I'm almost positive. I threw the third arrow at him. If we can confirm this, then Kawsay is right, and he or his grandson knows where the third arrow is."

"Are you sure it's the same person? Didn't he have feathers and face paint?"

"Well, I didn't get a good look at him that day, and he's probably older now," Ben admitted. "But the ear disks and that toothy necklace are the same – so is the clothing style. But what really clinched it was his big grin. It was unnerving then, and it still is."

"Maybe you should ask him whether he remembers a kid throwing an arrow at him," Alison counseled. "We could show him an old photo of you taken shortly after you arrived."

Ben appreciated this suggestion. "Well, he did say he wanted to talk about something. Sounds like he'd like to go home, if that's possible. He's probably worried about the rest of the family. They might think he's dead if he's been gone for three months."

That reminded Alison of something. "Remember how Helmut insisted that Kawsay get a series of inoculations after she arrived because she wouldn't have defenses against present day viruses? If her grandfather is going to spend any time around people, shouldn't he get the same shots?"

"You're right, honey," Ben agreed. "I need to talk to Helmut anyway about coming up here tomorrow. I'll ask him to bring the inoculations. I should call Herschel and see if he can come up here soon too. I know he'd relish meeting Kawsay's grandfather, and he could help with some translations that might be beyond Kawsay's ability."

Meanwhile, Nate and Kawsay enjoyed showing Grandfather around. Kawsay's prediction about the bathroom was right. Kusi was fascinated with the plumbing and wanted to know where the water came from and went to and how it was heated. He enjoyed sniffing the soaps and shampoos. His reflection in the mirror over the sink scared him a little, and he realized that some grooming was in order. He was amused as he bounced on his granddaughter's neatly made bed and closely examined her new clothes and shoes. He was also intrigued by the drawings she had made, and when he saw the scenes she drew of the village, he became quiet and sighed. He could not hide the tear that gradually emerged from his right eye. Nate was absorbed by observing Grandfather, who was both part of Kawsay's life and a living artifact. He also tried to pick out as many Quechua words as he could from their rapid conversation.

Kawsay saved the upstairs library and museum for last. She wanted Grandfather to look at the two arrows. "See here, Grandfather, this is the arrow that hurt Nate. Ben's brother, Helmut, had to break it to get it out of Nate's leg. And this other arrow is one that Ben brought with him when he came here. See, they are like the arrow you gave to Yachay."

Grandfather did not need to be convinced of the similarity, for they were virtually identical to Yachay's arrow. He could not imagine what they were doing here. He would have to ask Ben about them, but was also interested in what else Kawsay knew.

She told Grandfather Nate's wheat field story that preceded his arrival in the Hunters' cave. Kawsay then continued, "We learned that a young boy, a servant of the man who shot Nate, followed Nate into the cave with two other arrows and also fell into the tunnel. The tunnel took that young boy here too, but he arrived about 30 years earlier than Nate. On his way here, the young boy first stopped in another cave where he threw one of the two arrows at a strange person. He only stayed there a short time before jumping back into the tunnel with only one arrow. That young boy is a man now. It is Ben. We are wondering if you are the person he threw the other arrow at."

Kusi thought over Kawsay's unusual story. He looked at the arrows one more time. He did not smile, but a look of amusement appeared in his eyes. He was about to speak when they heard Alison calling up the stairs. "If the tour is about done, the food is ready."

Kawsay explained it was time to eat, and they quickly proceeded downstairs. Kusi walked past the set table and over to Ben, who was wiping his hands on a paper towel. Ben straightened up and turned, surprised that his guest was standing so near.

Kusi looked at Ben closely, particularly his face and hair. Satisfied, he said, "Ben Hunter, we met in another place – the secret caves in the mountains above my village. You were a young boy, and perhaps my appearance frightened you. You threw an arrow at me before you disappeared through the singing wall. It is curious that we meet again like this. I believe there are reasons we meet again here."

Ben looked to Kawsay for an explanation. She gave a rough translation, adding, "I showed him the arrows, and he knows they are the same as the one he gave to Yachay."

Ben looked intently at Grandfather, nodding and giving a confirming smile, which was immediately returned. "Tell him I agree it is right that he and I meet again at this time. Also tell him that after we eat, we will talk about the third arrow. Now, everyone, please join us at the table."

Ben helped Alison with her chair, and Nate wished he had done the same for Kawsay. Ben extended his hands to Alison on his right and Grandfather on his left. They joined hands in a circle while Ben gave thanks for the food and for the guest of honor.

Kusi noticed Kawsay's bowed head and her "Amen" and wondered. His attention was immediately diverted by Ben holding out to him a shiny white plate containing several thick pieces of hot orange-pink fish with some kind of seasoning on it. The aroma darted up his nostrils, and his mouth watered. Ben used a shiny two-pronged spear to transfer the largest piece to Kusi's plate. Kusi was then confronted by a plate of steaming corn on the cob and a spinach salad laced with peanuts. He looked at Ben and then at Alison in wonder. "How do you know my favorite foods? This is a wonderful feast!"

Kawsay explained, "They asked me what you liked best so I told them. Please pass me the corn."

Grandfather just shook his head at their special kindness and thought of how long it had been since he enjoyed a complete meal. He examined the delicate crystal goblets with invisibly pure water inside. Then he saw, in the center of the table, his carvings of Kawsay, Yachay, and Junior.

Alison noticed him eyeing them and wanted to put him at ease. "Your carvings look beautiful in the center of our table," Alison said graciously. "Thank you for all these generous gifts."

Kawsay told Grandfather, "They like to put beautiful objects in the center of their dining table. Alison appreciates your gifts very much." Grandfather was pleased and relieved to hear this and smiled at Alison.

They all grew quiet, enjoying the excellent meal. Grandfather studied their method of eating. As Kusi ate, he began to feel the nourishment revive his body. When the serving dishes were passed a second time, he was pleasantly surprised. "Kawsay, please thank them for generously sharing this feast and compliment them on how tasty it is."

Through Kawsay, Alison replied, "You have made this a special meal we will remember always."

Nate and Kawsay cleared the table while Ben scooped vanilla frozen yogurt into dessert bowls and topped each serving with some chocolate syrup. Grandfather knew about snow from the mountains, but had not encountered iced food like this before. A smile of enjoyment adorned his face, turning it youthful. "You saved the most wonderful food for the end of the feast! I wish you could visit my home and share a meal with Kawsay's family."

Through Kawsay, Ben answered, "We would enjoy that very much." Ben contemplated the logistical problems involved in attending a meal in Kusi's home.

Nate and Kawsay decided to show Grandfather the wonders of video recordings and selected a travelogue on South America. Ben and Alison had to consider what to do with Kusi. There was a small rustic cabin on the property, which had electricity and plumbing. It had seen little use in recent years. Ben and Alison decided Kusi might be most comfortable there since he would have privacy and freedom to come and go as he pleased. The harder question was what would happen after the first few days. How would Kusi fit into the modern world?

As the video ended, Ben and Alison joined the group. Ben looked at Kawsay and then at Kusi. "Will you be our guest? We have a small house nearby we use for special guests. May we offer it to you?"

Kawsay and Grandfather had an animated discussion that seemed to go beyond the narrow topic Ben had introduced. "Grandfather thanks you for asking him to stay as guest. I told him it is not good for him to live in the cold cave. He wants to stay in the small house. He wants to serve you in return. Also, he wants your help to return to our village. He cannot stay here for a long time."

"Good. That settles it," Alison stated. "I will get the linens, towels, and soap he will need. I hope the old cabin is not too dirty. Nate, will you help us by bringing a vacuum cleaner down? I wonder if there is a change of clothes we can offer him?"

Kawsay conveyed the gist of the plan, and the five hiked down to the guest cabin, which was on a spur trail part way to Helmut's cabin. The small cabin was well hidden in a stand of tall firs and cedars. The moss on the roof was getting thicker each year, but the forest had not yet reclaimed the stout logs. Ben attended to the pilot lights and checked the water supply. He ran the faucet until the rust bled out. Nate got busy vacuuming while Kawsay put sheets and blankets on the bed. Grandfather enjoyed watching all the activity and could not resist examining the vacuum, letting it repeatedly grab at the palm of his hand, the motor whining higher each time. "This really sucks!" he told Kawsay. She smiled, nodding.

When everything was ready, they rested, filling the available chairs. Alison asked

Kawsay to let her grandfather know they had brought snacks and fruit drinks for his refrigerator and clothes for him to wear while they cleaned his tunic.

Grandfather was overwhelmed by all they were doing for him. As they started to leave, he spoke up. "Shall we now talk about the third arrow?" Kawsay's translation stopped Ben in his tracks, and he immediately sat back down.

"Tell him 'yes', and we will also talk about helping him return to his village. And let him know that Herschel will come in a few days to speak with him in Quechua."

With Kawsay's help the discussion proceeded slowly, one sentence at a time. Grandfather first told a story. "After the handsome young boy threw the arrow at me and then disappeared through the singing wall, I thought it had a special power or purpose. I wondered who sent this little messenger with an arrow for me. And it was unlike any arrow I had seen – very well made. When Kawsay's grandmother and I returned to our village, I kept it with my most valuable objects and wondered why it had come to me. Many years later, when Yachay was becoming a man, I knew I must give it to him to protect him. I did not want him to use it to shoot an enemy, but to keep it close as a reminder of his eternal spirit. I told Yachay that his life was like an arrow that is shot forward in time, an arrow that will travel many places and fly forever. He must always go forward and not look back in fear. The arrow has helped Yachay. He is a young man of amazing strength and courage. Your arrow, Ben Hunter, is in strong and good hands." Grandfather grew silent and let his words have their effect.

Now it was Ben's turn to tell a story. Kawsay was pleased that she was able translate most of the words. "Kusi, as you know, we met a long time ago. I came to this place after I left the arrow with you and have aged 30 years since that day. Has Kawsay told you that I began my life about 3,000 years ago, long before you were born?" Kawsay had not fully explained this to Grandfather, but did so now. Ben continued. "Thank you, Kawsay. After I had been here for a while, I began to read a special writing given by our God to us. Part of this writing is a collection of stories from the early days of my people, the Hebrews. We understand that God's words to us are true and do not have errors. I am part of one of the stories in God's writings. In that story, it says that I returned to my master with the three arrows he shot, and he told me to return to my city. The story does not say that Nate was hit in the leg by one of the arrows and that he brought it here with him in a time tunnel. The story does not say that I tried to follow him and fell into the tunnel with the other two arrows. Also, it does not say that I left one of the arrows with you before coming to this time and place. I have thought about this a long time. All three arrows must go back in time, and the story must be completed because God's stories are always true. Nate brought one of the arrows to me. Now I hope Yachay will bring the third arrow. Then I must find a way to return them so the story will end as it was written. We have many challenges: to find Yachay and the arrow, to return the arrows to the past, to help you return to your village, and to help Nate return to the future. We must work together. All of these tasks are of utmost importance and seem beyond human ability."

Kawsay interjected a thought. "Yachay will not want to give you his arrow." Then she said to Grandfather, "Grandfather, if Yachay comes here, what can Ben give him in exchange for the arrow? It is a treasured possession. He believes it gives him power."

"I do not know about these writings, but if the God you describe to me has such great power, Yachay cannot fight against him." Grandfather then turned to Nate. "Why did you bring the arrow here? Did you have any choice?" Kawsay explained these questions to Nate.

"No, sir. A storm blew me out of a boat. I went through a time tunnel to the field where Ben's master was shooting the arrows, and one of them hit me. I went back in the tunnel to get away and arrived here not long ago." Nate thought more about Grandfather's questions while Kawsay translated. "I think my purpose is to warn my father about a sickness and also to give the arrow to Ben."

"Let's assume," Alison suggested, "that Yachay did show up with the arrow. How can we get the arrows back in time? How can we get Kawsay's grandfather back to his village? And what about Nate? We know he can't stay here indefinitely. I don't know the answer." She had been worrying that Ben might leave her by disappearing into a time tunnel.

Kawsay waved her hands so they would slow down while she briefed Grandfather on the direction of the discussion. Ben waited a moment and then spoke again. "Zevél told us that God works his purposes, and all we need to do is obey. He made it sound like jumping into a tunnel is like a step of faith."

Kawsay looked puzzled. "Why does God not tell us what to do? What if I stepped into the tunnel and went to the wrong place?"

Alison understood her concern. "Big steps in life can scare us, Kawsay, but when you trust God with your life, you can know for sure that He will care for you. You were delivered here safely."

Nate added, "Since God made the universe, then He must have made the tunnels too. So we're in His care even when we are in free fall and can hardly breathe!"

"Kawsay," Alison said, sensing it was time to go and let Kusi rest, "please ask if your grandfather has anything else he wants to tell us."

Kawsay explained the recent discussion. Grandfather listened thoughtfully and spoke sadly to Kawsay. They all sensed Kusi's weariness.

Kawsay reported his thoughts. "He says that we cannot trust Inti. Even when many sacrifices are made, sometimes Inti ignores our people or things get worse. He believes our world is ending. Our family is in danger and should escape, but he does not know where they can go." Kawsay had tears in her eyes. She slid over and embraced Grandfather.

Alison again spoke. "Let's agree to pray about these things. This is bigger than any of us. Now I think Kusi needs some rest."

Ben also thought it was time to adjourn. "Kusi, we understand how you feel. These are troubling problems, but I know we will find answers. We have to. Until we do, please stay here with us. I hope Yachay will arrive here just as Kawsay and Nate did. He may bring news of your wife and daughter."

Grandfather felt relief as Kawsay explained Ben's words. He had been carrying an enormous burden of care for those he left behind, and Ben's words brought him a ray of hope. He realized how tired he was. But he also realized that, as different as they were, Kawsay's new friends were people of integrity on whom he could rely. "Thank you for speaking to me from your hearts. I will stay with you until I can go home. Let me help you with your hunting and your gardens. Let us learn from one another."

Kawsay explained this to the others and added, "I will stay longer and talk more with

Grandfather. It is good that he is here with us."

As they opened the cabin door to depart, Junior, who had been their sentinel, bounded in and put two big puppy paws on Grandfather's lap, licking the side of his face. Grandfather returned the affection with a hug and a scratch.

"Well," Ben remarked, "Junior hasn't turned out to be much of a watchdog, but he knows how to make our guests feel welcome!" They left Junior with his secret friend.

Kawsay knelt by Grandfather and rested her head on his lap. He stroked her long hair. They both thought about times past – long past. "You have been happy here, Kawsay. Do you want to stay?"

She felt suspended between two worlds, so far apart, yet so close in her experience. "Yes, I like these people. They are like a family to me because they cared for me even though I was not perfect. I have learned so much about this huge world. They tell me I can choose to do with my life whatever I want to do. I can learn about whatever interests me. I could even visit our part of the world and find people who speak our language and may remember some of our ways. It all seems wonderful, but it feels empty without my family. I do not miss our village. Those people were hateful and stupid, except our Chief who was my friend. But I cannot go back and live there, even if my lip is better now. I must stay here. There is no other place for me."

Grandfather considered her analysis. "You are wise, little one. This is a good home for you at a time long after your people have all perished. I almost wish all of us could join you, but how would we live in this place? It is so unlike our home! Is there a place for me? For Yachay? For Asiri and Sumaq?"

"Why not, Grandfather? This is a very large world. Perhaps there is a place for every person. It may not be easy to find that place, but we must look." She was silent for a minute. "I wish we could all be here. It is not good for us to be apart. I thought it was not right that I was forced to leave the village. But maybe all of our family should have left with me. Should we not stay together?"

"Kawsay, the people of our village stay together because they fear living apart. They believe the jungle is a dangerous place, and they worry that the Invaders will find them and kill or enslave them. Their lives are controlled by their fears. Things we do not understand, we fear."

"I once felt that way too," Kawsay admitted, "but you and Yachay taught me to put away my fear and do what is necessary to live. Now I do not fear. And look what has happened to me! This new place is not bad for me at all! It is good for me. These people show me love and help me and teach me." She paused. "And their God is not scary like Inti. Their God knows them by name, even the number of hairs on their heads! And He has a beautiful place for them all ready when they die. Fear is a sickness of the heart. I will not be sick like that ever again."

Grandfather was again amazed at how Kawsay had changed in this short time. He wondered how Yachay would fare in such a place as this. *Did they need warriors like him?* "Earlier today we talked about the danger to the family because I am not there. If Yachay has left to find me, they are in even greater danger. I thought I needed to leave you here and return and hoped they would be comforted by my report that you found a new tribe. Today I have learned much about these people. I hope to learn more tomorrow and the day after. Now I must consider if it is better for our family to all come here. This may be a better place for all of us. Do you think this is possible?"

Kawsay understood time travel as a concept, but had no idea how it worked. At times she thought it was all a dream. "I cannot answer your question except with more questions. If you and I journeyed here, why can't the others do so too? If God brought me here and had you come to watch over me, why would He not also want the others to be here with us? When questions are too big for me, why should I not trust in a God who made me and has shown such care for me?"

Grandfather thought her answer was good. The gravity of the moment lifted, and his thoughts turned to more practical concerns. "We will talk more tomorrow, Granddaughter. Now I want to settle into my new house. Can you tell me again how to use these funny inventions? Let's start with the places where the hot water comes out and the good smelling skin cleaner. I want to smell like a flower just like you do!" They laughed together. Kusi was very pleased that Kawsay had found him that morning. With new hope, he wanted to live again.

CHAPTER 17

DESTINED TO CHANGE HISTORY

SEPTEMBER 1 – PRESENT YEAR
MENLO PARK, CALIFORNIA

I MUST LEAVE YOU SOON
SO I MAY JOIN YOU AGAIN
BACK WHERE WE PARTED.

John and Nate Diamond spent Tuesday afternoon in a luxury skybox at a Giants home game. For John, it was an opportunity to entertain the officers of a startup technology company seeking its first outside capital. For Nate, it was a last gasp of summer fun before returning to class. Not that his studies ever took a vacation. Over the summer he had continued to pursue his current interests, which included the Ottoman Empire, the North African campaigns of World War II, and differences between ancient and modern Hebrew and Greek. He was mystified why a group of men would spend hours in a private room overlooking the field, eating and talking, but barely watching the game. He enjoyed baseball very much and tried to anticipate each manager's strategy.

It had been a perfect late summer day, and they drove home with the sunroof open and the radio playing Golden Oldies. They reminded John of his high school days, and Nate thought they were funny. Over the last two weeks, the father and son had spent a few evenings shopping for school clothes and supplies, so Nate was ready for the first day of classes. He was eager to get through eighth grade so he could begin to select upper class courses rather than be compelled to follow a set core curriculum. At least he would have a class on European history and could continue studying Spanish. Compared to Hebrew, it was a breeze and handy to know.

The daily demands on John's time had crowded from his thoughts the topic of Sunday's phone call with "older Nate", but subconsciously he was processing the information day and night. In addition, young Nate's reports of ongoing vivid dreams reminded him of the need to solve the problem. Nate had recently reported a dream about being taught how to throw some rock and rope device at a tree by a pretty dark-skinned girl. John had not attempted to explain one theory of the dream. He wanted to insulate Nate from the possibly tumultuous future he may face three years down the road. John was both eager and anxious about the call scheduled for that night to confirm the Wednesday noon meeting. Not even the complex harmonies of the Beach Boys' *Good Vibrations* totally relaxed him. They did not reach home until almost 6:00 p.m. and were not hungry after gorging on chicken wings and egg rolls in the skybox. They each caught up on the day's e-mail and on-line headlines. John steered Nate toward an early bedtime and was free to call the Hunters by 9:30 p.m.

Up in the Sierras, Helmut had landed at his family retreat in a cloud of dust, just in time for the afternoon meal. He brought the inoculations for Kusi. Grandfather was very impressed with Helmut's size and presence, but skittish about the needles. Once Kawsay assured him that she had received the same treatment without ill effect, Kusi was challenged to endure Helmut's injections stoically. For the moment, though, he turned down the offer of a ride in the whirling bird, which appeared to be thoroughly unsafe.

Helmut was distracted the rest of the day gathering supplies for his Alaska adventure, which he planned to commence early Thursday morning, flying first to Anchorage and then to Iliamna. He still planned to search for the giant birds, but had added a second quest for monstrous fish reported to live in the uncharted depths of Lake Iliamna. He wanted to tell Ben and Alison all about his plans, but they were also distracted, not by strange animals, but by their strange new guest and the nagging questions of what to do with all the time travelers. Ben and Nate finally took time to work out the details of their meeting with John, including an outline of a plan.

In the midst of all the commotion, Kawsay felt a little left out, so she brought a special meal down to Grandfather at his new residence and stayed for several hours. She insisted on practicing her drawing skills by sketching him in an action pose. He insisted that she tell him more of the scientific and geographical facts she had been learning. He began to understand the value of written language and was excited to hear that Quechua had been put into written form so their people could communicate with one another at a distance. She taught him to write his name. He thought "Kusi" looked very elegant. He was excited to hear that the dark man who knew his language would be visiting in a few days.

The day was winding down when the telephone rang. Nate was still talking with Ben in his office. Ben answered. "Hello, Hunters."

"This is John Diamond. Is this Ben?"

"Yes, it is, John. May I put you on speaker? Nate is here with me, and we have been talking about tomorrow." He punched the button. "Can you hear us, John?"

"Fine. My son just turned in for the night. School starts bright and early. Are we still on for tomorrow?" John asked, still wondering if this was all just a strange dream.

"Absolutely," Ben responded. "We'll both be there, but I'll let you and Nate talk as long as you like. Then I'll join you."

Nate jumped in. "Are you still OK with the pizza place at the shopping center? I haven't had any real food like that up here. I think I smell it already."

John had to smile at this deep voice that nonetheless sounded just like his little boy. "Yeah, that's fine. Noon, right?"

"Right," Ben agreed. Ben and Nate looked at each other, wondering if they should get into the plan right now or let it wait.

John, of course, was not good at waiting, and the last two days had been difficult for him. "Look, I've been thinking about all this even though it's way outside my areas of expertise. I don't really understand it very well, especially all the side issues about arrows and the Bible. But I'm really interested to hear everything you have to say and want to assure you that I will help every way I can. Of course, part of me won't believe this is all on the level – all real – until I see you with my own eyes."

"You can even touch me!" Nate said. "Remember how mom used to kid you about your middle name?"

"Thomas? Well, I never faulted myself for wanting proof of things. When I have doubts, my instincts are to gather more facts," John admitted.

"Well, John, I think that's wise, so we'll have Nate and other 'facts' there tomorrow for lunch," Ben assured him. "My brother will fly us down in his helicopter. We'll probably land up Sand Hill Road from the shopping center and walk over. Weather reports are for a nice, clear day."

"Good. I've cleared my afternoon calendar. I want to figure all this out. Nate continues to have problems with the dreams, and I promised him we'd find a solution."

"Don't worry, Dad, it's all going to work out fine. The dreams go away soon – at least if we don't mess up history."

Ben wanted to prepare John for the meeting. "Nate and I have been talking a lot even though we've been a bit distracted up here. Remember the Inca girl who's staying with us? It turns out her grandfather has been living in a cave on our property keeping an eye on her. Yesterday she persuaded him to come out of the woods and meet us. Now we're not only trying to help Nate get back to your sailing trip in the future, but also trying to help the grandfather get back to his village about 400 years ago. Anyway, other than the medical checkup with your brother, Nate's uncle, your main challenge, John, will probably be to *not* tell young Nate what is going on and see that life continues just as Nate, the one I'm looking at, remembers it. In other words, we're trying to change as little as possible so that Nate's little detour back here from the future doesn't change more than is absolutely necessary."

"Right," Nate chimed in. "We don't want to disturb the Earth's orbit or destroy the universe as we know it."

"Well, that *will* be a challenge," John observed. "I'm good at making things happen, but not very good at making sure they don't happen."

Ben liked John. "We will keep in touch regularly and help each other. We're mostly doing this for Nate. You have a great son, and he deserves the best we can offer him. I can't say I'm optimistic, but … what's that saying? 'Failure is not an option'."

"I use that often myself," John responded, smiling to himself. "But it seems to me we're dabbling in things we absolutely don't understand. What makes you think there's a way to get Nate back where he belongs?"

"Dad, what did Martin Luther say?"

"What?" asked John, not following Nate's allusion.

"The just shall live by faith!" Nate prompted.

"Oh, that wasn't Luther. It was in Hebrews, and I think it's also in Habakkuk. So how does this relate?" John questioned.

"I think what Nate's suggesting," Ben said, "is that even working together *we* can't pull this off unless God helps us."

"Yeah, Dad. I figure that if God got me into this fix, He'll just have to get me out." Nate winked at Ben, who nodded back.

John was quiet for a moment. "I hadn't thought about this, um, problem in those terms, but I suppose there's no reason not to. Let me just say, Ben, that I'm really glad you take God seriously as I do. Maybe it's no accident that Nate ended up at your place."

"I don't think it's an accident at all that Nate came here, or that I came here," Ben agreed. "All the pieces are fitting together better than anyone could have planned."

"I'm not sure what you're talking about there, Ben, except when we talked Sunday, Nate was trying to tell me something about some arrows and Jonathan. I read 1 Samuel 20. What's that all about?"

"If there's time tomorrow, I'll give you the executive summary, John. Since you believe the fantastic story Nate told you about his time travel, let me just say that I'm the young kid in that story who retrieves the arrows." Ben waited, not knowing what response he would get to that piece of information. He did not have to wait long.

"OK. OK. I give up. These calls always seem to get more strange the more I probe. Let's just deal with what's on the front burner. If we get through that, I'd like to hear the rest." John looked up at the antique clock on top of his bookshelf. "We have a big day tomorrow; let's get our beauty rest. I'll be there early to get a good table for us, Nate. It will be very interesting to see you."

They completed the call. "Well, Nate," Ben said wryly, "better obey your father. Off to bed, and no reading past midnight!" As they exited his office, Ben noticed Kawsay entering the house through the laundry room. "Have you been down with your grandfather?"

"Yes, I think he likes his little log house. Here! Look at the pictures I drew." She held up a picture of what was obviously Kusi whirling a bola over his head, eyes trained on some target. Before he could pay her a compliment, she slipped a second drawing from behind the first. This one showed only Kusi's upper body, framed by the old wing chair in front of the cabin window. He was dressed in a loud shirt he had chosen from the old clothes closet and was looking at the artist with a smile and a twinkling eye. There was something about him that reminded Ben of a rock star. Maybe it was the long hair and earrings.

"Those are wonderful, Kawsay …" Ben began to say, but Alison came around the corner and finished his sentence.

"And she hasn't had any art lessons. I think it's a gift!"

Ben was very happy to see Alison. "Nate and I just finished talking with his father. It's all set for tomorrow."

Kawsay and Alison looked at each other. "I've been debating whether or not to go along," Alison said. "I'd love to meet Nate's father and participate in the planning session. But Kusi just had those shots today, and there's some danger of a negative reaction. I think I'd better stay here just in case, OK?"

Kawsay smiled at the thought of having Alison to herself. Ben agreed that it was important to watch Kusi for a few days to be sure he would be all right. "Before we go to sleep, I want to run our ideas past you to see if they make sense or if we're overlooking something." Alison and Ben did almost everything together, and they regretted days when they had to be apart. Ben understood this and added, "We'll hurry home. I'll give John your regrets."

Helmut barged into the house. "Are we still on for tomorrow?" he asked. Helmut was covered with a thin film of feathers. Everyone stared at him. "Oh, guess it was time to trash the old sleeping bag anyway. I'll have to get a new one tomorrow when we're down in the city. Nights in bush Alaska are already starting to get pretty chilly."

Wednesday morning was beautiful as promised, the mountain air cool. They planned to give John a written diary of all the important future dates and events Nate could remember from the three years leading up to and including the sailing trip. The idea was to help John keep to the script so as not to change anything except his medical care. At first it was difficult for Nate to remember all the details of his last three years, but little by little it came back to him. The diary was not yet complete. Ben assured him that he could continue to add to it, and they would supplement it later. Right now, John needed to know the events that would take place in young Nate's life for the next few months.

Helmut insisted they get airborne before 10:00 a.m. The trip would take a scant hour, but the landing site was almost two miles from the shopping center. Helmut had a lot of gear he was ferrying down including a pack, tent, firearms, and camera equipment. Nate had flown in a helicopter only once before. He was thrilled as the noise and vibration built, and they suddenly lifted from the world he knew to the magic world of the sky. With the Sun almost directly behind, the view was clear all the way to the foggy coast. He loved the feeling of being above it all – the traffic, the stoplights, and all the other obstacles. He felt like royalty and truly appreciated all that the two brothers were doing for him and his father.

Nate kept busy deciphering the landmarks as Helmut followed highways into the Bay Area. As they crossed the bay, he noticed remnants of a morning fog. He soon spotted the Stanford campus, the stadium, the dish, the golf course, and even the outline of the accelerator. He realized they had passed right over the shopping center. Helmut banked slightly and found his favorite parking spot on private land near Sand Hill Road. With a little pressure on the ears, they set down gently, and Helmut cut back the engine. Talking became minimally feasible again.

"I'll let you off here," Helmut shouted over the engine noise. "I need to refuel and run some errands. Unless we talk, I'll expect you back around five-thirty, OK?"

"Great, Helmut. Hope all goes well for you today," Ben responded. "We really appreciate your help." They quickly disembarked and scurried away, involuntarily ducking below the still spinning rotor. They were barely clear when the machine came alive again. It quickly rose, banked north, and disappeared from sight. "You know the way from here, right Nate?"

"Sure! I only live a few miles away, and my dad's office is right down the street. Aren't you coming with me?"

"I'll walk you part way. I have some errands to run on campus, and I want to pick up our mail. Sabbaticals are great, but the world goes on." Ben was energized to be in the city again. In controlled doses, civilization was welcome, even enjoyable. They walked quickly and quietly, each lost in his own thoughts. As they approached the campus, Ben announced, "I'm heading off. If you need me, you've got my cell number. Hope all goes well with your father. I'll see you about two o'clock." He extended his hand to his young friend, and Nate grasped it confidently.

"Thanks, Ben. It feels really strange to be doing this, but I know it's the right thing.

Everything will fit together. I just know it." Nate continued down Sand Hill Road skirting campus, excited to be seeing his father and somewhat lost in his thoughts. He had no premonition that he was about to save three lives.

The opportunity came in the form of a young man on a silver 21-speed road bike with racing handlebars and toe clips, who was rapidly catching up to Nate in the nearest traffic lane. Nate's attention was to his right toward the campus, not left toward the road. The cyclist had pulled out his water bottle and was sucking in a mouthful. He did not notice a two-inch diameter tree branch which had blown down, partially blocking the right-of-way. The bike ran over the branch. It veered left and tumbled over, sprawling its rider on the road, one foot still clipped to a pedal. Nate heard the crash and turned in time to see the bike and rider skid to an inelegant stop.

Without hesitation, Nate began sprinting toward the stunned rider. As he approached, an old green pickup truck pulled from the fast lane into the right lane to pass a slow-moving delivery truck and was bearing down on the cyclist. The pickup made a feeble attempt to stop, but there was insufficient distance. The cyclist, trying to sort himself out, was unable to move aside. He could only look at the rusty bumper approaching at forehead level and try to block it with his arms. Nate arrived, grabbed the cyclist's flailing left arm, and jerked him toward the curb, falling on his own arm in the process. The old truck swerved as far left as it could without hitting the larger truck it was trying to pass. Everyone was acting on reflex; there was no time to think. The maneuvers were successful, except for the new racing bike, which lost its front wheel under the passing truck's right tires. The pickup truck accelerated away from the scene.

No one stopped to help, and the two boys were alone on the ground at the curb, contemplating all the events that had been compressed into less than ten seconds. Nate was the first to recover and helped untangle the bike and rider. Then he moved the bike off the road and turned to the rider who had finally been able to move to a sitting position and was checking himself over.

Then the fallen cyclist saw his bike. "Oh, no! Did I wreck my bike? It's brand new." He crawled over to inspect the damage.

Nate looked on. He was more concerned with the blood on the rider's face than with the bent wheel. "I think it's just the wheel. Could have been worse," Nate observed. "I'm not so sure about you."

"I worked all summer to pay for this bike."

"Here, let me look at your face," Nate suggested. The rider took off his helmet and shook out his almost white blonde hair. He squinted up at Nate as Nate pushed aside the bangs, noticing a significant gash in the middle of the forehead. He also noticed the startling light green eyes. The rider was about Nate's age, maybe a year older, and several inches taller. "You have a bad cut there. You might need some stitches. Is there anyone you can call for help?"

"Yeah. I hit my head pretty hard when I went down." He shook his head to clear his thoughts. "I could call my mom. We live nearby. Maybe I could just walk the bike home. I don't want to miss work, though."

"Let's get out of the road." Nate pulled out the cell phone Ben had given him for the day. "What's the number? I'll dial it for you." After keying in the number, Nate handed the phone to the rider. He had a brief discussion with an instantly worried parent who insisted on coming to the scene immediately and taking her son to an emergency room.

Closing the phone, he handed it back to Nate. "Thanks. My mom will be here in a few minutes."

Nate extended his hand. "My name is Nate. That was a close call. Sure you're all right?"

"I think so, thanks to you. My name is Morrow. Guess you saved my life. I'm thankful you were here and acted so quickly."

"I'm glad I was. It all happened so fast there was no time to think. Where were you going?" Nate asked.

"Oh, I've been working for my uncle this summer. He owns a furniture store."

"Isn't this the first day of school?" Nate also wanted to know.

"That's right, but my parents home school me so we set our own schedule. Next year I hope to be a volunteer with the first responders. I really want to get into rescue work. Funny that you're rescuing me!" Morrow observed.

A light went on. Nate remembered the hair and eyes and strange name. He was speechless for a long moment as he stared at Morrow.

Morrow finally spoke. "Are you all right? I see you tore your shirt."

Nate looked down and saw that his skin was scraped too. "Oh. Yeah, I'm OK." He looked at his watch and saw that he needed to hurry to get to the restaurant to meet his dad. "Look, Morrow. It's been great to meet you, but I'm late. Have to meet my dad. Glad I was here. Please remember one thing, OK?"

"Sure, what do you mean?"

"I really think you should get into rescue work. Maybe God spared you today so you can save others later. That's the best way to thank me for helping you."

"No problem. Don't let me make you late. I'll be fine. See ya."

With a last look back Nate was on his way, examining his arm and picking some gravel out of the wound. Satisfied that it was superficial, he thought about what had just happened. *If I hadn't been here, Morrow might have been killed. But if he'd been killed, then maybe Jake and I would have been burned to death when we rolled the truck. Then, I would not have lived to return here through the tunnel, and I would not have been here today to help save Morrow.* He pondered the circularity of it all while he continued across the parking lot of the shopping center. *So, at the time we rolled Jake's truck and Morrow was there, it was already determined that I would be back here to save Morrow. The time tunnel wasn't a mistake after all but part of the plan for my life and also Morrow's and Jake's.* He continued to mull this over as he made his way past shops and then stopped just as he was approaching the pizza restaurant. *That means I really am here to change things and to make them better. That also means I can help my dad stop the cancer before it kills him. YES! We can do it!* Jubilant, he approached the restaurant, hoping his father would already be there. Nate was a few minutes early.

Then he saw his father who was never less than five minutes early for any meeting. He had his back to Nate and was talking to a waitress who was setting out menus and water glasses. *How should I handle this?* Nate hesitated and then plunged ahead. *Hey, it's just my dad.* He came around the table and quickly sat down. "Hi, Dad. We're both early!"

John should not have been startled, but was. Nate was suddenly sitting there before John had gathered his thoughts and prepared his opening remarks. It was very strange to look at the young man in front of him, totally familiar and yet remarkably different. Compared to his son he left a few hours ago, this individual was taller and more handsome. His nose and jaw were more pronounced and his shoulders and arms more muscular. And the voice. It was a man's voice, not that of his little boy. *So this is the future. This is what Nate will become.* John became aware that he was staring. "Sorry. I shouldn't stare. Is that really you ... Nate?"

"Yes, Dad, it's me. Have I changed that much?"

John continued to look him over. He was impressed. "Well, not really, but I see your mom even more in you now. And you are starting to be a heartbreaker." John smiled. "I guess I didn't know what to expect. I mostly wanted to see you in person. I supposed a phone voice could be some kind of hoax, but I trust my eyes. This is really fascinating."

Nate did not bother with the menu; he already knew what they would order. "Are you up for a pepperoni and sausage? That's what we always seem to order."

John began to relax. "Sure, what about drinks?"

"I've been staying away from sodas. It's Ben and Alison's influence. They've been encouraging me to eat better. There must be something to it. They're fit and don't look their age. I'll have some fruit juice or just water."

"Healthy eating – great. Let's skip the processed meats and try their veggie special." John waived the waitress over and placed their order. Then he noticed the torn shirt. "What happened to your arm, Nate?"

"Oh. I saved a guy who was about to be hit by a truck. He'd spilled his bike in traffic, and I just happened to be there when he needed me."

"That happened on your way here?" John asked.

Nate explained the events from the landing until his arrival at the restaurant and then added, "Just as I was arriving here, I figured out something really important. It affects what we're trying to do." He explained to his father his deduction that it was foreordained he would travel back in time to save Morrow today. "Otherwise I probably would have died three years from now in the rollover with Jake a few months before our sailing trip."

John thought he followed the logic, but was still skeptical. "Maybe I should take notes." John was concerned about protecting young Nate. "You say that three years from now you're in an accident? If you tell me which night, I can make sure you don't go. I want you to be safe."

"Oh, no, that would be exactly the *wrong* thing to do!" Nate protested. "See, I have a memory of Morrow rescuing me. In a way it's already happened, so you either shouldn't try to stop it or couldn't if you wanted to. I'm not sure which."

John had no counterargument. He had not thought as much about the oddities of Nate's position as had Nate himself. "So, you're saying that I shouldn't change anything? But you just changed something by being here – you saved the boy's life. Why is it OK in one situation but not the other?"

"I know it's weird, but trust me. See, when Morrow gets us out of the wrecked truck in three years, he recognizes me as the guy who helped him today, but I don't recognize him because I hadn't seen him before. It has already happened to me so I know about it, but it is still in the future for my younger self." Nate was pleased that his dad was nodding.

"Remember you told me on the phone that in the future I get brain cancer and don't get diagnosed until it's too late?" Nate nodded, and John continued, speaking slowly as he tried to apply the principles he was beginning to understand. "Why don't you tell me about the sailing trip and all that. I'd like to know exactly what is supposed to happen."

Nate leaned back and was pleased to see two cranberry juices arrive, vanguards of the pizza that was still baking. He started with the sudden decision to take the trip right after school was out, the revelation about the cancer as a storm was brewing, the frightening lightning strike, and the apparent drowning.

John commented, "Sounds like the storm gets me before the cancer. Why worry about the cancer? I suppose you're going to tell me we should still take the sailing trip and let the lightning hit the boat?"

Boy, Dad is really smart! It took me and Ben quite a while to figure out the plan. "I didn't like that idea at first either, but I think it's the right way. Since I know all this has already happened, we cannot or should not change it."

"OK, but then what about the cancer? We know that it happens, so we cannot or should not change that either, right? Maybe it's all futile." John felt a slight headache and had a pang of anxiety that something may be growing in his head already.

"Ah, this is where it gets interesting!" Nate leaned forward as if hatching a conspiracy. "See, I don't *know* whether you really had cancer or not. You told me you did, but it's not like I saw a brain scan or something. Ben and I think there's a chance that we can leave everything I remember the same, but still keep you from drowning or dying of cancer. You'll just have to work with us to pull it off. Even if it's not a sure thing, if we don't try, the future is terrible for both of us. Forget me for a second and think about your young son in school today. Do you want him to be an orphan?" Saying this sounded strange to Nate and his listener.

John was galvanized by the thought. "I promised your mother that I would stay close to you and help you all your life, especially during your younger years until you were independent. She wasn't afraid of dying, but she was desperate to stay with me and grieved that she would miss watching you grow up. You cannot imagine how much that bothered her." Both swallowed hard. "I would do anything to make sure that we're able to stay together. It seems ridiculous, though, to think that I would lie to you about a terminal illness and then take you sailing in a deadly storm in order to keep our relationship intact. You have to admit, it's totally counterintuitive!"

Nate was saved from answering immediately by the arrival of the pizza, his first in what seemed like ages. John thanked the waitress and pulled off a piece, placing the wedge on Nate's outstretched plate. Then he served himself. He was about to take the first bite when he stopped. "Nate, let's ask a blessing." Nate, chewing, agreed.

They bowed their heads. "Father, Nate and I thank you for this meal and this opportunity to meet. We acknowledge that our lives are in Your hands. We also recall that Your ways are above ours. Help us to know Your will in this unusual situation and obey Your voice. Heal our family and preserve us. Thank You for my amazing son. Please continue to preserve and protect him, and ..." John didn't know how to complete his petition.

"And help me to complete my mission and return safely to where I belong. Amen."

John added his "Amen" and looked up at Nate with admiring eyes. Nate smiled and then diverted his full attention to the meal, enjoying the luscious feeling of sinking his teeth into the warm chewy layers of cheese. When he finished the first piece and secured a second, he wiped his greasy fingers on a napkin and reached into his back pocket. He pulled out a small notebook.

"I started writing a forward diary a few days ago." Nate saw a questioning look from his father. "It has the main things I remember happening in our lives for the next three years. It was Ben's idea. He thinks it can help you avoid changing anything by mistake, even if his theory is right that you couldn't make a mistake. All you need to do is act naturally and everything will happen as I remember because it has to. Anyway, it can't hurt. I'm not done yet, but wanted to let you know what I'm up to. Once it's done, we'll give it to you."

John wiped his fingers, took a drink, and reached for the book. He flipped through it for a minute. "I see you've already made a good start. Looks as if we are planning a sailing trip two years from now also."

"We were," Nate responded, "but you got too busy at work, and we had to cancel. You wanted to take a trip the next year to make it up to me. You also told me later that you thought it might be our last chance to be together."

"And now I need to pretend all this; to lie to you?"

"Look, I know it's wrong to lie, but I give you permission to act this out, OK? See, once I return I'll know why you did it and will already have forgiven you." Nate thought this was a reasonable rationalization. "Besides, you really are going to get cancer. It's just that now you're going to get treatment early enough that it won't be a problem. Promise me you'll see Uncle Jack soon, OK? Just don't tell your young son anything about cancer until the sailing trip."

"All right, all right," John agreed. "That reminds me. How are you and Ben proposing to get you back to the sailing trip in three years? Do the tunnels go both ways?"

"Well, we think so – or at least hope so. There is a more experienced time traveler we've met named Zevél who tells us we can go both ways. Remember, before I got to Ben's house, I first traveled back to B.C. and then came forward to now."

John was still concerned. "If you go into one of these tunnels, how do you know you'll go to the right place or time?"

"I don't know, but I think it's one of those 'step of faith' things," Nate said, recalling their prior night's discussion. "If God doesn't want you or me to live beyond the sailing trip, there's not much we can do about it. But if He does, I'll be fine."

"So, what do you plan to do? Just jump back into the tunnel and hope for the best?" John wondered if he would be up to that kind of "step" if he were in Nate's position.

"Well, I don't see that I have any other choice, Dad. I can't very well stay here. By the way, if you look on the second page of the diary, you can see that in a few weeks, you and I pray the vivid dreams will stop, and they do. Ben and I think that's the time I need to go because that's when the dreams stop. I just wish I could remember exactly what day that is."

"I hope the dreams do stop soon. Your younger self is adjusting to them in a way, but I know they're causing him to lose sleep." John paused. "A few days ago, he dreamed about a girl with long, dark hair teaching him to throw something. What was that about?"

"Oh, that must have been Kawsay teaching me to throw a bola. You know, that weapon made from rocks and sinews that the Incas used to take down animals." Nate shook his head, amused. "She's determined to turn me into a warrior like her brother."

"Is her brother here too? Ben said something about one of her relatives hiding in the woods."

"No, Dad. That was her grandfather. He came through the tunnel with Kawsay. We don't know where her brother Yachay is, but Ben thinks he'll turn up because he has the third arrow that we need to get back to Jonathan."

John's understanding of Ben's situation was quite a jumble. "Nate, when is Ben joining us?"

"He said around two. He had some errands to do on campus."

"Well, before he comes, I would appreciate it if you'd explain his connection to the Old Testament and the business about the arrows. If we get through that, then tell me about Kawsay and her grandfather." John served up the remaining pieces of pizza and sat back to listen.

Nate took a deep breath. They had about an hour before Ben would arrive. "OK, you read 1 Samuel 20, right?" John nodded. "You know how much I like King David and all that stuff, so you can imagine how neat it is for me to talk with Ben, who spent his first twelve years in Saul's city of Gibeah. He even *talked* to David a few times! I just met him for a few seconds." Nate then told the story of the arrows in the wheat field. He explained the detour Ben had taken to meet Kawsay's grandfather before he ended up meeting Helmut in the Sierras about thirty years ago.

"And his brother flew you down here today?" John asked.

"That's right, and he'll be back around five-thirty to pick us up. He's getting ready for a trip to Alaska. When he's not working as an ER doc, he's somewhere in the world looking for bizarre animals." Nate continued the story about how the arrows had started to reunite, except for the one embedded in Yachay's spear.

John again interrupted. "How does Ben propose to get the arrows back where they belong? Is he going himself?"

"He's not sure right now. First he needs to get the third arrow. See, he's afraid that he's too big now to go back and finish the story. He says he was big for his age back then. Now he's about your size." Nate picked up his intertwined narrative with a summary of Kawsay's escape from her tribe and how well she was becoming a modern girl. Nate's eyes shone during this part of the story, and John could not help noticing that Nate thought a lot of Kawsay.

"How old is this girl?" John asked.

"Right now she's thirteen. You know, it's interesting. A few mornings ago, we were looking into the Inca calendar system online and comparing it to ours. She and I may share the same birthday. Wouldn't that be a neat coincidence, both born on Valentine's day? That would make her the same age as I am now, or the 'me' that's in school. Except, of course, plus about 400 years!"

The waitress had cleared their dishes, and the lunch crowd had dispersed. John ordered more drinks to secure the table a little longer. It was getting near two o'clock. "What are Ben and Alison going to do with Kawsay and her grandfather?"

Nate looked down for a moment. "Well, her grandfather is worried about what might happen to the rest of the family left in the village. I think they should all get away. It sounds like a terrible place." He filled in more of the details about the village, her cleft lip, and the ostracized family.

"You mean the rest of Kawsay's family could come here?" John asked. "Wouldn't that be a difficult transition?"

"I don't think they've thought about that. Right now I think they just need to survive."

John smiled. "Seems as if everyone's getting rescued. Think about it. You're here to save me from drowning and disease. You just saved the boy on the bike. He saves you later. Kawsay's mother saved her daughter from the tribe. Ben and Alison gave Kawsay a new home. Her grandfather wants to save the whole family. Ben wants to save the Bible story. Where does it end?"

Nate kept the story going. "Ben also wants to save his family. They're tight with King Saul, and he wants to warn them to get out before it's too late." Nate looked at his dad and gave him a grin. "You're part of this also, Dad. You'll be trying to rescue both of us in three years."

John had to agree. "So … what should we plan to do next for excitement if we pull this off?" Nate grinned, but did not reply because he saw Ben standing a ways off, waiting to catch his eye with a questioning look on his face. Nate waved him over. John saw him and stood up.

Ben arrived and extended his hand. "Hi. I'm Ben. Good to finally meet you, John."

"It's good to meet you too, Ben. I've heard a lot about you over the last two hours. Please join us. Did you eat?"

"Yes, I grabbed a bite on campus. Did you guys figure everything out?"

Nate looked at his dad, then at Ben. "Well, we made some good progress," Nate reported.

They all sat down. The day had warmed up. Ben took off his sweater and draped it over the back of his chair. There was a lull.

John abhorred a vacuum and stepped in. "Here's a summary of where we are." John quickly summarized his and Nate's discussion. "Nate also told me a lot about Kawsay and her grandfather and about you and the arrows. Do you have a good memory of your first twelve years? I detect a small accent even after all this time."

"You would think after 3,000 years I could lose the accent," Ben joked. "I don't notice it, but everyone else seems to. But yes, I do have a good memory about my early years. I think it helps that my work has often focused on that part of the world, and I've spent time in the region where I grew up. It doesn't seem like the same place; there's a totally different feel today. But the hills and ridges have the same profiles. I'm hopeful of nailing down the exact site of my parents' home and its stone foundation. Maybe we can even find the cave with the time tunnel, if it's still there. I'm not sure if the tunnels are hard-wired or get reprogrammed from time to time."

"The one on your property has been there for a while," Nate observed.

"Right," Ben agreed. "But thirty years is a short interval compared to three thousand."

"What about Zevél? Could he go back to where he came from?" Nate wondered.

"I asked him about that once, and he said that he could not. I think angels guard that place to keep everyone out!" Ben responded with a smile, though he was in fact serious. John almost asked a question about this, but Ben continued. "Anyway, I'm more interested in getting the arrows back to the wheat field, but first we need to find Yachay. Then I'll worry about getting them back."

Nate was still thinking about how the tunnels connected. He had an idea, which he expressed unfiltered. "You know, Ben, your cave seems to be attached only to early Peru and ancient Israel. Maybe I can't get to the Caribbean directly. Maybe I need to take one of those detours first."

Ben was startled at that thought. It had never occurred to him. He rubbed his chin. "That's an important idea, Nate. I know Zevél comes and goes to many places, but I doubt it includes the middle of the ocean. He probably doesn't like the water. But we don't want to send you on some detour or wild goose chase. This is going to be hard enough!"

John finally jumped in, his voice somewhat elevated and commanding. "Look, fellas. This entire plan sounds risky. This is my son's life you're playing with here." Ben and Nate looked at John, wondering if he had any better ideas. They waited. John wasn't sure he could do more than register his objections. "I'm not saying that I have the answer either, but this isn't a game. We need some guarantees." He was thinking of how he requires representations and warranties when putting together investment plans.

Nate sensed the tension. It seemed as if his dad was blaming Ben for all of this, which didn't seem fair. "Look, Dad, I didn't ask for all this to happen. I wish we could have had a nice sailing trip and lived happily ever after, but I didn't have any choice. You know I can't stay around here. I can't keep living two lives. I only have one soul. Ben and his family didn't have to help us, but look at all they've done. Don't blame him for all this."

John backed off, feeling ashamed at his outburst. "I'm sorry, but all this has me rattled. I don't know what to think. Ben, look, I can't thank you enough for being there for Nate and taking care of him. You didn't have to do that. I should reimburse you for all your expenses. For your brother's doctoring too."

"Believe me, John, there are more critical ways we'll need your help."

"Maybe this is bigger than all of us," John wondered out loud. "Ben, have you checked with any experts on this, gotten outside opinions?"

"Fair question," Ben allowed. "You can imagine, given my past, I've looked into the subject of time travel quite a bit. The problem is most of what's out there is fictional, unverified, or mere conjecture. Either we're pretty unique, or others who have had similar experiences are keeping quiet. I don't think there *are* any experts. The closest is Zevél, and he doesn't say much."

"Why not?" John inquired. "Doesn't he trust you?"

"Oh, I don't think it's that," Ben responded. "It's more that he wants me to find my own answers. His advice is usually to look within, to pray, to listen to God. He's pretty spiritual, if you know what I mean."

"Sounds as if he's some kind of guru. I'm not sure I would put a lot of stock in his advice." John did not like flaky people.

"Dad, he's no guru, but he is insightful. See, he's actually a really huge silver wolf that lives part-time in the Hunters' cavern. He looks scary, but he's a vegetarian because he came from before The Fall. I think it's neat that he knows all these different languages." Nate noticed Ben wincing and abruptly stopped his narration.

If John had not gone down the road so far with Ben and Nate already, he would have concluded they were both complete wackos and just excused himself. But he could not. He was stuck in the middle of their plot. All he could say was an incredulous, "*What?*"

"Sorry, John, we should have prepared you for that one," Ben apologized.

"Actually, now that I think of it, my young son related a dream to me about a huge talking wolf that was not dangerous," John said. "Being it was only a dream, I thought no more about it at the time."

"Once you realize that time travel happens, the possibilities are amazing," Ben said in a lowered voice. "I've known Zevél for a long time. He stops by my place from time to time. He helped me understand my own life better when I was young and missed my family. When Nate arrived with the arrow in him, Zevél carried him quite a distance from the cave down to our house. If he hadn't, Nate probably would not have made it. He'd lost a lot of blood."

"Hmmm, another case of deliverance," John observed wryly. "So, now I have to believe in giant antediluvian plant-eating wolves too?"

"It's a lot easier once you meet him in person," Nate offered. "Isn't it easier to believe in me now that you've seen me?"

"You've got me there, son," John admitted. "When I came here this morning, I would have been less surprised if you had not materialized so I could believe the phone calls were just a delusion. This is a difficult exercise for a hard-core realist."

"You like to say you're a realist, Dad, but you're the guy who taught me about miracles and the unseen eternal world. You also told me … well maybe you haven't told me yet but you will in a few years … that when you make your big business decisions, after you look at all the numbers, you go with your gut feel. You look the target company officers in the eye and ask yourself if you believe in them."

Ben wanted to be sure John was on board. He looked into John's cool blue eyes. "So, John, I've told you everything straight. What does your gut tell you?"

John knew how to make decisions. He added everything together, considered his options, and fought against the stifling logic of his mind. Ben and Nate were both looking at him. He met Ben's gaze and saw an intelligent and caring man. Then he looked into Nate's eyes and saw … his son, who always reminded him of his dear wife. His heart went out to Nate. "I'm your father. I won't let anything separate us. Let's get back to planning."

Nate really loved his dad at that moment. Ben wished he had a son like Nate.

For the next ninety minutes, they talked about all aspects of the plan and how to work together over the next few weeks. The hardest part was knowing when and how to send Nate back to where he belongs. They all decided to sleep on that detail. John wanted to pay a visit to the Hunters and meet Alison and the Incas. Ben appreciated John's open-ended offer to help any way he could.

The waitress had gone off duty, and the next shift had left them alone. The meeting was winding down when Ben's cell phone began playing *Somewhere My Love*. John wondered when he would see *his* love again.

"It's Helmut, just checking signals," Ben announced. "He's ready any time we are. What should I tell him?"

John looked at his watch. "We've probably taken this as far as we can for one day. I should hit the office and see what's going on before I head home. Nate will want to tell me about his first day at school."

"Helmut, give us about forty minutes, OK? … Right. Great. See you there." Ben folded up the phone. "Helmut is eager to get going. Says he has a lot of last minute things to do and wants to get to bed early. My eccentric brother is flying down to the airport tomorrow morning for a 7 a.m. flight to Anchorage."

"Let's stay in touch," John said. "I'll see if I can arrange a time next week to pay you a visit." Turning to Nate he added, "See if you can complete the forward diary in the next few days. I've made some notes from your first few pages I can use until then."

"I'll do that, Dad. It's been great today. Can't wait to see you again. Hey, when you get home, see if I need help with my homework. If I remember right, my new algebra teacher loaded us up every night."

They all stood up. Nate smiled at his dad, but that was not enough. It had not been that long since he was blown out of the sailboat. He had thought his dad might have drowned. Seeing his dad right now helped Nate realized how much he had missed him and needed him in his life. He gave him a big hug, and John was impressed with his strength.

"Sure that arrow wound is healing? It hasn't been all that long." John wished he could see it for himself.

"I keep it covered to be sure it doesn't get infected, but I think it's fine – just a little sensitive when I stretch the hamstring. Helmut thinks I'll be able to run full speed in a few weeks."

John extended his hand to Ben. "It's been a pleasure. Please also thank Alison for her hospitality to Nate." John stopped himself. "No, it's more than hospitality. Thanks for your love and care, Ben. You're an amazing guy." Putting a hand on Nate's shoulder he added, "I also want to meet your Inca friends. Guess they're part of this plot too. Kawsay sounds like an amazing girl."

"Yeah, she's great, Dad. She's a good student and teacher. It's been neat telling her all about the modern world and the universe. She's even interested in spiritual things. We talk for hours. You'll like her."

"We'll be on our way," Ben said, picking up his sweater.

"Let me give you a lift," John offered. He left a generous tip and asked the cashier to be sure the first waitress got her share. As he thought of his work responsibilities, they seemed easy and straightforward in comparison to the challenges he would face with Nate for the next three years.

After John delivered them to the landing spot, Nate and Ben had a few moments to talk. Nate described to Ben the incident with Morrow earlier in the day and how it confirmed to him that his presence was not random or meaningless.

Ben agreed, fascinated by this unusual confirmation of what he already believed. "So, it seems the day went well."

Nate nodded. "I'm glad we came. It helped my dad get a handle on everything that's going on. He gets very distracted by his work, but I know he'd do anything for me."

"Families are really important. In the final analysis, the only people you can really count on are your family and a few special friends," Ben observed.

"It must have been hard to get cut off from your family as you did."

"Yeah, and it's still hard," Ben confessed. "I do wonder what happened to them. I don't have any Bible or historical sources that mention them. All these years, I've wondered if somehow my family can be warned to get away from Saul so when his kingdom ends they'll be safe."

"Maybe when someone takes back the arrows, they can also deliver some message to your family," Nate suggested.

"I've wondered about that. Even if it were possible, I'm not sure how to convince them unless I go myself. But now I can't leave Alison. Maybe she should come along."

"But the story doesn't end with a grown up couple returning the arrows," Nate protested.

"Right, and I can't make myself twelve again."

They were distracted by the pulsing sound of a rotor just above the trees. Soon the machine hovered into view and set down lightly. A door popped open, and the passengers jumped aboard and belted themselves in. Ben gave Helmut a nod, and they were off. Rush hour was only a theory to them as they sped east toward the mountains, which were barely visible on the horizon through the haze. Helmut fished a small book out of his pack and handed it to Nate. It was a field guide to Alaska wildlife. It held Nate's attention for most of the trip. Ben was content to relax, enjoy the vistas, and write some notes.

As they approached the Hunter property, Nate paid more attention to the landscape. He could see the stream and bridge as well as the cluster of log houses. As they descended toward the landing pad by Helmut's cabin, Nate noticed a greeting committee. Alison and Grandfather stood at the edge of the clearing. Kawsay knelt beside them with one arm holding Junior and the other waving up at Nate. He returned the wave and felt a joyful contentment at being back at his new home. Then he remembered that he could not stay.

That night Ben and Alison each found little notes under their pillows as they went to bed. The one Ben wrote was a little wiggly because he had written it during the flight in turbulent air. Before recapping the day, they each read silently.

At the end of day
Past the end of all my life
There is Alison.

When you are away
I see signs of you and think
There is Benjamin.

They looked at one another with matching smiles and loving eyes. "We're never really apart, but I still hate it when we can't be together all day," Alison murmured. "Am I spoiled?"

"Sure, and so am I. It's our destiny to spoil each other." They exchanged a soft kiss.

Alison remembered something. "That was very sweet of you to send me the message this evening on Junior's chalk board."

"I did? What message was that?" Ben wanted to be sweet, but did not want credit where it was not due.

"You know: *I missed you!*"

"Honey, I *did* miss you, but I'm afraid I didn't write the message." They both were silent, thinking.

"Well," Alison began, "if you didn't write it then, it probably wasn't meant for me." She smiled a knowing smile that Ben returned. "Maybe we need to get Nate his own chalkboard. Guess the kids missed each other too!"

Ben reflected on the day. "John wants to come up here next week. He wants to meet you and our other visitors. I *do* wish you could have been with us today."

"Me too, but I'm glad I was here. Kusi was a little feverish, and it took both Kawsay and me to keep him still. He doesn't seem to have a word for 'relax'. He seems to like classical music, especially opera. *Madame Butterfly* put him right to sleep on the couch this afternoon."

Ben chuckled at the image that conjured. "Being down on campus reminded me that we'll be back in the thick of things in a few months. This sabbatical isn't turning out to be much of a rest. Maybe I'll try some Puccini tomorrow myself."

"Maybe things will calm down for a while now. Or do you have more time travelers arriving this week?" Alison joked.

"Well, you never know, so let's keep the place picked up. Herschel and Grace said they'll come up Friday. They couldn't wait for the weekend. After that, I don't know. But it's more the departures I'm concerned about."

"What departures?" she asked.

"Mostly Nate's. You know he can't stay here indefinitely. According to John, the dreams are wearing down young Nate more than the Nate we know. Apparently, Kusi was asking Kawsay when he should go back for the rest of the family. I don't see us getting a lot of our homework done for a while." Ben looked both worried and tired.

"Let's get a good night's sleep, dear," Alison cooed, kissing his forehead. "It's easier to cope when the batteries are charged. You say I preach too much about getting rest, but you know I'm right."

"Good idea, honey. And Helmut's helicopter will rise before the Sun. Hope I can get back to sleep after that racket!" Alison looked particularly darling right at that moment, so Ben could not resist offering another kiss. "Do you want to read before we turn off the light?"

Alison nodded. "Your reading always helps me unwind."

Ben had an idea. "When we talked with Nate's dad last night, he mentioned verses in Hebrews and one of the minor prophets. They have been on my mind all day. Let's see." He paged around for a moment. "I think this is it." He read from Habakkuk. It began with a cry for help and then despair at the slowness and apparent ineptness of divine assistance. As Ben started the second chapter, he felt the hairs on his neck stand up, and his senses became especially alert. He paused and then read verses three and four slowly.

For the vision is yet for an appointed time, but at the end it shall speak, and not lie; though it tarry, wait for it; because it will surely come, and will not tarry. Behold, his soul which is lifted up is not upright in him: but the just shall live by his faith.

Ben read it a second time to himself.

"Are you stopping?" Alison asked. She did not sound sleepy.

"I think this is important," Ben responded. "Here, listen again." Alison gave it her complete attention. "What does that tell you?" Ben asked.

"Well, it tells me that God may seem late, but we only think he's late because he doesn't conform to our timetable. If we're humble enough to let God be in control, He won't disappoint us." Alison did not see that this was controversial at all, but a good reminder.

"Does it apply to us, to Nate and Kawsay and Grandfather?" Ben inquired.

Alison thought for a moment. She furrowed her brow and then brightened. "I suppose it could mean that God will tell us when it is time to act. We shouldn't get impatient and do something before it's time. Do you think it relates to the departures?"

"Maybe it does. We know we live by faith. Right now, it's just more obvious how important that is." Ben put the Bible on the nightstand. "Zevél told us that walking with God doesn't have to be difficult. Just listen and obey. Honey, please, help me listen better. A lot depends on us right now. A lot of precious people."

"Ben, we've come this far. I don't think God will abandon us now, or ever." Alison gave Ben a gentle hug. "We'll be fine."

Ben could not improve on Alison's sentiment, so he just sighed and turned out the light. "I'm sure a lucky guy to have you."

A quiet voice came back through the dark. "I'd agree with you, except you say you don't believe in luck." She kissed his cheek, snuggled up to him, and became silent.

CHAPTER 18.

HERO'S QUEST

SEPTEMBER 2 – PRESENT YEAR
KODIAK, ALASKA

GREAT BEAST AWAKENS
FLAMING ARROW PIERCES SKY
A HERO'S WELCOME.

"You headed up to Launch Pad 1?" Sara tried to catch up with Loren, whom she had learned to admire the past two months during her summer internship at the Kodiak Island Launch Complex.

"Just need to check some numbers before the launch, Sara. It's getting close to final countdown. Did you get to see those auroras last night around 2 a.m.? It's pretty early in the year for auroras – what a treat!" Loren had lived in Alaska for nearly ten years, but became as excited about the auroras as she did a launch. "I love to go up to Fairbanks during the winter months to see the sky light up in color, but getting auroras down here in Kodiak in September is unusual."

"I did see the northern lights last night. I woke up, looked out my window, and was stunned! I wondered if anyone else saw them or if I was having a magical dream. Is the weather always so perfect here in September?" Sara looked around as the late summer green and brown carpeted terrain smoothed its way down to meet the azure blue ocean. "I really think I could live here forever. You have this amazing state-of-the-art spaceport on this remote, wild, exotic island. What could be better? Looks as if we have some folks out here to watch the launch." Sara could see a small line of cars and RVs approaching on the narrow paved road.

Loren looked at her young protégé. Sara reminded her of herself at that age – so full of enthusiasm. "I do love it here, Sara…"

"Yikes! Do you see that?" Sara was pointing into a patch of trees about fifty feet from where they were walking. "What *is* he wearing?"

Loren followed Sara's arm toward a cluster of trees where she could clearly see a teenage boy standing and staring directly at them. Loren was stunned by his appearance. He had long, thick, nearly black hair, camouflage markings on his face, what looked like round flat gold earrings, a tunic with some sort of geometric print, a few bags belted to his waist, bare tanned muscular legs, and strappy sandals. He was holding a spear, and some sort of pack was strapped to his back. His gaze was haunting and primitive, but not threatening. He almost seemed vulnerable. Loren and Sara were frozen in a stare.

"Twenty minutes to launch. Launch crew report now," bellowed from the speaker. Loren was jolted out of her fog and turned to Sara. "Come on, Sara. That means us. We'll have to examine Halloween-boy after the launch." When her eyes returned to the patch of trees, there was a space where the boy had been standing.

I have a bad feeling about this. Yachay was clutching his spear tightly as the vast darkness tried to pry it from his hand. He had already hurtled through one of these tunnels and had the breath sucked out of his lungs. Yet he had made it. Yes, he survived it once, and he will survive it again. He knew Kawsay and Grandfather had not been in the strange village with the big white temple, the stealthy man, the two cowards, and the men in red shirts. He had to move on and keep searching. He was going to find his sister and grandfather, and he was going to return to his mother and grandmother, and that was what he was going to do. Yachay held his breath, but his lungs were about to explode. He gasped. SMACK! He plunged into a lumpy, warm, furry object and sucked damp, thick, smelly fur into his mouth.

Yachay coughed the fur out of his mouth and lay there face down sprawled across the warm object, gathering his thoughts. He did not feel hurt anywhere. He was aware that his spear had flown out of his hand on impact. He needed to locate it. He lifted his head and opened his eyes. Dim darkness. Smelly darkness. The lumpy fur quivered and shifted below his torso. *Warm, lumpy, furry, moves, very big – not good. Better get out of here!* Yachay tried to lift himself gracefully without pushing on the furry whatever-it-was. His toes were against cold rock. *Another cave?* The fur made a deep, slow groaning sound.

Yachay slowly arose, using his muscles to lift himself like a snake. He did not want to push on the whatever-it-was. He looked around to see if he could spy a light source that might lead to an exit. He saw a faint glow in front of him and to the right, past where his spear must have landed. He thought he could feel an ever-so-slight wisp of air from that direction as well. Whatever-it-was moved, moaned, and snorted. The hair on the back of Yachay's neck was standing at attention. He sensed this was the biggest, most massive creature he had ever seen, encountered, or imagined.

"AARRRRRHH". Whatever-it-was lumbered to a vertical position. Yachay could see it towering at twice his own height, waving its head from side to side in the dark glow. "AARRRRRHH". The creature's fetid breath washed over Yachay.

Time to leave. Where is my spear? He did not think his spear would offer much protection unless he hit an eyeball, but he did not want to leave it behind. He strained to see in the near darkness. "AARRRRRHH". *Really time to leave*! Yachay began slowly backing up. The beast sniffed and snorted, and Yachay realized it was sniffing him! Still moving back toward the light, he caught a dim glimpse of what must be his spear. *That is where it would have landed.* He needed to move a bit closer to the beast and away from the light – just a bit – then he could reach down and pick it up, assuming it *was* his spear. He moved slightly forward.

"AARRRRRHH". He felt a strong wind as the beast ripped the air with its arm. In a single motion, Yachay dropped to the ground and reached out, grasping at what he thought was his spear. *Yes*! Yachay closed his fingers around the spear's familiar shaft. WWOOOOOSSSSSHHHHH. Another air-splitting swipe, but this one slashed his arm. *Crap!* He flinched, but did not release his grip, as he drew back his arm and slid backward toward the light.

"AARRRRRHH". The head was waving, and the beast was getting mad. Yachay was getting mad too. He wanted to get out of the darkness so he could see this aggressive enemy. WWOOOOOSSSSSHHHHH. He dashed for the light, running sideways, still partly crouched. He continued smoothly and quickly, eyeing the beast behind and the light ahead. The opening of the cave was in view. The beast was down on four legs now. "AARRRRRHH". It rose up again on its hind legs. It was taunting Yachay. It was going to charge. Yachay quickly observed that the beast had long brown fur, claws more than twice the length of his longest finger, and was two times his height and ten times his weight. Yachay had seen something like this before, but *this* thing was more than four times the size. *Yikes! It's really time to get out of here.* Yachay dove for the cave opening and veered off to the side, thinking *IT* would run straight out and past him.

The maneuver worked, at least temporarily, but for its size this creature was really fast – too fast. The creature flew out the mouth of the cave and barreled forward a distance of many times Yachay's height. It stopped and sniffed the air, then turned and looked back toward Yachay. By that time, Yachay had scurried most of the way up the cliff above the cave.

Yachay saw the creature beginning to turn toward him and squeezed into a crevice made by a protruding rock near the top. The creature could not see him. He heard it sniffing and snorting. Yachay held his breath. The creature stood for a while sniffing the air; it had nothing better to do. Yachay felt around behind him. He thought he could navigate the rest of the way up behind protruding rocks and stay out of the creature's sight.

Just as he reached the top of the cliff, his spear, which he held with the hand that was now mostly covered with blood, knocked a rock down from the cliff. *Crap!* The creature looked up and saw Yachay. It lumbered over to the bottom of the cliff. Yachay did not wait around to examine its climbing technique. If it was anything like its small cousin, it could climb.

Yachay began sprinting away from the creature, the cave, and the cliff. After traveling through brush and trees, he heard the "AARRRRRHH" sound a short distance behind. His arm was bleeding heavily, and the whipping it was taking from shrubs and branches was making it worse. Yachay's adrenaline level was so high he must have been running faster than he had ever run. He was climbing in elevation to a ridge which would be less populated by plants, allowing him to move faster.

As he crested the ridge, he could see vast blue water skirting the green earth below. He dared not stop and survey its spectacular, glistening surface, since the creature may be close behind him. He thought he could hear it growling and snorting and breaking brush, but he was not entirely certain what he was hearing. Maybe it was his own blood rushing in his ears. He did not know and did not want to stop to find out. He just kept moving.

He tried to stay above the tree line. He was mostly running on various types of ground cover including spongy plants, grasses, and wild flowers, as well as dirt and rocky outcroppings. The air was cool, but Yachay felt hot and was beginning to feel weak, probably from loss of blood or perhaps just from the events of the past few days. His thoughts drifted back to the pale, stealthy man he had followed to the river and the two cowards who tried to attack him. He still had the man's small oddly-shaped metal object with its strange markings,

.Я .Ꝗ, in his food pouch. He wondered if he would ever be able to return the object to its owner.

He continued to run as the Sun slid across the sky. The ridge eventually descended in elevation. He came over a slight rise, looked down, and saw a wide black path snaking into huge structures. *What world have I come to?* Yachay's mind was snatched away from the stealthy man and the large brown creature and was now occupied by something altogether stranger than either a man or a great beast. In an area where the sweeping hillside descended to meet the vast blue water, Yachay's eyes were transfixed on huge geometric structures, mostly light in color. There were several clumps of structures spread out over a large area; some of them had very odd shapes. They appeared to be constructed from peculiar materials. *This would be a place Kawsay would go if she were here.* The incident with the creature threw Yachay's intuition out of balance, and he did not have a sense if Kawsay and Grandfather were near him. *I will go find someone to ask.*

As Yachay descended, the brush and trees grew denser. He pulled his knife out of his sling and cut branches where necessary. He wondered about the creature, but felt it had undoubtedly gotten distracted and returned to its cave or wherever it chose. He had never seen or even imagined a creature that huge. *What was it and where am I? Are Kawsay and Grandfather near? If they are, perhaps someone will have seen them. There must be people near those structures.* Yachay bushwhacked his way to a clearing and spied down toward the structures. He blinked. "What?" he mumbled in an audible voice. He blinked again. There were small boxes moving along the wide black pathways. Yachay looked at his arm. Crusty blood was still oozing from the four gashes that cut across the top of his upper arm. It was throbbing. It needed to be cleaned and cared for. Yachay knew the cuts were deep, but he refused to look too closely. *What would that accomplish? I need to sleep.* Yachay worked his way down the wooded mountain until he reached an open, grassy area studded with small clusters of trees.

Yachay was feeling weary, too tired to be hungry. The throbbing in his arm was reverberating throughout his body. Using his spear as a cane, he began walking toward the structures. He could see a small field of huge, flower-like structures. He was too weary to care how strange and huge they were. He did not see anyone nearby, so he walked further. He noticed a number of boxes moving along the wide black path. Yachay realized these were some sort of moving boxes made of metal. He could see that they were moving along a road toward the tallest structure he had ever seen. There would be people to ask about Kawsay and Grandfather. That is where he would go.

As he got closer to the tall structure, he saw a smaller, pointed, cylindrical structure to its side. He was getting close to a road and was surprised to see that there were people inside the moving metal boxes. He could see people near the tall structure. He would ask about Kawsay; then he would sleep. He was weary but determined. As he approached the group of structures that included the tall structure, he decided to stop at a cluster of trees and reconnoiter. His eyes met those of two women. One was pointing at him. They were staring at him and he at them. They were wearing strange clothing that fit around their legs and arms. *Why are these women still staring at me? Have they seen Kawsay and Grandfather, people who look similar to me?*

"Twenty minutes to launch. Launch crew report now," bellowed into the air. Yachay was jolted from his thoughts of Kawsay. The women responded to the strange language. Yachay backed out of sight to think. *What are all these people doing here?* He sat down against the trunk of a tree to examine his arm. It looked ugly and was already getting hot, red, and sick. Yachay felt a wave of despair wash over him. Too much confusion, too many new experiences, yet he was not accomplishing his goal. He put his head back and began to doze. He jerked awake, pulled himself out of impending slumber, and stood, picking up his spear. *I will find those women and ask them if they saw Kawsay and Grandfather.* He walked toward the large building. He could not see any people near it. *Where have they gone?* Yachay came to a tall barrier made of loosely-woven, thin metal. He could see through its large square openings, but someone clearly did not want him to get any closer to the large building. He could now get a good look at the tall structure and the smaller, pointed, cylindrical structure to its side. The smaller cylindrical structure was still fifteen to twenty times Yachay's height. *Wow. What in the world is that?* Yachay sat down facing the perimeter fence of Launch Pad 1, staring, wondering.

"Ten, … nine, … eight," a man's voice pierced the air. Yachay jumped to his feet. ".. six, … five, … four." It was coming from the huge white structure. Suddenly, flames and white smoke burst out and poured from the bottom of the smaller cylindrical structure! *Yikes!* Yachay was thrown back by the force of the hot cloud of smoke and flames. He rose into a crouch and ran back from the heat of the smoke cloud and flames. The noise grew louder and louder, accelerating to a level Yachay had not even imagined possible! When he thought his ears were going to explode, the pointed cylindrical structure began to rise off the ground, dragging a cone of fire and smoke below it! As it rose higher it gained incredible speed! *How is this possible? What does this mean?* It created a streak in the sky and was gone! Into the heavens! Yachay stood looking up, mesmerized, frozen in wonder. He was so stunned by the events, he just stood staring at the sky. The thoughts in his mind jumbled into their own cloud of confusion – then nothingness. Yachay's mind was blank – he could not think at all. He just stood staring up where he had last seen the cylindrical structure.

"Hey! Kid! What are you doing?" Yachay heard the strange language. It was directed at him. Two men in some type of dark head-to-toe clothing were pointing at him. They did not look friendly. Yachay turned and ran toward a group of trees for cover. He looked back and could see the men going along the fence still looking at him. *They are after me. Why? What did I do? I need to find Kawsay, but these two don't look friendly. Somehow I don't think they would be helpful. I'll find other people to ask.* Yachay took off. He saw moving metal boxes in the distance and took off in that direction.

After getting a safe distance from the two threatening men, Yachay saw a group of people near some moving metal boxes. "Hey you!"

What? It was those two men again. They were still following him. *What is their problem?* They were still quite a distance away. Yachay was too tired to deal with them and decided to find a place to hide. He could easily outrun them, even in his weary condition. Yachay kept moving in the direction of the people. As he approached, he saw that there were a lot of people and moving metal boxes. There were adults and children eating and playing and looking out at the beautiful blue water. He did not want any of these people to tell the two unfriendly men about him. He decided to stay out of sight until the men lost interest in him – just as the creature had lost interest.

He saw some strange huts sitting up off the ground. They were on some sort of round, black rocks, yet they were not rocks. In fact, on closer examination, Yachay realized that all the moving metal boxes had similar round circles that appeared to be what moved them – by turning. *Wow! No time to learn about this now.* Yachay noticed one of the raised huts had a slightly open door. He looked in. *Wow.* There were a lot of unusual objects and surfaces inside. Yachay heard some people approaching. He slipped into the raised hut and climbed up to a high point. He pulled some soft blankets over him, covering himself, his sling, and his spear.

Yachay fell quickly asleep and was not awakened when the hut on wheels drove away.

Yachay suddenly awoke, opening his eyes wide into dim light. His ears were filled with a loud, deep rumbling. It sounded like an earthquake. The small elevated hut was moving. He must be in some kind of a massive, unceasing earthquake. He gathered his sling and spear, and climbed down into the center of the hut. The rumbling and rolling motion continued. Yachay's heart was racing and pounding, but the rumbling was so loud that he could not hear his heart inside his ears. He pushed on the door through which he had entered. It did not budge. He felt around and came across something sticking out of it and pushed, pulled, and turned it until the door opened. He stuck his head out and realized he was inside of a huge cavern crammed full of metal boxes. Everything was moving, rocking, and swaying – in fact, the entire cavern was rocking. *This is no earthquake.* A few of the metal boxes had dogs trapped inside them. *What is going on?* Yachay looked around. The metal boxes were attached to the ground, which was wet and made of some type of metal. *I need to get out of here.* Yachay saw steps leading up.

He ascended the steps onto a landing. He looked around at the strange colored materials and surfaces. He saw a doorway to the left. Everything was still rocking. He stepped outside. He was standing on the side of a huge boat! *That explains the rocking.* It was dark with a nearly full moon. There were dim lights – though nothing like the torches used in his village. He looked up the side of the boat and could see it was very tall and towered above his head. It had open walkways along its side as well as built-in steps going to its upper levels. In fact, it had at least two more levels above where he was standing. He saw people up toward the front of the boat and decided to head to the back.

He touched the cold metal fencing that protected people from falling off the huge boat into the water. He ran his hand along the fence as he crept to the back of the boat and onto a back deck that had a low raised fence. Yachay looked over the low fence down into the water. The huge boat made a splashy wake behind it. The air was full of the sound of the penetrating rumble. This sound must be coming from whatever was powering the huge boat. Yachay's ears were filled with the rumbling roar, the rushing of the water behind the boat, and the wind from the sea. It was a good place to think. There were two young girls nearby playing on some stools near the raised fence. They did not pay much attention to his presence. Their giggling voices reminded him of Kawsay.

He turned toward the front of the boat and did a double take. *What?* The sky gripped his eyes – it was luminous with intense bright green colors streaking and swirling from the horizon up and to the right. *Wow! That is what everyone is looking at – it is beautiful! What does this mean? Is the world ending? Or is this just what this strange world looks like?*

The girls looked closely at Yachay and giggled louder. "It's not Halloween yet! Halloween! Halloween!"

Yachay had no idea what they were saying, but it was not threatening. In the moonlight Yachay could see that one of the girls looked about six years old and the other maybe eight. They had yellow hair and pale skin. Yachay had heard of yellow hair and just yesterday he had seen pale skin himself. He wondered why the girls seemed to think he was so funny. They were now jumping around saying, "Ug, ug, ug."

Yachay looked back up the side of the boat at the luminous sky. He was glad he had slept and wondered for how long. His arm was crusted with dried blood and was still oozing. The girls were jumping around on the stools that were against the low fence that protected them from falling into the water. They were climbing from the stools up to the top of the fence and looking down at the water. Then they jumped back onto the deck and giggled. Yachay did not think it was safe for the young yellow-haired girls to jump around on the edge of a huge boat. Once again, they jumped down hard on the deck, looked at Yachay, and giggled. Then back up to the fence, whispering. Yachay was keeping an eye on the girls. He decided to take off his sling and tuck his spear as far into it as possible. He realized he was dressed very differently from anyone he had seen and decided the spear could not help the situation. He secured the pointed end of his spear into his sling along with the pouches that were tied around his waist. He wanted to keep all his possessions and weapons together and safely in his sling. There was not much he could do about his tunic and bare legs.

As he was about to strap the sling across his back, a loud booming horn pierced through the rumble. His eyes darted over to the girls, and he saw the younger one fly off the fence and down toward the dark water. In a single motion, Yachay dropped his sling, grabbed the older girl, whose scream joined the horn, and pointed her toward the front of the boat where the people were. He shouted "Yanapay!" as his momentum joined with a push-off from his feet and carried him off the stern of the boat right behind the small yellow-haired girl. Yachay had anticipated this type of accident so he was braced for it. The girl glided on the wind and splashed into frigid water, which silenced her scream. Yachay's arms were outstretched – he could almost touch her. Just as the force of her body hitting the water halted her flight, Yachay's hands reached her and his arms engulfed her small body. He did not want her to get away from him in the moonlit darkness. He clutched her to his chest as they both plunged beneath the frigid surface. He held his breath and hoped he had not knocked the air out of her small lungs as he landed on top of her.

He could not believe how cold the water was! It felt like icy daggers slicing his body. He needed to get her out. But first he needed to get her up to the surface. Yachay held her with one arm and fought to get to the surface with the other. He looked around under the dark, frigid water. There was enough moonlight to illuminate the bubbles on the water's surface, and he could feel the roughed-up turbulence from the boat's wake. He swam toward the faintly lit bubbles. His head broke the surface, and he took a breath. While kicking hard with his legs, he held the girl's head out of the frigid water. He could not tell if she was breathing. Yachay shook her shoulders. He did not know what to do. She coughed. Yachay could see her face in the moonlight. He could also see the huge boat moving away. The girl was sobbing. *A good sign,* Yachay thought. Yachay knew he needed to get the child out of the frigid water. He wanted her up on his shoulders. But how could he communicate that to her when he could not speak her language?

"Wichayman!" he shouted. She stopped sobbing. While using his strong legs to kick and tread water, he lifted her up part way out of the water and onto his shoulders. She grabbed handfuls of his long, wet hair. *Good. Good girl. You hold on tight.* He moved her hands down and wrapped her fingers around his chin.

She was young, but she realized what he was doing. She had sat on her father's shoulders many times. *Daddy would do something like this,* she thought, and felt comforted. Her small body was shaking violently from the cold water and air. She could see the ferry in the distance. She was too cold to scream and knew they were too far away to hear her.

What? Oh good, Yachay thought. The huge boat was beginning to turn. *The sister must have gotten help.* He could see big torches all over the boat as it slowly turned back toward them. The torches were lighting the water to its side and in their direction.

Yachay fought to keep his head above the surface. His flat sandals acted as flippers to aid in holding up the extra weight. His body was numb, and he was afraid of getting weak. He knew what cold temperatures could do to the body – he had heard stories of people losing strength in cold lakes or high in the mountains in the snow. They get sleepy and never wake up. He was not going to let that happen. The boat had turned toward them, and he heard its noise decline into silence. They had stopped whatever was powering them. *Maybe so they can hear us. Here, here!* Yachay began yelling to the boat, "Kaypi, kaypi!"

Julie knew she should not have let her little sister play where she could fall into the water. Her parents had told her more than once that evening not to encourage Cindy to play on the ferry's railings. She just had not thought something this awful would happen. If the boy in the short dress, earrings, and face paint could not keep Cindy alive, Julie would never forgive herself. She was the oldest, and she should have been acting more responsibly. When the strange boy shouted "Yanapay!" at her, she did not know the word, but it was clear he was instructing her to get help. Julie had only been on the ferry since early that evening when they boarded, but she had made her rounds and knew where all the important stuff was. She had ducked under the cables in the roped off areas and even snuck up onto the crew's deck on the side of the Bridge.

When Cindy went over the back of the ferry, Julie knew she needed to get to the Bridge and to the Captain, pronto. Julie also knew the fastest way up there – up the steps, up the side to the middle of the boat, in the door, up the stairs, out the door, under the ropes, up the outside stairs, onto the deck, and through the forbidden door onto the Bridge. Julie flung open the door and exploded into the middle of the small room, which was full of windows and computers. Three uniformed men turned to her in surprise.

"My name is Julie Stevens and my sister, Cindy, just fell off the back of the ferry. Cindy is only six. We need to turn the boat around and rescue her." Feeling the reality of her statement, Julie broke into tears.

Captain T. W. Roberts' attention was ripped from scanning his instruments by the young girl bursting onto his Bridge. Of all the events he may have imagined on this calm early September night, this would not have been one on them. His eyes were fixed on her, looking for clues to aid him in whether to believe her. If her story was true, he needed to turn his ferry around without delay. "Did anyone else see your sister fall off the back of the vessel?" Captain Roberts stooped down in front of the girl.

Julie wiped her eyes with the back of her fists and looked up into the Captain's concerned face. "Yes, there was a teenage boy with dark hair and brown skin, wearing earrings and a long shirt or dress. He jumped in the water after Cindy and shouted something in another language. He wanted me to get help, and he went in the water after her. If he doesn't save her, I will never forgive myself. I should not have let..."

"We're coming about now. Hit the GPS mark. Let's retrace our route – exactly!" Captain Roberts had heard enough to know it was unlikely the girl was making this up. If she was telling the truth, with this water temperature, the little sister and the teenage boy would not last long. Roberts had no memory of a brown-skinned teenage boy wearing earrings and a dress, however. He turned on the search lights, flipped on the PA system, "Attention all crew and passengers. We have a possible man overboard. We are turning around. All available crew ready yourselves."

After the Tustumena ferry had completely turned around and was retracing its route, the Captain cut the engines. He felt blind. He did not know precisely how long it took Julie to get from the stern to the Bridge, but figured she could have run it as fast as anyone – probably in under 20 seconds. Then he listened to her story and began the turn – maybe a minute. It took a few minutes to turn the Tustumena and get on track.

"We should see them now, Petrov. Dark haired teenage boy, blond six-year-old girl. Prepare for rescue. Drop an emergency lifeboat." The Captain's voice came through First Officer Petrov's radio, "Do you see those kids out there anywhere, Petrov? My guess is that it's been nearly ten minutes since they hit the water. We need to get them out. Make sure they are not directly in our path!"

"Lifeboat down with crew, Sir. We're scanning the water. Don't see anything – uh, wait a minute." Petrov had his night vision binoculars pressed against his eyes. "I see something – due south – looks as if the girl is up out of the water – on the boy's shoulders! He must be one strong kid." Petrov then shouted to his lifeboat crew, "Right in front of you! See them?"

"In sight," came a voice from the boat. Petrov heard the little engine rev up, and the boat shot south.

Yachay watched the small boat approach. He heard a whining sound grow louder as the little boat skidded across the water toward them. He was surprised how fast it was moving. His legs were beyond numb. He did not think he could keep this up. The girl shivered violently on his shoulders, but was otherwise silent – probably too cold and too shocked to speak. At least her grip on his chin was secure. Yachay felt her being lifted from his shoulders. He began to slip down under the water when a pair of hands gripped his upper arm and held him. Two pairs of hands dragged him over the side of the small boat.

There were two men and a woman in the boat. The woman was tightly clutching the yellow-haired girl. The girl had been wrapped in a large blanket, but Yachay could see that she was still shaking. The young girl's eyes were locked on him. Her stare communicated that she knew what he had done for her. One of the men had wrapped a blanket around Yachay and was holding him tightly. The third man was controlling the boat. They arrived at the huge boat.

Yachay thought about lying on his favorite rock. It was in a clearing in the jungle, and he loved to go there and think and sleep in the hot summer sun. That was where he wished he was now. His body was still shaking violently; he wondered if he would ever be warm again. The small boat had been attached to some type of rope Yachay had never seen before and was being lifted up into the air. There were people crowding around on the big boat looking down at them.

Yachay saw the older girl with a couple who must have been her mother and father. The girl and the mother were crying. Yachay knew they were tears of worry but also joy at seeing their baby alive. The father was saying something, but Yachay could not understand him. He was so tired; he thought he would just take a little nap. He was safe now. These people were caring for him. They had pulled him out of the freezing water and wrapped him in a blanket – it was safe to sleep now.

⇒ ⇐

Captain Roberts' crew had successfully pulled the six-year-old girl and teenage boy out of the Gulf of Alaska between Kodiak Island and Homer, and the M/V Tustumena was back on course, expected to arrive in Homer at 7:35 a.m. Captain Roberts wanted to meet this mysterious young hero for himself. There was no record that he should be on board, and no one seemed to know who he was. There were two high school-age boys traveling alone, but they were accounted for.

The boy looked as if he could be Hispanic or have some type of native ancestry, but he had no ID. Julie had retrieved his unusual backpack and brought it to the Bridge. His personal effects included a primitive spear, a knife, pouches with grains, an old stamp with the letters P.R., a woven sling with a few stones, three stones tied together by rope, and a jeweled dagger. *Our young hero is apparently quite the warrior,* the Captain thought. *Perhaps he is part of some strange survival game. Apparently he did survive a Kodiak brown bear attack – those claw marks on his arm were reported as very deep.*

The Captain's thoughts were interrupted by First Officer Petrov's arrival on the Bridge. "I can relieve you now, Sir. The boy is beginning to move and should be waking up."

"Thanks. I am looking forward to speaking with our young hero. How is little Cindy Stevens? Any after-effects from cold water or impact of the fall?" The Captain reached for the door.

"She seems to be doing fine. She is awake and talking quietly with her parents and sister, not four feet from the boy. I don't think she will ever forget that experience. Mr.

Stevens is anxious for the boy to wake up so he can properly thank him."

"Thanks, Petrov. Is Manuel in the infirmary in case this boy speaks Spanish?"

"He's there."

The Captain nodded and was out the door.

As Captain Roberts entered the infirmary, Joe Stevens stood and extended his hand. "Thank you, Captain, for your swift action in saving my daughter. I …"

A cough from Yachay interrupted the conversation. The boy blinked awake and met the staring eyes of the two yellow-haired girls, Joe and Lisa Stevens, Manuel the medic, and Captain Roberts. They were all looking intently at him, and he at them.

Cindy smiled broadly at the boy and said, "I love you for saving me."

Yachay was touched by her smile and knew she was somehow acknowledging what he had done.

Captain Roberts stepped a little closer to Yachay and quickly took stock. *Looks about medium height, maybe five-eight, long dirty hair, angular chiseled face, straight nose, well-muscled, overall a very untamed look to him.* The Captain smiled and said, "Do you understand English?"

Yachay knew he was being asked a question, but did not know what was said. He looked down and noticed his right arm was wrapped with a bright, white bandage. These people were taking care of him and being kind. He looked up at the man and smiled.

"Manuel?" The Captain nodded at his medic.

"¿Habla usted Español?" Manuel asked the boy. "Those gold disks in his ears are quite unusual, Captain."

This sounded a bit more familiar to Yachay, but he still did not understand what was being said to him. He looked down again and saw a tiny cylinder sticking out of his left arm. He immediately reached over with his right arm to pull it out.

Manuel slapped his hand over Yachay's right hand and said, "No! No!" while shaking his head. Yachay was looking at him in horror. "He is upset about the IV, Captain."

"Does he need it?" The Captain was trying to read Yachay's face and sensed the boy's fear.

"I used it as a precaution. He was dehydrated and his body temp was low. He also got a nasty bear gash. It was quite infected – I think he should be observed for a couple of days at a hospital."

"Is he still dehydrated?" the Captain pushed.

"Not seriously." Manuel still had his hand on Yachay's.

"Then let's take it out."

"Yes, Sir." Manuel gently lifted Yachay's hand and placed it on the sheet that was spread over his patient. He then carefully slid the IV out of Yachay's arm.

The Captain pondered why this boy reacted to a basic medical practice with such fear. Yachay was staring at the small puncture wound in his arm, wondering why they would do such a thing to him and what must they really be up to. He wondered if it was worth asking if they had seen Kawsay – he thought not. Manuel taped a cotton ball over the tiny needle hole in Yachay's arm.

Joe Stevens had been standing since the Captain entered the room. He cleared his throat. "Do you know anything about this boy, Captain, Sir? I mean, is there an address or any information regarding where he's from? He saved my daughter – risked his life – I would like to personally make sure he gets the medical attention he needs. He belongs in Anchorage where he can get full medical care and an interpreter, if necessary. I would like to take responsibility for him until we determine the whereabouts of his family, Sir."

"That is most generous of you, Mr. Stevens, and I'm sure the boy's family would appreciate your concern. However, it appears that this young man is a stow-away and must therefore be turned over to the State Troopers." Anticipating Stevens' reply, the Captain said, "I realize this doesn't sound right to you, but he will be turned over with a personal statement from me explaining that he dove into frigid water and not only risked his life to rescue Cindy, but held her on his shoulders to keep as much of her body as possible out of the water. I can also request that the State Troopers keep you abreast of his whereabouts. They will find an interpreter and locate his family."

"¿Habla usted Español?" Manuel tried again to communicate with Yachay.

Yachay did not think they were trying to hurt him. He looked across the tiny room and saw that the yellow-haired girl, whom he had been so worried about just a short while ago, also had one of those pointy objects in her arm and was looking quite healthy. They were caring for him in the same manner that they were caring for her.

She noticed him looking at her and her arm, and she held it up, smiled, and said, "It's OK."

He did not know what she was saying, but knew she was saying something reassuring. She must have seen him try to pull it out.

Manuel looked at Yachay, pointed to himself, and said, "Manuel." He pointed at each person in the room, stating their name as he pointed. Then he pointed at Yachay and nodded.

Yachay learned that they called the yellow-haired girls Julie and Cindy. He knew they wanted his name. He said, "Yachay." He saw the faces around him smiling.

"Well, Yachay, that sure is an unusual name," Captain Roberts said, smiling and reaching out his right hand toward Yachay. "Welcome aboard. I wish you had some papers so we didn't have to turn you over to the State Troopers, but we will ask them to treat you as a hero."

Yachay could tell this hand extending was a kind gesture and did not feel threatened. He reached out to the Captain with his left hand.

The Captain grasped Yachay's hand in both of his. "Where are you from, son?" The Captain glanced up at a large clock hanging on the wall of the infirmary and turned to Mr. and Mrs. Stevens who, along with Julie, had squeezed three small chairs into the corner of the tiny room between a medical cabinet and Cindy's bed. "It's nearly two in the morning. We will be arriving in Homer just after seven-thirty. Manuel will be right here observing Cindy and Yachay, and we have a security guard just outside the door. Why don't you try to get some sleep? We have a stateroom available two doors down if you would like to sleep there."

"You're right, Captain. Thank you. My wife and Julie can sleep in the nearby stateroom, and I will sleep in here next to Cindy, if that is permissible. I am very good at sleeping in straight chairs – just ask my wife." With a half smile Joe Stevens winked at his wife.

"If Manuel says it's OK – it's his infirmary." The Captain nodded at Manuel who returned an assuring nod. "We are requesting the Troopers provide the boy with medical care for the wound on his right arm. I guess the bear claws cut pretty deep?" The Captain looked at Manuel, who nodded in agreement. "We'll see if they can Medevac him up to Anchorage. I think they will be more likely to find an interpreter up there, perhaps at the University. He looks Hispanic or South American Indian, perhaps, but not Alaska native, and since he doesn't understand Spanish, determining his language could be tricky. I've not seen ear disks like those before, either. They do seem to go with his belongings. I assume Cindy has a pediatrician in Anchorage who can follow up with her?" Captain Roberts smiled down at the petite girl with heavy eyelids, tucked under the navy blue blanket. Then he looked up at her parents. "She's a lucky girl. Let me know if you need anything." With that, the Captain left the room.

The M/V Tustumena continued toward Homer without further incident. Yachay drifted in and out of sleep. His attention was on the girl. He still worried about her, yet reminded himself she was dry, warm, and in the care of her parents. She would be fine, but what about Kawsay? How would he find Kawsay? If she had entered the beast's cave, would she have ended up on a boat like this? Yachay tried to rest, knowing he would need his strength for whatever was before him. His arm hurt.

Manuel was happy that young Cindy Stevens was doing so well. When he was preparing the infirmary for her and the boy's arrival, he had not known what to expect. Cindy was adorable, and he could not help but notice her curious glances at her hero. Yachay was doing well too. Manuel wanted him followed up for the scratch wound, but he had managed to bring Yachay's body up to normal temperature. What concerned Manuel now was whether the infection resulting from the deep bear scratch would take his temperature up too high. Yachay was an interesting case – he acted as if he had never seen a syringe, a blood pressure cuff, an IV drip, or even a toilet! *Heck,* Manuel reflected, *there is not a single thing in my infirmary that this boy had ever encountered before!*

Officers French and Cole of the Alaska State Troopers boarded the M/V Tustumena at 7:45 a.m. in Homer, Alaska, and were escorted to the Bridge by the Tustumena's Chief Security Officer to meet with Captain Roberts. The Captain briefed the Troopers on the incident with Cindy Stevens and emphasized how the boy dove into the water behind her and held her on his shoulders to keep her from losing body heat. The Captain related that he did not know if the boy had identification that was lost in the water, but had no record of him as a passenger. He instructed the Troopers to give the boy medical care for his arm and advised them to take him to Anchorage where he could have an interpreter who could clear up many unanswered questions. He emphasized that the boy had not shown any aggressive behavior whatsoever and mostly seemed confused. Captain Roberts asked if they could gently escort the boy rather than treating him as a prisoner. Finally, he turned the boy's effects over to the officers and asked that, when they locate his family, he would be contacted so he could personally tell them of their son's heroic act. The Captain also alerted the Troopers that Joe Stevens was interested in looking after the boy and offered to take responsibility for him until his family was located. The Captain gave Officer Cole contact information for Mr. Stevens.

Officer French was stocky with thick black hair and large brown eyes. He was surveying with curiosity what he could see of the contents of Yachay's sling. He looked up at the Captain. "There is a Medevac plane available that can take him up to Alaska Regional Hospital right away. The chairman of the language department at UAA has been notified and given your description of the boy along with his name, 'Yachay'. They will send someone to the hospital."

"I'll take you down to meet the boy myself." Captain Roberts escorted Officers French and Cole to the infirmary.

A few minutes earlier, when Cindy's family retrieved her from the infirmary, Yachay wondered where she was going and what was about to happen to him. Cindy came over and gave him a big hug before she left. She said, "See you soon! See you soon!" But Yachay did not understand. After the Stevens family left, Manuel helped him into some strange clothing similar to what Manuel was wearing, and motioned for him to sit on a stool. He then put something around Yachay's arm that became very tight before loosening again with a hiss. He pulled Yachay's eyes open and looked at them closely using a tiny torch. Yachay was intrigued by his surroundings and did not feel like fighting or resisting, since he did not know what it would accomplish. He hoped that these people would take him either to someone with whom he could communicate or perhaps to where they had taken Kawsay and Grandfather – if they were anywhere near here.

Captain Roberts entered the infirmary with a man and woman. Yachay remembered Captain Roberts' name since he heard it mentioned many times since the water incident. Captain Roberts pointed at Yachay and said, "Yachay?" Then he pointed at the man and said, "French." He then pointed at the woman and said, "Cole."

Yachay noticed that "Cole" was carrying his sling. He reached for it. *Mine.* "Uqap," he said.

Cole raised her eyebrows and looked at the Captain. French started to reach for the sling, when the Captain put his hand on it and said, "Let's just let him look over his things. He hasn't seen them since we pulled him out of the water."

"Sir, what is in here? It looks like a spear or something," French cut in.

"There is a primitive spear and knife, and an odd dagger, along with some other old and unusual items. They are not modern-day weapons and would be no match for your firearms. They're probably family heirlooms. Why don't we let him look over his belongings; then you can carry them." The Captain lifted the sling from Cole's hands and handed it to Yachay.

French stiffened and put his hand over his holster.

Yachay cradled his sling on his lap and removed the spear so he could determine if everything was still there. It looked as if nothing had been taken. He slid his spear back inside so that the sling covered the tip and began to place it on his back.

Cole gently put her hand on Yachay's shoulder and looked into his eyes. "May I hold that for you?" She slowly put her hand on the sling and repeated, "Yachay? May I hold that for you?" She lifted it from him very slowly and noted the confusion on his face.

"You can't let him hold a spear, a knife, and a dagger during a flight – I don't care how 'primitive' they may be." French was getting annoyed by all this pussyfooting around with some kid wearing earrings.

Yachay spoke up again. "Yachay." He said it firmly.

The Captain nodded in agreement and put his hand on Yachay's. "Yes, Yachay's. It's OK, Yachay." The Captain looked at French. "Let Officer Cole keep the knapsack – she's a woman. It will seem less threatening, and this kid doesn't seem to understand certain customs. There is no reason to be aggressive with him until we find his family and figure out where he is from."

"I will keep the knapsack, sir," Cole said emphatically, casting an exasperated glance at French.

"If he doesn't understand 'certain customs', what's he gonna do in a tiny plane? The kid needs to be cuffed. It's for his protection as well as yours, the pilot's, and whoever else is on that plane." French was glad he was not flying up to Anchorage in a plane with that kid and Cole. He did not like being in a situation with a "potential hostile" teenager and a woman for a partner. He did not care if she was the most accurate sharp-shooter, she was relatively small and no match physically in many situations – especially one like this with an unpredictable male. *Heck, this kid treaded water in frigid Alaska waters for ten or fifteen minutes with a kid on his shoulders – they could be dealin' with Rambo in earrings here.*

Cole looked embarrassed by French's tone and behavior. She looked at French and said quietly, "I'll be right next to him. I'm sure he will be fine. If he gets excited before we get on the plane, I'll protect you – I am a black belt, you know." Cole loved springing that on her male colleagues, since she knew how many of them felt about being teamed with her. At age twelve, Cole had first shown an interest in going into law enforcement, which was when her mother enrolled her in karate classes. Cole extended her free hand to Yachay and helped him up from his chair. "Come on, Yachay. Let's take you on an airplane so we can get you an interpreter. I bet you have some interesting things to tell us. Come on." She smiled, urging him, as Yachay stood up.

The Captain walked them off the Tustumena to their awaiting squad car. Then the Captain took Yachay's hand and said, "I'm expecting a good report on you, son."

Cole helped Yachay into the back seat of the car, and they took the short drive up the Homer Spit to the small airport.

Yachay was mesmerized by his first experience inside a moving metal box. He could feel the vibration of whatever was propelling it. He was fascinated by the interior and how the moving metal box responded as French turned the circle-shaped object in front of him. Yachay began to look around outside. They were moving along a long narrow strip of land with water on each side. There were boats, a few of which had big white wings sticking straight up in the air. As they moved along, intermittent rows and groups of oddly colored and shaped huts captured Yachay's attention. There were also crowds of people scattered about in strange clothing getting in and out of the metal boxes, looking out at the water, and just walking around aimlessly. Yachay was captivated by all the strange structures – there were tall skinny ones, short fat ones, tall fat ones – and the colors were endless! His attention was redirected to a tiny, blinking torch in front of French. Just then their moving metal box turned sharply and stopped.

Cole began helping him out. There were oddly shaped moving metal boxes around… *What? One of them took off into the air like a bird!* Then he did a double take as one of them came down from the sky and slowed to a stop! *What is going on here?* Cole was holding his left arm and urging him forward toward one of the oddly shaped giant metal birds. Once they got to it, a door opened. Cole began urging him to crawl inside. He could see little stools inside. He could also see a person lying down and someone else attending the person. There also was a man dressed like Cole. *I'm not so sure about this,* Yachay thought, but Cole's firm hand was pushing him along. He climbed inside. The person lying down was a girl about his age with bandages on her chest and face.

Cole helped Yachay sit down, then sat herself and strapped something across her thighs. Yachay noticed that the woman attending the girl was also wearing a strap. The two men sitting in front of him were wearing them too. Then Cole reached over and gently attached a strap across Yachay. Before he could protest, the doors of the metal bird were closed, and it started to roar and shake.

Perfect, Cole thought when she saw that the patient was a girl about Yachay's age. *A girl his age will make him behave. He won't want to embarrass himself in front of a peer, even if they don't speak the same language.* Cole wondered how he would do in this situation. He looked uncomfortable, but he also looked tired. She wondered if the infection in his arm was making him more docile than he otherwise would have been. He did have a wild look to him, but he did not look bad. She had seen bad teenagers before, and Yachay was not one of those. *Heck, he risked his life heroically for a girl he didn't even know.* Cole smiled at the young girl with the bandages. The poor thing looked miserable but conscious.

She looked up at Cole and Yachay. "Hi, I'm Katherine. I was down here visiting some friends, and they had a motorbike and, well, you can see the results. My parents are going to kill me. They told me to be careful…" Her voice trailed off.

"Do they know you were hurt?" Cole asked.

"Yes, they know I'm being Medevac'd home. They'll be at the airport."

"I'm sure they are thankful you're not in worse condition." Cole was scanning her to see if there was anything else obviously wrong. She noticed Yachay staring at the girl with a compassionate look on his face.

Yachay was listening to the conversation between Cole and the girl as the metal bird was bumping along the ground. The roaring noise was getting louder. The voices were getting louder. Then he felt it lift – they were lifting! He could see the ground dropping below! He looked at Cole and the girl. They seemed entirely unconcerned with what was happening. He looked at the woman who was attending the girl, then to the man dressed like Cole, then the man apparently controlling the metal bird. They all seemed unconcerned! Yachay pressed his face to the window and looked down. He let out an involuntary squeak as his breath drew in. He had not been breathing. *Where are they taking me?* He felt fearful. *Yachay doesn't feel fear. Fear is for sissies. Yachay is not a sissy, and Yachay does not feel fear! No one is concerned that we have left the ground – that we are a bird. They are not concerned – Yachay is not concerned. Yachay is a man.* He squeaked again. *I am on a mission to find Kawsay and Grandfather – wait until I tell Grandfather about this experience!* Yachay smiled to himself and looked out the window. The world around him was quite beautiful and mysterious. He felt anticipation and excitement. He did not know what to expect next. The roar continued.

Yachay stared out the window during the remainder of the short flight from Homer to Anchorage. The loud droning of the airplane engine was soothing to Yachay as it washed over the comforting chatter of Cole and the others, conversing over the noise. The metal bird bounced around – up, down, sideways. Yachay could see that they were flying parallel to an aqua blue tongue of water surrounded by green land. He could see a mountain range with two prominent, white, icy peaks protruding higher than they were flying. Looking out the other side of the bird, he saw more mountains with patches of snow. It was comforting to him that he was not higher than the ground everywhere. Yachay noticed Cole pointing at a white tongue cut with blue on the side of a mountain, ending at a large turquoise lake.

"There's Tustumena glacier and its lake. The ferry you were on was named after the glacier," Cole said, smiling at Yachay, realizing he did not understand her.

Yachay had seen a couple of these huge blue and white tongues hanging from the sides of mountains on long trips with Grandfather. He saw that his sling was resting on Cole's lap. He wondered why she insisted on carrying it for him. Maybe she thought his wound made it difficult for him to carry it. His thoughts drifted back to Mother and Grandmother. They seemed so far away. He needed to find Kawsay and Grandfather and return to help Mother and Grandmother.

The metal bird jiggled its way past another turquoise body of water resting below a blue and white tongue. Cole was shouting, "And there's Skilak Lake with its glacier above. The color is so amazing!"

Yachay could see the others in the bird looking down at the lake. As they continued, the ground was peppered with small lakes. They soon reached a long ocean inlet, Turnagain Arm. Yachay looked up Turnagain Arm, amazed at the natural beauty. He pressed his face against the window. The water was swirled with gray and edged by sheer mountains on both sides, which eventually met, forming a forbidding wall. *Where is this amazing place?*

The man who seemed to be controlling the metal bird was talking. Yachay could see tiny structures all over the ground along what must be roads. He saw tiny moving boxes. He felt the metal bird begin to descend. He looked at the others, and they were all completely unconcerned and still chattering away. Yachay firmly gripped his armrests as the bird seemed to plunge toward the ground. The metal bird was turning! The green land and blue and turquoise water had transitioned into a huge grid of structures and roads. There was a mountain range right in front of them! As the metal bird dropped in altitude, the structures grew bigger! Some looked as if they were poking up into the sky! He had never imagined a settlement so huge! *Where did all these people come from?*

"OK, secure the patient – we're about to touch down at Merrill Field."

The loud voice in the unfamiliar language jolted Yachay. He saw the ground getting closer, and he closed his eyes. Then the plane touched the ground with a bump. The girl winced, but no one else seemed to notice the landing. He looked down and saw that Cole had placed her hand over his. She was still talking with the woman who was attending the girl, but must have seen his discomfort. Yachay felt a little embarrassed that a woman had noticed his concern, but thought that Cole must have been up in these metal birds many times before.

The plane stopped and Cole unstrapped herself, then reached over to help Yachay. She was holding Yachay's knapsack securely in one hand as she stepped down out of the small plane. She turned around, and Yachay was right behind her. *Cute*, she thought, *he must want off this plane fast.* She smiled at him and took his good arm. "Come on, Yachay, we're going to take a short ride over to the main entrance of the hospital." Cole had been assigned to remain with Yachay. It had been Captain Roberts' idea to keep the same person with him until his family could be located. Cole liked Captain Roberts and thought he had a lot of wisdom. She would definitely keep him informed on what was happening with Yachay.

Evans, the other Trooper who had been on the plane, was walking with them. "I'll run ahead and alert the staff we are here. Looks like your ride over there." Evans was pointing to a police car as he ran ahead and disappeared through a gate.

Cole liked Evans and thought he was "cool".

Yachay did not know where Cole was taking him and what was in store. She walked him over to one of the metal boxes that moved and helped him in. She had a firm grip on his arm and was saying something to him. *She must realize I don't understand her language. Maybe she just likes to talk, like Grandmother. Perhaps Cole knows something about my family and their whereabouts.* Yachay did not think so, but somehow he hoped.

Cole saw a media van parked close to the door of the hospital. *I wondered how long it would take those vultures to descend on this hero story. This is gonna be fun,* she thought. *Well, you never know when it may come in handy to have these clowns on your side, so I'll be nice. Besides, maybe, just maybe, someone is looking for this boy and will see a story.* Cole put her best friendly smile on her face as she opened the door and ushered Yachay inside the hospital. All lined up in a neat row headed by a smiling Evans were the Chief Nursing Officer, an obvious reporter, and a photographer. Cole could feel Yachay stiffen a bit. She squeezed his arm and said, "It's OK, Yachay. You'll get through this just fine."

The Chief Nursing Officer stepped forward and introduced herself. "Hi, Yachay. We have been expecting you. My name is Dawn." She reached out and took Yachay's hand and held it in both of hers, looked into his eyes, and gave him a smile.

Cole pointed at Dawn, looked at Yachay, and said, "Dawn." Then she nodded at Yachay.

Yachay was growing tired of all these new people; he just wanted to find Kawsay. He said, "Dawn." Then in his language, he continued, "Have you seen Kawsay? Or Grandfather?" He knew she did not understand him, but thought she may recognize the name Kawsay, just as he knew the names Cole, Manuel, Cindy, and Captain Roberts.

Not to be left out, Janie Briggs inserted herself between Dawn and Yachay, glanced back at her photographer, and said, "Get this, Kevin. Hi, Yachay. I'm Janie." Janie was pointing to herself. Janie Briggs embodied the word "reporter" with her rather pinched face, small dark eyes, neatly cut black hair, and well-tailored yet casual pantsuit. "We've heard what a hero you are. Interesting earrings. Zoom in on his face, but don't scare him, Kevin. Yachay. Do you understand anything at all that any of us have said to you? Gotta ask."

Yachay took an instant dislike to "Janie". Even though he could not understand her language, she did not seem like someone he could trust. He looked at Cole and then at Dawn. *These two I can trust.*

Cole could see Yachay's discomfort and did not want to push his patience. He had been through a lot, and she did not know his snapping point – everyone had one, and Janie was being downright irritating. "OK, Janie." Cole gently guided Yachay back a few steps to give him some air. "As you apparently have heard, Yachay has been through a lot. He has an infected arm, and we want to have him looked at. I will be happy to talk with you, Janie, and give you all the info you need. I am hoping your story can help locate Yachay's family. Let's help Dawn get Yachay to his room. Then you and I can sit down quietly and talk. Is that OK?"

"Sounds perfect." Janie smiled proudly. *This story is mine. Being just a little pushy always works. They'll talk to you just to get rid of you.* Her narrowed eyes twinkled.

Dawn smiled at Yachay and nodded at Cole. "Great. Yachay, can we take you to a nice, comfortable bed?"

Cole held Yachay's arm reassuringly as they walked down the wide corridor, accompanied by Dawn, Janie, and Evans. Yachay noticed people dressed in long white tunics that were open in the back. *What's that all about?* he wondered. His arm was hurting, and he was beginning to feel very weary. He realized he had not eaten since before he got off the boat. He and Manuel and Cindy had eaten some cereal, fruit, and flat round cakes. His mind was drifting back to breakfast. He was hungry. They entered a room with a bed. Yachay noticed one bed, yet there were four people with him. He thought he would go lie down on the floor so one of the women could sleep in the bed. He slipped his arm out of Cole's, sat down on the floor, and then lay down.

Cole and Dawn quickly reached down and helped him back up. "Come on, Yachay." They ushered him to the bed. He lay down, rolled to one side, and was asleep.

"We'll let him rest until the doctor arrives," Dawn mumbled.

The three women sat down in chairs in the corner of Yachay's room, while Evans took a chair in the hall. Cole told Dawn and Janie, and Janie's tape recorder, the whole story as she knew it. It turned out Captain Roberts had also spoken with Dawn and filled her in on Yachay's story. They answered as many of Janie's question as they could.

Janie had her story, and she had photos of Yachay standing in the hospital lobby, photos of Yachay sleeping, and photos of Yachay's belongings. *What a find this is!* Janie was intrigued by his primitive weapons and artifacts and was anxious to meet the family and find out why this boy was carrying such unusual effects.

A nicely dressed, slim, athletic man with a charming, comforting smile entered the room.

Dawn jumped up. "Dr. Menaker. Thank you for agreeing to see our unusual patient." Turning to Officer Cole, Dawn said. "Dr. Menaker is the best surgeon I know, and when I heard the boy's story, I didn't know what he would need so I asked Dr. Menaker to see him." Turning back to the doctor, she added, "The boy is exhausted, as you can see."

"Hello, Dawn. And you must be Officer Cole," Dr. Menaker said, extending his hand. "And you are Janie Briggs with the Anchorage Daily News. I've read your work. I'm Steven Menaker." Dr. Menaker shook hands with Janie and then walked over to Yachay. "I understand the boy had an uneventful plane ride from Homer. I'll need to take off that bandage and look at his arm. Can we get a temp and pressure on him, Dawn?"

Cole stepped forward. "Let me wake him." She gently touched Yachay's hand. Yachay tensed slightly, then opened his eyes to see Cole smiling down at him. He looked over and saw a new, gentle, reassuring face. Cole thought Dr. Menaker had a kind way about him and would not seem threatening to Yachay, since the boy seemed skittish and out of his comfort zone. Cole pointed at Dr. Menaker. "Yachay? Dr. Menaker." She thought for a moment. "Dr. Menaker, like Manuel." She nodded to Yachay. "Manuel was Yachay's medic on the Tustumena."

Yachay understood there was some sort of connection between Manuel and this man.

"Yachay, we're going to look at your arm," Dr. Menaker said. He slowly began removing the bandages on Yachay's right arm while Dawn took his blood pressure. "This arm looks pretty angry, Yachay. We need to give you some antibiotics, and we will keep you here for a day or two until we find your family."

Dawn started to slip a thermometer into Yachay's mouth.

"I don't think we should let go of that, or he might swallow it." Cole reached over and held the end of the thermometer that protruded from Yachay's mouth. "It's OK, Yachay." She smiled and raised her eyebrows in a sympathetic look.

Yachay was somewhat stunned by all this prodding and poking, though they were clearly not trying to hurt him. He got a good look at his wound. It hurt quite a bit, but did not look as bad as wounds he had seen on others during his life. It had minimal puss oozing from it. These people seemed to keep it clean and had healing techniques. He decided to accept their care. They kept presenting him with new people. Perhaps one of them would speak his language, and he could ask about Kawsay. They all seemed to know his name. Dr. Menaker tended to his wound and put a new bandage on it. He said something and left.

The women restarted their conversation, which was interrupted this time by a thin man with dark graying hair, wearing a burgundy sweater with elbow patches. *This must be the language professor*, Dawn thought.

"Professor Rios here to speak with Yachay – is it?" the man said. Seeing Dawn nod, the Professor walked into the room and looked over at the youth. "I understand the boy does not speak Spanish, but if I hear him, perhaps I can identify what language he speaks, even if it is not one I am proficient in. Then I can find someone who will be able to help." Professor Rios was staring intently at Yachay.

Cole pointed to Professor Rios, looked at Yachay, and said, "Rios. Rios"

"Let's begin with the Spanish. Yachay, ¿Habla usted Español? Yachay?" Rios asked hopefully.

Yachay knew this was an attempt to communicate, and if he ever wanted to find Kawsay, he better figure out a way to speak with these people. *What would we have in common? Inti? Surely they must worship Inti.* Yachay sat up straight and looked at Rios. He pointed up and declared, "Inti."

Rios perked up. *This boy is smart.* "Inti." He looked at Cole and Dawn. "Inca sun god." Professor Rios looked back at Yachay. "Inti Raimi?"

Yachay's face lit up. "Ari. Inti Raimi." Yachay had heard of the great festival. Yachay was hungry, and all he could think of was food. "Chuklu".

"What's he saying?" Cole asked.

"Corn, I think." The professor continued, "Food? Mikuna?"

Yachay looked confused.

"Mikuy?" the professor tried again.

Yachay thought. "Ari." He rubbed his stomach and pointed to his mouth.

"This boy is hungry. I'm just about positive he is speaking Quechua, but I am only weakly familiar with the language. Those ear disks are interesting. Let's try one more. Woman, talla?" He pointed at Cole.

"Ari, talla." Yachay smiled and pointed to himself. "Qari."

"Yes, Qari." Rios smiled at Yachay, then turned to Cole. "I will find you an expert who will be able to speak adequately with him. I'll look into it right away. I understand the boy is under your jurisdiction, Officer Cole? If you'll give me your direct contact number, I'll pass it along to the person who should be able to communicate with the boy." Rios looked at his watch. "I've got a class. The boy's hungry."

Cole pulled out a card with her cell number and handed it to Rios. "What were you two saying?" she asked.

"We mentioned the sun-god festival, corn, food, woman, and man." The professor smiled briefly and was out the door.

"Wow!" Janie expressed what they were all feeling. "Let's get that boy some lunch."

"I'm on that now." Dawn left the room.

Janie was scribbling notes when Dawn returned. She had a few more questions. After satisfying herself she knew as much about Yachay as Cole and Dawn did, she was finished. She left the hospital to file her story. It would be in tomorrow's paper.

Cole decided to camp out in Yachay's room. When he slept, she could sleep also, as long as Evans remained in the room and awake whenever she was asleep. She hoped the newspaper article would bring results.

Yachay spent the rest of the afternoon and evening eating. Cole began referring to him as the "bottomless pit". She was happy that he was so cooperative. *Heck, why shouldn't he cooperate. Everyone's waiting on him hand and foot and bringing him food.* She was surprised at his reaction to the TV. He was afraid of it at first, then he could not take his eyes off it. He fell asleep around 8:00 p.m. and slept until 8:00 a.m. It gave Cole a chance to call Captain Roberts and fill him in on the flight, the reporter, and day's events. Captain Roberts was relieved that the language professor was so helpful, and he reminded her that the Stevens family was likely to show up the next morning bearing gifts.

Friday morning Cole was curious to see what kind of job Janie Briggs did with the story. She and Evans read it together. They thought it was pretty good, but were surprised how thin Yachay looked in his photos and found a few errors. Cole demanded extra servings of food for him for the next few days. As Yachay was finishing his second full breakfast, the Stevens family marched in with flowers, cookies, balloons, and gifts. Cindy ran up to Yachay, handed him a helium balloon, and threw her arms around his neck and hugged him.

Her childish enthusiasm reminded him of Kawsay when she was little. He hugged her back and smiled at her. He held the string of the balloon out in front of him and looked up at the green ball floating above. He lightly jerked down on the string and watched in amazement as the balloon pulled itself back up, tightening the string. He continued to play with it as Joe,

Lisa, and Julie joined Cindy at his bedside. Lisa tied the remaining balloons to the foot of his bed. Julie handed Yachay a tin of cookies and then helped him open it after he began shaking it aggressively. He was visibly delighted with the cookies and began eating them. Joe set the flowers on the bedside table and handed Yachay a neatly wrapped package.

Yachay took the pretty box and began turning it and shaking it. Joe reached over and started the unwrapping process, which Yachay quickly understood. He uncovered something black, shiny, and hard. He was staring at it when Joe reached over and turned a knob. A loud sound broke out. Yachay was intrigued and began tuning the knobs himself.

Joe looked up at Cole. "Well, we know he doesn't understand English, but everyone loves music."

Cole smiled, realizing what her ears had in store for the next few days. *I sure hope Janie's article locates the boy's family.*

CHAPTER 19.

WHO IS YANKEE?

SEPTEMBER 4 – PRESENT YEAR
SIERRAS, CALIFORNIA

WE WAIT AND WONDER
IMPATIENCE GIVES WAY TO DOUBT
THEN WE ARE SURPRISED.

After Wednesday's meeting with John Diamond and Helmut's noisy early morning departure, Thursday had been a day without clear direction. In the morning, Kawsay and Nate explored the forest with Grandfather and Junior, and Alison and Ben tried to concentrate on their work. In the afternoon, Nate and Kawsay exchanged language and history lessons while Grandfather helped with gardening and deck painting. He had good instincts for both activities. Yet they all felt like they were just marking time. They knew they were not progressing on priorities – rescuing the family in ancient Peru, returning Nate to the future, finding Yachay and the third arrow, or returning the arrows to Israel. Waiting can be more challenging than doing. The hot, windless weather added to the tedium.

Friday began slowly. The Sun seemed reluctant to climb above the forest crown. The diverse residents of the Hunter estate shared a common lack of ambition and did not coalesce for breakfast until almost ten o'clock. The only anticipated event was the arrival of Herschel and Grace in the early afternoon for a visit and an interview with Kusi. Their arrival was the perfect tonic. They had not visited since before Nate's arrival, but had heard Nate's story from Ben and Alison, except for the episode with Ben as a boy in Gibeah. Herschel was eager to meet Kawsay's grandfather, certain he would be a trove of linguistic and cultural information. Grace also was understandably excited to meet an adult individual from what was essentially another planet. They planned to stay through Sunday and had a few small suitcases in the back of their silver Audi sedan.

As Herschel was opening the passenger door for Grace, the greetings began with Junior. Herschel was ready for the overgrown puppy this time and managed to stay on his feet. Kawsay was next to arrive. Grace saw her approaching on a run. Kawsay stopped a few feet short, hesitated for an instant, and then flung herself into Grace's warm embrace.

"Good to see you, child. How have you been?"

Kawsay held on a little longer and then let Grace go. "Hello, Grace. I am fine. Hello, Professor Herschel. Nice to see you again." Kawsay wanted to use her best English to impress her first instructor. Herschel also got a hug.

He held Kawsay by her shoulders. "It's nice to see you too. Have you and Nate kept up the language lessons?"

"Yes, but I am learning faster than he is. He has so many languages in his head. Maybe there is no space for my language!"

Alison and Ben then arrived with Nate a few steps behind. The two couples were genuinely happy to be together again and quickly exchanged warm greetings.

Nate stepped forward and announced, "I'm Nate Diamond. I've heard a lot about you from Kawsay. She really likes you guys."

Grace offered her hand to Nate. "She's one of our favorites too. I understand you two young people are both good linguists."

"Sure. We have a lot of common interests. You really taught her English quickly, Professor," Nate added, shaking Herschel's hand.

"Well, she was a great student *and* teacher," Herschel responded. "I learned things about Quechua that I could never have learned from textbooks. I found areas where the books were just wrong. I am very pleased to finally meet you, Nate. I understand we're almost neighbors."

Nate had to think for a moment. "Oh, right. But I came a long way to meet you here today!"

Alison thought they had stood in the sun long enough. "Nate and Ben will help you with your luggage. Why don't you two come inside for some refreshments? Then you'll have to meet Kawsay's grandfather. He's staying in that little guest cabin."

A short time later, as Grace and Herschel were standing in the kitchen finishing glasses of lemonade, they saw Ben and Nate enter followed by a very striking man who was smiling at them. He had a medium build, long black hair with a few streaks of gray, brown weathered skin, deep brown eyes, and a colorful, stylish sports shirt. He was looking at both of them with intense curiosity. Then he came forward with an outstretched hand and spoke in an extreme accent the words he had learned the night before from Kawsay.

"Hello, Professor Herschel. Hello, Grace. I am Kusi, taytaku of Kawsay." He gently shook Herschel's hand, then Grace's.

It was difficult to say whether Kusi or Herschel was the more enthralled. They both smiled as they looked each other in the eye.

Grace responded. "Nice to meet you, Kusi."

Herschel chose to respond in Quechua. "We are honored to meet you. Your granddaughter, Kawsay, told us about you and other members of her family. We are here today to talk with you about your life. We want to learn from you."

Kusi was ecstatic to hear his own language spoken, even in an odd accent and with unusual syntax. He had many concerns he wanted to discuss with this impressive-looking, dark-skinned man. He thought Herschel and Grace looked like royalty. "I also am honored to meet you and your wife. I am pleased that you know my language. Thank you for helping Kawsay learn your language. This is an important day for me. We have many important matters to talk about. My family is in danger and needs my help."

"I understand," Herschel assured him. "Grace and I came here today for that reason. We will be here for two days, but let us sit down now and talk." Herschel turned to Ben. "I don't know if you all want to be part of this. It will go more quickly if I don't need to translate. I can give you a summary when we take a break."

Alison had an idea. "Grace, Kawsay, and I have a lot to talk over. Ben, I know you wanted to finish the deck and Nate needs to work on the diary for his father."

Grace agreed. "That's right. I understand that Nate has been teaching Kawsay all about being an American girl, but I think I know more about it than he does."

Nate knew Grace was kidding. "Hey, she's been teaching me to be a warrior like her brother, but I promised to show her some of my martial arts moves."

Grace raised her eyebrows. "Martial arts? I rest my case." She took Kawsay by the hand and disappeared with the lemonade pitcher out to the deck. Alison followed.

Ben glanced at Nate. Both of them shrugged. "I'll get my work clothes on, and you can get your memory warmed up. Herschel, you and Kusi may use my office. Make yourselves at home."

As Herschel and Kusi started down the hall toward the office, Ben pulled Herschel aside and in low tones asked, "Did you get through to the guy in Peru that heads that cultural research institute? Does he think they'd have a place for our Inca visitors?"

Herschel's eyes twinkled as he answered. "Yes, talked with him last night. Once he got past the time travel story, which wasn't easy, he said that if he could validate our visitors' authenticity, he'd definitely want them. Actually, I think he was salivating at the prospect. Today he's on the horn to their Interior Ministry trying to arrange some kind of repatriation. He wasn't going to mention time travel, though. He thinks we should all be very careful about it and avoid publicity."

Ben was scratching his chin, thinking. "I think he's right about keeping things quiet. I'll be interested in what Kusi thinks about the idea. I have to believe he'd be happier among the descendants of his people than up here in California. I'm not as sure about Kawsay."

In a moment Herschel and Kusi were alone in Ben's office at the threshold of a verbal journey to ancient Peru. "Here, Kusi, have some lemon drink."

Herschel opened the two office windows to let in the day's light breeze, and the two men got comfortable. "Kusi, I want to understand the way things were in your village when you and Kawsay left. Kawsay told me about the agreement with the Chief that required her to leave. Why are you now concerned about the family's safety?"

Kusi leaned forward with an earnest look in his eyes. "When we sent Kawsay away, it was a very sad time for us all – her mother, her grandmother, her brother, and me. We knew life would be very difficult for her alone in the jungle. I had trained her all of her life to survive, but I questioned whether she would have a very long life. The jungle is cruel and dangerous. One of the rules made by the Chief was that her family could not help her. We were not to interfere with the gods. They alone would decide whether she would live. But we wanted to help her. I followed her to the secret caves. I did not plan to stay away very long. Once the tribe realizes I am gone, they will believe I am breaking their rule. They might hurt the family if I do not return quickly. Also, I am sure that by now, Yachay will have followed my trail. That would leave the two women without a protector. What if Yachay also fell through the singing wall and did not return? I have been gone for a long time, and the family will think I am dead. Kawsay tells me that I cannot travel home by walking, and I understand that a mystical event happened to us to place us many years into the future. Ben believes I can return home and perhaps even come back here with all the family. I do not know if this can be done. I do not believe Ben knows if this can be done. But I do know that I cannot leave my family in such danger. Every morning I awake and hope I can return on that day." His voice trailed off.

Herschel had only interrupted him a few times to clarify words or phrases that were not recognizable. There was an urgency, almost desperation, in Kusi's voice and a pleading in his eyes. Herschel wished he could help Kusi with a rescue, but had nothing to offer. So he moved on. "Kusi, I hope you can rescue your family and bring them here. Do you like it here?"

Kusi thought for a moment. "I do not know. I no longer like my village. It is a small and weak group that is alone in the great jungle. We are no longer part of a great empire. We fear our neighbors and fear the Invaders more. We may not survive. We will *not* survive if we continue to kill our babies and treat each other badly. But I do not understand this new place. Kawsay likes it very much, but I know very little about it. She has changed so much in her time here. She has grown in knowledge and in wisdom, but also has lost her respect for our traditions and beliefs. She is adapting to life here. I do not know if I can change at my age. I do not know where the family now belongs. I fear we are lost."

Herschel had thought about this in earnest since learning of Kusi's arrival. He wanted to test his idea. "Has Ben told you about people alive today who are the children of your people and who speak your language?" Kusi indicated he knew this. "They continue to grow food and raise animals, but they do not know very much about their great ancestors. They have forgotten who they really are. They are like a tree without roots."

Kusi was very interested to learn this. His furrowed brow indicated a great concern for his lost people. "If people forget their heritage, they lose their identity. They will be lost. What you tell me upsets my heart."

"I agree with you, Kusi," Herschel assured him. "Different people and tribes learn from one another. Now the world changes very quickly, and people need to change to survive. But it also is important to hold onto the wisdom and learning of the past."

Kusi wondered how Herschel could truly understand what he felt. "Since coming here, I also feel cut off from my people. I feel my spirit dying inside me. It is difficult for me to describe."

"Let me tell you of my people, Kusi," Herschel began, pleased he really could understand. "Shortly after the time of Pizarro, my people were brought to this land from a place far away to the east across another great sea. They were captured and enslaved. Many died. They were forced to work all their short lives. They were given new names and languages. They were sometimes treated like animals. After children and grandchildren were born, they lost a great deal of knowledge of their home and their past. Except for our old stories, we did not know who we were. This went on for a very long time. After a great war, we were made free and were no longer slaves, but still were cut off from our history. In recent years we have begun to study the old ways. Most do not want to return to them, but we value knowledge of our ancestors and their culture. Pizarro's Invaders enslaved many of your people, but now they are also free. Today your people are trying to learn about the old ways. They are desperate to learn their true history."

Kusi was fascinated. He was excited he knew things that people in this new world wanted to learn. "I could help them understand these things. So could my wife. She knows about the special healing plants. I know the ways of the jungle and of warfare. Do you think we could help the children of our people?"

Herschel saw that Kusi had grabbed this idea as if it had been his own. "Yes, I believe you could. Listen to what I learned yesterday. There are large teaching places where people work hard to discover the old ways of your people. They study places where villages once existed. They look at stone walls, pottery, even garbage. They try to fit all the pieces together, but there is much they cannot figure out. They cannot talk to the people of the past; now there are only dry bones. I have a friend who works with one of these teaching places. It is located close to your village. If you wish, you could talk with him. It will be difficult for him and those who work with him to believe a person from so many years ago could be alive today. Until I met Kawsay, I did not believe it was possible. But when he realizes you are a visitor from the past, I am certain he will want you to help him and his friends come to understand their history."

"Oh, I could help him very much. Yes, I want to talk with this man soon, but I cannot let this get in the way of rescuing my family. It is all I can think about now. Once we are all safe, I want to meet your friend." Kusi was enthralled by the idea of a possible place *and* purpose. "What is your friend's name?"

"Augusto Hurtado. I met him many years ago when we were both students."

"That is not a name I recognize," said Kusi, shaking his head.

"No, it is a name taken from the Spanish. Many of your people today have taken such names. They have some ancestors who are Spanish, so they have roots in both cultures," Herschel explained.

Kusi was somewhat dismayed. "Are you saying that my people and the Invaders have married each other?"

"Yes," Herschel answered. "The same is true of my people and people all over the world."

"I understand," Kusi remarked. "Kawsay told me that Ben is from a place called Israel and Alison from a place called Minnesota."

"Oh, I did not know that. I thought Ben and his brother grew up here."

Kusi shook his head and responded earnestly, "No, Kawsay says he came here when he was twelve years old. He came through the same sucking tunnel we did, but from a time long before my people."

Herschel thought Kusi and Kawsay must have mistranslated something, but determined to ask Ben about it. "Right now, Kusi, please tell me more about your early life, your family, and the life of your tribe. I have a 'tape recorder' here that will remember your words for me to study later. Tell me what is most important."

Kusi closed his eyes and envisioned his home. He smiled at a private thought and then began to describe his youth, his training as a warrior, his great battles, the founding of his village, his marriage, and his children. He told of the struggles to find and grow enough food, the dangers of the jungle animals, and the strife that had grown up within the tribe.

Herschel did not interrupt except to gain clarification of linguistic forms he did not know. He realized that Kusi was a natural storyteller, whose repertoire of tales was emblematic of a people with a strong oral tradition. He wondered if the older stories had been embellished over time.

As Kusi was beginning the second hour of his narrative and beginning to tell of Sumaq and her husband, there was a light knock at the door. Alison poked her head in. "I hate to disturb you two, but we'll be eating in about twenty minutes. Thought you'd like some advance notice." She smiled.

"Thanks, Alison," Herschel said, turning off the recorder. "We'll need a break soon anyway." Alison slipped silently out, closing the door with a quiet click. "Kusi, we will be eating soon. We can continue later. All that you tell me is of great interest. Also, listening to you speak helps me understand your language so much better. Is there anything you want to ask me right now?"

"I want to know how the great healer fixed Kawsay's lip. I understand you were there."

"I traveled with Kawsay to the healer's, or 'doctor's', work place because Kawsay did not yet know her new language very well. I wanted to explain to her what would happen so she would not be fearful."

"Kawsay is not fearful!" Kusi asserted.

Herschel was surprised by the exclamation, but recovered quickly. "I did not know Kawsay very well at that time. But you are correct about her. She is a very brave young woman." He then explained outpatient surgery, anesthesia, tissue reconstruction, sutures, bandages, and antibiotics. This strained his Quechua vocabulary beyond its limits, so it took some time to explain in a way Kusi could apprehend.

"So, this 'doctor' did not use any spirits to assist the healing?" Kusi asked.

"Ah, I see. We all prayed that God would help the doctor. But the doctor used skill she had been taught in a great learning place called 'medical school'. Kawsay's was a small treatment. Sometimes doctors open up people's chests and fix their hearts. If a person's heart is very sick, they can take the heart of another person who recently died and use it to replace the heart of the first person. They connect it to him and close his chest. Except for a scar, the person can live for many years like that." Herschel noticed the look of incredulity and open jaw that Kusi was displaying.

"This is too much for me to believe," Kusi said. "You must be joking!"

Herschel imagined how this must sound to Kusi. "Here, look at this." He stood up and untucked his shirt. He then moved his belt downward and pointed out a scar. "This is not a wound from a fight. When I was a boy, I had a problem with a small part of me called 'appendix'. It became full of poison and had to be taken out of my body or it would kill me. A doctor used a very sharp knife to cut through my skin and muscle. He found the appendix, cut it out, and sewed me up again. This doctor kept me alive."

Kusi was partly convinced, though the scar looked a lot like a knife wound in his own side. His nose caught an aroma that had snaked under the door. Herschel smelled it too, and they gave each other a conspiratorial look. Kusi spoke. "Thank you, my new friend, for spending this time with me. I hope we will talk more later. Now, I believe we need to help the other people eat some very good food!"

Alison and Ben had added two leaves to the table to accommodate everyone. With Kawsay's and Grace's assistance, they had taken available ingredients and made what they dubbed "Cuzco Casserole". The dessert was Grace's homemade apple pie. They were just finishing when the phone rang.

Kawsay liked telephones and began to rise before the others heard the ring. "Hello, Hunters." She paused. "Oh, hello, Helmut. How are you? Are you in Alaska now?" She nodded to the unseen Helmut. "Yes, I am fine too. We are eating Grace's apple pie. Shall I save a piece for you?" A pause. "OK, I'll get him." She held the instrument with extreme care as if it was occupied by a tiny Helmut. "Ben, Helmut says it is very important right now to talk to him."

Ben felt a small pang of anxiety as he rose from the table. It was unusual for Helmut to call so soon after the start of an expedition. "Thank you, Kawsay," he said as he took the cordless phone from her. All eyes were on Ben. "Helmut. What's up? Everything OK?"

"I'm fine. I got in late last night to Iliamna and spent the day making arrangements to travel into the bush. I hired a local outfitter. He hasn't seen the large birds himself, but knows someone who has. I had some time today to begin looking into the monster fish stories, but I'm going to concentrate on the birds first."

Ben was still not sure what prompted the call. "I'm sorry we didn't have more time to talk before you left. Sorry we were so busy."

"Am I interrupting anything right now?" Helmut asked.

"Not really. We were just finishing dessert. There's quite a group for dinner, including Herschel and Grace. Wish you were here!" Ben responded.

Helmut paused. "Are you on that cordless? Maybe you should put me on speaker. I ran across a newspaper article that might be of interest."

Ben brought the phone to the table and clicked the speaker button. The diners were pleased to have the opportunity to hear both sides of the discussion. "Can you hear OK, Helmut?" Ben asked, clicking up the volume.

"Fine. Sorry to interrupt your dessert, but I wanted to pass on something I saw in the paper up here. Here the morning paper doesn't arrive until afternoon. I saw an article about a kid that was a stowaway on one of their car ferries coming up from Kodiak. Seems a little girl fell overboard, and the kid jumped in after her. Saved her life. Those vessels are pretty tall. I'll bet they fell three stories or so. What's more amazing is that he apparently held her high out of the water for quite a while before they could turn around and pick them up. It's remarkable they found them since it was around midnight. I suspect the water was about forty-five degrees. An adult can last only fifteen minutes in water that cold, twenty at the most, before losing consciousness." Helmut stopped. "Oh, yeah, what's even more interesting is that he had an arm wound that looked like a claw mark from a very large bear, probably one of the coastal brown bears they have on the island. They Medevac'd him up to a big hospital in Anchorage."

"That's quite a story, Helmut," Alison said. "I hope he'll be all right."

"Sounds like he's in good shape," Helmut assured her. "He's quite a hero, but they don't know what to do with him. Seems he doesn't speak English, and they're not sure where he's from. Didn't have any papers on him. All they got out of him was a name, something like 'Yankee'."

"Helmut, this is Herschel. Did the article give any other clues about him? Anything about his language or dress?"

"Nothing about language, except that he *can* speak; they just don't know what. What most caught my interest, though, was the stuff he had with him. Seems he had a knapsack with some pouches filled with grain, a sling-like weapon with some stones, another device with three stones connected together, a spear, and ... oh yeah, there was also a fancy dagger with jewels on the handle."

"What was he wearing?" Kawsay asked, unusually excited.

"The article said he did not have pants and a shirt. They described it as a smock. He didn't have regular shoes but sandals. You know, Kawsay, all this reminded me of what you wore when you first arrived," Helmut said. "So I thought I'd let you all know. There were photos. The boy has long dark hair and earrings. Some people thought he might be Hispanic, but that didn't wash." He paused. "I think there's a website. You can look for yourselves. Let's see. ... Yeah, here it is. Oh, it's just ADN.com. Take a look and let me know. I'm curious."

"We'll do that right away, Helmut," Ben said. "Will you have the satellite phone with you so we can reach you?"

"Affirmative, though I won't be going anywhere until tomorrow at the earliest, and I might wait another day or two for the weather to clear. I'd rather not get soaked the first day out. There's plenty of time for that later."

"Got it. So we can reach you through the outfitter tonight?" Ben asked.

"Right. Nice little lodge. I'll let you go," Helmut responded.

Hearing the line click off, Ben turned off the cordless. They all looked at each other, except Kawsay who was trying to explain everything to Grandfather in a jumble of excited words.

"Let's leave the dishes," Alison suggested. "I think we should take a look at that website."

There was a chorus of chair noise as everyone rose to head for the office, interrupted by the phone ringing again. *Did Helmut forget to tell us something?* Ben wondered. "Hello, Hunters."

"This is Professor Rhodes secretary calling," said a formal woman's voice. "Is he there, please?"

"Yes, just a moment." Ben held out the phone to Herschel, who gave him a puzzled look. "It's for you; it's your secretary, Doris."

"Doris? ... Yes. ... Who? ... When? ... What did they say?" There was a long pause. Herschel was holding up an index finger as if asking everyone to stay put. "How did they know to call me? ... Oh, I see. ... Could I handle it by phone? ... Who is the contact person?" He signaled for a pen and paper. "I'm ready. ... Let me read that back. Officer Cole, State Troopers." He recited the number. "Oh, that's a cell phone? ... Good. Thank you, Doris. I'll take it from here. ... Yes, I still plan to be back Sunday night. I'll let you know if there is a change. ... Yes, it is unusual. Goodbye." Herschel turned to a room full of raised eyebrows.

"What was that about, dear?" Grace asked. "Doris wouldn't call if it wasn't important."

"I don't think this is just a coincidence," Herschel answered. "My office received a call this afternoon from a language professor from the University of Alaska Anchorage who had gotten my name from … well, I'm not sure where, but he tracked me down. My website lists many of the languages I know about. He'd been consulted by the police, or I guess the State Troopers, about a young man they have in custody. They need to communicate with him but cannot. This professor, I think Doris said his name is Rios, thought it might be a South American dialect from the northern Andes." *She said Rios thought it was Quechua, but I don't want to get everyone too excited here.* "He has spent time in Ecuador and recognized some of the boy's words. If I thought I could help, he told Doris I should call the Troopers to find out more."

"Before you call," Ben suggested, "let's take a look at the newspaper website." He led the group to his office, and they gathered around his computer screen as it blinked to life.

No one wanted to raise too much hope about the mysterious hero, but the air of anticipation was obvious. Only Kawsay spoke, again to insure that Grandfather was included. Kusi had not yet divined the difference between a computer and a television or between a DVD and the Internet.

The desired article was featured on the paper's opening webpage. The headline and initial paragraphs were on the first page.

"Ben, not all of us can see," Alison said. Will you read it to us?"

Ben adjusted the screen and began to read to a totally attentive audience:

STOWAWAY HERO SAVES GIRL FROM FRIGID WATERS
Mystery Boy in Custody of Troopers at Anchorage Hospital
By Janie Briggs
September 4

Shortly after midnight Thursday morning as passengers were on deck enjoying an early appearance of the Auroras, 6-year-old Cindy Stevens fell off the stern of the M/V Tustumena into frigid waters east of Afognak Island. The crowded vessel was traveling from Kodiak Island to Homer. According to Cindy's 8-year-old sister, Julie, a dark-haired teenage boy wearing earrings and a dress jumped into the dark water to rescue Cindy. Julie, who earlier had explored all the decks, rushed to the Bridge and alerted Captain T. W. Roberts.

The Captain turned the 296-foot ferry and retraced his route, lighting the water with searchlights. When the crew spotted the girl, she was being held out of the water on the shoulders of her rescuer, apparently to help prevent loss of body heat. Crewmembers used a lifeboat to retrieve them. Cindy and her rescuer were brought to the ship's infirmary and treated for hypothermia. They spent about 15 minutes in the water, and, considering the water temperature, would have soon gone under.

Who is this brave young man who saved the life of little Cindy? That important fact remains a mystery at this time. If he had identification, it was lost in the water. According to Captain Roberts there is no record of him as a passenger. Efforts to communicate with him in English or Spanish were unavailing, though he may have identified himself as "Yankee" or something similar.

He was wearing some sort of smock and sandals and had unusual gold disks in his earlobes. He also had a knapsack containing a primitive spear and knife, pouches with grains, an old metal stamp with the letters P.R., a woven sling, three stones attached to each other by cords, and a dagger with a jeweled handle. Perhaps most amazing, the young hero appears to have earlier survived an altercation with a Kodiak bear resulting in four deep claw wounds on his upper arm, which were treated on board during the remainder of the voyage.

Because of his status as a potential stowaway, the young hero was turned over to the State Troopers upon arrival in Homer. He was accompanied by Officer Marguerite Cole on a Medevac flight to Anchorage and was admitted to Alaska Regional Hospital for treatment of his wounded arm. Officer Cole describes the boy as curious and confused, as if he had never before seen an airplane or hospital but showing no sign of aggressive behavior.

Ben stopped reading long enough to hit "read more" to go to the next screen. The article quickly concluded and had three small photos along the right side of the screen. He was about to continue reading when he was interrupted by Kawsay speaking to Grandfather in rapid Quechua.

"Yachay! Look, Grandfather! Here, come closer. See? That looks like Yachay!" She was pointing to the first photo of a good-looking young man, framed by two women, one in uniform. He was looking into the camera as if it was a great curiosity. The images were small and Ben zoomed them to a larger size.

Grandfather peered intently at the screen, first where Kawsay pointed, and then at the next photo. He saw the second photo of the boy asleep in a bed and then a third of his earthly treasures arrayed on a table. He nodded his head. "Yes, I believe you are right Kawsay. It looks like Yachay. Why do we see him here? What is happening?"

"I think he was looking for us and got lost." She switched to English. "Where is Yachay now? Can we go to him?"

The rest of the group had figured out that "Yankee" was actually Yachay. Their thoughts were racing forward in different streams, imagining the implications.

Only Nate noticed Kawsay's questions. "I think he's in Alaska. It is a part of this country that is very far north. The people there are wondering what to do with him." Nate paused. "We have to go and help Yachay. Imagine what he must be going through."

"Are you sure it's Yachay and not someone who looks like him?" Ben asked Kawsay.

She looked again at the screen, which was filled with the photo of the table displaying the boy's possessions. She put her nose very close. "Yes, these are Yachay's." She pointed to one of the items. "Oh, look Ben! See, right here is his spear with the lucky arrow tucked into a place in the side. No one else has a spear like that."

Ben looked where she was pointing and saw a spear much like Kawsay's, except there was an arrow wedged into a groove along its side. His heart skipped a beat. *The third arrow. I never thought I'd see it! This is amazing!* "I see it. Yes, it's just like you said, Kawsay! Look everyone, Yachay's spear with the arrow!"

Alison and Nate shared Ben's excitement, but the Herschel and Grace did not understand what it was all about.

Herschel spoke up. "Let's hear the rest of the article."

Ben took a deep breath, shrunk the screen back to normal, and began reading again:

> *The State Troopers are trying to determine what language the boy speaks, so they can locate an interpreter and eventually his family and home. The chairman of the Department of Language at UAA, Professor Ernesto Rios, spoke with the boy soon after his arrival at Regional. Based on a cryptic word exchange involving "sun-god festival, corn, food, woman, and man", Rios suspects the boy's language may be an ancient tongue still spoken on a limited basis today in remote areas of Peru, Ecuador, and other South American countries. Professor Rios hopes to locate someone who will be able to serve as an interpreter.*
>
> *Where is "Yankee" from? Who is his family? What will happen to this stowaway hero who dove into icy Alaska waters to save a little girl and then held her on his shoulders to keep her from losing body heat? Why does he carry a primitive spear, wear "earrings and a dress", and speak an exotic language? Joe Stevens, Cindy's father, wants to thank the parents for the heroic act of their son. If you can identify Cindy's rescuer, contact the Alaska State Troopers.*

As Ben finished reading, Alison verbalized what they all were thinking. "I think we have just received *two* notices of Yachay's arrival – first Helmut and then the call from Herschel's office."

"Herschel," Grace asked, "don't you think you should call and offer your services as an interpreter?"

"Oh, I intend to do just that," Herschel responded, "but first I think we need to put our heads together and think this through. If we don't handle it right, our friend Yachay could end up in the hands of the immigration officials; who knows where that would lead." He paused and added. "I wonder what they would think of our other Inca visitors. This kind of publicity could spin out of control."

Kusi was still confused. "Kawsay, please, where is Yachay."

Kawsay explained that he was far away but at least alive and in the present time. He had been injured by a large animal, but was doing fine. He saved a little girl who fell off a large boat into cold ocean water.

"Yachay is brave and strong. It is good he did this deed," Grandfather said to Kawsay. "But he is looking for us. He will not stay in one place long, but will resume the search. Will he be able to find us here?"

Kawsay related Grandfather's concern to the group. Nate was first to respond. "No way. Alaska is far away. He'd never find us up here in the woods. We need to find him."

"And soon!" Ben added.

Kawsay related this to Grandfather who then asked through her, "How can we go to him quickly?"

Herschel answered Kusi in Quechua. "We will go in an 'airplane', which flies like Helmut's 'helicopter', but goes much faster." To the others he added, "I think I should check with the airlines and see if I can fly up there tomorrow. I'm not sure there are direct flights from the Bay Area, but I might be able to get there by late afternoon."

Ben understood the need for haste. "I think every minute counts. Maybe Helmut can get there in the morning or even tonight. He said he was delaying the start of his expedition for a day or two anyway."

Alison put her hand on Ben's shoulder. "Honey, I wonder if a member of Yachay's family should go too. It is essential the authorities allow us bring Yachay back here with us. How can we convince them they should? We don't have any official standing, and we're not his family. Yachay doesn't even know us."

"Maybe we can talk to the boy tonight by phone and set his mind at ease," Grace suggested in soothing tones. "You know, tell him to stay put until Herschel or Helmut or whoever can get there."

Ben was turning off the computer. "Let's go to the living room where we can be comfortable and figure this out. There are a lot of pieces to this and not a lot of time. We need to do everything exactly right."

They adjourned and soon filled the couch and chairs, with Kawsay and Nate taking up residence on the floor by the redwood coffee table. Alison said to the group, "I think our minds are racing. Let's stop and think. What is the best way to retrieve Yachay and get him back here."

They grew quiet for a few minutes. Then the suggestions began to emerge, with Herschel and Kawsay keeping Kusi in the discussion. The sticky questions seemed to be who should go on the mission and how to persuade the Troopers to turn over the stowaway hero to them. The initial idea was to send only Herschel and Ben, partly because commercial airline travel would not be possible at this time for Kawsay and Grandfather since they had no IDs and no legal status.

Then Nate had a proposal that changed the plan dramatically. "Hey, I just remembered. My dad has friends at a company he's financed who keep a corporate jet at the San Jose airport. When the executives aren't using it, they rent it out to others, complete with pilots. It isn't cheap, but there aren't security screenings either. Remember, my dad said he'd do anything he could to help us. Why don't I call him?" Despite objections that this would be asking too much, Nate insisted.

Ben placed the call and found John home. After greetings, Ben explained, "Alison and Nate are here with me along with Kawsay and her grandfather and also our friends Herschel and Grace Rhodes. We've had a surprising development here Nate wanted to tell you about. May I put you on speaker?"

"Sure. My son is at a football game with some friends and their parents. What's up?"

"Hi, Dad. Hope everything is OK. I have a favor to ask," Nate began.

"Sure, Nate. Good to hear your voice. I've been thinking a lot about you. How can I help?"

Nate related the story of Yachay's predicament and the need to transport a group of about seven up to Anchorage immediately, no questions asked. "I know this is asking a lot, and it isn't exactly about me and my problem. But it's really important to Kawsay and her grandfather, and if we don't rescue Yachay, who knows what the government might do with him! Besides, he has the third arrow that needs to be returned to Israel."

At this Herschel's eyebrows raised, and he looked at Ben. Ben did not notice, but

Herschel made another mental note to ask him about these references to Israel.

After some discussion, with John insisting on bearing the expense, they arrived at a plan. "OK, Ben," John said. "I'll call about the jet and get back to you in less than an hour."

Nate shrugged and smiled at everyone. "Well, looks like we all can go!" That allowed the preparations to proceed. John called back within twenty minutes announcing good news. They could have the jet for up to 5 days beginning the next morning. It would be ready to fly at 10:00 a.m.

In another thirty minutes, the plan was nearly complete. Ben handed Nate a pad of paper. "Nate, can you jot all this down?" The semi-legible handwriting read:

1. Herschel call Troopers to offer services.
2. Herschel call Hurtado: Peruvian government to authorize Yachay's release.
3. Ben arrange hotel and call Helmut to fly to Anchorage and pick up inoculations.
4. Alison supervise packing warm clothing.
5. Nate and Kawsay find clothes for Yachay.
6. Alison ask Robertsons to look after Junior.

Everyone went into action with great energy, and people actually answered their phones. Dr. Hurtado already had a contact in the Peruvian Ministry of the Interior who was very interested in helping repatriate nationals from the U.S. to their remote mountain villages, even if he did not know they were over 400 years old. There were private suites available at an Anchorage hotel, and the Robertson family would be delighted to keep Junior for a few days. Helmut was excited that he had helped find Yachay and would defer his expedition. He would also pick up the inoculations and meet everyone at the Anchorage hospital.

The most interesting call was made to Officer Cole, who was trying to catch a few winks despite Yachay's channel surfing on his new radio. He had settled on a classical station just long enough to put her to sleep. Her phone vibrated her awake. "Officer Cole," she said in a sleepy voice.

"Good evening, Officer Cole. This is Dr. Herschel Rhodes, a linguist from Stanford University. Professor Rios contacted me today about assisting as an interpreter for a young man who is in your care."

Marguerite Cole shook out the cobwebs and was at full alert in a matter of seconds. "Yes, Dr. Rhodes was it? Yes, do you think you can help?"

"I believe I can. From what the Professor told us, he believes you need an expert in the Quechua language. I have a good background in that language and have had occasion recently to refine my skills. I would be delighted to help out."

"That's great. Do you know the situation up here? Did he fill you in?"

"I read an article in your local paper about the young man." He paused. *Now for the hard part.* "I think Professor Rios contacting me was very fortuitous because I know the boy's family and believe I can help him return home."

Officer Cole was more than surprised by this development. Her primary concern was not Yachay's unauthorized presence on the ferry – Cindy's dad had already offered to cover the fare, and Captain Roberts had urged her to treat Yachay as a hero, not a criminal. Her primary concern had become what to *do* with her charge. He was due to be released from the hospital the next day, and she had already made an inquiry to the U.S. Citizenship and Immigration Office to help determine the options. "You know his family? Are you sure? Well, where is his family? Where are they from?"

Herschel had rehearsed this part in his mind several times. "They are from a remote Peruvian village that is not really part of the twenty-first century. I have a friend who is involved in cultural preservation for natives, and he is working with his government to repatriate the family."

"That's very interesting, Dr. Rhodes," she observed, becoming a bit suspicious about the "coincidence". "What is the boy doing in Alaska?"

Another good question Herschel had anticipated. "We were hoping you could tell us. His sister and grandfather showed up down here in California a few months ago at the mountain retreat home of some friends of mine, Ben and Alison Hunter. They're archeologists, also from Stanford, currently on sabbatical. Yachay's relatives will be returning to Peru soon, and they obviously want Yachay to go with them. They want to know what he's doing in Alaska."

"I can't help you with that," Cole responded. "Not that it's confidential; we just don't know any more than you probably read in the paper. And since we can't communicate with him, he hasn't been able to tell us anything."

"Can you tell me how his shoulder injury is doing?"

"Well, it looked pretty bad, but there's no nerve damage, and the muscles are still attached. Prognosis is good. From the spread of the claw marks, we believe the bear must have been very large. Some are over ten feet tall. An animal like that can take you out with one swipe."

Herschel ventured further. "Is he in any trouble? The family is concerned."

"Probably not, but we can't determine that until we're able to talk to him." Officer Cole was not sure how much to say. "We're not eager to criminalize anything given his age and also because he's becoming quite a local celebrity. The public likes heroes and mysteries. He's both!"

"So, things are up in the air?"

"Yeah, that's how it seems," she responded. "You know, he seems like a good kid. He doesn't complain about the pain or act like the rescue was anything unusual. He's been absorbed by gadgets, like the TV and a radio the girl's dad gave him. You said his village was remote. That doesn't surprise me. He acted as if he'd never seen a plane before or even a squad car. It's like he's from the past or another planet."

"I know what you mean," Herschel said as blandly as he could. "I thought the same about his sister and grandpa. But they're fine people. If you'd like me to help out, I can be up there tomorrow by mid-afternoon."

"Oh, yes, by all means. But maybe we can handle it by phone." Officer Cole was concerned about needless expenses.

"Well, if it was only a matter of translation, that would probably work," Herschel said, trying to sound casual. "But if things fall into place, we hope to have authorization in a day or so from the Peruvian government to take custody of Yachay. I'd like to bring along the Hunters and perhaps the sister and grandfather. We'll bear the travel expenses. Sounds like

Yachay has been through a lot, and I suspect his family would look pretty good to him right now!"

"Well, that would be fine. The little girl's father said he'd like to thank the family if he could. Do they speak English?"

"I've taught the sister quite a bit but not the grandfather. Shall I call you when I get to town? Where will Yachay be?" Herschel asked.

"He's slated to be discharged sometime tomorrow, but I could keep him here at Regional Hospital by Merrill Field until you arrive," Officer Cole answered.

"Oh, that reminds me. I almost forgot. Ben Hunter's brother is a physician and will be there by tomorrow morning. If necessary, he can take over the medical care of the boy. His name is Dr. Helmut Hunter. He's already in Alaska on a pleasure trip, and we asked him to meet us in Anchorage tomorrow."

"Well, you all have been very busy!" the Officer exclaimed, but then realized her remark could have been misunderstood. "I mean, we are grateful for all you and the others are doing and hope you can help us untangle this little mystery."

Herschel thought this was the time to ask a favor. "Do you think I could talk with Yachay to let him know that someone will be there tomorrow to help him communicate? It might relax him and help him rest easy." Herschel knew how to put people at ease.

Marguerite Cole found herself wanting to trust him and not exert unnecessary control. "Well, he's right here looking at me," she responded, using her softer, off-duty voice. "I think he's trying to figure out what a cell phone is. Maybe you can explain to him that I'm not some crazy person talking to my own hand." She brought the tiny phone over to Yachay placed it in his hand. She moved his hand up to the side of his face and smiled at him. Yachay's stare became one of surprise as he heard a voice come into his ear – a man speaking to him in his own language.

"Hello, Yachay. My name is Herschel Rhodes. You are hearing my voice on an invention called a 'telephone'. I am far away, but my voice is coming through the air into the telephone. If you speak, I will hear your voice. Tell me if you hear me and understand my words."

Yachay understood perfectly, but had never talked to someone in the air. He looked at Officer Cole with a puzzled look. She nodded encouragingly, so he responded, "Yes, I hear you very well."

"Good. Yachay, I am coming to see you tomorrow in an 'airplane'. Remember the invention that you flew in with Officer Cole? I will be there in the afternoon. I speak Quechua and also the language of the people around you there. I will help you talk with them. They want to learn how you came to that place and why you were on the large boat. You did a great thing to help the little girl who fell into the water."

Yachay thought it was a great thing too, but he was a warrior trained to do great things and then act as if it was nothing. "She is a beautiful little girl. I am pleased that she lives."

Herschel noted Yachay's humility. "Yachay, I will now tell you things that will bring you joy. It will help your thoughts to be peaceful. Do not show your feelings to the woman in the room with you, but listen to all I will say. Do you understand?"

Yachay wondered what this voice could tell him to ease his mind. "Yes, I will listen but not show my thoughts on my face."

Herschel took a deep breath. "Good. I know you have been looking for Kawsay and for your Grandfather, Kusi." Herschel heard a muffled gasp and then silence as Yachay remembered to mask his feelings. "They have been hoping to find you also. They are fine and want to see you. I will bring them with me tomorrow. We are planning to take you away from there and help you return to your home."

Yachay's face was like stone, but his heart was pounding. "I left my village to find Grandfather. He and I must return to the village soon because my mother and grandmother are in danger."

"Yes, I understand. Your grandfather is also eager to return to help them. He told me this earlier today."

"You talked to my grandfather today?" Yachay asked excitedly.

"Yes, please stay calm. He is here with me. He wants to talk with you now. Wait just one moment."

Herschel was sitting in the Hunters' living room using their cordless phone. The entire group was there, and he was flanked by Kawsay and Kusi. The others were listening intently to a one-sided conversation in Quechua. "He's fine. Let's let Kusi talk with him next." Herschel put the phone on the table in front of Kusi and pushed the speaker button.

Kusi began speaking very loudly at it until he was coached to speak in a normal tone. "I am Kusi, grandfather of Yachay." Kusi listened with tremendous anticipation.

"I am Yachay. Can you hear my voice?" Everyone heard.

"Yes. I do not understand how this invention moves our voices through the air. I do not understand many things about this new place." Kusi was staring at the phone, feeling foolish to be talking to a small shiny box as if it was his handsome grandson.

"Grandfather, I left our village after you were gone for seven days. I have had many strange experiences here, but I am pleased to find you now. We must return to the village at once. Grandmother and Mother will be in danger from the people. They will think we are helping Kawsay, which is forbidden." Yachay was speaking excitedly, but trying to look calm.

Kusi was not sure how to explain to Yachay that the trip home presented many problems. He knew he could only speak a short time and they would be together soon. "Yachay, tomorrow I will see you, and we will begin our journey home. Until then, stay where you are and heal from your wounds. I am very proud of your deeds." Kawsay was making gestures that it was her turn and time was short. Kusi nodded at her.

"Yachay, this is Kawsay. I am fine. My lip has been fixed. I am staying with good people who care for me. Thank you for coming to find us. We will come to see you tomorrow. You must heal fast so you can rescue Mother and Grandmother. Do you have any questions?"

Her confident, rapid-fire delivery was a bit overwhelming to her big brother who wondered if this really was his little sister. "Kawsay, you sound different."

"I have been in this new place for more than three months. I have new friends and have learned a new language. This is a wonderful new world. I hope you like it."

"Kawsay, I have a question. What *is* this strange place with these inventions that work like magic. What has happened?" Yachay was finally able to ask the question that had been on his mind.

"Oh, that is right, you don't know yet. Yachay, the sucking tunnel behind the singing wall moved us a long distance. It also moved us about 400 years into the future. To rescue our family, we need to go back through the tunnel and then bring them here with us. I will explain this more when I see you. First, we need to come and get you and bring you here where I am. Then, after you are stronger, we can go back for Mother and Grandmother."

Yachay no longer doubted that this was Kawsay's voice, but what she said was very troubling. He noticed that Officer Cole was showing signs of impatience. "Yes," he said, "we must hurry." Kawsay handed the phone back to Herschel, who took it off speaker.

"Yachay, this is Herschel again. Kawsay and your grandfather are eager to see you. In the morning, another doctor will come to see you. He does not speak your language, but he is a friend. His name is Helmut. He is the brother of Kawsay's friend, Ben. He will help you to heal. Now, please give the 'telephone' back to Officer Cole."

Yachay obeyed and offered the device to Officer Cole. She took it and asked, "Are you still there, Dr. Rhodes?"

"Yes, thank you. I explained to Yachay a little about returning to his home and told him not to worry."

"Well, he seemed pretty interested in what you were saying!"

"Wouldn't you be excited to talk to a person who could explain what was happening to you and to hear that your family was coming to take you home?" Herschel suggested.

"Of course. I look forward to meeting all of you tomorrow. Perhaps we can get this resolved to everyone's satisfaction," Officer Cole said.

"I look forward to working with you, Officer. You'll have to excuse me now. We're getting up quite early to get to the airport."

"It's been a long day for me too. I'll be here all night in case something comes up. I want to be sure Yachay is treated right. Good night, Professor."

"Good night, Officer."

Herschel set the phone down and looked around the room. Seeing curious looks, he gave a brief summary of the discussions with Officer Cole and Yachay. "I wasn't kidding about getting to bed. If the packing is all done, let's set a few alarms and call it a night." There was no argument from anyone. They had their plan and their objective.

Ben, as usual, made it into bed a few minutes before Alison. She knew he was not asleep when she emerged from the bathroom and slipped in beside him.

"Thanks for warming the bed," she whispered. "Do you think we're doing the right thing taking everyone along? I've begun to worry about what might happen if the whole story about our Inca friends gets out."

Ben noticed how Alison's thoughts often followed the same channels as his. "I'm concerned too. Who knows what our immigration people would do with people who claimed to be immigrants from another age. Would they lock them up or send them somewhere?"

"Will immigration officials get involved?"

"I don't know, honey. Herschel is hopeful that a communication from the Peruvian embassy will be enough. He's really stepped up to the plate on this and solved problems before I even thought of them." Ben finally rolled over and looked at her. He was always stunned by Alison's natural beauty and disarmed by her loving, searching eyes. "Um, what do you think about the idea of having Kawsay's family return to Peru and work with cultural anthropologists down there?"

"I think it's a brilliant idea," Alison answered, "except I'm not so sure about Kawsay. I was talking to her about it. She'd like to visit and even try to find the site of her old village, but I think she'd prefer to spend more time up here. She has bad associations with that area. Who can blame her? But I was thinking, if her mother and grandmother manage to get here and then settle in Peru, Kawsay may want to stay with them. After all, she's only thirteen."

"What about Nate?" Ben asked.

"What about.... Oh, you mean their attachment?" Ben nodded. "Ben, do you think there's anything serious there?"

"Actually, I do. I've been watching them, and they're very attentive to each other. They consult on everything. It's innocent and beautiful to see, but Nate will be leaving before long. It will be hard for them."

"You're right," Alison agreed. "But if all goes well, Nate will be back in a few years. Maybe they can meet again."

"Maybe it's something they can hope for to make the parting easier," Ben added. "We have a lot of planning to do. I just hope we are able to retrieve Yachay *and* my arrow."

"Darling, it's *his* arrow. Do you think he'll let you have it?" Alison had a way of finding important questions that he had overlooked.

"Honey, I don't know, but thank you for suggesting a question I can think about for the next three hours."

CHAPTER 20

UNION AND REUNION

SEPTEMBER 5 – PRESENT YEAR
ANCHORAGE, ALASKA

A NEW LOVE IS FOUND
A BRAVE HERO IS RESCUED
IN THE LAST FRONTIER.

Officer Cole woke up abruptly, and to her surprise Janie Briggs was standing over her with a cup of coffee in each hand. *A peace offering no doubt.* Scanning the room, still in a daze, Cole met two pairs of raised-eyebrows – first Officer Evans', then Yachay's. They each wore the same weak smile that spoke volumes about their collective opinion of Janie Briggs.

"Hi, Officer Cole, remember me, Janie Briggs from The Daily News? I really hope I didn't startle you." Janie giggled.

Cole could not tell if it was a nervous giggle or a well-crafted technique. Cole could not help but notice Yachay's self-possessed, almost noble demeanor. He had transformed from being an agitated boy into a confident, relaxed young man during his conversation with Professor Rhodes. *What did that professor say to him?* Cole remembered Janie. "Yes, Ms. Briggs?" she asked, rising to her feet.

"Janie, please call me Janie. I brought you a latte."

"Boy, you have no idea how good that sounds right now." Marguerite Cole began feeling guilty about her not-so-positive thoughts toward Janie.

"I *can* imagine." Janie winked at Cole. "I spoke with the Chief Nursing Officer, Dawn, early this morning and realized I had written Yachay's name as 'Yankee' in my article. I just wanted to apologize to everyone. I hope it didn't set anything back as far as finding his family." Janie was probing for information. *This boy is just too interesting to let this story drop.*

Cole did not know how much she wanted to tell Janie about her conversation with Professor Rhodes. She graciously reached for the latte, smiling at Janie. "You know, Janie, I don't think it hurt at all. Remember that Professor Rios from The University of Alaska who was able to communicate with Yachay yesterday? Well, he found another professor who spoke at length with Yachay on the phone last night and will be coming up to Anchorage to meet him. He thinks he can help us find Yachay's family." Cole decided to not say more to Janie until Dr. Rhodes arrived later that day.

Janie pulled a business card out of her blue blazer pocket, flicking her neatly cut hair back. Then she locked sincere eyes onto Cole's. "Officer Cole, I would really appreciate it if you would call me any time, day or night, with information on the boy. I really want to help him connect with his family."

"I will be in touch, Janie, and I do appreciate the latte."

Janie smiled and was gone.

As she slipped out to wash up, Marguerite Cole winked at Officer Evans, who was sitting in a chair with a magazine on his lap. When she was returning, she noticed a tall, burly, dark-haired man, carrying a large duffle bag, enter Yachay's room. Curious, Cole quickened her stride.

As she stepped through the doorway, she saw Yachay nod at the tall man. "Excuse me?" Cole spoke louder than normal at the man's back.

The man turned around to face Cole, and their eyes met. She felt a tingle race up her spine. *Would you look at those eyes?* Cole touched her chin to make sure her mouth was not hanging open.

"You must be Officer Cole?" Helmut put down his bag and extended his hand. "I am a friend of Professor Herschel Rhodes." Helmut was feeling a bit light headed and thought he better focus on getting himself some breakfast as soon as possible. *My blood sugar must be down.*

"Yes, good to meet you, ah…"

"Dr. Hunter. Helmut, if you will."

"I was expecting you Dr., ah, Helmut." Cole was tongue-tied. She had no idea what to say. Her mind was a complete blank. They stood there staring at each other for at least a full minute.

Yachay was amused. Hershel had told him to expect this new "doctor", and Yachay was wondering if there would be any further message from Kawsay, but these two were clearly charmed by each other. Yachay smiled. He knew the medicine man would be waiting here with him and Cole until Kawsay and Grandfather arrived. This obvious drama between them would pass the time in a more entertaining manner.

Cole noticed Yachay smiling at her. *Is this so obvious even the boy notices?* "Ah, Dr. Hunter." Cole cleared her throat and gathered her thoughts. "Let me introduce you to Yachay. His wound is doing well, and the infection is mostly diminished." Cole led Helmut over to Yachay's bed. Yachay had been sitting upright for hours and had already eaten two breakfasts.

Cole noticed that Evans looked tired standing next to Yachay's bed in his crumpled uniform. "This is Yachay and Officer Evans. Thank you for staying here through the night so I could sleep," Cole smiled at Evans. "I'll stay with Yachay until Professor Rhodes arrives."

Evans extended his hand to Helmut. "Good to meet you." Then he turned to Yachay. "You take care, son." Evans slipped out of the room.

Helmut was staring at Officer Cole, wondering what her first name was. She looked to be about five-six with big brown eyes and light brown hair. *The slim, athletic, outdoor type*, he thought. On the flight up to Anchorage from Lake Iliamna, Helmut had been preoccupied with how to get the first inoculation into Yachay at the hospital without the staff noticing or the boy freaking out. He had figured he would have to get this Officer Cole character out of the room long enough to get Yachay to accept a needle. Now he felt a little funny just being in her presence, yet did not want her to leave. *Maybe I should just tell her the truth: that I need to inoculate Yachay – family's orders. Would Cole buy that or would she alert the doctors? It may be easier to just sneak the inoculation. Just stick the needle in Yachay before he realizes what happened. Mmmh, that would work – the element of surprise.*

Cole wondered what this broad-shouldered man with wild-looking, blue eyes was contemplating. She was intrigued by him.

Helmut pondered his options. *Maybe if I offer to get her some coffee or food, she'll offer in turn to get it for me. Then she will leave for a few minutes, and I can inoculate Yachay.* "May I get you some coffee, Officer Cole?"

"Marguerite. Please call me Marguerite."

"OK, if you'll call me Helmut. And was that a yes on the coffee? Perhaps you can point me in the direction of a cafeteria." Helmut hated being deceitful.

"Oh, there is a little coffee bar down the hall and around the corner. I would be happy to get a cup for each of us, and you can get acquainted with Yachay – just don't let him leave the room." Cole thought a walk down the hall would clear the confusion out of her head.

That was too easy, Helmut smiled. "That is very kind of you, Marguerite. I will take good care of Yachay."

As Cole turned to leave, Helmut was already opening his medical bag. He picked up his stethoscope and gently put the earpieces into Yachay's ears while smiling and nodding at him. Then he held its diaphragm against Yachay's heart. Yachay looked intrigued. With one smooth motion Helmut slid his hand into his medical bag, picked up the loaded syringe, and slid the needle in and out of Yachay's arm, returning the syringe back into the bag. When he removed his hand, from the bag he was holding a small flashlight, which he turned on, swiveling the beam around to get the boy's attention.

Yachay heard a lub-dub beat when the doctor placed the cold disk against his chest. Then he felt a prick on the back of his arm and slightly flinched. Next, the medicine man was pointing a small torch around. He wondered what this supposed friend was up to. Helmut shined the torch into Yachay's ears, and then his nose and eyes. *What is he looking for?* Cole walked into the room, and the two adults began staring at each other again. *This is going to be an interesting day*, Yachay thought, as he began moving the stethoscope's diaphragm around his chest.

Whew! That went well. Helmut was happy his main mission to give Yachay his first inoculation was over so he could focus on this intriguing woman – who was not wearing a wedding ring.

Cole had reminded herself who she was and what her job was – to protect Yachay until he could be handed over to his family and to determine how he ended up on the M/V Tustumena without identification or reservations. This Dr. Hunter was most interesting, but she needed to keep her wits about the situation. As she entered Yachay's room, she could see the boy had a stethoscope in his ears and Dr. Hunter was waving a flashlight around in front of the boy. "Glad you two are getting along," Cole said, as she placed a cup of coffee into Helmut's free hand.

"Thank you, Marguerite. As you can see, your charge is discovering his *own* heartbeat." Helmut wanted to know everything about Marguerite Cole. "So, how did you get into being a State Trooper? Is it the family business, so-to-speak, or a childhood dream?"

Cole was surprised by the sudden focus on *her*. She felt her face begin to flush. *Great, Marguerite, now let's turn red. Good grief.* "Oh, neither really; well sort of a childhood dream. But I took a detour into microbiology first."

"Really? This sounds interesting. I would love to hear the story." Helmut handed Yachay the flashlight and began pulling two chairs over closer to Yachay's bed so they could sit near him but still focus on each other.

Yachay was enjoying the medicine man's tools, but was becoming interested in this dark brown liquid everyone was drinking. He pointed to Helmut's cup and said "Yachay?" That technique seemed to work well.

Helmut looked surprised. "You want my coffee, Yachay? Mmmh, let's see what you think." Helmut handed Yachay his coffee and waited for the response.

Being a warrior, Yachay took a large gulp of the hot liquid and held his breath.

Cole noticed the boy's face turned a little red; then she heard him swallow. A broad smile spread across Yachay's face. "He likes it," Cole laughed.

Yachay *did* like this hot, brown liquid. He decided this would be a drink he could enjoy. He took another less-large gulp and felt the warmth all the way into his belly.

Helmut refocused on Marguerite. "You were telling me about your microbiology detour on the way to becoming a Trooper?"

Those eyes are so intense – as if he is looking right into my soul. Cole felt herself turning red again. She smiled and decided to give him the condensed version of her life story. "OK, I wanted to go into law enforcement when I was a girl. But I did really well in school, especially science and math, so a few of my teachers said I should become a scientist or doctor. I didn't want to become a doctor since I don't like cutting things – animals – open, but I found I really was interested in biology. When I was a freshman at the university, I discovered microbiology where you are dealing with tiny creatures, usually unicellular, so I wouldn't have to cut animals open. So I stuck with it and got a master's."

Marguerite was aware that Helmut had not taken his eyes off her since she began her story. She continued, "When I finished school, I got a job in a lab down in California. I really missed Alaska – the grandeur, the mountains, the wildness, everything. So I came up for a vacation when I was twenty-nine to hike into Denali State Park with an old friend. Things went badly – we had unexpectedly foul weather. Everything went wrong. Anyway, we were out there for too long. My friend was badly hurt, so we couldn't travel. We ran out of food. I was hurt too, but not as badly. I didn't think we would make it. Then, I don't know how they found us, but the Alaska State Troopers rescued us – took really good care of us. When I was lying in the back of the helicopter, I thought about my little job in the lab and how insignificant it seemed compared to what these Troopers were doing. I decided to return to my girlhood dream and join the Troopers – and here I am."

"Wow, what a story." Helmut was staring at Marguerite.

Cole noticed Yachay holding his hands out in front of him, looking at them intensely. She looked closely and could see Yachay's hands shaking a bit. *What's happened to Yachay?* Then she realized Yachay had consumed all of Helmut's coffee – probably the first cup of coffee he had ever had. "I think he's gotten himself wired." Cole could not help but laugh, and Helmut shrugged.

Yachay was getting restless. He had been in this bed for almost two days. The pain in his arm was quite tolerable for a warrior – he just chose not to think about it; therefore he did not feel it. He was told by Kawsay and Herschel, who was supposedly with her, to stay put until they arrived. He certainly wanted to be where Kawsay and Grandfather would find him, though it was he who was supposed to do the finding. He knew it was best to wait just a little longer until they arrived, but it was going to be difficult. He was used to action, not waiting. A warrior needs his strength. Yachay was hungry again.

Cole noticed Yachay getting agitated. She figured his arm must have been hurting pretty badly for him to be as calm as he had been for the past twenty-four hours. *The coffee was probably not a great idea – it just wound him up a few notches. All I want to do is lose myself in Helmut's dreamy blue eyes. Stop it, Cole! You have a job to do. You need to keep it together, take care of Yachay, make sure he is successfully handed over to his family, and find out how he ended up on the Tustumena.* "I think Yachay needs some food to sop up all of that coffee." She turned to Yachay and pantomimed an eating motion.

Yachay's face lit up. *This Cole woman seems to be able to read my mind.*

Cole reached over and pressed the nurse-call button. She knew they were probably wearing out their welcome with all these special requests for food, but she did notice that his celebrity status and unique appearance – ear disks and all – seemed to bring a different face each time to deliver his meals. The word probably was out, and everyone wanted to get a close up look at this character.

Helmut was observing Marguerite's eyes as they darted around preoccupied with the boy's needs. *She would make a good mother. I wonder if she has any kids.* Without thinking further, Helmut blurted out, "So, do you have any children of your own, Marguerite?" *Watch it Helmut, don't pry too fast or you'll scare her off.*

"Ah, no, I, ah, never really found the right guy, you know." Cole felt like she was in a fishbowl.

"Look, Marguerite, you have been great at answering my questions. It's my turn to reveal my life story to you – keep things fair and all."

That sounds great, Cole thought, and responded, "Yes, please."

"Well, here goes. When I was young, I wanted to fly. I tried constructing wings, but my flights always ended rather abruptly – you get the idea. So I thought I would learn from the masters of flight – birds. That began my study of animals, which is why I ended up studying zoology and why I am in Alaska now. I was also very interested in people and healing. It really bothered me to see anyone or any creature suffer. I grew up in the Sierra Mountains of California in the forest. We had a fair amount of land, and the forest was my playground. I had a lot of opportunities to observe animals in the wild. Sometimes I would see a squirrel without a leg or a bird whose eye was gone. It cut deeply into my soul. I *had* to do something about suffering. I struggled with going to medical school verses veterinary school. About that time, my father had an accident with a chain saw. It looked worse than it was, but I felt so helpless in his moment of agony. I didn't know what to do. It was awful to hear him moaning on the way to the hospital, which was not close. The ER doctors became my heroes that night. That made my decision to choose medical school. But I could not give up my love of animals, so I decided to simultaneously enroll in grad school in zoology."

"You did a MD-PhD program in zoology? That's kind of unusual, isn't it?" Marguerite was falling for this sweet, unique, and intelligent man.

"It is a bit unusual, but not as unusual as my interest in exotic animals. But that's another story." Helmut saw a nurse enter the room.

"I bet the boy is hungry again, yes?" The short dark-haired woman had a playful half-smile on her face.

"Good guess," Cole smiled back at her.

"Be back in a moment with his first of, I'm sure, many lunches."

Yachay figured out the dark-haired woman probably stopped by for his benefit, and food was on the way. He wondered what unusual food they would bring. Everything he ate was new and different, just like this gigantic and strange house. Yachay had never seen so much white! *All these unusual surfaces and unnatural colors and textures – where did they all come from?* He enjoyed the food with its new tastes and smells, but missed his mother's and grandmother's cooking. How would he get back home and rescue them? He was so far away, and time was running out. He was thankful he had found Kawsay and Grandfather and happily anticipated their arrival. *I need to focus on getting strong and healing. Then I will be ready to recue Mother and Grandmother. Now, I must eat and rest.*

"Your interest in exotic animals? Can you explain?" Cole was staring intently at Helmut.

Helmut was imagining what Cole would look like in ten or twenty years. He felt drawn to her. *Why? Because she is pretty and confident? There are plenty of pretty, confident women. What is it about Marguerite Cole? There is something "right", something mystical about the way I feel – as if I have known her forever, but I don't even know her now!* "Exotic animals. Did I really bring that up?" It was Helmut's turn to blush. "Well, it all began with the leviathan in the book of Job in the Bible." Helmut was watching Cole's eyes squint as she was clearly concentrating and wondering where his story was going. "Have you read the Bible?" Cole nodded yes.

"OK. Well, when I was a teenager, my brother, Ben, was really into reading the Bible, so I became curious. Not to be outdone or outread by my younger brother, I had to read the Bible cover to cover as well. That's when I came across the leviathan. Have you ever wondered what those creatures really were? I mean, some people think they were dinosaurs, some say whales, some hippopotami, some sea dinosaurs, some crocodiles, some say they were angelic-like creations or even a yet-undiscovered species. But I wanted to know what they *really* were. That began the obsession, well, rather interest, in unusual and unexplained creatures."

"You mean like crypto-zoology?" Cole was wondering if this fascinating man was borderline insane.

Helmut could tell she thought he was nuts – it was written all over her face. "You have stories here in Alaska about birds with huge wing spans. They've been observed by reputable people. Have you wondered what they are?"

OK, maybe he's not nuts, just a big kid at heart. "I have heard of the giant bird reports. They were even in the newspaper. In fact, some type of huge fish has been spotted in Lake Iliamna."

Bingo. She knows about this stuff. "Have you ever given much thought to these sightings?" Helmut studied her. He could see the wheels turning behind those big brown eyes. *I could get lost in those eyes.*

"Well, I have to admit I love animals. And, well, as a matter of fact, I have wondered about strange things like that – you know, strange animal sightings – especially since I have spent a fair amount of time hiking. You hear the bigfoot stories and all. They make great campfire fables. But who has the time and resources to explore fantastical things like that!"

Helmut was feeling better about this conversation. *At least she doesn't appear to think I am completely nuts – just eccentric maybe, but that's OK. Eccentric is interesting, not certifiable.* "Well, you only live once, Marguerite, and sometimes you just have to follow your heart, your dreams, and your curiosity."

"I really love that sentiment, Helmut."

The short, dark-haired woman appeared in the doorway with a tray. "Here's lunch number one – or is it breakfast number three!"

Yachay sat up straight, a wide smile spreading across his face. The woman adjusted the tray in front of him, and he began his feast in earnest. His mind drifted off to his home.

"How are you able to find the time to pursue your curiosity of unusual animals?" Cole was intrigued. "You're a physician, and most physicians I know are pretty busy. Do you research creatures by reading, or do you actually go look for them – and where would one look anyway?"

She finds this stuff interesting. I cannot believe I am telling her this, and rather than having me locked up, she's interested. Maybe she's collecting more data before having me locked up. "Well, that's really what got me serious about learning to fly. I didn't just want to read what others observed; I wanted to look for unusual animals first hand."

"Are you a pilot as well?" *This is too much.*

"Well, I'm a do-it-yourself kind of guy. If I need it, I build it. If I want to go to unusual places, I better be able to get myself there."

"What do you fly?" *I keep on finding more amazing facets to this guy.*

"Helicopters mostly, but I can fly almost any small craft."

"Helicopter? Is there anything you can't do? And when do you have time for everything."

"I can't do a lot of things. But I have endless energy, and growing up in the forest and being a bit of a dork, I never had a huge social life. It's amazing how much you can learn and accomplish if you have an endless supply of both curiosity and energy."

"As long as you are also a genius." Cole was pondering Helmut's last statement. *What would I do with endless curiosity and energy? I have a lot of curiosity, and I don't lack for energy. What am I doing with my life? This guy is amazing – he just seems to follow his dreams wherever they take him.*

She thinks I'm a genius.

Yachay had turned on the little box with the people inside, but kept the sound very low. Cole and Helmut, however, were much more interesting to watch. He was imagining what they must be saying to each other.

Cole offered to get them some sandwiches from down the hall if Helmut would entertain Yachay again. For the next few hours, Marguerite and Helmut talked about their families and childhoods. Cole also was interested in Yachay's family and in who exactly was going to show up at the hospital that afternoon. She was enthralled with Helmut, but still had a job to do. Yachay needed to be handed over to his family, and she needed to find out how he ended up on the M/V Tustumena with no reservations. No one seemed to know why he was there or how he got there. Neither Marguerite nor Helmut wanted the day to end without having a "what comes next" conversation. Helmut told her his plans for being in Alaska for a few weeks and wanted to make sure they could spend more time together – if she was interested. He managed to slip in a dinner invitation. Marguerite did not hesitate.

Yachay's attention went back and forth between Cole and Helmut, his radio, and the television. He also spent time in the bathroom examining the water spout and the stool that drained and filled. His new world was amazing. He wanted to explore more, but first he was anxious to see Kawsay and Grandfather.

Saturday morning in the Sierras was crisp and clear, with just a whiff of smoke from the open burning in the Central Valley. The travelers brought breakfast snacks along in the cars so they could depart as early as possible. Grace drove so Herschel could try to call Dr. Hurtado about the naturalization issue, while Kawsay and Grandfather enjoyed the sumptuous leather back seat. Ben drove their black Jeep Rubicon with Alison as co-pilot, while Nate and Junior bounced along in the back seat. They hoped to reach the airport in time for their ten o'clock departure. The flying time would be about five hours, so with the time change, they hoped to land in Anchorage by two o'clock.

While short on sleep, everyone was buoyed with adrenaline. Nate was sorry he could not share a car with Kawsay, but she and Grandfather had a lot to talk over to get ready to reconnect with Yachay. Nate contemplated his own uncertain future while attempting to keep Junior from commandeering his peanut butter toast. He could hear Ben and Alison chatting about their next archeological expedition back to Israel scheduled for the following summer. *I wish I could go with them or, even better, return to that field where I met David. Maybe ...* Nate's thoughts were interrupted by Junior's eager mouth tugging on his toast.

Herschel explained to Kusi more about where they were going and how they would get there. Kusi was intrigued that their "jet" would fly them higher than the clouds and almost as fast as the sound of thunder. Kusi and Kawsay talked excitedly about a possible rescue of Mother and Grandmother.

As they reached a coverage area, Herschel turned on his cell phone and called Dr. Hurtado's office in Peru, where it was two hours later. The two men had not decided if it was easier for them to converse in Spanish or English.

"Hurtado," announced a surprisingly clear voice.

"Augusto, this is Herschel Rhodes in California. Can you talk now?"

"Sí, yes, of course. Thank you for calling. How are things going?"

"We're on the way to an airport and should be on the ground in Alaska by two, or about five o'clock your time. Without your help I doubt we could get custody of Yachay, at least not without bureaucratic delays and unwanted notoriety. I completely agree with your advice to minimize publicity. The problem is that there has already been newspaper coverage and the danger of almost celebrity status."

"Yes, it is wise to keep things quiet," Augusto agreed. "I am being very careful what I say to people here too."

"So, que pasa?" Herschel asked. Herschel appreciated how quickly Hurtado was moving forward.

"Well, I have good news and bad news. The good news is I am almost certain that my contacts at the Dirección General de Migraciones y Naturalización will be successful in forming an official communiqué that I can e-mail to you to give to the police. It will state that these individuals are Peruvian citizens who must be returned to their country and will authorize you to take them to California for further transportation. The bad news is that I do not believe I can get this authorization to you until Monday. Will that be acceptable?"

"We had hoped to take the boy back with us tomorrow," Herschel said, "but I don't expect your government to work on Sunday just for us. Do you have all the information you need?"

"I believe I do. I really hope this is a success, and I can soon meet your friends. If they joined our team, it would be a tremendous benefit to our work." Augusto paused. "Can you hear in my voice how excited I am?"

"Yes, I can. Remember, though, Kusi insists that his first priority must be retrieving the rest of the family. Don't ask me how he and Kawsay plan to do this, but if they are successful, you may have five new colleagues, not just three." Herschel paused for a moment to think. "Augusto, would you like to talk with Kusi? He's riding in the back seat with his granddaughter."

Augusto felt his heart jump, and he sucked in a quick breath. "Yes, I would like to do that. Is he familiar with telephones?"

"Yes, he's a quick learner, and Kawsay has been teaching him nonstop," Herschel said. "Be prepared, though, to hear Quechua the way it used to be before modern corruptions. I've been corrected very often for my errors." He turned to the back seat. "Kusi, this is Augusto Hurtado, the man from Peru who would like to meet you and have you help him understand the ways of your people. He is helping us get permission to bring Yachay back with us."

Kusi had begun to doze as the car rocked him along. As Herschel's offer registered, his eyebrows arched, and he gave an eager nod. Kusi accepted the phone. "I am Kusi. Do you hear my voice?"

Dr. Hurtado heard Quechua spoken with a strange accent, which in fact was no accent at all. "I hear you, Kusi. This is Augusto Hurtado. I learned about you and your family from Herschel Rhodes. I hope to meet you soon."

"Yes, and I will also meet you," Kusi responded with enthusiasm. "Herschel told me about you. You study the ways of my people. I can help you understand all about us."

"I am sure you and your family can help us very much. I wish we could get to work now, but I understand you first must rescue your family."

"So, you understand about our village and the danger my daughter and wife face?" Kusi appreciated this man's concern and understanding. "It is a large worry for me. I do not sleep well, but I have hope. Today is a special event for Kawsay and me. We will travel in a 'jet' to rescue my grandson, Yachay, who is a brave, young warrior. I learned that he saved a small girl who fell from a huge boat into cold water. He did this after being wounded by a giant bear. I want to hear his story and learn how he came to the cold place far to the north."

Augusto, who learned Quechua in his youth, had to concentrate to follow all that he heard. "You have a wonderful grandson, Kusi. His father would be very proud of him."

"Yes. I am sorry his father is not with us, but he died when Yachay was very young. He reminds me of his father, and Kawsay grows more beautiful each day and looks more like her mother, Sumaq." Kusi looked over at Kawsay, and they noticed each other's misty eyes, filled with care for the other.

Augusto noted that Sumaq's name meant beautiful or wonderful. "It was very brave of Sumaq to insist that Kawsay be given a chance to live." Augusto paused in thought. "Did she ever find another husband?"

Kusi sensed that this man truly cared about him and his family, so he was open with him. "Sumaq mourned her husband and worried about losing her daughter. She did not have joy in her life or room in her heart for another man. Our people shunned her much like they did Kawsay. Perhaps she will find a good life in this new world."

"She is still young," Augusto stated. "How do you like this new world, Kusi?"

Kusi pondered this. "It is so different and difficult to understand. I am curious about the strange inventions, but sometimes it is too much for me. And I feel cut off from my world, like a fish in a tree. I am with very kind and intelligent people who are helping us. But where can I find people who are like me – who speak like me and look like me? I miss my own small house and cooking fire, hunting in the jungle, telling old stories, …" His voice trailed off.

"Kusi, your jungle is still here in Peru, as are many of the animals you like to hunt. There are small villages where people all know one another and work together. Many of us are the descendants of the great Tahuantisuya. My family history shows that more than half of my ancestors are of your blood. But we do not remember what it means to be of the Incas. We also are cut off from our past. It is likely we share some of the same ancestors and are related as cousins."

Kusi warmed to this idea, as it made him feel more connected and gave him an added sense of purpose. "What you tell me helps me to believe that we are following the right path. First we reunite the family. Then we find our new brothers. I hope we can meet soon." He handed the phone to Herschel.

"Augusto?" Herschel said. "You and Kusi seem like long-lost friends!"

"It was amazing to talk with this man. It helps me believe all this is real." Augusto needed to complete more paperwork. "Watch for the e-mail early Monday, OK?"

"We all hope things will go smoothly. Thank you again for your help. I've never seen bureaucracy move so fast." When the call had ended, Herschel turned, looked back, and asked Kusi, "What do you think of Augusto?"

Kusi looked at Kawsay, thinking, and then back at Herschel. "I like this man. When we talk, it feels like he is already a friend. Our people today may be better people than the ones in our village."

After dropping off Junior, they arrived at the San Jose airport and parked by the private aircraft terminal off Coleman Avenue. They hurried inside and were met by a handsome, casually dressed young man. "Are you the friends of Mr. Diamond?"

Nate was about to answer that he was Mr. Diamond's son, but then thought better of it. Ben stepped forward. "Yes, we are. My name is Ben Hunter, and this ..."

"Yes, yes, we're ready to board. I'm Bill Pierce. Please follow me out to the aircraft. Just leave your luggage on the tarmac, and I'll have it loaded."

The sleek Gulfstream III-1 was being fueled, and the boarding ladder was down. They filed up the steps and past the pilots who were doing pre-flight checks. Bill soon secured the hatch and joined them. "Make yourselves at home. I'll be your steward today. This will be my first trip up the coast to Alaska. It should be clear after a while, and we should have some great views."

Nate and Kawsay sat together, wanting to make up for being apart during the car trip. After Kusi briefly explored the jet's posh interior, Herschel settled him into a big reclining chair and helped him with the seat belt. Just as everyone was settled, the engines came alive. After a short wait they quickly accelerated and were aloft, climbing smartly.

For the first half of the trip, most of the travelers tried to recapture recently lost sleep. Kusi, though, was glued to his window, enjoying the view from above the clouds. Three hours into the flight, Bill relayed information from the captain that there would be good views of the St. Elias Mountains, including Mt. Logan and Mt. Fairweather. He also said they would see the Malaspina and Bering Glaciers, which are giant shield glaciers rivaling Rhode Island in size. Their course took them along the coast in an ever more westerly direction. Bill also related that, according to the co-pilot, the only places on Earth with more glacial ice were Greenland and Antarctica. As they passed these stunning sights, there was competition for the starboard windows. Alison asked Ben why they had not explored this area as a change of pace from the torrid Middle East. Grace commented on the beautiful blue ice that was visible in the deep crevasses.

The last hour of the flight was used to finalize their plan for recovering Yachay. The jet could not land at the small airfield next to Yachay's hospital, so they had arranged for a large van to accommodate everyone and the luggage on the short drive from Ted Stevens International Airport to Alaska Regional Hospital and later to the Captain Cook Hotel downtown. They decided not to push too hard to get Yachay released immediately, but first to build trust with the authorities and, with Helmut's help, make sure Yachay was in good enough condition to travel.

After a smooth landing, they deplaned and collected their bags. It was just after two o'clock Alaska Time, but the bright sun did not impart much warmth, and the cool breeze was more than refreshing. They rummaged in their suitcases for jackets. Ben alerted the flight crew that Monday noon would be the soonest they might want to return.

As they got underway with Herschel at the wheel of the long, blue rental van, it hit them – they really were about to encounter the much-sought-after Yachay. This had a different meaning for each of them. Alison was curious to meet Kawsay's brother who was so brave and wonderful. Nate was worried that the great warrior-brother would look down on him. Kawsay stared blankly out the window at another strange city with small trees and square buildings, but inwardly was yearning to be reunited with her closest friend, teacher, and helper. Grace wondered how Yachay was holding up under the strain of his harrowing experiences and alien surroundings, while Herschel was concerned about how they were going to explain Yachay's undocumented presence. Kusi was eager to hear Yachay's stories and start planning the rescue of his wife and daughter. Ben's mind kept turning to the missing piece in his own life, the third arrow.

Herschel turned into the hospital lot, found a vacant parking place near the main door, and led them into the lobby. As they approached the desk, he muttered to Ben, "This should prove most interesting."

Marguerite Cole felt the intensity of Helmut's eyes on her. He seemed to be looking into her and searching her soul for information and connection. *Is he always like this? Does he intensely focus on everyone and everything, or is he truly interested in me? Is there a future here?* She could hear some commotion in the hall.

She and Helmut both rose at the same moment as a young, slim girl with long dark hair ran through the doorway and right past them to meet a leaping Yachay. As Kawsay and her brother were reuniting in unintelligible chatter, a distinguished-looking black man came through the door.

"Helmut, great to see you! And you must be Officer Cole; it's a real pleasure to meet you," Herschel said, extending his hand to Marguerite Cole. "Yachay's family and friends are deeply indebted to you for your expert care and protection of him."

Trailing closely behind Herschel were Grace, Ben, Alison, Nate, and Kusi. The room was a small, one-bed hospital room, but there was enough space for the group. Helmut was closely watching Marguerite's reaction to the onslaught and stepped closer to stand at her side.

Before Cole could say anything, Herschel continued. "Please let me introduce you to everyone. "This is my wife, Grace. To her right are Alison Hunter and her husband Ben. And this is a family friend, Nate, and Yachay's grandfather, Kusi. Sitting on the bed with Yachay is his sister, Kawsay." As Herschel gestured toward Kawsay, she slid off the bed and joined the group. Yachay was close behind her, his eyes scanning the new arrivals.

Kawsay reached out to shake Officer Cole's hand. "Grandfather and I thank you for taking care of Yachay. We were most worried of him. You are wonderful!" Kawsay beamed at this woman who she had learned from Herschel was like a modern-day warrior. "You are a brave woman like me."

Marguerite Cole's heart melted. "Thank you, Kawsay, is it? Your brother, Yachay, is a hero. I have been very anxious to meet you, all of you, and find out where he comes from. He is unusual in such a wonderful way." Cole was intrigued by Yachay's sister. She was a modern girl dressed in blue jeans, a tee shirt, a jacket, and athletic shoes, but there was still something quite mysterious about her. She also noticed the blond-haired boy watching Kawsay. Her grandfather, on the other hand, was not modern at all, even though he was wearing contemporary clothes – khaki slacks, a Hawaiian print shirt, a windbreaker, and new athletic shoes. His skin was rough and weathered. His wild eyes darted around the room, noticing everything, yet returning to her after each scan. It was more than the ear disks and shoulder-length hair that made him different – he had a primitive nobility.

Even though Kusi had agreed to let Herschel take charge of the meeting and get

Yachay set free, he felt he should affirm his patriarchal role. Kusi stood tall, looked reassuringly at Yachay, and began speaking in his native tongue. Herschel jumped in to translate. "Yachay's grandfather says he is deeply thankful to you for finding Yachay and keeping him safe. He wants to take Yachay back to the rest of his family and reunite everyone. Is Yachay well enough to travel? We know he was hurt by a giant bear. Can we take him with us?" Herschel smiled. "Well, Officer Cole, Kusi certainly gets right down to business, doesn't he?"

"We would like nothing more than to turn Yachay over to his family so he can go home. We need to establish how he ended up on the M/V Tustumena without reservations or identification. He was dressed in a rather odd manner and had with him some curious belongings. Once we receive answers to our questions, there should be no problem releasing him into the custody of his family." Cole scanned the group and noticed they all were staring at her.

"Well, let me respond to the questions you mentioned." Herschel was in charge. "Ben and Alison Hunter, Stanford professors in archaeology, are hosting Kawsay and Kusi. They have been searching for Yachay so he, his sister, and his grandfather can return to Peru. The Peruvian Ministry of the Interior will be sending me documents on Monday verifying that Yachay is a Peruvian National and should be released into my care, so that I can take him first to California and then on to Peru along with his sister and grandfather. Between now and Monday, if possible, I would like to ask you to consider placing Yachay into my care, so he can stay with his sister and grandfather at the Captain Cook Hotel where we are all lodging. I will accept full responsibility. We are staying in the Captain's Deck Suites, which are only accessible using an elevator key, so he will be secure."

Cole's head was spinning. "OK, let me ask a few more questions. Then we can check into getting authorization for you to assume responsibility for Yachay today." Everyone in the group nodded at Cole except Kusi who looked confused. She was momentarily transfixed by Kusi's ear disks; they were much bigger than Yachay's. *Who are these people?* "Well, the central question here is how did Yachay end up on the Tustumena, which would perhaps also explain how he ended up on Kodiak Island. If we can answer those questions and you provide documents from the Peruvian government verifying that Yachay is a Peruvian National, then I see no reason why he would not be released into your care. You understand, though, I am not the decision maker."

"Great." Herschel glanced over at Ben. "Perhaps it makes sense to ask Yachay to explain how he ended up on the ferry." Herschel noticed Ben's eyebrow shoot up. Herschel looked at Kawsay who had a slight smile on her face. In fact, everyone but Yachay and Kusi wore slightly raised eyebrows as if they were all waiting for the punch line of a joke. Turning his attention to Yachay, Herschel asked in the Quechua dialect he had learned from Kawsay and Kusi, "Hi, Yachay. I spoke to you yesterday on the 'telephone'. Do you recognize my voice?"

"I remember. You told me about the medicine man, Helmut, who arrived this morning and let me talk to Grandfather and Kawsay who were then far away with just their voices here." Yachay was learning about this new place, but all the little pictures and disembodied voices were still somewhat confusing.

Herschel continued in Quechua. "I would like to ask you how you got to the island and then ended up on the big boat. I know you encountered a huge bear. I want to explain your answer to everyone here who doesn't speak your language. Your grandfather and sister are also interested in your story, but they will be patient while I explain to everyone else as you are telling me. Kawsay has learned their language, so she can help me understand everything you tell me." Herschel winked at Kawsay. Continuing in Quechua, "We need to help Officer Cole understand how you got to the island and onto the boat so she can help you get released into our care and you, Kawsay, and Kusi can go to rescue your mother and grandmother. Do you understand?" Yachay nodded. Herschel explained to the group what he had said.

"Before he begins," Helmut interjected, "I'll grab a few chairs and bring them in here. I saw some down the hall." Helmut smiled at Marguerite. "Kawsay, why don't you, your brother, and grandfather sit on Yachay's bed. I have a feeling this will be longer than a couple of minutes, so we may as well get comfortable."

"I'll give you a hand, bro." Ben followed Helmut into the hall. "How did the day go? Yachay seems pretty calm considering what a shock this new world must be for him. Did you get the inoculation into him?" Ben excitedly fired off his questions.

"He got the inoculation. I distracted him with a stethoscope and pen flashlight, and he barely knew what happened. I think it made him a bit less trusting of me, but he seems to like Marguerite – ah, Officer Cole."

When Ben and Helmut arrived back with the chairs, Kusi, Kawsay, Yachay, and Nate were all sitting on the bed. The three chairs that had been in the room were pulled over near the bed making a partial circle for the remaining chairs to fill. Officer Cole was sitting on one side of Herschel, with Grace on his other.

"Everybody ready?" Herschel decided to be as honest as possible with his translation. Yachay's story would undoubtedly sound crazy to Officer Cole, but they could just say he has been through a lot, may have amnesia, and has a vivid imagination. "Yachay, tell me slowly what happened to you since you last saw your family."

Yachay straightened his back and cleared his throat. "Grandfather did not return from his journey to check on Kawsay, so I went to find him. When I got inside the secret cave, I found his dagger near the singing wall. I felt it was a sign from him, so I went through the singing wall into a sucking tunnel." Herschel translated.

"You did say 'secret cave', 'singing wall', and 'sucking tunnel'?" Cole's eyebrows were raised.

"I did. Kawsay, is that what you heard as well?" Herschel looked at Kawsay for verification. Kawsay nodded back. Herschel nodded at Yachay. "Pleases continue with your story."

"I smashed into a very dark, rock room, climbed out and up through some tunnels, and broke into a huge, white-walled temple with a very high ceiling. Once I got outside, I realized I was in a very different place – nothing was familiar." Yachay looked up, searching his memory. "There was a wide path covered with small round stones. Along the sides were many structures made of stones and wood. Then I saw a man with pale skin. He had brown hair that was pulled back, and he was covered from head to toe with fabric. He was acting stealthily, so I thought he might have seen Kawsay and Grandfather if they were there. I followed him to a river. Then I saw two cowards sneaking up behind him with knives. They were going to attack him from the back. A man fights face to face!" Yachay looked around. He had been using his hands to help communicate, since he knew only Herschel, Kawsay, and Grandfather could understand his words. "By the time I subdued the two cowards, the first man had gotten in a boat and was crossing the river. I saw that he had dropped an oddly shaped metal object with some sort of marking on it. So I picked it up."

Upon hearing Herschel's translation, Cole stood up and retrieved Yachay's sling containing his belongings from his bedside table and gave it to Yachay. "Can he show us what he found?"

Ben could not help but notice the end of Yachay's spear protruding from the sling, but the embedded arrow was not quite visible.

Yachay accepted the sling with a big smile. Herschel asked him to show the metal object he found. Yachay handed the metal object to Officer Cole.

She turned it over in her hand. "What strange markings, a backwards R and P." She held it out to show everyone. "It looks like an old engraver's stamp." She handed it to Helmut.

Helmut examined it. "P.R. Someone with the initials P.R. lost his stamp." Helmut handed the stamp to Alison's waiting hand.

Herschel nodded and Yachay continued. "I sensed that Kawsay was nowhere near. Nothing felt right. Then the cowards woke up and began yelling, 'Indian! Indian!' or something similar. I decided to return to the cave under the temple and try for a new place to look for Kawsay. I looked up and saw an extremely tall pointed structure sticking up from the roof of the temple – the one I first entered. Then two torches shone from near the top of the pointed structure just briefly. Then they stopped. I thought it was a signal. Maybe Grandfather." Yachay and Grandfather exchanged glances. Yachay continued, "But I sensed Grandfather and Kawsay were far away. The signal must have been for someone else. Then the two cowards yelled again, 'Indian! Indian!' and 'Church! Church!' Soon there were more men."

"What were people wearing?" Helmut broke in, and Herschel translated.

"The new men that began chasing me were wearing bright red clothing covering their bodies, white fabric on their legs, black headdresses, and black foot coverings. I ran back to the temple. I wanted to get back to the cave, so I could continue searching for Kawsay." Helmut and Ben exchanged glances.

Yachay straightened his back again and continued using gesticulations to describe what he was seeing. "I found the tingling wall and stepped back into the sucking tunnel. Before the air was completely removed from my body, I smashed into the great creature. My spear flew out of reach, and I had to retrieve it before I could leave the cave. The huge creature swung his claws at me." Yachay glanced at his arm. "But I was victorious and not afraid. I am a better climber and faster runner than the creature. So I got my spear and ran. I was on a mountain of green and there was a vast blue water below."

"Must be Kodiak," Cole butted in. "You mean – let me get this straight. You went from a 'sucking tunnel' to a place with a large white temple with two torches in the window above the building, found the P.R. engraved stamp, and were chased by men in red jackets and white pants. You went back into the sucking tunnel and landed on a great creature – a Kodiak bear? Is that what the rest of you heard?"

Herschel translated Officer Cole's question back to Yachay. Yachay smiled broadly at how well Cole had been paying attention. He looked directly at Officer Cole. "Cole would make a good warrior – she listens well, was very brave in the metal bird, and can sleep sitting up. I also notice that men give her respect. She has good instincts." Yachay waited while Herschel translated his high compliment to Cole.

Cole flushed and smiled at her charge. "You are a fine young man, Yachay. Your family will hear you tell about how you saved Cindy Stevens. You are a hero. I want to understand your story. Do you understand that it sounds a little odd?" She waited while Herschel translated.

"Many crazy things happened to me. But I had a mission – to find Kawsay and Grandfather. See, now I have found them." Kawsay began to tear up, but fought it back.

Helmut broke in. "Red jackets or coats, white temple or church, Indians, crossing a river, two lights in a steeple above a church, and a stamp engraved with P. R." Helmut softly chanted:

> "He said to his friend, 'If the British march
> By land or sea from the town tonight,
> Hang a lantern aloft in the belfry arch
> Of the North Church tower as a signal light,--
> One if by land, and two if by sea;
> And I on the opposite shore will be,
> Ready to ride and spread the alarm
> Through every Middlesex village and farm,
> For the country folk to be up and to arm.'
> Then he said "Good-night!" and with muffled oar
> Silently rowed to the Charlestown shore,.."

Ben gave Helmut an intriguing and reprimanding stare. Cole looked at the two brothers, getting insight into possible sibling rivalry.

Herschel prompted Yachay to continue. "I ran from the great beast. Much time passed until I came upon moving boxes and the tallest structure I had ever seen, with a smaller pointed cylindrical structure to its side. Then, to my surprise, flames and white smoke burst out and poured from the bottom of the smaller cylindrical structure! I was knocked back by a hot cloud of smoke and flames! It was very hot…and the noise! It grew louder and louder, until my ears were bursting! Then it rose off the ground, dragging a cone of fire and smoke below it! It rose higher and higher, created a streak in the sky, and was gone!" Yachay looked at Grandfather, who was clearly gripped by his story.

Yachay continued, "Two men began yelling at me in an unfriendly manner. I had had enough and took off. I was so tired – no sleep for days. So I found a raised hut, climbed inside, and fell asleep." Yachay took a drink of water from the bedside table. Kawsay was about to explode like a rocket herself. She wanted to question Yachay further about this strange event, but bit her lip and let him tell the whole story through Herschel.

Cole thought out loud, "Was there a launch at the Kodiak Island Launch Complex this past week? Yachay clearly has no idea what he witnessed. And if he was that close, he clearly attracted the attention of the guards. I still don't understand how he wound up on Kodiak Island from Peru. That is really the unanswered question. All he seems to know is that he went through a 'sucking tunnel'."

Yachay continued and told how he awoke in the boat, saw the two yellow-haired girls playing, and dove into the surprisingly freezing water after Cindy fell off the back of the boat. He told how he held her out of the frigid water until they were picked up. He talked about Captain Roberts and Manuel, his ride inside a moving metal box, and taking flight in the giant metal bird. He mentioned again how brave Cole was in the bird. He continued to this morning when Helmut arrived. He told Herschel how Cole and Helmut were sweet on each other, but Herschel did not translate that to everyone else. Kawsay and Kusi, however, understood and smiled at each other.

Dr. Menaker stepped into the small crowded room. "Well, we're having quite a party in here, aren't we?"

Helmut jumped up. "Pleased to meet you, Doctor. I am Dr. Hunter, Yachay's family physician. Please let me introduce you to Yachay's family and friends." Helmut made the introductions, while Dr. Menaker gave Yachay his stethoscope to distract him as he changed the bandage.

"I think you're going to make it, Yachay," Dr. Menaker said with a smile. "If Dr. Hunter will agree to keep an eye on you for the next twenty-four hours, you are free to leave the hospital." Dr. Menaker winked at Helmut, who was impressed that he used the old stethoscope trick to distract Yachay from pokes and prods.

Herschel stood up and turned to Cole, who was now standing. "Well, Officer Cole. Now that the good doctor thinks Yachay is out of the woods – so to speak – if the State Troopers will release Yachay into my care, Helmut will remain with us, and we will have the official paperwork from the Peruvian Ministry of the Interior by Monday morning."

"I still do not understand *how* Yachay got from Peru to Kodiak Island, Dr. Rhodes. Was there anything you could glean from Yachay's explanation of what transpired that would clue you in to how he arrived on Kodiak? That is the question my superiors will want answered. Having the Peruvian government vouch for his citizenship is helpful. And Captain Roberts is not pressing charges for Yachay being on the Tustumena without reservations or identification. No crime has been committed. Yachay is a hero, and I am very fond of him, but is there anything you can give me that will quell suspicions about him? He has these primitive weapons. It would be helpful to provide some sort of explanation about his belongings and how he arrived in Kodiak. I will recommend that he be released into your care while we await the official documents, but you need to give me something of an explanation." Cole was feeling exasperated. She really liked these people. She adored Yachay. They were all on the same side, but she needed something more concrete than "sucking tunnel"!

Herschel scanned the group. All eyebrows were up. *Here goes, dude.* "Well, he has these strange effects because he is from a very remote tribe in Peru. You know, there are some tribes that are still completely untouched by modern man. You are aware of that, are you not,

Officer?" Herschel noticed Cole's unconvinced expression. He continued. "Well, Yachay's tribe is so remote that he is unfamiliar with the modern world. He got lost from his sister and grandfather some time ago, and they have been searching for him. During this time, Kawsay has been in the care of Ben and Alison Hunter, and she has been becoming a modern girl, with the help of Nate." Herschel winked at Nate who had said almost nothing since they arrived at the hospital. He hoped that did not sound as convoluted to everyone else as it did to him. "As to how he ended up on Kodiak, well, how does one go from Peru to Kodiak? By boat or by plane? Yachay describes his mode of transportation as a 'sucking tunnel'. Gee." Herschel was stretching for creative truth. Something popped into his mind. "Well, there is another means of travel that a boy from a primitive tribe may imagine to be a 'tunnel' – that could be a submarine! And he did wind up at the launch site." Herschel looked around at everyone to see how his story was playing. Ben and Grace looked like they were suppressing laughter.

"A submarine?" Cole repeated. "How would a boy from a remote Peruvian tribe find his way to a submarine? Not to mention, how he would manage to board it dressed like he was – and carrying all that weird stuff?"

Herschel rubbed his chin. "Well, he managed to accidently stow away on the Tustumena by crawling into some sort of vehicle and falling asleep before the vehicle was loaded onto the ferry. Why couldn't he have gotten lost and crawled into something that was later loaded into a submarine?" Herschel was beginning to have fun with this story. He always had a secret desire to write fiction. Now, since his life had intertwined with these Incas, he was beginning to feel like he was *living* inside a fictional story.

Cole absentmindedly began rubbing her chin. "Submarines in Peru?"

"Well, he was lost. He could have been anywhere," Herschel suggested. "We just don't know."

"Are there any submarines that come near Kodiak?" Cole mused.

"I don't know. Submarines can go anywhere they want – I think it's classified." Herschel's tale of plausible reality had gone about as far as it could.

Alison could not hold back bursting into laughter any longer and excused herself from the room.

Cole cleared her throat. "Let me call my superiors. I'll do the best I can. Bottom line – you believe Yachay is sane and telling his story to the best of his ability since he has grown up isolated from the modern world. We have to speculate what he must mean by a 'sucking tunnel'. You suggest he may have accidently found himself on a submarine the same way he found himself on the Tustumena – by falling asleep in something that was brought on board? I'll see what I can do." Cole had a laugh-suppressing smile on her face as she left the room to find a private place for a phone call to her superior, Captain Boyer. She liked Boyer. He had a sense of humor and a sense of perspective. It was his sense of humor that was needed now.

Dr. Menaker had been standing back and enjoying the submarine story. "I'm sorry I missed the beginning of this chronicle," he said with a quizzical smile and a twinkle in his eye. "Dawn will help you check out when you're ready. Please tell Yachay how much we enjoyed having him as a guest here at Regional Hospital. He is a once-in-a-lifetime patient." Dr. Menaker shook Helmut's extended hand. "Take good care of him, Doctor. It's been a pleasure." He disappeared out the door.

They all began whispering to each other. Kawsay noticed that Nate had not said anything. She reached over and squeezed his hand. "I am very happy you are here with me. You and Yachay can get to know yourselves now. You are both favorite people of me." Nate and Yachay smiled tentatively at each other. Yachay knew there was something going on between these two and did not know how he felt about this light-skinned, light-haired boy and whether he was worthy of his sister's attention.

Ben, Alison, and Helmut were exchanging theories about the P.R. stamp. Alison mused, "Could it really be his? Wow, Yachay is more of a hero than he could ever realize. Cindy Stevens and …"

Officer Cole stood in the doorway, clearing her throat. "Well, Yachay, looks like you're in luck."

"Great." Herschel stood up.

Helmut jumped in, "How did you do it?"

"It turns out my boss went to school with Captain Roberts. What are the odds of that? And the Captain has been on the phone raving about Yachay – as if he is some sort of superhero. Since the Peruvian government will verify his citizenship and no crime has been committed, he can be released into Herschel Rhodes' custody today – now."

"We will need to thank Captain Roberts," Ben said.

"I just did." Marguerite Cole smiled. The chatter broke out as Herschel explained to Yachay and Kusi what had just happened. Cole leaned over and whispered in Helmut's ear, "See you at dinner."

CHAPTER 21

AN EVENING AT THE COOK

SEPTEMBER 5 – PRESENT YEAR
ANCHORAGE, ALASKA

AN AMAZING PLAN:
A YOUNG INCA WARRIOR
TO LEAD ME TO YOU.

Once the discharge papers were completed, Herschel led his growing army out the main door. They knew Yachay had gained an inconvenient local notoriety, so the clothing they brought along for him was something of a disguise, including sunglasses and a cowboy hat. Yachay had never worn either or any other modern clothing for that matter, but when he caught sight of himself in a mirror, he struck a pose and was very impressed.

What they had not anticipated, however, was that, thanks to Janie Briggs, plans were afoot to celebrate Yachay's heroism with a public ceremony. All Janie needed was an interpreter to complete the story of the mysterious hero. Fortunately the disguise worked well, because Janie was entering the hospital just as Yachay was leaving. She did not notice that her quarry was escaping. It also was fortunate that the suites they had reserved at the hotel were on a floor not open to the public and were paparazzi-proof.

The Captain Cook Hotel staff was cordial and quick, and the unusual guests were soon following two luggage carts and bellmen to their Captain's Deck suites on the 17th floor of Tower II. Their rooms had a South-Seas feel, and they liked the lounge area at one end of the hall where they could meet. They learned that they had the floor to themselves. The Hunters and the Rhodeses each had a room, and Helmut and Nate shared another. Kusi, Yachay, and Kawsay took a fourth room, which had been accented with a commodious portable bed. Two of the rooms had eastern views overlooking the mixed collection of buildings that made up downtown Anchorage. In the distance the high peaks of the Chugach Mountains had recently received their first layer of "termination dust" that marked the end of the brief Alaskan summer. The other two rooms faced west toward the sloshing brown tides of the Cook Inlet and Mt. Susitna, locally referred to as the "Sleeping Lady".

Helmut pointed out to Nate the ridgeline of the Alaska Range to the north-northwest, including Mt. McKinley, also known as Denali, the "Great One" in the Athabaskan language. "It's not only the tallest peak in the continent, it's the world's highest mountain measured from its base," Helmut stated. "That's why we can see it so well even though it's about 150 miles away. People die every year on climbing expeditions, but I heard that the first ascent was made a century ago by a sourdough trying to win a bet. All he carried was a thermos of coffee and a bag of donuts."

They quickly unpacked and gathered in the lounge to coordinate dinner plans and discuss how to spend their Sunday while waiting for the papers from Dr. Hurtado, expected

Monday morning. Since they needed to keep the Incas out of the public eye and make sure Yachay rested, they located a few room service menus and began compiling their orders. Helmut, however, seemed disinterested.

Ben offered Helmut a menu. "Here, Helmut. What sounds good to you?"

Helmut took the booklet, but did not look at it. Ben looked at him quizzically. Helmut shifted his weight a bit and cleared his throat before speaking quietly to his brother. "I'd like to try the Crow's Nest restaurant. I hear it is really good. It's in that other taller tower over there," Helmut said, pointing out the window.

Ben did not see the need to whisper. "Hey, we can go there tomorrow night. I'd like to keep everyone together tonight. Don't you have some stories to tell us?" Herschel, Grace, and Alison joined them.

"Are we all set to place the order?" Alison asked. "I think I finally convinced Yachay that he only needed to order one entrée. Even with Kawsay's help, I'm not sure I was able to fully explain to him about King Crab Legs."

"Good," Ben said, "but Helmut is thinking of going out to a restaurant."

"Really?" Herschel inquired. "I was hoping to de-brief you, Helmut, on your take on Officer Cole. You were able to spend time with her this morning. Do you think she's sympathetic to what we're trying to do here?"

Helmut continued to look uncomfortable. "Um, I ..." he began and then started again. "If you have particular questions, maybe I can talk to her. She seems pretty friendly."

"No, nothing in particular," Herschel responded. "I talked with her a little in the hall and think she wants this over too. She just needs to be sure that her final report ties everything up neatly."

"Officer Cole and I decided to meet for dinner tonight to talk more," Helmut admitted. "I think there's some special hospitality thing here in Alaska. You know, making people feel welcome. Besides, she is supposed to stay close to the family until Yachay is officially transferred."

"I hope you have a nice time, but be careful how much you tell her about Yachay," Ben cautioned.

Herschel said, "My instincts tell me that Marguerite Cole has a good heart. If we have any problems, it will be with her superiors."

Helmut looked around the room and spotted Yachay by the picture window with his sister. They were chattering away. "Yachay seems to be taking everything in stride. He certainly likes radio and TV. Let's make sure he doesn't discover video games."

Herschel asked, "Will Yachay be OK tonight while you're gone?"

"I think so," Helmut said. "I looked at the wound just before Dr. Menaker put on the new dressing this afternoon. The antibiotics came in time to prevent runaway infection. He just needs to be kept quiet so it can start to heal in earnest. Anyway, I'll just be a few steps away if anything comes up."

Alison noticed Nate sitting by himself. "Nate seems a little lost since Yachay came back into Kawsay's life," Alison stated quietly. "Not just that, I think he has a lot on his mind."

"Well," Ben added, "he's dealing with what's going to happen to him next. He knows that he has to leave us soon and has no assurance of how things will come out."

"Maybe it would do him some good to call his father," Grace suggested.

"I agree," Alison added. "We owe John a lot for making this trip possible for us. I don't know what we would have done without him. Let's call and let him know how we're doing. If he's able to talk, we can put Nate on."

"Sounds like a good idea," Ben said, "but first let's place our dinner orders. Helmut, what time is your reservation?"

Helmut consulted his watch. "Oh, I have about a half hour, but I think I might spend a little time downstairs in one of the gift shops. I'll check in on Yachay later before turning in." Helmut checked himself in a mirror and quickly disappeared.

Ben used his calling card to dial John Diamond's home. A somewhat familiar but surprisingly high voice answered the phone. "Hello? Diamonds."

"Is your father there, please?" Ben asked.

"Yes, just a minute."

There was a pause. "This is John Diamond."

"Hi, John. Ben Hunter here. Can we talk a few minutes?"

"Sure, Ben, let me shut my office door. Is everything OK? How was the flight?"

"Everything went very well. That's one reason I called. We all want to thank you. We could not have done this without your generosity. Wish you could have been here to see the family reunion of our Inca friends."

"Did you get the young man? Can he return with you?" John asked.

"Looks good, but we're not out of the woods yet."

"How's Nate?" John asked.

"That's the main reason I called," Ben said. "He's fine, but seems depressed. It's not like him. It may be that Kawsay has been focused on her brother, and he's concerned about what's going to happen to him next. We thought having him talk to you might be helpful."

John leaned back and ran his fingers through his hair. "Is he still having trouble sleeping? His younger self here isn't getting enough rest. The forward diary says I'm supposed to take him to the doctor after school Monday. The doctor will probably push some pills at us, but drugs won't cure a time warp!"

"Obviously they won't remove the cause, so let's keep working on that. When we get back home, I hope you can come up for a day so we can work on our plans," Ben said hopefully.

"I'll arrange something for the end of the week," John said. "If there's one thing I'm *not* good at, it's inaction."

"Let me put Nate on the phone." Ben handed the phone to Nate and moved across the lounge to give him space.

"Dad?" It was a muted voice.

"Hi, Nate. Good to hear your voice. How was your flight?" John asked.

"Fine."

"Do you like Alaska?"

"Sure."

"I understand you'll be there until Monday."

"I guess."

John noticed the flat voice. "What do you think of Kawsay's brother?"

"He eats a lot. He looks kinda wild."

"I'll bet his sister and grandfather were happy to find him!"

"Yeah. Kawsay hasn't stopped talking to him since we arrived," Nate complained. "I'm glad it's working out, but I'm not sure why I'm here in Alaska with everyone. They don't need me." John gave his son time to continue. "I'm not sure why I'm here in this time either. I can't stay here, but ...," Nate stopped and swallowed to soften the lump in his throat, "I don't know where to go. Dad, I'm really scared about getting back to meet you in the storm. What if it doesn't work?"

John wanted to encourage Nate, but was equally worried. "Nate, I'm scared too – for both of us. This tunnel thing is unproven. Even if I nip the cancer, thanks to your efforts, how do I know that I'll get you back? Maybe we ought to find a way to keep you here indefinitely."

"Nice thought, Dad, but you know that won't work. I know my other self is having trouble with the dreams because I've been having dreams about having dreams. It just can't go on. I don't want to leave you, or the Hunters, or Kawsay ...," Nate realized the other reason he was upset. "Of course now that Yachay is back, Kawsay hardly even talks to me."

"Son, it's only natural for Kawsay to focus on her brother at a time like this. They are very close, and she hasn't seen him for months. And that family has their own problems with the ones they left behind."

Nate looked across the room at Kusi and his grandchildren engaged in some fairly heated discussion. "Yeah, I see what you mean. But all I hear from her is about what a brave warrior and hero her brother is. She probably thinks I'm a wuss because I'm not an Inca warrior."

"Nate," John explained, "you're not Yachay, and he's not you. Would you want to be like him? Does he know several languages and all about ancient history? Does he know modern sports? Is he ready for college? Plus, you know martial arts. I'll bet you could teach him a thing or two."

"It's not that, Dad. It's the courage and bravery thing. Would I jump off a boat to save a little girl? Would I take on two men trying to knife someone? Maybe I'm too civilized or fearful to be a real hero."

"Well, a few days ago you saved Morrow. Doesn't that count? That showed great courage. You could have been hit by that truck when you rescued him." John paused. "I don't know where you'll get the courage to re-enter the time tunnel, but something tells me you'll pass that test too."

Nate remembered the feeling of his breath being sucked out of him. "Well, it's going to take courage and faith to jump into that tunnel. The last time, I just *fell* in by accident." Nate wondered if he should broach this topic now. "Dad, I don't think I can just return directly to where I fell out of the sailboat."

"What do you mean?" John's voice betrayed his alarm.

"Well, I've been thinking about the tunnels. Kawsay and Ben arrived in the cave in the Sierras from ancient Peru, and I arrived from Israel. As far as we know, no one has arrived directly from the ocean." Nate hoped his Dad could help think things through. "Maybe the tunnels are like a network. To get back to the ocean where I fell in, I may need to detour through Gibeah."

"I don't know about that. Wouldn't that be dangerous? Have you talked to Ben about this?" John pictured Nate getting shot at by the archer again.

"No, but I will. Actually, we both should." Nate wished he could see his Dad right now. "Can you come up for a visit when we get back to California? It's great how you helped them with the jet, but I need you to help them with me."

"Of course, Nate. Everything is happening so fast, but from what you've told me, the dreams end soon. So we need to get our plans together quickly because you're going to leave and go back to … somewhere. Make sure Ben calls me when you return."

"OK, Dad," Nate agreed. "Oh, you should see Ben. He can't take his eyes off Yachay's spear that has the arrow in it. I know he's trying to figure out how to get Yachay to let him have it and also how to return it to Jonathan. I think he'd also like to warn his old family about the need to get out of town before Saul's dynasty ends. Maybe I can help him." The last comment just hung there for a moment. John was about to object when Nate spoke again. "Oh, the food just arrived. I better get my dinner before Yachay eats it. Good to talk to you, Dad. Thank – just for being there."

John thought Nate was sounding more upbeat. "I'll always be here for you, Nate. See you soon."

As the group sorted out the covered plates and beverages, a calmer scene unfolded in the Crow's Nest restaurant atop the taller tower of the hotel complex. But under the surface things were actually quite tumultuous. Helmut had only paced back and forth in front of the maître d' a few times when a beautiful woman appeared from the elevator. She wore black slacks and heels and a shimmering, teal silk blouse, accented by a pearl necklace and earrings. She carried a black leather jacket over her arm. Helmut did not immediately recognize the elegant woman. She smiled and approached him with a confident air, speaking the line she had rehearsed on her way up from the lobby.

"Good evening, Helmut. I'm so glad to see you again." *There. I got it out without a hitch.*

The voice confirmed what was dawning on Helmut. *This is a policewoman?* "Marguerite?" he asked to be sure. He suddenly felt underdressed.

"Yes. Do I look so different out of uniform?" Their eyes were locked as they had been all morning.

"Well, as a matter of fact you do. The uniform doesn't do you justice at all." *There, I managed a decent compliment.* "Our table is ready. I asked for one on the west side so we could enjoy the sunset."

Marguerite took his arm as they were led a short distance past the bar area to a small table by an expansive window. Helmut assisted Marguerite with her chair and took the seat opposite. They were too absorbed with looking at each other to notice the panoramic view or to begin looking at the menu and wine list.

I had no idea she was quite this stunning, Helmut thought. Then he remembered the gift. "I found this for you," he said, handing her a small box.

Marguerite straightened her posture, smiled with delight, and began opening the box. "Oh, Helmut. It's a little carved puffin. Did I tell you I love puffins?" She turned it over. "It's made by a native in Hoonah. Thank you so much."

"I'm really glad you like it, Marguerite." They were interrupted by a waiter bringing water and a bread basket.

Marguerite was trying to focus her thoughts. She felt overwhelmed by Helmut's presence. *What is that power I'm feeling coming from this guy? It is strange but nice.* "How is your patient doing? Will he be all right without you for a few hours?"

"He's fine. They'll call me if there's a problem," Helmut quickly answered. "So, where did we leave off this afternoon?" *Easy, boy.*

"Oh, we'd just finished our life stories and were about to launch into our hopes and dreams," Marguerite answered with a smile and toss of her hair. "Maybe we should relax and get some wine."

"Sorry if I seem a little intense," Helmut apologized. "I'm only here for a short while and ..." *And what?*

"And you want us to make good use of the time?" Marguerite finished the thought.

"Well, sure. You could put it that way." *Should I tell her this? Why not? Nothing to lose.* "I had a picture in my mind – I sometimes see little pictures when I'm thinking – of two passenger ships passing in opposite directions. I was on one and you on the other. We saw each other and waved, but I could only partially hear what you were shouting. As the ships passed, we both moved to the sterns to stay close, but we soon drew apart and could not hear each other at all. I felt like we needed to jump into the water and swim to each other and not let the ships take us away. Funny, huh?"

The word picture mirrored Marguerite's feelings. "Do you ever get a strong feeling that something important is going on, and you need to stop and pay attention? I can see by your smile that you do. What causes that feeling?"

"I certainly felt that way today; still do. Seems to be affecting both of us. Did we meet just a little over ten hours ago?" *Is this really happening? Am I going too fast?* The waiter stopped by to take their order, but they had not even looked at the menus. "I suppose we need to order before they evict us!" Helmut said with a wink. "I take it you've been here before?"

"For some special occasions. Everything is good here, but you need to save room for their banana split. It's beautifully presented." Marguerite grew quiet as she studied the menu.

Taking a cue from her, Helmut began to read too. Helmut discussed the wine selection with the waiter, and they placed their orders.

Where do we take this now? Marguerite wondered. "So, Helmut, when does this ship of yours sail away?"

"As I mentioned this morning, I have a guide waiting for me in Iliamna. I had planned to get back to my animal tracking as soon as Yachay and the others leave. Could be as early as Monday morning. That depends on you, I suppose."

"On me? Oh, you mean the final official release. That decision will be made above me." *No official business tonight, Marguerite!* "What will you do tomorrow?"

"Not sure. I didn't even know I'd be in Anchorage until last night, so I have no plans at all." *Helmut began to flip through ideas of what he could ask Marguerite to do.* "Do you ever get any time off work for good behavior?"

"Sure. In fact, the State owes me a lot of vacation. I've been filling in this summer for all my colleagues who wanted time off for family trips." *Here goes.* "I'm off tomorrow and wondered if you might enjoy taking a hike in the Chugach."

"The Chugach?" Helmut asked. "Oh, you mean the big state park east of town. That might be a lot of fun, and I have more appropriate clothing for hiking than for fine dining. Did you have a particular trail in mind?"

Marguerite thought about this. "Well, how much time do we have, and what do you want to see?" Her eyelids fluttered involuntarily.

I'd like to see more of you, he thought. "I shouldn't be gone all day because my patient may need me, but I suppose we could be out five or six hours."

"Then we should do a hike near town, but not Flattop, which everyone does so it's always crowded. Besides, that area gives me a bad feeling. Hmmm. You know," she said, brightening, "we could hike from the Prospect Heights trailhead up to Wolverine Peak. It's a quick 10-mile round trip with about a 3,400-foot elevation gain. It's not too steep and rarely crowded. We won't see any wolverines, but there's a good chance of encountering some Dall sheep. It gives a nice view back toward town and also deeper into the Park. Are you up for that? I could bring some cheese sandwiches, fruit, and water…"

"And I'll carry the pack and bring some killer energy bars," Helmut cut in. He liked her initiative.

"Why don't I meet you on Fifth Avenue in front of the Cook at, say, nine o'clock? Will that give you enough time to take care of Yachay?"

Helmut was not troubled by the hour, but was wondering what he would tell his friends about a second date starting only a few hours after the first ended. Then he remembered. "Tomorrow is Sunday. But to tell the truth, I feel closer to God on a mountain top than just about anywhere."

"I've thought that same thing many times," Marguerite mused. "You know, I've been reading a great little book recently; I wonder if you've heard of it. It's called *The Practice of the Presence of God.*"

"Oh, sure, by Brother Lawrence. Yeah, I wore out my copy years ago re-reading it."

The wine arrived followed shortly by a large spinach salad they had decided to split. They were further distracted by the first tinges of a beautiful sunset. Helmut looked back to see Marguerite staring at him. No, it was more like gazing, lost in her thoughts. He was not accustomed to being an object of adoration and was not sure how to react, so he smiled and shrugged.

"Oh, was I staring?" Marguerite looked down, embarrassed. "I'm sorry, but I can see a sunset anytime, and …" She did not know how to finish the statement.

"No, that's fine," Helmut said, reaching out to take her hand. "I've been studying your face too when you're not looking. I want to remember … everything."

Marguerite was relieved not to be the only one feeling twitterpated. "Helmut, I have to ask you something, if you don't mind." He nodded. "You're a very accomplished and successful guy and very handsome … No, I'm sorry, but you are. Why are you, or how have you, managed to stay single all your life? It's rare to encounter a man like you."

Helmut leaned back and tilted his head. "Hey, 'all my life' hasn't seemed that long, you know. But I guess you're right. It is a little unusual, and I get asked that sometimes. My mother used to bug me about it."

"Are your parents …?"

"Oh, they're still around, but they don't live in the Sierras anymore," Helmut explained. "They're writers and travel all the time researching their novels."

"So," she continued prodding, "how *do* you usually answer the question?"

"Oh, I tell people that I've been too busy with my work, which has a grain or two of truth in it."

The policewoman was relentless. "So, are there other grains in there too?"

"Sure." He noticed her eyebrows arching, encouraging him to continue. "You might say I just never met the right person, but there's a deeper aspect to it. Ben and I used to talk about this. Our parents have an excellent relationship. They share interests and share their work. The two really are one. But so many other couples we knew were, well, it was like they were living two parallel lives that only touched tangentially. It was like they were role playing the parts of the husband and the wife…"

"Functions!" Marguerite interrupted, excited. "They were fulfilling the husband function and the wife function, but they weren't soul mates." She realized that she had interrupted. "I'm sorry, but I've thought the same thing about most couples – they aren't really joined at all, just working at living together. I've always been afraid that if I let myself enter into one of those *arrangements*, the next month I'd encounter the perfect man for me and find out that I'd made the mistake of my life by marrying in haste!" She stopped and took a deep breath to relax.

Helmut processed her theories for a while as he considered her intensity. *I think she nailed it. Who wants to be a "function"?* "Yeah, I think you're right, though I never thought about it in those terms. I used to think about the 'opportunity cost' of marrying the wrong person, which is missing out on the chance for the right person."

"Right," Marguerite responded. "I've tried to explain this to family and friends, and the usual response is 'That's too idealistic' or 'You're too picky'. I know they meant well, but I think they really stopped believing in the idea of a soul mate or perfect match, and they were afraid I'd be sorry if I waited too long."

"I have heard just the opposite from Ben and Alison. They've only been married a few years. They stayed single a long time. When I see how happy they are and how they bring out the best in each other and share so much on so many levels, I know I could never 'settle' for, what did you call it? Oh, being a 'function'. I believe it is way better to be single than to be hitched to the wrong person."

"Yes, Helmut," Marguerite said, nodding. "I believe that connecting with the right person is the most important thing in life, or second after God."

"I'd like to think so. Ben and Alison have described their experience to me, and I do take inspiration from them. They waited for each other. They couldn't *not* be together. Nothing else mattered. They hardly knew each other when they decided to get married. Yet they say it was like they had *always* known each other."

Marguerite felt a shiver up her back and rolled her shoulders. "Yes, I've heard it described that way too. It all happens so fast, as if everything else in life is immediately reoriented around the new core. Kinda scary, but it's exciting too."

Their meals arrived, giving them time to reflect and decompress. The western sky was intensifying as the Sun glided toward the "Sleeping Lady" across the inlet. Helmut mused, "I've always wondered if sunsets and sunrises are fundamentally different, other than the fact that we sleep through a lot more sunrises."

"They both can be beautiful," Marguerite observed. "But sunsets make me feel a little sad and wistful that the day is over. Sunrises are filled with quiet promises and hope. They're peaceful, but invite me to visualize what the day may hold."

"Which are we?" Helmut asked, leaning forward and again finding her hand.

Marguerite looked into his eyes for a long time. She thought she saw the answer and felt another chill. "Scary, isn't it?"

"Well! Hello, Officer Cole." The jarring voice caused Helmut and Marguerite to retract their arms and straighten up. "Am I interrupting anything important? You must be Dr. Rhodes."

Cole could not believe the intrusion. "Janie! How did, … What are you doing here?"

"Oh, I was hoping to talk a little to Dr. Rhodes about Yachay, hoping he could fill in a little more of my next story. Aren't you going to introduce me?" she said with a little pout.

Helmut rose, sharing Marguerite's distress at this development. "Hello, I'm Dr. Helmut Hunter, and you are…?"

"Oh, I'm so sorry," Janie said in a fluster, taking his hand. "I thought you were another doctor." Helmut kept waiting for her name. "Oh, yes. I'm Janie Briggs with the Daily News."

"I'm pleased to meet you, Ms. Briggs. I read your excellent article about Yachay yesterday," Helmut stated with a small bow and then sat down again.

"Janie, we just talked a few hours ago. The family has asked not to be disturbed," Cole said with a stern stare. "What brought you up here tonight?"

"Well, I just checked with the better hotels and then called Dr. Rhodes' room, but got no answer, so I thought I might find him in one of the hotel's restaurants." Janie was proud of her cleverness.

"I'm sorry, Ms. Briggs, but Dr. Rhodes isn't here," Helmut said evenly. "Officer Cole and I were discussing hiking trails in the Anchorage area. What's your favorite?"

"Oh, I'm afraid I'm not much of a hiker or anything like that. Did you say you know Dr. Rhodes? Do you know where he is?" Janie said returning to her agenda.

"Yes, I have met him. I think he may be dining in tonight," Helmut responded.

Cole took control. "Janie, Dr. Hunter was vacationing in Alaska and agreed to assist with Yachay's medical care so he could be released from the hospital. I believe he's prescribed bed rest until the wound heals, isn't that right Dr. Hunter?"

Helmut's brows furrowed as if considering the question. "Oh, yes. Best thing for him right now is peaceful rest. His family is nearby, and he's very happy to be with them right now."

Janie sensed the opportunity closing. "Well, when could I get a short interview with

Yachay or Dr. Rhodes? I'm so disappointed that I just missed them as they were checking out of the hospital. I presume he's been able to translate, so you know how the boy got here and where he's from."

Marguerite hoped a little more information would satisfy Janie, at least for tonight. "Like I told you when you stopped by the hospital, Yachay and his family are from a remote village in Peru and hope to return there soon. We're still trying to verify how he got to Kodiak. He's not sure himself. There may be some amnesia problem. Maybe if we give him a few days, his memory will improve."

"This can't wait long," Janie explained. "People want to know the rest of Yachay's story, and I've missed the Sunday paper cutoff already. Maybe I'll just leave a message for Dr. Rhodes to contact me. *He's* not under any doctor's orders to rest, is he?"

"I'm sure Dr. Rhodes would be happy to talk with you," Helmut said with an encouraging smile. "If you leave a message with the desk, he could return it tomorrow."

"I guess I have no choice," Janie lamented. Then with a wicked smile she added, "Marguerite, you look beautiful tonight. I don't recall seeing you out of uniform before."

Marguerite returned her smile with narrowed eyes, "Well Janie, unlike you busy reporters, I do occasionally go off duty."

Janie knew it was time to go and apologized for her intrusion before leaving them alone. Marguerite and Helmut returned to cold food and a broken spell. "I'm sorry, Helmut."

"It's OK, Marguerite. I think we handled it right, don't you?" Helmut responded.

Marguerite looked out the window with a worried expression. "I just know that she's going to research you tonight and start asking me about our relationship. I wish I could just hide or leave town for a while."

"Well…" Helmut looked out the window to the southwest toward the volcanoes of the Alaska Peninsula and Lake Iliamna beyond. His eyes returned to hers and, raising his eyebrows, he said, "Maybe you should. Let's explore that tomorrow. Do you think Janie will be a problem for Yachay and the group?"

"Usually giving Janie a short interview is better than blowing her off. But you heard Yachay's story. What can he tell her? It makes no sense – unless you think she believes in mythical submarines."

Helmut was reluctant to tell Marguerite too much too fast, but also sensed that she was very bright and completely trustworthy. "Marguerite, have you learned in your work and in your biology research how preconceptions can interfere with the testing and analysis of hypotheses?"

Marguerite had to pause to change gears into her investigator mode. "You mean, if we're not open minded, we may miss the pattern or dismiss the clues?"

"Exactly. What troubles you most about Yachay's story?" Helmut asked quietly.

"Well, it's not that he seems unreliable or, you know, making up a story. But there he is in a remote Peruvian cave, and he falls through a musical wall and ends up in a basement somewhere, so he jumps back into some hole and ends up in a bear cave on Kodiak Island. Of course, that's impossible, but Yachay believes it happened that way. So… What? Why are you looking at me like that?" Helmut was smiling at her. "Oh, Helmut, you're not saying that it *is* possible, are you?"

"Wasn't it Sherlock Holmes who suggested that when you eliminate all the other possibilities, then the one remaining, no matter how improbable, must be the truth?" Helmut posed.

"Really, Helmut. There's a world of difference between improbable and impossible," she protested. "Besides, we haven't begun to look at all the possibilities."

"What if I told you his sister and grandfather and others had been through similar experiences?" Helmut added. "Wouldn't that blur the improbable-impossible distinction?"

Marguerite sat back and searched Helmut's face. She weighed another possibility, the one that Helmut was concerned about. *Maybe this beautiful man is also a fruitcake. That would be just my luck!* "What are you saying?" she asked.

"I'm not saying anything," Helmut dodged. "I'm just encouraging you to be completely objective and not imprisoned by presuppositions that may be wrong."

"Fine! I'll keep a completely open mind even if my brain falls out," Marguerite said. Leaning forward, she added just above a whisper, "But I need a little assurance, OK? You're not crazy, are you?"

"Me?" Helmut stated in mock protest. "No more than Ben and Alison and Herschel and Grace. Besides, don't all the ER docs you know go searching for mythical creatures and give aid and comfort to severely displaced Inca warriors? All the policewomen I know are trained in microbiology, are incurable romantics, and are drop-dead gorgeous."

Marguerite gave him a sly glance. "Look, you crazy, wonderful man. I'll cut you some slack because I'm a little strange too, but I don't want you to toy around with me. If you know something important about this matter, I want you to tell me. Not as an officer assigned to a case – there is no case here – but as a friend. I care about Yachay, and I care about you. If you don't trust me, why should I trust you?"

Helmut pondered how to proceed. She waited. "Marguerite, I think you're the real article. As a person, I feel you're completely trustworthy. But because of your official role in this matter…, well, it's not up to me. I'm just here to help Yachay and his family. All they want to do is take Yachay back with them. I don't want to do anything that would prevent that. Wherever he belongs, Yachay doesn't belong in Alaska."

Marguerite perceived Helmut's difficult position and did not want to pressure him too much. "Darn it, anyway."

"What?" Helmut was surprised. "Did I say something wrong?"

"No, Helmut. It's just that, well, if you've never been a cop, maybe you don't know how it is. People just don't ever let you step out of the role. It's like the uniform is tattooed to your body. I'm sitting here losing my heart, and you're all defensive. And I can't criticize you for it either. It's so frustrating!"

Their waiter stopped by with water and, noticing the untouched food, asked if everything was all right. They looked at their plates and smiled conspiratorially, but assured him that everything was fine.

"Look, Marguerite, we'll have more time to talk tomorrow, and all this wonderful food is getting cold," Helmut reasoned. "Believe me, I'm really interested in you – just you without the tattoos – and my instincts are to tell you everything and trust you 110 percent. We're moving pretty fast here. Let's sleep on it and see how we feel in the morning. Just being with you has me a bit off balance, so I don't know if I can trust my own instincts."

"Just out of curiosity, what are your instincts?" Marguerite asked.

Let's see, this is just about me, not the others. I can say what I want. "Oh, nothing much. Just to never be away from you for more than five minutes for the rest of my life."

"Is that all? What happened to eternity?" she teased. She saw his eyes twinkle and added, "Can you get along without me until nine tomorrow morning?"

They finally focused on their dinners and topped it off by sharing an exquisite banana split with berries and multi-colored syrups swirled across the plate. They let their eyes do most of the talking. As they rode down the elevator and walked to the main lobby, they made final plans for their hike, deciding to defer the start until 10:00 a.m. Helmut escorted her to her car in the adjacent parking garage. She opened the car door. Before she could get in, Helmut gently turned her toward him, holding her hands in his.

"Are you still scared?" he asked.

She looked up at him, so close and so real. "Yes," she sighed, "and I love it."

"Thank you for a great evening, Marguerite. Do you see the dawn yet?" he asked, looking for answers in her eyes.

"I feel it," she whispered, returning his gaze.

"Yes, so do I." Helmut tried to coalesce his thoughts. "Marguerite, I *really* want to find out what this is all about. It's so unusual, really unique. I don't want to let something perfect slip away from us."

"So much has happened in a very short time on one very busy day. Let's make the most of the day we have together tomorrow," she replied with a hopeful smile.

Helmut returned to his room shortly after 10:00 p.m. to find Nate reading on one of the beds. "Hi, Helmut. I got a good book downstairs about Alaska history. Did you know that there are reindeer here? They aren't native, but were brought over from Lapland by a missionary named Sheldon Jackson because he thought they would be useful to the native people."

"Yeah, I think I heard about that. How did the evening go?" Helmut had only been away a few hours, but felt like a different person.

"Fine. Everyone is pretty tired. Ben said you should give him a call if you got back before eleven."

"I'll just knock on his door."

Ben answered in pajamas and invited Helmut in. Alison was also dressed for bed.

"Helmut," she said cheerfully. "How was your evening?"

Helmut's smile said it all. "Very nice. Marguerite is very, hmmm, very special. We're going hiking in the morning."

Ben was surprised. "Really? Where?"

"We had more to talk about, so we decided to climb Wolverine Peak. It's just a few miles to the east. She'll pick me up after breakfast." Helmut found a comfortable chair. "Goes to show, when you get up in the morning, anything can happen. I've been up since before six, but I'm not tired. I feel like a kid."

Ben and Alison looked at each other. "According to Yachay, you and Officer Cole hit it off from the beginning," Alison asserted. "Apparently, he is very perceptive."

Helmut was impressed. "He must have read our body language; I suppose that's universal. Anyway, Nate said you wanted to talk to me before we turn in tonight. Anything wrong?"

"No, at least I hope not," Ben said, sitting down opposite his brother. "Yachay seems to be doing fine, though you might want to look in on him. Herschel has gotten two recorded phone messages from the reporter who did the original article you found. She wants an interview with him and Yachay and anyone else who can shed light on what she calls 'our young hero'. I can understand what she's trying to do, but things are delicate. This kind of publicity could endanger Yachay and the others. It might scuttle our plan to get out of town Monday. Maybe, as the doctor, you can help keep Yachay away from the press, but Herschel can't use you as an excuse."

"Janie – she's the reporter – tracked us down in the restaurant. She's good, and she's persistent. Marguerite had told her earlier Yachay was from Peru and was going back, and she's still investigating how he got here. Marguerite thinks the reporter is going to look me up on the internet. For all I know, I'll turn up on some gossip column."

"Did Officer, I mean, Marguerite ask you more about Yachay?" Ben inquired.

"A little. I debated how much to tell her because of her official involvement. She's already decided there's nothing for the Troopers here other than to get some paperwork to allow them to close the file. She really took a liking to Yachay. I think she is just naturally curious. If you were in her shoes and heard his story today, wouldn't you wonder too?"

"Of course we would," Alison stated. "But isn't it risky to tell anyone the whole story?"

"She heard the whole story," Helmut clarified. "She wonders if I know the *real* story. I don't want to lie to her, but I don't want her to think I'm crazy either."

"Why is it so important what she thinks of you?" Ben teased.

"Maybe I *am* crazy, Ben. But I think you of all people would understand. She may be my 'Alison'." Helmut glanced over at Alison and then back at Ben. "It's pretty much like you described it to me. You don't plan it or even invite it. You just know something has turned or changed inside, and you will never be the same again."

Ben looked at Helmut for a long time, while Alison watched them both. "How does Marguerite feel about this?" Ben finally asked.

"Well, I think she feels the same. She says it feels scary, but she loves it," Helmut recounted.

"Yes," Alison interjected. "It is scary, probably like disappearing down a time tunnel, totally out of control, but I loved it too. I still do!"

"Helmut, you don't need our advice," Ben admitted. "You're no kid, and you've been very careful about relationships all your life. If Marguerite is the one, I'd be thrilled, but I'd worry about her trying to fit into your lifestyle. What would she do when you go out searching for mythical birds and fish?"

Helmut offered an impish grin. "I was thinking of using a little test, you know, like a fleece." They both looked at him skeptically. "No, really! Why not let God have a say in this? I was thinking of inviting her to go with me back to Iliamna. She's accomplished at outdoor living. We'll have the guide for a chaperone. If she agrees to go, I'll take that as an indication that I should pursue the relationship seriously."

"Oh, Helmut, that can be dangerous," Alison said with concern. "It's like forcing God's hand. Don't do it unless you really feel led to do so."

"Well, it's just that I don't want to get involved if it's a dead end. Don't worry; I'm being careful. In fact, to be sure, I was thinking about a second test of the relationship's potential, but wanted your opinions first," Helmut said. "I think I should ask her to promise to keep a confidence, and if she agrees, then I'll tell her what I believe is the full Yachay story. If she believes me – well, most people wouldn't –that would be a second confirmation."

Ben's cautious side came out. "We cannot let this involvement of yours jeopardize Yachay and his family. It's not fair to them."

"That's what I thought," Helmut quickly responded. "But I figure it this way. If she doesn't believe me, then she'll just write me off as a nut. Her report will simply leave Yachay's arrival a mystery. If she does believe me, she'll realize how important it is to protect Yachay and the others and will help us any way she can. She obviously won't tell her superiors that she thinks her charge arrived through a time tunnel after first meeting Paul Revere. And, of course, if she believes my story about the Incas, she might also believe me when I get up the courage to tell her I love her." He smiled at his own brilliance.

Alison mediated. "Guys, it's been a *really* long day. Can a final decision on this wait until morning?"

"Sure," Helmut allowed, "but she's picking me up at ten in the morning. I need to have a good breakfast so I can keep up with her on the hike."

Ben set his mind at ease. "We'll talk this over in the morning. Let's get some sleep."

"Fine. OK." Helmut got up to leave and looked back as he opened the door. "One question: Is it five-seven-five?"

"What do you mean?" Ben asked.

"Yes, Helmut," Alison answered. "Haikus are five-seven-five."

CHAPTER 22.

MISSIONS ACCOMPLISHED

SEPTEMBER 6 – PRESENT YEAR
ANCHORAGE, ALASKA

RESTING AND WAITING
WHILE ACTIVE MINDS FORGE ONWARD
SEARCHING THE FUTURE.

"You're going on a hike today? May I come along?" Nate asked Helmut as they were walking down the hall to the lounge for a communal breakfast. "Maybe Kawsay would like to come too. She's probably feeling cooped up."

"Nate, I'd like to have you come along, but this is more like a date. Officer Cole and I have important things to talk over. I'm sure you understand," Helmut answered carefully.

"A date? Didn't you two just have dinner last night?" Nate asked with surprise.

"Sure we did, but I'm only here a short time, so we wanted to get to know each other better while we have the chance," Helmut answered.

"OK. I understand. Hope you have a good time," Nate said. He still felt a little glum. *I'm only around a short time too. I want to spend more time with Kawsay, but then what? I may never see her again.*

As they entered the lounge area, aromas of hot breakfast delicacies greeted them. Herschel and Ben were already there. It was 8:30 a.m., and Helmut was surprised to hear his satellite phone ringing.

"Dr. Hunter," he answered.

"Good morning, Helmut. Did you sleep well," said the now familiar voice of Marguerite Cole.

"Hi, Marguerite. Yes, just fine. You too?"

"Yes, though I was up a little late thinking about things. Are we still on?" she asked.

"I hope so," Helmut responded. "Should I bring a fleece?" *Funny, I'm bringing two fleeces!*

"I would," Marguerite said. "The weather can be very changeable. Say, I had a message on my cell phone from Joe Stevens, the father of the girl Yachay rescued. He'd like to meet Yachay's family and thank them in person. I know everyone is concerned about publicity, but Joe is a good guy and has paid for Yachay's medical bills. Do you think the Stevens family could visit later today?"

Helmut paused. "It's not really up to me. I think Herschel and my brother, Ben, need to make that decision. If Joe left a phone number, they can call him and arrange something."

"That's fine. I better hurry now; I'm still trying to find some gear I haven't used in months," Marguerite said. She gave Helmut the Stevens' number, and they ended the call. Helmut conveyed the gist of the call to the other men.

"I think it would be fine to meet up here with the Stevens family," Herschel said. "It's a big event in their lives – especially the little girl's. They will always remember it. I'll confirm it with Kusi and the kids first, though."

Ben agreed. "From the sound of it, Joe's a good guy and isn't likely to probe too much like a newspaper reporter."

The breakfast aromas had made their way down the hall, and within minutes everyone was gathered around the food. Yachay allowed Helmut to change the dressing on his wound, which was healing quickly.

This gave Nate the opportunity to talk with Kawsay as they ate together in a corner. "I tried to get Helmut to take us on a hike with him and Officer Cole today, but he said it was a date," Nate whispered.

"A date? Is that some kind of fruit?" Kawsay whispered back.

Nate smiled. "Yes, but the same word means different things. A date is a special time that a man and woman spend together when they want to get to know each other better and have fun. Boys and girls start to go on dates together when they are fourteen or fifteen. They stop when they get married."

"Why do they stop?"

Nate thought about this question. "I don't know. They just seem to stop. Maybe they don't have fun anymore, except some married people like Alison and Ben seem to have fun all the time."

"Should we have a date?" Kawsay asked. "I like to spend time with you and know you better and have fun."

Nate was very happy to hear this. He looked closely at his best friend. "Since Yachay was found, we do not talk or spend time together. You are with him all the time."

"Nate, Yachay is my brother. He was lost, and now we find him. He also was my teacher. I am happy to be with him now. I must explain more to him about moving in time. We must plan how to go and save Mother and Grandmother. I am very busy now. Maybe we have date later?" Kawsay stopped.

Nate noted that she was not only speaking English better, but faster, stringing thoughts together. "Sure, I understand," Nate said. "But, Kawsay, I will not be here much longer. You know I cannot stay, but I must return to where, or when, I came from. Maybe I will never see you again."

Kawsay saw the troubled look in his eyes. "Nate, it is only three years in the future to your boat in the ocean. I will live that long. We will have many dates when we get to the future."

Nate smiled and hoped Kawsay was right. But he continued to feel small and weak compared to her heroic warrior brother. *What can I do to show her that I am brave and strong too? Maybe I need to join the Marines or something.*

As breakfast was ending, Ben announced that he and Alison were planning to take a short walk on the nearby Coastal Trail and that Herschel and Grace would be coming along. Herschel added in both languages that it would be dangerous for Kusi, Kawsay, and Yachay to appear in public and that Helmut had prescribed a day of rest for Yachay before tomorrow's hoped-for trip back to California.

Nate thought of tagging along, but decided to stay with his Inca friends. *I need to get to know Kawsay's brother better. Maybe if he gets to know me, he will like me.*

It was a cool, 48-degree morning, so the four walkers wore extra layers under their jackets. As they waited for the elevator and rode down to the lobby, Ben explained that they could access the Coastal Trail at the bottom of Fifth Avenue. "The trail follows the shoreline for about 10 miles, where it ends at Kincaid Park, a large urban wilderness south of the airport. According to the concierge, people often see moose and, on rare occasions, bear along the trail but mostly walkers, bikers, runners, roller bladers, baby strollers, and many dogs."

Grace looked at Ben dubiously. "You're taking me on a 20-mile stroll to see wild animals? On a Sunday morning?"

Ben smiled back. "Don't worry, Grace. There's a pretty lagoon only about a mile down the path. Then I guess it goes by some parks and nice oceanfront homes. A little past three miles is Earthquake Park where there is a memorial to the 1964 earthquake. Sounds like a whole neighborhood slid down into the ocean there."

"Herschel, Ben's trying to make me feel better by telling me that around here whole neighborhoods fall into the ocean!" Grace teased.

After they exited the elevator and strolled down the hall toward Fifth Avenue, a voice called out to them from behind. "Oh, Dr. Rhodes, Dr. Rhodes." They all turned around to see a slightly disheveled woman in slacks and a tailored sweater. She was hurrying toward them with a laptop computer under one arm and an open cell phone displayed in her other hand. She came up to Herschel, slipped her cell phone into her pocket, and extended her right hand. "Hello, Dr. Rhodes," she gushed. "I'm Janie Briggs with the Anchorage Daily News. I hope you got my messages. I need to talk with you about Yachay." She saw Dr. Rhodes' confused look.

"Have we met? You seem to recognize me," Herschel said.

"I recognize you from your website. Please. I really need to talk with you. It's important. I learned that you were staying here and have been waiting to see you for over three hours."

Ben tensed, and Alison gave Grace a worried look. Hershel was confused for only a moment. "Oh, yes. Janie Briggs. You wrote the article in the paper about the rescue of Cindy Stevens."

Janie smiled. "Yes, that was mine. I hope to write another for tomorrow's edition now that you're here to complete the story."

Herschel was not pleased, but was nonetheless gracious. "My friends and I were just heading out for a stroll. You have a beautiful city and …"

Janie cut him off. "Please, Dr. Rhodes. The people of Alaska want to know the rest of Yachay's story. He's a hero, you know, but he's a mystery too! You talked to him yesterday. Tell me. What did he say? How did he get on the ferry? How is that nasty bear wound healing?"

Herschel noticed Helmut, dressed for his hike, moving silently behind Janie toward the door. Helmut signaled them to keep his presence quiet as he slipped away. Herschel gave Janie a serious look through narrowed eyes. "Look, Ms. Briggs, I'm only a translator. I'm really not at liberty to discuss police matters or divulge medical information."

"Dr. Rhodes," Janie said, cocking her head to one side. "I have learned that you are here with members of Yachay's family and plan to return him to Peru. I believe you could tell me a great deal."

Herschel thought about his options and quickly decided. "OK, Ms. Briggs. I'll ask my friends here to wait a few minutes while we talk. I'll give you ten minutes."

"Thank you," Janie replied graciously. "Let's sit over there so I can take some notes while we chat." Ben, Alison, and Grace slipped quietly down the hall before Janie attempted to question them too. Sitting down and opening a new document on her laptop, Janie began her fishing expedition armed with rumors she had picked up from her sources. "So, it's quite a coincidence, isn't it, that the translator whom Professor Rios called turned out to be a friend of Yachay's family. How is it you know the family?"

"Yes, it seems to be a coincidence," Herschel replied. He decided not to volunteer information. "I met other members of his family in my interpreter role as well. There aren't too many people who speak their language."

Janie looked for another opening. "What *are* these people doing here in Alaska or in the U.S. for that matter?"

"As far as I know, they are just trying to get back home," he replied, again keeping it brief.

"Yes, but how did they come to be here in the first place?" she persisted.

Herschel gave her a perplexed look, shaking his head. "Maybe you can explain it, Ms. Briggs. They all say they were in the mountains near their village and fell through a hole and ended up in our country. Have you ever heard of such a thing?"

Janie just stared back for a few seconds, not knowing what to say. "I, um, no, I haven't. Do you believe them? What do you think really happened?"

"I'm just a linguist and have no first-hand observations I can relay," Herschel said apologetically. "It seems that they just showed up. Beyond that, I really don't know."

"So you can't tell me how Yachay got to Kodiak Island," Janie remarked, more a statement than a question. Herschel just shrugged. She continued, "Well, it sounds like they all may have entered the country illegally. Will they be allowed to return?"

"I don't think we can assume they came here illegally, and I certainly hope you don't create problems for Yachay. After all, he saved Cindy's life despite his serious injury," he responded somewhat indignantly. "It's my understanding that the Peruvian government wants Yachay and his family to return home, and they're eager to return, so I don't see any problem here at all."

Janie was a bit flustered. She wanted to push the hero story, not create problems. "Well, how soon will Yachay be leaving? Some people are planning a ceremony to honor him."

Just as I feared, Herschel thought. "There's some paperwork that needs to come through from Peru. You tell me how long that might take – you know bureaucracies."

Janie did know bureaucracies and thought it could take a while. "So, how is Yachay doing today? Could I interview him and his family? Our readers would be very interested in hearing more about their, let's call it, fantastic journey."

"All I know is that Yachay's doctor has prescribed full bed rest today. We all want him to recover as quickly as possible, don't we?" Herschel said, nodding.

Janie involuntarily nodded along. "Of course," she responded using her sympathetic voice. "When do you think he'll be strong enough to attend *his* ceremony? We're trying to schedule it."

"Oh, you are? I'm not sure. Maybe in a few days. We'll just have to see, won't we?" Herschel was nodding again.

Janie began nodding again and then cleared her head. "Well, this is all very interesting, but I'm not sure you have really helped me understand the real story here. Aren't you curious or even concerned about these Peruvian villagers just showing up here? What does it all mean?"

Herschel shrugged again. "Ms. Briggs, I agree with you. This is a mystery that seems to defy natural explanations. I have to admit I've never encountered anything like it. I wish I had all the answers." Janie seemed to have run out of questions, so Herschel took the opportunity to add, "I don't want to keep my friends waiting any longer. I've enjoyed visiting with you. Thank you for helping Yachay."

"Oh, you're welcome," Janie responded, wondering exactly what she had done to help. "Here's my card. Please call me if there are any developments, or if you recall something you forgot to tell me."

Herschel took the card and stood up, effectively ending the interview. "Goodbye, Ms. Briggs. It was a pleasure to meet you this morning. Hope you enjoy this beautiful day." With that, he strolled down the hall where Grace and the Hunters had recently disappeared. He found them being invisible in a crowd of late-season tourists waiting to be loaded onto a bus. "It's safe to come out now," he whispered loudly.

"How did it go?" Alison asked.

"We'll see. I know I didn't give her the story she wanted, so who knows what she'll print," Herschel responded, aiming his friends toward the door. "She still wants an interview with Yachay and his family, but I hope we can avoid that. I just hope that the publicity will end here in Anchorage."

They left the hotel and followed Fifth Avenue down a hill to Elderberry Park. It was a quiet morning with only a few couples and families in the park and one dog chasing a Frisbee.

"Let's see. I was told the Coastal Trail entrance was to the right by the old house," Ben said, leading them down some steps. They turned left onto the trail, which immediately brought them to a tunnel under railroad tracks and then out close to the shore. Across the inlet were the shimmering white peaks which begin the Aleutian Range. The morning's high tide was already receding, revealing an unusual, brown mud bottom.

"Honey, what's wrong with the beach?" Alison asked. "It's all muddy."

"According to Helmut, these inlets are full of glacial silt – rock ground fine by glaciers. It just keeps coming down the rivers, and not even the thirty-foot tides are able to wash it all out to sea. When it's wet, it can be like quicksand," Ben replied.

The two couples continued down the narrow paved trail, enjoying the fresh breeze coming off the cold water. The calls of gulls reminded them that this muddy water was ocean, even though there were no breakers. After walking nearly a mile, they passed through another tunnel under the tracks and came to a lagoon harboring several fleets of ducks, grebes, and other waterfowl. They enjoyed the view east across the water toward the Chugach Mountains and wondered which peak Helmut and Marguerite were climbing. They were struck by the large number of small planes overhead, which they had read was typical in Alaska where many towns and settlements are not on the road system. They continued past the lagoon and through one more tunnel, which echoed as a small, dark blue passenger train with gold trim passed overhead.

They decided to turn around by a half-mile marker on a bridge over a spillway. Passing back up through the park toward Fifth Avenue, they heard an extremely raucous but plaintive "meow" sound being uttered repeatedly, apparently for their benefit. They were soon accosted by the author of the noises, a gray and white tomcat who blocked their path. The bold animal looked right at each of them in turn, continuing to meow loudly, opening his mouth so wide that his ears moved down with each iteration. The creature was quite arresting.

"Are you getting Minged?" The voice belonged to a young-looking woman with very long, dark hair, a long-sleeved white top, black stretch pants, and wrap-around sunglasses topped by a black visor. A tall man wearing a similar outfit who sported a short beard accompanied her. Both wore running shoes and appeared to be finishing a run on the trail. They were both smiling as if they knew some inside joke.

"Are we what?" Alison asked.

"Minged," the woman repeated. "Ming is Minging you."

"You may be right," Grace agreed, "but I'm not sure what you mean. Is this your cat?"

"No," answered the man, "Ming belongs to our friend, Daniel. But Ming has a whole string of people in the neighborhood he has trained to feed him." The man crouched down, and Ming sauntered over, turning his head sideways to be scratched. The cat was finally quiet.

"He certainly knows how to meow!" Alison observed.

The woman offered an explanation. "We decided that it's not just meowing; it's 'Minging'. It is a special way that Ming communicates, and it's always the same message."

"Which is…?" Alison asked.

The man answered, "What we think he's saying, in so many words, is 'I'm not happy, it's your fault, and what are you going to do about it?' So we made a new verb in Ming's honor." He continued to scratch and pet the temporarily uncomplaining beast. "You're welcome to add it to your lexicon."

"That's a very generous offer. I'm sure we all know people we'd like to 'Ming' from time to time," Ben quipped.

"I think that's enough scratching for today," the man said, standing up. "Honey, we need to get back and clean up so we can get some writing done today."

"Thanks for the local information," Ben said with a smile. "So you're sure Ming wasn't unhappy just with us?"

"No," said the woman. "He's an equal-opportunity Minger. Take care." With that, they ran off up the path. Ming wandered off in search of his next encounter.

Grace asked Herschel, "What time did you say the Stevenses are coming over to the hotel?"

"I told them about three o'clock," Herschel replied. "Kusi was excited to meet them. I think he's very proud of Yachay."

"Isn't he proud of Kawsay too?" Grace asked. They hiked up the street toward the hotel as they continued talking.

"Oh, I'm sure he is," Herschel replied, "but I think he's also a little in awe of her. He's never met a twenty-first century girl before. You and Alison have been putting a lot of ideas into her head, and she seems to be taking to her new modern identity with relish."

"Herschel, why shouldn't she take to her life here?" Grace asked. "Ben and Alison have been so good to her. She had the operation to correct her lip. She has found a great friend in Nate. Kawsay has a future here."

"Don't misunderstand me, dear," Herschel said, putting his arm around her. "I think Kawsay's coming here was, well, providential. But then it was Providence that brought you to me too."

Ben and Alison looked at each other and winked.

It was hard not to notice Yachay's muscles ripple under his skin. Nate figured he would need to spend eight hours a day in the gym for at least a decade to even begin to look as strong as Yachay. Nate continued to berate himself. *Now that her brother is here, especially with his hero status, how can she not notice what a wuss I am compared to Yachay? Twenty-first century men are wussies and sissies compared to Yachay's brand of man.* "What?" Nate realized Yachay, Kawsay, and Kusi were all staring at him. *I didn't say anything out loud – did I?* "What?" Nate repeated.

"Yachay said he has never seen anyone think so hard. He worries your head may explode!" Kawsay was giggling as she spoke.

Nate smiled and went back to his thoughts. Nate looked up again, and his Inca friends were chattering away – apparently making plans for Yachay to rescue his mother and grandmother. Nate's thoughts moved away from his desire for Kawsay to admire him and transitioned to the arrows and the need to return them to Jonathan in 1 Samuel Chapter 20. *There's no way Ben can return those arrows at his age. I wonder if I really do need to go through Israel to get back to Dad and the future where I belong.*

"What difficult thoughts do you have now?" Kawsay's question held a more serious tone this time. Nate had a befuddled look on his face they all could not help but notice.

"I was thinking about the arrows – and my return to the future. Have you told Yachay about his arrow and where it belongs? Does he know where it's from and where it needs to be returned to? We know it somehow gets returned because it's in the Bible. Does he know he is part of such an important history? In fact, does he even know where he is now in relation to Peru, and that he's from the past?" Nate's brows were furrowed as he spoke.

"That is perfect, Nate! I did not have good idea how I would make Yachay return the arrow to Ben. But that is perfect. When Yachay knows that his lucky arrow is part of the Bible, he will want to help." Kawsay smiled at Nate in admiration.

"Yachay does not know what the Bible is, does he?" Nate missed the compliment and continued his questions.

"I told him about your God and that Inti, the Sun, is only a star. I can tell him about the Bible and the arrows, but what do I say?"

"Let me check our room for a Gideon Bible." Nate got up and disappeared down the hall.

Kawsay began explaining to Yachay and Grandfather that Nate's God has a book through which He communicates. That precipitated questions from Grandfather and Yachay on *her* beliefs. Did she not believe in Inti anymore? Did she believe what Nate's God had written in this book?

Nate returned carrying a Gideon Bible. "OK," he said, setting it open on the table around which they had gathered. "Tell Yachay this is the book that God uses to speak to us."

Kawsay translated this unusual concept to her brother. Yachay had seen so many strange and seemingly magical things in the past few days, he did not know what to expect from this object. He laid his ear against the Bible and closed his eyes, listening.

Nate smiled. "We all should listen to God with such expectation. Tell him it is like God's quipu, only our God has coded it for us. Here." Nate pointed at 1 Samuel Chapter 20. "See the little marks? They are like knots on your quipus. See?" Nate pointed to one of the passages mentioning the arrows. "This word describes your arrow, Yachay. God is telling the story of a message that one man is giving to his friend. He used *your* arrow to communicate his message. There were three arrows, and they all need to be returned to these men. Only these men lived over three thousand years ago. You are from about 400 years ago." Nate looked at Kawsay. "Have you and Kusi explained to Yachay that you are from an Empire that existed over four hundred years ago?"

After a few minutes, discussion in Quechua, Kawsay turned to Nate. "Yachay does not understand how your God can speak from the Bible. So much is new to Yachay. He is a bold warrior and is not surprised by anything, but to him the Sun is god and the idea of God speaking with marks like a quipu is not easy to understand. I told Yachay you are the smartest person I know and to think about everything you say."

Kusi and Yachay were talking again. Nate looked at Kusi. He realized that Kusi had been unusually quiet the past two days. Nate had been so absorbed in his own thoughts he had not considered how Kusi must be feeling with his wife and daughter alone and at risk in their village. *Kusi must still be adjusting to all this time travel stuff and wonder if he will ever see his wife and daughter again.* Nate could relate to that fear. He watched as Kawsay explained the time issue to Yachay. Yachay got up and walked over to look out the window. *He must be trying to see beyond the present.* Kusi began talking, and Yachay turned and looked at him with an expression of shock. The two were exchanging words with emotion. "What are they saying? I recognize a few words but not much," Nate asked Kawsay.

She explained, "Grandfather just told Yachay that Ben threw the arrow at him in the secret cave many years ago before Yachay was born. But Ben was a young boy at that time. When Grandfather arrived a few months ago at Ben's home, he realized Ben was the boy now grown up. Yachay said he needs the lucky arrow to rescue Mother and Grandmother. He wonders why Grandfather did not tell him before that the arrow was not really Grandfather's. Grandfather explained he had said he got the arrow in the secret cave, but just did not say that it came from a strange light-skinned boy – Ben. He always told us there were strange things about the secret caves – that is why they are secret. Then Yachay asked if the lucky arrow belongs to Ben or to God. Yachay just wants to get back to Mother and Grandmother – he has been gone seven days."

"He is not grasping the time separation between where he is now and where he came from," Nate mused. "I have an idea. Ask Kusi and Yachay to explain to each other when they each last saw your mother and grandmother and how long they each have been away. I think Yachay will begin to understand that you and he have traveled on different pathways through time." Nate watched grandfather and grandson explaining their realities to each other.

Kusi already had come to terms with how he had stepped into the tunnel in the secret cave and ended up in another place many hundred years later. But Yachay was trying to make sense out of why Grandfather thought he last saw Yachay and the women about four months ago, yet Yachay saw Grandfather leave ten days before he left, which was about seven days ago. *I may be a bit fuzzy, but I know I did not leave home four months ago, which is about how long Grandfather says he has been gone,* Yachay thought, looking at Kawsay and Grandfather suspiciously. Then he looked at his arm and realized it took time for a wound to heal and scars to fade. He looked at Kawsay's lip and knew it would have taken time for the opening in her lip to close and heal. She had explained the doctor and surgery to him. It could not have been done in the past few days! His sister and grandfather must have been here for a while for her lip to heal and for her to learn the new language. She seemed older and more confident. She was not the same girl he had seen seventeen or eighteen days ago. More time had passed for her – but how?

"Grandfather and I arrived about four months ago, and Yachay arrived about seven days ago. But we all left at close times to each other – days, not months." Kawsay was repeating this to herself. "You tell me many times, Nate, that we can return at a time we choose. We can return any time – even the day after Yachay left. But how?"

"We will need Zevél's help," Nate said pensively. "He will have to help us."

Kawsay explained to Yachay that they can arrive back home any time – even the same day he left – but they will need the help of the silver wolf. She turned to Nate. "We make a plan that Yachay will go back to our village alone and will make our people less angry when he tells them that Grandfather is gone and will not return – never. Grandfather and I wait in the jungle until night, and Yachay will bring Mother and Grandmother to us. Then we all return to the secret cave."

"Why not just sneak them out in the middle of the night?" Nate wondered out loud.

"Because they may be watched. Yachay can put everyone at rest by going in and seeing what is going on with his eyes. After he explains and no one suspects anything, he can bring them out," Kawsay explained.

"That makes sense. I hope it works smoothly."

"Yachay says you are a smart teacher and good at planning. He wants to know what *our* future will be."

"Tell him thank you. What did you tell him about our future?" Nate felt good that Yachay would say something positive about him.

"I told him you have a big mission to do and need to return to your future. I also told him I want to have many dates with you after you return and I am older."

Herschel, Grace, Ben, and Alison had returned from their Coastal Trail walk around 1:00 p.m. and lunched in their seventeenth-floor lounge with Nate, Kusi, Kawsay, and Yachay. During lunch, they talked about the funny grey and white cat, Ming, they had met as well as the two runners, the cat's self-described interpreters. Yachay loved the definition of Ming as "I'm not happy, it's your fault, and what are you going to do about it?" He decided that most of the people in his village could be described as "Mings".

Kawsay relayed their conversations about time travel and Nate's idea of explaining to Yachay that his lucky arrow was part of a Bible story. Kawsay noticed Herschel and Grace's eyebrows shoot up. She told them about Nate's suggestion of helping Yachay understand time travel by having Yachay compare notes with Grandfather. "I believe Yachay plans to give Ben his lucky arrow so he can return it to the God story in the Bible, but first wants to take it with him to rescue Mother and Grandmother."

Kusi had begun to ask questions about how they could return through the sucking tunnel when a phone in the lounge rang. It was the front desk alerting them that the Stevens family had arrived at the hotel.

"It's three o'clock. They are right on time. I'll run down and get them," Hershel said as he left the lounge. He brought them up for a reunion with their hero.

The Stevens family had learned from Officer Cole that Yachay was from a remote village in Peru and that his sister and grandfather were here to reclaim him and take him back home. Joe Stevens had wanted to get Yachay another token of their appreciation and bought him a fine sports watch – not realizing the significance of *time* in his life. When they were selecting Yachay's watch, they thought his sister and grandfather may appreciate watches as well.

When Cindy Stevens entered the lounge, she saw her hero's face light up and ran and threw her arms around his neck as he stooped down to greet her. Cindy was followed by Julie bearing a tin of cookies; their mother, Lisa; and Joe, carrying the gift-wrapped watches.

When Yachay saw Cindy, his thoughts returned to the water which had seemed to cut him like icy knives. The two of them could have died that night. He looked into Cindy's happy face and up at her parents. They wore broad smiles. He felt their appreciation. He reached out and squeezed Cindy's sister's hand. *I am glad that Julie does not need to go through life blaming herself for Cindy's death.*

Hershel introduced everyone and ushered the guests to chairs they had previously arranged in a circle. They were surprised at the size of Yachay's entourage. The Stevens family was eager to learn how Yachay's wound was healing, all about his home and family, and if he had a mother and father. Hershel answered their questions in a totally honest manner while protecting their time travel secrets, a previously unknown skill for which he seemed to have quite a knack. Ben and Alison were happy to sit back holding hands and let Herschel take the lead.

Cindy could not wait any longer and retrieved the gift bag from the table in front of her. At Joe's prompting Cindy handed Yachay, Kawsay, and Kusi their boxes. They contained fine sport watches that were good to high pressures and had chronograph functions

Joe thought they would enjoy. Joe explained that the watches were "automatic" and would wind with arm movements – no batteries were required.

"Wow," Grace gasped. "Those are exquisite."

Joe explained. "The value of these watches is nothing compared to the life of one of my daughters. Yachay risked his own life in the frigid blackness of the Gulf of Alaska in the middle of the night to save my daughter's life. He would have done it for either daughter or both daughters – I have no doubt. He not only saved Cindy, but saved Julie from a lifetime without her sister and the guilt she may have put on herself, since she is the oldest. He saved Lisa and me from a lifetime of loss and guilt as well. So, these timepieces are a reminder of the time and joy Yachay and his family have given to us. Yachay's family raised and developed him into the hero he is. Now that we know more about his family, we would like to give his mother and grandmother watches as well. And we would like to keep in touch with him and his family and visit them in Peru sometime."

The conversation continued as they learned more about each other. Kusi was full of pride and was ecstatic that other people were seeing the amazing grandson he knew so well.

This was the first time Kawsay had been around other young people except Nate since her lip surgery. Julie and Cindy said she looked like a "beautiful princess" and that Yachay was a "handsome hero". It felt so very odd to have young girls think of her as beautiful after a lifetime of being shunned by her peers for being an ugly "cat-face". She wished her mother and grandmother could be here and see how much their son and grandson was being praised. She missed them and looked over to Nate who had been sitting quietly and smiling at the happy occasion. *How does he feel?* Kawsay wondered. She would miss him terribly when he left. After the Stevens family left, Kawsay tried to engage Nate in quiet conversation.

Ben was interested in steering the conversation to the topic of Yachay's arrow. *Seems that Nate and Kawsay laid some serious groundwork with their explanation that Yachay's arrow was part of a Bible story. Perhaps he now will appreciate how important his lucky arrow really is*, Ben thought.

"Ben, how can we get from your cave through the sucking tunnel back to our secret cave so we can rescue Mother and Grandmother?" Kawsay's questions interrupted Ben's thoughts. "And how can we get Nate back to his time in the future so he and I can go on dates?" Kawsay reached over and squeezed Nate's hand. "When do you need to leave, Nate?"

"Well," Nate said, looking at Kawsay's small hand on his, "I've been thinking a lot about that the past few days. I really think I should return the three arrows to Jonathan." He took a breath. "And I also really think I should go and warn Ben's family to get away from King Saul and join up with David. We know the arrows get back to their rightful time and place because it's in the Bible, but we don't know about Ben's family. Watching the Stevens family and their happiness over Cindy's life because of Yachay convinced my brain of what I have been feeling lately – that I am the only person who can warn Ben's family. Ben is too big and too old to go back and return the arrows. Besides, I may need to go through Israel to get back to where I belong." Nate looked at Yachay. "A few minutes out of your life saved Cindy and her family for a lifetime. You really inspired me." Nate looked down as Kawsay squeezed his hand and waited while she finished translating his words to Yachay and Kusi.

Herschel and Grace were both looking directly at Ben with eyebrows raised.

Kawsay looked at Ben again. "But how will we get to our cave at the right time to save Mother and Grandmother? Can Zevél really tell us what to do?"

Ben noticed Herschel and Grace staring at him and felt sorry he had still not told them his story. *They have done so much; they deserve the truth.* He made a mental note to tell them tomorrow on the plane.

Alison knew Ben was anxious to resolve the arrow issue with Yachay and decided to speak up. "You know, I've been thinking." She looked around to make sure everyone was paying attention. "As Nate pointed out, we know the three arrows get back into Jonathan's possession since 1 Samuel 20 states they are returned. So, since you were responsible for the arrows, Ben," Alison gave Herschel and Grace a we'll-explain-later look and continued, "it's logical that they will be returned under your direction – perhaps by Nate. Now, Yachay is willing to give his lucky arrow back to the Bible story, but first wants to have it along during the rescue of his mother and grandmother. If we let him take it with him during the rescue, then we can be assured that Yachay, Kawsay, and the whole family will return safely to us – arrow in hand."

"And how can we be assured of that?" Ben pressed.

"Don't you see, dear? Jonathan's arrows get back to where they belong, so for that to happen through Nate – which seems logical – Yachay will need to return his arrow to Nate after he rescues his family. Then Nate can take all three arrows back to Jonathan and return to the future to get back in his own time." Alison was sure everyone would agree with her logic.

"I wonder what Nate's dad would say about all this," Ben mused.

Nate jumped in. "He knows I cannot remain here. My younger self is having increasingly confusing dreams. Dad has a lot of faith in God and the truth of His Word. I'm sure I can convince him it's the only way."

Kawsay had been translating all this to Yachay and Grandfather. Yachay cleared his throat and began to speak with Kawsay translating. "Alison is very smart like Kawsay. She can convince well and thinks fast like Grandfather." Yachay paused, smiled at his grandfather, and continued. "What I understand is Ben's God needs Yachay's arrow back so His Bible will work right. Ben's family needs to be warned of something, and Nate needs to do it. I need my lucky arrow to rescue Mother and Grandmother. Alison agrees that my arrow will bring all of us back safely. So I will take my arrow back and we will rescue Mother and Grandmother. After we come back here, I will give Nate my arrow so he can take it back to God's book. Then, Nate can warn Ben's family and be a hero like Yachay." Yachay was satisfied with his plan and looked around for approval. Then added a final thought, "Kawsay likes Nate so he must have potential. But Nate will be a man if he goes through a hard test and saves Ben's family and returns arrows to God. Then he may be good enough to be friend of Yachay's sister."

Later that evening Herschel called Dr. Hurtado to see if there was any news on the immigration papers. He learned that Hurtado hoped to transmit the e-mail with attachments the next morning. Herschel planned to forward them to Officer Cole's superior and follow up immediately with a phone call. He suggested that the group be ready to check out by 11:00 a.m. and alerted the Gulfstream flight crew of the tentative plans. He was sorry they did not have more time to enjoy their northern adventure. But classes would soon begin, and Grace had some Tuesday appointments.

Alison and Ben were starting to pack their bags at about 7:00 p.m. when there was a quiet knock at their door. Ben opened it. Helmut and Officer Cole were looking back at him with youthful grins on their faces.

"Hi, Ben," Helmut began. "Marguerite wanted to check in on Yachay and also say goodbye in case he leaves tomorrow when she's not on duty."

Ben thought something about Helmut looked different. Alison came to the door and asked, "How was the hike? Did you see those Dall sheep?"

Marguerite answered, "Yes, a mama and a kid." She turned and beamed up at Helmut. "Isn't it amazing how they scampered over the ridge and down the north side, almost straight down a cliff?"

"They have no concern for heights," Helmut agreed. "It was a great hike. Great views from the top. I could see our hotel from there with binoculars and a panorama of peaks. There was so little wind that we were able to spend a couple of hours by ourselves at the summit."

"That's great. Did you two want to come in for a minute?" Alison said.

"I know it's getting late and I wanted to see Yachay," Marguerite stated. "Then I have to get home to do some packing." She and Helmut paid a short visit to their Inca friends. They all hoped to meet again one day. Helmut walked her to her car.

Soon there was another knock at Ben and Alison's door. "Now what?" Ben asked. It was Helmut, alone this time.

"Do you have a few minutes? I wanted to tell you a little more about my day and coordinate our plans for tomorrow." Helmut did not await an answer, but took the same chair he had occupied the previous evening.

"Of course, Helmut," Alison said, sitting on the edge of the bed next to where Ben had perched. "We'd like to hear all about it. Sounds like we may not see Marguerite again because she's off duty tomorrow and has a lot to do."

"I'm wondering about those tests you planned, Helmut," Ben added with concern. "We forgot to talk about it at breakfast. What were they again?"

"Nothing to worry about," Helmut stated with satisfaction. "Everything turned out fine. The first test was that she'd say yes to my invitation to go on the expedition, and the second was that she'd believe the truth about Yachay and not run away screaming because I was certifiable."

They both gave him looks that said "So?"

"So," he continued, "we had a great hike up the mountain and had a nice lunch at the summit." Helmut shifted in his chair and noticed the "So?" looks still on his listeners' faces. "So, I started to tell her I thought she was special but wondered if needed to go slow. She asked how I proposed to do that since I was leaving town. So I casually suggested she take some time off work and join me on my expedition."

"Well," Alison prompted, "what did she say to that?"

"She didn't say anything at first," Helmut responded. "She just looked at me searchingly, and finally asked, 'Really?' I nodded, and she said she thought it was very sweet of me to invite her along, which I took as more or less an affirmative."

"You must have found that encouraging," Ben suggested.

"Yes, I did." Helmut agreed. "I hoped my first test was passed. We talked a little about how quickly she could get ready and how long we'd be gone. But then she abruptly changed the subject and said now that it looks like Yachay is free to go, did I want to tell her all I knew about him and did I believe in Herschel's submarine story."

"Whatever you told her, I hope it wasn't another tale like that!" Ben said smiling.

"No, I followed my plan and asked her if she would keep what I told her in confidence. She said that for our relationship to work, we'd need to learn to trust each other, so why not start right now. Good enough, I thought, so I started with Kawsay's story about her lip, leaving the tribe at age thirteen, and how the evidence indicated she had fallen through a time tunnel from the Inca Empire. I couldn't tell if Marguerite actually believed the story. So I continued with the Kusi piece and finally told her that we all thought what Yachay related was probably entirely accurate."

"So?" Alison prompted.

"Well, she looked at me for the longest time, as if she was searching my face and my eyes for something." Helmut paused. "I think she finally realized I was dead serious, and she wanted me to confirm that you, Herschel, and Grace also believe these stories. Then she just looked off in the distance for a while. Finally, she said I was right about what I'd said about presuppositions last night – that they can imprison our thinking. In other words, she said, unless she presumed that the tunnel story was impossible, it fit the facts perfectly, while nothing else did. Then she asked me why I told her a story that I knew she probably wouldn't believe. I told her it was because I was falling in love with her and wanted her to know that nothing would keep me from telling her the truth, no matter how difficult it might be."

"Helmut, that's beautiful!" Alison remarked, holding one of Ben's hands in hers and massaging it. "Don't you think that's beautiful, dear?"

Helmut waved his hands, laughing a little. "Wait, it gets better. As soon as I told her how I felt, she stood up and walked a few feet away from where I was sitting, muttering something about how it all was just 'too much'. I didn't say anything, and she finally came back to where I was sitting and told me she had a confession to make."

"A confession?" Ben asked.

"Yes! Listen. She said last night she had been examining why we have such strong feelings for each other so quickly and the fact that I was going to leave in the next day or two, and she didn't want things to suddenly end. She hoped I would invite her to take some time off to join my expedition, but wasn't sure that it was the right thing to do or even if it was safe. So she decided that even if I asked, she wouldn't agree to go unless I trusted her enough to level with her about Yachay. If I didn't trust her, she didn't think she could trust me either. She said even though she was still wondering whether to believe the time tunnel stories, at least she was sure I was telling her what I thought was the truth, which must have been difficult for me considering how preposterous it was. She also kiddingly suggested some of the missing person cases she handles – guess there's a lot of them up here – might be people disappearing through time tunnels."

"Sounds like she had the same two tests that you did," Alison said, shaking her head. "Maybe God is leading you both in the same way!"

"Well, that's what just blew me away. I'm not as mystical as you two about things like that, but I must say Marguerite and I were amazed how it all fit together. If she gets permission for the time off, we'll be out of here tomorrow afternoon. I don't know if we'll find any big birds and fish, but we'll have lots of time to get to know each other better, with the guide and his assistant as chaperones, of course." Helmut gave a shrug and a grin, signaling the end of his account.

"Well, Helmut, thanks for sharing your good news with us," Alison said, standing and pulling him up for a hug. "We're really happy for you and hope things finish as well as they have begun." Releasing him and beaming up into his face, she added, "Ben and I have always hoped you would find your special person…"

"I was beginning to doubt I ever would," Helmut interrupted, "which also confirms this could be the real thing. I wasn't trying to make anything happen and neither was she. It just happened. It is a gift out of the blue."

"Well, my most fortunate brother, if Marguerite *is* your soul mate, you will find your feelings growing even more wonderful. But remember," Ben added, "even if she is, you can still mess it up. Love and care for her in every way you can."

"I'm on that, Ben. After all, I've had a good role model," Helmut said with a look of admiration. He quickly left to begin his packing, wondering if the rest of his life had just changed.

Herschel arose early on Monday, eager to check if Dr. Hurtado's e-mail with the immigration documents had arrived. He noticed that clouds had moved in overnight and the surrounding mountains had disappeared from view. Seeing no e-mail, he decided to take his morning shower and plug in the coffee maker. When he checked again thirty minutes later, it was there accompanied by a note from Augusto saying he hoped the attached documents would be sufficient. The documents looked official, with letterhead of the Dirección General de Migraciones y Naturalización on dual documents, one in Spanish and the other in English. He scanned them. *Good,* Herschel thought. *Straight to the point. Says they're Peruvian, should be returned home, and appoints me to make it happen.* He quickly returned a note of thanks to his friend in Peru. He then forwarded the documents to Cole's supervisor, Captain Boyer, requesting immediate final clearance so they could begin the return of Yachay to his home that morning. Though it was still early, he wanted to alert Ben and Alison.

"That's great news," Ben replied over the room phone, "and just in time. Check out the front of the B Section of the newspaper outside your door."

Herschel hastily hung up the phone and retrieved the morning paper. He quickly found the article in question, adorned with two photos, one taken on Yachay's first day in the hospital and another of himself, Grace, Ben, and Alison in the hotel lobby just before they left on their Coastal Trail stroll. The caption read: *"Dr. Herschel Rhodes (second from left) and others in Anchorage to take custody of Yachay."*

Herschel snorted. "How the," he muttered under his breath. "She must have shot us with her cell phone as she approached me for the interview!" Herschel sat down to study Janie's article.

TUSTUMENA HERO IN HIDING
Yachay's Family and Friends Arrive But Cannot Dispel Mystery
By Janie Briggs
September 7

More has been learned about the mystery boy who performed the heroic rescue of 6-year-old Cindy Stevens of Anchorage after she fell into the Gulf of Alaska from a ferry early last Thursday morning. Unfortunately, the more we know, the more questions arise. Perhaps the full story will become available at the award ceremony scheduled for 7:30 p.m. this evening at the Captain Cook Hotel.

Here is what we have learned so far: Cindy's rescuer, Yachay, apparently comes from a remote mountain village in Peru. He speaks an ancient native language, Quechua, and is not familiar with the trappings of our modern world. He is a very strong boy of about sixteen and is recovering from wounds apparently inflicted by a Kodiak bear just hours before he performed the rescue. Members of his family had been in California looking for him. They, along with Stanford University linguist and interpreter, Dr. Herschel Rhodes, and other unidentified persons, arrived in Anchorage Saturday afternoon and have provisionally taken custody of Yachay from the Alaska State Troopers. They have been keeping him on a restricted floor of the Captain Cook Hotel, so Yachay and his family have not been seen since he left the hospital early Saturday evening. No charges are being pressed due to Yachay being on the M/V Tustumena without a ticket or an ID, apparently in deference to his heroic and selfless service to Cindy Stevens and the State of Alaska.

But what was a young man with primitive weapons and clothing from a remote and untouched village in Peru doing on the ferry from Kodiak to Homer last week? How did he get there? What are he and his family doing in the U.S.? According to his interpreter, Dr. Rhodes, who coincidentally is a friend of the boy's family, Yachay reported that one day he just fell through a hole near his village and came out in a bear cave on Kodiak Island. He could provide no credible explanation and neither could Officer Marguerite Cole of the Alaska State Troopers, who said this aspect of Yachay's story remained under investigation. (continued on B-2)

Herschel opened to B-2 and immediately saw another somewhat fuzzy photo of Helmut and Officer Cole sitting at dinner. The caption was: "Trooper dines with Yachay's personal physician". The article continued:

Another interesting member of Yachay's entourage is Dr. Helmut Hunter, a physician based in San Francisco known for his expeditions in search of unusual animals throughout the world. He also is coincidentally a "friend" of Yachay's family, and Yachay was released into his care. Asked why he was dining in the Crow's Nest restaurant Saturday night with the officer who had been guarding Yachay up to that time, Dr. Hunter said they were discussing Anchorage-area hiking trails. It is Dr.

Hunter who gave the orders that Yachay was to stay in bed and out of the public eye while his wounds heal.

It is not known how soon Yachay and his family will be leaving Anchorage and returning to Peru or what their immediate plans might be. No doubt Yachay and his family can fill in the gaps in this incredible saga at tonight's reception, which is being held in their hotel to facilitate Yachay's attendance. Despite the aura of mystery that surrounds this young hero, it is inspiring to find a young person with such amazing strength of body and character willing to risk his life to save a stranger. Anchorage is honored to have Yachay here with us, and we have a chance to express our appreciation to him at tonight's award ceremony.

Herschel's mind had shifted into high gear. His primary conclusion was that under no circumstances should they attend any public ceremony with three undocumented time travelers. They needed to get out of town, preferably back to California, right away. Herschel related his concerns to Grace, who readily agreed.

Meanwhile, Ben had alerted Helmut, who was concerned about how the article put his favorite Trooper in an embarrassing position. Helmut was steamed at Janie for violating their privacy. He told Nate about the article, which Nate skimmed before calling Kawsay to tell her. Kawsay relayed the news to the rest of her family. Kusi understood the danger, while Yachay thought the award ceremony sounded fun and thought he would wear his new cowboy hat and sunglasses.

Herschel alerted the front desk that they planned to check out that morning. As they were gathering in the lounge for breakfast, Herschel received a call from the manager on duty regarding developments in the hotel lobby. The manager reported that several print media reporters, three TV news cameras, and a loose assortment of gawkers had gathered and were asking if they could talk to the famous guest, Yachay. He was wondering what to tell them.

Herschel brought the problem to the group. They were bouncing around ideas when Marguerite called on Helmut's satellite phone. He apologized to her for the article. She also was upset at Janie's tactics, but her real concern was for Yachay and his family. She agreed they needed to get away, if possible, adding that she was glad to be leaving for a few weeks too. She volunteered to push Captain Boyer to get final clearance immediately.

Helmut offered a plan. Assuming they could get final clearance for Yachay's release in the next hour or so, Helmut would agree to meet with the multitudes in the hotel but away from the elevators to their tower. He suggested he could distract the reporters while everyone escaped. Helmut would give them an update on Yachay's medical condition and answer questions as best he could. The hotel staff would fetch the van and quietly transfer everyone's bags. When all was ready, the group would journey down the stairway to the lobby and quickly jump into the van and head for the airport. Helmut would later retrieve his things, meet up with Marguerite, and help her finish packing for Iliamna.

Herschel spoke to the hotel manager, who affirmed that the wishes and privacy of guests come first and agreed to assist with the plan. In testimony to Officer Cole's persuasive powers, the official clearance from Captain Boyer releasing Yachay to depart came at about 9:30 a.m. As a result, Helmut's first-ever news conference was scheduled for ten. They quickly finished packing and alerted the flight crew.

"Let's talk tonight, Helmut," Ben suggested. "We'll let you know that we got back OK, and you can tell us where you are. When will I see you again?"

"Well, I think I'll stick to my original schedule unless events unfold differently. I planned to dedicate about two or three weeks to the expedition, and Marguerite has that much vacation time coming. By the way, I've briefed Alison on the care Yachay will need for the next few days. If anything comes up, I'll have my satellite phone."

Thanks to the efforts of the hotel manager, the growing crowd was ushered to an empty ballroom away from the escape route of the reluctant celebrities. At precisely ten o'clock, Helmut gave final hugs and handshakes to family and friends and disappeared down the elevator. As he entered the ballroom, he noticed a small podium had been set up against the far wall, with people and recording equipment fanned out in front of it. Janie Briggs noticed his entry and signaled for him to hurry over. "Hello again, Dr. Hunter. As you can see, interest in *our* story has been growing," she said with delight.

Helmut's response was not audible as he made his way around the little podium and tapped the microphone. He wanted to let the session take enough time to allow his friends to exit the hotel and start toward the airport. He began with a detailed and very boring explanation of Yachay's wound and how it was healing, along with estimates of when Yachay might be able to resume normal activities. He continued by thanking Ms. Briggs and her newspaper for their wonderful coverage of the story, Regional Hospital and Dr. Menaker for their excellent care, Professor Rios for helping find a good interpreter, and the hotel staff for making Yachay's stay very nice. Finally, he mentioned the touching visit Yachay had with the Stevens family the prior afternoon and their interest in Yachay's welfare. All the while, he observed the crowd grow increasingly restless as he talked about everything except what was really on their minds. When he received a signal from the head bellman through the door in the back of the room indicating that the van was leaving, he stopped and said he would take a few questions.

There was a rush of loud voices. Helmut raised his hands to ask for quiet and then called on Janie because of her special relationship to Yachay.

"When will you allow Yachay to leave his room? Is he well enough now?" Janie asked.

"I believe that Yachay is well enough now. He's made wonderful progress because he followed my orders to rest," Helmut replied in a matter-of-fact way.

Another voice quickly shouted between two TV cameras, "How did this boy get here? Do you believe his story about falling into a hole?"

Helmut looked thoughtful. "I have found Yachay to be an intelligent and truthful boy. Since I was not there at the time, I cannot add to or subtract from what he has reported. While his story is strange, a lot of strange things are reported in the press."

There was a lull for a few seconds while the reporters thought about what other strange stories he was alluding to. The next question came from the back of the group. "Will his family join him at the ceremony tonight?"

"To my knowledge," Helmut spoke slowly, "neither Yachay nor his family was consulted about the ceremony mentioned in the morning paper. I don't even think they were invited. I have no idea who is planning the event, though I'm sure they mean well."

That caused a lot of murmuring. Janie found many eyes looking at her and was relieved when another question was asked. "How long will Yachay and his family be here? When will he be able to return to Peru?"

Helmut braced himself. "It is my understanding that papers arrived earlier today from the Peruvian government and the Alaska State Troopers have given him permission to leave at any time."

Janie felt her story slipping away. Another voice asked, "Do you know when he's leaving? Are you going with him?"

Helmut knew it was time to redirect the discussion. "I will not be going with Yachay to Peru. Later today I am returning to Lake Iliamna where I happened to be at the time I first saw Ms. Briggs article about Cindy's rescue."

Janie was getting suspicious and asked, "Just what were you doing at Lake Iliamna, and what is your relationship with Officer Cole, the Trooper assigned to Yachay's case?"

"Oh, I hardly think that would interest your readers," Helmut began. There were several voices saying it *would* be of interest to them, so he continued. "I had read in the press about two mysterious animals that caught my interest. One is the large bird with a wingspan of over fourteen feet sighted in western Alaska. The other is a very large fish that's been sighted in the lake. One of my interests is cryptozoology, the study of rare and yet-to-be documented creatures."

"What about those creatures, Dr. Hunter. Do you think you'll find them?" asked a new voice. It was not long before the group split between those interested in large birds and fish and those not interested at all. The latter half dispersed.

Janie hurried to a house phone and tried to call Dr. Rhodes' room, but got no answer. She then made inquiry at the desk. "Dr. Rhodes, … let me see," said the clerk. "Oh, yes. He checked out about ten minutes ago." Janie's jaw dropped, and then her eyes narrowed as she ground her teeth. Her stomach tied itself into a knot. How was she going to undo the ceremony she had so carefully orchestrated?

A few miles away, a van was pulling up next to a Gulfstream III-1 jet that was fueled and ready to take Yachay and his friends south on the first leg of his rescue mission to ancient Peru. Bill Pierce helped transfer the baggage to the aircraft as the pilot began to warm the engines. There was a damp chill in the air with a few wisps of light rain. Without looking back, everyone boarded the plane. Herschel made a point of sitting by Ben.

Bill made sure everyone was comfortable as the aircraft began its taxi. He indicated that they would be over heavy cloud cover for most of the trip, so the spectacular views they enjoyed on the flight up would probably be obscured. Within a minute of leaving the ground and flying over the Cook Inlet, they disappeared into thick clouds. They emerged about five minutes later into the ever-sunny world above. Nate and Kawsay sat on either side of Yachay, explaining to him the *Sports Illustrated* magazine Nate had purchased in the gift shop. Ben started to doze off.

"Excuse me, Ben," Herschel began, "but before you nod off, could you explain to me all these references to arrows and Israel I keep hearing? Sometimes I feel like Grace and I are missing a piece or two of the plot."

Ben opened one eye, then the other. He opened his mouth to speak and then shut it again to think. Then he said, "OK, Hershel. You've passed the initiation test with all you've done to help us. After all you've weathered in the last few days, I think you can handle a few more shocks. It's no big deal, really. It's just that I'm a character from the Bible, and I threw an arrow at Kusi in his secret cave over 400 years ago. Oh, and my closest childhood friend was a 500-pound talking wolf. Now everything seems to be turning out fine." He smiled, turned, and pretended to go back to sleep.

Herschel cleared his throat. "Ben, that's fine. But I'd like a few more details. After all, you have a captive audience for the next several hours. And let's have Grace join us. I'm sure she'd like to hear all about this from the horse's mouth."

Along with Alison, they gathered at the quad of seats that surrounded a table on the port side of the cabin. Ben began his tale at the beginning and brought it through to the present, with a little prompting and coaxing from Alison. At first the audience was quiet, just listening, but then Grace and Herschel began to find the entire story both amazing and amusing. The conversation was peppered with questions and laughter. It continued through the sandwiches that Bill brought around.

When Ben's narrative wound to its end, Grace provided a summary. "Well, Hershel, don't we have interesting friends? And they tell *such* fascinating stories. I have to say, though, that I was very relieved Ben didn't mention anything about submarines."

CHAPTER 23.

DELIVERING THE DELIVERERS

BY FAITH WE WILL FLY
BUT WHO WILL GUIDE OUR LANDINGS
AND SHEPHERD US HOME?

Two big paws landed on the bed next to Alison. She woke to see Junior's happy face looming over her. The chalkboard dangled from his mouth. In the morning light that filtered through the curtains Alison read, "Breakfast!" She gave Junior's ears a scratch as she looked at the clock. *Nine-thirty already? Well, at least I caught up on some sleep. I didn't even hear Ben get up.* "Hey, Junior, I missed you!"

Yachay slept soundly in the little cabin with Grandfather. The quiet of the woods felt more like home to him than a hospital or hotel. He awoke refreshed, at first disoriented, but famished. Yachay noticed Grandfather's bed was empty. As he sat up and cleared his head, Kusi entered from outside, silhouetted by the morning sun.

"Yachay. You slept well, but talked during your dreams. You spoke of the Chief and others in the village."

"Did I?" Yachay asked, eyebrows knitted together. "Ah, yes. I remember parts of a dream about our village." With a look of concern he added, "There was a ceremony of sacrifice. I ran into the center and shouted that it must stop."

Grandfather became concerned too. "Do you remember who was being sacrificed? Was it Kawsay or maybe your mother?"

Yachay thought for a moment. "No, Grandfather. It was a man, a young man. I think maybe it was me."

"Yachay, sometimes our dreams can teach us, sometimes not. Perhaps there is a special danger for you in our plan to rescue your mother and grandmother."

Yachay shook his head. "That is not important to me. We must go for them – and soon. If I perish, I perish."

Kusi admired Yachay's bravery but not his bravado. "I agree, Grandson, but how tragic it would be if I lost you during the rescue. We must be wise and clever in our plan." Kusi put a hand on Yachay's shoulder. "Here, put on your clothes, and we will go up to the big house and join Kawsay and the others." He smiled conspiratorially and continued in a low voice. "Alison and Ben prepare very wonderful meals."

Ben served Herschel and Grace a quick toast and juice breakfast before they departed for home. Kawsay and Nate arrived in the kitchen in time to say goodbye and help Herschel and Grace to the car with their bags. Ben carefully handed Herschel a box, which he explained to the young people after the car disappeared down the driveway.

"That box I just gave to Herschel – he and I talked with your Grandfather last night, Kawsay," Ben began. "I still was wondering where the jeweled daggers that you and Yachay brought came from and also your pretty necklace. They are a mystery. Kusi told us the daggers were spoils of a battle and said the necklace was one of the 'jewels of the earth'. We're not sure what he meant. Herschel volunteered to take them to experts at the university, and Kusi consented providing we promised to return them. We want to find out about their materials, likely origin, and value. Who knows? Your secret cave may have links to other times and places."

Actually, Ben did have some idea what the objects were. The daggers were European, inlaid with precious stones. The necklace was different. He suspected it was late Incan. But he wondered how their little castaway obtained the necklace made from equal parts of solid silver and gold.

Kawsay had wondered about the origin of her dagger and necklace too, but this morning she was more interested in showing Yachay her new mountain home. As she ran down the path to retrieve him and Grandfather for breakfast, she saw them in the distance exiting the little cabin. "Yachay! Do you like your new jungle?" she shouted.

Yachay smiled when he saw Kawsay dashing toward him, reminded of their many hours and days of wilderness training. He looked up at the large trees and took a deep breath. "Yes, Kawsay," he shouted back. "It is a wonderful place. It is quiet here like at home – only bird sounds."

Kawsay reached the two men and positioned herself between them, taking them by the hands and tugging them toward the big house. "Nate and I have prepared a nice meal to give you strength for this day. Well, Ben helped some. Later we can explore together. Grandfather, you can come with us. Nate and I have favorite places to show you."

Kusi liked her youthful enthusiasm, but had serious matters on his mind. "Can we spend our time like that when your mother and grandmother remain in danger? Do we not need to begin our rescue mission very soon?"

Yachay was still thinking of his dream. "I agree with Grandfather, Kawsay. We must not delay any longer."

Kawsay felt ashamed that she did not share their impatience to get back to the village, but then she remembered. "We already talked about this in Alaska two days ago. When we travel back, we will arrive at the right time even if we do not begin today or tomorrow. When I met with the large wolf in the cave near here, he told us that his God would show us the right time to enter the tunnel."

"This God talks to people?" Yachay asked. "Has He talked to you?"

Kawsay thought about the God that her new friends had explained to her. "Well, I talk to Him, and He answers me but so far not with a voice. He answered me by bringing my brother and grandfather back to me. Now He will bring the rest of the family together."

Yachay looked at his little sister with curious eyes. "All this may be so, Sister, but it is not right for us to delay our mission. My dreams tell me the time to go is soon. My arm is healing fast, and my strength has returned." He pumped his arm up and down, trying to use his will power to speed its healing.

As they approached the house, Junior came out to meet them, still carrying his breakfast sign. He had not had much opportunity the previous evening to check out Yachay, the newest addition to his human family. The wagging tail indicated that any friend of Kawsay was a friend of Junior too.

Kawsay, seated between Yachay and Nate, was kept busy during breakfast with translation duties. Despite the stress they experienced in Anchorage related to unwanted publicity and Yachay's release from custody, no one felt a need for a day of rest to recover from their travels. They felt energized and sensed it was important to move forward.

"Yachay and Grandfather want to start the rescue right away," Kawsay related. "I tell them that God sends us to the right time, but we must get ready to begin the trip when He says 'go'."

"I think the time to go is soon," Nate suggested. Everyone looked at him, waiting for a reason. "See, I can't leave until Yachay returns with the arrow, and we know that I can't stay here very long. So, they get to go first."

"Is Yachay well enough to go yet?" Alison asked.

Yachay reach for a heavy pitcher of juice with his injured arm. "This morning my arm is much stronger. Kawsay tells me we must wait for the right time to enter the tunnel. When is the right time?" Yachay waited, but nobody had an answer. He looked at Kusi. *Grandfather always knows what to do.*

Prompted by Yachay's inquiring glance, Kusi shared his thoughts. "Yachay is a warrior, trained to think and act quickly. I am older and know sometimes it is wise to wait. Kawsay and I told Yachay about the great wolf who travels in the tunnels. Zevél may help us travel to our village. We must seek him at the cave and request his aid."

As they coalesced around the idea of a cave visit, they heard rain begin to fall. It soon intensified. "Don't worry," Ben said. "They say the more intense the rain, the shorter it lasts. Let's wait a while until it clears up."

After helping with the dishes, Nate and Kawsay found Yachay sitting outside on a covered portion of the deck watching the rain. Kawsay took a companion chair while Nate sat on the deck and leaned against a support post. They were quiet for a moment.

Yachay eyed Nate, trying to figure him out. *He seems like a good person, and Kawsay likes him a lot. He knows about so many things but not about fighting for survival. Why?* So he asked. "Nate, you learn about many things, but you are not trained as a warrior. Are there no warriors at this time?"

Kawsay wondered how Nate would answer.

"The world is divided into many countries, and each country has people trained to fight and protect them." Nate explained about modern military training, weapons, and warfare. "Some say there are too many people trained to fight and too many die. But when there are bad people and countries in the world, I think we must be ready to fight to protect ourselves."

Yachay was pleased to learn that his warrior training was not outdated.

Nate continued, "When I was younger, I asked my father to give me training called 'martial arts'. This taught me to fight with my hands and body. It made me stronger and able to protect myself, even against a large attacker."

Kawsay had heard about Nate's training, but did not know much about it. "Can you tell us more about this training?" she asked. She hoped Nate would be able to demonstrate to Yachay that he knew something about fighting.

Nate began to explain, but decided a demonstration would be better. Excusing himself, he went inside to ask Ben if he could borrow some small pieces of wood from the storage shed. He soon returned with an assortment of one-inch thick pieces of sawn pine carried on top of two small concrete blocks. "This takes strength but also surprise and accuracy," he explained. Nate removed his shoes and performed a quick series of stretching exercises for his attentive audience.

For dramatic effect, Nate drew a scowling face with a black marker on one of the squares of wood and directed Yachay to hold it out with stiffened arms a little higher than his head. Nate faced Yachay and looked up at the face on the board. "Now hold it very firmly." Nate turned as if to leave. Then his right leg flashed upwards toward the leering face on the board. As Yachay's eyes blinked, he felt the impact of Nate's foot on the board, which exploded into two pieces in his hands. Yachay also felt a shooting pain in his injured arm, but did not mind. He was intrigued.

Before Yachay could comment, Nate took three of the boards and bridged them between the concrete blocks. Kneeling before them, he took concentrated aim with his arm. Accompanied by a loud "Hyaaah", Nate's hand flashed down and through the boards. This time Nate felt the pain, but maintained a stoic heroic expression. *Boy, I must be out of practice!* His audience again was delighted.

Kawsay regarded Nate with a new dimension of respect. Yachay thought about how Nate managed to focus his strength so completely, since Nate did not look particularly strong. "Nate, you can teach me these things, and I will teach you to be a warrior."

Nate smiled at his new Inca friend. "I hope we will have time to learn many things from each other."

Kawsay bent down to inspect Nate's deadly hand, noticing it was a little red. "He already knows how to throw a spear, and I have taught him about the bola."

Alison appeared at the door. "Is everyone all right? I heard some strange noises out here."

"Nate was showing Yachay how to be a ninny," Kawsay answered.

Alison looked puzzled. Nate said, "I think she means a Ninja. We were talking about modern warriors, though my martial arts are probably older than the Inca Empire."

"Well, it's good to see you two young fellows getting to know each other better," Alison said. "Ben and I are ready to go to the cave, and the rain seems to be stopping. Your grandfather has been relaxing on the sofa listening to opera music on headphones, but I'm sure he won't mind being interrupted." She turned to go and then stopped. "One more thing, Nate. Your dad called Ben and plans to come up here tomorrow morning. He said that you're going to stay with your friend Jake while he's here."

Nate saw Kawsay's confused look. "She means my young self will be with Jake. I'll be here. My dad and I have a lot to talk about."

Yachay was struck by the subtle differences between this jungle and his own. Even though it had just rained and the ground was slightly damp, the air was dryer. Yachay noticed the sun dancing on the raindrops that still remained on the leaves. He noted that the trees were taller, the foliage less dense, and the bird sounds unfamiliar and less frequent. He breathed in deeply sensing that this midday jungle smelled both fresh and earthy.

Kawsay had explained to Yachay they were going to the cave where she and Grandfather had entered this new world, with Grandfather holding on to her ankle. He was looking forward to meeting the great beast who could help them rescue Mother and Grandmother and also help Nate return to his time. Yachay was still intrigued that he had left home only days after Kawsay and Grandfather, yet arrived months later.

The six of them plus Junior had been walking in silence since they left Ben and Alison's house. Yachay could understand why Kawsay was happy here. Even Grandfather was enjoying all the new comforts, especially hot running water and warm soft beds. Grandfather appeared deep in thought. *He has been less talkative the past few days. I guess being here away from home these many months has changed him – it must have been difficult for him to have been stuck in this new land with Kawsay living in the big house as he watched from outside. Even being the great warrior and protector that he is, he must have felt fear of an unknown place with no way to return. He said the wolf made it clear he should not try to return through the tunnel. All he could do was watch Kawsay becoming friends with Nate – how strange for Grandfather. He will be happy when we get back and help Mother and Grandmother out of the village. He does not know if they are even alive.*

After they crossed the bridge, Ben led his small convoy up the trail as it narrowed and became more obscure from intruding tree branches and bushes. Kawsay followed close behind Grandfather. Kawsay imagined Grandfather had been up and down this trail countless times. *The last four months must have been a very dark time for Grandfather. I wish he had let me know he was here – did I somehow feel his comforting presence? I should have known he would be close, making sure I was safe. He was so depressed when I finally found him.* Kawsay had noticed the change in him from his smart, quirky, funny personality with pride in his abilities as a stealthy warrior to the sad man she found in the cave a few days ago. *He seems to have hope again. I hope Zevél can help us. I hope the wolf can take Nate back to his time. I want to be friends with Nate in the future. I wonder what it is like for Nate to be living at the same time as his younger self.*

Nate was cogitating on the question of how he would know when to step into the tunnel, both here and in old Israel. *Will Zevél be with me and tell me when to leave? Will Zevél help Kawsay, Yachay, and Kusi?*

"Be careful guys – the trail's a bit slippery here." Alison's voice broke the silence and everyone's thoughts. She returned to her thoughts. *What had the wolf said? He made an impression on me with that statement – what was it? Oh yeah. He said, "I sense in my spirit when I am to travel and step through with confidence that I will be directed to the intended destination. Obedience is a simple concept."*

Alison said to Ben, "Remember the other night we talked about the idea that 'the just shall live by faith'? I think Zevél navigates the time tunnels by faith. He had made that statement about obedience and that he sensed in his spirit when it was time to travel. He must be walking with God, or he wouldn't be able to reliably sense God's promptings."

"Reliably sensing God's will is one of those great challenges to faith that one who tries to walk with God struggles with throughout his life – perhaps coming from Zevél's pre-fall age makes that walk easier," Ben remarked.

Ben led the group through the mouth of the cave, stopped a few steps inside, and let everyone gather around. "OK, it is dark in here. Let's let our eyes adjust for a moment. Kusi knows this place well. Kawsay, I'm sure you will explain to your brother and grandfather what is being said if Zevél is here. I once asked him if he was always here. He said he traveled much, but sensed when I needed him and returned to wait for me. I hope he senses our need for him now. OK, step carefully." Ben turned on a bright flashlight and led them into a dark, dank-smelling rock hallway.

They wove their way through near darkness toward the main chamber. When they finally entered it, they were all taken with its luminescent beauty, especially Yachay who had not seen it before.

"This place seems even more beautiful than the last time I was here," Alison said. The cavern was a magical world of sparkling, glittering rock, lit by tiny jets of light that came in through overhead vents and were magnified as they reflected off the crystalline ceiling and walls.

Kusi was whispering to Yachay, explaining the subterranean waterfall and stream, which had been his water supply for the many months he called this cave home.

Ben noticed Junior slink behind Alison knees and sensed they were not alone. He looked toward the rock outcropping where he and Zevél used to talk. "Zevél?" Ben called out. He noticed Yachay freeze and Kawsay's hand slip around her brother's arm.

Kawsay whispered to Yachay, "Remember, this beast does not eat people."

Just then, Ben detected the shimmering form of Zevél lying in the dusky shadows of the rock throne where they always held their meetings. Ben was relieved to see his old friend and led the group over to the majestic silver wolf. Ben looked back over his shoulder and noticed Nate just standing there staring blankly at Zevél.

"That's it!" Nate's voice was barely above a whisper.

"What's it?" Ben responded without realizing it.

The light blue eyes surrounded by a shimmering silver coat rose to a standing position.

Nate slowly walked toward his friends, still looking at Zevél, yet not really seeing him. He absentmindedly sat down on Ben's old rock throne, and the others settled into surprisingly comfortable rock perches surrounding Nate. Yachay was vigilant, keeping an eye on the huge wolf. Kusi put a comforting hand on his shoulder. Zevél sat, but still looked huge. Junior crouched down submissively with his head resting on the ground between his paws.

"I just remembered when my dreams stopped! That's when I need to leave. It was Zevél – a great beast – who reminded me." Nate stopped and realized what he was saying. "Oh, I'm sorry, Zevél. I don't mean you're a beast." Nate felt embarrassed at his inappropriate outburst.

The huge silver face spoke. "Do not be troubled my young friend."

Yachay's jaw dropped. He had never imagined an animal speaking, especially one so magnificent.

Everyone was silent for a moment, and Nate continued, trying to choose his words carefully. "Well, when I saw Zevél, I remembered my last dream – well actually a nightmare. It was the night before Dad's birthday when I was thirteen. I had a terrible nightmare about a grizzly bear." Nate turned to Yachay and waited as Kawsay translated his words. "I must have incorporated what I'm thinking about now into my dreams, and I've been thinking about Yachay's bear encounter. Anyway, my younger self had the nightmare about a cave with the huge bear clawing at me. I guess when I saw Zevél, my brain recalled a large furry creature in a cave."

Nate took a breath and noticed everyone's rapt attention on him. Zevél looked like he already knew what Nate was going to say. Nate wondered if he always looked like that. "Don't you see? This means I'm going to leave on Dad's birthday, which is September 19th! Dad and I prayed extra hard on his birthday after the bear nightmare, and I never had another one of those dreams. This means Kawsay, Yachay, and Kusi need to leave and return before Dad's birthday, so I can leave with Yachay's arrow and the other two arrows on that day." Nate looked pensively at Yachay. "I still don't know exactly at what moment on Dad's birthday to enter the time tunnel or when to leave Israel and re-enter that tunnel." His eyes rested on Zevél.

Zevél shifted his weight. He noticed Yachay staring at him and turned his attention to the young Inca boy. "You must be the grandson of my friend, Kusi. Your arrival has been eagerly anticipated by your sister and grandfather. I am glad you are here." The silver head nodded at Yachay as Kawsay translated.

Ben decided to update Zevél on developments since their last visit a few weeks ago. "Somehow you always know when I need you, Zevél." Ben smiled at the intelligent eyes. "I want to introduce you to our newest time-traveler, Yachay. He speaks Quechua, like his grandfather and sister. Kawsay's English has further improved since you last saw her, and she is translating well for Kusi and Yachay. Of course, you already know Kusi. He thought his Kawsay would integrate into our family and world with greater success if he was not in the picture. We found a place for Kusi and his family in Peru, their home country. They have been invited to live there by researchers who are eager to learn the rich history of the Incas from them."

Gesturing toward Yachay, Ben continued, "Yachay traveled from his time in ancient Peru to what we think was Boston 1775, where he saved the life of Paul Revere. He re-entered the tunnel and ended up on Kodiak Island in Alaska. Then, after being attacked by a grizzly bear, he saved the life of a young girl. We finally caught up with him in Anchorage with the help of my brother, who was nearby hunting for giant birds." Ben noticed Zevél actually looked surprised. *That's a first,* he thought, wondering if it was Paul Revere or Helmut's bird search. He continued, "Anyway, Kawsay, Yachay, and Kusi are anxious to go back home, rescue Kawsay's mother and grandmother, and return here with them. And here is a coincidence…" Ben stopped. "I guess with God there are no coincidences. Well, it turns out that after I left Israel as a boy, I passed through ancient Peru and threw one of Jonathan's arrows at Kusi – of all people!" Ben noticed that Zevél did not look surprised. He continued, "Kusi eventually gave the arrow to his grandson, and Yachay has the third arrow. Now, the three arrows can *finally* be returned to 1 Samuel 20."

Nate jumped in. "And since I need to go back to my time and we thought I may need to first go to the cave by the wheat field near Gibeah, I believe I should take Ben's arrows back to Jonathan. After all, I'm the one who messed up everything to begin with." Nate noticed Zevél's compassionate eyes. "Yachay wants to take his lucky arrow with him. Alison figured out that having the arrow will insure he and his family return here safely because the arrows all are returned to Jonathan in the Bible. That means Yachay's trip needs to happen before I can leave with the arrows."

Zevél interrupted, "You believe you are appointed to return the three arrows, do you? Why do you think so? Tell me what you sense in your soul, Nate."

Nate looked across the sparkling cavern. "Well, it's like I can't *not* do it – I just have to."

Zevél breathed deeply. A low rumbling sound in his throat could be heard. "Most decisions are made from either a sense that something feels like it is the right thing to do or by an intellectual calculation. There are a few matters in life, however – such as a marriage decision, a rescue, or a life-affecting journey or endeavor – which require a deep and overwhelming conviction. There is a wholly overpowering awareness that the matter is somehow settled in your heart, yet your mind has to catch up. As you say, Nate, a deep conviction that you 'can't not do it'."

"Like you know that you know," Kawsay chimed in. "That is how Yachay and Grandfather talk about the strong feeling they have to get Mother and Grandmother out of our village – even if it takes their lives. It is a very deep feeling. This is much greater than they feel about most all things."

"It is important to test your heart, mind, and soul when decisions having life-altering consequences are made. Never, never take such things lightly." Zevél's voice seemed to be booming through the cavern. "Even if a person's intensions are good – that alone does not necessarily make something divinely right. When I hear 'I can't not' and 'know that you know' I sense you may be in His will. I cannot judge for you what you must do – only you can truly know what His will is for you."

"How do we know the exact moment when we are to enter the tunnels?" Kusi asked through Kawsay.

Zevél looked at Alison. Alison felt everyone's eyes follow the wolf's to her, and she cleared her throat. "Well, the last time we were here speaking with you, you said you sense in your spirit when you are meant to travel and that you are obedient to God's prompting – like walking in faith."

"Binyamin has a wise wife." Zevél shifted his weight. He was not comfortable in a sitting position, but maintained this formal demeanor with such a large group. "It is not a matter of the moment you enter a tunnel. Traveling through time is similar to living one's life. If you walk with Elohim or are in His purpose, you are guided by Him in all things – even to *when* or *where* you need to be. Someone not in Elohim's purpose or who does not walk with Him moves haphazardly in life or in time."

"How does someone truly walk with God?" Nate asked. He had wondered about this most of his life.

Zevél looked up pensively at the sparkling ceiling. He spoke slowly. "To walk with Him you constantly remind yourself of His presence, so that everything you think and do reflects His will. If you desire His presence, learn of His Son. To know Him, read His Word with the constant intent to know, understand, and have a relationship with the Author. No one is capable of fully understanding Him, but sincere ongoing seeking will be rewarded with His presence and a great peace with eternity."

"You have compared traveling through the tunnels with living life," Ben mused. "If you step into a time tunnel and you are not in His will, the result would be unpleasant at best. As an experienced tunnel navigator, would you be willing to pilot our friends through their journeys, Zevél?"

Zevél had anticipated this question. "Nate's faith is young but developing well. I will help him with a good part of his journeys. Kawsay's faith is a bud, and I sense her family will grow behind her. I will take them through the tunnels. Just as Kusi arrived with Kawsay by holding on to her ankle, you will hold on to me and to each other as we travel. I will serve as your pilot. Nate must leave on his father's birthday and will need time to ready himself." Looking at the Incas he continued, "Your rescue will be completed before Nate's journey. You have a strong and deep conviction to leave soon. I will come for you – go and ready yourselves. Rest for two nights, prepare yourselves, and rest in God's care."

CHAPTER 24

THE SACRIFICE

SEPTEMBER 9 – PRESENT YEAR
HIGH SIERRAS, CALIFORNIA

WE GAVE YOU TO GOD
NOW I HOPE AGAINST ALL HOPE
HE WILL RETURN YOU.

While his three Inca friends huddled down at the small cabin, Nate asked Ben and Alison if they would help him prepare for talking to his father. They expected John by eleven o'clock, less than an hour away. As they settled in the living room with Junior curled up at Alison's feet, Nate explained his concerns. "I've almost finished my forward diary. You can give the final version to my dad after I'm gone. I know he's worried about allowing me to return to Israel on my way back to the Caribbean. He believes complicated plans are more likely to fail."

"Well," Ben responded, "he makes a good point. But the detour to Israel probably is not optional. There may not be a direct tunnel connection from here to the Caribbean."

"I think he will be OK with having me return the arrows because he knows the Bible is true, so he believes that will turn out fine. It's pretty obvious that I'm the person to do this, right? But Dad probably will want me to get the job done quickly, circle around, and jump back into the tunnel. He'll want me to minimize the risk that something might go wrong."

Alison empathized with John. "I think you shouldn't take any chances, Nate. Think about this from your father's standpoint. You're all the family he has. He would never get over losing you. Even if you're totally successful, he'll have to wait three years to find out if you will return to him."

"Yes, I know. But I *really* think I have two missions, not just one." Ben and Alison looked at each other and back to Nate. Nate continued, "We haven't talked about it too much, Ben, but I know you're worried about your brother and the rest of your family. You want to warn them before King Saul is killed, but don't know how to do it. I can to do it for you while I'm back there. If I don't do it, no one will."

Ben sat forward, troubled. "Nate, I know we talked about this to some extent, and I was excited about the idea at first. Now I don't think it's such a great idea. It's too risky. Times were very different back then. If something happened to you, I could never forgive myself. Isn't it enough that you'll be returning the arrows?"

Nate knew adults would try to prevent him from being a hero. *Yachay didn't ask permission before saving Paul Revere or Cindy Stevens.* "We already know that I'll succeed at returning the arrows. But you don't know about your family. Look how Yachay is going to save his family, and look at everything you and Alison are doing to save my dad from cancer and from drowning. Isn't your family just as important? They are no more dead right now than Kawsay's family, right?" The conversation was not going the way Nate had hoped. He wanted Ben on his side to help with his dad, but now he needed to convince Ben.

Alison was impressed that, despite his apparent need to prove his bravery, Nate also was showing an amazing empathy for Ben, not a trait common to young people. "Ben," Alison said quietly, "I know you have always wondered what happened to your brother and the rest of your family, and I can only imagine they wondered what happened to you. They probably concluded that you had been killed or else captured and sold into slavery. Isn't there something Nate could do that would let them know that you are all right and also that they need to get away from Saul before his downfall? Would it have to be that complicated and dangerous? Couldn't Nate just give them a letter or something?"

Ben heard every word Alison said. From his troubled look she suspected he was reliving the pain of being torn away from his loved ones. Ben put his hand over his eyes and slowly shook his head, his chest heaving with emotion. After a moment he composed himself and looked up at Nate with caring eyes, as he would look at a son. "But I can't let you do this for me. It wouldn't be fair to you or your father."

Nate understood Ben's dilemma. "Ben, I *want* to do this. It isn't just that you and Alison have done so much for me. I'm not just doing it for you. I'm also doing it for your family. Aren't they just as important as I am?" Nate paused. "I also want to do it for me." He saw Ben start to object. "Oh, I know. You think I'm just trying to compete with Yachay, the big hero, and trying to impress Kawsay. I'll admit that was what I was thinking at first. But I've prayed a lot and really believe God wants me to do this. I'm no expert at knowing God's will, but, well, it's like Zevél described to us – I just know that it's right. Yachay cannot do this rescue. I know I'm sixteen, but I'm still not too tall. I know Hebrew, and I've already been back there once. Wouldn't God protect me when I'm doing what He wants?"

Ben listened to this argument and thought if Nate did not become an archeologist, he could try being a lawyer. "Well, if you were there just a short time, the risk may not be too large. After all, last time you were there for thirty minutes and only got hit by *one* arrow! You could deliver a letter from me to my family. I could tell them what has happened to me, but how would we make them believe it? They might think you had done something to me – and then stolen my cloak!"

"But if it worked, I could tell you about it when I return." Nate continued with a scenario he already had run through his mind several times. "See, I would stay with them until they took off to meet David in the wilderness. Then I'd take a bunch of photos of David and his men and bring them back with me to show the world. It would be the greatest archeology story of all times! And I could give David a Hebrew Bible to help him so he'll know that he eventually gets to be king. Maybe he can avoid some of his big mistakes too."

"Hold on, Nate," Ben interrupted, waving his hands. "Just a minute. You're getting carried away. No way are we going to have you trying to change Biblical history like that. I let Helmut and Alison convince me we should let you warn your father about the cancer, and since my family is not mentioned in the Bible, it may be OK to give them some warnings. But it has to stop there. Remember, the only reason you are being sent back to Israel is to fix the arrow story, not to create new problems."

"But Ben," Nate persisted, "we could save *more* lives – like, well, what about Uriah, the guy David basically killed to get his wife? Isn't Uriah's life important too?"

"Look, Nate, you're not using your head," Ben shot back with a hint of anger. "You have been able to understand a lot of the time travel issues, but you are not thinking all this through. Sure, it's terrible what happened to Uriah and terrible that David took Uriah's wife like he did. But God was present even in those events with his plans. There was a purpose in Uriah's death."

Alison asked, "There was?"

"Sure," Ben answered. "I believe it is important for people to understand that even a person anointed to be king – a man 'after God's own heart' – is still capable of committing terrible acts. Could David have written Psalm 51 unless he had first been confronted by Nathan with his sin? And, even though his first child by Bathsheba died, their second child, Solomon, not only became the next king, but the lineage of Christ includes Solomon. Do you want to *fix* all of that, Nate?"

Nate got the point, and his enthusiasm subsided. "OK, Ben. You win. But I still think it would be neat to get some photos of David to help prove the Bible is true."

"Nate, we don't need photos to prove the Bible is true," Alison said. "You and I already know it is true, and a DVD of David singing with his harp to Saul and dodging a spear wouldn't convince anyone who didn't want to believe. It certainly would be fascinating to see photos like that though. I wish I could make a trip into history and experience it personally."

"Honey," Ben said, taking her hand, "Nate obviously shares our strong interest in ancient history. I can understand he would like to explore while he's back there to learn all he can and then share it with the world. But it's not up to me."

"It's not?" Nate inquired, sitting straight. *Maybe it's up to me!*

"No, Nate, strictly speaking, whatever century you may find yourself in, you are still under the authority of your father. He may allow you to pay a visit to my family, or he may not. Do you really think he'll turn you loose in ancient Israel at your age all by yourself? Does he even let you go to San Francisco on your own?"

Nate took a deep breath, exhaled, and shrugged. "I see what you mean." Then Nate brightened. "But maybe this won't be our last chance to travel back there or to travel to other times! Wouldn't it be fun for all of us to do some archeological research while all our subjects are still alive?"

Ben smiled. "I agree, and I've thought about it too. But Zevél discouraged me from attempting any more time travel, and I've never felt right about it."

"Well, dear," Alison added, squeezing his hand, "maybe he'd make an exception if we went together."

Junior's sharp bark ended their discussion, and they heard a car in the driveway. John's black Mercedes was disguised by dirt and dust. His fast driving had reflected his eagerness to see Nate and the Hunters' haven for time travelers. From their last phone call, John knew Nate was worried about having to re-enter the tunnel, but also had some grand ideas of playing the hero by going back through Israel. John did not like that idea at all, but also knew that the arrows needed to get back.

Before Nate could get outside, Kawsay ran up the path and opened John's car door. She stepped back, and John looked at her as he slowly got out of the car and stretched his back. He was wearing jeans and a plaid shirt, and so was Kawsay. He smiled, and she smiled back. *What a charming girl.* "You must be Kawsay. Nate has told me wonderful things about you. I am so pleased to finally meet you."

Kawsay stepped forward and offered John her hand. They shook hands like they were sealing a business transaction. "Hello, Mr. Diamond. I am happy to finally meet you. Before you talk to Nate about his trip, please meet my father and brother. Thank you for giving us the big jet to bring Yachay back to here from Alaska. You are very kind to us."

John was impressed by Kawsay's good manners and strong handshake. John saw Nate running from the large log house and opened his arms. Nate gave him a strong welcoming hug. This Nate was a lot bigger and more solid than the one back home.

"Boy, is it good to see you, Dad! We have so much to talk about. I'm leaving on your birthday next week!"

"What?" John exclaimed, holding Nate at arm's length and looking him over carefully.

"Yeah, I just remembered yesterday when we were talking with Zevél that my last bad dream was the night before your birthday. It was a real nightmare, so we prayed extra hard that they'd stop, and they did. You told me later it was funny that it was *your* birthday, but *I* was the one who got the best present."

"Did I say that?" John asked.

"You will next week!" Nate proclaimed. "I added it to the forward diary last night. I need to finish it soon 'cause I'm almost out of time. But first Kawsay is leaving to rescue her family. We think they're leaving tomorrow."

John was trying to catch up on all the news, but he had not had time to get his briefcase from the back seat. As he reached for it, he heard Ben's voice.

"John, good to see you. You seem to have found our hideaway OK. I'd like you to meet Alison."

John bumped his head as he pulled it out of the car, still without his case. He laughed at his clumsiness. "Hello, Ben," he said, rubbing his head. "Alison, it is great to meet you. I really want to thank you for your kindness in taking care of Nate and helping him."

"Nice to meet you too, John," Alison replied. "You have an amazing son, and I do not think it's an accident that he came here."

John's attention was drawn to two figures approaching on the same path that earlier brought Kawsay, both with ear disks that flashed in the sun. *Amazing. These people are over 400 years old!*

As they drew near, John observed that the younger wore a cowboy hat and denim shirt and had exceptionally alert eyes. The older wore a modern sports shirt and a necklace of human teeth John hoped did not come from the jaw of anyone in the neighborhood!

The elder flashed a big grin, extended a weathered hand, and said with a strong, accented voice, "Hello, Mr. Diamond. I am Kusi, I am grandfather Kawsay." After a firm handshake that had the air of an important ceremonial greeting, Kusi continued. "Here Yachay, my grandson." He looked at Kawsay, who nodded approval.

Another hand was extended to John. "Hello, Mr. Diamond. I am Yachay. Good I meet you."

"It is an honor to meet you, Yachay, Kusi," John said, looking at them with a casual but observant eye. *What do you say to people from another age?*

Kusi spoke something to Kawsay that was completely unintelligible to John. "Grandfather says he enjoyed flying in your jet, and he appreciates your help to bring Yachay back to here." Kawsay stopped as Yachay spoke up. "My brother wants to know where he can learn to break pieces of trees with his hand like Nate."

John looked at Nate who smiled. "I showed them some martial arts moves yesterday. We were just fooling around. Yachay is a trained warrior, you know, so he's really interested in things like that."

"Kawsay," John requested, "tell your brother that when he returns from your village, we'll see that he gets all the lessons he wants."

Upon hearing this, Yachay smiled at John and nodded. Yachay liked Nate's father. John's quick and piercing eyes reminded him of a bird of prey.

Alison thought John looked weary. "John, you probably want to relax after that long drive. Why don't you come in? Would you like some refreshments? We have iced tea, lemonade, or just water."

"Water is fine for now. Let me try again to get my briefcase." But Nate had it in hand already and led his dad up the steps and into the house with Ben following closely.

Alison stayed behind. "Kawsay, Nate and his father have a lot to talk about, and Nate asked Ben and me to be part of the discussion. I feel bad that you're leaving tomorrow, and I haven't been helping you as much as I would like."

"I understand," Kawsay said quietly. "Nate tells me his father wants him to go to the future and not to the past. If Nate gets lost, maybe his father will not see him later. So it is good they be together today."

"Well, I think he'll be fine, don't you?" Alison remarked. "Will you help with our afternoon meal?"

Kawsay smiled. "I do better. You are busy today, so Yachay and Grandfather and I will make you a special meal. It will be a surprise."

Alison thanked her in advance and turned toward the house. *This is going to be hard for John. I hope we can work things out,* she thought. She saw that Ben had brought a pitcher of ice water into the living room, and he and Nate were already settled. She sat down next to Ben on the couch and gave him a hopeful look. John joined them, poured himself a glass, took a long drink, and looked carefully at each of his companions.

"Well, where shall we begin?" John asked. There was no immediate answer. "I assume we are here to reach agreement on a plan for Nate's return to, ah, the future. I've heard various proposals; what is your latest thinking?"

Nate spoke up. "Dad, relax, OK? This isn't a board meeting."

John turned quickly to look at Nate and realized that he was acting authoritarian. "Sorry." He turned back to Ben and Alison. "I'm sure you can understand this is difficult – having two sons and not knowing if in a few years I'll have any. I just want us to do the right thing."

"I've been watching Nate, and I sense it's really hard for him too," Ben said, turning to look at Nate for a moment. "After all, *he's* the one who is about to embark on a very difficult undertaking. For him, life itself is on the line. We owe it to Nate to do all we can to help him make it."

"Yes, but what *can* we do, dear?" Alison asked. "Once he disappears into the tunnel, it's out of our hands."

"You can help me," Nate interrupted, "by not wigging out over this. I know I have to leave, and there's only one exit I know of around here." Nate looked at his Dad and took a breath. "Dad, we all know I have to step into a time tunnel in ten more days. It feels like I'm either on death row or about to be launched to Mars. The way I see it though, God got me here OK, and He will just have to get me back. Our job is to get me ready for whatever is coming."

John thought about Nate's position. "Well, I agree there are only a few options open to us, and I certainly want you to be fully prepared for the trip." He turned to Ben. "For me, the goal is to have Nate return to me in three years. Is there any way I can know before then if he's going to make it? I don't know if I can live with that uncertainty for three years!"

"There may be," Ben answered. "If Nate could leave something in Israel at an agreed-upon place and we could find it 3,000 years later, he could tell us that he was doing all right. That would not guarantee he would successfully complete the rest of the trip to the Caribbean, but at least we would know something."

"I think getting some kind of indication like that would help, Ben," John said. "Yet if Nate is able to leave a positive message but for some reason we don't find it, then we'd be even more worried." John knitted his eyebrows for a moment and then brightened. "What about that old wolf you told me about? Couldn't he tell us if Nate makes it?"

"Maybe," Ben answered, "but Zevél didn't say that he planned to accompany Nate into the future and then come back to us and tell us what's going to happen. In fact, come to think of it, he has never told me *anything* about the future, though he may have traveled there many times. I just don't know."

"Isn't this one of those times where we're not in control?" Nate inquired. "Dad, you taught me that the testing of our faith is good for us!"

John was surprised by Nate's comment, but had to agree. He smiled. "Fine, son, and we intend to pass the tests, but that doesn't mean we have to enjoy it. I promise to do everything I can to get through the next three years with your younger self and to *not* get cancer. But *you* need to promise to use your head and not take unnecessary risks. If everything works out, we'll have a lot to celebrate."

"Yeah," Nate agreed, "but let's not celebrate with another sailing trip!" Everyone laughed, and a lot of the tension seemed to dissipate. "By the way, do I need to wear your long brown dress or cloak or whatever it is? If I do, I want to wear my own underwear."

"We might have to alter it a bit," Ben replied, "but the more you look like me when you return to Jonathan the better. For instance, we'll want to dye your hair. The coat has a mantle though, so you can probably hide your face. I'm really not too worried. Jonathan was very distraught that morning, and he is about to send away his best friend. With so much on his mind, he won't be thinking about what you look like, and there's no reason he should be suspicious."

"Doesn't that depend on whether there is a delay with Nate returning the arrows?"

Alison asked. "Jonathan might be suspicious if he sees you, Ben, disappear into a cave and not come back out for a long time."

Nate had an idea. "Well, I can check with Zevél, but maybe we should arrive a few minutes early, hide in the back of the cave, and then as soon as you fall into the tunnel, Ben, I'll take off out of the cave and run back to Jonathan."

"If I heard him right yesterday," Ben replied, "you cannot necessarily control exactly when you arrive."

"Then I'll just have to peek out of the cave to see what's happening before I start running back," Nate reasoned. "I don't want to run into myself!"

John felt left behind in this discussion, which seemed to him premature. "Hold on just a minute, Nate. How can you be so sure when you step into the tunnel you will end up back in Israel? And, when did we make a final decision that you even *are* going back to Israel? I'm worried about your safety and really wish you could return directly to the Caribbean. We know the arrows get back somehow. If you don't do it, Nate, presumably someone else will."

His father's remark took Nate by surprise. *I thought this was settled. I just know I'm supposed to do this!* "Dad, we already talked about this," he pleaded. "We think the way back to the Caribbean goes through Israel. And there *is* no one else around to bring back the arrows. And I just know that I'm supposed to do this. When God gives us a job to do, we can't assume that if we wimp out someone else will do it. Maybe they will, but that doesn't make it OK for us to disobey, does it?"

"Did God give you this job or are you just doing it because you want to have an adventure or be a hero?" John shot back. Ben and Alison wanted to calm the waters between the father and son, but knew it was not their part to do so. "Well?" John added.

"Dad, I'll admit I want to do this, but what's wrong with wanting to do God's will? I remember a book I read about guidance that said to look at three things – the Word, your heart, and the circumstances." Nate was thinking fast. "Well, the Word says the arrows get back there, right? And my heart tells me I should be the carrier." Nate began to count out his points on the fingers of one hand. "And the circumstances are right: all three arrows are here now; I'm here but can't stay in this time because I'm already here three years younger; we have the tunnel nearby and Zevél to help; we have Ben's old clothes for me to wear; and we have Ben to coach me on how to do it because he knows the area around ancient Gibeah. How much more clear does it need to be?"

John was not accustomed to losing arguments and did not want to argue in the first place. "I can't dispute what you say, but I still don't like it." John continued voicing his thoughts. "And if you are right about the tunnels not connecting directly back to the Caribbean, then there may not be any way to avoid a stopover in Israel. And if you're there, well, why not drop off the arrows? Someone has to do it, right? If you just stay there a few minutes, maybe the risk isn't too great."

Ben observed that John had reached a good conclusion in his own way. "Remember, John, I know the territory and people, so I can prepare Nate thoroughly for what he will be doing. Also, keep in mind that Zevél will be there if there is a problem. I imagine a 500 pound wolf makes a good body guard."

"All I hear about is this huge wolf!" John said, a bit exasperated. "I've never seen or heard of a creature like this. You expect me trust a giant wolf to protect my son?"

"I wish you could have been here yesterday when we were up at the cave and visited with him," Alison said earnestly. "He has some kind of inner strength or peace that gives me confidence in him. I get the feeling that he's seen and done a lot, and he seems dedicated to helping people. Remember, if it weren't for Zevél bringing Nate here, your son would have bled to death."

John just nodded slowly, realizing that he owed a debt of gratitude to a seemingly mythical creature as old as Adam. "Yes, I think if I had been there it might have helped me feel more at ease. As Nate's father, I wish I could take this trip for him. I feel helpless. It's really hard to let him go."

"Dad, it's hard for me to leave you too," Nate said desperately, tearing up a little. "I really wish I could just go home with you right now and have everything go back to normal. But we all know I can't."

Ben empathized with Nate and John. "I remember after I arrived here, I wished every day that I could return to my family. I thought about jumping back through the tunnel, but Zevél told me it may not take me home. I knew he was right and, somehow, I felt I was supposed to stay here. It was really hard though, to think about my family. They did not know what had happened to me and probably in time gave me up for dead, but I'm sure my parents grieved for the rest of their lives." Ben's voice trailed off. Then he added, "They may not have mourned very long because it was only a short time later that the House of Saul fell, and they were probably killed."

"Yeah, if they somehow survived the battles with the Philistines where Saul and his sons were killed, they would have been in trouble when David's forces took control of the country," Nate blurted out. "Wasn't your older brother Jonathan's shield bearer?"

"We all were servants of the royal house in one way or another," Ben answered.

Alison had seen the deep sadness surface in Ben from time to time. She despaired that there was no way to help other than to love him completely.

John was reminded of his loneliness. "I came to realize when Nate's mother died that death is just *wrong*. Can we ever really accept the separation it imposes between us and those we love? Even Jesus wept at Lazarus' tomb right before bringing him back to life. The way our hearts refuse to accept death points back to God's original plan." He saw the curious looks on everyone's faces. "Nate, we talked about this when you asked why your mother had to die. We were not designed to die and be separated. It's only as a result of sin we need to pass through death to reach a better place where death is banished."

"Well, Dad, even if I don't get back to you in the future, we'll be together with mom in eternity." Nate gave his father a hopeful look. "But I'm not ready to give up on this life yet."

"Neither am I, son." After a pause, John returned the discussion to the immediate topic. "I suppose we've settled things pretty well. What else do we need to talk about?"

"Well," Ben offered, "we do need to work on keeping you two from drowning in the storm, but that can wait until later. We have three years to figure that out."

"Um, there *is* one more thing I need to talk to you about, Dad." Nate observed that his dad did not look like he really wanted any more difficult issues to handle just then, but he had to forge ahead. "After I return the arrows, I think I should go to Ben's family, tell them that Ben is alive, and warn them to transfer their allegiance to David before it's too late. It wouldn't take too long, maybe just a day or so, and …"

John stood up, interrupting his son. "Do you really expect me to allow you to wander around Israel at one of the most dangerous times in its history all by yourself?" he said in a loud and authoritative voice. "This plan is getting more dangerous by the minute." He turned to Ben. "Ben, did you know he was concocting this?"

"Yes, John, Nate brought it up. I appreciate that he wants to help my family, but I did not suggest or agree with it. In fact, we tried to talk him out of it."

"And, Dad," Nate added, coming to Ben's aid, "Ben said it wasn't up to him or to me; it was up to you as my father."

All eyes were on John, who began to feel awkward just standing there, so he walked over to the window. No one spoke as John considered his dilemma. His eyes saw nothing; he peered only inward. *I don't like being boxed into a corner like this. If something happened to Nate, I don't think I could handle it. But if I just say "no", it will seem as if I'm uncaring about Ben and his family, particularly after all he's been doing for Nate and me. No, it won't just **seem** uncaring, it will **be** uncaring. I can imagine how Ben's family wondered about their son, and I can understand Ben wanting to get them out of harm's way. It's interesting. They've been dead for 3,000 years, but he still worries about them just as the Incas worry about their family all those years ago. I care for Nate more than everyone else in the world put together, but from God's viewpoint everyone's life is important. So far on his journey, Nate has saved Morrow's life who later saves Nate's life in return. Nate also warned me about cancer and probably saved my life. Now Nate wants to save Ben's family just like Yachay and Kusi want to save their family. And Yachay also saved that little girl's life without thinking of his own safety. Who am I to limit God? But Nate's only a kid! And he's the only son I'll probably ever have and all of his mother I have left. I just can't give him up. This is too much! I don't know what to do!* John rubbed the tension he felt in the back of his neck. *When I have a difficult decision, I don't rush it. But I don't have much time either.* "Ben, I need to think about this a little more. Is there somewhere I can go and be alone?"

Ben was immediately at his side and gently placed a hand on John's shoulder. "Sure, John. I think that's a good idea. Let me suggest a little bridge over a stream just a short walk from here." Ben gave John directions, pointing out the window to where the path went into the forest.

John finished his glass of water. "Nate, I'll be back in a while." He strode out of the house and across the clearing. John followed the path through a beautiful section of the woods and down a long hill to a stream. While not flowing heavily after the long dry summer, there was still enough water to produce refreshing moist air and a relaxing burbling sound. John stood at the center of the little bridge and leaned on the railing, looking down at the water curling around the rocks.

As he brought back his competing thoughts on his difficult decision, his attention was drawn to something moving through the underbrush about one hundred feet upstream. John's studied the moving object, not willing to believe his eyes. The form emerged from some bushes and stopped by the stream, bending down to drink. It was a large animal, larger than a mountain lion. Was it a bear? No, too slim. And bears are not silver. Then the animal's head rose from the water and turned toward John. Its eyes locked with his for a very long moment. John felt a shudder of fear and considered his escape routes, but he was riveted to the spot. *That must be the wolf. He's looking right at me. He's starting to walk this way. His strides are very long. My Lord, he's way bigger than I imagined! Does he know who I am? No use running. He's obviously coming over here. What a magnificent creature!*

The wolf was by the bridge, looking at John with his piercing blue eyes that reminded John of the color of his own. Time seemed to stop. "May I join you?"

John was not prepared to be spoken to by this otherworldly creature, and the deep resonant voice only added to his shock. He felt his pulse race. A whispered "yes" was all he could muster. The silver wolf stepped back, as if to invite John to approach him. John moved to the end of the bridge and sat down only a few feet from the creature who then lay down on a soft patch of long grass. John crossed one leg over the other, and the wolf crossed his paws in a pose that looked like an enormous puppy.

"Might you be Nate's father?"

"Yes." This time John's voice was a little stronger.

"You have met the others? Ben and Alison? Kusi and his grandchildren?"

"Yes."

The wolf continued. "They have told you about me?"

"Yes. You are undoubtedly Zevél," John stated, regaining some of his composure.

"I do not know your name, Mr. Diamond."

"Oh, it is John, sir."

"God is gracious."

"What?" John asked.

"Your name. It means 'God is gracious'."

"Well," John responded, still feeling very strange talking to such a creature, "I am in need of His grace right now."

"Why did you name your son Nathaniel?"

John looked at the large blue eyes. "His mother and I believed he was a gift from God, given to us to enjoy and care for."

"Did you dedicate him to the service of Elohim?"

John had to think about the name Elohim for a moment. "Oh, yes, we did, when he was very young."

"So you have given him back to the One who made him?" Zevél asked.

John realized that Zevél in some way knew his dilemma, his travail, and was helping him find the answer. "Yes," he answered, again very quietly.

Zevél gave him a brief respite from his gently targeted questions. Then he spoke simply. "Abraham had one son by Sarah."

"Yes," John agreed. Then he remembered a key part of the story. "And God commanded him to offer Isaac as a sacrifice, and he ..." John could say no more. They both understood the lesson.

"And God had one Son?" asked Zevél.

"Yes." John paused, thinking. "And He gave His Son as a sacrifice."

"That you may live. That Nathaniel may live. That all who believe may live." Zevél waited a minute to continue. "Did God return Isaac to Abraham? Did God's Son return to Him?"

John looked at Zevél intently and felt something break inside himself. "Yes, I understand. The ram showed up immediately, and the Lord rose on the third day. Are you sure God will return Nate to me?"

Zevél seemed to smile and then turned his head to one side. "When we are called upon to sacrifice, our only job is to place what we value on the altar and give it to Elohim. It is His choice whether to return it to us or to bless us in other ways. It is an act of worship and an act of faith."

"You know, then, that Nate wants to return those arrows *and* bring messages to Ben's family? That he is asking my permission to take these risks?" John asked.

"Nate was very excited yesterday when they visited me. He explained how these matters were settled in his heart."

"He said it was up to me whether he does this. I came down here to think," John explained.

"You will do what is right. I can tell you that I have agreed to accompany him to the past and set him on his path to the future." Zevél stirred as if preparing to leave. He rose to a sitting position and seemed to smile. "You have a father's heart. Perhaps you have found your way through your time of questioning. May I be of further assistance?"

 John was somewhat startled by the abrupt end to the interview. "You will watch over my son?"

"Yes, John. I will be with him as long as he needs me," Zevél replied. "It seems both you and I were chosen to help Nathaniel." The great wolf nodded briefly and turned away, loping at surprising speed into the forest.

John was alone with his thoughts and a feeling of unreality. He stared meditatively at the tumbling water and went over in his mind what he had learned. *The wolf really did not tell me anything. He just asked me to think more clearly about what I already knew!* He felt at peace.

John returned through the forest and entered the big log house just as the mealtime began. "Oh, John! Nate was about to go and fetch you. Please join us," Alison said.

John smiled as he caught a very warm and inviting aroma. Then he heard the haunting sound of panpipes on the stereo. "Looks like my timing is impeccable! And the atmosphere is very Andean," he commented, sitting down next to his son.

Nate looked at his father with a questioning look. John smiled and winked, which told Nate all he needed to know. "You'll love this casserole, Dad. Kawsay made it with help from her brother and grandfather. She says it's similar to what her mother makes on special days."

Kawsay smiled at John. "Today you are guest of honor."

John smiled as he took a good helping and a hearty bite. "Mmmm. It's great."

Everyone ate in silence, wondering if things had been resolved between Nate and his dad. John caught them looking at him from time to time and then quickly looking away.

"OK. You're all wondering what I decided about Nate's trip, right?" Kawsay translated, and Kusi nodded earnestly, ear disks flapping. "Well, I had some help. Your friend, Zevél, stopped by to ask me some probing questions. He reminded me that while I am Nate's father, so is God. I also recalled that the measure of a person's life is not how long he lives but what he does with the time he has. I thought about the amazing journeys through time many of you have made. I realized these events have not been random or without purpose, but had a theme: to bring about extraordinary changes in peoples' lives, including the saving of lives. I just needed to get my own ideas and desires in line with God's. I've decided that allowing Nate to deliver messages to Ben's family is the right thing to do. His family deserves a chance to live just as much as Nate and I do. I have been very impressed that our Inca friends do not hesitate for a moment about rescuing their family. These events are bigger than any one of us, and we should all be honored to be part of them. I have to believe that God will honor Nate's and my faith and obedience and return him to me, to us, in three years."

"So I can go?" Nate asked with enthusiasm, wanting to be sure he could believe his ears.

"Yes, *but*," John answered, "I have a few conditions. First you will obey Zevél. Second, you are not to take unnecessary risks. And third, you are to remain in Israel only two days. I know you will be tempted to stay longer and learn as much as possible. After all, this is a dream trip for an amateur archeologist and Bible scholar like you, Nate. But your mission is for a limited purpose, and it is not *your* mission, but God's. We cannot have you changing Bible history, or we'll have to send Alison and Ben to put things back together!" Everyone laughed, and Nate gave his dad a big hug.

John was ready to leave by seven o'clock that evening. He spent the last hour talking with Nate alone, as they both realized that they would not meet again for three years, if ever.

John had a few parting words with Ben and Alison. "I won't be here the day that Nate leaves because the forward diary says I'm with his younger self the weekend of my birthday. I wish I could be here, but then again, seeing my only son about to step into a time tunnel might make me change my mind, or I might grab his leg like Kusi did to Kawsay!"

"We'll let you know what happens," Alison comforted him.

"John, we need to keep in touch with you during the next three years, especially if things get tough for you," Ben said. "Also, we need to figure out how to keep you two guys from drowning."

John gave them both a hug. "Ben, Alison, I'm sure we'll work out something."

Nate gave his dad one more hug. "I'll miss you, Dad," he said tearfully.

"Not for long," John said. "For you it will only seem like a few days." He noticed that Kawsay had appeared out of nowhere and was standing beside them.

"When Nate comes back, we will be the same age," Kawsay said with a hopeful smile, looking up at Nate and slipping her arm inside his.

John looked from Kawsay to Nate and back. He smiled and cocked his head. "I think you will be as happy to see him again as I will be. What will you do for the next three years?"

"I go with my family to Peru to teach people the old ways. But I want to visit Alison and Ben and help them dig up old pots and bones," she answered, looking to Alison for approval. "I must learn Spanish words in Peru and also learn about numbers and sinus."

"She means science," Nate added, nudging Kawsay.

As he drove slowly away, John saw Nate and Kawsay together in his rear view mirror. *What makes them look like they belong together?* he wondered.

Ben and Alison and the two young people watched the black sedan disappear down the drive, pursued half-heartedly by Junior. Then they turned back to the house to face the future – and the past.

As he put his head onto his pillow that night, Ben heard a telltale crinkling sound. He removed a small piece of paper. *Amazing that Alison thought to do the same thing I did.* He read:

> *Our lifelines have joined*
> *We travel onward as one*
> *To eternity*

Ben added this to his precious collection in the drawer by the bed, pondering what adventures might lie ahead for them until eternity arrives. Alison soon joined him as he feigned sleep. As she cuddled up, she heard the familiar sound of crinkling paper. *Did I put it under the wrong pillow?* She reached under and removed a small piece of notepaper. *When did Ben write this?* she wondered. It read:

> *They all fly away*
> *To distant times and places*
> *Will we have a turn?*

"Have you made reservations?" Alison asked.

Ben turned and opened one eye into the glare of the reading light on her nightstand. "Reservations?"

"Yes," Alison replied playfully. "To take our turn to visit another time. You said you would take me along."

Ben opened the other eye to verify whether she was serious. "I tried, but the tunnel office said they wouldn't let us bring Junior."

"That's ridiculous!" she protested. "I'll have to sic Zevél on them."

"Seriously, Alison," Ben inquired, searching her face. "You'd be open to an experience like that?"

Alison looked down thoughtfully. "You know that I have a sense of adventure, but it also would have to have an important purpose. And I think I'd want to eventually return to our life here. Being totally uprooted like you and the Incas seems very disorienting."

"But we'd be taking our world along with us," Ben said. Seeing her confusion, he added, "You are my world."

CHAPTER 25

YACHAY'S PROMISE KEPT

SEPTEMBER 10 – PRESENT YEAR
HIGH SIERRAS, CALIFORNIA

I HAVE TRAVELED FAR
BUT ALWAYS MY PATHWAY LED
BACK TO RESCUE YOU.

"I will return. I promise," Yachay declared to his grandfather and sister outside the small cabin he and Kusi had called home the past few days. "Those are the last words I spoke to Mother. It is time – I just sense it." Yachay stood tall in his camouflage tunic and sandals, exactly what he had been wearing the night he left home. He had his llama hide sling securely holding his knife, bola, and the small spear in which he had embedded the lucky arrow. "I am taking the food and water bags up to Ben's house to fill for our journey. We should eat breakfast and go. I am sure the silver wolf will come for us."

Kusi and Kawsay had been sitting in the warm morning sun discussing their expectations of the future and what may await them after they rescue Mother and Grandmother. "I feel it too," Kawsay said as she stood up. "See, I am wearing my clothes that Mother made, so I will be camouflaged in the jungle. I think I have grown – my tunic seems shorter. Grandfather and I were talking about our return to here with Mother and Grandmother. Herschel said we can go to live near our home but in this time. We can live under the care of Herschel's friend Hurtado. Herschel trusts Hurtado, and I trust Herschel. Hurtado will provide us all with education of this world, and in return we will teach him about our home. Yachay, you and Grandfather know weapons and military tactics as well as farming. Mother knows all aspects of domestic life such as cooking, weaving, and making clothing and shoes. She even learned about stone cutting from Father. Grandfather, you know the most – not just weapons, military, and farming, but also construction, art and metal work, and the quipu. Grandmother knows domestic life, medicine, and planting. I have learned from each of you and am the best interpreter of our language to English language."

Yachay was getting impatient. "Your thoughts are of this time. Why do you not worry about rescuing your own mother and grandmother?"

Kawsay was startled. Yachay never spoke curtly to her before. He had always been her greatest defender. Kawsay stared at the ground for a moment trying not to cry. Perhaps Yachay is not happy about her friendship with Nate. *I better not mention his name,* Kawsay thought. "Yachay, we will return at the right time to rescue them. Zevél will help us. Besides, I am planning with Grandfather for the life and future of Mother and Grandmother. Herschel has made sure there will be a safe and happy place for all of us to live. Our lives will have a great purpose. That is what I have been worrying about, Brother. You are being a 'Ming'!" Kawsay stood frozen.

Kusi was the first to laugh, remembering the story of Ming, the small grey and white cat from Alaska. "Enough, you two. You are both warriors, but have each grown and changed in the past days and months. We must grow and change together and look after each other – both at our old home and in our new home. Kawsay is right to plan for the future. But you, Yachay, are right to ready yourself and plan for the rescue that is before us. Let us now focus on our mission of bringing your mother and grandmother back. Later we will think about our new life. Kawsay, let's gather what you need and go to Ben's house. I hope Zevél will come for us today – we cannot travel the tunnel without him as our guide"

The three Incas, outfitted for the rescue, headed up the wooded path. Kusi looked back at the small cabin the Hunters had entrusted to him these past days and then over at his brave grandson. He wondered if letting Yachay take the lead and enter the village without him was the best way to ensure the safe escape of his beloved wife and daughter. *I cannot simply go in and demand that everyone allow me to take my family and leave. The agreement was that Kawsay was to live alone in the jungle after the age of thirteen, and that she was to fend for herself – alone. They have no idea how well she has fended for herself! Not only has she gone into the jungle and survived, but she has traveled through time and excelled in a new world – a very different jungle. Her learning at age thirteen surpasses most of the elders. She has not only learned the ways of our people and become a better warrior than most of our young men, but she has learned a new language and about a new and very advanced world way beyond the imagination of our people. Kawsay has far surpassed the expectations of the Chief and elders who decided to give her a chance at life. Now even her lip is healed, and she is no longer deformed. I will let Yachay go in according to plan, but I will be watching and ready to step in.*

As the path wove around the side of the house, depositing them in the front yard, Kusi noticed Junior lying on the front porch. He could smell breakfast cooking. Kusi liked the Hunters and appreciated all they had done for Kawsay and Yachay. *Imagine if we had arrived at a hostile place rather than this sanctuary of kindness.* Junior led the way into the house, and they could see Ben and Alison busy in the kitchen.

"Great timing," Alison greeted them. "Look, I pulled out three of our backpacks and packed some food for your trip. Kawsay, you and Kusi will be on your own in the jungle so no one will see these packs. Yachay will be in your village, so he can leave his pack with you and Kusi and then use it to help you carry your mother and grandmother's belongings back here in the tunnel. I made twenty-five almond butter sandwiches for you to take," she said, placing her hand over a mountain of sandwiches. "You can divvy them up between the three of you. I also put in apples, pears, four pounds of mixed nuts, fifteen power bars, and a water purification filter. Kawsay, you and Kusi have been away from home for a while, and your bodies may not be able to handle the water. Here, let me show you how to use it." Alison noticed Yachay eying the sandwiches, nuts, and other food items.

Ben was putting breakfast on the table while Alison gave Kawsay and Kusi a water filter demonstration at the sink. Yachay began rummaging in the refrigerator to see if anything looked like it belonged in his smaller food pouches. He felt sorry he had snarled at his sister. She had changed a lot and did not seem to need him as much. She was learning from other people rather than from him. He looked over at her listening intently to Alison. Kawsay was smart and had learned the Hunters' language so well. He had needed to rely on her in this new world in order to communicate. He was proud of her and wanted her to grow up and be a happy woman. He hoped they would always be close to each other. Their relationship was special and unusual. Yachay looked up to see Nate wander into the kitchen. He looked tired and distracted. *He is just my age and is caught in his own battle with time.*

"Great, we're all here." Ben pointed at the table. "Everyone sit down." He slipped into the laundry room and returned with some ropes and rock climbing harnesses. "I only have four harnesses, so you will have to jury-rig a bit using rope in order to secure five people and Zevél together. For your trip home you will have enough harnesses for the three of you, but you will need to secure your mother and grandmother on the way back. You can tie the ropes around Zevél's shoulders and back. I think he will be OK with that." Ben smiled weakly, picturing the great silver wolf with climbing ropes tied around his dignified and imposing body.

Grandfather reached for the ropes and began sizing up the situation in his mind. "Grandfather knows the quipu and is good with knots," Kawsay said. "He will connect us all together for the return trip through the sucking tunnel. You think Zevél will be happy being tied to us?"

"He would probably prefer that to having you all hold on to his tail," Nate said, smiling as he reached for the large platter Ben had covered with slices of nut-butter-lathered toast. Nate was in a funny mood that morning.

"Here, let me put those ropes up on the counter away from Junior's reach," Alison said as she got up. "We haven't heard from Zevél yet this morning, but his presence will be confirmation that your journey is to begin today. I know you three are eager to go. We will be equally eager for your safe return. I only hope it is well before Nate needs to leave next Saturday. It would be nice for Nate to be able to get to know your mother and grandmother a bit. The next time he will see them, three years will have passed for all of us except you, Nate. We will have aged three years and you three days," Alison mused.

"Yes, but I already aged those three years before I met you," Nate assured her, knowing that adults are always worried about aging too fast. "You're just catching up with me. Our bodies age at their own rate no matter what time we're in – it's in our cells, even if we jump around from one time to another."

"I think these tunnels bypass time and jump from one location in space-time to another rather than moving through it," Ben added. "I've thought the tunnel openings must move around very slowly over time as well. It doesn't seem as if they would remain static – nothing in this universe is. We know the tunnel between here and that field in Israel has been in place for at least thirty years, but who knows where those portals will be in another thirty years. Remember we talked about whether the portals are always in caves just below the surface of the Earth. I mean, what if some exits are in the middle of the Earth or some random place in outer space."

"Yeah, we know one of them shows up in the ocean!" Nate added.

Ben, Alison, Nate and the three Inca sojourners finished their breakfast while discussing Zevél and time travel. They wondered how many other Zevél-like animals may be roaming the time tunnels, if he has a female counterpart anywhere, and where he spends most of his time. After breakfast they filled the backpacks, securing Yachay's sling and lucky spear inside one of them. Alison put a fresh dressing on Yachay's wound. She prepared two more dressings for him to take along, including one made of cloth that would not look out of place in his village.

They went outside to the porch to wait for Zevél and spotted him lying in the sun-drenched grass near the path to the cave. "He's already here – waiting for us!" Kawsay exclaimed with youthful delight.

Kusi and Yachay looked at each other and smiled. They were happy to see that the little girl was still inside the new, more sophisticated teenager.

"We are ready." Kawsay spoke clearly to Zevél, once again taking on her role as interpreter for her family.

"Yachay and Kusi ready," Yachay asserted himself. *It is time I master this language.*

"I believe you are ready." Zevél carefully scrutinized his charges. He continued, "Good to see you, Binyamin, Alison, and Nate." The wolf looked down at Junior who was hiding behind Alison on a taut leash.

Yachay still thought it was odd for this huge animal to speak as a man. He had needed to rely on Kawsay for interpretation and the medicine people for care of his arm, and now the very lives of his family depended on a talking wolf who must weigh as much as three men. Yachay preferred to be in charge.

Zevél stood, turned toward the path, and began walking to the cave. Nate's head was full of the questions they had discussed at breakfast, and he quickened his pace to catch up with Zevél. "May I ask you a few questions while we walk, Zevél?"

The others crowded forward to hear any answers the wolf may grant. Zevél seemed to nod. That was all Nate needed. "Great. How many portals do the tunnels have? In fact, how many tunnels are there? I mean, ten, a thousand, ten-million? You know – order of magnitude?"

Zevél considered this. "I have been through many tunnels, but the number of them is unknown to me." The great wolf continued a steady stride along the trail. He seemed to glide rather than walk.

"Do the tunnels move around?" Nate jumped in with his next question.

"The way to my home is no more. The universe is dynamic, Nathaniel. Would you expect one part of a changing world to be static? Only Elohim does not change."

Nate was considering Zevél's answer when Kawsay broke in. "The door to the tunnel at home sings, but this door does not sing. Why?"

Zevél smiled to himself. He liked this innocent girl with so much spirit and courage. "Do you have music-making instruments that use breath to make sound, Kawsay?"

"Yes, we have panpipes and flutes. I learned how they play music."

"You need to have your breath hit the hole just right to make a noise, do you not?" Zevél asked.

"Yes. You are saying the air in our cave hits the tunnel door just right and plays music? That makes our secret cave special." Kawsay was happy that she finally understood the mystery of the "wailing lady". She explained this insight to Grandfather and Yachay.

"Are there other animals from your home that travel the tunnels like you, Zevél? You know, people often think of a noble lion." Nate hoped that question was not offensive to his friend.

"Cats are inherently unreliable, Nathaniel."

"What I meant was, have you ever encountered other animals who navigate the tunnels as you do?" Nate realized the canine-feline thing must go back eons.

"Well, there is this annoying parrot – but that is another story. Besides her, others may have mastered the tunnels, but I have not met them. There are many different places and times. I have noticed that most animals have an innate sense to stay away from tunnel entrances."

Nate was looking at Zevél profile and thought the wolf looked sad for a moment. "Are you ever lonely?"

Zevél briefly slowed his pace and looked over at Nate. "I am never alone, Nathaniel. I have a constant companion who gives me peace and security."

As the small entourage crossed the bridge, the trail narrowed forcing single file travel. They each were in thought about the days ahead. This was the first goodbye for Nate and Kawsay, and they each were thinking about the other.

The trail climbed up through the sun-speckled forest toward the cave entrance. As they entered the cave, Ben turned on his flashlight and pointed the wide beam ahead onto the cool rock floor. They wove through the rock maze in silence. The air was cool and moist compared to the dry, late summer mountain air. Zevél led the group into the large crystalline cavern. The small dark room with the portal was just beyond. The wolf stopped. He assumed there would be some parting conversations – humans were like that.

Nate had one more question he had been hoping to bounce off Zevél. On a subconscious level he was delaying saying goodbye to Kawsay. He wished things did not have to change. But now Kawsay was leaving, and as soon as she returned he would leave. When they meet again in three years, things may be different between them. "Zevél, may I ask you a question about time?"

Zevél sat down to listen.

Nate took a deep breath. "I believe time is speeding up. I know adults say it only *seems* like time is speeding up since, as you live longer, your perspective changes, because one day is a smaller percent of the life of a sixty-year-old than it is of a six-year-old. Therefore, a day for the sixty-year-old *seems* shorter. I understand all that, but I think something different is happening. I think time really *is* speeding up." Nate thought he saw Zevél raise his eyebrows – if he had any. Nate continued, "Well, we know the universe is expanding. And not only is it expanding, but its expansion is accelerating. Dad says he thinks time is a function of the expanding universe so that as everything moves, time is created from that movement since time and velocity are intertwined. Well, if time is caused by the expanding universe and the expansion of the universe is accelerating, then the passing of time must also be accelerating. Therefore, time is actually speeding up." Nate felt confident he had made his case in a logical manner. He realized Kawsay was not able to properly translate his thesis to Kusi and Yachay, and they each looked confused and distracted. He would have to explain it to them at some later date. *Hey, by the time I return to the future, they will probably be speaking fluent English, and I can talk to them about it directly.*

A soft, low rumble could barely be heard in Zevél's throat. "You must think I am Steven Hawking. This question of yours reflects deep insightful thinking, Nathaniel. Elohim gave you a good mind. I do not have sufficient answers for such profound questions as the definition of time. I am a humble servant of my Master. I am called to navigate in and out of this mysterious domain, but I do not fully comprehend it."

Ben and Alison smiled. They often discussed similar questions with each other. In fact, one of the characteristics that had attracted them to one another was that they each pondered the great questions of the universe and eternity, at least to the extent of their understanding.

Kusi sensed it was time to move on and removed the climbing harnesses and ropes from one of the backpacks he planned to later fill with treasures from home. He said in English, "Ready."

Ben realized he had not discussed the harness and rope idea with Zevél. He pointed to the gear and said, "Zevél, Alison and I were thinking we need to somehow attach everyone for the trip through the tunnel. You will have three people – Kawsay, Yachay, and Kusi – to take to their home, but there will be five returning. Alison and I were trying to imagine the logistics of keeping everyone together and touching. We have some climbing ropes and harnesses we thought could be used to attach everyone to you." Ben smiled weakly.

Zevél looked at the harnesses and ropes and said, "Are you trying to domesticate me?"

"Of course not!" Ben quickly responded, thinking he had somehow offended his friend.

"He's making a joke, honey." Alison winked at Zevél.

"You and Alison understand the importance of staying linked in the tunnel," Zevél observed. "You and Kusi can attach the harnesses and ropes. A body feels great forces in the tunnels. Kawsay, you may each hold on to me and to each other and use the ropes and harnesses to secure us together." He waited for Kawsay to translate, then continued, "We can now go to the small cavern with the portal."

Ben used his flashlight to illuminate the small room. Alison turned on a smaller flashlight she had slipped into her pocket before they left the house. Kawsay put on the empty backpack, Kusi had the food-filled pack, and Yachay had the third pack filled with his sling.

Kawsay looked small and vulnerable in her Inca clothing. Nate smiled down at her. He felt so much for this mysterious enigma from the past. He reached down and gave her a long hug. He looked into her pretty face. "I will see you in a few days." In the dim light he noticed she was wearing the watch that Joe Stevens had given her. "You guys are wearing your new watches?"

"Yes. We will use them to set a time to meet so Yachay can tell us Mother and Grandmother are fine. Yachay will hide his in a pouch while he is in the village." Kawsay turned to Alison and Ben. "We love you and thank you. We are happy to have a new home to return to together. I want to spend time with you and go on your digs. I asked Grandfather if I can come and spend time with you while we are living in our new home in Peru. He said, 'Yes'." Kawsay hugged Alison, Ben, and Nate for a second time. Kusi and Yachay also hugged them. The two boys had begun to feel a kinship, as they were the same age and in similarly odd life circumstances.

Ben and Kusi tied a rope around Zevél's shoulders and chest. Zevél moved toward the wall in the back of the room that hid the portal. The back wall of the nearly round cavern folded back on itself forming a hidden narrow hallway that sloped slightly downward. The portal, which was at the end of the short hallway, was perpendicular to the back of the room and well hidden from the cavern's entrance. Ben thought of it as entering a hidden spiral staircase to other worlds.

"We must be careful and enter together. Tie yourselves to me and hold on to my body and each other. And remember to take a deep breath just before entering and hold it," Zevél instructed. "I sense it is time."

Ben helped his Inca friends to the entrance of the small hidden hallway. "Kusi and I will secure everyone together. Let's go."

They stepped into their harnesses and cinched them tightly. Kusi pulled the rope linking them as close as possible. Kawsay climbed onto Zevél's back and put her arms around his neck. Grandfather and Yachay put their arms around each other, Kawsay, and Zevél. They awkwardly squeezed into the narrow hallway.

"Is the tunnel wide enough for us to hold onto Zevél?" Kawsay asked.

Alison, Ben, and Nate heard Zevél's low voice respond. "The tunnel has no walls. Breathe in now! You must trust Elohim in the tunnels." The word "tunnels" was clipped off with a whoosh. They were gone.

Kawsay did take a deep breath. Her arms were wrapped tightly around Zevél's neck. She thought of Mother and the Chief's jaguar stool. *I am so excited about seeing Mother and Grandmother!* Kawsay's eyes were tightly closed, but she could feel tears welling up. Her face was buried in the wolf's fur. She could feel Yachay's and Grandfather's arms over her arms and back. She did not feel the effects of the sucking tunnel as much being sandwiched between the wolf, her brother, and Grandfather. She was overwhelmed by what had happened to her life, her lip, and herself. She felt grown up and confident with her lip fixed. But she also felt like a young girl going home to Mother.

Kusi felt his young, strong grandchildren as they flew through this mysterious tunnel that crosses time and distance. He held his grandchildren and himself securely against Zevél with his strong arms. What an amazing adventure he had experienced in an unimagined world! He was eager to tell his beloved Asiri his story. He was happy that in her world he had only been gone for days rather than the months he had actually been away. *Asiri will be ecstatic to go on such an adventure as moving to the future! She will jump at the chance of a new and exciting life beyond what she could ever imagine. My dear Sumaq, you have much excitement ahead of you! You have children for which you can boast with pride. You have a new life with many surprises.*

Yachay felt Grandfather securely clutching his arm and Kawsay's back under his shoulder. He hoped the landing would be softer than his others. *When will we arrive, and will it be before the suspicions of the troublemakers in the tribe are aroused? Are Mother and Grandmother being watched? Will they be ready to leave their home forever? How will the people of the village respond when I tell them Kusi is never going to return? Will they be happy, or will they feel sad they drove him away to another world?*

Zevél's body stiffened as they decelerated. The great wolf lunged out of the tunnel and slid across the rock floor, dragging his three passengers. Their mild collision with the far rock wall was sustained mostly by Zevél's front paws and head.

"Are you OK, Zevél?" Kawsay quickly asked, rolling off his back and untangling herself from the harness and ropes.

Their pilot shook himself. "I am well."

Kusi and Yachay gathered themselves, stepped out of their harnesses, and checked their backpacks. Kusi found a place up on a rock to stash the ropes and harnesses for their return home. "I am not sure of the time, but I recognize our secret cave!" Kusi stated.

Zevél noticed the anticipation on his charges' faces, looked at Kawsay, and said, "I will stay with you and Kusi in the jungle. First, I will lead the way out of the cave."

"But the opening is over there." Kawsay was pointing in the direction that Yachay and Kusi were already heading. "Grandfather, Yachay, wait," she called in Quechua. "Zevél knows another way."

"I think you will find it preferable to bringing your mother and grandmother up a sheer cliff." Zevél trotted off down a rock hallway.

"I worried about that cliff," she answered.

The three of them hurried to catch up with the wolf. After a series of descending tunnels, turns, and tight squeezes through some barely visible openings, the four emerged slightly above the jungle floor. It was an easy jump for Zevél, and the others climbed down.

Once on the ground, Kawsay instinctively drew in a deep breath, taking in the old familiar smells. The tall trees offered shade from the warm sun. It appeared to be midmorning. Kawsay could feel the difference in humidity. She heard familiar bird calls, and she and Grandfather exchanged glances. The two of them had been away months.

"You have been to our secret cave before, Zevél." Kawsay declared, wondering why the wolf would have come here. Perhaps she could probe further while Yachay was in the village.

"I have. I do not know your jungle though, so I will follow you from here." Zevél looked at Kusi, expecting him to lead.

"Does he know what day it is?" Yachay asked Kawsay.

The wolf's answer was, "I do not know the day, but am confident it is correct."

Kusi took charge. "We will travel as fast as we are able. Let us get a good distance in; then we can have a quick meal." The four of them began a smooth jog into the jungle.

Kawsay followed closely behind her grandfather with her brother jogging silently behind her. The great silver wolf followed, alert to sights, sounds, and smells. Zevél had been traveling this planet through eons – even deep into jungles. He decided ages ago bugs were not creatures with which he would choose to share breathing space. He also thought himself more suited to cooler, slightly dryer climates due to this thick fur. *A cool, dry climate – now that would feel good just now,* he mused.

Yachay was rehearsing in his mind how he would handle the announcement that Grandfather would not be returning. He wanted to tell the Chief about the new world they found, but Grandfather was not sure that was wise. Grandfather trusted the Chief and thought it may be nice for him to know that the secret cave houses a time tunnel, but he did not want to encourage him to attempt to follow them. Grandfather had said a person cannot know where he may end up or what kind of trouble he may get into or cause. Besides, what good would it do the Chief to know they went off to some exciting future world when his duty was with his people?

As the hours passed and the four of them continued at a constant pace, Kusi began to wonder when the warm sultry air would impact their furry tunnel-guide. *Dogs are excellent runners, but this wolf looks to be better suited for the cold.* He thought a lunch break was in order and slowed to a stop. Kusi still had the food pack, which had some water Alison had slipped in so they did not need to filter stream water right away. Kusi pulled out a sandwich for each of them, gingerly placing one into Zevél's intimidating muzzle. "You eat, I give you more," Kusi said in beginning English, knowing one sandwich would not be enough to fill such a large animal. The four of them ate quickly not wanting to waste daylight.

Yachay was watching Zevél's large mouth contend with almond butter when his attention was drawn to his sister. "What are you doing, Kawsay?" Yachay began laughing at his sister who was furiously swatting herself.

"It's the bugs," Kawsay said. "I believe they have gotten worse during the past months since I've been gone."

"You left just twelve days ago," Yachay said. "But I guess for you it seems like months. Anyway, you have spent your entire life in this jungle with its bugs, and they never bothered you before." He noticed Grandfather fanning the air in front of him. "You too, Grandfather? The future is making you both soft," Yachay laughed.

"I also do not like them," Zevél defended.

Yachay could see all manner of flying insects buzzing around Zevél's eyes and ears. "What did he say?" Yachay asked with a half smile.

"He doesn't like them either – and the huge wolf is not 'soft', brother," Kawsay said, taking the last bite of her sandwich.

Kusi furnished Zevél a second sandwich and gave everyone else a handful of nuts. He mused, "It is odd that we notice the bugs now, but never gave them much thought before. I wonder what else will seem different. It is good you have only been away a few days, Yachay. You will be able to act completely natural. Let's finish up and go. We have had plenty of sleep the past days and should be able to travel late into the night – even those of us who are *soft*." Kusi smiled at his grandson.

For the next two days the three Incas and Zevél passed swiftly through the jungle. They slept only a few hours each evening. Kawsay slept nestled against Zevél while Yachay and Grandfather preferred tree branches. Zevél was happy to travel during the nighttime and early morning hours when it was noticeably cooler. The Incas had spent their lives in this jungle at night so they were comfortable journeying in the darkness. They were all thankful for the sandwiches, nuts, power bars, and fruit Alison had prepared for them. The water filter even worked as it should.

Zevél's ears perked up, and he shot ahead of Kusi. "Stop," he said in a growling whisper. "We must hide for a moment." Kawsay quickly translated as Zevél steered them behind a large moss-covered tree trunk that had fallen. "Stay quiet. I thought this may happen," Zevél whispered.

"I hear it," Yachay breathed.

"Me too," Kawsay added in a whisper.

The soft footsteps grew louder, and a boy came into view. They all froze in stunned silence. After the boy ran past them and out of ear range, Kusi looked at his grandson and said. "You run well, Yachay. I don't think we would have heard you in time if Big Ears, here, hadn't stopped me."

Yachay was stunned by the sight of himself running past. He tried to remember what he had been thinking at that moment. Had he sensed that anyone had been watching him? Perhaps. Then he thought of where he was going and what fantastic and unbelievable experiences lay before him. "Ask Zevél if I will have to live all that again, Kawsay."

"He says you already lived it, Yachay. You only live it once. We just overlapped time a few days in order to get you back to our village in time for whatever you need to do there." Zevél knew how disorienting it was to overlap with oneself.

The four rose from their crouched positions and continued their journey in silence. They were now only about a day away from the village. The terrain along the river had become increasingly familiar to Kawsay. She had traveled to the secret caves along this route once with Grandfather over a year ago as a trial run and then again on her final journey a few months ago. Will she find this same trail again after they return to Peru with Hurtado? Will they look for the secret cave again? She felt strong and confident. She had always felt strong, but her lip had always made her feel insecure and inadequate. Now she was whole and healed. She had learned of a new world and a new language. She could hardly wait to show her new lip to Mother and Grandmother and anticipated their surprise and happiness. She was eager to tell them about Nate and the Hunters. So much had changed for her, and she felt so different. *Will Mother notice how different I am on the inside too?*

Kusi eventually stopped. "This is far enough. I think the three of us should stop here and let Yachay go forward alone." Kusi took a deep breath of the familiar jungle air, warm and soft. He looked around searching for anything that should be of concern, but saw only the jungle as it had been for many years. *No reason for alarm.* "It is midmorning. We must tend to your wound and replace that white patch with Alison's medicine cloth." Kusi began rummaging in the side pocket of the backpack to find the cloth dressing. Kawsay carefully removed the old bandage from Yachay's arm. The wound looked like it was healing well. There was no angry red sickness to be seen. She helped Grandfather apply the new bandage.

Noticing Yachay's watch on his wrist, Kusi said, "Put your new time clock in your pouch, Yachay. But first let's agree to meet late tonight right here by this huge old tree when the clock's little line points right and its big line points up. You can sneak out and give us an update even if you cannot get your mother and grandmother out yet. My preference is that you will return here with your mother and grandmother by then, and we will all leave here forever." His words sounded final.

"What will you do here while I am gone?" Yachay wondered aloud.

"I will teach Grandfather English language!" Kawsay said excitedly. "He will benefit if he knows English. Zevél can help. Maybe we can teach Zevél our language too!"

The wolf yawned and decided a full day of sleep would be more welcome.

Yachay removed his twenty-first century backpack and gave it to Grandfather. He affixed his nearly empty sling to his back. He was saving room for personal possessions from home. *What we take from home now is all we will ever have of our possessions,* Yachay thought. He, Kawsay, and Kusi had decided what they wanted to retrieve and bring to their new world. They figured Mother and Grandmother had been preparing lists in their minds in case Yachay did not return quickly and they needed to leave on their own. Yachay had his spear with the lucky arrow embedded in it. He looked at the arrow in a different way now that he knew it had a remarkable history and was from a book written by Ben's God. Yachay looked solemnly at his sister, grandfather, and a sleeping Zevél. "Take care of each other. I will not let you down." He quickly disappeared toward home.

He arrived where the dense jungle meets the village and, after a few more strides, slipped silently into his house. It was near the edge of the village and adequately spaced from its neighbors.

"Yachay!" Sumaq said in a loud whisper, turning from the soup she was cooking. "You are home so soon!"

Before she could say more, Yachay hugged her and whispered in her ear. "Kawsay and Grandfather are safe. I have much to tell you that will be difficult for you to believe, but I will soon show you. I will tell everyone that Grandfather will never return here. Then I will take you and Grandmother to him and Kawsay. We have a new home. It is in the future."

"Yachay, you only left yesterday. Where is your grandfather?" Asiri said with surprise in her voice as she entered their house. She noticed her daughter looked stunned, and her heart began to sink with worry.

Yachay could see her fear. "No," he whispered and drew close to her. "He is safe and healthy. They both are. But as I just told Mother, I will tell everyone he will not return, which is true. They can think what they will. But we must leave. We have found a new home for all of us. We can be together." He stopped for a moment and studied their confused faces. He was about to confuse them even more. "Kawsay is healed. Her lip was fixed."

Sumaq noticed the cloth tied to Yachay's arm. "You have been hurt, son. That is why you are delirious." She touched the dressing. "What happened, Yachay?"

Yachay stiffened. He noticed Grandmother looking at him with a dubious expression. He had not anticipated they would not simply believe what he told them. He needed them to believe him and support him in telling his people about Grandfather not returning. He took a deep breath and sat down, signaling them to sit close to him. "I will tell you exactly what happened to Kawsay, Grandfather, and me. It is an unbelievable story, but you must believe me. I am not delirious. Their lives depend on you believing me." Yachay noticed his spear with its embedded arrow leaning against the wall and thought of Nate, Ben, and Ben's family. They needed the arrow. Yachay had not paid full attention to Ben's story, but he knew Ben's family was in trouble. He also knew Nate needed the arrow back so he could take it on his journey to help Ben's family and then return safely to his time. "There are other people you will soon meet whose lives and families depend on you believing me. Please listen and understand me." Yachay could see in their eyes that they were now earnestly listening to him.

He told them about Kawsay falling through the wailing lady's wall into the future and about how Ben and Alison took care of her and fixed her lip. He told them how Grandfather had been right behind her, and that he fell through the tunnel holding on to her ankle. After he arrived, however, Grandfather hid and watched her, believing Kawsay could integrate into a new life better without him. Then she discovered him. Yachay then told them about his own wild trip and how he first arrived under a huge white temple in another time and stopped two cowards from killing a man. Then he went back into the tunnel and landed on a massive bear in a different time, which is how he got the wound. Then there was the great bursting of smoke and flames and a huge pointed cylindrical structure rose off the ground dragging a cone of fire and smoke below it. Then he ran from that, fell asleep in a raised hut, and woke up on a huge boat, which he dove off of to save Cindy Stevens from drowning in frigid water. After that, he rode in a metal bird to a medicine house and talked to Kawsay and Grandfather as their voices traveled through the air and came out of a little box. The next day Grandfather and Kawsay came to the medicine house. They rested for two days, and then they all flew to Ben and Alison's house in a different metal bird. Finally they came back here, and Kawsay and Grandfather are now waiting for them in the jungle. *The time clock*, he thought, *that will convince them I am telling the truth.* He slipped the elegant chronograph watch out of his pouch and handed it to Mother.

"It is moving all over. Look Mother, the little lines are moving around." Sumaq showed the watch to her mother.

"It's beautiful" Asiri said. She mostly felt relief to hear her husband and granddaughter were safe.

"Listen to it," Yachay said as he pushed it up to his mother's ear. He saw her face light up as she heard the fast ticking. She let her mother listen. *My wound is not new,* Yachay thought. *That will also convince them I am telling the truth.* "Look," he said pulling his cloth bandage aside. "This wound happened about eleven days ago. I landed on the great bear eleven days ago! You say I left yesterday, but I have been gone at least sixteen days. I must tell you. Kawsay and Grandfather have been gone from here and living in the new world for months, yet you saw them leave here days ago. Traveling through time is very confusing. But, as you will experience yourselves, it is real. I was four hundred years in the future."

Asiri was carefully examining her grandson's wound. "These are huge claw marks, Yachay. A creature with such claws … you are lucky to be alive. You are correct though. This wound did not happen within the past two days. It looks to be healing well, but it has been here for over ten days. And you did not have it when you left." Asiri looked at her daughter for acknowledgement of this strange phenomenon of a deep scratch that was not here yesterday but was not a new wound. Sumaq's eyebrows were furrowed as she too examined the wound. "The medicine that is on your wound – it smells strange," Asiri added.

"One more thing." Yachay remembered another proof. "Grandmother, do you remember when you and Grandfather got the strange arrow in the secret cave?" She nodded, and he continued, "The boy who threw it at you has also traveled to the future and has grown up. He is the man who owns the house where Kawsay and Grandfather have been staying and to where we will be traveling. You will meet him again!"

"When did you learn about the boy who threw the arrow?" Asiri asked.

"I didn't know until I met him a few days ago," Yachay said.

"I always wondered what happened to the boy," Asiri mused.

"Well, you will soon meet him. His name is Ben." Yachay could see the women's faces deep in thought, trying to imagine the reality of what he had told them. He figured it was best to warn them about Zevél now rather than have them frightened by him later tonight – assuming they could leave tonight. "There is one more thing I should tell you. The tunnels are tricky to navigate. We need help with them and, uh, this is going to sound strange, but I don't want you to be frightened when you meet Zevél. He knows the tunnels and helped us get here at the right time. He is a rather large wolf." Yachay had a weak smile on his face, bracing for their reaction and thinking perhaps he should not have pushed his luck by bringing up Zevél.

"A wolf," Sumaq said blankly.

"You will soon meet Zevél. For now, here is Grandfather's plan." Yachay thought that by presenting it as Grandfather's plan, they would comply with it. "I will tell the Chief that Grandfather will never return – that he has, in fact, gone to a new world. Grandfather hopes when the word gets out, it will remove all the suspicion our people have about our family. Everyone will feel sorry for us and not be suspicious we are helping Kawsay. Grandfather expects the Chief will hold a ceremony for him, and our people will become intoxicated. That will give us the opportunity to sneak away. Today, we must gather what we can carry to take with us. It will be all we will ever have of our possessions, so we should choose carefully. If the Chief holds the ceremony tonight, it will give us the opportunity to sneak away once everyone is asleep. If the ceremony is not until tomorrow, we will leave late tomorrow night. We will meet Grandfather, Kawsay, and Zevél in the jungle and begin our journey to the secret cave."

"Your mother and I had been preparing in case you did not return. We have gathered what we want to bring with us," Asiri said. "Have you eaten, Yachay?"

Yachay was eager to talk to the Chief and get the plan into action, but thought a quick meal with his mother and grandmother would be nice – especially after what he had just told them. *Perhaps they have questions I can answer.* "I am hungry. Then I can visit the Chief."

Sumaq jumped up and served the three of them the soup she had been preparing. They wanted to hear more about the girl Yachay had saved from drowning and where he got the time clock. He filled them in on what he understood about their future, about Hurtado, and about the new land that will exist here in four hundred years.

After they finished eating and Yachay answered all their questions, he stood up. "I will go and talk to the Chief. You can imagine the response once the word gets out. You do not need to speak to anyone. You can mostly stay in the house. If you see anyone, just look sad. I will come back and tell you about my conversation." Yachay started to leave, but stopped, turned to the women, and said in a near whisper, "Grandfather misses you both terribly. His heart has been breaking without you, Grandmother. And Kawsay is so excited with anticipation to see you she may burst if we do not get to her quickly." He saw their eyes begin to tear and smiled, feeling a bit misty himself. He turned and stepped into the bright midday sun. He stood tall and proud, hoping to be noticed. He sauntered over to the Chief's house and presented himself in the doorway.

"Yachay, please come in." The Chief was talking with the two elders he most trusted.

Good, Yachay thought, *a wider audience for faster spread of rumors.* "Thank you, Chief." Yachay stepped into the Chief's house.

"Please, sit down and join us. We are discussing weather and crops – what else is there?" the Chief said, trying to be cheerful at a time he knew was difficult for Yachay's family. It had not been that many days since young Kawsay had been sent away. The Chief was wondering how the small family was holding up. "I have not seen your grandfather for a few days. Is he well?" The Chief hoped for a good report, knowing how suspicious his people were becoming since Kawsay left.

Yachay sat down and looked at the floor. *Here goes*, he thought. "That is why I have come to speak with you. My grandfather will not be returning. He has gone to a new world. He will not ever return to us here in our village. My mother and grandmother are shocked by this news."

The Chief sat there stunned. He could not believe his friend, Kusi, was gone. Perhaps the strain was too much for him, and he had not been vigilant in the jungle. The Chief did not need the gory details from a boy who has lost so much. "Is his body with us for a proper honoring?" was all he could ask.

"There is no dead body," Yachay responded still looking down. Yachay was thankful there was no dead body. He could not bear the thought of seeing his grandfather dead. He wanted a long life for his mother and grandparents. *Grandfather seems invincible – he is the best at everything.*

"We will give support to your family and honor Kusi. He will be deeply missed. Your mother and grandmother must be grieving. I will visit them after I make arrangements for a ceremony. We will do it immediately – tonight." The Chief looked at the two elders, and they nodded. Their weathered faces looked sad and strained. They felt sympathy and sadness for this family that had endured spurning from most of the tribe's members since the birth of Kawsay.

Out of the whole village, these three men are the most decent, Yachay thought. *It is unfortunate I cannot tell them the truth of the tunnel in the secret caves and of the new world in another time.* "I will tell Mother and Grandmother of your plans," Yachay said. He continued to look down, not wanting the Chief to read his eyes and suspect there may be more to the story. *It is true that Grandfather will never return and has gone to a new world. It is also true that if this tribe was not a bunch of barbarians who murder their babies because of a small dimple on an infant's lip or send a thirteen-year-old girl out to the jungle alone to die, we never would have found the new world or be trying to sneak away.*

Yachay worried about the Chief and his close allies and what would happen once it was discovered that his family snuck away. He hoped the villagers would go on with their lives and maybe be influenced by the goodness of the Chief. *Perhaps there are other good people in the tribe, but none of them went out of their way to be kind to my family since Kawsay's birth.*

Yachay stood up, nodded at the Chief and two elders, stepped outside, and took a deep breath of the familiar midday smells. He noticed a few of the boys near his age in the distance. They saw him. He did not want any encounters or conversations. He walked away from them and took the path that skirted the outside of the village over to his house where

Mother and Grandmother would be awaiting his report. He quickened his pace as he noticed them eying him suspiciously. *They'll hear the news, then maybe they will back off – and then we'll be gone.* Yachay slipped into his house. He noticed Mother and Grandmother jump a bit when they heard him enter.

"Yachay, it's you," Sumaq said, relieved. "How did things go?"

"Why did you jump? Has anyone been bothering you?" Yachay asked protectively.

"No, well, we saw some of the boys hanging around. They must have been looking for you. But they said nothing to us." Sumaq looked weary.

"I saw them. They will soon hear the news about Grandfather. I told the Chief. He said he will hold a ceremony for Grandfather immediately. I think it will be tonight. The Chief will pay you a visit and tell you very soon. If you are packed, it would be best to hide what we are taking. Then we can act like we are grieving. People may come by, and we do not want to raise suspicions." Yachay was thinking out loud.

"You are a wise young man, Yachay," Asiri said. "Your grandfather and I have always been very proud of you. Sumaq and I have hidden what we plan to take to this new world. We are ready to leave without sadness." She paused and looked at her grandson and daughter with a slight twinkle in her eye. "This will be a great adventure for us. We will have a better life and future. I just know it."

Yachay smiled at her courage. She and Grandfather had been the strength of this small family. Their good-natured spirit and optimism had always made life seem fun, even through the struggles the family had endured. Yachay looked around at Grandfather's metalwork and at Mother's and Grandmother's pottery and weavings, and he felt a hint of sadness. He noticed some of Grandfather's gold and silver masks, plaques, and animal figurines were missing. Yes, most of the gold and silver dishes were missing too. Yachay smiled. In fact, they had collected the family's most precious valuables and then spread out other items so that the house appeared normal. "Very good. At first even I did not notice. I hope we will be gone by this time tomorrow. Now we wait for the ceremony and rest for the difficult travel days ahead." Yachay smiled at his cohorts, and the three of them sat down.

A short time later the Chief presented himself in the doorway of the modest home of his friends. He saw the jaguar stool he had given Kawsay on her tenth birthday. *This is all so wrong*, he thought. He could see Asiri, Sumaq, and Yachay sitting quietly looking up at him.

"Please, come in," Sumaq rose, motioning to the Chief. Asiri and Yachay stood to greet the Chief.

"We will honor Kusi tonight. Plans have been made for sundown. I am so very sorry to lose my dear friend, Kusi. Kusi is a good man. I cannot yet speak of him in the past. He is as a brother to me. His wisdom and courage are unmatched." The Chief looked sad. "I will go and continue the arrangements. Please let me know if there is anything I can do for you."

Kusi's family stood quietly, listening to the Chief. They did not know what to say.

As the Sun was setting, Yachay led his mother and grandmother down the broad, intricately-cut steps Yachay's father had chiseled during his abbreviated life. The people were gathered in the outdoor amphitheater they used for meetings and special events. Yachay felt everyone's eyes on them and slipped his hands through the arms of his mother and grandmother. He knew this had to be a very strange experience for each of them. Mother had lost Father when Yachay was a young boy. She had endured a ceremony such as this for her husband's death. They walked down to the front near where the Chief was standing.

"Please be silent and sit down," the Chief began. "I will say a few words in behalf of my good friend, Kusi. You have all heard by now that Kusi is gone. He has gone to the next life. Most of you know Kusi as a great warrior noted for his stealth, but our younger people may not know he served with me under Túpac Amaru when we were sixteen and seventeen. Kusi and I later met up in the jungle. Kusi found and chose this land that we now live on and designed how our village would be laid out. Because of his choice of this land, we have been able to live safely from the Invaders. I was not sure this was the best place, but Kusi insisted we would remain safe here. He was right. Kusi married his beautiful bride, Asiri, when he was eighteen and became a father to his daughter Sumaq at nineteen. Kusi has guarded our people and kept us safe from Invaders and animals of the jungle for all these years. Many of you were trained by Kusi. He has been a teacher for our youth and has made improvements to our bola as well as our crop management. Kusi's wisdom and courage are unmatched. He has been a friend and brother to me, and I encourage all of you to show compassion to his family."

The Chief looked at the faces of his tribe. Many looked shamed, obviously thinking about how they had shunned Kusi's granddaughter, Kawsay, because of her tiny deformity. If the Chief could read their thoughts, he imagined they figured the stress of Kawsay's recent exile must have had something to do with Kusi's end. "I will leave you with a funny story. Then you can pay your respects to Kusi's family and celebrate his life with a drink of Chicha."

The Chief paused and looked around at the burning torches. The air was pleasant and smelled of smoke and food. He continued, "One night not too long after Kusi and I met up, we were in the jungle searching for a site to build a village for the people who escaped the Invaders. It was very late and dark. We heard a cry. Kusi said, 'It's a baby! Maybe its mother is dead. We must help it.' I said, 'Uh, I don't know about that, Kusi. It could be an animal.' We heard the noise again, and Kusi insisted we determine where it was coming from. So we hunted around in the dark listening and eventually spotted a little cave in the dim moonlight. 'That looks like an animal's den,' I said. But Kusi insisted we enter it after we again heard the cry. Well, the 'baby' turned out to be a baby jaguar, and the mother followed us into the cave. Kusi grabbed the baby, and we wedged ourselves into a deep crevice in the rock wall of the small cave. We spent the night squeezed into the crevice with Kusi gently holding the jaguar cub between us and its mother. It was very clever of him. She didn't dare attack us since her cub was between her and us. The baby was enjoying Kusi scratching its neck and ears throughout the night and fell asleep in his hands. Eventually the mother also fell asleep, and we crept out, leaving cub with mother." There were smiles on the tribe members' faces. "That, my friends, is Kusi – always the hero and defender. Go and celebrate his life. And be kind to his family."

So far everything is going as Grandfather had hoped, Yachay thought. *We will just sit here, let everyone say a few words to us, and smile and thank them. We will encourage everyone to drink up. Then, late tonight we will leave.* He nodded at his mother and grandmother. They had discussed the plan to just sit for a while. Slowly everyone came over to speak nice words about Kusi. Grandmother felt sad just thinking about losing her beloved Kusi. She could not wait to see him again and wished this evening would end so they could flee to the jungle and join Kusi and Kawsay. Sumaq sat silently, nodding at people who offered kind remarks about her father. She, too, just wanted to go.

Once in their house, the three quietly placed the bags containing the possessions they most valued near the door with a blanket over them. They were ready. Now they just needed to wait until it was quiet and everyone was asleep. They sat in silence as the revelers carried on. It was getting later and later. Yachay put his time clock on his wrist and sat staring at its luminescent dials. It was getting late and approaching the time he was to meet Grandfather, Kawsay, and the wolf. He guessed he could sneak out alone, but wanted to get Mother and Grandmother out of the village tonight. Besides, he did not want to leave them alone. He was becoming disgusted by the drunken whoops and hollers of the tribe members. *Soon they will all be asleep. What will Grandfather think? We should be meeting them now.*

Asiri reached over and squeezed the hand of her visibly stressed grandson. She knew it was near their meeting time, and there was still too much commotion outside to risk being seen. "Your grandfather is very wise, Yachay. Do not worry; it will work out," she quietly whispered.

Yachay watched the big line go around the clock face as the village became quieter and quieter and people slowly went to their homes for what was left of the night. Finally, all was quiet. Yachay could hear only his ticking clock. He put his sling on his back, gingerly picked up his spear, and stuck his head out the door. Silence. The air was cool. He could hear nothing but the typical jungle night sounds. Asiri and Sumaq stood up, ready to embark on their new future. The women picked up the two bags they had packed and followed Yachay out of their house – for the last time. They silently followed Yachay to the edge of the village where he had entered the jungle nightly during Kawsay's years of preparation. As he stepped under the jungle canopy, he took a deep breath of relief.

"What have we here? If it isn't Yachay and his mother going for an evening stroll," laughed the boy.

"And his grandmother too," another voice chimed in. "Isn't that sweet? We knew something didn't smell right." The obnoxious voice made a sniffing sound.

Yachay could not see them, but knew who they were – sissies. He was calculating their demise when two more voices taunted, "Where is your *pretty* sister Yachay? Are you going to find her?"

CHAPTER 26

GET READY, GET SET

SEPTEMBER 10 – PRESENT YEAR
HIGH SIERRAS, CALIFORNIA

HOW DO WE PREPARE
TO RESTORE WHAT HAS HAPPENED
AND FULFILL WHAT IS?

"They're gone – just like that!" said Alison in astonishment, looking at Ben and Nate. "I hope they'll be all right." Junior was sniffing around, wondering where his friends had gone. The abrupt departure of Zevél with the three Inca travelers seemed to leave behind a vacuum.

"We won't know until they return," Ben said, "which may be any time between now and the end of next week. But we can't wait here."

Alison was not eager to leave and kept looking back as they moved toward the cave exit just in case the travelers would return immediately. They slowly and quietly followed on the trail back to the house. Nate felt a strong sense of loss; he missed Kawsay already. The longest they had been apart since his arrival was the day he visited his father for lunch at the shopping center. He also pondered how he would feel in just nine days when it would be his turn to depart.

The house seemed unusually quiet and empty. "I'll clean up the breakfast dishes," Alison offered, happy to have something to take her mind off her feeling of loss and disorientation.

"I don't know what to do," Nate lamented. "I suppose I should finish my forward diary, though it seems that if my dad just acts naturally, he does OK."

Ben, however, was feeling restless. He retrieved a pencil and a few paper tablets from his office. "Nate, there's a *lot* for us to do."

"There is?" Nate asked, wondering what Ben had in mind.

"Absolutely," Ben said forcefully. "Alison, Nate and I need to spend the day planning his time in Israel. I'd really like your input, honey. Nate, let's sit in my office and put our heads together."

"You know, Ben," Nate confessed, "I've been so busy thinking about how hard it's going to be to leave next week that I haven't really thought much about what exactly I'm going to do when I get there."

"Returning the arrows should be the easy part," Ben suggested. "Your visit to my family presents far more difficult problems." Ben pulled out notes he had made the previous night after John left. "Let's see. I need to map out for you the way to get from the field to my house in Gibeah. I want to tell you about my family. Alison and I should prepare letters and photos for you to give them. We want to send a camera and a waterproof container to use when you come back through the ocean. You'll need a way to prove to them that the impossible story is not only possible but true. Otherwise, they may think you've hurt or killed me, and you'll end up in big trouble. Let's think about the best way for you to transport everything through the tunnels. We want to dye your hair dark brown, make sure my tunic fits you, and find new sandals that look old. You need to memorize the entire plan and brush up on your Hebrew. Maybe from now on you and I should speak mostly Hebrew to give you immersion practice. Finally, let's agree on what you can tell people and what you can and can't leave behind so as to minimize the impact on historical events."

Nate was feeling somewhat overwhelmed. "This is going to be a bigger deal than I thought! I hope I have time to get ready." Then he had an idea. "Ben, you mentioned a camera?"

"Yes, some little digital camera so you can take some pictures for me of my family."

"Well, that's fine, but why don't I take a camcorder?" Nate asked. Ben looked startled. "No, really. Wouldn't you also like to have me bring back some video of everyone and maybe some shots of the neighborhood? I think that would be fun."

"I can't believe I didn't think of that!" Ben said shaking his head. "Guess I've had too much on my mind." He held up an index finger with an idea of his own. "You know, that would let us *send* a video message so they would have more than just writing on paper." Ben was getting excited over the possibilities. "We could show them the house and Junior, and I could just *talk* to them. Once they get over the future shock, maybe I'll seem more real to them." He thought more about it. "But, maybe the electronics won't time travel well, or maybe some magnetic field will erase everything, so we still need the letters as a back-up. Also, you can't leave the hi-tech stuff there."

"But Ben," Nate observed, "remember what we learned from the incident with that guy, Morrow? By coming back from three years in the future I'm not interfering with history, I'm fulfilling it. Maybe it's the same with your family. They might be destined to change allegiance to David and help him, and I'm just part of that plan. Do you think it is really possible to change history? Maybe it just all has to happen – because it already did!"

Ben absorbed Nate's digression. "I understand what you're saying, Nate. I don't know the answer. But I am naturally cautious about introducing something into the past that shouldn't be there. Maybe I'm destined to be that way." He shrugged. "I *do* know, though, that we need to assemble the things you need." Ben took a deep breath and smiled at Nate. "Putting all this together will be an interesting challenge. Now, let's see," Ben continued, his mind racing, "I think we could send along a digital camcorder with a hard drive that can be backed up onto memory cards. The cards can travel in a small lead-lined box for protection from any fields you might pass through."

"If it's a special new model, I want to practice using it. I only have one chance to do it right!" Nate said, again feeling overwhelmed by his responsibilities.

"And," Ben added, "we don't know how much time we have to get you ready. Kawsay's entire family could return any minute, and then it will be difficult to focus on your preparations. There are items we need to purchase too, so I think we need to get as much as possible done in the next few days. Also, I need time to compose my letter." Alison joined them, smiling, not wanting to interrupt. Ben continued, "Alison, you said you wanted to send a letter to my family…"

"Thanking them for you, dear," Alison added, sitting down near Ben.

Ben liked that idea. "Right. And I'd really like to get a message back from my family once they're safe, but you won't know about that by the time you leave, Nate. I've been racking my brain trying to think how they can send us a message later after David is established as king. I wonder if we could use a strong container and durable paper and specify a place they can leave it for us. Then, next time we're in Israel we can try to find it."

"It has to be small," Alison said, "so Nate can carry it along with everything else. He'll need some kind of backpack."

"Whatever he uses has to be at least three feet long to hold the arrows and also waterproof for his return," Ben said.

"I've seen waterproof backpacks. They come in big sizes, and I think some models have floats built in. That would be good to have when I return to the Caribbean," Nate suggested. "If I'm carrying around a lead container, I'll need help staying afloat!"

"Sounds like just what we need," Ben said with enthusiasm. "I also was thinking you ought to have a radio transmitter so your father can locate you in the water."

"Remember, my dad was in the water trying to rescue me. I saw him swimming down to me before I was sucked away," Nate recalled. "You and my dad have to figure out some way to make sure he gets back into the boat!"

"Right. Don't you worry about it, Nate. Your dad and I will figure that out." Ben's mind flitted along. "What could Nate give my family so they can store a return message for us? Anyone have ideas on some kind of container that would remain intact for 3,000 years?"

"Isn't that what time capsules are all about?" Alison proposed.

"Of course. Why didn't I think of that?" Ben remarked.

"How would you be able to find it?" Nate asked. "Israel is a small country, but you'd have to dig a lot of holes!"

Ben smiled. "Well, we'd use a good metal detector once we were in the right area. There must be some landmark that is the same now as it was then – some place that won't have a shopping mall or townhouses built on top of it!"

"And that is fairly dry and where archeologists are not likely to disturb it," Alison added.

"Right," Ben agreed. "Israel has probably been explored and probed more than anywhere. Maybe on a mountaintop? That would have good drainage."

"But won't it still be hard to find? How deep would they have to bury it?" Nate wondered.

"I think a top quality metal detector could find a large capsule as deep as six feet so long as the soil isn't too mineralized," Ben answered. "I just want us to be the first to find it, so it needs to be in an out-of-the-way place."

"Did you and your brother have any special places you explored near home?" Alison asked.

"Well, there were some low hills, but nothing that's a very distinct mountain," Ben replied. "I'm thinking that something to the north would be best, maybe Mt. Tabor, Mt. Moreh, or Mt. Gilboa."

Nate perked up. "Isn't Gilboa where King Saul had his last battle and fell on his sword?"

"Yes, that's correct," Ben nodded. "I'm not sure my family was familiar with Mt. Gilboa or knew it by that name. But they *will* be certain to know about it after Saul is killed and beheaded there! I think that will work! I'd have to be careful with my directions though, because the summit is very gradual, and I recall there's a military installation up there. Since there hasn't been the incessant digging by archeologists, there is a good chance no one would disturb the capsule."

"This is interesting, honey, but is it the main thing we need to do to Nate get ready?" Alison asked gently.

"You're right. But I would really love to find out if my family heeds the warning."

"When I get back I can tell you if they seemed convinced," Nate suggested. "But the message in the time capsule could also let my dad know I made it out of Israel alive. Then he would not have to wait three years to find out."

"Since we'll be in Israel next summer, we could try to find the capsule then," Alison said. "Kawsay might be with us. She'd be very excited."

The mention of Kawsay's name brought them back to the present and to their feelings of unease. "I wonder how they're doing?" Nate said wistfully. "Funny how it seems like they're just away on a trip and might give us a call to say they arrived OK."

"It does seem like they're just on a little trip," Ben agreed. "I remember that my trips in the tunnels seemed to take less than a minute. So the distant past isn't all that far away."

Alison looked at her watch. "It's almost two o'clock! I suggest that you two make a shopping list and also a task list. I've been thinking about my letter and want to start writing. I'll write in English first and count on you, dear, to help me put it into perfect ancient Hebrew."

"Alison," Ben remarked, "Nate suggested we send along a camcorder so he can play video messages from us along with the letters. You'll get to read the letter to my family on camera."

Alison smiled. "That would add a real personal touch, but they might find my accent amusing." She turned to leave, but then looked back. "Maybe I can send them one of my special butter cakes too! It might help break the ice."

Nate and Ben got busy with their lists. Ben made phone calls and located an outlet for diving gear that had waterproof backpacks and pouches and an electronics store with the compact camera equipment. Finding a small lead box took the longest. Alison found a few companies on-line that could provide small time capsules and e-mailed them a specification for one with a "3,000-year guarantee".

"Let's alert Herschel that he may have the opportunity to meet the rest of Kawsay's family at any time," Alison said. "I know he will want to invite Dr. Hurtado to fly up here to meet them."

"I'll call him tonight. I was wondering if we should also call and see how Helmut and his new colleague are getting along. They've been in the bush for a few days now, I presume."

"That reminds me," Alison said. "Who will provide Kawsay's mother and grandmother with inoculations? We've been fortunate so far with the others."

"I'll mention it to Helmut when I call him," Ben said. "If he doesn't plan to be back here in time, he probably can call and have prescriptions delivered here, and you can give them the shots."

During the evening, Ben drew a map of the Gibeah area and wrote directions to his house. Nate finished the diary for his dad and pulled out a Hebrew language primer. Alison labeled several photos of Ben that might help validate the preposterous story Nate would tell them. Alison and Ben went to bed with some anticipation that Zevél might wake them in the night with a group of tired travelers.

There were no knocks on the door that night – or the next night – so the preparations continued without interruption. Alison and Ben completed their letter drafts and helped each other edit them. It proved to be a challenging task, since they had to cover so many difficult topics in a convincing manner. Ben and Nate conversed at length, mostly in Hebrew, about each member of Ben's family and about the neighbors, the layout of the town, and important customs. They tried to imagine everything that could go wrong and develop contingency plans.

Alison joined them much of the time and convinced them that Nate should *not* show up at Ben's house in the old brown cloak. "It would be very difficult for parents to accept someone telling them their son was lost forever if that person is standing there wearing the very same clothes their child had put on that very morning," she counseled. She also suggested sending along water purification tablets.

Ben alerted Herschel who, in turn, alerted Hurtado, who immediately began checking for flights to San Francisco. After leaving a message for Helmut on his satellite phone, the return call came in Saturday evening. "Hello," Ben answered.

"Helmut here. Is everything all right? How's Yachay doing?"

"Yes. As far as we know he's OK," Ben answered. "But I haven't seen him for two days."

"Why not, have you been gone?"

"No," Ben responded. "Things have been happening fast which is why I called. The three Incas departed Thursday morning with Zevél. There's no way to be sure when they will return, but we're pretty sure it will be before next Saturday."

"Was his wound healed well enough?" the doctor inquired, concerned.

"To my mind, no, but there was really no way to keep them contained any longer," Ben explained. "Yachay and Kusi were totally focused on getting the rescue accomplished. I don't think Yachay even thought about his personal well-being. Alison managed to send along some extra bandages and ointment, and also a lot of almond butter sandwiches."

"I could use one of those right now!" Helmut chuckled. "Anything else to report?"

"We didn't talk about this before, Helmut. Assuming the rescue is successful, we could have two new visitors here at any time with incomplete immune systems. If you're not coming back any time soon, I was hoping you could call in to a pharmacy down here. Alison could give the injections."

"I plan to be in the bush for about three weeks, so I probably won't be back in time. Why don't I just call them in and have them delivered to the house."

"Sounds good," Ben remarked. "So you're not thinking of cutting the expedition short?"

"No," Helmut answered. "The weather has been pretty horrible unless you're a duck. But we've made some interesting discoveries. Based on the latest sightings, we were dropped upriver from Togiak and have been traveling by inflatable kayaks. I decided that any motor noises would work against us. Probably traveled about 30 miles against a slow current. We're up at Togiak Lake tonight. No bird sightings, but we've learned a lot from some natives who have a fish camp up here. They've had a lot of sightings and don't buy the idea that they're just big sea eagles. They say the birds have long necks and remind them of flying dinosaurs. One guy told me he had a friend who located a large abandoned nest in a white spruce tree near the lake. He found some shards of eggshell in the area and estimated the size of the eggs at about six to eight inches across. Surprisingly, they didn't seem to think it was a big deal and didn't report it. If the weather doesn't clear up though, I'm pessimistic about sightings. The low-hanging mist cuts visibility."

"Glad you've made some progress, Helmut, especially considering we caused you to get a late start," Ben stated, leaning against the kitchen counter. "So everything's OK?"

"Sure, but, well, it's a little uncomfortable out here, and there's more to life than looking for rare animals."

Now Ben knew something *was* wrong or at least different. "Alison will kill me if I don't ask how Officer Cole is doing."

"Oh, she's a real trooper!" Helmut reported. Hearing no reaction, he continued, "I'm really glad she came along, and even the two guides are impressed with her. Haven't heard any complaints about the bugs or weather, and she is a natural at wilderness travel and knows the Alaskan flora and fauna like a, well, like a professor. Turned out she knew one of the native women we met. Marguerite had a tour of duty in this region so she knows some of the people. You know, out in the bush the only real law enforcement are the State Troopers, and they have to cover many towns over a large area where there is no road system."

"So, you're getting along OK?" Ben prompted.

"Yeah. We've had a lot of time to talk. We paddle our kayaks side by side, and the guides do a lot of the work around camp so we have some down time." Helmut stopped and decided to add more information. "Actually, Ben, to tell you the truth, I'm finding it hard to concentrate on the expedition. It's not that I can't focus when I need to; it's more like it just doesn't feel all that important. I don't feel the usual passion for it. Funny, huh?"

"I wouldn't call it funny, Helmut. I remember that happening to me on the dig where I met Alison. I continued with the work, but my 'passion', as you put it, was focused elsewhere. And I don't just mean physical attraction. I mean, well, prime motivation – my first priority. Everything changed so fast I had a hard time keeping up with my heart."

"So, I'm not losing it?" Helmut asked in a soft voice.

"No," Ben replied. "Sounds like you're finding it. Have you talked with Marguerite about your feelings – and hers?"

"Sure. A lot. She says her focus has totally changed too. It's amazing to me, but she keeps looking over at me and telling me how beautiful I am and that I'm the most interesting man she's ever met. Of course, I know I'm somewhat interesting, but I *never* thought I was beautiful. I've never had anyone treat me this way, but I like it."

"The eyes of love," Ben said quietly.

"What?"

"She's seeing you with the eyes of love. Things look different. How do you see her?" Ben asked.

"Not as a police officer!" Helmut chuckled. "Actually, I think she's the most beautiful and graceful creature I've ever seen – the way she moves, tosses her hair, sticks out her tongue when she's trying to get a zipper to work, … I could go on. Hey, I even like the way she hums little tunes when she's paddling!"

"Sounds to me like you've both already found the most exotic and alluring creatures in the universe," Ben summed things up. "Why are you still looking for birds and fish?"

"We talked about bagging it," Helmut responded, "but decided we're having too much fun together. I think being totally away from our normal lives gives us a chance to find out who we are in relation to each other. Besides, Marguerite isn't too eager to go back to Anchorage and deal with that newspaper woman."

"Thanks for the update, Helmut. I'll relay it all to Alison. She'll be happy for you – as I am. Keep us posted. When the Incas return, I'll give you a call." After hanging up, Ben checked on Nate who was using the computer and printer in the office.

"Look what my dad sent us!" Nate said with obvious excitement. "When he was here last Wednesday, he and I talked about all the different time travel experiences everyone was having, and I sketched mine on paper. We thought it would help him keep everything straight. Look," Nate continued, turning over the pages from the printer. "Dad made this on his computer! Neat, huh?"

Ben looked at the schematic. He studied the lines and markings and immediately understood. "Nate, this is very well done. It reminds me of our discussion that a person's life is like a vector – like an arrow. From your perspective and mine, our lives have been arrows flying forward to the future. But compared to the Earth's vector, we have made some leaps and, in your case, some U-turns. Let's make some extra copies. If we ever write a book about our experiences, this would make a good illustration."

Later Ben found Alison. She had begun work on a change of clothes for Nate to use when visiting the family in Israel. "Look, dear," she said. "I've patterned this after your old cloak, but made it a little bigger. I found this old, rough, off-white cotton cloth. Do you think it will do?"

Ben looked it over and judged it to be close enough to blend in. "Could you also make a little bag for him out of the extra material – something to carry the camera and letters and other items? He can't take that bright green backpack that arrived today down Main Street in Gibeah without attracting a lot of attention."

"Good idea. Who was that on the phone?" When she heard it was Helmut who had called, Alison was wide-eyed with curiosity. "Tell me. How are they?"

Ben summarized Helmut's report, leaving the best to last. "It reminded me of how I felt after we met, honey."

NATE'S TIME TRAVEL MAP

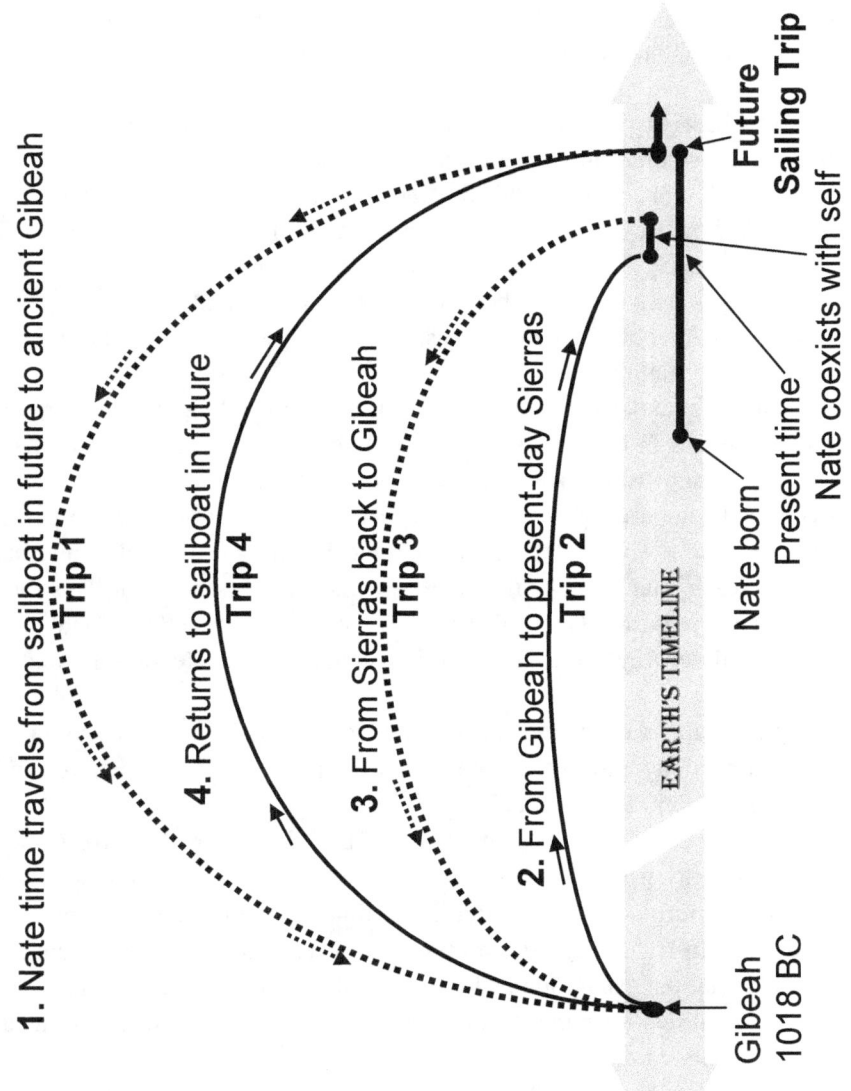

"That's wonderful," Alison agreed, "but we can't expect that their relationship will follow the same path as ours. I'll be interested to hear what they have to say after another week in the rain and bugs!"

When Alison climbed into bed that night, Ben was staring studiously at the ceiling. "You look like you're pondering one of the great mysteries," she observed.

Ben gave her a somewhat stricken look. "I just realized something. We've been going to a lot of risk and trouble to warn my family so they survive the fall of King Saul, right?" Alison nodded, and he continued. "That is all well and good, but is that all we have to say to them?"

"Well," Alison responded in her simple yet profound way, "you should tell them that you miss them and love them and hope to see them in heaven."

Ben took a big breath and exhaled. "You hit it, honey. My family wasn't particularly focused on keeping the Law. At that time there was no temple in Jerusalem and the oldest scriptures, the Pentateuch, were not available to common people." He gave her a grim look. "Anyway, I'd *like* to see my family in heaven…" His voice trailed off.

Alison thought about Ben's concerns. "So, you are thinking about giving them some encouragement in their faith?"

"Yes, but I'm not sure what to say. It risks meddling with history to tell them everything that happens in the following thousand years. Besides, my family has been dead for three thousand years. Maybe it's too late for prayers to reach them."

Alison understood his point – she had been taught a person needs to put faith in God *before* death. "Honey, I feel pretty humble and lacking in wisdom right now, but I can say this. If Nate can reach your family with a message that will preserve their lives for a few more years, why can't we pray that God will preserve their lives forever? If Nate can visit them while they're still alive, why can't God's spirit also visit them? He's not limited by time; He created it."

Ben gave her hand a squeeze. "I see what you mean. It just seems strange to send our prayers back in time along with Nate. The more I think about all this, the more I realize there are a lot of things we don't understand."

"That's true, dear," Alison responded. "But I find we really have some interesting conversations, especially when I'm half asleep." In five minutes they were both asleep.

On Sunday morning Nate and Ben spent time trying to remove bloodstains from the arrow that had been in Nate's leg. Then they glued it back together, reinforcing the shaft by inserting a small metal pin. Ben found a long piece of plastic tubing in which the arrows could be protected from further damage during their return journey. Nate practiced using the camcorder and memory cards.

John called that night to talk with Nate to see how the preparations were progressing and to ask if there was anything he could do to help. The father and son bolstered their hopes for a future together by making tentative plans about what they would do after Nate's return.

By Monday morning, the Incas still had not returned. With Nate's preparation largely completed, time dragged. They made the final recordings of their messages to Ben's family. Nate thought the messages were very good, and he was proud to serve as the messenger. "You two have said everything that needs to be said. Maybe I won't need to talk much at all," Nate said.

Alison disagreed. "Nate, you'll *be* there and can interact. They will have a lot of questions for you. And you will have the chance to learn from them too. I really wish I could be there with you. It's an archeologist's dream."

By Tuesday noon they were as prepared as they were going to be. Everything fit nicely into the big green waterproof backpack, which Nate could heft without too much effort. Nate had the main and contingency plans memorized.

By Tuesday night, everyone's nerves were becoming frayed. It was tediously difficult to wait without knowing, worry without relief, and wonder without answers. "I wish Kawsay and the others would come back," Alison lamented. "I miss them, and I'm eager to find out how things went. Every time I hear a noise outside I jump to look, but no one's out there."

"We need to do something to occupy our minds," Ben stated.

Nate had an idea. He pulled a few videos off the shelf. "Let's look at one of these."

Alison brightened and agreed. "Let's make some popcorn and get into our PJs. I think we've earned a little time off!"

The idea worked, and they all went to bed later more relaxed. The next morning though, the sense of time dragging returned, accompanied by a greater sense of urgency. "I know the longer we wait, the closer we are to the time they'll get back here," Alison said as they were finishing breakfast. "But the longer it takes, the more I can't help but wonder if something's gone wrong."

Ben took her hand. "Honey, I feel that way too, but it reminds me what a good idea it was to let Yachay take the third arrow back with him."

"I have an idea," Alison said, brightening. "I don't want Kawsay's family getting hurt when they arrive in the cave by crashing into the rock wall. We should set an air mattress by the tunnel opening to break their landing."

"That's a good idea," Ben agreed. "It seems like the tunnel delivers its travelers in the middle of the night! Let's leave the battery lantern for them to use."

"Do you want to come along, Nate?" Alison asked.

"No thanks," Nate responded. "I had a scary dream last night about the cave. It felt like I was heading to my own execution. I don't think going there today will help."

"We understand," Alison comforted. "It makes sense for you to take things easy from now until Saturday. You need to be strong and rested."

"I know," Nate agreed. "I think I'll sit on the porch and finish a few books I started before our trip to Alaska."

Alison and Ben left for the cave. Junior was happy to be included without his leash. Nate read for a while and then went inside for a glass of lemonade. He noticed some of Kusi's carvings on a shelf nearby, including the small statue of Kawsay. Nate examined it closely. Turning the carving's face toward his, he looked it in the eye and spoke earnestly. "Kawsay, you just have to come back. You just have to! I miss you, and I want to see you again before I go. Bring Yachay and his lucky arrow, but mostly just bring *you*." Nate blinked back some tears, though one escaped down his cheek.

Alison and Ben soon returned.

"Find anything?" Nate asked.

Alison shook her head and looked down.

Ben answered, "Nothing. It's just like we left it. Other than the dripping of the water, it was quiet as a crypt." Ben regretted using that particular simile in Alison's hearing.

Junior, however, was undaunted and went for his tennis ball, dropping it at Nate's feet. "I'm being summoned!" Nate remarked. "I think I'll play a little fetch with Junior." As he reached the door, he stopped and added, "I wish Junior could fetch the Incas!"

"I hope Zevél will fetch them!" Ben responded.

That night Alison left the outside light on "just in case". They went to bed at the usual time, but did not talk about what was on everyone's mind. But they all silently prayed that their dear friends, so far away, were safe and would soon return with a report of a successful rescue.

CHAPTER 27.

A MESSAGE FROM THE FUTURE

YEAR 1609
SMALL VILLAGE NEAR VILCABAMBA, PERU

STRONG AND HEALED SHE SPEAKS
RETURNING GOOD FOR EVIL
A MESSAGE OF HOPE.

A deep rumble increased to an overpowering growl, reverberating through the predawn jungle.

"I may not be able to see you, but I assure you – *he* can," Yachay warned, scanning the murky tangles of trees and shrubs. Yachay could now barely see the sissies who were cowering with their backs together, each holding his spear out in front. He had almost rescued his mother and grandmother out of the village. In fact, he had just ushered them into the protection of the jungle canopy. Everything had been going according to plan until the sissies showed up.

"What was that?" One of the boy's voices had a slight quiver in it.

Yachay could barely discern the outline of Zevél with Kawsay close behind his right hind leg. "That is my sister's guard. I don't think he likes you very much. He is a great and terrible beast, and you have angered him." Yachay's mind flashed to the great Zevél eating an almond butter sandwich and complaining about bugs. He pursed his lips so as not to betray his thoughts with less than a serious tone. This situation *was* serious, and sneaking away was getting more problematic. He heard noise from the village. *Of course, now the whole village will show up. Who could possibly sleep through that roar?*

The commotion materialized in the form of some twenty or thirty torch-carrying men including the Chief. The flickering torches revealed the escaping Yachay, Sumaq, and Asiri, along with the four sissies, the huge silver wolf, and Kawsay. *Good, Grandfather is not here,* Yachay thought. Yachay knew Grandfather was most certainly watching them from somewhere, but he was careful not to look around and betray Grandfather's hiding place.

Mother and Grandmother realized it was Kawsay standing behind the beast, cried out with joy, and ran to her. Zevél did not move a muscle.

Yachay was glad he had told the women about Zevél so they did not have any fear of him.

"My beautiful daughter!" Sumaq hugged Kawsay so tightly that for a moment they both forgot where they were. Asiri wrapped her arms around her daughter and granddaughter.

"I am so happy, Mother. I have missed you so much – both of you." Kawsay looked at her mother and grandmother with tears running down her cheeks. "I feared I may never see you again." The three hugged once more.

It was obvious to the Chief, elders, and gathering tribe members that Kawsay had not seen her family – at least not her mother and grandmother – since her exile from the village. Their attention, however, was increasingly focused on the massive silver wolf positioned between them and the women. This creature clearly *was* Kawsay's guard. The torches, along with the increasing morning twilight, not only revealed the magnificence of Zevél but also something very different about Kawsay. She stood tall and confident. She was beautiful like her mother. She was no longer deformed.

The Chief wanted to get a closer look, but did not want to challenge the wolf. "May I come closer to you, Kawsay?" the Chief asked timidly.

"I like the Chief," Kawsay whispered to Zevél in English. "Yes, Chief. I will keep him from ripping your face off." Kawsay decided having her people fear Zevél could be helpful.

The Chief approached her slowly staying as far from the beast as possible. "I am sorry about your grandfather, Kawsay. I love Kusi. He has been a brother to me." The Chief was confounded by Zevél's magnificence, yet he was almost equally puzzled by this very different Kawsay. *Is she standing straighter, or is she actually taller? And her lip – it's healed!* The Chief closed his eyes for a moment. It seemed like a dream – a giant silver wolf and the Kawsay he loved like a granddaughter since she was a tiny baby. *I just saw her days ago. She was small and frightened with a deformed lip. Now she stands straight with a healed lip that speaks commands to a huge beast.*

"I would like to speak now," Kawsay said to the Chief. She exchanged glances with Yachay who raised an eyebrow and nodded.

"We will listen to what Kawsay has to say." The Chief edged further away from the wolf toward Yachay.

Kawsay stepped forward to stand next to Zevél's shoulder, leaving her mother and grandmother safely behind the wolf. More people had arrived and were gathered around the curious spectacle. Kawsay began with a strength and confidence that was surprising to her people. "You treated me poorly during my life and then exiled me. Thanks to the Chief and elders, I was allowed to live, which I truly appreciate. The Chief is a good and wise man. You are fortunate to have him as a leader. My family upheld the agreement that I go into the jungle alone. I have gone far away, survived, and become strong. This confirms that the decision of the Chief and elders to let me live was wise and correct. After my exile, God brought me to people far away who showed me compassion and love. They healed my lip and gave me food, clothing, and a soft, warm bed. They also taught me what will happen to our people in the future. You may find this difficult to believe, but I have traveled to the future. I do not mean in my spirit but in my body. My lip is proof of this fact. The Chief can see me up close and can testify that it has been healed." Kawsay looked at the Chief for confirmation. He nodded to his people.

She continued, "I will show my lip to any of you who do not believe it is healed, but the dawn light allows most of you to see it from where you are standing. You know this is not possible with our medicine. In the future, our people and other people of the world fix many deformities. In fact, in the future, our people live peacefully with the Invaders." She heard murmurs from her audience. "Yes, it is true. Our descendants survive. Our people are oppressed and ruled over for more than two hundred years. But we survive, regain control over our lives, and again rule ourselves and our land. Our language also survives and is still spoken four-hundred years from now. Along with our language, much of our culture survives. We learn from the Invaders, and they learn from us. We learn of their technology, and they teach us about their God. We in turn teach them about our culture, agriculture, food, art, and metalwork." Kawsay took a breath. She could tell many of the people listening thought she was crazy. But how could they deny her lip?

She decided, whether they thought she was crazy or believed her story, the goal was the same – that they allow her and her family to leave peacefully. She continued, "There are many things I have learned about the future. For example, Inti is a star like all the others we see at night." Kawsay heard a few gasps. "Your descendants will learn all of this. My message now is to encourage you by telling you your descendents survive and also to urge you to not sacrifice your babies. Take care of them. Many of you wanted to kill me as you have killed others because you thought I would not have a good life, but your wisdom was not great enough to foresee the outcome of my life. God in His wisdom has given me a wonderful new life. We should leave the life of the innocent in the hands of God. Do not assume someone with a deformity cannot contribute to our people. A child may not be strong of body, but he or she may possess wisdom and become strong of mind. Your children will judge you by how you treat the weak among you. We all have strengths, and we should use those strengths to better ourselves and those around us. We all have weaknesses too – though some are more visible. My family taught me to be strong and to think for myself so I could be self-reliant, even at age thirteen. Many of you are old and are still not self-reliant. I urge you to protect your children and also to teach them to think for themselves and be self-reliant so they will not be victims of oppressors. This beautiful animal you see standing next to me is going to help my mother, grandmother, brother, and me leave and go far away. You cannot follow us to where we are going. If you try, you may be killed or lost. There is a God who loves you." Kawsay looked at the Chief and said in a quiet whisper. "We will miss you, Chief. Thank you for all you have done for me. Grandfather loves you."

The Chief cleared his throat and spoke loudly. "It is evident that Kawsay has surpassed the expectations of the elders and me when we decided to give her a chance at life. She has survived alone in the jungle and even, apparently, in a far away world. Some of her words are strange – and I suspect fodder for gossip as well as many late-night conversations. Nevertheless, I know Kawsay to be a truthful young woman, and she has spoken to us with strong conviction. And I can verify that her lip is, in fact, completely healed. It is quite remarkable and unexplainable. This family has paid a great price for her tiny imperfection. Now that her lip is completely healed, there is no further reason for any of you to treat this family any differently than you would treat any other family. This village is not a prison. We will allow Kawsay and her family to live the life they choose, even if it is to go off into the jungle alone."

The Chief turned his head toward Yachay who was standing between him and Zevél. He lowered his voice to a soft whisper, "I hope your grandfather is in this new world your sister speaks of." Yachay turned slightly toward the Chief and winked in response.

Kawsay turned to her mother and grandmother and nodded at her brother. She touched Zevél's coat and whispered in English, "Let us go now." The five of them backed up into the jungle, turned, and disappeared from sight. They walked quickly in silence with Yachay in the lead and Zevél at the rear, ears up and alert. Yachay did not know where Grandfather was, but set a course for the old tree where they had previously agreed to meet.

Kawsay eventually broke the silence. "Zevél, have you ever ripped anybody's face off?"

Just then, Grandfather cut in front of them from behind a cluster of trees. Yachay stopped abruptly and Sumaq, who was not paying close attention, smacked into the back of her son. Asiri dropped her bag, ran past Yachay, and threw herself into her husband's waiting arms.

"I've been silently following you. We are far enough from our village to speak." Kusi eyed Zevél over his wife's shoulder, wondering if the wolf had heard him following close behind.

"He steps lightly, undoubtedly unnoticeable to the human ear," Zevél said, knowing Kawsay was the only one who knew English well enough to completely understand his words.

Kawsay smiled, not wanting to tell Grandfather that Zevél had been aware of his presence.

Sumaq set her bag down, turned to her daughter, and began closely examining her lip. "Mother, come and see our baby." The two women ran their fingers across Kawsay's upper lip. Their faces were full of joy and disbelief. "I cannot wait to meet these wonderful people who healed your lip, Kawsay," Sumaq said, cradling her daughter's face in her hands. "Can you believe this, Mother?" Sumaq asked in stunned disbelief. "You also seem taller, Kawsay, and I saw such confidence and maturity in you during your speech to our people. You reminded me of your brother," she said, smiling at Yachay. "I am so proud of both of you. I wish so much that your father could see his children." Sumaq noticed her mother staring at the huge wolf who was calmly sniffing the air.

"Are you certain he is perfectly tame and friendly?" Asiri asked.

Kusi looked at Zevél. "He does seem intimidating, doesn't he? But to put your mind at ease, I can tell you he does not eat meat and seems to be a close friend of the God of the future. I spent time with him in a cave. He carried Kawsay from that very cave to Alison and Ben's house when she first arrived in the new world and needed human care. I followed him closely, ready to protect Kawsay if needed. I watched him carefully in the beginning as I was not sure what to expect from such a beast, but he will not hurt you. I am certain of it. You have no reason to fear him. In fact, we are depending on him to take us safely through the tunnel to our new home."

Kawsay translated her grandfather's words for Zevél who was beginning to understand their Quechua language. "Thank you for your kind words, Kusi. If it is God's will, we will arrive safely at our destination. We should move on now," Zevél suggested.

Kusi had begun transferring the bags his wife and daughter had taken from their home into two of the backpacks. He shouldered the heaviest and gave Yachay the other. Kawsay took the lighter third backpack with what remained of their food. Yachay put his sling on one shoulder and the backpack over both shoulders, which secured the sling in place. Yachay had his lucky spear with the embedded arrow in hand.

Kusi looked at his wife and daughter. "We will go as quickly as you are able. We can travel for a while and then break for lunch. Yachay will lead; you two follow him. Kawsay, Zevél, and I will be close behind you."

The five Incas and the wolf began their journey to a new life and home. Kusi and Kawsay had so much to tell Asiri and Sumaq and were each wondering how the two women would react to the future. Yachay had already had the opportunity to tell his mother and grandmother about his adventures in the new world. For now, what mattered to each of them was getting safely through the jungle and to the secret caves as quickly as possible.

They maintained a fast pace, but, as the day wore on, Kusi began to feel hungry and knew the others would need food and rest. "Let us stop for a bit. We can rest, eat, and fill our water pouches." He noticed Yachay's bandage looked frayed. "Let's change your bandage too, Yachay." The six travelers found a perfect lunch spot in a small clearing near the stream. Kusi presented power bars and nuts while Sumaq and Asiri unpacked their food stash from home. Kawsay explained the water filter to her mother and grandmother and gave them a demonstration. She told them about her surgery, Helmut's helicopter, automobiles, toilets, showers, light switches, refrigerators, and her new friend, Nate. Kusi put a new bandage on Yachay while telling the women about his life during the months he kept his presence secret from Kawsay. Kawsay felt warm and happy, finally being together with her whole family. She was eager to introduce them to Nate, but felt a twinge of sadness realizing Nate would be leaving soon after they returned.

Zevél had asked Kawsay about which plants were known to be safe, and Asiri took on the job of helping the wolf forage a meal of plants and fruit. Yachay also put a large pile of nuts on a rock for the wolf to eat. After he ate, Zevél stretched out on the rock for a short snooze while the others talked.

Over the next few days, the six voyagers sustained the pace of a fast walk. Kusi and Yachay were impressed with the stamina of the women who had not spent their lives training in the jungle. Kawsay knew her mother and grandmother were of strong spirit and determination and was not surprised by their fortitude. Nevertheless, compared to the journey from the caves, they did sleep longer at night and stop for a long lunch each day. Zevél was happy to travel at a slightly slower pace, particularly because there was light rain accompanied by humidity and bugs. The bugs were buzzing his eyes and ears, and his wet fur made him feel heavier and less spry. It was times like this that made him long for either his first home or his final home. In the meantime, his long life was a walk of faith that continued to touch the lives of those brought into his care.

"The cliffs are near. We should see…" Kusi was interrupted by a low growl from Zevél who ran past his friends and blocked them from continuing.

Zevél's voice was barely audible to Kawsay. "We are not alone. I hear men's voices, four or five, maybe. I will scout ahead. Do not move or speak until I return." Zevél waited while Kawsay whispered a translation. He then silently moved ahead of them about a hundred steps away. They saw him crouch behind a tree several paces short of where the forest canopy ended near the foot of the tall cliffs. After a few moments, Zevél backed up, turned, and silently returned to his friends. "There are four men who appear to be camped at the cliff base near our entrance. I will lead them away from their camp while you climb up and enter the caves. Wait for me there until I join you."

Both Yachay and Kusi had some idea of what Zevél said, but waited for Kawsay to translate. Kusi did not want Zevél alone and unprotected from whomever may be out there and asked "What color is their skin?"

"Light," Zevél answered.

"Kawsay will take Sumaq and Asiri into the cave. Yachay and I will stay out of sight, but serve as your backup," Kusi announced. He waited for Kawsay's translation and the wolf's response.

Zevél realized he needed to explain his plan. "I will lure them away from their camp. I will quicken my pace until they are running behind me. Then I will accelerate out of sight, loop back, and join you in the cave. I can run three times the speed of a man. I will be back to the cave quickly. I do not want you left vulnerable."

Kusi protested. "They surely have crossbows and guns, and there are four of them. We will wait until you lead them from the cliff, but will remain where we can help you if they attack. We care about your safety. You are very unique. We also need you, Zevél. Besides, Yachay and I are exceptionally fast runners too."

"Their guns are primitive, and crossbows are difficult to fire while a person is running," Zevél whispered. "But I appreciate your concern. If I can lure them away from the cave, I can run back to the cave long before they will know where I have gone."

"What if they do not all follow you? What if there are more than four of them?" Kawsay asked.

The wolf thought for a moment. "That is a concern. I will convince them all to follow me. If there are others nearby, I will deal with them. What I care about is your safety and your return to the future." Zevél took a pensive breath. "Can you find your way back up through the cave to the tunnel entrance if I am not leading you?" He waited while Kawsay, Yachay, and Kusi deliberated.

Kawsay answered, "We think we can find it again. Grandfather is pretty familiar with the cave. How would we get to the correct time and place in the tunnel if you are not with us?"

"You have learned about God from Nate and the Hunters, Kawsay. You would need to trust Him. You also need to harness yourselves together." Zevél paused and thought for a moment. "I will be with you, Kawsay. Do not worry about me – just get yourselves into the cave." Zevél waited for the inevitable counter.

Kusi's final response was, "We will get the women into the cave as soon as you lead the men away from the entrance. Yachay and I will wait just outside the cave entrance for your return."

"As you wish." Zevél was honored by their care for him, but somewhat annoyed by the stubbornness of the human spirit.

Silently the six of them crept to the edge of the jungle. The four men were sitting at the bottom of the cliffs under the cave's entrance. Zevél glanced back at his friends as if to remind them to stay out of sight. He calmly strolled up to the four Spanish men clad in long-sleeved shirts, trousers, and long leather vests. The men looked up at Zevél in stunned silence. Their jaws gaped open. Their bodies were visibly rigid. *Fortunately, I speak Spanish*, Zevél thought.

In his best Spanish, Zevél said, "The ruler of Spain, Filipe the Third, is your ruler. Do you serve your ruler?"

The four men could not believe their eyes and ears. "That creature is at least the size of three or four wolves," one whispered.

"Those teeth!" another said with a slight squeak in his voice.

"Did you hear him speak?" the third asked.

"Wolves do not speak," the fourth whispered slowly.

Zevél cleared his throat and repeated himself louder, adding, "Please follow me. Stand up and come with me. Now. Do you understand? This is not a request, but a command."

The men slowly rose looking at each other. They tentatively began following Zevél into the trees and brush. When they were out of sight, the Incas quietly ran to the cave entrance. Kawsay climbed up first, and Kusi and Yachay transferred their backpacks to her. "Put this in a safe place," Yachay said, handing her his spear, but retaining his sling, bola, and a knife. They helped Sumaq and Asiri up the rocky bottom of the cliff to the cave entrance. When the women were out of sight, Kusi and Yachay climbed up to the small ledge near the entrance and then inched sideways to where a rocky protrusion mostly hid them from the jungle.

A moment later they heard approaching voices coming from the jungle, but from a different direction than Zevél had led the four men. Just then, three men dressed similarly to the first four, but wearing helmets, walked into the open. *Just what we need*, Kusi thought. The men began talking and gesturing. They clearly noticed that their fellow soldiers were no longer sitting at the base of the cliff.

Suddenly an approaching rushing sound could be heard, and all eyes looked in its direction. As Zevél's silver body broke from the jungle, two crossbows and a gun were trained on him. Kusi and Yachay immediately began swirling their slings with almost simultaneous releases of stone missiles, which knocked the two crossbows from the soldiers' hands. As the gun fired, Zevél launched himself up into the air toward the cave's entrance, dodging the low shot. Yachay and Kusi glided across the ledge and into the cave just behind Zevél whose momentum sent him skidding through the cave's entrance into the dark interior. After a hard thud, the wolf's pained voice said, "I'm getting too old for this. Come. Follow me."

They gathered their packs and closely followed Zevél into the darkness. They each touched the person in front as they wove their way through black passageways, making tight turns and squeezing through small openings. Kawsay did not believe she could have found her way up to the time tunnel entrance in the blackness if they had not been following Zevél. Before they arrived at the tunnel entrance, Kusi called out, "Zevél, I need to grab something."

The small group waited and listened while Kusi went down a small side corridor and crawled up to a shelf and into a crevice which opened to a small cavern. Kusi retrieved a large bag and returned to the group. They ascended in the darkness a little further before reaching the dimly lit hallway housing the elusive time tunnel portal. They could hear the faint wail of the tunnel.

"Quickly," Zevél whispered. "They will be looking for us and will not give up easily.

You need to secure yourselves to me and to each other."

Kusi stuffed the bag he had retrieved into a nearly empty backpack. He then retrieved the four harnesses and ropes and helped Kawsay, Sumaq, Asiri, and Yachay each into a harness. Kusi thought he heard voices in the distance. In the dim light, he glanced at the others to see them each intently listening. He noticed Zevél's ears at attention.

They inched toward the tunnel entrance, but it was difficult to move. They squeezed even closer as Kawsay climbed onto Zevél's back with her mother and grandmother at her sides. Kusi was behind Asiri, and Yachay behind his mother. Kusi tied himself and Zevél with the rope that linked the harnesses together. Yachay had his spear secured in his backpack with its tip poking out. Kusi cinched the rope tighter once more. "Ask Zevél if it is too tight on his throat, Kawsay," her grandfather requested.

Zevél looked back, "The portal in Ben's cave is narrow. We need to squeeze even closer."

Kusi realized his backpack was too big, took it off, and held it tightly in one hand behind Zevél's tail. *This is not good. I really should secure this, but we must hurry,* Kusi thought.

They heard voices again, closer than before. Zevél's voice was at a low whisper. "Ready? Kawsay, tell everyone to take a deep breath and hold it. They may also close their eyes. Hold on tightly." Zevél waited for Kawsay to translate and for each of them to take a deep breath. He then stepped into the tunnel, dragging his passengers.

Once in the tunnel, Zevél felt the burden of having five people tied to his frame – never had he taken so many through time. He usually focused only on Elohim when he was in a tunnel, not allowing his mind to drift or be occupied with anything but Him. He was thankful Asiri and Sumaq had been prepared for this experience. Everyone seemed secure. He returned his focus to God and waited.

Just before reaching their destination, Zevél felt a jostling. Then he decelerated, braced for the inevitable hard landing, and skidded into something – *padded*? When Zevél opened his eyes, he could see a small battery-powered lantern sitting in the middle of the small cavern. It appeared that Ben and Alison must have also positioned an air mattress against the impact wall. Zevél looked over his shoulder at his travelers who appeared shaken, but were slowly unclipping and untying themselves from him.

"Oh no, no!" Kusi was quietly lamenting.

"What happened?" Kawsay asked.

"My backpack was not secure and flew off in the tunnel. It had my treasure."

"It did?" Asiri asked her husband. "That's terrible."

Zevél was trying to understand the Quechua, but wanted clarification. He looked at Kawsay.

"Grandfather lost his backpack. It was very important. Is it possible to go back and get it, Zevél?" Kawsay did not know what was in the bag that Grandfather had retrieved before they left the cave, but could tell from his tone that it was of great significance to him. "Is there anything you can do?" she asked Zevél again.

Zevél looked at Kusi whose eyes were downcast. He looked miserable. "I will do my best. It could take a while."

"I would appreciate that very much, Zevél. It is of great value to my family," Kusi said.

"Let's get you to the house," Zevél said. His body felt battered from the past week of jungle travel and impacts with cave walls. He could use a few days of rest on the Hunter's porch.

They finished untangling themselves, and Kawsay picked up the lantern. They left the small room. As they entered the main chamber, Kawsay noticed it was dark except for the light from their lantern. "It must be nighttime. There is no light coming in from the openings in the top of the cavern." They could hear the water streaming down the far rock wall and lightly splash into the stream.

"I spent much time here wondering how I would get back to you," Kusi said, looking at his wife in the dim lantern light.

Zevél slowly led the way out of the cave. Kawsay followed with the lantern, and Mother and Grandmother walked closely behind her. They stepped out of the cave into warm velvety air.

Sumaq looked up and saw unfamiliar stars. "The sky is different," she said pointing up.

"It does look different. And it smells different too," her mother added.

Zevél sniffed the air, happy to be in a dryer climate. He liked this part of the world. He felt good about bringing this family together and to a new world that held the promise of happy, new lives for them. "Kawsay, tell them to watch their step on the first part of this trail. I will go slowly," Zevél said.

The five Incas followed behind quietly, lost in their own thoughts of the harrowing escape and of what may await them. The forest floor was soft, and the smell of pine seemed to welcome them.

Yachay finally felt at peace. He had rescued his mother and grandmother, and they were all together. Now he could plan for the future. He had his lucky spear in hand. *I will deliver its embedded arrow to Nate.*

After they crossed the bridge and the trail opened up, Kusi hurried forward to talk to Zevél. Zevél's eyes were about eye level for Kusi. Kusi whispered in English, "Thank you, Zevél." Then he whispered, "Backpack, for Kusi people." Kusi did not want his family to know about its contents until it was returned, assuming it could be found.

Zevél looked at his friend, nodded, and said, "Ari."

Kusi wished he could communicate better with Zevél. *I will learn languages so I can communicate. That will be my first goal for my new life in this new world.*

They stepped into the clearing and could see Ben and Alison's porch light shining. Zevél trotted ahead to the porch and gave his characteristic knock on the Hunters' door.

THUD … THUD … THUD.

"Ben, did you hear that?" Alison awoke abruptly, trying to focus on the glowing clock face. "It looks like 2 a.m." She heard a growl from Junior who had been sleeping on a rug at the foot of their bed.

THUD … THUD … THUD.

"There's only one person – um wolf – who knocks with such enthusiasm," Ben said, as he helped Alison out of bed and reached for his robe.

"This is great! It must be Kawsay and her family," Alison said excitedly, putting on her robe. Junior was now whining and pacing at the bedroom door.

Alison and Ben raced to the front door, nearly colliding with Nate who was already there. Junior let out a yelp. Nate looked at Ben and then opened the heavy wooden door. The bedraggled but smiling faces of Zevél, Kawsay, and her family greeted them.

"We are so happy to see you! Please come in," Alison said, reaching for Kawsay with a warm hug.

Kawsay looked over Alison's shoulder into Nate's smiling eyes. He winked at her, and she felt a twinge of delight in her heart.

Ben began ushering everyone into the house. "What can I get you? You must be hungry and thirsty! I bet some baths and showers are in order too. Zevél, you too. Come in and let's get you something to eat and drink." Ben noticed Junior take a submissive posture to the huge wolf. Ben smiled to himself, wondering when Junior would ever get comfortable around his giant cousin.

Kawsay was watching her mother and grandmother react to the house. She remembered her first night after Zevél brought her to the front porch. She had entered their strange house and walked through the living room to the large kitchen. Everything had been new and amazing. She imagined what Mother and Grandmother must be thinking as they saw the house for the first time. She was eager to show them everything this new world had to offer.

"Kawsay, is it safe to assume everyone is hungry?" Ben's question interrupted her thoughts.

After a quick discussion with her family, Kawsay answered, "We did not sleep a lot the past days on our journey back to the cave. A light meal, a bath, and a comfortable bed – perfect."

Alison and Ben prepared French toast for the Incas and a large bowl of granola for Zevél. Sumaq and Asiri were overwhelmed by the house and the kitchen. Kawsay had tried to describe the place she had been living to her mother and grandmother, but they had not imagined all the niceties of a modern home.

Sumaq felt deeply grateful to Alison and Ben for their kindness toward her daughter. "How can I express how thankful I am, Kawsay? I am in debt to Alison and Ben. Please tell them how much I appreciate the way they cared for you and for finding Yachay," Sumaq said earnestly and waited for Kawsay to translate.

"It was our pleasure," Alison said. "We love Kawsay and Yachay too. We are thankful Kawsay, Yachay, and Kusi came into our lives. We are so happy you are here too. You are our family now."

Kawsay translated. Her mother and grandmother were slightly tearful at the warmth and love shown by their hosts.

Kusi looked around the kitchen, remembering the nights he clandestinely rummaged around looking for food before he had been discovered. He quietly recounted to his wife the story of how he had made carvings for Ben and Alison in exchange for food he had taken for himself and Zevél.

Nate asked Kawsay to tell them all about the trip back to their Inca home. Kawsay explained the whole journey including when Yachay saw himself running in the opposite direction and their encounter with the Invaders requiring Zevél's heroic gambit to get them safely back into the cave. The group looked over at Zevél who was sleeping soundly in the doorway between the kitchen and living room. Kusi and Yachay, who were intent on becoming fluent in English, understood about a third of what Kawsay said.

After they finished eating, Yachay got up and retrieved his lucky spear from its resting place just inside the kitchen. He brought it to the table, sat down, and carefully began removing Ben's arrow from the groove cut along the length of the spear. He looked over at Grandfather who nodded and smiled. The group was silent except for faint snoring sounds from Zevél and Junior. Junior had positioned himself on the opposite side of the kitchen from Zevél. Yachay gently slid the arrow out of the spear shaft, set the spear down, and presented the arrow to Nate. In English, he said, "Ben's arrow for God story."

Nate glanced at Ben and then at Yachay. The boys' eyes locked in respect and understanding. Nate accepted the arrow from Yachay. "I am happy you rescued your family and brought them here safely, Yachay," Nate said. "You inspire me. I hope we will always be friends. When I return to my time in a few days, you will already be there. I will still be sixteen, but you will be nineteen." Nate smiled at Kawsay who was sitting next to him.

Sumaq and Asiri exchanged glances. They could see the special connection between Nate and Kawsay. Sumaq was confused how Nate, now sixteen, will still be sixteen in three years.

Kawsay saw her mother's eyebrows furrow and explained Nate's upcoming mission to the past and then to the future. "For Nate, only a few days will pass, but we will live three years of our lives. When you time travel, you jump in and out of different times, but your age does not change."

Alison realized the concept of time travel was a bit much to lay on Kawsay's mother and grandmother tonight. "Kawsay, why don't you take your mother into the hall bathroom for a bath? You can tell her about your first night here. I put a nightgown in the bathroom. I think Kusi can help Asiri bathe in his cabin. I left a nightgown, robe, soap, shampoo, and a hairbrush for her in the cabin." Alison looked at Kusi for confirmation.

After a short discussion, Kawsay reported, "That will be fine."

"Great," Alison continued. "Ben and I thought Yachay may want to share Helmut's old room off the living room with Nate."

The group scattered, leaving Alison, Ben, and the two somnolent canines in the kitchen. Junior had migrated across the room and was now sleeping quietly against the wolf's large flank. Alison nudged Ben, pointing. "Looks like Junior is finally adjusting to Zevél. Isn't it exciting to have Kawsay's whole family here? We can call Herschel in the morning, and he can make arrangements for Hurtado to fly up from Peru to escort Kawsay's family to their new home. I really want to stay in close touch with them, dear. Do you think we can see them often? I know they need to begin productive lives for themselves, but they are our family now."

"I've been thinking the same thing. I ordered a satellite phone for Kawsay when I was buying stuff for Nate's trip. That way she can call us regularly from anywhere. It should arrive any day," Ben said as he rinsed the dishes Alison brought from the table. "It's going to get pretty quiet around here – just you, me, and Junior again."

Alison kissed her husband on the cheek. "I love you, Ben." She noticed Zevél stand up and stretch.

"Do you mind if I sleep on your porch tonight?" Zevél's voice was low and raspy.

"You are welcome to sleep on our porch every night, Zevél," Ben answered. "I'll open the door for you."

"Perhaps if tomorrow is a sunny day, someone wouldn't mind hosing the Peruvian jungle out of my fur," Zevél said sheepishly.

"You mean a bath?" Ben asked, surprised. "We would be delighted to help you bathe." Ben winked at Alison who was smiling at the thought. Ben closed the door softly behind Zevél, and he and Alison tiptoed to their bedroom to seize the few remaining hours of the night.

Nate was the first to wake up. He looked over at Yachay who appeared to be in some sort of dream state. Nate was leaving Saturday and wanted to spend as much time with Kawsay as possible. He also wanted to get to know her mother and grandmother. *Three years of Kawsay's life will pass before I see her again. What will she be like after spending three years in the modern world without me? She will be sixteen – not a little girl anymore. Will she look different? Will she still look up to me? Will she have a boyfriend?*

Nate slipped out of bed, grabbing his jeans and a sweater. He crept lightly across the hardwood floor, trying not to make creaking sounds. He gingerly opened the bedroom door. From the living room he perceived the house was quiet. The old clock on the wall opposite the large living room windows read 8:15 a.m. Nate quietly changed out of his pajamas and carefully slipped out the front door to the porch. Zevél twitched and woke up.

"Good morning, Nathaniel." Zevél yawned and closed his eyes again.

Nate smiled a hello to Zevél, breathed in the crisp morning air, and sat on the small loveseat under the window. While he had been planning for his trip back to ancient Israel the past several days, he had consciously tried to block out any scenario of things going wrong. His accent was less than authentic, and he sort of knew the customs but not on a detailed level. He would have to travel a short distance from the cave to Ben's house and then back again by himself in a strange, new – or rather old – culture. Zevél would be there, but would need to remain out of sight. Nate felt his pulse begin to quicken when the front door creaked.

Kawsay stuck her head out the door. A big smile washed over her face, and her large eyes sparkled. "I hoped to find you up." She closed the door softly behind her and joined Nate on the loveseat. She reached down and stroked Zevél's silver fur. "It will be odd to be your age when I see you again." She did not look into his eyes but out into the forest. "How do you think we will feel about each other, Nate?"

Nate thought she may be as concerned as he was about their future. "I will feel the same about you as I do now," he said without reservation. It will only be a few days for me. But you will have lived three years without me. I won't be an older guy anymore but someone your age." Nate took a deep breath. "Yachay will be nineteen, and I will still be sixteen."

Nate looked pensive.

"I will always love you as I do now," Kawsay said confidently. "You are Nate, my best friend. Our life is tied together. But promise me you won't color your hair brown again." Her eyes twinkled.

Nate felt relieved that Kawsay wanted their relationship to continue as it was now. He hoped nothing would change that during her next three years. "Maybe we can go to the same college? We will be the same age, and you will have had three years to catch up with school. Have you thought about what you want to do with your life and if you want to remain in Peru?"

"Oh, I have thought about it much. I do not know if I like Peru, but I know I want to be an archeologist like Alison. I looked through her books, and I think I like to study ancient writings. What do they call it?" she asked, searching her memory for that strange word.

"You mean hieroglyphics?"

"Yes, that is the word. I want to learn about hieroglyphics and ancient writing. Our people did not write, but used quipu. I want to know why other ancient people did writing and we did not."

"That's very interesting," Nate mused. He liked her curious mind. It was not just her striking looks that attracted him to her, but she had a curious mind like his. Most girls he knew only thought about themselves or silly things. They were boring. But Kawsay was different in so many ways. He really felt a connection to her on many levels. He could not imagine how that would change even when she was three years older. He thought she would probably be even more interesting in three years, not less. "I want to see you soon after I return to my future."

"Then we can date?" Kawsay asked, looking at him with a cute half smile.

The front door opened, and Junior shot out like a missile. By the time he realized the giant wolf was lying on the porch, Junior was already airborne. Zevél opened one eye, then closed it again. Alison stepped onto the porch after Junior and was surprised to see Nate and Kawsay already up. "Good morning! It looks like a beautiful day. I hope everyone slept well."

"Sleeping in a bed feels wonderful," Kawsay said, yawning.

"I think we've spoiled her with modern comforts." Nate smiled and winked at Alison.

Alison squeezed Kawsay's shoulder. "I think you're right, Nate. We're making her soft, and we're about to make her whole family soft."

Kawsay reached over and stroked Zevél's back. His fur twitched, but he showed no sign of waking up. "His fur is a beautiful color, but it is full of the jungle." Kawsay stood up. "I see if Mother is awake. She maybe forget where she is."

"Ben and I are going to start preparing breakfast." Alison took a deep breath of the smooth, pine-scented morning air and disappeared into the house.

Thursday proved to be a perfect day. Ben alerted Herschel that Kawsay and her family had arrived safely early that morning. Herschel contacted Hurtado who made arrangements to join Herschel in San Francisco and drive up to meet Kawsay's family on Sunday. Hurtado scheduled a charter to fly the Incas back to Peru. Kawsay acted as translator for her mother and grandmother so they could get to know Nate, Alison, and Ben. Kawsay and Nate took Sumaq and Asiri on a long walk in the forest. Kawsay's mother and grandmother understood Nate had become a special person in Kawsay's life and wanted to learn everything they could about him before he left. They asked Nate all about his family and his plans for the future. They also asked probing questions about his feelings for Kawsay. Nate was delighted at their interest in him and eagerly told them how he thought Kawsay was smart, beautiful, talented, and admirable, and how fast she mastered the English language and the modern world.

The warm, late-summer sun flooded the Hunters' yard making it the ideal afternoon environment for outdoor bathing. Alison and Ben recruited Kusi and Yachay to help bathe Zevél. Ben, Alison, and Zevél had been steadily learning basic Quechua, while Kusi and Yachay were adding English words to their vocabularies. The bath afforded the opportunity for language practice. Zevél endured the bath with as much dignity as he could muster, After the final rinse, however, he involuntarily shook out the water as all dogs must, creating a small rainstorm for his groomers.

Late Thursday evening, Nate spent an hour on the telephone with his father after his younger self went to bed. Their conversation was rich and intimate, and they both talked about how they were deepening their father-son friendship. They wondered if John would notice the difference in maturity between the Nate that falls into the water in the Bahamas and the time-traveler Nate who comes back up. John told Nate what a special and unique young man he was and noted that Nate's maturity and fine character were especially evident in his good judgment and lack of egocentricity.

Nate was up early again on Friday, but was happy to know the vivid dreams would soon end. It was the last day he would have with Kawsay and her family. Tomorrow he would step into the tunnel – destination ancient Israel. After a few days with Ben's family, he would attempt to return to his own time. He imagined Kawsay's memory of him during the next three years would be colored by conversations she would have with her family. He wanted to make certain he left the best possible impression on all of them. He decided to just be open and honest and to show his genuine interest in them.

Alison and Ben had discussed how this was Nate's last full day with them. They thought a leisurely picnic up at Ben's special "Window to Heaven" overlook would provide a perfect setting. Alison left a large salad and some nuts for Zevél, and everyone else headed up the trail. They enjoyed a day of white fluffy clouds, warm sunshine, and short excursion hikes in smaller groups. Kawsay translated stories from her mother and grandmother to Nate, Ben, and Alison and in turn translated stories from Nate's background to her family. Nate felt a special connection to Kawsay's mother.

While Kawsay felt certain her future would be in archeology, Yachay had no clue what he wanted to do with his life in this new world of what seemed to be endless possibilities. He probed Ben and Alison for descriptions of any and all fields he should consider. Yachay had always assumed he would follow in Grandfather's footsteps, but now everything was different. He felt confident and optimistic, yet he had twinges of being overwhelmed and insecure – a new feeling for him.

Nate and Kawsay stole away for a climb up the rocks behind the overlook. Nate's leg was still tender, but had regained most of its strength. It felt good to be out climbing with

Kawsay. He imagined a lifetime of exploring the world with her – and that mental image seemed right to him.

Late Friday night, Nate received the final call from his dad. They knew if something misfired in the tunnels or in Gibeah, Nate may not reappear in the Caribbean storm. As a result, it was very difficult to say good-bye. They reminisced about Nate's early years and shared how much they both missed Nate's mother. John kept reminding his son to be very careful. Nate reminded his dad not to be so careful that he prevented young Nate from attending the football game when he and Jake rolled the truck or to fail to position the sailboat correctly to take the lightning bolt. John agreed to keep the forward diary close at hand and not let young Nate find out his older self had visited.

Early sunlight scattered through the open window, gently reminding Nate of the day ahead. *It's Saturday morning, the 19th of September, Dad's birthday*, Nate thought. He dressed in the clothes Ben had planned for him to wear to Israel. Alison and Ben were already up gathering Nate's supplies and preparing breakfast. The breakfast conversation was mostly about Nate's trip. Nate felt butterflies in his stomach and had to force himself to eat.

After breakfast, Nate slipped out onto the front porch. Nate had not seen Zevél earlier when he stuck his head out before breakfast. *Where are you, dude? Oh.* Nate then saw the wolf standing across the yard near the trailhead to the cave. The sight of Zevél standing there as a regal escort flooded Nate with feelings of anticipation and apprehension. *What?* Nate thought. *Is that a bird standing on Zevél's back?* What appeared to be a small white parrot cocked its head toward Nate and then flew into the forest. *Did I really see that?*

"Are you ready, Nathaniel?" the deep voice echoed softly across the yard.

"Yes," Nate said barely above a whisper. He stood immobilized, staring at Zevél. Then he felt a presence and turned to see Kawsay, Yachay, Alison, and Ben standing behind him on the porch. Nate could see that Ben was carrying the waterproof backpack containing the three arrows, cameras, clothing, gifts, and time capsule.

"We would like to see you off, Nate," Alison said.

Just then, Kusi stepped onto the porch followed by Sumaq, Asiri, and Junior. "We say goodbye now, Nate. We you wish safe," Kusi said in his best English.

Nate understood. "I look forward to our reunion in three years for you and three days for me." Nate sequentially hugged Kusi, Asiri, and Sumaq. He looked Sumaq in the eyes and said, "Take good care of my Kawsay." He studied her face, seeing strong hints of Kawsay. He felt sad he would never know Kawsay's father. Nate leaned down and scratched Junior behind the ears. "You take care of the humans for me, Junior."

Zevél led the small contingent to the cave, Nate and Kawsay hand in hand. On the way up, Ben ran through Nate's itinerary – again. Alison pointed at the passing forest milieu and quietly spoke descriptive English words to Yachay. Zevél was quiet. He felt a peace about the upcoming mission.

The moment had arrived. The small cavern with the tunnel portal was dimly lit by the lantern Alison held. Nate secured the waterproof backpack tightly to his back and turned to Yachay with a half smile. "I cannot wait to hear about the new adventures you will have during the next three years. The world needs more heroes like you. Take care of Kawsay." Nate then turned to Ben and Alison. "You two have changed my life and inspired me. Thank you for giving me a home. You are second parents to me." He hugged Ben and a teary Alison.

"We will always be here for you. And don't worry about your dad. We will stay in close touch with him over the next three years," Ben assured him.

Looking at Kawsay, Nate said, "Never doubt my feelings for you. Never." They gave each other a long and tight hug. Nate kissed Kawsay's forehead, winked at Ben, climbed onto the strong back of Zevél, and wrapped his arms around Zevél's neck. He whispered, "Thank you," into Zevél's ear and took a deep breath. With a last look at Kawsay, Nate saw her lips move and heard, "I love you, Nate." A smile washed over his face as he felt the black void of darkness envelop them.

Ben put his arm around Alison and looked at Yachay. "Well, let's go see what kind of trouble your mother and grandparents have gotten themselves into."

As they approached the house, Ben could hear his favorite Tchaikovsky CD resonating through the walls into the surrounding forest. He smiled at Kawsay who broke into a gallop toward the front door. The remainder of Saturday was filled with intimate conversations between Ben, Alison, and their Inca family. Late Saturday night, Ben called John Diamond to wish him a happy birthday and tell him of Nate's departure. Young Nate had a peaceful, dreamless sleep.

Sunday morning began with a call from Herschel. "Good morning, Ben. I picked up Dr. Hurtado at the airport early this morning, and we should be at your place within an hour or so."

Ben looked at the clock, thinking that it was still early. "Great. We are looking forward to your arrival. You're bringing Grace, aren't you?"

"She wouldn't miss it. See you in a bit."

Ben heard static and the connection dropped.

As Ben and Alison finished cleaning up the breakfast dishes, they heard barks coming from the living room. "That must be Herschel," Ben said.

Kawsay took the hands of her mother and grandmother and dragged them out the door to meet Herschel, Grace, and this new Hurtado person she had heard so much about. "Hershel! Grace! This is my mother and grandmother, Sumaq and Asiri."

Herschel and Grace greeted the women, shook hands with Kusi and Yachay, and gave Kawsay a hug. "Let me introduce you to my good friend, Augusto Hurtado. He is very excited to meet you."

"We meet in phone," Kusi said in English, shaking Hurtado's hand vigorously. Kusi instantly liked Augusto. *He seems a fine young man, very handsome and confident. Looks to be just a little older than Sumaq.*

Augusto Hurtado was surprised by Kusi's quarter-size ear disks. Yachay's disks were slightly smaller than a dime, but still quite noticeable. Hurtado responded in Quechua, "Yes, we did already meet on the phone. I enjoyed our conversation and anticipated meeting you in person. We have much to discuss. You have a beautiful wife, daughter, and granddaughter – and a most handsome grandson." Augusto Hurtado was especially taken with Sumaq's beauty and poise. In fact, these Incan ancestors of his people were extremely impressive. They stood with an aristocratic posture and were each striking in appearance. *It will be difficult to protect their true identity as their mere presence will draw intense curiosity and attention. I need to impress upon them not to mention that they are from the past but only to reveal that they are from a remote village whose location must be protected.*

Ben and Alison ushered the group to the back deck. They began a conversation about what Hurtado had been envisioning for Kusi and his family. Augusto explained his ideas on helping them develop modern language skills. English and Spanish would be a must. Then they would want to learn as much as they could about the modern world, especially geography, history, world politics, basic science, and medicine. Augusto had been studying these interesting people – relics really – though his eyes seemed to rest mostly on Sumaq.

Kusi was interested in how he and his family could teach their modern relatives. "We can tell the people of today about their ancestors and how some of us survived the Invaders. People will want to know what the last battle was like and how a group of us started our own village deep in the jungle."

"Did you say the 'last battle'? As in 1572 when the last Inca stronghold under Túpac Amaru was conquered? You were there, Kusi? Were you in Vilcabamba?" Augusto raised his bushy eyebrows, eyes round with excitement. His questions hung in the air for moment.

Kusi sensed the surprise of this man who shared part of his bloodline with Kusi's people and part with the Invaders. He *did* feel he could trust Hurtado though, and gave him an honest answer. "Yes, Kusi fought bravely." Kusi touched his necklace of human teeth. "Kusi defended his people and protected women, children, and possessions."

With Kusi's disclosure about the "last battle", Augusto's interest turned to the necklace displayed across the front of Kusi's throat. "Your necklace. Dare I ask who owned those teeth?"

"They were from the last battle." A broad smile grew on Kusi's face.

There is more to this man than meets the eye, Augusto thought.

Ben interrupted Augusto's thoughts. "That reminds me. Alison and I have a present for Kusi... sort of a going away gift." Ben stepped into the house and was back before anyone spoke. He presented Kusi with a small black box.

Kusi lifted the lid, revealing a masculine, 14-carat gold chain suspending a hefty shark's tooth.

Alison stood up and helped Kusi place it around his neck. "We thought you may want to wear a shark's tooth rather than human teeth – at least some of the time."

Kusi was impressed and showed it first to Yachay and then to each family member to admire.

"This is a good time to give you the results on the two daggers and the necklace," Herschel said, removing a box from the briefcase he had set next to his chair. He opened the box and handed Yachay the dagger with the oval cutout and Kawsay her dagger and necklace.

Hurtado's eyes lit up. "May I look at those?"

"Last battle," Kusi said, pointing to the jeweled daggers.

"Well, that explains why they are of Spanish sixteenth-century origin," Herschel reported.

"Qué interesante... ¡Estos son exquisitos!" Augusto gently swiveled the daggers, watching the inlaid jewels twinkle in the afternoon sun. "And this necklace of peanuts... they must be pure gold and silver. The necklace is of your people. And the daggers, yes, they are Spanish. Interesting that you would have this combination of Incan and Spanish artifacts."

"Did you get an estimated value on those, Herschel?" Ben asked.

"Well, that's what's so interesting." Herschel leaned forward. "See those markings near the base of the handles? It says PLVS VLTRA, or Plus Ultra. That means…"

"Further beyond – in Latin," Hurtado mumbled.

"That's right." Herschel's voice went up slightly in pitch. "It was the motto of Charles V of Spain. Your friends in the archeology department," Herschel nodded at Ben and Alison, "think these two daggers are from a private collection of Spain's leader, Emperor Charles V, also known as King Charles I." Herschel paused. "As far as value? This stuff is museum quality. The Spanish daggers and Inca necklace … extremely valuable."

Kusi looked at Herschel with a questioning gaze and reached over to retrieve the necklace and daggers Hurtado had gently laid on the table.

"Yes, Kusi, these belong to your family." Herschel gestured. "They are yours to do with what you will. I wouldn't flash them around, though."

"Good advice," Augusto agreed.

For the remainder of the day and evening, Hurtado spent time with each member of the family individually. He talked with them about their interests and answered their questions. Ben and Alison helped Kawsay and Yachay gather their belongings and new clothing and ready themselves for their journey to Peru the next day. Hurtado had chartered a jet to fly them from San Francisco to Lima.

It was all happening so fast. Kawsay already missed Nate. How would she survive the next three years without him? She and Yachay took a final walk around the property. They both felt at peace being there and were each a little apprehensive about leaving. They thought that going to Peru was the best situation for their mother and grandparents, but they thought the U.S. was probably where they wanted to be long term. Kawsay wanted to go to college with Nate. Yachay was not sure what he wanted to do, but unless he found Peru as exciting as the U.S., he thought he may want to return. One thing was for sure – they both wanted to visit the Hunters often. Yachay decided Nate was a good guy and very smart. He was especially impressed with Nate's martial arts moves. He vowed to himself to stay close to Kawsay in the coming years, as he always had. When Nate returned, he would have to see what developed between them. Both Kawsay and Yachay had noticed Hurtado looking at their mother, and neither had a problem with him if something developed. Their mother had been so sad since Father died and had never been interested in any other men. They giggled about a possible romance between them.

That night, Hurtado bunked in Yachay's room, which gave Yachay a chance to talk more with him and determine if he thought Hurtado was someone he could trust.

Early Monday morning after a quick but ample breakfast, everyone congregated in the driveway around the large van Herschel had driven. Alison and Ben reminisced about the first time they saw Kawsay after Zevél had deposited her on their porch. Kawsay pulled the satellite phone out of her bag and promised to call them regularly. Ben told Kawsay and her family that if they were unhappy for any reason in Peru, they were welcome to return here. They made plans to get together for a Christmas visit either here in the Sierras or in Peru.

They also agreed on a reunion in three years when Nate returned.

As the dust of the van settled in the driveway, Alison and Ben walked hand in hand back to the porch. Alison reached down, petted Junior's head, and said, "It's just the three of us guys. I really wonder what is happening with Nate right now and if he made it."

"We'll need to go and dig up that time capsule on Mt. Gilboa." Ben took in a deep breath of morning air.

"When?" Alison said with eyebrows raised.

"I'm not sure. We've been so focused on getting everyone launched, I haven't thought about when we would go to Israel to dig up the capsule."

"Well, what are we waiting for?" Alison looked up at Ben. "It should be there already."

"You're right, honey." Ben looked down at her smiling. "How long will it take you to pack?"

CHAPTER 28

ARROWS HIT THE MARK

1018 B.C.
NEAR GIBEAH, ISRAEL

THOUGH I FLEW AWAY
BEYOND THE DAWN DO NOT MOURN
FOR I LIVE AND LOVE.

Nate's anxiety about again entering the time tunnel turned out to be misplaced. Taking and holding a large breath reduced the feeling of suffocation and holding on to Zevél imparted confidence of a safe arrival. The landing, while not soft, avoided any bruising impacts. *How does he decelerate like that?* Nate wondered. When they came to a stop, everything was quiet for a moment.

"Nathaniel, you may get off my back now. Please leave those handfuls of fur behind," Zevél requested.

"Sorry. Are we here? Do you know the local time?" Nate asked.

"Let us assume we have been delivered to the correct time and place. I suggest you get yourself ready," the wolf stated. "I will remain hidden here during the daylight hours. I will come for you if necessary." With that, Zevél found a dark corner of the cave and curled up to rest.

I think Zevél is still recovering from his journey in the jungle. With fur like that he must have been very uncomfortable, Nate thought. Still wearing the large backpack, Nate felt his way across the cave floor toward the dim light and slowly and cautiously made his way up to the craggy entrance. He recognized the aroma of newly cut wheat and saw a familiar sight. *The field with the rock piles!* The stubble was wet with dew, and the Sun had just risen. *Assuming this is the right day, I'm here a little earlier than last time!*

Nate looked around and then retreated back into the cave entrance. Using the light of the new day, he removed the plastic tube from his pack and carefully withdrew the three arrows. He removed his wristwatch and stowed it in the waterproof pack, noting that only a few minutes had elapsed since he had entered the tunnel. Then he took out the mantle and arranged it like a hood on his head. Adjusting Ben's old brown cloak and checking his new tan sandals, he decided he was ready.

Nate lugged the backpack down into the recesses of the cave beyond the tunnel opening and set it next to Zevél. "Hey, Zevél!" Nate whispered. "I just thought of something. I'm about to run into myself again, and for a while there are going to be six arrows here! Pretty funny, huh?"

The half-slumbering wolf raised his head. "Yes. That is why I am careful not to take a tunnel to a time and place where I already am or will soon be. When I was very young and new to time travel, I encountered myself on a narrow rock ridge. My younger self was startled and began to growl, but my older self remembered the encounter, backed up, and yielded the right-of-way."

Nate did not remember seeing himself in the cave on his first visit, so he hid deep in a dark recess. Crouching against the cool rock, his legs began to ache. He began to shiver, so he nestled against Zevél's silver fur for warmth. Nate's began to feel moving air against his face and then heard a rushing sound. Suddenly, not ten feet from where he hid, a blonde boy in light-colored pants and shirt erupted from the tunnel and sprawled across the floor. The dripping figure seemed stunned for a moment, tried to stand, and then spun to the ground. Nate, the sailor, slowly rose again and felt his way toward the cave entrance. After a moment, he was gone.

Nate remained immobile next to the wolf and resisted the temptation to watch the scene unfold outside, partly out of caution and partly to avoid watching himself get hit by the arrow. Instead, he listened intently while making sure he was ready to spring into action. For several minutes everything was quiet. Then he heard some shouting, followed by the approach of running footsteps. His freshly-wounded self crashed into the cave, hobbling and feeling his way down to the recesses, eyes not accustomed to the dark. Nate recalled the excruciating pain of the arrow. Another figure was soon at the entrance, pleading in a small voice for his arrow to be returned. The wounded Nate moved closer to the hiding Nate, but then with a gasp disappeared back into the tunnel.

Easy, Nate counseled himself as he relived the scene. *One more to go.* Young Ben, two arrows in hand, came closer, again asking in Hebrew for the arrow. For a fleeting second, Nate thought of giving the boy one of the arrows that he was holding and telling him to run home, but then remembered both Ben's admonition not to tinker and Alison's love for her Ben. Only a minute after the first figure disappeared, young Ben gave a gasp and was also engulfed by the tunnel. That was Nate's cue!

Remembering Yachay's selfless courage, Nate flew out of the cave and headed toward the tall archer with the regal bearing. He carried the arrows in his right hand, obscuring where the broken shaft had been repaired, and held his mantle around his head with the other hand. He slowed as he approached Jonathan, careful not to show his full face. He held out the retrieved arrows.

Jonathan scarcely looked at Nate. He handed the bow and quiver to Nate. "Go, carry them into the city," he directed. Nate did not hesitate, but without looking back ran quickly toward town on the path. Once he was around a bend out of sight, he darted off the path and up onto the long ridge above the cave. He found a cluster of large rocks and hid where he would be able to see Jonathan returning to town.

Nate caught his breath. Then he waited. While Jonathan and David were talking, Nate had time to think. *All right! Mission accomplished! Jonathan's arrows are finally returned! Ben worried about this for thirty years. I wish I could tell him right now! I guess this couldn't have failed. I don't think Jonathan suspected anything! Actually it was really easy. The first half of my mission is a success!*

While keeping an eye out for Jonathan, Nate went over the plan one more time. Before long, he saw Jonathan pass by, listless and downcast. Nate thought Jonathan must be sad and distressed; he pondered the tragedy of the prince's life. *I wish I could help him.*

When Jonathan was out of sight, Nate climbed down from the ridge and darted quickly back to the cave. He found Zevél asleep. *My 500-pound protector must have a lot of confidence in me!* Nate thought. He changed into his new cloak and placed the key items into the matching carrying bag. He quickly ate the snack Alison insisted he take along and read over the directions to Ben's house one more time.

"I'll be going now, Zevél," he whispered.

"May God bless your mission," Zevél stirred and replied in a low, quiet voice. "May I have a map to the home of Ben's family?" Nate dug out an extra copy, unfolded it, and slipped it under a giant paw.

It was about two miles to the center of Gibeah, and Nate was worried about meeting people along the way. *I just need to relax and act natural.* Coming around a curve, he saw two men approaching. As they passed by, the taller man eyed him closely and nodded his head. "Greetings, stranger," he said evenly.

Nate smiled and nodded back. *This must be one of those small towns where everyone knows everyone else. I need to keep cool.* He looked for a large tree and bore right on the larger pathway. Then he found the beginning of a low stone wall and angled left. Nate's progress was interrupted by a herd of fat-tailed sheep crossing his way, guided by a man and two small boys, one of whom smiled at Nate. Nate paused to look at a tree similar to ones he had seen in California and noticed the figs were ripe. He was startled by a sharp pain in the side of his foot. He looked down and saw he had been accosted by a small cactus. *Glad it wasn't a snake!*

Coming over a small hill, he saw what must be Gibeah – a large grouping of flat-topped adobe buildings of various sizes arrayed on an east-sloping hillside. A small wall surrounded the settlement. Carrying a large bow and quiver of arrows belonging to the king's son made Nate feel conspicuous. As he approached the main gate, his pulse began to race. All the people milling around seemed to be looking at him. *I hope they don't find me too strange-looking!* Maintaining his courage, Nate continued to the center of town and passed the community well and the largest building, which Ben had said was Saul's palace. Nate counted 120 more steps and arrived at a small two-story house with a flat roof. It appeared to be constructed from baked mud bricks with pieces of straw protruding in a few places. He knocked on the arched wooden door.

A pretty woman in her late thirties came to the door. Her hands were white with flour, which she was wiping on a rough apron. She wore a brown high-neck tunic tied at the waist with a sash, which Nate recognized as being cut from the same cloth as Ben's old cloak. Her long, dark brown hair was tied back. She smiled at Nate.

"Yes?" she inquired.

"Greetings. I am a friend of Binyamin."

"I am Tirzah. You are a friend of my son?" the woman asked, not recognizing Nate.

Before he could reply, a deep voice inside the house spoke. "Who is it, mother?" A young man of about seventeen years also appeared at the door. He had the strong and fearless look of a soldier, but reminded Nate of a younger version of Ben. He joined his mother in gazing at Nate with a questioning look and immediately noticed at the armaments.

Nate focused on his mission. "Your brother, Binyamin, asks that you return these to

Jonathan." He held them out to the young man he assumed was Ben's older brother. "He is sorry he cannot return home at this time." Nate had practiced this part many times. "Please return them before Jonathan comes to look for them."

The young man began to question Nate. "Why does my brother not return the weapons himself?"

The mother interjected. "Shimon, it is best to return them quickly. We will question Binyamin when he returns." Shimon was not pleased to perform a chore for his younger brother. She turned again to Nate. "You have a heavy burden. Please enter my home, Nathaniel. I am preparing the Shabbat meal for this evening."

"Thank you," Nate said, entering through the low doorway. He found himself in a small courtyard containing a cooking fire, a grinding stone, shelves with a small supply of fruits and vegetables, and a few benches. Across the courtyard was a gate to a walled area that contained two goats. Tirzah led Nate through another doorway into a long common room with two windows on the far wall. It contained low wooden chairs covered with thick wool blankets. The floor was made of odd-shaped flat tiles, and the mud brick walls grew up from a one-course stone foundation. The ceiling was held up by rough wooden cross-beams and four thick stone pillars. At one end was a wooden ladder leading to the upper level and doorways that presumably led to other rooms. At the other end was a complex device Nate concluded was a loom. He noticed shelves with a few decorative items and felt how cool the interior was compared to the sun-drenched courtyard.

"You may place your sack in the corner," Tirzah said, gesturing with her hand. "Then join me outside. I have much to do."

He removed a small piece of notepaper from his sack and joined her outside. Ben's mother returned to grinding barley. Nate settled on a wooden bench by the south wall, which was still partly in the shade. He said nothing and tried to look inconspicuous.

"Do you know when Jonathan will send Binyamin back?" she asked, continuing to work with her strong arms. "I do not like him to be so far away from the city. There are dangers from animals and outsiders."

Nate hesitated. "Binyamin sent me to deliver a message to you and your husband. Is he nearby?"

"Jokim is with the flocks," she answered. "Doeg, the King's head shepherd, is away at Nob on a religious errand and directed Jokim to stay with the flocks last night. Jokim should return soon. He must bathe before the start of Shabbat."

Nate realized it must be Friday, because the Sabbath would begin at sundown. That meant the family would likely be together all the next day. "I must wait to deliver the message," Nate announced, trying to sound authoritative.

"Tell me, Nathaniel, where did you see Binyamin this morning?"

"I saw him at a wheat field east of Gibeah that is next to a long cliff. Jonathan was shooting arrows," Nate answered slowly, trying to avoid linguistic errors.

"I hope they return soon," she said with a sigh, looking up from her work. "My son has not mentioned your name to me. Have you known him a long time?"

"I met Binyamin more than a month ago. We are good friends now," Nate said. "Your son is a very admirable person."

Tirzah was surprised to hear her unruly young son referred to in reverential tones. "I have great hope for him, but do not believe he will be happy herding sheep or fighting with the army. I think he is a dreamer like Jacob's son, Joseph. Where is your family from?" Tirzah asked, taking a break from her meal preparation to focus on Nate.

"Far away, across the water," Nate answered as if he found the question uninteresting.

Tirzah pondered his vague answer with suspicion. "So you are not a Benjaminite?"

"No," Nate answered. Seeing Ben's mother grow suspicious, he added, "But I am a son of Abraham by adoption." She seemed to accept his response and began stoking her fire.

After a moment, Tirzah asked, "Why are you sojourning here? Where is your family now?"

Nate wondered how much longer he could keep up this conversation and was growing tense. "I was sent with important messages I must deliver today and tomorrow."

Before she could probe further, they heard the door from the street open. Ben's brother strode in followed by a bearded man carrying a shepherd's crook and wearing a dirty blue coat and yellow mantle. Tirzah rose and went to him. She stood before him for a moment, and they gently embraced.

"It is well you have returned home early, Jokim," Tirzah said. "I hope you spent a peaceful night in the hills. Look. We have a visitor from afar, a friend of Binyamin."

Nate stood. "I am Nathaniel. I am pleased to meet you, sir."

Shimon had little interest in the visitor and continued inside, but Jokim looked at Nate with a keen eye. The father was a little smaller than Ben, with weathered and tanned skin. A full, dark beard prevented further comparisons. "Welcome, Nathaniel. I am Jokim, son of Benaiah." He turned to his wife. "I will wash first, then converse with our visitor. Where is Binyamin?"

"He is with Jonathan. I do not know when he will return," she replied.

"May I wash also? I am dusty from my travel," Nate requested.

Jokim motioned for Nate to follow him. In a back room Jokim picked up a jug of water and poured it into a basin. He began to wash. Jokim anticipated Nate's need and pointed him to a small outhouse. When Nate returned, Jokim was finishing by rinsing his feet and drying them with a long cloth. He put on a clean, light-colored robe. Nate washed his face and feet and felt better.

They returned to the courtyard through the long common room. Tirzah addressed her husband. "Nathaniel has come to Gibeah from a distant place with messages. He will stay the night with us." Turning to Nate, she continued, "You and Binyamin may sleep on the roof since the weather is fair."

Nate felt the notepaper in a pocket of this cloak. *Here goes.* He took a deep breath and removed the paper. "This is one of my messages," he announced. "It is for you and your family. It is from your son, Binyamin."

Jokim took it and looked at his wife with a mixture of curiosity and alarm. Shimon appeared at the courtyard door dressed as if he planned to depart. "Shimon, Nathaniel has a written message from Binyamin." Jokim looked at the text. "Yamin wrote this? You and your brother have learned to read and write like scribes! Will you read it to us?" Jokim asked.

Shimon took the paper and examined it. Its texture and straight edge was unusual, and the writing was very fine, though it looked somewhat like Binyamin's hand.   Ben's parents sat on the bench by the south wall to listen.   Shimon read the letter:

From Binyamin to his father, mother, and brother:

Shalom.   Please take care of my messenger, Nathaniel.   He is a good and loyal friend who has braved great dangers to bring you important messages from me.   I ask you to receive him as you would your own son and help him to return quickly to his family.   His people do not speak our language, but through study he has learned it well. I have sent him with additional messages and gifts for each of you.   The purpose of the messages is to explain what has happened to me this day and to give you timely warning to save your lives.

Shimon paused and looked up with a furrowed brow.   *What is this?* he wondered.   He saw his parents impatient for him to continue.

What I will tell you will make you question the truth of my statements and perhaps the soundness of my mind, but please withhold judgment until you hear and see everything I have sent with my messenger.   You will be upset, but do not take any action against Nathaniel.   He is not a Hebrew, but he is a person of strong faith in God.   If you are upset, bring your complaint before God because all that has happened to me has been from His hand.

"What is this about?" Jokim asked Nate.   "What is Binyamin talking about?"

"Binyamin told me to let his letters answer your questions," Nate replied quietly.

Shimon continued:

So you will know this is from your son, I tell you these things: My first meal today was goat's milk and old bread with honey.   Since my birthday, I have insisted that you stop calling me "Yamin".   I have a large collection of Philistine arrowheads in a small urn by my bed.   My father brought me an addition to my collection which he found in the fields west of town four days ago.   I have been hoping for an opportunity to study with the priests.   My grandfather died on the day I was born, but not before giving me a special blessing for a happy life.   My father chipped his tooth during last year's Pesach meal.   If this is not sufficient, Nate can give you the brown cloak I wore this morning.

Tirzah gave Nate a questioning look, and Nate nodded to her.

My story is incredible.   Listen with the ears of your hearts.   You will see that Grandfather's blessing came to pass.   I am happy in all ways but one – I am not with you today.   It may not be possible for me to ever see you again unless one day God allows me to take the same journey as my messenger, Nathaniel.

Nathaniel must leave in two days.   Use the time he is with you to learn all you can about me and to prepare messages for him to bring back to me.   Most important: Listen carefully to my warnings.   I want you all to live long lives, but if you remain in Gibeah, you likely will not.   I will tell you events that will occur in the next few weeks, and when they do, you will know that I speak true words.   Do not dismiss my messages as the trick of an unruly boy.   As I write this to you, I am a man of forty-two years.   Do not be downcast and do not mourn for me.   Only mourn for the separation that has occurred. I hope my words and pictures will comfort you.   When you learn all that has happened

to me, I hope you will be proud of your second son and will feel the great love he has
for each of you.

God be with you forever.

Shimon looked up. "It is signed 'Binyamin'. It looks like his writing."

Jokim and Tirzah both began talking rapidly at once. Shimon moved in front of Nate, breathing on him. "What sorcery and witchcraft is this?" he demanded.

Nate felt very vulnerable and did not know how to reply. Shimon pushed him and shouted, "What have you done with my brother? Is he your prisoner?" He pushed again.

"Stop that!" commanded Jokim. "Nathaniel is making no demands. There are more messages. I want to hear everything before making any judgment."

Ben's mother looked bereft. "Will I never see my little boy again? I want my baby!" Jokim put an arm around his wife to comfort her.

"Your son is fine!" Nate blurted out. "He is a great teacher and has a good wife who also is a great teacher. He lives on the other side of the Earth. He knows that King Saul and his reign will soon end, and many of Saul's people will be killed. He wants you to give your allegiance to David, whom Samuel has anointed to be king. Men from all tribes will join David soon."

"You speak like a fool!" Shimon objected. "My brother was here this morning. He cannot live on the other side of the Earth and cannot have a wife. He is only a boy!"

Tirzah put her hand on Shimon's sleeve. "Son, Binyamin's letter warned us that his story would be strange. I also want to hear his entire story." Shimon continued to glower.

Nate wondered what to do next. He thought about the plans and the contingencies. *I think it's time to show them the photos. That will help them understand that Ben has grown up.* "I will show you pictures of Binyamin that he sent with me."

"What are these pictures?" Jokim asked.

"Where he lives, there are small boxes with tiny windows that let in light for a short time. The light paints a picture of the scene. These pictures will interest you very much," Nate promised.

Jokim spoke. "We are confused and do not know what to say or do. We are worried about Binyamin. Tell us everything you can."

"I will do my best," Nate offered. He quickly retrieved a packet from his sack. "Come. Look at these pictures." Nate sat on the ground in front of the bench in the warm sun of the early afternoon and motioned for Ben's family to sit. The parents sat together on the bench, and Shimon pulled up a stool.

Nate removed the first picture. It showed a young and confused Ben on the day he arrived at the Hunters when he was still wearing his brown cloak. "Does this not look like your son as you saw him this morning?" He handed the photo to Tirzah who looked at the likeness of her son and felt the smooth shiny surface.

"Of course, this is Binyamin. It shows every detail of our son," she observed.

Jokim looked at the photo intently and silently. Then he handed it to Shimon.

"Look," Shimon said. "There is a message written on the back of the picture." He read:

This is a picture of me on the day I left my home in Gibeah and arrived at my new home. I did not know where I was or what had occurred. I wanted to return home, but could not.

Nate pulled out the next photo. It showed Ben about a year later in front of the large log house. Shimon read the caption:

This is a picture of me one year after I arrived at my new home. My hair and clothes are different, and I have grown larger, but you can see that it is your son. This is a dog that my new family kept at their home. Her name was Abigail, and she was my friend for many years. I still live in the large house that is made from tree trunks laid on their sides.

"I don't understand how Binyamin can be older," Tirzah remarked.

"He will tell you how this happens," Nate promised, handing her the next picture. This showed Ben, Helmut, and Helmut's parents dressed up standing in the front of a church sanctuary. Shimon read the narrative on the back:

This is the family that found me wandering on their land and helped me. At first they tried to find where I came from, but could not. Later they adopted me and gave me love and care until I grew to manhood.

There were many more photos, including shots of Ben by his first car, at a graduation, working on an addition to the log house, standing atop Mt. Whitney, on archeological digs in modern Israel, under the Statue of Liberty, on a sailboat, and on a beautiful beach in Tahiti. They were arranged chronologically to illustrate that the bewildered young boy in the first photo had morphed into the handsome, strong man who looked like a clean-shaven version of Jokim. There were two photos left. Nate pulled out a wedding photo of Ben and Alison.

When Tirzah saw it, she caught her breath. *What a beautiful woman,* she thought. *What a beautiful garment she wears! Is this a marriage ceremony? Who are her people? They look very nice together!* She was not eager to pass the photo to the others.

Finally Shimon reached out for it and read:

This is a picture from my wedding. My beloved wife is Alison. I believe God brought me to this far-away place because he wanted Alison and me to be together in this life and forever.

Nate handed her the last photo, which had been taken the previous day in the Hunter's living room from a tripod. Nate was standing in front of Ben and Alison by the stone fireplace, with Junior seated regally in front showing a large pink tongue. Nate was wearing the same outfit he now wore.

Silence reigned. Ben's family pondered what they had seen but without understanding how it could be. Yet their eyes could not lie, could they?

Shimon had lost his belligerence, and his brows were knitted in thought. "Nathaniel," he said suddenly, breaking the silence. "I have read that the Lord God made the Sun stand still in the heavens for a day to help Joshua prevail in battle over the Amorites. Has the Lord God made the Sun over my brother to move quickly forward? Has time moved fast for him?"

Nate smiled at Shimon, pleased he was using his head instead of his brawn. "The next message from your brother explains this. Where he now lives time does not move faster. Your brother traveled through a tunnel that moved him to a different time many years in the future. He has been there for thirty years and grown to be a man. He sent me back to talk with you because he could not come himself."

"That is impossible!" Jokim remarked. "There must be another explanation."

"Sir, not long ago I would have agreed with you," Nate replied. "But I have traveled to different times too. I was born three thousand years in the future and have traveled here two times."

Tirzah had heard all she could absorb for the moment. "The Sun will set in a short time, and we must prepare for Shabbat. We will talk more after our meal. Nathaniel will sit in the place of Binyamin." She rose and began the final preparations for the meal.

"Binyamin's wife, Alison, sent a cake for you to enjoy. I have it in my sack."

A low dining table was set in the long room, lit by several large candles and an oil lamp. Nate had attended Sabbath meals at a friend's home and was familiar with the reverent prayers offered by the mother and father and sometimes by one of the children. The tradition was not as well formed in Ben's family. Jokim offered a short prayer of thanks for the food and a Sabbath blessing. He ended with a brief prayer for their guest and a request for wisdom regarding their missing son.

As they began to pass the dishes around, Tirzah cast glances toward the door as if expecting Binyamin to enter and end the strain of her ordeal. Her eyes were red. Shimon, quiet and thoughtful, eyed Nate, trying to figure him out. Their conversation drifted to the small topics of daily life – work, neighbors, the royal family, and even the weather.

Nate suspected it was a relief for them to *not* think about their lost son. He was getting an invaluable glimpse into life in this time. While he listened, Nate analyzed each of the foods offered. The spicy vegetable dish was a little strong for his taste. He had refused both diluted wine and goat's milk, preferring just water into which he slipped a small piece of a purification tablet. In addition to more grapes and figs, there were melon, dates, olives, and excellent bread. At the end of the meal, Nate shared the cake. Tirzah was fascinated with its translucent sealed container.

As everyone was finishing the meal, Jokim asked, "Are there more letters from Binyamin? There is time to read more before we sleep."

"Yes," Nate assured him. "I will give you the letters, but also have a special box that will allow you to see and hear Binyamin and Alison speak to you and read the letters. I will make things ready."

Nate set the camcorder on the table and brought the oil lamp close so he could see what he was doing. "Please sit here where you can all look at this small window. You will see and hear Binyamin, but he is not inside the box, just a memory of him. Here is the letter he asked me to give to you." Nate hit "play". After a few flickers, Ben appeared on the screen, eliciting three small gasps from his audience. When Ben's image spoke, there was a hushed awe.

Father, Mother, Shimon. Shalom. I am your son, Binyamin. I want to explain what has happened to me. Since I left this morning with Jonathan, I have traveled to a place far away in distance and time. I have now lived here thirty years. Every day of those thirty years I have thought of you and grieved that I left without even a parting kiss or kind word. While you may grieve with me that we are no longer together, rejoice that I am alive and living a good life.

I have three requests of you while Nathaniel is with you. First, please care for him and make sure he returns in two days. Second, allow Nathaniel to make a record of you with this "camcorder" and a "camera". This will allow me to have pictures of you to keep always. Finally, Nathaniel will leave with you a small round "time capsule". Wait three or four years and then write a letter to me using the special paper and writing tools inside the container. I will give you directions to bury it on a mountain to the north. Then, when I find your letter in three thousand years, I will know that you are safe and well.

So why was Jonathan shooting arrows this morning? It was neither for practice nor for hunting. Confidentially, it was to warn David to flee. As you know, King Saul is not right in his mind. He has tried more than once to kill his son-in-law, though David has not lifted a hand against him. Samuel has anointed David as the next king, but Saul presumes to fight against the will of God. Jonathan discovered for certain that his father intends to kill David and used the arrows as a sign to warn him. But an unplanned event occurred that proved to be the beginning of my journey. It involved Nathaniel.

Shimon looked at Nate who nodded. Ben's narrative digressed to a description of the time tunnels and then proceeded to the accidental wounding of Nate. Nate showed Shimon the scar on his leg as corroborative evidence. Ben described how Nate and he fell forward in time, his inability to return, integration into his new family, education, career as an archeologist, and courtship with Alison. He then explained the dispersion of the three arrows and the recent gathering together of the arrows for return to Jonathan. The narrative continued:

The activities of Jonathan and David this morning will be chronicled and preserved for all time. It will be told how a young boy returned the arrows to Jonathan who instructed him to return the bow and arrows to Gibeah. I discovered this story some time after I arrived in my new home. It helped me understand who I was because I was mentioned in the story. This story is part of the collected writings that were inspired by God, including the books of Moses which are already known to you. I knew the words were true and could not be broken, which meant the arrows would be returned. I could not return the three arrows until recently because I only had one of them, and now I am too big to be the boy who returns them. Today Nathaniel has completed this important task. He wanted to stay for two days and bring you my messages so you would not spend the rest of your lives wondering what happened to me. His service to our family can never be repaid.

Ben quickly finished his story and introduced Alison, explaining that he believed God made them for each other and that he loved her more than his life. He added that he believed the main reason he was brought to the future was to be her husband. Alison entered the field of view and sat close to Ben, somewhat embarrassed by the effusive introduction. Alison's letter described her and Ben's love for each other and for God, how Ben was the perfect husband for her, and her thankfulness to them for bringing him into the world.

Ben then concluded, asking that his warning message be played next. Tirzah asked if they needed to hear everything that night, as it was late and she was exhausted and overwhelmed by all she had seen and heard. Nate assured her that tomorrow would be fine. After Nate put away the equipment and wished Ben's parents a good night, Shimon helped him arrange a bed on the roof. He rolled out two woven mats along with some thick woolen pads and blankets.

"I will join you up here tonight. The sky is clear, and the air will be cool and pleasant," Shimon explained. The two young men from different worlds were soon lying side-by-side, peering into a vast starscape that drew their minds upward.

"Nathaniel, I was wrong to threaten you today," Shimon said. "I am sorry."

"You are very strong, Shimon. I realize you wanted to protect your brother. I hope you understand I am here to help."

"I do not know you, but I know my brother. Even aged thirty years, I recognize his way of speaking and moving. What I have seen and heard today changes how I view my world. I am curious about the warnings we will receive tomorrow."

Nate saw a shooting star blaze across the sky. "Did you see that?"

"Yes. Is it a sign?" Shimon asked.

"I do not know if it is a sign, but what we saw was a meteor – a large rock from far beyond the Moon that heats and burns when it gets near the Earth," Nate replied. He then launched into a tutorial about meteors, stars, planets, moons, galaxies, and space travel. He went on for many minutes before he stopped, wondering if he had put Shimon to sleep. He looked over at his companion whose eyes were still roving the heavens.

Shimon spoke slowly. "Nathaniel, I do not know if you are making up these stories. You tell me the Earth is a sphere spinning in empty space, supported by nothing. You tell me men have walked on the Moon. Next you will tell me men have traveled to the bottom of the sea and have built temples as tall as the clouds!"

"Well, actually, this also is mostly true." And Nate was soon explaining nuclear submarines and skyscrapers. He was turning to fiber optics when he heard some snoring sounds begin to rise from Shimon. *I guess I overdid it!* Nate thought of Kawsay back in California and of his father waiting in a Caribbean storm. He finally drifted off into a deep sleep, for the first time in many weeks untroubled by vivid dreams.

In the middle of the night by scant moonlight, a large creature climbed stealthily up the outside stairway to the sleeping deck. A large silver head appeared over the railing, shimmering in the moonlight. Two tall ears tilted forward, listening. Two large eyes surveyed the young men curled up under their blankets. Nodding his head, the ancient wolf spoke in a low, almost inaudible voice, "You have done well thus far, Nathaniel." Then Zevél vanished back to the cave.

Before dawn, as Nate shivered under his blankets, Gibeah's animals began to stir. As he cleared the cobwebs, trying to remember where he was, his first thought was of a barnyard. He saw the large mound next to him that was Shimon and everything flooded into his consciousness. His back was stiff, but otherwise he felt strong and rested. He lay quietly and planned his day.

Voices came up from the street and woke Shimon. He sat up quickly and stretched. He smiled at Nate. "You slept well?"

"Yes. What will happen today?" Nate asked.

"I hope nothing," Shimon replied. "On Shabbat, I rest and relax and do not apologize for it. You have more messages from my little brother. I am eager to hear them."

The young men arose and folded up their bedding. They climbed down the ladder to a quiet house. Ben's mother was already busy in the courtyard milking the goats. She wore a lavender tunic with tassels and a scalloped hem, clearly not designed for hard work.

"After you young men wash, we will eat. I have milk, fig cakes, and pomegranates."

Nate washed his face and then pulled out his toothbrush and toothpaste. He was foaming at the mouth when Jokim came up to him with a look of alarm.

"Nathaniel, are you all right? What has happened to your mouth?"

Nate spat out the foam. "I am cleaning my teeth." He showed Jokim his brush. "It keeps my teeth white and healthy."

Jokim took the toothbrush and smelled the residue. He raised his eyebrows and smiled. "Yes, you will smell like a sprig of mint!"

As they finished the meal, there was a knock at the outside door. Shimon rose from the table and returned with a young man about his age but taller with very broad shoulders and a chiseled face. He had the bearing of a military officer. Jokim rose and embraced the visitor. "Ah, Ittai. Good Shabbat to you. How are Ribai and Jarusha? You have been away?"

"My parents send greetings to your family," Ittai responded. "We returned yesterday from a visit to my uncle at Ramah. My cousin's wedding celebration lasted for three days!"

Shimon was pleased to see his best friend. "Ittai, we missed you at our exercises the last two days. An army needs to keep strong."

"Yes, yes, I know," Ittai said impatiently. "I perform my drills every day, even when I am away visiting and meeting beautiful young girls." His eyes flashed with confidence.

"What brings you to our home this quiet morning?" Tirzah asked. "We have a visitor with us," she said, extending a hand toward Nate. "He is Nathaniel, a friend of Binyamin."

Ittai gave a curt nod in Nate's direction and then turned to Jokim with a serious look. "King Saul sends me and others to tell everyone in Gibeah to watch for his son-in-law, David, and to report any sightings. He is missing, and Saul is concerned for his safety."

Shimon gave a sideways look at Nate and then at his father. "We have not seen David."

"If you do, tell him the King requests his presence at the palace. The King desires a song from David, and his wife misses him and is worried." Ittai lowered his voice. "It is my duty to tell you this. If you *do* hear of David's location, do not tell anyone. And if you see him, tell him to run for his life for Saul intends to kill him. Jonathan is in seclusion, and we are concerned about the King's mind. Saul's kingdom may not survive. Tell Binyamin when he rises. He was with Jonathan and David only yesterday morning. Pray that we can survive these troubled times! Now I must go." He looked everyone in the eye to be sure he was understood and could trust them to use discretion. He turned abruptly and departed, leaving them in stunned silence.

Shimon spoke first, very agitated. "Ittai plays a dangerous game and puts us all at risk. Like me, he is a soldier in King Saul's army, sworn to do his duty to protect the kingdom with his life. What does he expect me to do?"

Jokim looked angry. "Do you think this is your problem alone? I am also a servant of King Saul, and I am the head of this family. But every day my fear grows that we are supporting a leader who no longer has God's approval and who rules by force and intimidation! Yesterday we lost your brother when he went out to a field with Jonathan. If we lose you too, Shimon, it will be the death of your mother and me. You talk of loyalty, but are our leaders worthy of our loyalty, or will they lead us to defeat and death?"

"But what choice do we have, Jokim?" Tirzah asked, trying to remain calm. "This is our home; these are our people. If we were to serve David, could that upstart provide us food and clothing? Does he rule a city where we can live? Does he command an army that can protect us?"

"If I desert from the army, I am as good as dead!" Shimon protested. "Ittai speaks boldly to us behind the walls of our home, but has he made any move to change his allegiance? No. He is only talk, dangerous talk."

"Shimon, I am not saying we should do anything precipitous, only that we think and plan and be ready," Jokim reasoned. "I tell you; I knew the King when he was a young man and was not impressed with his wisdom and character. I was shocked when Samuel anointed him to be our king. He may look like a king because he is tall, strong, and handsome. And he won some important battles in his early days. But so many times he has not shown good judgment and has even presumed to act as a priest! Can we really trust him with our lives?"

Shimon considered what he knew of the King and realized his father was right. But he loved his life as a soldier and dreamed of excelling in battle against the enemies of his people. He thought he would not fear even the giants.

Nate followed the heated discussion despite some expressions he did not know. He cleared his throat loudly. Everyone looked at him. "If you please, I believe you will find what Binyamin tells you in his next message will help you at this difficult time."

Tirzah had heard her husband and son argue like this before. "Yes. Let us hear what Binyamin has to say. He told us yesterday he had a warning about our future. Nate, can we hear the next message?"

They assumed the same seats as the previous evening. Within a few minutes, Ben reappeared on the small screen, sitting at the desk in his office with a serious look on his face.

I again greet you all. You have had time to consider my story. Now I want to give you a timely warning that might save your lives. Please hear my words and put them to the test.

You are already aware that King Saul's kingdom has been torn from him and given to David, yet Saul remains in power. His loyal servants and soldiers continue to follow him, but the time is coming when that loyalty will cost them their lives. Once the House of Saul falls, do not presume that you will be spared. Many of Saul's followers will lose their lives.

Living in the future, I can read the history of our people. I am no prophet, but I have studied the events that will unfold during the remainder of your days. It is not for me to shine a light on all these events. I only seek to tell you enough so you will survive and have the chance for long lives. Listen to me, please!

Saul will hunt David like an animal, but David will prove his loyalty and not kill

Saul even when he has the opportunity. David knows that the kingdom is not his to seize. David will live in caves, forests and deserts. Yet brave people will join and help him. Before long, Saul and his sons will be killed in a battle with the Philistines in the Vale of Jezreel and the western slope of Mt. Gilboa. After a struggle, David will consolidate his authority as the new king, establish a dynasty that will last for many generations, and help prepare the way for God's kingdom on Earth. Many people who remain loyal to Saul will perish in his last battle with the Philistines or in the transition to David's rule. Those who transfer their allegiance to David will escape that fate. Do not wait too long to escape from Gibeah and from Saul. Your only hope is to join David and suffer with him until he becomes king.

I know you love your home and life in Gibeah, and I expect your mind will resist my warning even if in your heart you know I speak the truth. So you can be confident in my words, I will describe events that will soon take place. When they happen as I describe, you will know with certainty that my advice is reliable.

Doeg will return soon from Nob, the city of many priests. While Saul is sitting under the tamarisk tree with his officials, Doeg will tell him that David received help from Ahimelech. Ahimelech knew nothing of David's flight from Saul and was guilty of no disloyalty. Saul will send for Ahimelech and his fellow priests. Despite their innocence, Saul will command that they be killed. His soldiers will fear to obey. But Doeg will obey and kill eighty-five priests. He will then go to Nob and kill all the men, women, and children and even the cattle, donkeys, and sheep. Only Abiathar, a son of Ahimelech, will escape and flee to join David. Let this be your signal that you also must flee.

It would not be wise to discuss your plans with anyone. Confide in no one, except in Ittai, Shimon's fearsome friend. He will be a great and mighty warrior for David in the future. When you see Ittai make his move, tarry no longer!

You may feel it your duty to warn Ahimelech or try to prevent the murder of the priests. Do not do this! These events must be allowed to happen. From where I am in the future, the written words of God state they did happen. If you interfere, you will gain nothing, but will put yourselves in needless danger.

I ask one favor. After David's kingdom is established and there is peace, send me a message. My mind will not rest until I know you heeded my warning and escaped. My messenger, Nathaniel, has a strong metal container and special paper and writing tools that will last for millennia if buried in a safe place. In a written message I will explain how to close the container properly and instruct you where to bury it. Alison and I will find and read your message and, if all is well, will rejoice that my beloved family lived through these dangerous times.

My last message will speak of matters more important than escaping death.

Ben's face revealed his concern and hope. The screen went snowy, and Nate turned off the camcorder. Ben's family was not sure how to react to the ominous message that echoed what Ittai had just told them. They remained quiet to see what else Binyamin had in store for them.

Nate took the time capsule out of his sack and set it on the low table. It was like a giant bullet, about one cubit long, with an impossibly shiny silver surface. Nate slowly unscrewed the top, revealing several rolls of hard-surfaced paper, six pens containing permanent ink, a tube of sealant, and a set of directions translated by Ben into Hebrew. Then he read Ben's instructions:

> *Go to the highest point on Mt. Gilboa, the low mountain to the north in the land of Issachar, west of the Jordan River. Follow the river northward, turning west at Beth-Shan, and follow a small stream for about three hours. Local people will know the mountain as the place where King Saul lost his final battle.*
>
> *From the highest point, walk five hundred long steps in the direction of the high point of Mt. Moreh across the valley. If it is too rocky to dig, go another five hundred steps in the same direction and see if the soil can be excavated. Repeat this process until you find soil that can be excavated. Dig a hole four cubits deep. Place small stones at the bottom of the hole and put the metal container in its white sack at the bottom. Refill the hole and restore the surface to hide your work.*

Jokim rubbed his beard thoughtfully. "I cannot comprehend all that has happened to Binyamin. It is difficult for me to accept that these messages are real."

Shimon also was unsure. "Father, I know my brother, and that man whose image I see and whose writings I read – I do not doubt that he is my brother! But I am not prepared even on his word to run from my duties. I think of him only as a small boy."

Unimpressed by their gainsaying, Tirzah spoke. "Listen to me! You think I do not know my own son? These messages are from Yamin. Does not your heart go out to him? Do you not still love him as he loves us? He knows it will be hard to abandon our home, our friends, our duties, our very lives! He knows because he was torn away from his entire world and, after thirty years, still feels the loss as if it happened yesterday. He has counseled us to wait and test his words. If the awful events he predicts take place, will not our way be clear? Will we have any choice? We wait and test his words, but we must begin to prepare today. I know in my heart that God has sent us a deliverer, and we must not reject his message!" As Tirzah finished, her eyes shone as if she saw beyond the room and beyond her current peril.

Nate felt a shiver down his spine. This confirmed to him that his instincts to connect with Ben's family had been right. "Before we look at Binyamin's final message, he asked me to give you small gifts." Nate distributed brightly wrapped packages. Each contained a note of explanation.

Shimon's contained an Israeli Defense Forces knife with a leather-wrapped handle, riveted sheath, and an eight-inch dark carbon steel blade. Jokim's gift was a monocular, which Nate demonstrated on the roof, where they viewed the hills that surrounded the town and spied on Saul pacing on his roof. Tirzah's present was a fine gold chain holding a beautiful six-pointed gold Star of David, studded with small diamonds. An accompanying note explained the star was the symbol for their country in his time and appeared on their blue and white national flag.

Nate's mission was not quite over. "Can we listen to the last message from Binyamin?" he asked.

They gathered in front of the camcorder. Ben was sitting on the high escarpment where he had often gone to think. The camera panned the beautiful mountain views before it settled on Ben sitting on a rock near the precipice. The wind ruffled his dark hair.

Father, Mother, Brother, I speak to you one last time from an overlook I call my Window to Heaven. When I was grieving the loss of my family, I came here to think and pray. I never found answers to all my questions, but did find peace in my heart and hope for the future.

Our father Abraham was tested. God commanded him to sacrifice Isaac on Mt. Moriah, which is not far from Gibeah. Abraham obeyed, believing that God could raise up Isaac and fulfill the promise of many descendants. During the journey to the mountain, Isaac asked what sacrifice they would offer. Abraham assured him God would provide the sacrifice. And God did, at the last moment stopping Abraham's hand and revealing a ram with its horns stuck in a thicket.

The Law teaches that our sins separate us from God. The blood of animals covers our sins for a time, but the Law requires endless new sacrifices. As God told Abraham, I tell you with certainty from the truth of God's written words: God will provide the perfect sacrifice without spot or blemish that will take away the sins of all who believe.

I was an unruly child, as you all know very well! When I tried to be good, it did not last long. The harder I tried, the more I found that in my strength I could not keep the Laws or even obey my parents! But when I asked God for help, he changed my heart. God puts a conscience inside us and calls us to lead a life centered on love – love of God and love of other people. When we ask God for help to lead upright lives, He gives us this grace. If we ask for wisdom, He bestows it. And if we ask Him to take us to be with Him after death, He makes a place for us with Him.

I am not a priest or rabbi, so why do I tell you these things? Because I may never see you again in this life. Our only opportunity to be reunited is probably after death in the place God prepares for everyone who has faith in Him. Please ask for this eternal blessing!

When I was twelve years old and went out to a field, I fell through a tunnel into a new life. Had I fallen to my death, I do not know what would have become of me. God gave me many chances to come to Him, but His door does not remain open forever.

Thank you for your love and care. You gave me a solid beginning that carried me through the unusual challenges of my life. Never, never forget your little Yamin. He will carry you in his heart always. Goodbye for now. I hope to see you all in a new world.

Just before the picture went blank, Ben took out a handkerchief to wipe his eyes, and Alison came over to embrace him. Then it was over. As Nate turned off the camcorder, Tirzah stood and motioned for her family to come to her. They all embraced and quietly wept together. Nate thought of how much he yearned to be with his father again. Tirzah looked up and motioned for Nate to join them. It felt good to be included in their circle of love.

"Nathaniel," Tirzah said, "Binyamin is not here with us, but we ask you to take back to him our love and blessing."

"And assure him that his messages have touched our hearts very deeply," Jokim added.

Nate thought of the time and said, "Before I leave, Binyamin requests that we make pictures and messages from all of you to him and Alison." Nate began with photos of everyone with their gifts and then did several candid shots. After lunch, Nate took some photos of Gibeah from the roof, including Saul's small palace, and then recorded the video messages in the sunny courtyard.

Nate spent a memorable day. He told his hosts everything he knew about Alison and Ben and their lives in California. He also told them more about his life and dreams and about his first trip when he was shot by the arrow. He explained what he knew of modern Israel and the continuing conflicts with the Philistines. Ben's family told Nate stories of their history and of Ben's childhood. Nate realized how similar Ben's family was to Ben himself – intelligent, caring, curious, and kind. He was gratified they were starting to adjust to Ben's disappearance.

Jokim left the room, returning soon with several objects. "Nathaniel, will you have space in your sack for these? This is Binyamin's arrowhead collection. He will want to have it. And here is a shofar, a ram's horn, which belonged to Binyamin's grandfather who gave him his dying blessing. Jokim demonstrated its haunting sound.

Shimon added his old dagger, which he no longer needed. "My knife is not equal to the one my brother sent to me, but so far in the future I think it may be of interest to many people."

Tirzah wanted to give a gift to Alison. "Here, Nathaniel. This is for Alison from me." She handed him the intricately designed silver and ivory pin she had been wearing.

"Have you determined what you will tell everyone about Binyamin's absence?" he asked.

"No," Jokim replied. "We have not solved this problem. People will assume Binyamin returned from his morning in the field. We don't know how to explain his absence."

"Yes," Shimon agreed. "People might even think Binyamin has defected to David's side. Then we would be under suspicion."

Nate appreciated their dilemma and thought of the problems of explaining Yachay to the people of Anchorage. "Why don't you tell them the truth?"

"They would think we have lost our minds!" Shimon objected.

"Here is an idea," Jokim stated. "After Nathaniel is gone, we simply will tell people he was sent by Binyamin to return Jonathan's property. We will say Nathaniel was a strange boy – please pardon me, but this is true, Nathaniel – who said Binyamin had disappeared into a secret tunnel into the distant future. We will not say whether we believed the boy, but will have no other explanation. They will think our visitor was crazy or a liar. They will sympathize with us. There will be some talk and even some mourning, but after we leave what will it matter?"

"So, husband, we are leaving?" Tirzah asked.

"Well, we will await the outcomes of the events Binyamin predicted," Jokim replied. "But I will not be surprised if they happen exactly as he states. I never liked Doeg and believe he is capable of murder if he thought it would win the King's favor."

Nate failed to stifle a yawn. "I may leave very early while you are sleeping. You have been very kind to me. I will always remember you."

After last words of encouragement and embraces, Nate went up to the roof with

Shimon, bringing along his large sack. They arranged their beds, checking the sky for any sign of a storm. He promised not to bore Shimon with more science lectures. Settling under the heavy wool blankets, he tried to banish foreboding thoughts of re-entering the time tunnel. Instead he thought of Kawsay, wondering what she would be like at age sixteen. He smiled to himself.

Shimon asked quietly, "Why did God choose you for this mission back through time?"

Nate had wondered about that too. "I am not sure. Maybe He chose me because I am small and I speak the Hebrew language. Perhaps because I have studied the history of God's people, He knew I would be excited to make this journey."

"There may be another reason, Nathaniel," Shimon suggested. "God looked at your heart and found you to be a courageous and faithful servant. I also observe that you have wisdom and maturity that is rare is so young a man."

"Thank you, Shimon," Nate responded. *That compliment feels very encouraging coming from someone like Shimon.* "I do not doubt that God has important missions for you too, including helping your parents during these dangerous times."

They were quiet, but continued to stare upward. After a few minutes, a shooting star streaked across the heavens toward the eastern horizon. "I know," Shimon stated. "It is just a big rock from a place beyond the sky." Shimon paused. "Nathaniel, you must tell my little brother I will meet him out there beyond the sky!"

"I'll be there too," Nate added with a smile. Shimon and Nate looked at each other in the dim light and clasped hands as if to seal the promise.

Nate enjoyed another deep sleep, free of troubling dreams. As the eastern sky began to show light, he was jarred awake by an unearthly howling sound. He heard another howl that made the hair on the back of his neck stand up. *I wonder if that is Zevél impersonating a wild animal. I'd better be going.* Shimon stirred, but did not seem to wake. Nate hastily put on his sandals, rose quietly, and hoisted his sack. He stepped carefully to the railing and swung his feet over onto the top of the stairs. He looked back at Shimon. *Ben has a great brother and family. I wish he could have made this trip!*

Nate made his way to the dark, quiet street, past the well, and to the main gate. He thought he heard footsteps behind him. But, when he looked back, no one was there. He slowly slid the massive latch, opened the creaky wooden barrier, slipped out, and hurried on his way. The air was still and moist. The sound of his footsteps seemed exaggerated. In a few minutes, as he passed a small grove of olive trees, he heard his name spoken quietly but insistently.

"Nathaniel." Nate froze in his tracks, but quickly relaxed and exhaled as Zevél stepped out into view. "So you heard my call?" Zevél asked, his head tilted to the side.

"I'm sure half the people of Gibeah heard it!" Nate replied in a scolding whisper.

"Yes, but only you would be motivated to leave the protection of the city at such a sound," the wolf observed, changing to English.

"I hope you're right, Zevél. I don't think I was followed," Nate said, still whispering. "I didn't know that you could howl like a wolf."

"Actually, Nathaniel, that is one kind of speech I did not have to learn," Zevél said, showing his teeth with an impressive grin. "Come, we must move quickly."

Nate moved as fast as he could, somewhat hampered by his sack. They reached the wheat field without seeing a soul and turned down the ridgeline toward the cave opening. "How much time do I have?" Nate asked, a bit out of breath.

"You need not act in haste, but neither should you delay," was the typically cryptic reply.

Nate removed a small flashlight from his sack and entered the cave to retrieve his waterproof backpack. He stepped back out into the pre-dawn light with his pack. The flashlight beam revealed that one side was covered with a layer of silver fur. "You must be shedding!" he declared.

"The Peruvian jungle was not to my liking," Zevél replied, somewhat embarrassed. "I prefer cooler climates."

"Well, I can't promise it will be cool in the Caribbean." There was just enough light to work by. He removed what he needed for the return trip, including a wetsuit Ben had prescribed in case he was left in the ocean for more than a few minutes. He also retrieved the radio locator that would signal his location, flipped it on, placed it in a sealed box, and slid it into a side pocket of the pack. He struggled into the wetsuit. Nate efficiently stowed the contents of his sack, carefully securing the delicate items and inserting the electronic gear and recordings into waterproof bags for an extra measure of safety. He inflated the flotation chambers on the backpack and sealed it up. "There. I think I'm ready."

"I think you are ready too, my friend," Zevél agreed. "That is why I am not making the journey with you."

"Oh, you just don't want to get wet," Nate joked.

"That is true. I normally do not swim in the ocean far from the shore," the wolf agreed. "But that is not the reason you will travel alone. While your missions through time have aided many people, remember God provides good works for you to perform for your benefit as well."

"He does? For *my* benefit?" Nate asked.

"Nathaniel," the wolf urged, "think how much you have grown in character and understanding since you were in the lightning storm. Have your experiences not prepared you for even greater missions in the future?"

Nate could not disagree, but was not eager to brave the tunnel alone. "Are you sure I'm ready to solo? The first times were accidents. Now I'm stepping into the tunnel deliberately."

"Yes, stepping in faith. If you keep your mind focused on God and do not doubt, you will do well. If you take your eyes off God or let your doubts control you, you may not arrive as you should," Zevél admonished him. "Can you remember that?"

"I was hoping all I needed to remember was to grab your fur and hold my breath!" Nate replied. "So you're saying I only need to hold onto God and believe?"

"This has worked for me so many times I have lost count," Zevél encouraged him.

Before Nate could extend their discussion, they were distracted by the sound of gravel cascading down the cliff from above. Zevél's piercing eyes immediately saw a person crouched on an outcropping not twenty feet above them. "Come down here!" commanded

Zevél. The figure did not move until the command was pronounced more menacingly a second time.

Nate watched the figure deftly clamber down the cliff face, jumping the last six feet to the ground. The person, dressed in a dark hooded cloak, cautiously approached them. As the hood was lowered, Nate gaped in recognition. "Shimon! What are you doing here?"

Shimon was totally distracted by Nate's companion. Zevél assumed his least threatening pose, retreating and sitting. Shimon calmed himself. "Nathaniel, I followed you to protect you. I wanted to ensure that the beginning of your return journey was successful." He paused, eyeing Nate's unusual companion. "I do not know if I can protect you from a wolf of this size."

"Shimon, it was good of you watch over me, but I don't need protection. I already have a great bodyguard!" Nate smiled. "This large wolf knows Binyamin and has assisted me in my travels. Since you believed your brother's messages, perhaps you can accept that this wolf, whose name is Zevél, also travels the time tunnels and speaks many languages."

Zevél cleared his throat. "Shimon, Binyamin told me all about you after he first traveled to his future." He paused to let Shimon adjust to the experience of a talking wolf. "He spoke of you with admiration. Many times he wanted to attempt to return here, but I discouraged him from doing so because he did not have a conviction in his heart that God had ordained the trip." Zevél paused again. "Shimon, did you not have another reason for following us here? Are you not curious about the location of the tunnel and tempted to travel to another time?"

Shimon was a bit stunned that the wolf had read his mind. "How do know my thoughts?"

"I know Binyamin. You are like him, having an inquisitive mind and a boundless sense of adventure," Zevél replied. "I will explain to you the dangers of the tunnels and the conditions that must precede any voluntary attempts to use them. With Binyamin gone, your family needs you here at this time. But our discussion must be deferred for the moment." Turning to Nate, he continued, "Nathaniel, your time of departure is at hand."

Nate had been engrossed in Shimon's discussion with the wolf. His pulse quickened as he thought of what lay ahead. He donned his pack and strapped it on tightly. Nate stepped over to Shimon. "I must look very funny dressed like this!"

"Yes," Shimon agreed. "Everything about you is strange, yet I feel we are connected. May God protect you!" He embraced Nate and stepped back. "May I watch as you depart?"

Nate looked at Zevél, who nodded. Nate flipped on the flashlight and led them down into the cave to the mysterious opening that connected to both known and unknown places. Nate reached out and put his hand through what appeared to be a rock wall, though it shimmered as if alive. *I guess there's no way to wait any longer,* Nate thought. *The only reason I can do this is that there is no other way to get my life back together. My life is with my father and with my new friends, especially Kawsay. They are waiting for me.* He turned to look at Shimon, who looked at Nate as he would a person about to jump off a cliff, and then at Zevél, who nodded slowly.

"We will meet again, Nathaniel," said the great wolf with confidence, encouraging Nate.

"I'll hold you to that, Zevél!" Nate responded jauntily. He hyperventilated three times, took an enormous breath, looked straight ahead, and stepped through the shimmering opening. There was a rushing sound. Then the cave was silent except for the sound of breathing.

Shimon turned to his unusual companion and again felt threatened. The wolf was huge. Shimon noticed the shining flashlight Nate had left on the cave floor by the tunnel opening. He picked it up, shining it around the interior in search of an exit. The beam came to rest on Zevél's enormous face, causing his cold blue eyes to narrow. Shimon drew in a breath.

"Shimon, please. That hurts my eyes!" the wolf protested. "Please use the light to guide us outside." Zevél followed Shimon out of the cave. Zevél carefully looked around to insure they were still alone. "I must depart soon. Now that you know the location of the tunnel, I must inform you more fully of its dangers and the conditions that must precede its use."

Shimon was curious, though after watching Nathaniel disappear into thin air, he was no longer tempted to follow.

EXCEEDING OUR HOPES AND PRAYERS

SEPTEMBER 28 – PRESENT YEAR
MT. GILBOA, ISRAEL

TO KNOW YOU ARE SAFE
THAT YOU HEEDED MY WARNINGS
WHAT MORE COULD I ASK?

The drive in the blue rental sedan from the Tel Aviv airport to the parking lot near the summit of Mt. Gilboa took about ninety minutes. Ben and Alison had learned that nothing in Israel is ever far away. Not even the past. In a land punctuated with archeological excavations, time is measured in millennia. They also had learned that "Mount" often really meant "Hill" by Sierra standards. The summit, though only 1,700 feet above sea level, afforded pleasing vistas of the patchwork of fields and orchards in the Jezreel Valley and of Mt. Moreh beyond. Below to the east was the Jordan River. Several settlements of varied sizes dotted the landscape.

Alison and Ben decided to handle this particular "dig" by themselves, aided only by a shovel and a new metal detector that had traveled as their third piece of luggage. They were fatigued from their overnight flight, but could not rest until they at least tried to find the capsule. Ben had consciously avoided thinking about the odds of finding it. Parking at the picnic area near the summit, they removed the metal detector, quickly assembling and testing it. They looked at each other slyly, like partners in crime. They felt conspicuous and a little uneasy, knowing Israel strictly controlled digging for artifacts. They quickly positioned themselves as close to the summit as the military fencing would allow on the side facing Mt. Moreh. They moved northwest until they were about 500 paces below the summit.

"Let's check our alignment and mark off a search area," Ben suggested.

Alison donned the earphones and adjusted the detector's settings. She combed the area, listening carefully. Nothing. Not even a false alarm. She gave Ben a disappointed look. "The ground is very rocky here. I don't think this is where they buried it."

Taking their bearing again, they moved another 500 paces down the slope, which grew steeper. Ben tested the soil with his shovel. "This looks more promising."

Alison began the search, going at a slower pace. "Ben, I have something here."

"Let's see what's down there," Ben said.

Before he could turn more than a few shovels, they heard footsteps approaching from above. It was a man dressed in a khaki shirt and green slacks that looked a bit like a uniform. He carried a dirty white bag in one hand and held a cell phone to his ear with the other. As he approached, they observed his salt-and-pepper wavy hair and weathered complexion. He appeared to be in his early sixties and very fit for his age. He was clean-shaven and wore metal-framed glasses. He stopped in front of them, silhouetted by the sun. "Yes, I found them," he said, finishing his call. Flipping the phone shut, he inquired, "Dr. Hunter?"

"Yes?" Alison and Ben answered simultaneously.

"Ah, I am very pleased to find you," he continued in flawless Hebrew. He reached into the sack and pulled out a long, shiny object they could not help but recognize. "Might you be looking for this?" He held it out to them.

Ben was too stunned to react. He looked at Alison for reassurance. She nodded at him. "Um, well, perhaps," Ben stammered. "Let me see." He took what appeared to be, except for a few scratches, the same time capsule Nate had taken into the time tunnel just over a week ago. He and Alison were thinking fast. "Maybe. May I open it?"

"You will find it empty," the man replied.

Nevertheless, Ben unscrewed the top and looked inside. It was indeed empty. Alison took the lid and inspected it closely. "Look, Ben. It looks like it was never properly sealed shut."

Ben furrowed his brows. "You're right." Turning to the man he continued, "We are looking for a time capsule like this. Where did you find it? Where are the contents?"

"I did not find it," he replied. "It was given to me many years ago, and I have been waiting to return it to you."

Alison tried to make sense of this. "I don't understand. *Who* gave it to you?"

Ben had been staring at the man, wondering where he had met him before. "Are you with the Israel Antiquities Authority? We are not performing any unauthorized excavation." They knew the IAA's jurisdiction extended over all archeological matters in the country. Alison and Ben had often been to the IAA's headquarters in the magnificent old limestone Rockefeller Museum located outside the old wall of Jerusalem both to examine the collections and to deal with permits for their site work.

"Yes, I am with the IAA, and we have been working on your case for many years," the man replied with a quizzical smile.

"Our case?" Alison asked with concern.

"Yes," he replied, nodding. "Oh, do not be concerned. You are not in any trouble. As you know, the capsule is not an ancient relic but of recent American manufacture. I have been waiting a long time to talk with you about it."

"What do you mean wait?" Ben asked, recalling how they had purchased it only two weeks ago.

"We had no choice," the man replied. "We did not want to disturb any important events in your life. We waited until you came to look for the capsule. We are aware that the capsule was brought by a friend of yours to a time in history near the end of the reign of King Saul."

Ben could not believe his ears. "Perhaps you can appreciate how important it is to us to learn how you came to possess this capsule. We are very concerned about the safety of the young man who transported it for us and the outcome of his mission."

"Of course. I understand," the man responded sympathetically. "I cannot tell you very much about the young man. I do not know where he is at this moment, but I can report his mission was a success." The man stared intently at Ben as if looking for something behind his eyes. Then he saw a light go on, and he nodded. "Ah, Binyamin, it has been a very long time, has it not?"

Alison looked at one man, then the other, and asked in English, "Ben, do you know this guy?"

Ben asked just above a whisper, "Father?"

"Of course! Who else? Oh, that's right. You have never seen me without my beard – and with these glasses!" Jokim answered with a hearty laugh. He stepped forward toward Ben, who was still immobilized by shock, and kissed him on the cheek, giving him a great bear hug. "I have waited too long to greet you."

The two men found themselves crying with joy. Ben was overcome with emotion. He was again twelve years old and felt like a lost boy who had been found.

After a moment, Jokim let his son go and stepped back. He wiped his eyes with a handkerchief and turned his attention to Alison. "And this is my daughter, Alison. You are more beautiful in person than in your photographs!"

Alison was not much better than Ben at finding words. "You are Ben's *father*?"

"Yes, though I have neglected my parental duties for many years!" Jokim said, flashing a smile and giving her a kiss on the cheek and a brief hug. "I have a lot of explaining to do and much news to give you."

Ben continued to stare with disbelief. "Father, please. Do not keep me in suspense. What are you doing here? How long have you been here? Where are Mother and Shimon? Are they all right?"

Jokim held up his hands to curtail Ben's stream of questions. "Yes, yes, Binyamin. We are all very well. We have lived here about twenty years. Our home is in the Pisgat Ze'ev neighborhood, not far from our old home in Gibeah. Your mother, brother, and his wife are waiting for us there. They wanted to come here to meet you, but I assured them I would bring you directly. A colleague came here with me and can return the staff car. May I ride with you?"

Alison handed Ben the time capsule lid. Ben looked at his father questioningly.

"Oh, we never buried the capsule and never wrote any letters," Jokim explained. "It spent the last twenty years in my bedroom closet. I preferred to report our activities to both of you in person. I hope you do not mind"

"Mind!" Ben protested. "Father, you have been here twenty years and did not let me know?"

"Believe me. We wanted to!" Jokim said, lifting up his hands. "But we were persuaded that we must wait and not dissuade you from sending your young friend, Nathaniel, to warn us. You of all people should appreciate the need to not disturb such important events. If you knew we were already here, would you have sent your messenger to us, which resulted in our journey to this time?" Ben's and Alison's eyes showed the light of understanding. "Ah, I see you appreciate the problem we faced. Of course the wait was difficult for us. We regret the strain it has caused, but what could we do?"

"How did you know we would be here looking for the capsule today?" Alison asked.

"Our government contacts let us know when you were scheduled to arrive," Jokim explained. "It is an amusing story. We arrived here twenty years ago, but did not know exactly when you had first arrived as a young boy or from what year Nathaniel had come to us. And we did not know your full name or where to look for you. A few years after we arrived here, just by chance, I found a paper in the bottcm of the box holding my monocular you had sent with Nathaniel. It was a packing slip from the company that sold you the instrument containing your address, full name, and date of purchase, which was earlier this month. We expected you to come looking for the capsule soon after that date." Jokim shrugged and smiled. "By the way, we liked your family name, so we adopted it. Now I am Jokim Hunter!" He looked at his watch. "Come, we must not keep your mother waiting."

Jokim took Alison on his arm and started up the slope. Ben replaced the dirt, gathered the equipment, and followed. Back at the parking lot, Jokim introduced them to his colleague, Nuri Zahavi. "Nuri is one of the few IAA people who is aware of my origins."

Nuri smiled and said, "We have been so fortunate to have Tirzah and Jokim as staff members. They have been invaluable in identifying and classifying artifacts and explaining life in their time period. Were their story not so incredible and requiring secrecy, I think they would be national heroes!"

They drove down the mountain toward Bet Shean, an ancient town with a history pre-dating the Hebrews. Then they turned south toward Jerusalem. Jokim insisted they hold their questions until the family was together. Instead, he asked Alison all about her family and her early years. He was delighted to learn the details of how she and Ben met while working in Israel a few years earlier. "We were so sorry that we could not attend your wedding. We could not even send a gift!"

"Meeting you here today is the greatest gift we could imagine!" Alison assured him.

In less than two hours, they arrived at the Hunter residence, a small two-story house similar in color to their former Gibeah home. Before Ben could turn off the engine, his family swarmed out the front door to greet them – Tirzah, followed by Shimon and his wife, who carried a small boy in her arms.

Ben's mother embraced him before he could shut the car door. "Yamin! My little boy! This is the happiest day of my life. We have waited so long for this; you have no idea!" Tirzah held her boy at arm's length to look him over. She wore a white skirt and blue blouse. Her graying hair was held back by a blue headband. She wore her Star of David necklace prominently around her neck. "Yes, you look like you did in those beautiful videos that Nathaniel brought to us. But you look too thin. We will begin to fix that tonight. Now, please introduce me to my new daughter who is the most beautiful woman in America."

Alison stepped forward, beaming. "It is such a wonderful surprise to meet you. Never in my dreams did I expect to see you in this life."

Tirzah embraced her warmly. "Ah, my Alison. I feel I already know you. Welcome to our home."

"So, when is my turn?" a man's voice asked.

Ben turned to his big brother who wore a knitted green golf shirt and sharply creased gray slacks. Ben embraced him strongly. "Shimon, somehow I think you are behind all this. You have a lot to answer for!" Ben joked. "I think we are about the same size, my big brother."

"Yamin, it is most interesting," Shimon observed. "You have been here thirty years, but I arrived only twenty years ago. So, my little brother is now several years older than me.

Maybe it is time I gave you some respect."

The greetings continued. Alison and Ben learned that Shimon had met his wife, Sarit, while they attended Hebrew University. They had a common interest in science – Sarit in biology and chemistry and Shimon in astrophysics. Ben was surprised to learn that Jonathan's shield bearer had not followed a military career.

"It was your young friend, Nathaniel, who first stimulated my interest in the heavens," Shimon explained. "His first night in Gibeah, as we camped on the roof on a beautifully clear night, he told me everything he knew about planets, stars, meteors, comets, black holes, and space telescopes. He stopped after I finally fell asleep!" Alison and Ben were very impressed that Shimon had continued following this passion, eventually becoming Dr. Hunter, and that he was now associated with the Racah Institute of Physics in its Astrophysics and Relativity Group.

Alison and Ben learned that Shimon and Sarit married after graduation. Little Jonathan had just celebrated his third birthday, and a second child was due in January. "Dear, is this another sign for us to get serious about starting our own family?" Alison asked Ben with a smile.

Tirzah began ushering them inside for dinner. They filled all the places at the small dining table, and Jokim asked a blessing. While their hands were yet joined, he remarked, "Now that we have bridged the years, let us often bridge the miles!"

Alison assured them she and Ben would be back in the summer for at least six weeks and hoped to get together often.

Shimon told of his one visit to America for a symposium at Cal Tech in Pasadena and how difficult it was not to drive up and spy on his brother while he was there. "I even thought about setting up a webcam outside your house to keep tabs on you," Shimon admitted.

Alison and Ben told the family about their lives in California and also related tales of Kawsay's and Yachay's adventures. They floated the idea of a family reunion at the end of the summer in the Sierras. Ben remarked, "Seeing my family around the table here this evening, I finally understand why it was important I never try to return to my original home through the time tunnel."

"This is a meal we always will remember!" Jokim declared. "We have much more to tell you about our adventure." They moved to the living room. Jonathan alternated between laps and toys, but kept looking quizzically at his new aunt and uncle.

Tirzah related how Nate arrived unexpectedly and introduced himself as a friend of Binyamin. Jokim and Shimon added their pieces to the story. Alison and Ben listened with fascination.

Shimon told how he followed Nate to the cave, was discovered, watched him disappear into the tunnel, and then talked to Zevél. "Once I adjusted to his imposing appearance, he proved to be a very interesting character. I never met anyone who answered my many questions by just asking me questions! But he vouched for the authenticity of Nate's messages and your warnings and provided me a primer on the use of the tunnels. I figured he wouldn't give me all that information unless he thought I might need it in the future. He finally sent me home with the admonition to await the coming of the events you had predicted would soon occur."

"We are relieved to hear Nate got away, but why didn't Zevél go with him?" Alison asked, showing great anxiety.

"The wolf told Nathaniel he was ready to travel on his own," Shimon reported.

"We were skeptical at first of Shimon's tale of the wolf," Tirzah related. "We tried to go about our lives as if nothing had happened. But you know Gibeah – there are no secrets. Everyone wanted to know where you were. We stuck to our plan to just tell them the incredible truth. Our neighbors insisted we conduct a search, but of course it availed nothing."

"Except for questions about some giant dog prints in the dust!" Jokim interjected. "We endured a parade of people expressing sympathy about our loss. I think they were afraid if they started official mourning, you might suddenly return and make them look foolish!"

"In about two weeks, we ceased being the center of attention because of the turmoil at the palace over David's escape," Shimon said. "There was a crescendo of rumors. Saul's temper was ready to explode. He questioned everyone's loyalty and had spies everywhere to catch anyone trying to escape and join his rival."

Jokim continued the story. "I was with the flocks when the slaughter of Ahimelech and the other priests took place. From the reports I heard, I don't think the Biblical account highlights its grisly reality. I knew Doeg was a snake. I had worked for him for many years, but could not have anticipated his brutality. Not even the King's hardened soldiers would lift a hand against the innocent priests.

"That night we huddled indoors," Tirzah explained. "People were wondering if a divided kingdom could stand. We knew it would not."

"We finished preparing for our escape," Jokim continued. "We knew that we would need to travel light. It was very difficult to leave our family treasures, but we could not carry them. So we buried our valuables under the fire pit where vandals would be unlikely to look."

"But we took the time capsule," Shimon added. "We wanted to send you our message once we were safe. The next morning, Ittai and his father came early to our house and invited us to leave with them that night. Ittai had encountered young Abiathar, Ahimelech's son, who was the only priest to survive. Abiathar was terrified that Ittai would turn him in. Ittai had to calm him down and assure him that he meant no harm. Then Abiathar told Ittai that David was hiding in the caves at Adullam, but may have to keep moving to be safe. Abiathar had an ephod and planned to offer his priestly services to David. He urged Ittai to go with him. Of course, Ittai would not leave without his family, but promised to follow as soon as possible."

"So, did you escape with Ittai's family?" Ben asked, enthralled by the account.

"God works in unexpected ways, Yamin," Tirzah replied. "We had decided to go with Ittai's family. That evening, however, we all became very ill with some kind of food poisoning. When it was time to depart, I could barely move at all, so we sent our friends away. Two days passed before we felt strong enough to go anywhere. Soon there were rumors that David was at Keilah, and Saul planned to trap him there. The King was wroth that Ittai, one of his best soldiers, had defected. Saul doubled his spies and threats. We had to lie low until a better time."

"A few days later we heard David had fled Keilah for the wilderness of Ziph," Shimon explained. "Saul and Jonathan were preparing to go in search of him. I had orders to go along, but did not want to leave our parents. I asked Jonathan what he would do if he encountered David in a battle. He gave me a pained look and told me he had made a covenant with David. I think Jonathan believed David would eventually become king and would make him second in charge."

"So what did you all do?" Alison inquired.

"God made a way of escape," Jokim stated with conviction.

"It was suddenly clear to me," Tirzah agreed, smiling radiantly. "Yamin, God had sent you ahead to prepare the way to our future. What was there for us at home? Years of danger and strife? Saul's Kingdom was ending and with it the life we knew. People would always be suspicious of anyone from Gibeah. So I suggested escaping through the tunnel."

"Father and I realized at once she was right," Shimon asserted. "I remembered what Zevél had told to me about the tunnel, especially the danger if a person enters without God's invitation. We prayed earnestly for an entire afternoon and waited for an answer."

"We all had the same strong feeling and conviction in our hearts that we belonged in another place or time," Jokim said, his eyes shining. "Tirzah remembered a recent dream in which she had seen a star that looked like her necklace on a blue and white flag. Your message accompanying the necklace said a flag like this was used by our people in your time."

Tirzah ran her fingers through her hair and shuddered. "Yet the entire idea frightened us. Could we stake our lives on the words of young Nathaniel and a talking wolf? Then Shimon was ordered to prepare for a morning departure with the army. It was our last chance to get away."

"So you left that night?" Ben asked.

"Yes," Shimon answered. "Thankfully, Saul's men were busy preparing to leave and were not on high alert. After midnight, we slipped out a small gate on the east side of the wall, the side closest to your wheat field and cave. Nearby trees and rock outcroppings gave us cover until we were some distance away. Our luck held most of the way."

Alison cocked her head. "Most of the way?"

"We got a little careless and were seen by a small group of soldiers just as we approached the wheat field. We ran for the cave," Jokim explained. "We were carrying some of our belongings and could not outrun them. They were gaining on us. Shimon did not see the cave entrance, and we ran right past it."

Tirzah picked up the narrative. "Then we heard a terrible snarling sound. It made my heart stop! Shimon stopped us, and we turned in time to see a huge dark form chasing the soldiers back toward the road. They were yelling in panic." She now could laugh about it.

"I knew immediately it was Zevél," Shimon clarified. "Though even I was amazed at his ferocity, since he told me he was a vegetarian!"

"We heard about his occasional use of intimidation tactics," Alison said. "Apparently he held Kawsay's entire village at bay by expressing himself that way."

"That doesn't surprise me," Jokim said chuckling. "When he emerged out of the darkness with his shimmering coat, I stood frozen to the spot. He quietly trotted back and stopped in front of us, looked at Shimon, and chided him for not making proper introductions!"

"Well, I apologized for my poor manners," Shimon said, "but then quickly explained our situation. He said he understood, but pressed us to explain why we presumed to use the tunnel. I was tempted to tell him that it wasn't *his* tunnel, and he should help us rather than stand in our way or waste time talking. But I realized he was just testing us before deciding whether to aid our escape in this way. We explained we had prayed and were certain this was the right thing to do."

Tirzah added, "Then he put us at ease by telling us he had expected this encounter. He explained he had seen us a number of times in the future visiting at Binyamin's house in the mountains, though we were much older then!"

"We hope you can visit us soon," Alison said, smiling. "Seems you have no choice!"

"It also seems that Zevél was destined to help you," Ben observed.

"I think you're right," Shimon agreed. "Zevél said God will bring us to the right place and time. I told him we were not interested in going to another *place*, just to a time when we might find you and Alison. Of course, at that time, I did not yet know that Sarit was in my future."

Sarit smiled. "I remember when I was twelve years old asking my mother if she thought I would ever find the right man. Maybe that was the very day Shimon arrived."

"There was little preparation for the journey," Jokim explained. "We felt our way down into the cave and wrapped our arms around Zevél. He told us to take deep breaths and not lose our grip. Then he just gently stepped through the wall."

"Part way into our journey, we seemed to decelerate to a stop and then immediately accelerate in the opposite direction," Shimon elaborated. "Next thing we knew, we made an unceremonious stop and found ourselves sprawled on a rocky floor."

Jokim added, "Thankfully, we only had a few scrapes and had all our belongings. We made our way up and out of the cave and into blinding mid-day sunshine. The cave opening was in the side of a cliff like the one we had entered a few minutes earlier, but the wheat field was gone. A few feet in front of us was a metal fence with barbed wire on the top. I had never seen anything like it. Beyond the fence was an open area with weeds, and further away we saw a busy road and buildings. A jet flew low over us. We had no idea what to do next!"

"Zevél was not sure exactly what day or year it was," Shimon said, "but explained we had done a U-turn and come back to the same place, though much later in time. He gave us stern instructions to ask a policeman, whatever that was, to take us to Ze'ev Borot at the Immigration and Absorption Department of the Jewish Agency. He made us repeat it back to him so we'd remember. He said to tell Mr. Borot that Zevél had sent us and everything would be arranged. He also cautioned us not to try to contact you until after Nathaniel left on his mission to warn us."

"That's amazing," Ben observed. "Zevél seems to have thought things out carefully. And I had no idea Zevél had contacts in high places!"

"We're glad he did, or we may not have been allowed in the country," Jokim said. "It was surprisingly easy to find Mr. Borot. He asked us where we were from. We told him Gibeah. He looked at our clothing and luggage and rubbed his chin thoughtfully. He asked us who sent us. We dropped Zevél's name. He asked us what time period we were from and why we came. I explained the danger we were in back home due to political unrest. He seemed to understand. It made me wonder if he had met other travelers like us in his job, which he said was to help Jews from all over the world return and get settled in their homeland."

"He placed us in a kibbutz up in the Jezreel Valley in the shadow of Mt. Gilboa. How's that for a coincidence!" Tirzah laughed. "Mr. Borot insisted we not tell anyone where we were really from. Soon Jokim was tending sheep and goats, and I was getting acquainted with their kitchens and craft shops. Shimon enrolled in a school and received intense lessons. We quickly learned about life in modern Israel. We worked hard, which was nothing new to us."

"You already know I became quite a student," Shimon explained, "but Mother and Father were great. They took to modern life amazing well and soon learned to drive. A few years later they got a big break when the Israel Antiquities Authority made them a good offer."

"I think I missed something," Ben protested. "How did the IAA find you?"

"Sorry, we left that out," Jokim apologized. "About a year after we arrived, Mr. Borot, Zevél's friend who first helped us, stopped by to see how we were doing. We told him about our desire to find you. We didn't know where or exactly *when* you lived. We showed him your photos, letters, and gifts. That's when the packing slip fell out of the monocular box. He noted the name and address and also the date of the purchase. We told him how you had sent the gifts along with warnings that saved our lives. He insisted that we avoid contacting you until after you sent Nathaniel to us. We explained Zevél had told us the same thing, but persuaded him to help us find out about you. He made inquiries and found a graduate student with your name studying archeology in California. We've been following your career while keeping our distance ever since."

"Well, we did interfere somewhat," Tirzah interjected. Everyone turned to her. "We prayed often that God would preserve you until this day when we could meet again."

Alison blinked back tears. "We prayed about meeting you in this world or the next."

After a quiet moment passed, Jokim continued explaining their IAA connection. "We asked Mr. Borot to tell us about archeology. He told us of the extensive archeological activities that were ongoing in Israel. We wondered if we could help find sites, understand artifacts, and explain life in ancient times. Mr. Borot was reluctant to let our true origin become known beyond his small circle, but said he'd look into it. A few months later, he introduced us to the then-director of the IAA."

"The Director had dedicated his life to studying the past and couldn't believe we might know more about it than he did!" Tirzah recalled. "He asked if we could prove our claims."

"IAA had located historical Gibeah, including Saul's fortress," Shimon stated. "But we did not know how to persuade a doubter that we had once lived there."

"Then we remembered the stash of valuables we had buried in the courtyard under the fire pit," Jokim said. He went over to a display shelf and returned with a small stone sculpture and a metal candlestick. Handing them to Ben, he asked, "Remember these?"

Ben held them reverently. "These belonged to Mother's grandparents, if I remember right," Ben replied in astonishment. "You were able to find the family heirlooms? That's amazing."

"Not so amazing. Digging up relics runs in our family, Son," Jokim said, chuckling. "Saul's palace gave us an easy reference point! Having finally been convinced of our authenticity, the Director treated us with utmost respect and spent the rest of his career making sure nothing happened to us!"

"How many people know of your origins?" Alison asked.

"We are under orders to tell no one," Shimon explained. "We are all considered state secrets. Perhaps a dozen people know. Our files contain the documentation, but are off limits absent the Director's approval. For the same reason, we are not acquainted with any other displaced people like us, except I suspect there may be a few others."

"It's been the second most amazing day of my life," Ben said. "Maybe even equal to the day I went to California by way of Peru. But I confess I'm tired and jet-lagged."

"So let us bring in your luggage. I have our guest room ready," Tirzah said. "I am sorry, but our roof here is not designed for sleeping."

Alison and Ben extended their stay and did not leave for home until Friday. Shimon and Sarit were with them every evening, including one spent at their home. There was a lifetime of events to catch up on. Shimon gave them an English-language copy of a book on theoretical physics he co-authored. Ben promised to read it and pass it along to Nate when he returned."

As they were driving to the airport, Alison mused, "Ben, I wonder what we will tell your parents and my family. None of them know anything about your ancient roots, and now your Israeli family will be spending at least a week at the house next summer."

"Hmmm. Could we continue our policy of telling the truth?" Ben wondered. "We'll just tell them that we found my biological parents after all these years. It's a beautiful story."

"That's wonderful, dear. Then we'll tell them that one sunny day thirty years ago you were swimming in the Mediterranean. You were caught in an undertow, picked up by a submarine, and deposited in the Sierras where Helmut almost landed on you wearing a bird suit."

"Honey, you've been spending too much time with Herschel," Ben responded. "But I agree we'll need to work on some of the details!"

CHAPTER 30

ARROWS POINT NEW DIRECTIONS

LIKE LIVING ARROWS
WE TRAVELED THROUGH TIME FOR LOVE
AND FOUND OUR FUTURE.

As Nate stepped out of 1018 B.C. Gibeah and was sucked into the inky darkness, he repeated Zevél's parting words in his mind: "We will meet again, Nathaniel." *That certainly means I will survive and see Zevél again,* Nate told himself. He had filled his lungs with as much air as possible, knowing it would have to carry him through the tunnel and up to the surface of the ocean. He wondered how close the tunnel's portal was to the surface of the water and how far up he would need to swim. Nate's mind began swirling with questions. *How long will I need to keep holding my breath? What if Dad didn't make it back up to the surface after he jumped in behind me? What if something happened and Dad didn't take the sailing trip at all? What if ... Oh no, I am doing exactly what Zevél warned me against. Navigating the tunnels requires faith – walking with God. I'm not trusting God, I'm freaking out!* Nate felt himself decelerate. His lungs felt like they were about to explode. He felt frightened. *Help me God! You know I am weak. Help me trust You.* Nate tried to calm his thoughts and rest in faith. Then, he felt a wave of peace rush through his body. It seemed he was accelerating again. *That's funny.* He broke from the blackness into a world of dark turquoise. *I must be there!* As he shot toward what must be the surface, the water grew lighter and lighter. He broke the surface, gasping for air and coughing. The Sun was shining brightly. *Uh-oh. Where's the storm? Where's Dad?*

It was déjà vu. John was going through the motions with his son aboard the 32-foot *Second Chance,* just as Nate from the future had described in his forward diary. But now it *was* the future, and Nate's timeline would reconnect and again move forward. John would no longer need to follow the cryptic warnings jotted into a diary from his sixteen-year-old son's memory. John had charted his course naturally, by instinct, realizing he could not deliberately intersect with the lightning bolt. They just finished the discussion about brain cancer, which John had caught and treated early – and apparently cured. Then he saw the approaching storm Nate had warned him about in the forward diary, but it was the piercing crack of lightning striking the mast and shattering the cabin roof that shocked John fully into the reality of the present – the reality where he had to allow his son to catapult back in time.

John saw Nate disappear overboard, heard Nate's splash, then heard his own splash. John swam hard down toward his son, not knowing if he was aiming for the Nate who was falling into the tunnel or the Nate he was expecting, hoping, to shoot back to him from the past. It really did not matter; he just wanted his son. Nate's blond head faded into the gray-green darkness, then suddenly disappeared. But there was no returning Nate to greet him. John swam furiously, searching. He wanted to scream, but knew he would lose what little air he still held in his lungs. He needed a breath before continuing his search and kicked his way up to the surface. The sea was violently whipping him. Gasping for air, John caught sight of the *Second Chance* smoking in the distance. He dove back into the gray depths to search for Nate.

John knew something had gone wrong. He just felt it. He had worried about this moment for three long years. He and Ben must have spoken a hundred times. They covered everything. They had reserved the Zodiac rescue boat a year in advance. *Where is Ben? Is he picking up Nate's signal?* Ben had assured him Nate had a radio transmitter. He knew Nate had accomplished his mission in Gibeah, but no one had seen hide nor hair of Zevél since Nate supposedly stepped into the tunnel alone. *Where is Zevél, and why didn't he go with Nate? Where's Nate?* John looked up through the murky foam and saw what must be the Zodiac overhead. He swam toward the surface. He felt weary.

Ben had only been getting one signal on his receiver. He checked his watch – about 9:00 a.m. He could barely see a smoking sailboat off in the distance through the whipping mist. *It must be the Second Chance, but the signal was not coming from the boat. It was in front of them – no, below them.* "Stop!" Ben shouted to the Zodiac's Captain. "We must be over him." But Ben did not know if it was Nate or John below them.

Helmut had been watching the receiver too. "Whoever's down there has been down too long. I'm going in to look around," Helmut shouted over the crashing waves and rain.

"Then we'll have three missing people, Helmut," Ben shouted back. "Wait, the signal's getting closer."

A head popped out of the water on the port side of the bow.

"It's John!" Alison yelled, grabbing a life preserver and struggling toward the bow with Ben, Helmut, Marguerite, and Kawsay clambering after her. "John!" Alison's voice was drowned in the fury of the sea and wind.

When John broke the surface, he could see his friends hanging over the bow of the rescue boat. His face was being pelted by hard rain. He grasped at a life preserver and felt two sets of strong hands pulling him out of the water.

Kawsay wrapped a blanket around John and ushered him to a sheltered area of the swaying vessel. She, Alison, and Marguerite huddled close to John to shield him from the pounding storm. John's eyes betrayed that he had not seen Nate. Ben and Helmut resumed staring at the receiver waiting for Nate's signal to appear. But there was no signal.

Over the next few hours, the storm receded and the Sun reappeared, but there was no Nate. While waiting, they captured the damaged *Second Chance*, retrieved John's and Nate's belongings, and secured the sloop with a tow line. Helmut and Marguerite occupied themselves staring at the GPS, quietly discussing everything that could have gone wrong. Ben and John pondered whether Nate was there but in a different year. Alison and Kawsay stared out at the sparkling turquoise water, waiting, hoping, still optimistic.

By noon, Nate was officially three hours late. The Captain of the Zodiac, thinking they were waiting for a boy to "pop up" who had fallen off the sloop, was not optimistic anyone would survive swimming alone in the water for more than three hours. He wondered how long they would expect him to putter around in one spot. He also was intrigued about the whole plan to hurry to a certain nondescript location where a sloop would coincidentally need their help.

John was visibly anxious. Too much time had passed. He announced they were not going anywhere until they retrieved Nate, and he would make it worth everyone's time to sit there. He, Ben, Helmut, and Marguerite had a lively discussion of the odds of Nate being in another place or time or both. They also debated why Zevél had not escorted Nate safely to them. Alison and Kawsay defended Zevél saying the wolf would not have let Nate go alone if he was not certain Nate would make it. Kawsay said she was certain Nate would be here soon.

Alison looked around at the glum faces of her companions and stood up to get their attention. "When you think about how many years he had to travel through and then break that into hours, it's not reasonable to expect he would arrive exactly at the right moment."

"I think Alison is correct," Marguerite agreed. "If you break three thousand years into hours, you get, let's see, 3,000 years times 365 days per year times 24 hours per day. That's about …"

"26,280,000 hours," John interrupted.

"Wow! That was fast." Alison was impressed.

"I've been over it in my mind a thousand times," John said, looking at his watch. "It's 12:30."

"I feel him. I just know he's OK," Kawsay proclaimed into the breeze. She stood up and walked to the bow.

Nate was treading water and trying to spot the sailboat. The water was still choppy from the departed storm, and Nate rolled and bobbed in the swells. He just could not get a clear look around. At least the flotation chambers in his backpack seemed to counteract the pack's weight. It was not dragging him down, but it did not have much buoyancy either. He began to wonder if he was in the right time and place, but stopped himself and decided to trust God and not worry. He had placed his transmitter in a metal box in case it was sensitive to whatever forces may exist in the tunnel. While trying to stay afloat, Nate reached back with one hand, unzipped a side pocket on his pack, and removed the box. He was trying to pry open the box when the lid suddenly popped off. "Oops. Crud." Nate dropped the box containing his transmitter down into the water. He dove down after it.

"I got something! Captain! That way!" Ben was jumping up and down pointing behind them, trying to peer over the waves of the still choppy sea. He still could not see anything.

The Captain turned the Zodiac around and began moving slowly in the direction Ben was pointing.

"Wait a minute. I think he's below us," Ben warned, looking over the side. They stationed themselves around the deck, staring into the water.

"This is ridiculous. I'm going in," John announced. "Ben, where exactly is that signal?"

"Ah, starboard, and straight down."

John dove in, scanning the turquoise water through the bubbles he had created. *Wait a minute. There he is! Brown hair? Yeah, that's right. He died his hair.* John swam toward the figure.

Nate looked up and saw his dad. *Dad!* The two embraced and kicked toward the surface.

As John and Nate broke the surface, Kawsay, unable to contain her excitement, jumped into the water to greet Nate. Nate hugged his dad, looked into his eyes, and said, "I love you, Dad." He turned to Kawsay. "I love you too, Kawsay." The two embraced.

Once on board, Nate scanned the faces of his relieved rescuers. "How late am I?"

"Hours," John said, helping Nate out of his wetsuit and motioning for his son to sit between him and Kawsay.

All eyes were on Nate, waiting for an explanation. "I don't know what happened. I mean, I … Well, I started to worry when I was in the tunnel. Then I just decided to trust. But the spiritual wavering must have slowed me down. It all happened so fast. The last thing Zevél's said to me was, 'We will meet again, Nathaniel,' so he knew I would make it." Nate looked at Kawsay, who was staring intently at him. She definitely looked more grown up, more womanly, though still the athlete. Her face was slimmer and more beautiful. She appeared to be one or two inches taller. She even seemed more graceful.

The Zodiac accelerated for the marina with the *Second Chance* in tow. John used Helmut's phone to alert the Gulfstream they would be at the airport within an hour. As they slapped across the uneven water toward shore, a wave of relief settled over them. Nate and Kawsay managed a mouth to ear conversation through the noise. She told him how she had compared his two days in Gibeah to her thirty-three month wait. She explained how she divided her 990 days by his 48 hours so that each hour for him was about 21 days for her. "That is how I got through. Ben told me what he thought your schedule would be, and I pictured what you may be doing each hour you were away."

Nate was blown away that Kawsay had gone to all that mental effort to be with him in spirit. She was the Kawsay he loved when he left, but he was growing more impressed each new minute he spent with her. He whispered, "I love you," through the roar of the engine and the smacking of the boat's fabric on water. "We need to have lots of dates this summer, Kawsay."

Kawsay smiled back, remembering when he had first explained to her the concept of dating.

John settled up with the boat rental companies, insisting on more than covering the damage to the sloop. During the flight to California, Nate recounted the details of his Gibeah adventure. He was excited about bringing Ben his arrowhead collection, gifts from his parents and brother, and the video he had taken of Ben's family and their home. Ben seemed grateful, but not as thrilled as Nate had expected. What Nate did not know was that his Gibeah hosts had traveled from ancient Israel to the twentieth century after he left.

They arrived at the house early evening before sunset. The air was warm and dry. Nate stepped up to the Hunters' familiar porch followed closely by his dad, Kawsay, Ben, Alison, Helmut, and Marguerite. He heard Junior barking from inside the house. When he opened the front door, he was greeted by, "Surprise!" Lined up before him were Hershel, Grace, Kawsay's whole family, and Ben's family from Israel – Jokim, Tirzah, Shimon, and Shimon's wife and children.

What? Nate squeezed his eyes closed for a moment in disbelief. "What's going on? How you get here?" he exclaimed, reaching for Tirzah's outstretched arms. He hugged her, wondering if she was really there or would evaporate in his arms.

"We left Gibeah a few weeks after you," Tirzah responded to Nate's obvious confusion. "We arrived at the same place we left but about 3000 years later. Nate, we've been living in modern Israel for over twenty years waiting until Ben sent you back to warn us. We didn't want to contact Ben and mess up your rescue – or we may never have come." Nate noticed Jokim and Shimon nodding in agreement.

"You mean you guys were already here, in the present, while we were going through all the plans to go back to Gibeah and warn you?" Nate asked incredulously. Then he thought for a moment. "You know, maybe I should have seen this coming." He winked at Shimon, remembering his interest in time travel. "You have been living here since before I was born! And Shimon, three days ago you were close to my age. Now you're old – I mean all grown up."

Nate greeted and hugged each person in the group.

"Maybe we should migrate out to the deck," Helmut suggested.

"We set up chairs out there," Kusi offered, leading the way outside to tables already set with snacks, pitchers of iced tea and lemonade, and an oversized arrow-shaped cake.

Ben stood looking at the cake for a moment. "It's remarkable. I spent most of my life worrying about getting the three arrows back to Jonathan. I knew they were somehow returned – it was just a matter of when and by whom. But never in my wildest dreams could I have imagined getting my parents and brother out of Gibeah and having them in my life again. On top of that, neither could I have imagined who else the arrows would have brought into my life – Nate, John, Kawsay, and her extraordinary and delightful family. All of you are now Alison's and my family. I am happy my adoptive, twentieth century parents will be here tomorrow to join in this reunion celebration."

After everyone settled into chairs, Nate looked at Helmut and Marguerite. "I really want to hear everyone's news. I learned on the flight here that Helmut and Marguerite got married, and she went back to school and is now a Physician Assistant. She and Helmut are working together part-time in California and part-time in Alaska. You know, I wouldn't mind if you two wanted to take me on an Alaska hike one of these days."

Nate then turned his attention to Yachay. "Like I said a few days ago, Yachay, I cannot wait to hear what you have been up to for the past three years. I can already see that you removed your ear disks."

In perfect, though accented, English, Yachay said, "Yachay has been taking care of his sister, mother, and grandparents, of course. I remember you said the world needs more heroes, Nate, so I've been doing my part." Yachay's voice had become more full and resonant, and his face was more chiseled. Nate also noticed he was a good two inches taller and even more muscular.

"My brother still speaks of himself in the third person. And he is still a hero." Kawsay reached over and squeezed Yachay's arm, then continued, "Augusto thought Yachay would integrate better into the modern world without the ear disks, so Yachay had them removed by Dr. Salazar, who fixed my lip. Grandfather likes his disks and decided to keep them." Kawsay smiled broadly at Kusi.

Sumaq spoke up. "Yachay and Kawsay have mastered both English and Spanish languages. In fact, we all have worked on language and learned geography, history, science, and reading. After we moved to Peru, Augusto spent all his time teaching us. After a long day of learning, he rewarded us with what he called 'story time'. He read us many books on all subjects. Lately, he has been making each of us read out loud. When we are not learning, we have been teaching people in Peru about their ancestors and our ancient culture and ways. They listen to us because they know we are from a remote tribe and believe we have much ancient knowledge to give them. Mother teaches about our medicine; Father teaches about, well, everything. He has so much knowledge, and by teaching it he keeps it fresh in his mind." Sumaq looked at Kusi with admiration. "Everybody loves Kusi," she added.

"We are very proud of our daughter and grandchildren, Nate," Kusi said, wanting to take the spotlight off himself. "Kawsay and Yachay have been learning languages, but they also are preparing for great futures. Kawsay is still interested in ancient writing and archeology, and Yachay believes his next conquest is space."

"Space?" Nate questioned. "You mean like an astronaut?" Yachay nodded to Nate, somewhat shyly. "It's perfect!" Nate laughed, slapping his knee. "You are the most fearless person I have ever known, Yachay. I cannot think of a more perfect future for you than as an astronaut! I can see you exploring other planets with gusto!"

"Maybe you were intrigued by the Kodiak Island Launch Complex you visited, Yachay?" Marguerite asked, remembering Yachay's description of the missile launch he had experienced up close.

Yachay thought for a moment, reliving the experience of watching and feeling the pointed cylindrical structure rise off the ground dragging a cone of smoky fire below it and then suddenly shooting out of sight. "I think that did make an impression on me, Officer Cole, I mean Marguerite. By the way, I really appreciated how you were so kind to me when I could not speak for myself and was in a strange world." Yachay smiled broadly at Marguerite. "I hope you and Helmut will live a long, happy life together and have many adventures." Yachay then turned his attention back to Nate. "What will you do with your future, Nate?"

Nate took a drink of lemonade, looked at his dad, and thought for a moment. "I'm still interested in Biblical archeology and history. I could see becoming a professor like Ben. In fact, I could see Kawsay becoming a professor like Alison." Nate studied Kawsay for a response.

"I think Ben and Alison are our role models," Kawsay said, happy that Nate envisioned spending their futures together as professors. She was still feeling a combination of contentment and exhilaration now that she could finally interact with him again.

"I was hoping Kawsay and I could go to the same college and grad school," Nate said, looking a Kawsay.

"The Bay Area has some great universities," John contributed. "I hope you two will consider going to school close to here."

"That would be wonderful," Grace said. "You'd have a large support system, and Kawsay's family could come and stay in California for long visits."

"Our house is too big for us and could use some visitors," Herschel added, nodding at Kusi.

"How have *you* two been the past three years?" Nate looked at Herschel and Grace.

"Oh, we've been good," Herschel answered. "We haven't had to tell too many wild, yet true, stories lately. We did escort little Cindy Stevens and her family down to Peru once to see Yachay and his family. They gave Sumaq and Asiri the fine watches as they had promised. Other than that, we've been working and enjoying ourselves. In fact, I've even begun studying Aramaic. And I should tell you, Ben, Alison, Grace, and I have snuck in a few enjoyable lunch dates with your dad." Herschel said, nodding at John.

"You'll be happy to know, Nate, that the Hunters and Rhodeses kept a close eye on me the past few years to make sure I followed your forward diary," John added.

"Any other news I should know about?" Nate asked. He slid his hand over and placed it on Kawsay's.

"Well, I think Dr. Hurtado likes Mother," Kawsay blurted out.

Sumaq felt conspicuous and quickly looked down and busied herself by petting Junior's head.

Alison decided to come to Sumaq's rescue. "I have some news." She looked at Ben, who nodded back. "We're expecting a baby around Thanksgiving!"

There was a collective cheer followed by several people talking at once.

After a few minutes, Shimon slipped a long cylindrical package out of a bag next to his chair and stood up. "I would like to present a gift to Nate on behalf of my family. As you all know, Nate fell off that sailboat and endured the pain of an arrow, which he promptly delivered to an adult Binyamin three thousand years later. We are alive and here with you today because Nate brought all three arrows back in time, conveyed Ben's warning, and even introduced me to Zevél. The morning Nate arrived, I was taking the bow and three arrows back to Saul's palace when I felt a rough spot along the shaft of one of the arrows. I examined it and saw it had been broken and repaired, and there appeared to be some blood stains. I saw no reason to return a broken arrow and thought I'd ask my brother about it later." Shimon looked at Ben, who smiled knowingly, and then continued, "When I showed the arrow to Ben a few years ago, we both agreed it belongs to you." Shimon handed the package to Nate.

Nate was not sure he wanted to see the arrow that had wounded him. After removing the wrapping, he did not see an emblem of pain but rather a vector of hope and life – a vector that circuitously brought his and Kawsay's lives together. Nate looked at Kawsay and then at her mother. He felt his eyes water slightly and realized everyone was waiting for him to speak. "Sumaq, thank you for your courage in pleading for Kawsay's life, and, with the help of your family, developing her into the young woman she is today. The small mark on her lip that seemed a tragedy led to a new and better life for her whole family."

Nate slid his hand along the arrow's shaft and continued. "It's funny but the 'problem' created when the arrow pierced my leg turned out to be similar to Kawsay's lip. Both seemed like tragedies, but wound up affecting many lives for the better and bringing us all together. Who would have thought?" Nate looked at all his new friends. "After I handed the three arrows to Jonathan, I realized an important mission had been accomplished. The three arrows were finally together and where they belonged. If this arrow had not hit me by 'mistake', everything would have been different. I may not have returned to the cave and ended up on Alison and Ben's front porch. Ben would not have ever gone to California to be Helmut's brother and Alison's husband. He would not have been there to help me or to help Kawsay and her family. I would not have been able to save Morrow and warn my dad about cancer. Dad and I probably would have ended up drowning in the lightning storm. Helmut would not have gone to Anchorage to stay with Yachay, where he met Officer Cole. And I would never have met Kawsay. It's amazing! The Bible tells the simple true story of the three arrows, but God's purposes and plans ran deep and intertwined in every direction. We could never have figured out beforehand how it all was supposed to work out."

Everyone was silent for a moment as they pondered Nate's insightful words. Junior broke the silence with loud barking and dashed into the forest after a chattering squirrel. The party soon broke into smaller groups. Yachay and Shimon found they had a lot in common since Shimon's forte was astrophysics and Yachay would need to pick a college major befitting his astronaut aspirations. Kusi and Asiri enjoyed getting to know Jokim and Tirzah and sharing the mutual and amusing experiences they had adjusting to a future culture. Alison huddled with Grace, Sumaq, and Sarit to discuss the baby news. Ben and Herschel went upstairs to the library to look over Ben and Alison's artifacts from their latest dig.

Nate, Kawsay, and John found flashlights and took Junior on a walk to the bridge to discuss Nate's and Kawsay's future plans for finishing high school and planning for college. Kawsay had been getting an intensive private education from Dr. Hurtado and his team in Peru and was preparing to take standardized exams. Nate was slated to graduate high school at the end of his junior year. Nate and Kawsay lamented they would continue their next school year apart with Kawsay in Peru and Nate in California. They promised to talk on the phone or e-mail every day. During the year, they would apply to the same colleges and go to the one that admitted them both. In the meantime, they had all summer to be together, as Kawsay was planning to spend it in California.

John observed Nate and Kawsay interact. He could see that Nate had grown and changed during his foray into the past. He could also see the maturity in Kawsay since he first met her three years earlier. "Nate, before you left Ben's to travel back to Gibeah on your way to the Caribbean, we talked on the phone about whether I would notice any changes in you. Well, I can tell you, before you fell off the boat you were sweet and bright, but still a bit naïve. Now, since you took your excursion into the past, you are still sweet and bright, but you have also developed wisdom and maturity."

That night the house and two cabins were full of happy guests. Alison and Ben had even outfitted their upstairs library with air mattresses as an extra sleeping room. By midnight, the house was finally quiet. Ben held Alison tightly as they ran through possible baby names and drifted into a peaceful sleep.

Zevél had been quite busy the past few weeks. He had helped his Inca friends rescue family members from their village, and then he had spent a few days in Gibeah helping Nathaniel return the arrows and warn Binyamin's family about Saul. He had thought it a good idea to pop back to Gibeah to make sure Binyamin's family had heeded the warning and were all right, when he found them being chased by soldiers. He escorted them out of danger and into the future. Now it was time to go someplace where he could just rest for a while. He thought Binyamin's cave with its sparkling cavern and Alison's refrigerator nearby would be the perfect refuge. He wanted to arrive at a time he had not been to before so he would not run into himself.

He landed gently in the familiar small cavern, made his way into the larger cavern, and took a long drink from the subterranean stream. It was dark and obviously nighttime. He stretched out on the cool floor and began to relax. He took a deep, slow breath, rested his chin between his large paws, and slipped into much needed slumber.

Zevél was jolted awake by a "Brawk", then a squeak as Tzippa-el's small body hit the rock wall of the adjacent cavern, immediately followed by jangling noise and a loud crash.

Undaunted, the small white parrot blinked and waddled out of the familiar small cavern into the larger room. "Zevél? Brawk. Zevél? Are you here? Brawk. Zevél! Help! I was chased in the tunnel! Zevél! Hurry!"

Zevél smiled to himself. *What was Elohim thinking when he gave me this funny, annoying little parrot for a friend?* "I am here, Tzippy. What happened?" Zevél stood up and started toward the small cavern.

Tzippy ruffled her feathers and flew toward her friend's voice. She skidded across Zevél's back, grasping his soft fur in her claws. "Brawk. As I was coming through the tunnel to tell you that you need to learn a new language, I was chased by a huge clanging monster! It's here! I am very busy, but wanted to talk with you. And then this monster came at me!"

Zevél, with Tzippy on his back, entered the small cavern. Zevél sniffed the air and continued to where he had landed only a few minutes earlier. *What's this, I wonder?* He nudged the object.

"Be careful! Be careful! It could be dangerous!"

Zevél picked up the object and carried it into the larger cavern. It was too dark to see anything. He sniffed the object closely. "Hmmm, this must be Kusi's missing backpack."

"Brawk. Who?"

"Our Inca friends. Kusi lost his backpack. I need to take it to Ben and Alison's house."

"I am very busy, but will wait for you here. But please hurry! I must teach you a new language."

"I will return soon, Tzippy." Zevél felt Tzippy lift off his back.

"You be careful! It could be dangerous! Brawk."

Zevél wondered what dangers his two-pound friend thought awaited so large a wolf. He secured the strap of the pack in his mouth and began the short journey to the Hunters' house.

THUD … THUD … THUD.

"I hear it," Ben said in a sleepy voice.

THUD … THUD … THUD.

"Maybe he's bringing us more travelers," Alison said, getting out of bed.

Junior was pacing and whining. By the time Alison and Ben made it to the front door, their guests were streaming out of their bedrooms. Ben opened the door to find Zevél holding a backpack.

Zevél set down the pack. "Good evening Binyamin, Alison, my friends." He nodded to Alison. "I believe this is Kusi's missing pack."

"Zevél, it's great to see you," Ben said, genuinely happy to see his old friend. "Nate, why don't you run down to the cabin and get Kusi. You may want to drop by Helmut's cabin too. He may find this interesting. Zevél, please come in. Are you hungry?" Ben ushered Zevél into the living room.

Nate grazed Zevél's fur as he stepped out the door. "Good to see you, Zevél. You were right. We meet again."

Zevél brought in the backpack. Within minutes everyone was gathered in the Hunters' living room. Helmut's eyes were riveted on Zevél. He had heard of Zevél, but not realized his magnificence until he finally stood next to him. *All these years I've searched for unusual animals, and this giant wolf has been chitchatting with my brother.* Helmut turned his attention to an obviously elated Kusi.

Kusi was ecstatic! He waited until everyone was quiet and began ceremoniously opening the backpack. There was an Inca cloth bag inside which he gingerly slid out of the pack. He opened the top and slowly removed its contents, laying each piece reverently on the large coffee table. He glanced around at the astonished eyes of his audience. After all the pieces were carefully displayed, he announced, "This is a small part of the 'jewels of the Earth'. These pieces are a portion of what some now call the 'Inca Treasure'. I hid this for my people after the last battle." Kusi looked at the wolf. "Zevél, how can I ever thank you for bringing this to me?"

"I can claim no credit." Zevél looked almost embarrassed. "It arrived while I was resting. I had not yet begun searching for it."

Kawsay began gently examining the artifacts. "Wow, Grandfather. Why didn't you tell us about all this before?"

"Your grandmother and I planned to tell you, either when we grew old or if we needed to trade these for our lives. We thought of them as an asset of our people to be protected and passed down through generations. Then, when I lost the backpack in the tunnel, there was no point in mentioning them."

"You say this is part of the 'treasure'," Kawsay mused. "Is this what you retrieved in the secret cave when we rescued Mother and Grandmother? You didn't mention it when we found the caves again last year."

"You found the cave near your old village?" Ben asked, surprised.

"We did. Asiri and I believe the caves should *remain* secret," Kusi said. "Kawsay, Yachay, and I studied maps and searched much. Finally, we found them. Sumaq and Asiri kept Hurtado and his friends busy and without suspicion. They understand we do not want to lose our skills of being alone in the jungle. They have learned to trust us and not try to control us."

"May I look at these?" Herschel asked, motioning toward the shining array of artifacts.

"Yes, of course," Kusi replied.

"Astounding," Herschel said in a hushed tone. "Beautiful gold and silver jewelry, figurines, masks, plates, and bowls. This is really amazing, Kusi. I had heard legends of this lost treasure. I imagine Augusto Hurtado will be completely blown away by this."

Janie Briggs was engaged in her favorite morning ritual – sitting in her office combing through the news wires with two half-caff lattes and one doughnut hole. Janie finished the wires, then moved on to her favorite online newspapers. She clicked to a new page. *They look really familiar*, she thought. Janie increased the zoom a few percent on her computer screen and squinted at the photo. Staring back at her were none other than Professor Rhodes and Yachay! *What are they doing in the newspaper?* She checked the source and found that whatever was happening – was happening in Peru. Janie took a long sip of her latte, settled into her chair, and began reading the article – an article that should have been hers. It even used *her* phrase "stowaway hero" in its title.

GRANDFATHER OF ALASKA'S "STOWAWAY HERO", YACHAY, DELIVERS INCA TREASURE TO PERU
Lima, Peru
June 22

The mystery family who emerged from a remote tribe in Peru not only produced hero Yachay, who three years ago fought off an enormous Kodiak bear before braving icy Alaska waters to rescue a six-year old girl, but now has donated part of the splendid lost Inca Treasure to our government. The Inca Empire possessed great wealth including gold and silver. Much of it was believed to have been stolen or destroyed by Spanish conquistadores. The whereabouts of what may have remained of the Treasure has been a mystery for centuries. The small family's patriarch, Kusi, said he had "rescued part of the Treasure for his people and kept it safe." Apparently the Treasure went missing for a time but somehow ended up in California in the United States. The mystery of how the Treasure made its way to California is similar to the one that shrouds how Yachay found himself on Kodiak Island in Alaska after last being seen by his family near his remote village in Peru.

Attending the ceremony honoring Kusi were his close friends and family, as shown in the photo: Dr. Augusto Hurtado, Professor Herschel Rhodes, Dr. Grace Rhodes,

Professors Ben and Alison Hunter, Dr. Helmut Hunter, Marguerite Hunter, and Kusi's wife Asiri, daughter Sumaq, granddaughter Kawsay, and grandson Yachay. Kusi's family has been awarded an undisclosed sum of money for bringing the Inca Treasure to the people of Peru. The Treasure is currently on display at the Museo de la Nación.

*When probed further about how Kusi's Treasure ended up in California, Kusi said his friend Professor Rhodes seems to always have a theory about such unanswerable questions. When asked, Professor Rhodes said, "How **could** such an item get from Peru to California ... an airplane or ship? ... ah, or maybe a submarine?"*

Janie diverted her attention from the computer screen and looked to her doughnut hole for solace. She ate the doughnut hole in ten small bites, chewing slowly. Then she indulged in a long deliberate sip from her second latte. Janie took a restrained deep breath and then exploded, "A submarine?!"

DISCUSSION QUESTIONS

1. TIME TRAVEL: What are your arguments for or against the possibility of time travel? Are the distant past and the future necessarily "far" away? Is the past really "over" if we are able to travel there? Hasn't the future already "happened" if we can travel there, return, and explain what we saw? From a viewpoint outside of time, might all times appear to be happening at once? Is Eternity a long time or is it beyond time?

2. DISTURBING HISTORY: Were Ben's concerns about disrupting past and future events valid – or was it impossible for Nate to change something that was not meant to be changed? What is the difference, if any, between changing history and fulfilling it? If you traveled to the past and saw a person in mortal danger, would you attempt to save his or her life? Would it make a difference if you knew the person from studying history so you knew about their life story or their good or bad character?

3. INCREDULITY: What evidence would it take to persuade you that another person had traveled to the present from another time? In what ways are you captive to your presuppositions about life, the universe, and ultimate reality?

4. FLYING BY FAITH: Is stepping into a time tunnel analogous to living a life by faith? Did you ever just "know that you know" something with certainty that is beyond logic and reason – if so, did it turn out you were correct? Where does that knowledge come from? How can you test whether an idea or a calling is from God rather than just your own imagination or desire?

5. THE TENUOUSNESS OF LIFE: Nate learned about his father's cancer and then was blown out of the sailboat by lighting in a matter of a few minutes. How do you cope with the fact that your life is never secure?

6. GOD'S PRESENCE AND CONTROL: Might the times when your life seems tumultuous and beyond your control be the times when God is most in control? Do you have a sense of God's presence in your life moment to moment? What does Zevél mean when he says he is never lonely?

7. ADVERSITY: Kawsay's adversity taught her to be strong and self-sufficient. How has adversity affected your character? What life survival skills do we fail to teach our youth?

8. SOUL MATES: Do you believe some or all people have one (and only one) true soul mate? What is the basis for your belief? Do you need to search diligently for your soul mate or will destiny bring you together at the right time? How can you know if another *is* your soul mate? What distinguishes a soul mate relationship from all others? Was Ben and Alison's whirlwind courtship ill-advised? Is it wise to wait to marry until you find your soul mate, even if that takes years or decades?

9. ARROWS: An arrow is similar to a geometric vector having a beginning point and direction but no end. How is your life like a vector or arrow? Can a life change direction? What sets the direction of your life? When your life is launched, can you really know where it will fly? Do you believe people's lives are intertwined in hidden ways?

10. DELIVERANCE: Do we have a duty to save people in peril? Was Yachay's and Nate's heroism unusual or is everyone a potential hero?

11. LUCKY OCCURRENCES: Was it just luck that allowed Nate to save Morrow's life? Do we sometimes use luck and coincidence to explain positive occurrences that may have a plan or cause? Have you experienced unfortunate events or detours that eventually led to good outcomes?

12. BAILING OUT: If life in your world became intolerable, would you consider traveling to a past or future time? Where and when would you go? Could you adjust and survive being totally cut off from your family, friends, and culture? Do you expect life in the future will be better or worse than today?

13. CONNECTION TO HERITAGE: What do you know about the values and aspirations of your ancestors? If you could visit your ancestors 5 or 10 generations back, what would you most want to ask them? If you could visit your descendants in future centuries, what life messages would you communicate? How are you passing along your wisdom and values to future generations?

14. THE VALUE OF ONE LIFE: What does the way a society treats its vulnerable members tell you about the society? Why do children pick on their most defenseless peers? On what basis can we assume that people with disabilities cannot contribute to society or do not have lives worth living? Do you know the purposes of your life or how to discover them?

ABOUT THE AUTHORS

DEBRA ANNE ROSS LAWRENCE is the author of the popular *Master Math* series: *Basic Math and Pre-Algebra*, *Algebra*, *Geometry*, *Pre-Calculus*, *Trigonometry,* and *Calculus.* Debra is also the author of *The 3:00 PM Secret: Live Slim and Strong Live Your Dreams* and *The 3:00 PM Secret 10-Day Dream Diet.* Debra's career encompasses R&D management in the areas of engineering, biology, chemistry, biosensors, pharmaceutical drug discovery, and intellectual property. Debra earned a double BA in biology and chemistry with honors from the University of California at Santa Cruz and an MS in chemical engineering from Stanford University. Debra's passions range from cosmology, Bible prophecy, finding one's destiny, and practicing God's presence to cute dogs, glaciated mountains, and David Lawrence.

DAVID ALLEN LAWRENCE cut his literary teeth drafting legal briefs, regulatory orders, and contracts. He holds Bachelor and Master of Science degrees in Management from the Massachusetts Institute of Technology and a Juris Doctor *cum laude* from the University of Minnesota. His legal career includes: director of law for a Fortune 500 energy company, senior vice president and general counsel for an engineering consulting company, and chief judge for a state regulatory commission. David has led church and school boards and taught classes in law, business, and apologetics. He is an accomplished wilderness explorer, wind surfer, distance runner, and accordionist.

DEBRA AND DAVID currently reside in Alaska. Their extra-literary activities include all-season mountaineering, the pursuit of an ultra-healthy lifestyle, following their dreams, and living happily ever after.

They are working on a sequel to **ARROWS THROUGH TIME**. Debra and David enjoy receiving questions and comments from readers of their books.

You can email them through: glacierdog@glacierdogpublishing.com.

www.ingramcontent.com/pod-product-compliance
Lightning Source LLC
Chambersburg PA
CBHW080951020726
47505CB00009B/2159